CHAMPION
OF THE
SCARLET WOLF

BOOK TWO

GINN HALE

BLIND
EYE
BOOKS

blindeyebooks.com

Champion of the Scarlet Wolf
Book Two
Ginn Hale

Champion of the Scarlet Wolf
Book 2
By Ginn Hale

Published by:
BLIND EYE BOOKS
1141 Grant Street
Bellingham, WA 98225
blindeyebooks.com

Edited by Nicole Kimberling
Cover Art by John Coulthart
Interior Art by Dawn Kimberling

First print release October 2015
Copyright © Ginn Hale

Digital ISBN 978-1-935560-35-7
Print ISBN 978-1-935560-34-0

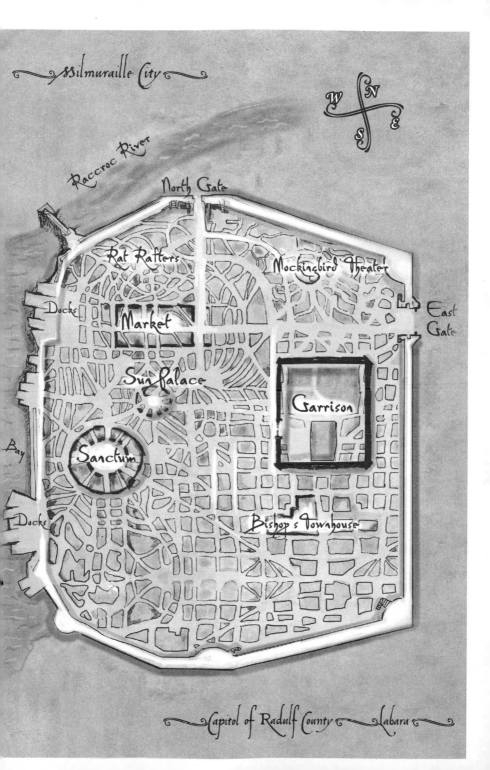

CHAPTER
ONE

Clouds of granite dust swirled through the narrow lanes, throwing a haze over the few rush torches that lit the nighttime street. The grit irritated Elezar's eyes and caught in his throat but he didn't have time to wait until it settled. He gripped Skellan's limp body with one hand and held his reins in the other as he urged his charger farther into the chaos of Milmuraille city.

In the gloom, the great heaps of newly fallen rubble and the jumping shadows cast by distant fires lent an eerie uncertainty to every form Elezar glimpsed as he rode through the maze of streets. The deathly pale faces of stunned onlookers peered from windows, while parties of irrepressible drunks hooted and screamed like wild devils from overhanging balconies. Exhausted city guards stumbled through the wreckage, escorting clusters of filthy, bloodied folk to the shelter of temples.

The few bell towers still standing in the city clanged out alarms as fires lit the stormy night sky. And all around bizarre creatures pulled themselves from the shattered stone walls that had held them captive for generations. The strange beasts fled through the crowds and confusion like the damned racing from the three hells.

Lightning crackled across the sky, silhouetting the smoky forms of ghostly horses as they bounded over the roofs of guild houses. A buck with a crown of six antlers and snakeskin for a hide darted across the crooked street as if making way for Elezar and his wounded charge.

Far in the distance the gray edifice of the Cadeleonian garrison loomed. It had been erected too recently to harbor wild spirits within its structures. It would stand through this madness and if need be its cannons could be turned against all the unknown that crept and slithered and flew free now that the Labaran sanctum lay in rubble.

Flocks of white bats with dangling strings of flickering tentacles winged overhead, squealing and screeching like excited children. Cloud imps, Javier had called them.

Ahead of Elezar, two long-limbed women scurried from the remains of a bell tower, racing for the river. As Elezar's charger barreled down the broken road, lightning filled the sky. He caught a clear view of the women's gaping, frog-like faces and the mats of green hair that draped from their heads down to their webbed feet. Their huge toad eyes caught the light of lamps shining from overhanging balconies and glowed orange even after darkness closed in again.

"Frogwives," Javier shouted from the behind Elezar. He ran a hand soothingly along the neck of his small dark mount. Dust powdered his long black hair to gray and his clothes hung in tatters. Elezar doubted that he himself appeared any more presentable. He'd crossed a courtyard of ash and clawed through the wreckage of the sanctum, tearing his clothes and bloodying his body in the race to reach Skellan. He'd walked over dead bodies and listened to a ghost whisper of a plot to destroy his homeland.

But right now all he seemed able to care about was the faint, living heat that radiated from Skellan's battered body. Elezar dug his fingers into the bearskin cloak that he'd wrapped around Skellan.

He's still alive, Elezar silently assured himself.

Somehow, Skellan had survived his lone battle against a fiery serpentine demon lord. Just remembering the sight of that immense monstrosity rising up over the sanctum tower where Skellan had stood set Elezar's heart pounding hard.

Skellan had looked so small—a lanky witch dressed in rags and standing barefoot, his red hair swirling in the hot wind of the demon lord's breath. Yet he hadn't wavered, not even when a cascade of flames poured down upon him from the demon's molten jaws. He'd fought, rending the demon lord down into darkness even as his own life had faded away. It humbled Elezar to think of Skellan's courage and infuriated him to realize that the witch had seemed all too willing to simply sacrifice himself.

He'd survived. Barely. But he'd not opened his eyes or spoken a word. He hung limp against Elezar.

"Stay with me," Elezar whispered. "I'll get you to help, Skellan, I swear." It seemed so little to promise but at the same time so difficult to accomplish in the chaos of this night.

Elezar's mount shied suddenly as the cracked facade of a small Labaran tavern collapsed. Hundreds of tiny black shadows scurried from the rockslide, hissing.

Javier pulled his own mount to a halt beside Elezar's. He hurled a shining white light ahead of them. It spun and shone like a comet, casting its cold illumination across the faces of people staring from their windows and balconies.

On the ground, some hundred yellow speckled lizards hissed in alarm, and then spreading insectile wings, lit up into the air like a swarm of beetles. Cloud imps swooped after them, snapping them into their tentacles and pursuing them beyond the eaves of the surrounding buildings.

Elezar glowered at the rubble filling the street. He didn't have the time or strength to shift so much stone. They'd have to turn back and try yet another of the winding side streets. At this point, he'd take a mugger's alley if it stood clear.

I will shift the little rocks. You protect our Hilthorn.

The words rumbled through the air like the crashing of distant waves. Then Bone-crusher, the craggy four-story troll whom Skellan had freed from the walls of the sanctum, stepped gingerly forward. Even the raving drunks fled from their balconies as the troll squatted down. His rocky thighs brushed the buildings on either side of the narrow street and a musky smell rolled off his pendulous genitals in waves. The odor caught in Elezar's throat, tasting sweet as the wild grasses that sprouted all across Bone-crusher's body but also pungent as a prison cell. The long spikes jutting from the troll's back caught the light as he scooped up the spill of cracked granite.

His eyes were black pits and the glow of distant fires lent a red cast to the ragged crown of his mossy skull.

"Fascinating company you've fallen in with since we last rode together," Javier remarked. He glanced up at the troll then cast a much more concerned eye over Skellan's slack body, then Elezar himself. "You know you're bleeding?"

"Scratches," Elezar said with a shrug.

Bone-crusher heaved the ruble aside with a force that shook the ground beneath them. Then he straightened and stepped back. Javier's horse tossed his head in fear as the troll's body passed over. Both horses bolted ahead the moment they were given free rein. Bone-crusher followed them, passing through the city like a walking fortress.

Soon the collapsed maze of old Labaran streets gave way to the neat grid that marked the Cadeleonian district of the protectorate. Here the garrison dominated the skyline even in the darkness. In comparison to the bright paint and ornate decoration of Labaran structures the massive walls of the garrison appeared imposingly drab and ugly. It occupied four times more land than Count Radulf's Sun Palace and had been built to house an army and repel an invasion. Though after decades of corrupt leadership, abuse, and desertion, the number of Cadeleonian soldiers inside numbered only seventy-five and of those hardly twenty remained fit to fight. Walkways and watchtowers, which should have blazed with lamps and torches all along the massive walls, stood dark and empty. Only a few lights flickered beyond the portcullis. Two near the stable, one at the gate, and another just beyond at the entry of the headquarters.

All four of the men guarding the gate wore Labaran uniforms: three attired in the colors of Count Radulf's personal guard while the fourth displayed the white badge of a deputy to Sheriff Hirbe. These men owed Elezar no allegiance and he feared they might refuse him entry. The garrison had all but fallen into Labaran hands this evening, and though Elezar still held the keys entrusted to the garrison's commander, he'd only come into their possession by chance and with the complicity of the Labaran sheriff.

Then Elezar's gaze fell on the young deputy. He wore his brown hair a little long but didn't sport the mustache favored by the majority of Labaran men. His hands and feet seemed oversized, like those of a wolfhound pup. Likely he would fill out to a brawny man in a year or two.

"Magraie!" Elezar called to him. "I've brought Ske—Count Hilthorn Radulf. He needs the care of a sister-physician."

At the mention of Skellan's birth name the deputy leapt to the winch and cranked the heavy gates open.

Elezar and Javier rode in easily. But Bone-crusher had to crouch low to pass beneath the massive portcullis.

Magraie and his fellow guards stared in wide-eyed shock as Bone-crusher emerged and straightened from the shadows. The count's guards raised their spears and the young deputy stepped forward to halt the troll's advance, though he had no more chance of doing so than a sparrow might have of stopping a landslide.

"Let him pass!" Elezar shouted. "Master Bone-crusher is faithful to Hilthorn."

Magraie and the other three guards looked immensely relieved to obey Elezar's command. The troll stepped around them with a surprising grace.

Faithful I am, but I cannot make him well nor are my hands enough shelter for him now. Bone-crusher bowed so that his huge rocky face hung over Elezar. His breath felt like the vapor of a hot spring. Something bright gold glowed within the depths of the troll's eyes. His teeth were iron spikes and lichen and moss crusted the tattoo of swirling patterns carved across his cheek. *You must take Little Thorn inside and see to him. I will take my rest near the well where I can hear the water running deep.*

Elezar couldn't see the well but he knew where it lay at the back of the headquarters, near the open training grounds and the cavalry arena. How Bone-crusher knew the well's location,

Elezar couldn't say. Perhaps he indeed felt the currents of water pooling deep underground and filling the cisterns beneath. Bone-crusher straightened and then strode away, his footsteps quiet as falling snow.

"Shall I take your horses to the stable, Lord Grunito?" Deputy Magraie asked.

"Yes, thank you. And have the sister-physicians sent for." Elezar tossed the deputy his reins and then swung down from his saddle with Skellan cradled in his arms. "We will be in the first floor rooms at the end of the east hall of the headquarters."

Javier dismounted and handed his horse over to the deputy's care as well and followed him as he made for the austere headquarters. Two more of the count's men guarded the entrance, though one went pelting off to the infirmary on Elezar's orders and the other merely held the door for him.

Elezar chose the humble chamber that overlooked the well. It held a bed, but no bedding or pillows of any description. Char, but no wood nor embers, lay in the cold fireplace. Past the open iron shutters he spied Bone-crusher's silhouette curled like a mossy hill. Cloud imps flitted over the troll's jagged spine like nighthawks hunting mice.

Elezar laid Skellan down on the straw-stuffed mattress. The rickety bedside table offered neither wash water, nor a lamp. But at least the mattress stuffing smelled fresh. Javier laid Skellan's dog skin cloak over the white bearskin. The scarlet fur stood out glaringly against the white ticking of the mattress and glossy bearskin.

For a while neither Elezar nor Javier said anything. Both stood staring down at Skellan's still body. He wasn't elegant in his spill of dirty, tangled hair, and bloodied limbs. Crusts of dried blood speckled his nose and mouth. Ash and mud streaked his skin. He looked an utter mess and Elezar found it nearly impossible to pull his gaze from him. He wanted to take Skellan's hand in his own but felt ashamed of the impulse. Now was no time to act like a distraught suitor.

"I expect he'll live," Javier said at last. Flickering white light danced between his fingers.

"He has to," Elezar responded. The raw emotion in his own voice alarmed him. Javier arched one of his black brows and Elezar turned away. "He's Count Radulf now. If this city is going to stand against the grimma, we'll need him."

Still fearing what his expression might reveal, Elezar strode to the writing desk standing in the corner of the room and picked up the oil lamp sitting atop it. He found a tinder box along with a pen and bottle of old ink in a drawer then busied himself coaxing a warm flame from the short wick of the lamp. Shadows jumped and fled into the corners of the room like startled roaches.

When he turned back he found Javier studying him with the expression of a man who had amassed a long string of unspoken questions.

"Something wrong?" Elezar demanded. They'd known each other since they'd been twelve and Elezar didn't see the point in making small talk if there was trouble.

"You mean aside a sanctum being shattered and half of ancient mythology climbing up out of the wreckage?" Javier inquired. "Apart from the troll we left in the courtyard and the fact that there is nothing now standing between this city and four armies of giants and monsters?"

"Yes, aside from the obvious," Elezar replied.

"No, I suppose that's about all that's troubling me. Well, that, and the fact that I stink like the inside of a dog." Javier laughed at himself and then with a soft clap of his hands extinguished the white lights he'd kept rolling between his fingers.

The room dropped into a dim golden glow. Elezar stretched, feeling the pull and aches of his body.

"Do you truly intend to stay here and attempt to defend this city against four armies?" Javier asked softly, as if someone might overhear.

"I do."

"This isn't your country and these aren't your people," Javier said. "Why would you risk so much for them?"

"Because… I was sent to keep Cadeleon from being dragged into a war. That means the grimma and their armies need to be stopped here." Elezar wasn't lying but he knew his motivation wasn't so simple as serving his king and country.

Prince Sevanyo wished to avoid bloodshed, but neither the king nor the royal bishop opposed a war so long as it was fought on Labaran soil. A hundred years before, similar circumstances had given Cadeleon dominion over the southern Labaran counties. The taxes Labarans still paid to maintain Cadeleonian garrisons and soldiers in their lands amounted to fortunes. As far as Elezar's exact duties went, he'd accomplished all that Fedeles had entrusted to him—he'd breached the Sumar grimma's sanctum and delivered Prince Sevanyo's gifts. He'd even done all he'd promised for the Sumar grimma. He had located her abducted child and placed her ring upon his hand. Elezar glanced to Skellan and noted how the ruby stone gleamed against the dusty skin of his index finger.

No, his urge to stay stemmed neither from duty or obedience. He knew that. But he declined to acknowledge the stirrings that inspired him to protect Skellan's city. Particularly not to Javier, who already knew too much of the desires lurking in Elezar's heart.

He suspected that if Javier were in his place he wouldn't have hesitated to speak. But that was why Javier now lived as an impoverished, heathen holy man, exiled from his home, friends, and family. Elezar admired him no end for his courage and honesty but he didn't think he could make the same sacrifices that Javier had.

"Defending Milmuraille is the honorable thing to do," Elezar said flatly. "There's nothing more to it."

"Of course." Javier offered him that smug smile that had made Elezar want to put him in a headlock so often back at the Sagrada Academy. And it didn't help that Javier still looked like the handsome, fine-featured nineteen-year-old of their school days. But they weren't the boys they had been and Elezar quashed the urge.

If he hadn't been so exhausted he might have flicked Javier in his sharp pretty nose just for appearing so young and energetic while Elezar felt like a battered old man.

"If you're planning on surviving a four-army siege you're going to have to start taking better care of yourself." Javier stepped closer and frowned at Elezar's chest. "That gash is still bleeding."

"It's fine." Elezar wiped at the narrow cut. It stung a little. He'd been scraped and bruised but hadn't endured anything that wouldn't heal completely in a week.

"The last time you claimed you were fine you were dying of a poisoned wound."

Kiram had brought the incident up as well. It embarrassed Elezar that both men had seen him in such a moment of despondency.

"And because of that mistake I now know the difference between a harmless scrape and a wound that will cause imminent death by muerate poisoning," Elezar replied. "I assure you, I'm fine."

"I suppose you are." Javier sounded tired all at once. He eyed the chair beside the desk and then dropped down into it. He kicked his legs up on to the desktop and sprawled back in his seat. "What a damn day."

Elezar leaned back against the wall.

"Hell of a night as well," he commented. Then he stole another glance to Skellan's body. Elezar watched his chest rise ever so slightly as he drew a shallow breath. Oesir had said that he would live, but then how well could a ghost judge the difference between the living and the dead?

Javier might know, Elezar thought, but as he turned to his old schoolmate Javier asked his own question.

"How much do you really know about him?"

"Skellan?" Elezar asked, though from the direction of Javier's dark gaze he knew well enough. Still it bought him a little time.

The urge to confide just how intimate he'd allowed himself to become with Skellan arose but Elezar couldn't seem to find the words. Then he thought better of it all together. What would the point be? Why struggle and stammer in front of Javier about a liaison that wouldn't last longer than Elezar's remaining time in Labara?

"Yes, Skellan." Javier pointed to where the man in question lay. His expression reminded Elezar of their old war master pointing out the obvious to a particularly dense pupil.

"I haven't kept his company long," Elezar admitted.

"Only a few days, you said before."

"That's right." It felt like much longer and still not time enough. They'd just begun to truly know each other—only shared a fleeting day of intimacy and yet Elezar couldn't allow it to be meaningless in his own mind. He couldn't just discount Skellan, not after all the other man had done for him and the city.

"I've not known him long enough to be sure but this last week alone has shown the true quality of his character," Elezar replied. "And tonight… It's not just any man who would have stood on that tower and faced a demon lord. He knew better than anyone that it could cost him his life and still he went. He went alone."

Guilt and a strangely deep pang pierced Elezar's heart and he found his throat had grown alarmingly tight. He knew too well what it was to be alone in the darkness, wounded, and bereft of any hope. He hated to think that Skellan had chosen to face such a death rather than call upon his aid.

Elezar turned his face away from Javier and his gaze fell again upon Skellan. His pallor nearly matched the white bearskin wrapped around him.

"He does seem like something from a bedtime story," Javier commented. "You know the sort—a valiant heir disguised as a beggar but still somehow true and pure through and through. That sort of rubbish. Though in this case..."

"They call them troll stories here in Milmuraille and the troll that brought Skellan up on them is out in the courtyard." Elezar indicated Bone-crusher with a gesture of his thumb out the window. "That might explain where his high ideals come from. But it doesn't make him any less brave or sincere."

"Brave without a doubt, but beyond that, on a practical level, what do you know? For example, what school of magic was he trained in? Does he draw his strength from the pooled power of a coven or does he call on his witchflame alone?"

Javier's cavalier question took Elezar aback. Clearly, five years traveling with Irabiim Bahiim through wild lands ruled by witches had allowed his friend to forget the prohibitions of the Holy Cadeleonian Church. Even in a city like Anacleto people didn't go around publicly discussing magic.

At the thought of his home and the danger posed to Cadeleon's deemed heretics there, Elezar touched the pendant that his little brother, Nestor, had given him. Nestor was safe he assured himself. His finger brushed over the incised surface then dropped away. He doubted that Javier missed the gesture but he wasn't likely to have understood it.

"I have no idea," Elezar said at last. "Why do you want to know?"

Javier swung up from his slouch in the chair and paced to Skellan's bedside. He reached down toward Skellan and Elezar tensed despite himself. But Javier simply smoothed out the ragged edge of Skellan's dark scarlet cloak. Then he stepped back. He met Elezar's gaze with a wry smile.

"Because if I'm going to consider fighting for his county I'd like to know what assets—"

"You?" Elezar demanded. "This isn't your fight. You and Kiram were going to retreat to safety."

"I know, but... Well, I may not be a storybook hero brought to life," Javier replied with a slight smirk, "but how can I just abandon my best friend to fight the Mirogoth grimma on his own?"

"But—"

"You're all going to need me so there's really no point in arguing," Javier stated.

Somehow in the past five years Elezar had forgotten how breathtakingly arrogant Javier could be in his sweeping decisions, but now it came back to him.

He said, "I'm not arguing. This just seems sudden."

"Well, I have to find some way to amaze Kiram after you took command of an entire garrison, don't I? He was far too impressed with you and with your bold appropriation of all that payroll. And you've gotten even taller," Javier added with a playfully aggrieved expression. "Which, by definition, makes it difficult to demonstrate your comparative shortcomings."

"Maybe we should just take out our dicks and see which is bigger?"

It wasn't the best line for Kiram to walk in on, but it did elicit a laugh from Javier. Saddlebags and several packs weighed Kiram's slim body down, making him seem delicate, though in truth he stood nearly as tall as Javier. Rock dust and soot powdered his weathered traveling leathers and speckled his dark skin. He looked tired, smelled of fire, and sported flecks of straw throughout his golden curls.

Atreau followed on Kiram's heels. Ash dusted his fine black sable coat and dulled his emerald green silk trousers to olive. With his perfectly groomed black hair, handsomely draped figure, and two teenaged pages trailing at his heels like pups, he looked every inch the powerful duke he'd been impersonating for the past six months.

The taller of the two pages closed the door while Atreau raised his brows and offered Elezar and Javier a theatrically lewd smile.

"I had always wondered how the two of you settled your arguments." Atreau strode forward and threw his arms around

Javier, embracing him so tightly that Javier's face flushed.

"God's tits, Javier," Atreau said when he at last stepped back. "I can hardly bear to see you like this! Dressed like a wild man and your hair grown out longer than Queen Marenya's. Fedeles would weep if he saw you."

"I've missed you as well," Javier said. The affection in his expression shone.

"I'm just so damn glad you're alive." Atreau glanced to Elezar. "Both of you. When Kiram and I saw that serpent rising up over the sanctum, we feared that you were both... lost to us."

Kiram none too gently dropped the saddlebag from his shoulder—Elezar recognized that it was his—and then lobbed the pack to Javier, who barely caught it before it hit his face.

"With all the fires we decided to move the horses to the stables here in the garrison. Eski is insisting on staying there with them," Kiram informed them in a terse voice. "Also there's a live troll in the courtyard just behind this room."

"That's Bone-crusher," Elezar said. Then he added, "He's a friend of Skellan's who followed us from the sanctum."

"Yes, the sanctum. Did you get Skellan out before..." Kiram trailed off as he took note of the body sprawled beneath the furs on the bed. He went to the bedside and placed his hand first against Skellan's throat and then to his brow. His fingers looked like polished bronze against the gray pallor of Skellan's complexion.

"No fever. If anything he feels too cold," Kiram said. He scowled at the blood that caked Skellan's nose and mouth.

"I've already sent for the sister-physicians to treat him," Elezar said.

Kiram nodded and then turned his attention to Javier. He pinned the other man with a sharp, accusatory stare.

"It was you up on that tower, wasn't it?" As much anguish as anger sounded in Kiram's voice. "Damn it! You promised me—"

"It wasn't. I swear." Javier held up his hands as if to surrender. "Believe it or not, Elezar's managed to dig up someone who's even more reckless than I am. Skellan challenged the demon lord on his own." Javier threw his arm around Kiram, embracing him.

A brief silence filled the room. Elezar glanced to Atreau, whose gaze drifted between Javier and Kiram. The corner of his mouth twitched up, and he smiled as if confirming a long-held suspicion. The pages, however, just seemed confused by the turn of conversation.

"The gigantic, flaming snake, you mean?" the older one asked.

"Exactly," Javier said.

"I'm not sure I've ever been quite so terrified in my life, and I only saw it from a distance." Atreau studied Skellan. "He's either braver than any man I've known or utterly daft."

"I thought we were all going to die," the younger of the pages confessed with a shudder. The other boy attempted a brave face but Elezar could see fear lingering still in his wide pupils and shaking hands. Neither of them would sleep well tonight, he suspected.

"It's gone now," Elezar assured the pages.

"Back in the box?" Atreau inquired.

"What box?" Elezar wasn't certain if he was just too tired to think anymore or if Atreau was babbling. But then Atreau went on to describe how Skellan had asked him to search Bishop Palo's chapel for the golden coffer that once severed as the demon lord's prison. Atreau had discovered many copies but he'd sent the original to Skellan. Javier added that he'd seen Skellan take the coffer with him into the sanctum.

"No, Zi'sai isn't trapped in some coffer. He's dead." Elezar had witnessed Skellan strip the demon lord down to bone and then dust. "But, listen. There's more. The demon lord wasn't meant to be released here in Milmuraille at all."

Elezar quickly laid out all that Oesir had confessed to him up on the tower: that he Rafale and Bois had intended to use the duke of Rauma's body as a vessel to carry Demon Lord Zi'sai into the Cadeleonian court at Cieloalta. There the violent deaths and ensuing chaos would have ensured that neither the Cadeleonian king nor the church could raise arms against Count Radulf when he at last disclosed the identity of his long-lost heir as the only child of the Sumar grimma.

At the mention of the possibility of a demon lord possessing Fedeles, as a shadow curse had once done, Kiram and both the pages looked horrified. Barely restrained fury lit Javier's expression. Atreau appeared disgusted but he nodded.

"I knew it." Atreau spoke to the taller of the pageboys. "Didn't I say, after meeting Skellan at the theater, that I feared Fedeles hadn't been invited into the bishop's home by chance?"

The page nodded solemnly. From his slightly guilty expression Elezar guessed that the youth hadn't believed Atreau at the time.

"I discovered some rather suspicious symbols carved into the boards beneath my bed that very night," Atreau went on with a wry smile though it didn't reach his eyes. "Fortunately, I had already found a number of other beds to sleep in by then."

"You should have said something sooner," Elezar told him.

"I didn't know anything for certain until just now, did I? I had only suspicions and strange symbols, so I brought the coffer for Skellan to decipher." Atreau's gaze shifted to the bed. "I didn't think it would bring him to this."

Kiram rubbed the palm of his hand against his eyes as if trying to scrub exhaustion from them. Elezar knew exactly how he felt. Tired to his very bones and yet an uneasy agitation kept him from rest.

"Do we have a plan?" Javier asked.

"Does getting some sleep count for a plan?" Kiram replied and Javier smiled at him with such undisguised sympathy that Elezar felt like an interloper.

"We have the new count in our grasp and a ship that could easily carry us and him back to Cadeleon before any of the courtiers or the sheriff were the wiser," Atreau said. "Why not leave these treacherous, back-stabbing priests and courtiers to face the ruin they've brought down upon themselves?"

Elezar scowled and shook his head but it was Kiram who responded.

"Javier and I can't return to Cadeleon—"

"You could if you brought the Sumar grimma's only child to Prince Sevanyo. Once the king learned of this Labaran plot to unleash a demon upon him, you'd be saviors of the entire Cadeleonian court!" A boyish delight lit Atreau's handsome face. "Even the royal bishop would have to recognize that. This is just the opportunity that Fedeles and I have been praying for. You could come back to us and the Hellions would ride again!"

The joy in Atreau's voice was painful to hear, and though Elezar understood it, he couldn't share it. Even if Javier and Kiram were welcomed back into Cadeleon the time of the Hellions was done. They were none of them boys anymore. Javier wasn't even a lord since he'd converted to become a Bahiim.

And then there was the question of Skellan.

"Neither the king nor the royal bishop would forgive Skellan for his father's plot or his mother's blood. If we take him to Cadeleon we doom him." Elezar's voice came out rough, sounding too raw for his own liking. He was too tired to have this argument but it had to be settled.

Atreau frowned down at Skellan's pale prone form but then looked quickly to Javier. They both knew where Atreau's alliance fell. Elezar's should have been the same. Hadn't he once sworn to fight to the death to defend Javier? Of course, that had been before he'd actually died while doing that very thing. Did that release him from the oath, he wondered.

"Neither Prince Sevanyo, the king, nor the royal bishop is stupid," Atreau said "They'll want to keep Skellan alive. As the Sumar grimma's only child he would make a powerful tool for controlling the Mirogoths. With Skellan in our grasp, Cadeleon could even parlay a greater peace accord with the grimma. This could work, Elezar."

It could, Elezar realized, but only at the cost of Skellan's freedom and only after the Mirogoth grimma overran Radulf County. Certainly with armies of Mirogoths on the move, the three remaining Labaran counts would sacrifice even more of their sovereignty and wealth for Cadeleonian protection. Hell, if the Labarans were desperate enough, Commander Lecha might even worm his way into control of another garrison.

"A few hours ago you were volunteering men and cannons to defend this city," Elezar reminded Atreau.

"That was before I really knew what they meant to do to our country—to Fedeles."

"Both Grimma Oesir and Skellan's father have already paid with their lives for their plotting," Elezar replied.

"What about Sacrist Bois—"

"You'd condemn this entire county over the actions of one man?" Elezar demanded.

"I would! For Fedeles, I would murder him with my bare hands!" Atreau seemed as startled by the stridency of his own tone as Elezar was. Javier, Kiram, and both of Fedeles' pages stared at him, shocked.

"The duke would not wish for such a thing, I do not think," the taller of the two pages suggested softly. Atreau shook his head but the anger seemed to have gone out of him. His dark eyes looked hollow and he leaned back against the door as if he was too exhausted to stand.

They were all of them too weary to be having this argument. None of them wanted to fight, Elezar knew that.

The room remained quiet. Elezar was suddenly aware of the slow deep rhythm of Skellan's breathing. He sounded stronger. Elezar glanced down at the witch's drawn, pallid face and the mess of his soot tangled hair. Briefly, he thought he saw Skellan's eyes flutter open, but it could have been a trick of the flickering lamplight. Still it made him realize that they needed to settle this and be done with it before either Skellan woke or a sister-physician broke in on them.

"Fedeles sent us here to stop a war. I don't know if it's too late for that," Elezar said. "But I will do my damnedest to keep the Mirogoths from taking this city and this garrison."

Javier nodded as if he'd known as much, and Kiram just sighed. He ran his hands through his curling golden hair and dust rose up around his face.

"And what will you do to keep me from taking Skellan anyway?" Atreau asked into the quiet of the room.

Alarm lit Kiram's face and he stood as if to say something but Elezar cut him off.

"I don't know what I'd do," Elezar replied honestly. "I don't want to find out. Do you?"

Atreau met his gaze—it wasn't fear but sorrow that Elezar thought he recognized in Atreau's expression. Then Atreau offered him a strained smile and waved Skellan aside as if to dismiss him.

"He looks like just the kind to jump overboard before we even cleared the harbor in any case," Atreau muttered.

Elezar nodded. Doubtless Skellan would jump whether he knew how to swim or not. In the quiet Elezar thought he heard footsteps echo through the empty hall beyond the bedroom.

"Are we to stay here?" the smaller of the pages asked. "I mean, in the garrison for tonight?"

"It would probably be for the best for us all to keep close." Javier hefted his pack onto his shoulder. "Kiram and I will take the room across the hall."

Atreau nodded again then straightened from the support of the doorframe. Just as he did so a knock sounded and three red-robed sister-physicians hurried in with wash water, bandages, and pots of astringent smelling poultices. Elezar remembered all three of the women from the brief supper they'd shared. The eldest of them offered him a smile, which stretched into a yawn, and then she turned her attention to Skellan. A plump novice trailed in after them, her arms loaded with blankets. Tangled locks of dark hair hung from beneath her rumpled red snood.

Atrcau offered the women charming smiles and warm greetings but seemingly more out of reflex than any genuine interest. A short conversation later he and the pages accepted two blankets and withdrew to the adjoining room. The older sister-physicians shooed Elezar from the bedside while they settled around Skellan to wash and tend his wounds. Javier bid Elezar goodnight and started for the door. Kiram, however, paused at Elezar's side.

He held out a sheathed hunting knife and Elezar recognized it at once as the one he'd earlier given to Skellan.

"He forgot this on the steps outside the kitchen," Kiram said. "I think you should give it back to him."

Elezar accepted the curved hunting knife, feeling strangely dazed, because here was Kiram again presenting him the the same knife that he'd given Elezar years ago as a solstice gift.

"Get some rest if you can," Kiram told him.

Elezar set the knife aside on the small desk. He considered slumping down into the chair but was startled be a loud knock at the heavy oak door.

The stocky, white-bearded Sheriff Hirbe offered Elezar an off-handed salute. Soot darkened the multitude of fine wrinkles lining his face. Singe marks showed on his leather armor and patchwork cap.

"Deputy Magraie tells me that you brought our Hilthorn back to us," Sheriff Hirbe said. "And that you looked a filthy wreck for your effort. Here."

He handed Elezar a clay jug of wash water with a clean rag stuffed in the top. In his other hand he held a bottle of the harsh liquor of Elezar's Hellion days: white ruin. Elezar took the water and went to the desk and rinsed his face and hands as best he could. The sheriff stepped into the room to crane his head around the sister-physicians, attempting to catch a glimpse of Skellan.

"He'll live, Hirbe, don't you fear," the eldest of the sister-physicians commented over her shoulder. "He's stronger than even his father and aside from cleaning up his wounds the best thing we can do for him is let him rest and heal himself."

The sheriff nodded then glanced to Elezar and held up the bottle of white ruin invitingly. Blisters dotted the back of the sheriff's hand.

"No, thank you," Elezar replied. He guessed, from the sheriff's surprised expression, that even in northern Labara his history of drunken binges following bloody duels preceded him.

The sheriff asked after Elezar's injuries, which Elezar assured him were slight. Then Sheriff Hirbe informed him that his fire guard had doused the flames in the old section of the city before much more than a few thatched roofs could be destroyed. This close Elezar could see perfectly where flecks of black soot hung through the sheriff's thick white beard. He smelled like a bonfire and sweat and looked exhausted, but he made no move to take his leave.

At last the sister-physicians drew away from Skellan. They'd cleaned him and bandaged the deepest of the gashes that crisscrossed his arms and chest. One of them had obviously made an attempt to untangle his hair and comb it back from his face. The novice carefully laid a pillow under his head and then stepped back to follow her elders from the room.

"Let him rest as long as he needs." The oldest of the sister-physicians paused at the door to cast a hard look at the sheriff and then Elezar. "Sleep certainly wouldn't hurt the two of you either."

After the sister-physicians retired, Sheriff Hirbe gave Elezar a particularly measured look.

"Certain you wouldn't like a drink, Lord Grunito?" The sheriff offered the bottle a second time.

"I'm not always good company when drunk, so no. Not tonight," Elezar responded. "But feel free if you're thirsty."

"No, no, not for me. It's too late an hour and I'm too old a man." The sheriff set the white ruin aside on the writing desk. His gaze shifted to where Skellan lay, gleaming with oily poultices, his arms and chest swathed in bandages. Tired as he was, Elezar suddenly thought that the sheriff's bright round eyes and wild hair lent him the look of a ruffled owl as he bobbed his head in Skellan's direction.

"I heard that you charged into the sanctum to battle the demon lord."

Elezar shook his head, feeling ridiculous. "I climbed through some rubble to try and get Ske—Hilthorn out of there. He was the one who fought the demon lord."

"Well, you've done rightly by him in any case. More than should have ever been asked of you in the first place." The sheriff flashed Elezar a cursory smile. "After all you have your own business to attend to. And Hilthorn now has his own people to look after him. His rooms have already been prepared for him at the Sun Palace. And his sister will be delighted to meet him at last."

Elezar didn't laugh out loud at the thought of a courtly young noblewoman delighting in the company of a man who pissed out windows and ate with his bare hands, but it took an effort.

The sheriff said, "The count's golden carriage awaits to carry him home."

"It can keep waiting," Elezar replied.

The sheriff scowled at him.

"Hilthorn will decide for himself where he will go and who he wants at his back," Elezar said. "Right now I'm the one he named as his man and I say he stays here until he can speak for himself."

"A little high-handed for a foreigner, don't you think?"

"High-handed is a damn sight better than dealing him a

low blow," Elezar returned. "I don't know how much faith I'd put in all those attendants who happily abandoned him to live like a beggar for ten years."

The sheriff's face flushed.

"He lived like a dog," Elezar said. "And not one of you came to his aid—"

"No one knew where he was—"

"How hard could he have been to find?" Elezar replied. "He was a child, for God's sake! You have an army of grown men at your disposal. He wasn't found because it didn't suit you or any of the count's court to find him. Oesir told me everything."

The sheriff went very still, glowering into Elezar's face and Elezar met his gaze with his own anger.

"You're tired, Lord Grunito, and so am I. We'll discuss this further after we've both rested." Sheriff Hirbe stepped back from Elezar and started for the door. He paused just before leaving. "You cannot keep him locked up in this little room forever. In the coming days you and he may need all the friends you can find. Remember that."

CHAPTER TWO

Skellan lay in a frigid darkness. Far away he thought he heard voices. Then more alarming sounds of latches catching, bolts sliding, and locks closing tight. He wanted to open his eyes but he couldn't seem to move. His witchflame—his very soul—felt as if it had been scraped thin as gauze. An icy wind cut through him, reminding him of that first winter he'd lived on the streets of Milmuraille, starving in the body of a dog. But even then the heat of his witchflame had protected him from the worst of sleet and snow.

Now he shivered and shook like he'd been turned entirely to ice. He wondered if he'd died. This seemed a strange sort of hell.

Nothing but cold and endless darkness.

Was this where broken souls went when neither paradises nor hells had a use for them?

Then a small flare of heat ignited around his finger.

He concentrated on that, urging it to grow and offer him some hope. A ring of gold light flared through the dark sky above him. At its center a tiny ruby star flickered to life, radiating warmth across his naked body. Skellan reached up and to his surprise the star fell into his palm and became a stone. He closed his fingers around it and all at once a melody seemed to rise through his body. He caught the rich fragrance of a summer garden and a sweet, merciful heat sank into his flesh. Overhead the shining gold ring broke into a long sinuous line. It curled and twisted like an eel swimming through a black sea. It seemed to grow more green and immense as it drew nearer. Skellan wanted to step back from it but he could only open one outstretched hand. When he did, an emerald flame shot up and cascaded over the serpentine form that surged towards him, lighting each of its scales like sunlight illuminating panes of stained glass.

All at once Skellan's line of sight filled with undulating green scales and the taste of flowers and honey. Then, with a hiss, the huge scaly body slipped behind Skellan and out of his sight.

He wanted badly to turn and look behind him but couldn't. Warm breath brushed across the back of his neck.

My precious abomination lives still.

Skellan didn't know the woman's low voice and yet it seemed somehow deeply familiar. He knew her and yet he couldn't remember a name or face to pair with her resonate voice. The faint refrain of a lullaby rolled over him.

You will know me soon enough though it may cost you dearly.

Skellan shivered despite the warmth surrounding him. He felt the hard edge of a talon curl around his shoulder and heard scales clattering against each other like stone tiles.

Rest and gather your strength.

Skellan managed to lift his face to stare up at the angular, almost equine, face that gazed down upon him with burning green eyes. Membranous jade wings stretched over him and flecks of starlight seemed to shine through them. Skellan felt too awed to register how terrifying it truly was to realize that a dragon cradled him against the hard scales of her breast. She bared white teeth and exhaled a soft breeze across his face.

Tonight I show you the mercy you will not know when we come to conquer your lands, child of mine. So, rest while you can.

Elezar slid the bolt then went to the window and locked the shutters closed.

Alone with Skellan he pulled the battered chair to the bedside and slumped down in the seat. He watched Skellan sleep, wondering why it was that he was making such a fool of himself for this man who was all but a stranger to him. He had no answer—Skellan was not the most handsome, nor the wisest, nor the most elegant man he'd ever laid eyes upon. He knew next to nothing of Elezar and seemed to possess less common sense than a crow keeping company with hawks.

And yet as Elezar gazed at him, lying there, spilled out on tattered furs, bandaged and bloodied and artless in his sleep, that deep tenderness welled up in Elezar again. It grew so strong it felt like a physical pang.

He recalled the shock and exhilaration of tasting Skellan's mouth, the joy of caressing his naked skin and sinking deep into the welcoming heat of his body. Staring at Skellan's bruised face and split lip, he wished he possessed some power to wipe away those hurts. He wanted to hear Skellan's loud brash laugh and feel his strong hands.

How could he feel so mesmerized and affected by the other man's mere existence? How could a near stranger move Elezar as if he were something perfect and precious? Elezar felt utterly ridiculous for his impulse to cherish and protect the other man. Skellan was hardly a wilting flower. He was strong and brave and quite capable of killing a man in a fight—or killing a demon lord if it came to that.

And still that intense longing to shelter this reckless, half-feral man remained in Elezar. If anything the desire seemed to grow fiercer the longer Elezar assured himself that he was not needed at Skellan's side.

Skellan had probably had a good reason for leaving his hunting knife behind.

The lamplight flickered low, and Elezar realized that he shouldn't be trying to think about anything in this state of fatigue. His intellect was burning lower than the lamp oil, no doubt.

He closed his eyes and leaned back in the chair. He needed to sleep. His whole body ached for rest. The hush of the night seemed to blanket him. Then he heard a strange skittering noise from the adjoining room. He didn't recognize the sound and that brought him awake at once. He stiffened in the seat and strained to catch the noise again.

Scuttling whispers and perhaps the scratch of something fine and sharp against stone. A creeping quiet stretching out nearly long enough to lull Elezar into thinking himself mistaken. Then the faint scrape and whisper sounded again.

What the hell was Atreau up to?

Elezar stood and crept to the door that divided the two rooms. Taking up the lamp, he whipped the door open to glare into the smaller bedroom. A rag rug lay at the foot of the bed, but nothing else adorned the room. On the bed Atreau slept fully dressed with one of the page boys nestled into each of his arms. The sight reminded Elezar of the nights, years ago, when his frightened little brothers invaded his bed during summer thunderstorms. Elezar shook his head at himself, wondering if his brain was going soft or if sleep deprivation always rendered him so nostalgic and sentimental.

Then he spied the rat.

She was large and her pelt shone golden in the warm light. She hunched on one of the flagstones, her eyes shining deep orange as she watched Elezar.

"Queenie?" Elezar whispered.

He didn't know why it surprised him that the rat sat up and scuttled to him upon hearing her name called. That was why he'd called it. Still, it seemed so counter to everything he knew of rats for her to scurry into the glow of the lamplight.

Elezar led the rat back to Skellan's room and closed the door. When he returned to his chair Queenie scrambled up the writing desk and stared at him like a soldier awaiting instruction. She was the witch Cire's familiar. Elezar knew that, but he didn't know exactly what that meant. Was she a part of Cire—in the way that certain Bahiim could extend their minds and bodies into those of their crows—or was she simply an animal in Cire's thrall?

"Can you understand me?" Elezar asked.

The rat nodded.

"Has Cire sent you looking for Skellan?"

Another nod, though it was interrupted by a brief period of frenzied ear scratching.

"Can you relay a message to Cire?" Elezar asked. Queenie stared at him then scratched her other ear. Elezar wondered if that indicated anything other than the fact that rats suffered from their own share of mites, ticks, and lice. He tried again, "Can you carry a note to Cire?"

This time Queenie nodded.

Between his own saddlebags and the abandoned contents of the desk Elezar managed to find a scrap of birch paper, a split quill, and a leaking bottle of ink. Considering the limited paper and the rat's carrying capacity Elezar deemed it best to keep the message short.

Bring everyone to garrison, not Sun Palace. At gate, say Hilthorn called for you.

The birch paper naturally coiled into a tight scroll and Elezar handed it over to Queenie. Then he gently lifted the rat and took her to the window and dropped her onto the grounds. She scurried into the deep shadows far beyond his sight. In the darkness Elezar could almost mistake Bone-crusher's slumbering mass for a hillock, dotted with mounds of moss and wild flowers, except for the slow rise and fall of the troll's breathing.

Across the grounds Elezar noted that armed men still straggled into the garrison a few at a time. Most wore dress of the city patrol but others were from Count Radulf's private guard. Elezar didn't know if Sheriff Hirbe had summoned them all or if this was the doing of some other nobleman from the count's court. Either way it didn't put him at ease.

He closed and barred the shutters.

Between the designs of Elezar's own friends and the count's courtiers, Skellan might very well need the aid of every street witch in the city if he hoped to maintain his liberty. Even so, Elezar wasn't certain that would be enough.

The rest of the night Elezar took his sleep in snatches, sitting in a chair at Skellan's bedside. He watched the door, his sword resting across his thighs and his eyes red-rimmed and aching. Thin rays of morning light filtered between the slats of the shutters and lit the bare walls. One beam flared across a battered brass mirror that had been left on the back of the door.

A bird sang so loudly that Elezar suspected it had alighted upon the windowsill just to torment him. Elezar closed his eyes and let his chin droop down against his chest. Then he caught himself just before he nodded off.

He gazed across the bed to Skellan. He'd slept restlessly, working free of many of his bandages. Only thin scratches remained of the deep lacerations that had marred his arms and chest. The black bruises that had colored his nose and mouth had gone completely. The dead, gray pallor had left his skin and somehow even his dog skin cloak appeared more glossy this morning.

He looked a hell of a lot better than Elezar felt at the moment, certainly more relaxed.

As Elezar watched Skellan cracked one pale green eye open.

"Elezar?" he murmured, though he didn't sound awake or certain.

"I'm here."

"Come to bed, my man." He worked one hand free of the blankets and patted the mattress beside him.

"I'm your man, am I?" Elezar asked. His voice sounded rough and dry. "Even though you forfeited my knife?"

Skellan's eyes popped wide open. He stared at Elezar as if only seeing him now for the first time. "I'm alive?"

"You are," Elezar assured him.

"I thought..." He stared up at the ceiling for a moment as if trying to fix its exact distance. Or perhaps he saw something up there in the wood and plaster that eluded Elezar. "You really did come for me."

"I did," Elezar replied. Then he asked, "Do you still want my knife?"

"I..." Skellan turned to look at him and Elezar guessed that the morning light rendered him none too lovely a sight. He'd rinsed his hands and face but blood, ash, and dust still clung to his hair and clothes.

"You really mean to present it to me?" Skellan asked. "Knowing what it means?"

"It's on the writing desk and it's yours if you'll have it."

"Yes, of course I want it!" His voice went soft, almost shy. "It would be an honor to accept your blade, Lord Grunito."

Elezar snickered at the turn of phrase and Skellan scowled at him.

"I'm sorry. I meant no insult. Honestly," Elezar said. "My mind's a little filthy at the moment."

"Oh." Skellan smiled then. "Yes. Well, come to bed, my man, and we'll see what we can do."

"I doubt very much that you're in any condition to—"

"Oh, hush and get into this fine bed with me!" Skellan gave a kick to the blanket the sister-physicians had laid over him. "You're obviously about to fall over anyway. Come lie beside me and be mine."

Elezar considered the prospect briefly. He had wanted to lie down beside Skellan the whole night. Only anxiety had kept him awake so long but now even that felt dull in comparison to the draw of Skellan's warm body and the comfort of a bed.

Elezar left his sword on the chair and joined Skellan beneath the blankets and fur cloaks.

"If we're seized and thrown into the brig of a Cadeleonian ship in chains, it's your own fault," Elezar murmured.

"All right." Skellan shrugged. "Let it be my fault."

He stripped away Elezar's clothes and laid his bare skin against him. Despite his exhaustion Elezar couldn't have felt further from sleep. Desire rushed through him, as if following the path of Skellan's hands over his body. When Skellan bent over him and kissed his lips it sent a shock of arousal coursing through him. He drew Skellan closer to him, caressing and kissing him with a care he rarely practiced. Skellan's hands and mouth felt molten and radiant as they traced over Elezar's skin.

Elezar allowed himself the delight of touching Skellan in return and this time, unlike the last, he lingered and took pains to watch Skellan's responses. He allowed himself to admire the other man's naked body instead of simply seizing all he could claim in a frenzy of lust. As he kissed and stroked Skellan he explored his own desires.

He enjoyed the smell of Skellan's skin and the taste of his spit. Elezar hadn't suspected that he would find freckles pleasant to trace or that the glint of morning light across copper red curls and a jutting erection would move him more than any art. He wouldn't have thought that simply gazing into another man's eyes, as they stroked and worked each other, could have set his heart pounding so hard. The scrape of Skellan's callused hands took his breath from him. Skellan's broad smile and unashamed responses to Elezar's touch soon stripped away Elezar's own inhibition. He shared Skellan's grin and climaxed with a laugh at the milky spills of pleasure they'd drawn from one another.

Then he lay back, spent and filthy and unwilling to regret any of it.

Skellan sprawled out, his eyes nearly closed, absorbing the heat of Elezar's body. He drew in a slow deep breath of the musky air and listened to the steady breath of his man. He cracked one eye open—took in the tousled mass of Elezar's dark hair amid the red fur of his own cloak—and let his lids fall back closed.

Skellan lifted his hand and poked his own sticky chest, just to feel the solidity of his flesh. He was alive. Never before had that simple realization felt so powerful or so like a miracle. He'd been certain that he was dying when he'd collapsed on the tower. Just recalling his desolation at that moment sent a chill through him now.

He remembered crushing the black void he'd summoned and holding it himself as it churned and shredded his flesh. His mouth had filled with the blood bubbling up from his lungs. But he'd forced the void back down into the shell of a pearl. And then he'd lain against hard stones, gazing up at the stars and dying.

Nothing, not even his first winter alone on the streets of Milmuraille, had ever made him feel so defeated and lifeless as those minutes.

A vague image floated back to him. Oesir bowed over him, with an inexplicably gentle expression and somehow the stars of the night sky had seemed to shine through his face. Skellan thought Grimma Oesir had laid his hands on Skellan's shoulders but his touch had felt as insubstantial as a breeze.

And then Elezar had been there. His broad body and dark hair cutting a solid dark silhouette from the field of constellations. He'd taken Skellan's hand and a rush of warmth and well-being had flooded Skellan's whole body.

Skellan thought he must have slept because what he could remember next seemed to have taken place indoors He'd caught the impression of Cadeleonian men arguing in angry hushed voices. The recollection collided with strange fever dreams. A green dragon had coiled around him but he hadn't been afraid.

Skellan closed his eyes and let his thoughts drift back towards that sense of warm security. But the dragon didn't return. Instead he'd found himself fleeing strange men dressed in costly brocades who hunted him through a dark cave. He didn't dare call for help but Elezar arose to his defense unbidden. Though Elezar looked already beaten and bruised. Blood poured from a gaping wound in his thigh. The six men turned themselves into grizzled mordwolves as they circled Elezar's hunched, bleeding form. Elezar glanced over his shoulder to where Skellan found himself crouched atop a throne of polished bones.

Is this how you would use me?

Skellan bolted upright in the bed, his heart pounding and a cry choking in his throat. Next to him Elezar grumbled, but didn't open his eyes.

Skellan wasn't certain if he'd dreamed of waking up before or if he'd just fallen back asleep briefly. Not that it mattered. He was up now and not just pleased to be alive, but also half-starved.

He didn't recognize the bed or the room he shared with Elezar, but from the rough gray stone of the walls and the almost empty quiet of the place he guessed that they'd returned last night to the Cadeleonian garrison. Someone had carved a crude drawing of breasts into one of the bedposts and the scratched writing desk across the small room appeared to sport a number of initials and childishly profane words. A small tarnished mirror hung on the close door. It threw a dim glow of morning sun across Elezar's empty chair and saddlebags.

Oddly, Skellan couldn't feel Oesir's witchflame. He wondered if that was some enchantment of the garrison or perhaps due to the lack of it. Not even the faintest scent or color of Oesir's presence filtered in on the shafts of morning light that trickled in through the closed shutters.

Skellan jumped up from the mattress, bounding towards the window.

"Skellan!" Elezar called out. He sat up and almost fell from the bed as he groggily attempted to grasp Skellan's arm. Skellan truly hadn't expected that he would be so alarmed, but then he'd endured a bizarre and disturbing night. Most everyone in Milmuraille probably had.

"All's well." Skellan dropped back to the mattress.

"No." Elezar rubbed his eyes. Skellan thought he'd seen staggering drunks with less blood-shot gazes and haggard faces. "There are things I have to tell you before you go out."

A smug pleasure lit Skellan, assuaging the isolation he'd felt so keenly last evening.

"You already told me this morning." Skellan ran his hand over Elezar's chest, stroking the thick black hair. "I accept your knife, my man. I was wrong to leave it, but I won't again."

"That's good…" Elezar scrubbed at his face. "But that's not… Have you ever heard the name Hilthorn before?"

After ten years his old name seemed more like a lost milk tooth than anything he owned. Still, Skellan nodded. "I was called Hilthorn when I was a boy. Only Bone-crusher and Oesir call me by that name, though."

He wondered if this had to do with Oesir. Even after Skellan had restored the sanctum to him, would he have he tried to bribe Elezar into doing away with him? Very dimly Skellan recollected someone snarling that they should ship him to Cadeleon… But it wasn't Oesir's voice that Skellan remembered.

"So you know that much. Good." Elezar sounded near delirium. He really should go back to sleep, Skellan thought. Instead he kept his grip on Skellan's arm. "You remember when we discussed the Sumar grimma's abducted child, and you said that it had been Count Radulf's son that Lundag had taken for ransom."

"Yes, that's right." Skellan shrugged, feeling relieved at this new direction of the conversation. His attention shifted to the coat that Elezar had left on the floor. The fragrance of spice-cured meat rose off up from the folds of cloth. His mouth began to water and his belly let out a growl. "Do you smell sausage? Yuanese sausage."

"What?" Elezar blinked at him. Then he sighed and said, "No, I can't smell them but they're in the pocket of my coat. I bought them for you yesterday. Go on and help yourself. But listen to what I'm trying to tell you, as well."

"I'm listening." Skellan snatched up the coat though he nearly hurled it from him when he slid his fingers into the deep right pocket and felt the numb emptiness of the void trapped inside the pearl at the bottom of the pocket.

After the previous night he could hardly bring himself to lay a finger upon the thing.

He pulled his hand back and turned his attention to the other deep pocket where he found the coil of bright orange sausages. His hands shook with excitement as he tore into the first greasy link. He wolfed the second down as quickly as he drew a breath. Elezar watched him with his dark brows raised as if he'd never seen a man eat sausages before.

"You were saying, about the count's son," Skellan prompted around a mouthful of delicious oily pork and fragrant, fiery spice.

"Yes, I was saying that you insisted it was the count's son that Lundag took while I believed it was the Sumar grimma's son. Well, we were both correct."

"So, Lundag kept both children locked away. I never laid eyes on either of them, but then I spent most of my days out among the trees or climbing over Bone-crusher," Skellan said.

"No, I mean we were both right because they were the same person. Apparently, the count made a secret pact with the Sumar grimma. He fathered her child, intending their son to become his heir and doubtless hers as well, thus uniting Radulf County the Sumar domain and freeing his lands from

Cadeleonian control—" Elezar raised his hand to cover an enormous yawn and then added, "Children have two parents, you know."

"Some do. Some don't have any." Skellan felt compelled, as a foundling, to point this out. Still, even to him Count Radulf's plan sounded like it forged a dangerous allegiance. Not only would it infuriate the Cadeleonians, but the southern Labaran counts weren't likely to be pleased with it either.

That wasn't even considering the danger of turning Radulf County over to the son of a Mirogoth. If the boy followed his mother's way, then he'd raze the city for wild forest to reclaim and likely turn most of the populace into his beasts.

Skellan cocked his head and eyed Elezar's tired face.

"Are you certain? Breeding such a brat seems like dangerous plan for the count even if he were taken with the Sumar grimma in some way." Skellan caught the odd expression on Elezar's face and thought he must have overlooked something. "Unless... Could Oesir have kept the hostage child to maintain his hold over the count after he fell for the Sumar grimma? Is that it?"

"No. Not even close." Elezar shook his head. "How can you not see where this is going?"

"I don't know." Skellan found Elezar's grumbling tone almost charming—maybe because he seemed so intent upon tactfully leading Skellan to a particular conclusion. "Why don't just tell me where it's going?"

"Fine. It's you. Your are twice named, a member of Labaran nobility. You are Hilthorn Radulf," Elezar told him. "You're the Sumar grimma's child and Count Hallen Radulf's heir."

For a moment Skellan stared at Elezar, unable to make the words he'd spoken resolve into a statement that made any kind of sense. Then he burst into laughter. He couldn't help himself.

"Did this come to you in a dream, my man?" Skellan teased, because he felt sure it must have. "With my temperament I'm more likely the son of a wethra-steed and a wolverine, don't you think?"

Elezar scowled at him and then caught his hand. Skellan glanced down, taking note of the ring on his third finger.

"That's the ring that I brought back from the Sumar grimma's sanctum. The ring she made for her child. Last night it led me to you, and it fits you perfectly because it was made to be yours. You even asked me for it at the inn that first morning." Elezar's expression turned wry. "I should have realized."

Skellan stared at the ring. How could he have not seen it there? Or felt it? The red stone glowed with the inner fire of an ember and the gold band clung to him as if it were embracing him. Skellan ran his thumb over the ring and felt it warm in response to his touch. Nothing since his dog skin cloak had ever felt so much a part of himself.

But it couldn't be… That was madness.

"But…" Skellan foundered, trying to find the words to convey the incongruity—the impossibility. "This is a mistake… I'm a foundling, a street witch and a mongrel. I'm not… You can't seriously think…" He felt his pulse quicken as if in preparation for flight.

"It's much to take in, I realize that. But I swear it's true," Elezar said. "And I'm sorry that I can't give you more time, but I'm not the only one who knows about this."

"What do you mean?" Skellan asked. "Who else knows?"

"You remember when Bois and Rafale seemed so desperate to take you with them to the Sun Palace? It's because they knew who you are. Sheriff Hirbe recognized you as well. I suspect that a good many more courtiers are aware that Count Radulf's son wasn't dead or as lost as was claimed."

Skellan scowled at his own battered hands. He couldn't believe this. It sounded like half the damn city had known about his heritage while he ran wild in the streets.

He jammed a finger into his mouth, sucking up last of the sausage grease, and then noted that Elezar had gone quiet, watching his tongue and lips work over his fingers. Was he remembering the feeling of Skellan's mouth on him? Yes, Skellan felt certain he was. Seeing the color rise in Elezar's face, Skellan grinned.

Somehow, looking at Elezar's flustered face, Skellan felt more at ease; he wasn't the only one who found himself out of his depth. He eyed the gold ring again, allowing himself to take in the faint gold spells that it wove around his third finger. *Strength. Courage. Power.* The repeated Mirogothic symbols encircled the scarlet stone, which gleamed with the bright symbol of his own name.

"Even if this were all true, what does it really matter?" Skellan asked. Then he lifted his gaze again to Elezar. "Unless—is there money in it for me?"

"Are you joking? Of course, there's money—we're talking about the entire northlands, all of Radulf County." Elezar threw his big arms wide. "Money is the least of it."

All of Radulf County was too much for Skellan to ever contemplate, though being a lord Elezar probably wouldn't have understood that.

Skellan reached out and caught up his beaten dog skin cloak and pulled it around his shoulders. A white bearskin lay across the bed as well but Skellan's eyes darted from it. He was too occupied with his conversation with Elezar to do more than briefly note its presence.

"I'm not going to demand lordship over Radulf County, am I?" Skellan asked.

"That's exactly what you must do," Elezar told him.

"What? Why would I ever?" Skellan objected. "I'm a witch. I might challenge for a territory or a sanctum at most but not—"

"The count is dead. The violet flame killed him." Elezar caught Skellan's hand as if to offer him comfort. But what loss could Skellan feel at the death of a father he'd never known? Then he met Elezar's eyes and saw that it wasn't compassion in his expression. Elezar went on, "Right now Milmuraille faces invasion. The county needs a lord to rally around."

"There's not going to be any invasion. I destroyed the violet flame and saved Oesir. It killed… nearly killed me, but I did it." Skellan shuddered despite himself, just the memory of that freezing black chasm seemed to waken an ache within him. Elezar must have read something of that in his face because he gentled his hard expression.

Skellan caught himself. What was there to feel melancholy about? He'd fought and been hurt, but in the end he'd won. He was here with his man while the demon lord was less than dust scattered in the frozen black hanging between distant stars.

He hadn't thought he would, but he even took pride in the fact that he'd spared Oesir. Bone-crusher and all of the other wild spirits held captive by the sanctum were free and Oesir had already suffered far greater pain that he'd ever inflicted upon Lundag. Since Oesir's witchflame kept the Mirogoth grimma at bay, why not let him live?

Then Skellan's gaze fell again on the white bearskin draped across the bed. Oesir had worn such a cloak at all times…

Again Skellan reached out with his witchflame but could feel no hint of Oesir's presence.

"Did you speak with Oesir last night? Is the sanctum too broken for his witchflame to burn?" Skellan asked.

"You were very badly hurt," Elezar said. "Oesir healed you but I think it cost him what little strength he still possessed. His witchflame died with him."

"No!" The word burst from Skellan. After everything he'd endured last night, Oesir couldn't be dead. He couldn't. "That fool!"

"Skellan, I'm sorry but—"

"No!" Skellan drowned him out. "Don't—just don't say anything more…"

Elezar went still and quiet.

Skellan stared at the far stone wall, drinking in the emptiness of it and very slowly allowing himself to feel all that was now absent from the air around him. Neither the scents of flowers nor the verdant warmth of summer washed over him. Each breath he drew tasted strangely cold and colorless. He closed his eyes.

He'd gone and fought and given his life to protect his city, and still, he'd failed.

"Why the fuck would Oesir die to save me? He hated me!"

"Oesir was your father's man. He told me so himself. I think he loved your father a great deal," Elezar said. "He knew he'd done wrong by you and also that he was to blame for the demon lord breaking free in the first place. Last night I promised him that I would tell you everything."

Skellan drew in a deep breath of the cool morning air, willing himself to remain calm.

"All right, tell me everything. But just tell me. Don't beat about, trying to spare me."

Elezar nodded and then he told Skellan more than he would have believed possible. That Oesir, Bois, and Rafale had intended to use Duke Quemanor as a vessel to carry the Demon Lord Zi'sai into the Cadeleonian court and that they had done it for his sake—so that Skellan could at last be reunited with his father, Count Hallen Radulf, and rule both Labara and the Sumar lands.

"With the both Count Radulf and Grimma Oesir now dead, the county needs a leader. The count's heir must step forward and call both his subjects and vassals to arms," Elezar finished.

"Rally them? Are you joking? I'm not a leader of men. I don't even feel right commanding a familiar."

"Last night most of this city witnessed you destroy a giant, fire-breathing serpent with a gesture. If there's anyone who they'll believe could lead them to victory against the grimma, it's you."

Skellan shook his head again but this time his hands were trembling and his gut felt like it was packed with ice.

"But I can't do that." He bowed his head to hide his face

from Elezar. "I don't know how to lead an army."

Elezar said, "You won't need to. This time you won't fight alone."

He caught Skellan's chin and then lifting his face, kissed him. He was becoming quite good at it—more assured—and this morning he comforted as well. But one kiss didn't alter the magnitude of what he suggested.

"How can you ask this of me?" Skellan didn't want to sound like a frightened child but the prospect of being responsible for the lives of soldiers terrified him.

Elezar drew back and looked him in the eye. This close Skellan could see the thin line of an old scar that marked the bridge of Elezar's hooked nose. A dark scab colored his ear and another beaded the thick column of his neck. Skellan remembered the thick scar bisecting Elezar's thigh and the other that marked his heart. His was not the body of a coward. Skellan felt no doubt that if their positions had been reversed Elezar would not hesitate.

"I'm not *asking* you to do anything. I'm *telling* you what the circumstances are," Elezar replied and Skellan felt certain that they both knew he was lying, but he played along.

"And what do you want me to do with that information, then?" Skellan queried. Elezar eyed him and then sighed heavily.

"I want you to tell me what you intend to do, if you aren't going to take your place as count." Elezar's heavy black brows rose. "Are you going to abandon Milmuraille and flee south?'

"No, of course not," Skellan answered. "I never said anything about leaving Milmuraille. This is my city."

"Then by default you must intend to stay and fight." The corners of Elezar's mouth quirked up just slightly.

Skellan scowled at Elezar's smug expression but then nodded. In spite of the sharp memory of his agony at the edge of death Skellan knew he would accept even that before he would abandon Milmuraille and all of his friends.

"Then what is it that we're arguing about?" Elezar's voice sounded rough with exhaustion. His red-rimmed eyelids drooped as he continued to stare at Skellan. "I might be delirious from lack of sleep but I honestly can't see what the problem is."

It was all too much at once, Skellan thought, but that wasn't reasoning so much as the reflexive resistance of an animal feeling himself being dragged by a collar.

Skellan tried to find a word for what troubled him, but if it had a name he didn't know it. He only knew that last night when he'd learned that Elezar was actually Lord Grunito, he'd felt as if a chasm had opened up between them. He'd known instinctively that he did not belong in the elegant and perfumed company of nobles. He hardly possessed the manners or poise to keep the friendship of street witches.

"How am I supposed to rally forces, as you say?" Skellan asked softly. "Or take my place as the count's heir? I don't know any nice words or fancy manners about forks and hats. I don't even know how to properly address you now."

"You're worried about making a breach of etiquette?" Elezar gave a tired laugh. "You faced down a monster the size of a forty-gun ship. How could a few rules of civilized dining and proper conversation intimidate you?"

Skellan fixed him with a glower, which appeared to amuse him all the more. Elezar fell back on to the mattress, pulling the white bearskin over his naked shoulders. His dark eyes fell shut.

"You correctly address me as Elezar because we're… friends… intimates…" Elezar's voice rumbled up but he didn't open his eyes. "Formally, I suppose I would be introduced as Count Hilthorn Radulf's… *man*, Lord Elezar Grunito."

Count Hilthorn Radulf's man. So few words and yet they implied so much about them both.

"What about you being the Baron of Navel and Count of Odd Something? Wasn't that what the duke called you last night?" Skellan persisted.

"Baron of Navine, Count of Idara," Elezar corrected with a laugh—soft, half-asleep. "Far away holdings… and best forgotten about…"

"What do you mean?" Skellan asked.

"I'm here now. I don't want to think about there," Elezar mumbled. "Etiquette lesson over for now…"

Skellan watched him draw in deep slow breaths, the tense lines of his face softening until he looked surprisingly young despite his thick beard and harsh features. Knowing he'd schooled with Javier, Kiram, and the duke, Skellan realized that Elezar couldn't be much older than himself. He just carried himself like a man who'd endured a lifetime of trouble.

Skellan leaned over him and very lightly ran his hand over Elezar's lined brow.

Elezar cracked one eye open then let it fall closed again.

"Queenie came. I forgot to tell you…" Elezar murmured. "I told her to tell Cire to bring everyone here."

"You think any of them have stayed in the city after last night?" Skellan asked but Elezar had obviously drifted too deep into sleep to answer him.

Skellan brushed some of the dust from Elezar's dark hair and watched it rise in a fine halo. He felt hesitant to leave Elezar lying here alone and unguarded. At the same time his own restlessness would ensure that he would soon wake Elezar again if he lingered in this small room. Already he felt the temptation to play with the thick dark hair of Elezar's chest and to run his finger along the delicate pink curve of his ear.

If only he could lay a ward over Elezar…

Then he realized that with both Oesir and the violet flame gone he could work any magic he wished.

His gaze again slid across the white bearskin of Oesir's cloak. He could still smell the hint of summer flowers wafting from it but not so strongly as the scent of sweat and dark forests. Before Oesir had taken the skin as his mantle it had hung from the broad shoulders of a Sumar champion—a man who, in the form of a huge bear, had fought for an entire night before Lundag's own champions had killed him.

Lundag had told Skellan the story herself, and he'd always wondered why. Now Skellan wondered if the hide might have once belonged to his own guardian. Had the man fought against Lundag's wolves to keep Skellan from Lundag's clutches? Was that why Lundag took such pleasure in relating the tale to Skellan, time and time again? Skellan couldn't know. But he felt certain that the Sumar champion had been brave—even Lundag had acknowledged that of him.

Few men were worthy of such a hide and yet the thick white fur and black leather beneath seemed to suit Elezar.

Skellan wondered how easy it would be to bind the cloak to Elezar, armoring him in heavy animal muscle and thick skin. Even sleeping, a great white bear would terrify most men. Who would dare even approach Elezar, much less wake him?

Of course when Elezar woke in the flesh of a bear...

No, it would be the wrong thing to do for a great number of reasons. The foremost of which was that Elezar hadn't in any way agreed to it. Skellan was simply uneasy and longing for the company of the huge, quiet creatures that so often had comforted him in his childhood.

Instead of transforming Elezar, Skellan slipped off the bed and called his witchflame up over his body. Heat flared through him and his senses seemed to roll out, licking the stonework surrounding him and curling over Elezar's bruised body. He drank Elezar in, feeling the solid weight of him as though it played over his tongue. He grinned, tasting traces of his own body spilled across Elezar's skin.

Skellan circled the bed once, blazing fiery red wards into the flagstones and laying his protection and well-being over this man... *his man.*

For just a moment Skellan let the full implication of that sink in. Lord Elezar Grunito had agreed to become his man—not as a joke or in ignorance but in truth. The formality and gravity of it unnerved him a little. Never before in Skellan's life had another soul entrusted so much power to him.

An image from his morning dream flickered through Skellan's memory—Elezar, streaked with sweat and blood and surrounded by wolves and fighting for his life, while Skellan himself simply looked on—but he refused to think it prophetic. Dreams could just be dreams.

At last, he closed the circle of curling red flames and shining scarlet spells. No one meaning Elezar harm would be able to lay a hand upon him while he slept.

Skellan sighed and smiled at his own handiwork. He'd almost forgotten how good it felt to light the air and infuse wood and rock with the power and purpose of his own spirit. Then he strode to the small writing desk. Elezar's curved hunting knife waited for him there.

Foreign, beautiful and deadly, the blade embodied everything Elezar entrusted to him. He didn't know that he could live up to such a blade and yet he couldn't bring himself to give it up a second time. He wanted it. Perhaps a more honorable man would have left it there, knowing that he would not do it justice, but Skellan couldn't resist.

He snatched up the knife and sheath and secured them on his belt.

"By this blade and by your word I bind you to me, body and soul." As Skellan whispered the words, he crafted a scarlet spell. Then with a wave of his hand he released it to curl over Elezar's sleeping body and roll into him on his breath. Elezar shuddered, but he didn't wake. He exhaled a long wisp as white as smoke. Deep inside him Skellan's scarlet spell already took root.

Skellan smiled. He might not have a sanctum, but today he'd claimed his champion. He felt as though he'd been entrusted with a treasure. Skellan allowed himself a few pleased dancing steps to the window, wisps of magic still trailing off him like red smoke.

He pulled open the shutters and had to stop himself from calling out in joy. Just beyond the window Bone-crusher lay bristling with wild grasses and spring flowers. Willowy saplings threw sparse shadows over his curled back. Even studded with broken harpoons and tattooed with stretches of sculptors' decorative flourishes, he looked wild and alive.

Freed from the sanctum he'd even regained his natural coloring. Skellan could clearly see the green moss and red iron inlay decorating his protruding crown of ivory horns, and he grinned at the faint blushes of pink that colored Bone-crusher's earlobes and knuckles. The sight reminded Skellan of dogwood blossoms in an otherwise vast expanse of green.

The few men-at-arms who crossed the courtyard kept clear of the troll.

And well they should, Skellan thought. Bone-crusher was not a ravening monster but he'd slaughtered and devoured his share of soldiers in his time. Though at the moment he looked to Skellan like nothing so much as a huge hedgehog, all curled up to protect his tender underbelly.

Skellan bounded out the window and rushed to the troll. He clambered over the big mossy arms and swung himself up Bone-crusher's shoulder and snuggled his face against the velvet heat of the troll's long earlobe.

Bone-crushed cracked one dark eye open and sighed.

How lively you are this morning, Little Thorn.

As always, Skellan felt as much as heard the troll's inhumanly low voice rippling through him .

"How could I be any other way with you here, Master Bone-crusher?" Skellan teased as he ran his hands over the troll's ear. The thick flesh flushed warm beneath his hands and Skellan grinned. "Shall I tickle the back of your neck as well?"

He felt Bone-crusher's soft laugh reverberated through his body.

How jealous your new man will be if he sees you making so much of me.

"He'll count himself lucky that I don't hang off if his ears, more likely," Skellan replied.

Bone-crusher sighed again, but this time more heavily, as if discomforted. Skellan swung up onto the troll's broad back and clambered between the pale green saplings growing there down to reach the cracked shafts of harpoons jutting up from the troll's flesh. Thick gold scars and turquoise lichen mounded at the bases of the two iron harpoons. Given time the lichen would overgrow them. Spells of dominion that had glowed like emeralds in the sun now looked dull brown and cracked. They flaked off the raw iron shafts and drifted on the breeze like autumn leaves. But the metal of the harpoons themselves remained strong and buried deep in Bone-crusher's heavy muscles.

"They pain you still, don't they?"

How could I notice any small hurt when your good hands are upon me, Little Thorn?

"Ah, you flatter me better than any lover," Skellan said, laughing.

If you were but a bit taller, Bone-crusher teased him in response. *And much more green.*

Skellan laughed but then crouched down and ran his hands over the troll's tough olive skin, scratching between the clusters of moss and meadow flowers. Sparrows flitted into the saplings as Skellan stood and scowled at the harpoons.

Bone-crusher took pride in his fortitude and Skellan respected that, but he wouldn't allow the troll to suffer. He carefully laid one hand against the iron harpoon, and wrapping his witchflame around it, he sank his senses and will into the iron. The metal—cold forged by witchflame alone—retained the raw quality of the wilderness from which it came. Skellan placed his will against the structure of the iron and reforged the harpoon's forms into those he caught fluttering on the wind. The shafts split into supple branches, deep-buried shanks receded to a tangle of shallow roots, pale green leaves, and white blossoms burst open. Two plum trees bowed where once the harpoons jutted up.

Skellan hadn't been certain that he was capable of so much and felt exhilarated that he'd succeeded. Though a moment later a wave of vertigo rolled over him and he had to steady himself against the trunk of one of the plums. He'd done too much too soon. He waited the few minutes it took for his balance and strength to return.

Then Skellan plucked a cluster of flowers from the plum tree, tossed them into the air, and grinned as the wind showered them across Bone-crusher's brow and nose. The troll gave a pleased sigh and Skellan felt Bone-crusher's relief shiver up through the balls of his bare feet.

He climbed back to the troll's shoulder and stroked the curve of his ear.

Thank you, Little Thorn. I am more in your debt than I can say.

"I'm only repaying the care you gave me long ago, Master Bone-crusher."

Not so long ago. You are a child still in the ages of trolls.

"Maybe, but not in the world of men, I assure you," Skellan replied. He gazed at Bone-crusher's weathered face. "Did you know that my mother is Drigfan, the Sumar grimma?"

Know? No. But I felt her fire in you and heard her pride when you came to keep me company on so many lonely nights. There has always been something of the ancient ages about you. Even when you were smaller than my tooth.

Skellan nodded. He gazed across the garrison courtyard and noted the wind hawks perched above the stables as well as flashes of silver light playing through the clouds overhead. All across the city newly awakened wild spirits and ancient creatures flittered, slithered, and hid.

Their freedom came at a price for the city. The vast wards they had powered with their radiant souls now lay in crumbled heaps of rubble. That wouldn't have mattered if Oesir hadn't died. The grimma would have been bound by their word not to attack. But now Milmuraille retained neither the fire of a grimma's witchflame nor the vast enslaving spells that had stood from ages before Lundag even raised her sanctum.

Still he couldn't regret freeing those creatures who'd been locked away for so long.

Skellan wondered how welcome they were to most of the population of the city.

Somehow he could imagine Bishop Palo finding a school of cloud imps at play in his lily pond amusing, but few other Cadeleonian holy men were likely to agree with him. And doubtless Labaran fishermen wouldn't much appreciate clever frogwives raiding their nets, traps, and lines. Still, he had to believe that in this city where so many different peoples found ways of living alongside each other, these last survivors from ages of myths would find homes too.

Beneath him he felt a shiver pass through Bone-crusher.

Can you sense them marching from the north?

Skellan stilled, taking in a breath of the chill northern wind and drawing in the taste of distant forests and hungry beasts. Huge gray mordwolves, snow lions, wethra-steeds, and even shackled trolls, all cloaked in the glow of shining witchflames. Even marching so far from their sanctums the raw power of the grimma stung Skellan's senses.

Onelsi—whose domain of winding rivers and vast lakes lay northeast of the Sumar lands—proclaimed her presence with a flickering yellow green witchflame, the faint perfume of reeds and spring rain.

Ylva—her vast highland territories rising to the northwest—burned an orange witchflame, the color of the setting sun and autumn leaves. She filled the wind with the pungent tang of ripe apples and blood. Lundag had hated her above all the others, calling her Auntie Wolf-Bitch.

Naemir—ancient ruler of the blue forest far, far north of Labara—whose witchflame shone blue as the shadows of snow and whose voice filled the air with slivers of frost.

Only Drigfan did not cast her presence on the wind to announce her intention to invade. Skellan wondered if he should take heart in that or if the most powerful of all the grimma was simply biding her time. Would it matter to her that he was her son?

As far as that went, did it mean anything to him that she was his mother? He'd never known her and felt only an emptiness at the thought of possessing a mother. Still… Skellan ran his finger over his ring and felt it warm. He decided to take reassurance from the ring, if nothing else. Why would she have sent it if she intended to destroy him? Why make it at all? The notion emboldened him and rekindled his confidence.

"Let them come. I'm not afraid of them," he said. "I've defeated a demon lord. They are the ones who will find themselves quaking with fear."

And will you keep their spears from my hide? Bone-crusher's question rose soft, low, and a little teasing.

"I will defend you like my virgin daughter," Skellan replied lightly. But then he added in all seriousness, "Not one of those witches will lay a hand upon you so long as I live."

How gallant you've grown, Little Thorn.

"Indeed I have…" Skellan felt almost embarrassed by his own earnestness. He ran his hand over his dog skin cloak, then asked, "Did you know that I'm to become a count?"

No. I thought only that you would be a grimma like none before you.

"Like none before me indeed." Skellan laughed. "I'm not sure there's enough of the sanctum left to even bother with attempting to claim the title."

No, perhaps not. But the empty grounds have become a shelter of the two little trolls that used to hold up the Souge bridge.

"They may want to shelter farther from here with the grimma coming," Skellan replied.

No, you are their protection as you are mine.

Skellan shivered, feeling the complete responsibility of Bone-crusher's words. He possessed far less assurance in his own ability to defeat three grimma than Bone-crusher did. So many lives were at stake.

Fear not, Little Thorn. Many of us who were trapped in the stones know that we're in your debt. The wards defending the city may be broken now but we are here in their places. If you face war we will stand by your side. The wethra-steeds only await your call to take up their riders. They dance overhead even now.

Skellan considered the shattered wards that had protected the city but then turned his thoughts to the silver spirits flashing through the clouds. He didn't know how to command an army of men, but he remembered enough from his early life in the sanctum to know that leaders retained heralds and messengers. His would need to reach the Sumar grimma's sanctum and assess her intentions as soon as possible. If she sided with the other three grimma, then Milmuraille could expect an attack any day. If she took Skellan's side, then perhaps they had a chance of stopping the other three grimma before they even reached Labaran land. Only a wethra-steed could travel so far so fast. So at least Skellan knew his first order of business, if nothing else. He'd call the wethra-steeds down and strike what bargain he could to win their service.

This one decision helped Skellan feel less adrift—less like he'd wandered from his vei and stumbled into some other man's destiny.

I smell witches at the gates.

From atop the troll's shoulder Skellan surveyed the grounds. He spied the familiar faces of his fellow street witches. Behind them, Sheriff Hirbe rode on a handsome gray horse closely followed by a number of costly, gilded carriages. Nobles or merchants? Skellan couldn't be certain. It occurred to him that whomever they were Elezar would be better suited to deal with them for him.

Skellan's attention shifted back to the witches.

"These are our friends. Perhaps even the beginnings of our army," Skellan told Bone-crusher. "Shall we go invite them in and see if one of them doesn't pique the interest of a wethra-steed?"

Bone-crusher's laugh rolled over Skellan like a wave.

You have the makings of a count after all, Little Thorn, mark my words.

CHAPTER
FIVE

"Elezar?"

The familiar voice drifted over him but he didn't feel quite ready to force himself awake yet. He'd been dreaming something and for once it seemed to him to have been a pleasurable dream. A supple strong body had curled against his. The sensation of soft lips and rough stubble lingered on his skin.

"Elezar, are you asleep?" Atreau sounded closer, but it didn't alarm him. He'd grown quite used to Atreau intruding upon him over the course of the last few months. He didn't think he'd ever known a man or woman less able to abide being alone for any length of time.

"Elezar?" Weight settled on the mattress beside him. Atreau's hand touched his bare shoulder. "Are you truly sleeping or feigning?"

Elezar felt warm breath blow across his face perfumed by the distinct rose water that Atreau favored for sweetening his words.

"Elezar..." This time soft and almost melodic. "Elezar? Elezar... Elezar?"

"God's teeth," Elezar growled, though he refused to open his eyes. "You're worse than any of my little brothers."

"I knew you weren't asleep."

"Well, not any more."

A cool breeze carried in the scent of spring and Elezar thought he could hear birds singing. It seemed so peaceful. He could almost forget that the sanctum lay in ruins and war was at hand.

Cannons, he thought. He needed to see Kiram about repairs to the cannons and also to take a tour of the city walls. He prayed that after last night they remained standing. But surely he could sleep another hour before all of that. Just one hour more.

"I need to talk to you." Atreau's grip on his shoulder tightened.

"Can you do it while I sleep?"

"I would never do it while my partner slept," Atreau replied. "You mistake me for those artless rogues and robbers you've spent so many nights with on the open road."

Elezar took a moment to make peace with the fact that he would have no more rest nor any more sweet dreams. Even if he laid Atreau out flat on the floor, he wasn't likely to get back to sleep afterwards. He opened his eyes and jerked back, discovering Atreau leaning far too close to his face.

Atreau pulled back at once, looking equally startled.

"I was going to bite your nose," Atreau proclaimed, as it that would somehow reassure Elezar. "I wasn't attempting to kiss you."

Elezar stared at him in silence, wondering if perhaps he was still asleep.

"Why would I think you were going to kiss me?" Elezar asked at last.

"Because I was—just as a jest, to shock you awake—but then I realized that it wouldn't—so I thought I might just nip your nose instead."

Elezar suppressed the urge to flick Atreau's forehead as he would have when they'd been boys at school together.

He didn't normally wake up so irritable but abandoning the warm comfort of rest for the company of man who seemed only moments from chewing on his face made for a poor exchange. Still he had to leave dreams behind some time; if not for Atreau, then it would have been to see to the garrison. Much as he wanted to, he couldn't lounge in bed all day. Particularly since Skellan had dashed off to God only knew where.

"All right, I'm awake." Elezar sat up and glanced to Atreau. "So what do you need?"

Elezar waited while Atreau seemed to reconsider what he wanted to say.

"I need to know what it is that you're doing here," Atreau said.

"What I'm doing here?" Elezar repeated. "Aside from attempting to steal a few hours of sleep, you mean?"

"I mean, what are you playing at with taking command of garrison and keeping company with that red-haired witch boy?"

Elezar didn't think he could have answered Atreau, even had he been so inclined. He didn't know himself what he was doing, exactly, only that for the first time in years he felt as if he had a place and a purpose that he could be proud of.

"If you have some long-ranging plan, then I need to know."

"I told you last night. I intend to stay and hold the garrison."

"For that witch?" Atreau scowled at Elezar.

"And others," Elezar allowed but Atreau cast him a knowing look.

"How can you take some stranger's side at the cost of winning a reprieve for Javier?" Atreau asked and now Elezar frowned.

"I thought we killed this conversation last night." Elezar shoved his hair back from his face. He needed to trim it and his beard as well.

"You were tired and aggrieved last night, so I let the subject drop but I can't see how I could simply let it go." Atreau rose from the bedside to pace to the desk and then turned back. "Didn't you see what pathetic rags Javier has been forced to don for the sake of hiding and how worn Kiram looks? How could you, of all people, condemn them to that life for the sake of some shifty street witch?"

"He's not a just a street witch. He's Count Hilthorn Radulf, the son of the Sumar grimma. You may recollect that Fedeles sent us here to win a peace with his mother. Handing her child over to the royal bishop is not going to do that." Elezar tossed the bedding and bearskin aside and pulled on his trousers. "More to the point, what fantasy have you dreamed up for yourself wherein the royal bishop welcomes Javier back to Cadeleon, after Javier has taken the vows of a Bahiim and been excommunicated? And by the way, those rags he's dressed himself in are his holy robes or something. Don't criticize them."

"The royal bishop won't care about the embarrassment Javier caused him five years ago, not if he compares it to the outrages the Sumar grimma has committed." Atreau cast him a defiant glower. "Fedeles would support us, as would Prince Sevanyo. You know as well as I do that this could work."

He did, and yet he couldn't even bring himself to think of taking such a course of action. He'd killed men face to face in combat, but he'd never connived against them in secret while pretending friendship. Elezar felt repugnant even discussing this betrayal of Skellan—not to mention the people of Radulf County, who would find themselves leaderless and at the mercy of the invading grimma. He couldn't do it, not even for Javier.

Elezar snatched up his shirt. The cloth smelled of sweat and ash but was hardly the worst thing he'd worn since he'd arrived in Labara.

"I don't care what argument you offer me. I will not deliver an innocent man to the royal bishop's torturers," Elezar said.

"Are you joking?"

"No, I'm not."

"When in the three hells did you become so conscientious?" Atreau demanded. "For five years, you've done nothing other than cut down your own countrymen—noblemen—over the most insignificant slights! Men who were friends to your family and yet you killed them without batting a lash. Lady Gaddo begged you on her knees to spare her brother and you still gutted him like a pig. But now you won't dirty your hands for Javier's sake? What's happened to you?"

Elezar's hand tensed on his sword belt. "You have no idea of what you're talking about."

"No, of course I don't. I'm only the fourth son of nobody. How could I understand what it means to stand by the man I've given my oath to?"

Elezar shook his head.

"You aren't even willing to try!" Anger colored Atreau's pale face. "You've let yourself fall under the spell of a bent witch and now you're willing to just forget all about your friends. You're just as bad as Morisio, sailing off on his own, or Javier, running away to the north and leaving us!"

The aggrieved fury in Atreau's voice and expression took Elezar off guard. What did Morisio have to do with any of this?

"We swore oaths to each other! We promised one another friendship forever, you bastard! And you won't even try—" Atreau cut himself off short as he met Elezar's glare. Then he raised his chin defiantly. "What? Will you cut me down too?"

"You know I wouldn't." Elezar met Atreau's gaze. He'd always assumed that it was the drunken orgies of their Hellion's youth that had mattered to Atreau, not those foolishly sentimental promises they'd all made to each other in the aftermath.

"You might not kill me with your own hand. But you'll let us both be dragged into a war against witches and monsters! Those creatures last night were just a taste of the armies coming to crush this city." Atreau glowered at Elezar, his dark eyes shining as if he were on the verge of furious tears. "We came here to escape death at the hands of assassins. I came here to survive, not to die for some witch you've fallen—"

Elezar caught Atreau and pulled him to him, holding him as he'd held his brother, Nestor, when his wife had lost their first child and the whole family had all feared for her life as well. For an instant Atreau was stiff in his arms, seemingly too startled to respond, but then he drooped into Elezar's chest. He closed his eyes, leaning into Elezar in silence for a long while.

"I don't want to die," Atreau whispered.

"I know," Elezar replied. "None of us do."

Elezar expected Atreau to draw back from him then but he remained with his head laid against Elezar's shoulder and his arms hanging limply at his sides. He reminded Elezar of a heartbroken child burying his face in his father's chest—a large child who smelled of a libertine's cologne.

"Ever since Javier left us it's seemed like you've been seeking your death," Atreau murmured. "All those duels you fought..."

On the few occasions that he'd considered Atreau sparing a thought for him, he'd imagined that the other man had simply accepted him as the bad-tempered beast that so many courtiers believed him to be. It was what Elezar's own mother had called him the last time they'd spoken.

"There are easier ways for a man to do away with himself," Elezar replied.

"But not for you." Atreau's eyes remained closed but he lifted his hand to Elezar's chest and laid it over Elezar's heart. "You'd let yourself die in battle before you'd admit..."

Elezar waited but Atreau didn't go on.

"Is that what you think I'm doing here?" Elezar asked at last. "Using a war for suicide and dragging you down with me?"

"I don't know," Atreau replied. "First those duels against so many experienced swordsmen and now this."

Elezar patted Atreau's back and then purposefully stepped away from him, so that Atreau could look him in the face.

"I killed those six noblemen because they murdered my brother Isandro," Elezar admitted.

Atreau stared at him, aghast. "They killed your brother? But I thought highwaymen waylaid the two of you."

"I thought they would kill me if I told the truth," Elezar said. "And I didn't want Mother to know her own friends' sons had committed the murder." It was not exactly the truth, but close enough. The whole truth was more than Elezar wanted to share and he suspected it would be more than Atreau wanted to know.

"And your leg?" Atreau asked. "They did that to you as well?"

Elezar nodded and Atreau's expression grew more troubled.

"All this time I thought you were just being a merciless bastard." Atreau looked guilty. "Why didn't you ever say?"

"I had to let them think that they'd gotten away with it until I was old enough and strong enough to make them pay," Elezar said. "But I wasn't trying to kill myself then or now, and I promise that I'll do all I can to keep you from harm."

"But you won't leave here with me if I asked, would you?" Atreau inquired.

"No, but I wouldn't stop you from going. I don't want you to be hurt, I swear."

Atreau shifted his gaze to the view outside the window. Elezar looked in time to see Skellan dancing on Bone-crusher's green shoulder as the troll rose slowly to its feet. In a single step the troll was beyond the view allowed by the window.

"Somehow it seems unreal to see that thing move in broad daylight," Atreau commented. "How can you not feel terrified of this?"

"You think I'm not terrified?" Elezar managed a dry laugh. "If I ponder it too closely my heart starts pounding like a drum in my chest. But I just have to remember that men before us fought the grimma for this very city and they won."

"You're just like that witch of yours," Atreau muttered. "As far as I can tell he's not afraid of anything."

"So I thought, but that's not the case," Elezar replied. "This morning he confided a fear to me."

"Oh yes? What was it, a sausage too thick to fit down his throat?"

An entirely different image came unbidden to Elezar's mind and he felt a flush color his cheeks.

"I see." Atreau actually laughed then. "Trolls aren't the only giants whose company he enjoys."

Elezar's skin burned as the flush spread across his entire face. Atreau grinned at him, obviously relishing the moment.

"It's nothing like that," Elezar managed.

"No? I should have hoped that he would be more amenable to you, if you're going to fight a war for him."

"I am talking about his fear," Elezar said. "He's intimidated by the etiquette and formal propriety that will be expected of him now that he's Count Radulf."

Atreau cocked his head. "Truly? He's so unconcerned about the coming grimma that he can trouble himself over fish forks and salt spoons?"

Elezar didn't think that was quite the case but the idea seemed to comfort Atreau, so he simply shrugged.

"I could offer to tutor him," Atreau suggested.

"I thought you wanted to shove him in a sack."

"Not because I hold a grudge against him personally. It was just the course of action that could—would have—gotten us away from here." Atreau sighed heavily. "He did go out of his way to warn me about the coffer and he sheltered you... In truth I found him pleasant company. I'm just loathe to die for his sake."

"I wouldn't stop you if you took Fedeles' ship and sailed back to Cadeleon," Elezar told him.

Atreau made a face like he'd just smelled shit on his shoe.

"I'll not sail off a second time to leave you and Javier to fight monsters on your own. I can hardly look Kiram in the face as is. What sort of cur do you think he'd take me for if I fled again?" Atreau went to the window, leaned out, and then ducked his head back inside. "There's a parade of street witches, grand carriages, and men-at-arms out at the front gates all standing around Skellan—Count Radulf—and his troll."

So it has begun, Elezar thought. He did his best to pull an unconcerned smile and then asked, "Well, shall we join them?"

Atreau's gaze flickered to the mirror hanging on the back of the door. He ran his hand through his tousled hair and then catching Elezar's study of him, smiled and said, "It looks like we haven't much choice. The other side wouldn't have us, would they?"

CHAPTER
SIX

Elezar had to admit that what Skellan lacked in grandeur of dress and refined poise he more than made up for simply by standing on the shoulder of a troll the size of a hillside.

Wind lifted Skellan's long red hair and bright morning light glinted off his scarlet cloak. No shirt clothed his chest and his breeches presented the appearance of tattered ribbons more than clothing and yet Elezar felt transfixed by the sight of him. How many other men could bare such a lanky, battered body and still flash such a wide, triumphant grin? He was like no one Elezar had ever known.

Elezar felt his heart quicken just a little. Skellan appeared no less ragged or wild than when Elezar had first laid eyes on him but now his bravery and daring seemed to gild him in an aura of valor. At least that was Elezar's impression. Atreau's pages reacted as if confronted by a profane vision of witchcraft from chapel school.

"Savior protect us!" The older page made a holy sign over his chest. The smaller youth gaped at Skellan and Bone-crusher while edging behind Atreau.

"He is truly a witch, isn't he?" the younger page whispered and Elezar understood the wonder in the boy's tone. Last night chaotic marvels had come in dark glimpses and fleeting impressions—more like theater tricks than reality—but now in the bright light of day Skellan and his troll loomed over them, solid and compelling.

"Yes, he's quite a talented witch, as well as the new Count Radulf, which makes him our ally." Atreau chastened the pages with an easy-seeming bravado. "And so is his big friend, apparently."

"The troll is called Master Bone-crusher," Elezar supplied.

The boys attempted to muster as much assurance as Atreau, but neither of the youths was as consummate an actor.

Though they weren't alone in their wary demeanor. As Elezar started across the courtyard, he noted that both Cadeleonian soldiers and the Labaran men-at-arms stared up, slack jawed, at Skellan.

Skellan appeared largely unconcerned with the impression he made upon anyone but his fellow witches. He waved and smiled at the twenty-five street witches gathered at the troll's feet.

Elezar wasn't surprised to recognize Cire, Merle, and Navet among the crowd. He picked out Ogmund and Clairre as well, but then paused as he realized that Rafale stood beside Cire. The dramatist might have fled when the sanctum walls fell to pieces, but he obviously hadn't gone far. Elezar wondered what he was playing at presenting himself in such company.

"Don't we know him?" Atreau inquired with a discreet gesture towards jaunty gold plumes billowing up from the red velvet hat propped atop Rafale's head.

"We certainly do."

"He was one of the fellows who plotted to use those coffers, as I recall." Atreau's placid expression betrayed only an instant of contempt.

"We'll settle that after all this is done," Elezar assured him quietly and Atreau gave a brief nod of agreement.

As they came around the corner of the mess hall, Elezar noted that the witches weren't the only ones who'd come calling upon Skellan. At the open portcullis gates and beyond a parade of carriages, riders, and onlookers crammed the road.

Sheriff Hirbe, his men, and a sizable contingent of stately nobles watched from the backs of their horses inside the garrison courtyard. Others peered from the windows of carriages. Beyond them Elezar noted a pair a carriages bearing Bishop Palo's crest. On the street beyond the portcullis a dozen or more of the brightly painted carriages favored by Labaran guild masters vied for first entry into the garrison. Servants in pied liveries lounged alongside their masters' carriages while clots of cider vendors and sweets mongers gathered to hawk their goods, look on, and gossip.

Elezar couldn't pick out any single exchange from the rumble of so many conversations but he caught a general tone of anticipation. As much as the battle last night must have unnerved the city's populace, those gathered here this morning seemed less afraid than excited. Curiosity lit the faces he observed. He supposed that those inclined to flee the city had probably done so during the preceding weeks. These people had already stood their ground in the face of crumbling bell towers and witches spontaneously burning to ash. Clearly, these weren't flighty folk.

Five years before in Anacleto, when the night sky had come alive with tiny golden lights of Haldiim blessings, several of their noble neighbors had not been so stalwart. His mother's cousin had locked herself away in her chapel for days afterwards, fearing the Holy Judgment Day was upon them. He had, himself, thought the light unholy and Javier blasphemous for being able to call and wield it.

He could only imagine the panic that would ensue should griffins come bursting up from beneath the almond tree lined streets of his hometown.

Living among so many witches on the border of the Sumar grimma's domain lent the citizens of Milmuraille a much greater of immunity to the strange. Elezar admired them for that. He could see why Skellan loved this place and its people.

From atop Bone-crusher's shoulder, Skellan regarded his fellow witches with a welcoming smile. Not all of the witches returned Skellan's happy expression but that hardly surprised Elezar. Clairre's hung over scowl seemed as much a part of her normal appearance as old Ogmund's badger seemed part of his.

"Was it you that brought down the violet flame then?" Cire shouted up to Skellan. She mirrored Skellan not only with her coils of wild red hair but in the happiness of her expression.

"And destroyed the sanctum," Clairre accused.

"It was the only way to finish off the Demon Lord Zi'sai's violet flame," Skellan said. He shrugged and whether by chance or twist of magic his scarlet cloak billowed up behind him as if he were a heroic figure in some epic painting.

"What were you thinking, killing Oesir?" Clairre demanded.

"Fuck if that was me, Clairre!" Skellan responded. He did have a way with words, Elezar thought dryly to himself.

"He did that on his own," Skellan went on, "and may the wethra-steeds over my head strike me dead if I'm lying!"

Skellan held up his arms as if challenging the heavens to do their worst. The witches in the courtyard gazed up at the few gray clouds with expectant expressions. Only a soft breeze stirred and after a moment Skellan let out a sharp laugh.

"So that's that!" Skellan shouted. "Any other complaints you'd like to lay against me for saving your lives?"

Silence settled over the gathered witches.

"Right! Then here's how it is," Skellan announced. "We're free of the violet flame but it means we'll have the grimma to contend with very soon. I mean to fight them and any of you who will stand with me are welcome to share in the glory. Those who can't or won't fight, well, you'd better get yourselves gone, because Milmuraille will be at war, whether we like it or not!"

"Who are you to say, Skellan?" Clairre shouted. "Who made you master of the city?"

Before Skellan even opened his mouth to reply Bone-crusher turned his massive craggy head to Clairre and let loose a bellow like the boom of thunder. Elezar felt the sound rock through his guts and the horses all around went stiff and tremulous. Directly below the troll, Clairre collapsed, clutching her head in an attempt to shield herself from the onslaught of sound and spittle. Witches near her scattered away.

"Enough, Master Bone-crusher," Skellan called and Elezar noted how he gentled the command by stroking the snarling troll's ear. Bone-crusher snapped his immense maw closed but continued to fix Clairre with a glare. She lay wet and motionless for a moment. Then slowly she pulled herself to her knees.

"The truth of it is that I'm Count Radulf's son." Skellan's words carried through the profound silence that had followed Bone-crusher's roar. "I've not lied or misled any of you. I only learned of my parents this morning, but there it is. Count Hallen Radulf died in the grip of the violet flame some days ago and now... I'm your count."

"Is that a good enough answer?" Cire inquired of Clairre, though Elezar sensed that she meant the question for all those gathered round. It also struck him that this was not the first time Cire had heard this news. With Rafale standing at her side, Elezar easily guessed who'd told her but he wasn't certain why. Unless Rafale hoped to use Cire's obvious affection for him to shield himself from the revelations that might expose his duplicity.

Clairre nodded but remained on her knees in the spattered dirt. Merle reach out and helped her up to her feet. Elezar didn't hear what the old woman said to Clairre but she seemed to take some consolation in it.

"Well, that's that then!" Cire proclaimed with a grin. Beside her, Rafale smiled up at Skellan like he was a ham hanging on a hook.

Farther back, courtiers and merchants peered from their coaches to get a better view while the garrison guards gaped at Skellan and his troll with expressions of awe verging on terror. Elezar studied the courtiers and merchants. Invoking wethra-steeds and Bone-crusher served to impress witches, but Elezar didn't think that alone would move the city's most powerful men to put their trust, as well as their troops and wealth, at Skellan's disposal. He wished that Sheriff Hirbe hadn't brought these people to Skellan so soon—before Elezar had even managed to convince the wild witch to put on a proper shirt or shoes.

The door of the armory opened and Elezar saw Kiram lean out to take in the scene. Catching his eye, Elezar offered him a brief wave and Kiram returned the gesture, but then his attention shifted back to Skellan.

"Some of you know this already," Skellan's gaze settled briefly on Rafale, "but for those who don't, I'll tell you all. It turns out that I share blood with the Sumar grimma as well. In the name of peace I intend to send envoys to her sanctum."

A gasp carried through the air at the mention of the Sumar grimma, but Elezar's concern lay more in the practicality of sending an envoy. He wondered if he ought to volunteer. After all he'd made the journey once already—though it had nearly killed him. He started closer to the gathered crowd, aware that Atreau and his pages hung back. From his perch atop Bone-crusher's shoulder Skellan caught sight of Elezar and met his gaze with a delighted smile.

"Lord Grunito!" From high atop Bone-crusher Skellan executed a dramatic half-bow. He should have struck Elezar as absurd but somehow Elezar felt his face warming and he smiled back at the glee in Skellan's expression. "What do you say? Who shall I send to treat with the Sumar grimma?"

"Your envoy will need to be a strong rider who can travel light and fast," Elezar suggested. "They will need to ride hard indeed to reach the Sumar grimma before her forces start their march upon Milmuraille."

"Truly spoken, my man. Fortunately for us, two of the multitude of wethra-steeds set free last night have remained here. They feel their chosen riders are among the folk of this city. So I've decided to invite them down to find their riders."

At Skellan's announcement the air came alive. The word wethra-steed hummed through the surrounding crowd like the buzz of bees. Far back on the street Elezar heard men and women shouting it. A moment later Eski pelted out from the stables, straw falling from her white blond hair.

Javier appeared as well, though he stepped out from the armory apparently just to scowl at Elezar's chest. The concern in Javier's expression struck Elezar as far too intense. Elezar himself studied his shirtfront, expecting to discover some terrible stain. Streaks of ash and dirt marred his shirt but nothing worse. The gash Javier had earlier noticed had already healed to a thin scab. Elezar shrugged at him but had no idea what the arcane hand signal Javier offered in response was supposed to mean.

He'd ask later.

For now Elezar kept close to Skellan. The mention of we-thra-steeds had drawn more of the crowd into the courtyard. All around Sheriff Hirbe and his mounted deputies, curious courtiers pressed in. Merchants with their sea of footmen and varlets also edged into the circle of witches gathered around Bone-crusher. Elezar couldn't imagine the garrison yard ever accommodated such a diversity of people. Certainly street witches wouldn't normally have stood shoulder to shoulder with lordlings dressed in velvet and silk. Even a few Cadeleonian priests squeezed their way forward. As the crowd closed in, Elezar caught bits of conversation and speculation.

"Look at him," a neatly coiffured older man whispered to the young men standing at his side. "He's the spitting image of the count. But where has he been hidden away all this time?"

"Among common street witches, if you believe the story Sheriff Hirbe's telling," one of the young men replied.

The older man nodded. His certainty seemed to impress the two younger gentlemen. Elezar overheard them disseminating the information through the crowd moments later.

He, himself, kept quiet and shouldered his way nearer to Bone-crusher's massive calf.

Skellan didn't seem to take note of any activity down on the ground. Eyes closed, he lifted his bare arms to the sky and a wind rose up around him, spinning through Elezar's hair and tossing aside the velvet caps and plumed hats of the gathered courtiers. Overhead, the silver clouds roiled as if stirred by Skellan's hands. Slowly, a gray wisp of cloud spiraled down between Skellan's arms as if he were pulling a tornado into his embrace.

Then two silver lights flared between Skellan's hands like falling stars and he hurled first one then another down to the flagstones below. The lights crashed to the ground at Bone-crusher's feet like hot cannon shot. The impact rocked through the soles of Elezar's boots. Cire and Rafale staggered. A few courtiers even fell. Smoke rolled up from the blasted stones but didn't obscure the flashing silver hides of two very big horses.

As the smoke thinned across the courtyard, Elezar took in the animals—a mare and a stallion, with eyes as orange as flames, bodies that blazed like quicksilver, and glossy cloven hooves. Each stood at least a hand taller than Cobre and when the stallion barred its teeth, Elezar noted that they were long and sharp as a wolf's. Breezes stirred as they shifted and turned, taking in the gathered crowd. Elezar thought he could see patterns of lightning flickering across the big animals' legs.

While he and the rest of the onlookers gawked at the big animals, Eski let out a cry of pure delight and dashed forward.

"Eski! No!" Elezar shouted but his warning did nothing to slow the girl.

Catching sight of Eski, the silver mare suddenly sprang towards her. Men and women threw themselves clear. Elezar started forward, terrified that the mare would crush Eski, but the wethra-steed drew to a halt just short of the gangly Mirogothic girl. Eski didn't hesitate a moment, throwing her arms around the mare's neck and leaning her whole body into the wethra-steed.

Then the mare knelt before Eski, allowing the girl to climb atop her back. Mounted, Eski laid her head against the mare's arching neck and closed her eyes as if she were lost in some kind of bliss. Oddly the wethra-steed also closed her flaming orange eyes. The two of them remained like that, while everyone around, including the stallion, looked on in silence.

Then Eski lifted her head. Her pale eyes gleamed golden and silver streaked her blond hair. Beneath her the mare's hide seemed to have dulled to a warm gray and her eyes darkened to a soft gold.

"She's called Nottsol, and she stood at the temple gates, imprisoned in stone for a hundred years before you freed her." Eski's voice rose as if carried on a whispering wind. She craned her head up to gaze at Skellan. "For that and this reunion of our spirit, we gladly offer our loyal service to you, Hilthorn Radulf."

"Thank you," Skellan replied. Again he gave that half-bow. "But what of Nottsol's brother?"

Both Eski and the mare turned their heads to regard the stallion. The beast stamped one of his hooves in a manner that reminded Elezar of Cobre when his advances at a mare had been frustrated. A low rumble rose from his mouth sounding like distant thunder.

Eski laughed and again Elezar heard a whispering voice intertwined with hers.

"Well, go get him then," she said. Then she looked back to Skellan. "Rigni is sulking because his other half has not come forward to welcome him."

"But his chosen one is here in the city?" Skellan asked.

"Of course," Eski chirped. "It's his vei to ride with Rigni. Even if he'd been born in the jungles of Yuan, his vei would have called him to this place at this moment. He is here."

Skellan nodded and scanned the crowd, searching through the sea of witches, soldiers, merchants, and courtiers. As he did this, the massive wethra-steed stallion gave one final annoyed grumble and then strode into the crowd, pacing directly toward Sheriff Hirbe and his men. Men and women scurried aside. The sheriff kept close rein on his own nervous mount. The silver wethra-steed only spared a glance at the sheriff before pacing past him to where the young Deputy Magraie sat astride a roan gelding.

The sheriff and all the other deputies stared at Magraie and the young deputy's lean face darkened deep red. The stallion wethra-steed snorted and plumes of white mist rose from his flared nostrils. He glared at the deputy. The young man bowed his head and then glanced to Sheriff Hirbe. The sheriff's heavy sigh carried through the surrounding quiet. Nearly everyone in the entire courtyard now watched the young deputy in silent expectation.

"I'm sorry, sir." The deputy kept his gaze downcast. "I thought they were just dreams... I should have said."

"Sorry doesn't come into it now," the sheriff said. "We each must go when we are called. You have most certainly been called."

"Yes, sir." Deputy Magraie saluted the sheriff then dismounted from his gelding and handed the animal's reins to another of the deputies.

He stepped up in front of the wethra-steed and Rigni lowered himself before Magraie. The young deputy climbed onto the stallion's back and Rigni stood. Instantly the sorrowful expression disappeared from Magraie's face and his eyes lit to a shining bronze. He ran his hands over Rigni's mane and broke into a joyous grin. Silver streaks shot through his dark hair while the stallion's gleaming coat dulled to pewter gray. Rigni turned and cantered back to Nottsol's side, alongside Bone-crusher's knee.

"Hail to you, Hilthorn Radulf!" Magraie saluted Skellan and his words, like Eski's, seemed to be carried on a resonant wind. "Rigni and I swear our service and loyalty to you."

"Thank you both," Skellan replied. He bounded down Bone-crusher's arm like a mountain goat springing down the ledges of a sheer cliff, coming to a stop atop the troll's craggy hand. He waved Elezar closer. Only when Elezar drew near did he spy the signs of fatigue that Skellan doubtless wished to hide from the rest of the gathering. The faintest sheen of sweat shone on his brow and dampened his hair. The palms of both his hands bore red welts. The remaining scrapes and bruises from his previous night's battle looked black against the pallor of his skin.

Still he grinned at the two wethra-steeds and their new riders.

"You know that I mean to send you both to the Sumar grimma," Skellan began. Then he lowered his voice so that both Eski and Magraie leaned forward on their mounts and the wethra-steeds pricked up their ears. "I can't offer you a stone of passage, but Elezar has traveled to the Sumar grimma and he knows the way—"

"I have a stone of passage." Elezar spoke without even really thinking. He'd all but forgotten the stone in the days since he'd returned to Milmuraille.

"You do?" Skellan raised his dark red brows.

"I do. I kept it." Elezar dug the white river rock out from the pocket of his jacket. Its polished surface gleamed like a pearl in his palm as he held it out.

"Eski's aunt gave it to me. I followed a white path of river rocks that lit in its presence…" His journey to the Sumar grimma's sanctum felt like it had taken place a lifetime ago, but now Elezar recollected that Elrath had helped him with the hope that he would prevent a war and keep Eski from becoming embroiled in battle. Now the very same stone promised to send Eski into the very heart of this conflict.

He suddenly wished he hadn't spoken so quickly but Skellan snatched up the stone and held it up to the morning light. For just an instant Elezar thought he saw tendrils of red light curl around the stone. Skellan grinned and then folded his hand around the stone almost tenderly.

"Yes, this is definitely hers. Elezar, you are a gift without end, you are!" Skellan leaned out from Bone-crusher and handed the stone to Eski. "Never stray from the path that this stone offers and remember you and our Magraie are brother and sister now, so protect each other out in the Sumar lands."

Eski and Magraie exchanged an uncertain glance but then the wind seemed to rise around them and Elezar was certain he heard soft voices speaking low in a language he didn't know. Eski smiled and Magraie nodded.

"We'll look after each other," Magraie assured Skellan. "And we'll carry your word wherever you wish it to be heard."

"All right then. You two tell the Sumar grimma that her son sends his greetings and needs her to know that he has sworn himself to the defense of Milmuraille." Skellan spoke slowly and carefully. Elezar imagined he'd been working out this wording for some time. "Her son, Hilthorn, hopes that neither she nor I need shed the blood of our own lineage. I would have peace between out lands and ask her aid in par-laying a peace between Radulf County and her sister grimma." Skellan drew Elezar's hunting knife from his belt, and with a quick motion, caught and cut off a lock of his own red hair. He handed the lock over to Magraie.

"Give her this as proof of who I am and tell her that I wear the signet she forged for me with great pride... I think she must have felt my presence the moment Elezar brought me her ring but still that lock of hair couldn't hurt."

Magraie nodded and clenched the long coil of bright hair in his fist.

Skellan glanced to Elezar. "Anything else you can think of that needs being said?"

"Only that time is short and this must to be resolved before the other grimma arrive," Elezar replied.

"So it is," Skellan agreed. He turned his attention back to Eski and Magraie. "Ride fast."

Then Eski asked, "Is that all then?"

"That's it," Skellan said, shrugging.

"We take our leave and carry your will to the Sumar grim-ma, Hilthorn Radulf." The words came from Magraie's mouth but a low resonant rumble rolled through his voice and Elezar wondered if that wasn't Rigni speaking with him.

Both wethra-steeds turned and in three great strides carried their riders across the courtyard. Then suddenly both sprang into the air. Elezar craned his neck to watch them, noting how their forms flared like shards of glass flashing in sunlight only to vanish into the wind.

Elezar kept his eyes on the sky, tracking the faint distortions that danced on the air like heat mirages, and wondering how he might bring an enemy's wethra-steed down when Skellan leaned close to him.

"What are all these fancy hats doing in the courtyard?" he whispered. "I thought you only sent word to Cire?"

Bone-crusher's hard gaze fell upon Elezar as if mirroring Skellan's annoyance. Did the troll imagine himself as Skellan's guardian or his servant, Elezar wondered.

"I didn't send for them. But the count's courtiers and guild masters are naturally anxious to meet his long-lost heir."

"What am I supposed to say to them?" Skellan muttered.

"What did you think you'd say when you became grimma?" Elezar responded.

"I'd though I'd gloat a bit and... I don't know. This is nothing like I imagined it would be. Look at them all." Skellan's pale eyes shifted as he stole a glance out over the assembly. His frown deepened into a scowl. "They aren't going to give me the respect they'd favor one of their turds, are they? And we need them, don't we? We need their money and soldiers, more than fleas need blood."

"Neither you nor I are fleas," Elezar said. He didn't bother to survey the gathering of nobles and merchants. Neither gilded carriages nor costly raiment intimidated him. He'd been born to such frippery. What he understood, and what he suspected that Skellan did not, was that all the comforts and niceties afforded to the landed and wealthy bred profound desperation in the face of the probable ruin caused by war.

"We need them but remember they need you as well, Skellan," Elezar assured him. "You're their liege lord now. More than that, you're the witch we all saw defeat a demon lord last night. They know the grimma are coming. And they understand that if they hope to retain their properties and prosperity you'll be the one who'll save them."

Skellan nodded but uncertainty lingered in his expression. He ran his hand across Bone-crusher's mossy thumb and the troll bowed his craggy head down over them. The pungent smell of wilderness wafted over Elezar as the troll blocked out the sun overhead.

Shall I crush them and scatter their bodies like kindling, Little Thorn?

Somehow Skellan simply pulled a tired smile at the alarming suggestion.

"No need, Master Bone-crusher. We'll have fighting enough to do later, I think."

Bone-crusher sighed a heavy earthy breath and then straightened, though Elezar noticed the way the troll drew Skellan just a little closer to his rocky chest. Skellan absently caressed the troll's hand but looked to Elezar.

"Can I send them away, then?" Skellan asked. "I have enough trouble before me just returning these witches' children to their natural forms. I'd rather not break my own spell with half the city ogling me."

Elezar considered dismissing the gathered onlookers. How many of the men in the garrison would obey him if he ordered the grounds emptied? Certainly none of the men Sheriff Hirbe had brought were likely to send the sheriff off on Elezar's command—not yet at least.

As deeply as it chagrined him, Elezar realized that he was going to have to approach the sheriff for his help in this matter. No wonder the sheriff had left so easily the night before. Doubtless he'd known that both Elezar and Skellan would need him, if only to discern who among so many officials, merchants, and courtiers could be trusted to support Skellan. Despite months spent in Labara, Elezar possessed only a passing knowledge of most of the upper crust of Milmuraille society.

Atreau, on the other hand, would probably know nearly all of the women and a fair few of the men as well.

"Let Atreau and I speak to the sheriff," Elezar said. "We'll work out who you should allow to call upon you and who can wait. What do you say to a group of nobles, city officials, and merchants being invited to sup with you tonight?"

Skellan paused, scratching his foot as he considered Elezar's proposal.

"Can't it be tomorrow? After I've returned the children to their natural forms I'd like to have a few words with your Javier about the way he's tugging at my spells just now."

"What?" Elezar glanced to the armory but both Javier and Kiram had withdrawn from sight. Elezar lowered his voice. "What's he doing? Do you need me to talk to him?"

"Tugging and nipping. Nothing I can't manage myself." Skellan scratched the back of his hand. "I'd rather you took on the nobles. Javier and I would do better settling this ourselves."

Elezar didn't like the sound of that and for an instant an old reflex to protect Javier arose within him, but then he cautioned himself. He hardly knew enough of magic to guess whether Skellan or Javier presented the greater threat to the other. Nor could he know which of them was in the wrong. Though if he had to put his money on either he'd have guessed that Javier had intruded with a former duke's arrogance upon Skellan's spells.

"I don't think that the two of you need an entire day to have a conversation, do you?"

"No," Skellan admitted. "But a dinner with all these elegant sorts. I need a little time just to…"

Skellan didn't have to finish for Elezar to recognize the extent of his discomfort. And the truth was that none of them were at their best just now.

"It has to happen. But you're right. Another day would give us all more time to take stock of our resources and clean up," Elezar decided. "I'll put them off until tomorrow night."

"Thank you, my man." Skellan favored him with a relieved smile and then reached out, and to Elezar's shock, stroked his cheek. Elezar felt his entire face flush at the contact. God only knew what all these men and women surrounding them must have thought of that. Out of the corner of his eye, Elezar noted exchanges of knowing smirks. Outrage flared through him and he had to stop himself from spinning back on one particularly smug-looking young man and knocking him to the flagstones.

For all he knew the smug lordling was some baron in command of a battle-worthy battalion. Now was not the time or place to take offense.

Elezar bowed back from Skellan and turned away from the embarrassingly open affection in his gaze. Only as he withdrew did Elezar realize that anyone witnessing that brief caress would not be wrong in assuming an uncommon intimacy between himself and Skellan. It wasn't the amused young man, swathed in yellow brocade, who had it all wrong.

It was Elezar himself.

Somehow, before this moment, he'd managed to keep himself from really thinking about it. Glancing past Atreau to his wide-eyed pages, Elezar realized the enormity of his error. He might be standing in Labara but more than a few of his fellow Cadeleonians looked on and now no doubt suspected him of being not only a deviant but a traitor to his country.

It took an immense effort for him to hold his head up high and stride across the courtyard. But if he hadn't let his brother's murderers or the Sorrowlands break him, he certainly wasn't going to give that satisfaction to a crowd of strangers.

Skellan envied the easy way that the sheriff, Elezar, and the dissolute duke of Rauma handled both men-at-arms and the horde of wealthy onlookers. In a matter of minutes the majority of people departed, most smiling as if they'd been paid a high compliment by being evicted from the garrison.

There had to be a skill to such flawless handling of other folk—insights and nuance that struck Skellan as more mystifying than any spell. Magic, he could see and feel—even hear and taste drifting through the air. He reached out with his witchflame and pulled apart the shining little spells that bound young human flesh into animal bodies as simply as he might have unlaced one of Elezar's boots. Far across the city he felt Sammi and Sarl straighten, a little startled, as their kidskin cloaks fell from them. He caught the warmth of their giggles before moving on. His witchflame washed over dozens of other children, freeing them as easily as he blew out a breath.

Even those pesky white sparks that Javier sent winging out from the armory like hungry swifts fell beneath Skellan's will. He might not be able to catch them all, but with a flare of his witchflame, he could burn away those interlopers that alighted upon the threads he'd woven around Elezar. Skellan scowled at the armory and wondered what the Bahiim was playing at. Javier had his own man, but that didn't mean he couldn't wish to claim Elezar as well. Maybe the Bahiim hadn't put the past behind him as much as Elezar seemed to think. Well, he would just have to have it out with Javier. At least that Skellan understood.

Curses and spells. One witch against another, everything settled by pitting the raw power of his exposed soul against another's will. But all these strangers with their fine silks and formalities—with their political interests and private armies— they were a strange language and their manners might as well as have been alien incantations for all that Skellan could understand them.

Was he really supposed to lead these people—or lead anyone for that matter? Nothing in his life had prepared him for such a role and he honestly didn't know how he was supposed to inspire an entire city of strangers, particularly when just glancing around him he could so easily see real leaders already taking charge. How exactly they managed it Skellan wasn't certain.

How could a Cadeleonian duke inspire an entire circle of elegant Labaran men to smile upon him like one of their own and even kiss his cheeks? The white-bearded sheriff shepherded nobles from the grounds as amiably as if they were a docile oxen. Even Elezar, dressed in dirty theater togs, seemed to command respect and admiration with just a word and a glance.

How did they do it?

Skellan glanced down from Bone-crusher's arm and caught Rafale watching him. No doubt Rafale understood every aspect of high society just as he so perfectly manipulated the society of the street witches he stood among now. Cire leaned into him with such a pleased expression that it hurt Skellan to see it. She looked so happy, basking in the Rafale's company. Skellan understood; he'd once imagined Rafale as his lover and faithful friend.

Under other circumstances Rafale would have been the first man Skellan turned to for advice about merchants and nobles. But he'd held that coffer in his hands last night and felt the spells wrought through the gold. Rafale had planned the deaths of every one of the witches he now stood beside.

A betrayal far beyond petty lies and infidelity, that was.

Watching Rafale drape an arm over Cire's shoulder filled Skellan with dismay. How could Rafale have plotted the deaths of all these people and still stand here wearing that charming smile and looking so guileless? Was he so superb an actor or did he truly feel no guilt?

Perhaps he hadn't known what the coffers would do—maybe Bois had kept that from him? Skellan wanted to believe as much but no longer trusted his own judgment in the matter. He ran a hand over the soft moss of Bone-crusher's arm, reassuring himself. Distressingly, it was Rafale who seemed to read his uneasiness and who offered him a reassuring smile.

Skellan wanted to call him out and hear him explain himself but he knew this wasn't the time or place. Clairre and the rest would be only too happy to tear Rafale to pieces before he got out a word in his defense and no matter what Rafale said it would probably break Cire's heart to know that Rafale hadn't thought to spare her when he'd attempted to whisk Skellan away.

No, if he was going to confront Rafale, it would have to be later when they were alone. Then he and Rafale would have it out about those golden coffers.

"Cire was asking me how we should address you now," Rafale called. "Are you still our own Skellan or will you have your old friends address you as Count Hilthorn Radulf?"

Cire wasn't alone in eyeing Skellan uncertainly. Clairre scowled at him while Ogmund squinted up as if meeting him for the first time and trying to fix his features in his memory. Of all the gathered street witches only Navet and Merle beamed at him like proud mothers. Meeting their gazes, Skellan felt suddenly absurd, poised up here over their heads and putting on airs. He wanted to scramble down between them and let them walk him back to the quiet anonymity of their stable.

But that was no way to inspire confidence in anyone, Skellan realized, and Navet and Merle as much as anyone else needed to think that their Skellan knew what he was doing—that he was a match for the grimma's armies.

So Skellan simply offered them a friendly wave of his hand and answered Rafale's question with a grin. "Now, you all know me. I'll answer to any name if I'm being called to supper."

A roll of laughter and relieved expressions rewarded him.

"But you are Hilthorn Radulf," Cire asserted, as if she couldn't quite credit what she was saying herself. "You're the count's firstborn."

Skellan hardly believed it himself but kept his calm as he replied, "I am."

Cire stared up at him like he was a golden plum growing on a branch of her crab apple.

"You'll be expected to join your sister at the Sun Palace." Cire exchanged a glance with Rafale before returning her attention to Skellan. "You wouldn't want to go there alone, would you?"

"For fuck's sake, Cire." Merle shook her head. "Just ask him to get you appointed to the count's court and have done with it, will you?"

Cire scowled at both Merle and Navet, but her own uncle laughed at the comment. Skellan didn't take offense. Cire had never made a secret of her higher aspirations.

"I don't know where I'll go just yet," Skellan answered. "To be honest I've been too occupied with the demon lord and now the grimma to think about palaces. Most likely I'll stay here until the fighting's done. But once that's over you know I'll see right by every one of you who stands up for our city."

At this, Navet gave a decisive nod.

"So what is it you'd have us do for the time being?" Ogmund swung his badger up onto his shoulder and patted its grizzled back like he was burping a baby.

"We must rebuild the city's wards," Skellan said.

"I'm not certain that any of us could raise a ward strong enough to hold off a grimma—not without binding a great creature such as that troll of yours," Merle commented.

Skellan felt Bone-crusher's whole body tense.

"No," Skellan snapped. "None of the wild creatures are to be enthralled again. We'll offer alliances to those willing to stand with us but I'll not allow any of them to be enslaved again."

"It's not as though any of us would truly know how to enthrall a creature so powerful as your Master Bone-crusher in any case," Navet answered with an easy smile. "But it does beg the question, Skellan. How are we to rebuild wards that were laid down in ages before with spells no one any longer recollects?"

Some spells were better lost, Skellan thought, but he didn't say as much. Even he realized that now was not the time to argue over the ethics. Now they needed to be unified and focused on the city's defense.

"We don't need to raise an entire wall of immense wards. Remember when I used all those tiny abandoned incantations to distract the demon lord?" Skellan paused as those gathered nodded and murmured their recollections. "I mean to do something like that again. Light the city with hundreds of little spells that appear to be one immense tapestry of wards."

"So you need us to…?" Cire asked.

"Bless everything you can lay your hands on in the city. Set the place ablaze with spells." Skellan could see it in his mind, a vast ambient glow shining across towers and temples. That radiance would backlight the actual wards that he himself would have to build around the walls of the city. If he wove his spells just right it would all seem as one.

"You think this can truly work?" Clairre wiped her thin nose with the back of her hand.

"Of course it will work," Rafale responded and he offered Skellan one of his dashing smiles. "I believe in our dear Skellan so completely that as of today I am offering up the grounds of my theater for whatever uses he sees fit. And I am myself completely at his service as well."

Skellan knew Rafale's words were too dramatic and his admiring gaze too staged. Still they did set his pulse tripping with a delighted rhythm. The gathered witches appeared impressed by the declaration. Even Clairre.

At Rafale's side, Cire beamed.

"We will all do our part," Cire told Skellan.

"Thank you," Skellan replied and he meant it. Then thinking of the importance of allies he added, "And if any of you happen upon a wild spirit wishing to make its home here send it to me. If the frogwives and cloud imps will keep watch from the air and river the grimma won't have a chance of taking us by surprise."

"Consider it good as done," Merle promised.

Skellan thanked them all again and then in a matter of minutes they'd taken their leave of the garrison. Skellan guessed that only about half of them would bother with blessings—the rest would get straight to packing. Still, half was better than none and he felt certain that between Merle, Navet, Cire, and Ogmund, the spells laid down would blaze true and strong.

But what to make of Rafale's offer—or of Rafale himself? Skellan frowned up at the blue sky overhead. A white cloud imp flitted past like a drifting cloud.

He could too easily remember how glorious it had felt when he'd been nothing but a scrawny beggar boy and Rafale had called him beautiful and fucked him on a feather mattress. For a few weeks he'd stumbled about in a stupor of devotion. But then he'd met Rafale's kind wife and found his happiness at odds with the guilt of eating the pastries she offered while the taste of her husband's cock still hung in his mouth.

As he had learned of the long string of Rafale's dalliances his disillusionment had grown. Yet in some small chamber of his heart affection persisted like a pox. He wanted to trust Rafale and yet he knew he could not.

Another white spark whipped past Skellan's face. He flared his witchflame up, engulfing the blazing Bahiim magic. The sparks stung like a fistful of nettles and filled his mouth with chill of ice. Skellan exhaled a cold breath that reminded him just a little of the demon lord's violet flame. Perhaps Javier's power also arose from another world—most likely a haunted, deathly realm. Two more sparks darted past Skellan only to evaporate as they fell against the wards Skellan had wrapped around Elezar.

"What is that damn Bahiim up to?" Skellan muttered.

Bahiim gather and become trouble, Little Thorn. Does this one need crushing? Bone-crusher asked.

"No," Skellan replied. "We haven't come anywhere near that yet." He gazed up at the troll but Bone-crusher's attention had already shifted. He lifted his big head and drew in a deep breath. The saplings on his back rustled as if tossed by the wind.

There are two little trolls I would see to and river full of fish that I would bring them food from, were I free to do so.

"Certainly. Are you not free, Master Bone-crusher?" Skellan couldn't sense so much as a charm that still restrained the verdant troll.

I would not leave you, if you have need of me. You are so small and these armed men all about you here seem too many. You have only me and your man to look after you.

The almost motherly tone of that made Skellan laugh.

"I can manage," Skellan assured him. "Go on. Tend to the little ones. You and they should eat and drink your fill. I'll still be here when you return."

I could carry you with me, Little Thorn.

"You could, but then how would I settle matters with the Bahiim?"

Bone-crusher's corbelled brow wrinkled.

Have a care with the Bahiim. They walk the paths of the dead and cannot be laid low so easily. Once, long before your time, an army of them came into the far north and made war against the Black Fire. I saw many witches fall then, Little Thorn... Mayhap I should stay—

"You worry too much." Skellan cut Bone-crusher's offer off. "Javier is no army. He's my man's friend."

Bone-crusher scowled again at the armory building but then a pungent wind once more rose from the river and that seemed to decide him.

I will return to you before night falls.

"Good fishing, then, Master Bone-crusher." Skellan slid down from the troll's arm and dropped to the ground. Bone-crusher inclined his massive head and then straightened and in a few steps he'd cleared the courtyard and passed through the garrison gates.

Barefoot, ragged, and bruised, Skellan half-expected to pass as unnoticed among the men-at-arms and garrison guards as he had the night before. But it came as an unnerving surprise when first one than another four of the men he walked past on his way to the armory bowed down as if he were their liege.

Even reminding himself that he was Count Radulf's heir, Skellan felt like some kind of imposter having these men bow. He was still the same dirty street witch they'd ignored the night before. Couldn't they all just go back to that? He stole a glance back over his shoulder to see Elezar and the sheriff standing with one of Bishop Palo's attendant priests. All three of them had been watching his back, he realized.

They weren't the only ones. All across the grounds, sister-physicians, pages, guards, and grooms studied him. An uneasy feeling washed over him. He'd spent a decade hiding from just this sort of thing and in his experience only goose fat pies and winter cherries ought to have inspired such unwavering interest.

Skellan squared his shoulders and continued on his way to the armory, willing himself to ignore the surrounding attention and yet feeling more and more self-conscious with each step he took. At the armory door a weathered guardsman dressed in the count's colors met Skellan's gaze with an expression so like hope that Skellan nearly turned around to see if there wasn't someone behind him. Then the guardsman bowed low and pushed the door open for him, as if it were Skellan's right to enter where he wished without question.

Skellan smiled but said nothing, imitating the entitled assurance that he'd witnessed in both Bishop Palo and the duke of Rauma. When at last he slipped into the shadows of the armory Skellan sagged back against the heavy door.

Inside, narrow beams of light passed through the barred slit windows to illuminate a long gallery of stone walls and half-empty racks of weapons. The shafts of spears and pikes threw long black shadows across the unadorned expanse of the flagstone floor. Skellan felt the solidity of the stones surrounding him. Neither breezes nor magic easily penetrated the still, dim air here.

Then some six yards away a flare of white sparks swirled up, lighting the massive, glossy black barrels of two cannons. The sparks rose near the vaulted ceiling and then hung in the air like newborn stars. Even through the muggy warmth of the armory Skellan felt the deathly chill of those shining lights. He picked out Javier's pale figure beneath the sparks, leaning against a hulking cannon, head bowed.

Kiram's voice drifted up from the deep shadows below.

"That's Elezar's business. You should let it alone."

"Letting it alone is not my strong suit," Javier replied. "And I'm not certain that Elezar even understands what he's getting himself into—" Javier broke off as he caught sight of Skellan.

"He seemed to understand well enough last night." Kiram's reply distorted and echoed slightly. Skellan wondered if he wasn't conversing from inside one of the cannon barrels.

Drawing nearer, Skellan saw that Kiram lay beneath a cannon with dismembered pieces of machinery and tools spread out all around him. A jar of flickering lights flashed and sparked near one of his legs and made the shadow of Kiram's discarded vest seem to shudder like an anxious hare.

"And speaking of what Elezar's gotten himself into, here's Skellan," Javier announced. Then he arched one of his sharp black brows. "Or should I call you Count Hilthorn Radulf, now?"

"Skellan is fine."

Kiram rolled from under the cannon and straightened to greet Skellan. For just an instant Skellan thought the handsome Haldiim man wore a series of pale bandages around his waist. Then he realized that the white bands that stood out so starkly from the dark bare skin of Kiram's lean torso were thick, ragged scars.

Skellan didn't mean to gawk. Even he knew that was rude, but he couldn't look away. What kind of injury left such immense scars—flesh sliced from navel to spine—and how did any man survive afterwards?

Kiram's friendly smile wavered as he followed Skellan's stare. Then he caught up his vest and pulled it on to hide his exposed body. It hadn't been Skellan's intention to make Kiram feel self-conscious but saying so now wouldn't make anything better.

Javier scowled at him. "Is there something you needed?"

"Yes," Skellan snapped back, annoyed to once again find himself in awkward social territory. "I need you to stop picking at my spells."

Javier's gaze narrowed.

"Maybe you shouldn't place them where they're not wanted then." Javier snapped his fingers and a wave of cold white brilliance seemed to burn up from within him, searing his features to shadows and exposing the hollows of a grinning skull.

The hair on Skellan's arms rose and instinctively his witchflame flared around him.

"No Bahiim tells me where I lay my wards," Skellan replied. He didn't want to fight Elezar's friend but the spells that Skellan crafted were to protect himself and his city. He wouldn't compromise them.

"No witch enthralls my friend. I don't care if you are—"

"If the two of you are going to flare up like torches do you think you could do it somewhere further from the gunpowder?" Kiram favored them both with the tired gaze of a man who found himself in the company of imbeciles.

"I wasn't—" Skellan drew his witchflame back into the hollow of his chest. Then he pointed to Javier. "Your man started it. I came here to have a reasonable conversation with him."

"You've bound Elezar to you!" Javier grumbled, though the deathly skull no longer leered up from his youthful features. "What's reasonable about that?"

"He's not your man," Skellan told Javier. "As far as I can tell he never was, so how is this any of your concern?"

"There's a good question." Kiram gave a dry laugh but then just crouched back down beside the barrel of the cannon. He ran his hand along the metal. "This one's scratched and gouged but not cracked..."

"I don't have to be fucking Elezar to want to keep him from being enslaved by a witch." Javier seemed to speaking as much to Kiram's back as he was to Skellan. "He's my friend—"

"He's also not enslaved," Skellan interrupted—because if they were going to fight they should at least both know what it was over. "He chose to be my man—my champion. My life and strength are as bound to him as his are to me."

"So you say, but I've seen the fate of grimma's champions." Javier's dark eyes bored into Skellan with accusation. "They fight and die like animals."

Instantly, Skellan remembered his dream of Elezar bleeding and outnumbered.

Is this how you would use me?

Skellan shook his head to clear it. That vision would never come to pass. He wouldn't allow it.

"I'm not some twisted old grimma with a stone for a heart. Nor is our Elezar a guileless dupe. We're—" Skellan couldn't think of a single word to sum up what he and Elezar might be to one another. Words didn't come into it. And damn Javier for making Skellan think that he needed to justify anything to him. "—We're grown men and what's between us isn't your concern."

"Not even if it costs Elezar his home and title?" Javier demanded. "You can't be so ignorant that you don't know how his fellow Cadeleonians will react when they learn about the two of you."

That thought did take the wind out of Skellan. But then he noticed the smug curve of Javier's lips and realized that the Bahiim was playing a kind of bait and switch with him.

"You picking at my spells has nothing to do with what rumors travel back to Cadeleon or how my Elezar chooses to face them." Skellan took a step closer to Javier. "What I came here for was to get it straight between you and me. You don't undermine my spells, whether I lay them over the stones of my city or the flesh of my people."

Javier's dark brows rose but Skellan went on before the Bahiim could knock him off his course. "I may not be fancy mannered or well-heeled enough for your tastes, but I mean to defend this city and these people from the grimma and their armies. I won't allow you or anyone else to endanger that just because you don't like the look of me."

Oddly, Javier smiled. He glanced to where Kiram had straightened from his study of the cannon.

"I like the look of you just fine, Skellan." Javier paused, seeming to study Skellan's face intently. Then with a resigned sigh he went on, "Hearing you just now, I think you do mean what you say about protecting Elezar and this city. But there's something about you… your wildness, I suppose, that I don't quite trust."

"My wildness? That means fuck all. I'm city bred as the next gutter rat. Nothing of the wilderness about me. You want wild? Try that Mirogoth girl, Eski, who served as your guide. There's a creature that's never known the inside of a house," Skellan replied.

"I don't mean wild in the sense of…" Javier sighed then seemed to take a different track. "Last night you called the Black Fire down into the city you were protecting. You could have killed us all—"

"No, only myself." The memory of raw agony knifed through Skellan but he held it with a kind of pride.

So that killing nothingness had been the Black Fire of legend? No wonder he'd nearly died last night and no wonder that the Bahiim was looking death at him.

Skellan met Javier's gaze and held it.

"What I did last night to destroy the demon lord was desperate, I'll give you that, but the emptiness—that Black Fire—never left my grasp, not even when it was killing me. I held it in me to the end and I would have died before I ever let it loose on Milmuraille."

"But you were willing to take the chance," Javier said.

"And you wouldn't have?" Skellan demanded. "If it had been your friends and family that the demon lord threatened, wouldn't you have done everything—anything you could to stop him?"

Javier looked almost troubled by the question. He exchanged a brief glance with Kiram.

"I would have fought him with all my strength. But to summon the Black Fire?" Javier shook his head. "It wouldn't have even occurred to me to do something so... impossible. And I don't know how it occurred to you. That's exactly what makes me uneasy about you."

"What? That I thought of something you didn't?" Skellan couldn't help his amused grin. "Haven't you ever been outwitted?"

"More often than I would care to admit." Javier cast another brief, meaningful glance to Kiram. "But in those cases I can follow the reasoning back to an origin. I can see the logic in the method. But you and your spells are like... like one of those half-mad stoats that capers and dances through a meadow and seems so, so playful up until just the moment that it rips the throat out of a rabbit."

Skellan wasn't certain if the comparison was a compliment or an insult.

"I believe what Javier is trying to communicate is that you don't seem to do what's expected in a way that one would expected it to be done," Kiram said. "He keeps feeling at your spells because he can't work out what they do or how they function."

"All witches craft spells in their own ways," Skellan said but then he had to concede. "I wasn't schooled by any one coven, so maybe mine are appear more... unique than some."

"Unique?" Javier snorted. "Troll runes and archaic Miro-gothic spliced with tracks of Labaran slang and an incomprehensible pigeon of Cadeleonian blessings and Yuanese curses and that's not even counting all the random rocks. Last night you strung together a couple dirty pebbles and a dog collar to somehow resurrect the Black Fire."

Javier pinned Skellan with a hard, searching gaze. "Since the age of the Old Gods the Bahiim have scoured the world for every shred of that ancient magic to ensure that it would never be resurrected. Some sorcerers and mystics have spent their entire lives attempting to rekindle even a shadow of the Black Fire. Then you—you just summon it back like you're calling a lapdog."

"My intention wasn't to resurrect anything," Skellan defended. "I'm not out to defy the Bahiim or proclaim myself a new god. It just happened."

Skellan didn't know why but this answer inspired a quiet laugh from Kiram and an expression of even greater aggravation from Javier.

"I was there. I saw the stones and the coffer and the collar." Javier narrowed his gaze at Skellan as if trying to look through him. "Early this morning I hunted down more of those topaz pebbles for myself. But there's nothing to them. Nothing at all."

"Exactly. It's nothing," Skellan responded.

"Is that supposed to be some kind of a riddle?" Javier asked. "Are you trying to be clever about this?"

"Clever doesn't come into it," Skellan answered. "If it did, no doubt every cockscomb and playhouse wit could call down the Black Fire. No, it's just as I said. The stones hold nothing." Skellan studied Javier for a moment. "Why are you so keen on knowing how to call the Back Fire anyway?"

"I'm not keen to call it into existence, but it's my duty to ensure that no shred of it remains in this world."

Javier's frustration suddenly made much more sense to Skellan. How was the poor pretty bastard to destroy a spell that was at its very core nothing? Then Skellan remembered the pearl in Elezar's coat pocket and he took a moment to consider both Javier and Kiram. He knew from just breathing the air swirling around Javier that the youthful-looking Bahiim commanded an immense power. He sensed that Kiram was not so common a man either. He obviously understood these Cadeleonian cannons like Skellan understood spells—he also possessed enough skill with mechanisms that he'd warranted the attention of Grimma Naemir and remarkably he'd survived the cold, old witch's attentions when no other man Skellan knew of ever had.

The last time four Mirogothic grimma had threatened Milmuraille they had not been driven back by witchcraft alone. Cadeleonian armies with their solid mechanisms had stood against beasts and curses. Skellan didn't command a Cadeleonian army but perhaps he could get possession of mechanisms.

That was, if he read Kiram and Javier correctly.

From all their talk the day before he knew neither of them had been born to the lives of ragged vagabonds. They traveled between bands of nomadic Irabiim now only because they were wanted men in their homeland. But the two of them had schooled with Cadeleonian dukes and earls. Skellan imagined that in their lives they'd both slept on feather mattresses and dined on suckling pig. Skellan would have wagered a whole duck that they missed their refined comforts and fine dinners.

"What would you be willing to do for me if I could hand a remnant of the Black Fire over to you?" Skellan asked.

Kiram looked up from his study of the cannon's breach. Javier crossed his arms over his chest.

"Do for you in what sense?" Javier asked.

"In the sense of staying here and helping to defend the city," Skellan replied. "Yesterday, Kiram, you spoke of leaving before the grimma arrived."

"I did," Kiram said. "And I still think that would be the wisest course for everyone to take. But particularly us. We aren't citizens of Radulf County—"

"But you could be," Skellan cut in. "You could be much more. You're wanted men in Cadeleon, aren't you? Southern Labara can't be too safe for you either. That leaves you nowhere to make your home but the north. And here there's only Mirogoth wilderness or Radulf County."

"Actually, the majority of maps demonstrate that there's quite a lot of land beyond Cadeleon." Kiram seemed to be answering Skellan but there was something in the way that he looked at Javier that made Skellan think this was some part of an old argument between them. "Even discounting the Salt Islands, there are still the kingdoms of Usane as well as all of the Yuan."

"Our friends and family are in Cadeleon. It makes no sense to travel so far that news can't reach them or us," Javier replied, clearly to Kiram. Then he turned his attention back to Skellan. "Are you telling me that there is a remnant of the Black Fire in this world?"

"There is, and I can give it to you." Honestly he'd be only too happy if Javier took that terrible pearl and destroyed it. Skellan's fingertips ached just at the memory of touching that thing this morning. "But in exchange for handing over the remains of the Black Fire I want you, both of you, to accept..." Skellan scraped at his memory for the term he needed and then recalled Cire. "I want you to accept appointments to the count's court—my court."

A caliper actually slipped from Kiram's hand. He caught the tool before it hit the floor but his expression remained slightly stunned. Javier blinked at Skellan, opened his mouth, and then closed it again without speaking.

"Appointments?" Kiram asked. "You mean that you wish to offer us positions in your court? Paid positions?"

Elezar had assured him that money came with his title. Skellan took a chance and nodded.

"Count's own master mechanist is a title, isn't it?" Skellan asked.

"It is," Kiram replied. "A highly coveted title, in fact."

Skellan grinned. "So what do you say? Are you interested in staying here and helping us? Not just to repair these cannons but to build something—a mechanism that might knock the wind out of the grimma's armies? Something that common folk up on the city walls can deploy without need for magic."

"Mechanisms can't just be whipped up out of thin air," Kiram responded but even as he spoke, Skellan saw a sudden thoughtfulness bloom through his handsome features. Kiram ran his hand over the cannon barrel. "There isn't much time. I would need space and workmen, smiths…" Kiram's blue eyes seemed to actually light up as some inner inspiration radiated through him. "The city foundries would be the place, but we may have to melt down every iron pot and pan we can lay our hands on…"

"Done," Skellan said.

Kiram laughed dryly. "Skellan, I think that count's actual master mechanist will probably have something to say about this. He may already have drawn up plans."

"Count Radulf didn't trust mechanisms or mechanists. He put all his faith in his astrologer and Osier. Every few years there's gossip about visiting scholars that he might appoint to the post but he never does—never did." Skellan corrected himself as he remembered that the man he spoke of was dead. He was now Count Radulf. "I need something up on the city walls that a grimma can't undo with a word."

"I…" Kiram looked uncertainly to Javier.

"If anyone in this world can come up with the weapon you need, it's Kiram," Javier proclaimed.

"Then we have an agreement?" Skellan asked.

Again both of them were quiet, each seeming to contemplate Skellan through the pale shafts of afternoon light.

"You argue just the way you craft a spell, don't you?" Javier said. "I have absolutely no idea how we got to this point from when you first came through the door, but… But yes. If you're willing to offer us sanctuary and income as well as allowing me to destroy what remains of the Black Fire then we have a bargain. I'm willing to stay and defend this city."

Kiram nodded slowly but then cocked his head and eyed Skellan. "What appointment are you offering to Javier?"

"Astrologer?" Skellan offered. "The astrologer's mansion is standing empty and it's a grand house with stables and gardens and all…"

"As a matter of disclosure I must tell you that Javier doesn't know anything about astronomy," Kiram stated. "And he can't do math."

"It's astrology," Javier countered. "Who needs math to peer up at the sky, make a few dramatic gestures, and then murmur something mysterious and vague? 'There are clouds but these will pass and all will become clear then.'"

Kiram laughed and Skellan smiled. With his soft voice and dramatic flair Javier would likely make an outstanding astrologer even if all he did was offer obvious commentary on the weather.

Kiram turned to Skellan and asked, "I don't suppose the astrologer's mansion is plumbed as well?"

"Plumbed?" Skellan had no idea what the word meant but took a guess. "Oh no fears, there's any number of fruit trees that grow in the garden there, I'm sure. If there aren't any plums it shouldn't be too hard to plant some."

Kiram frowned and a rich, deep laughter burst from Javier.

"If all goes well against the grimma then perhaps we could import some of the bountiful plumbing of Anacleto." Javier clapped Kiram on the shoulder. "I imagine Elezar's missed it nearly as much as you have, Kiram."

Kiram ignored him, pointedly focusing his attention upon Skellan. "You have a bargain."

Skellan rocked back on his heels, feeling an odd sense of triumph. He'd managed something like the forging of an alliance. Not so bad for having been Count Radulf for less than a day.

Though as a result he spent the next hour looking on as Kiram leaned over a cannon barrel sketching out the design of a strange new mechanism. Now and then Kiram muttered something that sounded like a string of garbled numbers. Skellan stole a glance to Javier who offered him an amused shrug.

"More math that I know nothing about," Javier stated. "But if you'd like I can concoct an inaccurate weather prediction for you."

"Storms?" Skellan guessed.

"Certainly, of one kind or another," Javier agreed.

Skellan studied him a little while he turned a golden lotus charm through his hands.

"You don't have any crows that I've noticed," Skellan said at last. "I thought all Bahiim kept crows."

"Not all. The masters of many Bahiim choose to forsake their rebirths and remain with their students to aid them. But my master isn't dead so all those who instructed him remain with him as his crows."

"You mean their souls?" Skellan asked.

Javier nodded.

"It's a great sacrifice." Javier dropped his charm, letting it fall on its gold chain against his chest. "But some Bahiim are dedicated enough to protecting this realm that they forfeit new lives."

Skellan tried to imagine abandoning his flesh entirely and living only through the fluid blaze of his witchflame. Never to touch nor taste or feel anything of the physical world. He couldn't imagine it. The Bahiim truly were strange, he decided. Though Javier was obviously not without his charm and wit.

Then Elezar came through the armory doors and Skellan forgot entirely about the prospect of souls drifting from bodies and the realms of the dead that the Bahiim traveled. The sharp ray of sun lent Elezar's strong jaw and hooked nose a chiseled appearance and cast his eyes into deep shadows. His hair looked damp and Skellan wondered if he hadn't indulged in yet another dangerous dip in wash water.

He called out to Elezar and after they exchanged greetings he asked Elezar to turn the black pearl buried in his pocket over to Javier's keeping. Javier took the pearl and rolled it over in his palm. Skellan didn't know what he felt from the thing. He wouldn't have touched it himself any more than he would have grasped a white hot poker.

"I see," Javier murmured. "This I will lay to rest beneath the Old Road."

Elezar scowled at the pearl but made no comment. Instead he turned his attention to Kiram's plans.

"These aren't cannons," Elezar said.

"No," Kiram replied. "Cannons we can repair from what we have here and hopefully add to them by stripping some from ships. This mechanism is one that the count has just commissioned. These are lighter and will demand less time and ore to build."

Elezar frowned at the fine lines and Haldiim notes that Kiram had scribbled all across the weathered parchment. Skellan peered at the design as well but couldn't make much sense of what he saw. Some little part looked almost like a bellow.

"Will that work?" Elezar asked.

"It had better," Kiram replied. For the first time Skellan recognized absolute assurance in Kiram's expression. "I'd hate to lose my position as master mechanic to Count Radulf on my very first job."

"Master mechanic, eh?" Elezar glanced back over his broad shoulder to Skellan.

"I've given Javier the court astrologer's position," Skellan informed him.

Elezar turned back to study Skellan, a slight rueful smile curved his mouth. "For someone who had no idea how to be a count you're certainly assembling your court quickly enough."

Skellan didn't know what to say. He wasn't even certain if Elezar meant the comment as praise or criticism.

Perhaps Elezar read something of his uncertainty, because he added, "It's good that you're beginning to act as the count. Now I think you just need to put a little effort in trying the look the part as well. You need a bath and raiment that's more suitable your new station."

"A bath?" Skellan drew himself back from Elezar's grasp out of instinct. He'd allowed his Cadeleonian to dunk and soak him once while in a dog's body but a second washing struck him as almost reckless. Out of the corner of his eye he noticed Javier's cool expression curl into an amused smile. If Elezar asked it of him, Skellan had no doubt that Javier would assist him to wrestle Skellan into some water trough.

"Are you thinking of bolting from the threat of washing?" Elezar sounded incredulous and appeared as amused as Javier. Even Kiram looked up from his work to study Skellan like he was some sort of curiosity in a glass case.

Skellan guessed that his intention was all too clear from his expression of dread. Still he attempted to play it off.

"Not at all. But perhaps it can wait," Skellan said. "I need to build my wards around this garrison before I can expand them out over the rest of the city and that will mean a mess of dust and sweat. Could the... bath wait?"

Elezar considered for a moment, his expression skeptical. "It could wait, but you will need to be presentable by tomorrow evening."

"Of course," Skellan replied, though he suspected that he wasn't convincing anyone of his willingness to submit to a washing. Still he decided to take advantage of the respite. "I'd best get to work. I'll see you later, my man."

Skellan quit the armory at a quick clip but one that he hoped didn't betray his dread. Outside, he found his way to a staircase leading to the top of the wall surrounding the garrison. Despite his awareness of his altered rank and the deferential manner of the men standing guard, Skellan still felt like a sneak thief invading the space of the watchmen's posts. He couldn't keep himself from slinking across the granite flagstones as he peered down upon the grounds below.

Wagons and carriages rolled through the huge portcullis and groups of folk in liveries and common dress seemed busy unloading mountains of furnishings, tapestries, and carpets. Workmen and maids hauled dressers, chests, and long mirrors into the headquarters like streams of ants ferrying their spoils into their hill. Skellan wondered if all this finery could belong to Elezar. Did his man travel with an entire kitchen staff and great barrels of beer? It seemed unlikely.

Skellan noticed the sheriff directing a group of men in scarlet liveries. Then Elezar appeared from the armory. The two men greeted each other, and following the direction of the sheriff's indications, Skellan realized that the sandy parade grounds of the garrison now held at least another fifty troops. Something in the way Elezar observed them made Skellan think that they were now under his command.

Then Elezar looked back from his survey of the troops to where Skellan stood gawking down at him. Caught out doing nothing, Skellan pretended to make an arcane sign over the stones nearest him and then ducked down below the line of Elezar's sight. Briefly he gazed off to the northeast where Ylva's witchflame streamed up into the distant clouds like an orange geyser. Skellan wondered what she was up to, but even he wouldn't be so foolhardy as to cast his witchflame so great a distance from his body in an attempt to spy on her. Perhaps luring him out so far that she could snatch his soul from his flesh was exactly the point of her display in the clouds.

He couldn't know. All he could do was be prepared for whatever came.

Skellan turned his attention to the real labor of laying new wards in stone that had never known a spell. He flexed his feet against the granite and sank his witchflame down to the cold mineral beneath him. His will spread like a spill of red ink, curling and pooling through the rock, making it his. Skellan leapt to the next patch of cold stone and again impressed the heat of his soul and the intensity of his drive into the rock, making it just a little less inanimate, more alive and all his own.

Stepping, bounding, and skipping in his own rhythm Skellan circled the entire wall twice, driving his will deep into the granite and down to the cobbles that filled the garrison courtyard. The stones warmed, as if heated by his hammering pulse and behind each of his footsteps a scarlet spell lit up like an ember catching fire. He felt only distantly aware of the sun sinking across the sky and Bone-crusher returning to the garrison. His witchflame and all his senses flooded the stones, leaving only a red thread tying him to his aching body. But steadily his strength drained and even the slender thread holding his flesh and soul wavered. Skellan pulled his witchflame back and found himself stumbling and staggering over his own sweat-damp footprints. His legs shook and his arms hung nearly as emaciated as those of a corpse. He tottered to a stop, shaking with ravenous hunger, exhausted but also proud of his accomplishment.

Beneath him the garrison wall burned with his wards and the stones warmed at his touch. The garrison knew him now. Skellan sank to his knees and ran his hands over a block of the dark gray rock. Soldiers in Labaran uniforms passed him as they made their rounds guarding the wall but Skellan paid them little heed and concentrated instead on how their steps reverberated to him from far across the grounds. Reaching deep he sensed mice scurrying across the rock as well as some man beyond the stable pissing on the wall. On a wicked impulse Skellan called up the smallest spark and let it course across the matrix of stone to flicker up the stream of urine.

A startled yelp rewarded Skellan.

"Piss on my wall…" Skellan mumbled to himself. He started to rise to his feet but found himself too tired to bother. Better to just nap here. He closed his eyes and ignored the ache of his hungry stomach.

Then a strong hand shook his shoulder. Skellan recognized the tenderness of the touch and rolled over to gaze up at Elezar. Skellan had been so long and so deep in the dark lattice of stones that he felt like a bit like a mole suddenly brought above ground. Elezar's towering form looked like a column of black marble backed by the brilliant red, gold, and green streaks of a vibrant sunset. Skellan blinked at the beautiful, bright sky and then looked to Elezar. He soothed Skellan's eyes and tired mind.

"You wouldn't have another sausage in one of your pockets, would you?" Skellan asked on the off chance that he might be so lucky twice.

"I've got better to offer tonight." Elezar crouched down beside him. The firelight of the torches on the watch posts lent a ruddy hue to his tanned face. He smelled of leather, sweat, and straw. "Can you stand and walk to the mess hall or shall we repeat last night with me slinging you around like a sack of onions?"

"Onions sound delicious… fried in duck fat… or with sausages…" Skellan's mouth began to water at the thought. He roused himself enough to push to his feet. Elezar rose easily beside Skellan but then frowned at him.

"Something wrong?" Skellan wondered if he didn't have dirt all over his face from lolling on the ground. He considered wiping it away but the motion didn't seem worth the effort.

"You look like you've wasted away." Elezar reached out and

touched Skellan's chest but then with a glance back at the men standing guard he withdrew his hand. His expression turned almost angry. "What are you doing to yourself?"

"Nothing that a few good meals won't undo. Never fear." Skellan scratched his sunken belly. He'd been far more gaunt in his life and he'd seen other witches in worse condition after working easier magic. All in all he felt rather proud of the flesh he'd managed to retain. Still, it would have been a lie if he'd claimed that hunger didn't gnawed at him painfully. He'd happily have eaten a cat's corpse if there had been one lying on the ground. When this emaciated, his few restrictions on what constituted food vanished. He'd eaten river clay more than once just to fill his belly.

But today he hoped he might claim something more nourishing.

"You said something about a better feed than even this morning's?"

"I did. Lady Hylanya Radulf sent cooks and stores from Count Radulf's Sun Palace." Elezar started for the stairs that led down to the grounds then paused to glance back. "Come along before you wither and drop like a damned autumn leaf."

Skellan snorted at the idea and managed several fast strides to bound past Elezar. He lost a little speed on the steps but Elezar's steady tread behind him kept him from slumping down for a rest.

On the grounds the perfume of meat and spices curled around him and drew him into the headquarters. Dazed, he took little note of the elegantly uniformed men standing guard at the doors. He hardly registered the gleaming furnishings or the costly candelabras filled with beeswax candles that provided illumination for the wide halls.

Lengths of gold cloth covered the tables and red banners depicting snarling wolves hung from the walls, but Skellan took little note of anything but the overpowering aroma of food. Only the veritable army of men in various uniforms seated at the tables brought him up short. He wondered where he might squeeze in unobtrusively. How much of their food could he lay claim to before one of them took offense?

Elezar stepped in behind him and startled Skellan with a bellow that echoed across the mess hall.

"Attention!"

All at once the hundred or more men looked to the doors and silence filled the large chamber. Then all the men rose to stand. Skellan glanced over his shoulder to Elezar. It struck him as a little bullying to demand hungry men break off their meals and acknowledge him, but likely Elezar wished to remind the men that he now commanded the garrison.

Skellan started to edge back but Elezar blocked his retreat. Then a roar rose up from the gathered men. "Hail Count Radulf!"

The words boomed over Skellan with a stunning report. Feeling like a dullard, he belatedly realized that Count Radulf was now his title and that these men stood at attention for his sake.

"What do I do?" Skellan whispered as the echo of voices died down.

"Walk to the head table directly in front of you and take the carved chair at the center. I'll be on your right." Elezar spoke softly and close to Skellan's ear. The sensation of his breath tingled over Skellan's skin, though the forceful forward nudge that followed struck Skellan as less charming.

Having so many soldiers observe his progress filled him with a nearly irresistible urge to hunch and slink his way between the ranks of men standing at attention. But he knew Elezar wouldn't have done any such thing and he doubted that many other nobles would have either. Skellan squared his shoulders and did his best to stride, straight and tall, to the table and take his seat. Elezar followed him and once he'd reached Skellan's side he ordered the men to return to their seats. The men surrounding them sank back to their chairs though their voices remained subdued and many stole side-long glances to where he sat at the head table. Elezar surveyed the men before with an assessing gaze. Then he dropped down into the chair to Skellan's right. He leaned back as if he might kick his feet up onto the table but then seemed to think better of it and straightened. Moments later a strapping dark-haired youth carried a platter heaped with food from the kitchen. Dishes of eel, goose, and duck delighted Skellan as did the heaps of roasted nuts, creamed spinach tarts, and slabs of bread and butter.

The youth offered the cook's apologies along with some explanation about the time required to stoke the kitchen fires and roast piglets. None of this sank in to Skellan. He simply ripped into the rich fare, gulping it down like the starving man he was. Elezar gave the youth a reassuring reply and accepted the serving of table beer proffered to him by another kitchen boy.

Skellan devoured two of the three eels and took fistfuls of the nuts. He ate slices of bread but then helped himself to a great chunk of butter. As he fed he felt his bones and muscles growing dense and flooding with strength. The flesh of his forearms filled in before his eyes and his desiccated skin recovered its natural luster.

He wrenched a leg from the roast goose in front of him and tore into the fatty, rich meat. He didn't think he eaten this well even when he'd lived in the sanctum.

"You know, there is a place setting for you," Elezar commented.

Skellan glanced down and noted the little dish and varied array of silverware but decided that this was not the day to test his patience with spindly forks and dainty spoons. He made quick work of the rest of the leg and licked the salty grease from his fingers. Elezar watched him with an expression Skellan couldn't quite read.

"Maybe later you can teach me how to use all these little things, but right now I'd rather just eat the way I know best." Skellan snatched up a thick hunk of smoked eel, laid it across a slice of buttered bread and then gobbled it down in a few bites.

Elezar took up his silverware and served himself a four slices of duck as well as spinach, nuts, and goose. He used his silver with an expert ease that fascinated Skellan and for an instant delayed his realization that he'd been eating from serving dishes as if they were all his own.

"I'm sorry—"

"Please, eat all you need, Count Radulf. I'm heartened to see you recover so quickly from your exertions." Elezar cut him off then added much more quietly, "You shouldn't apologize to me in front of the men. I'm in your service."

Skellan nodded but then tore free the second goose leg and placed it on Elezar's plate. That won him a smile.

"I suppose you'll learn a few table manners someday," Elezar told him.

"Mayhap after we've defeated the grimma, you can teach me how to present myself as elegantly as your duke," Skellan teased.

"Maybe." Elezar's expression turned unduly troubled.

Skellan wondered if it was the thought of the grimma or if it was the idea of the time after that bothered him. The time when Elezar would leave Radulf County and return to Cadeleon felt far off and yet too near at hand.

Skellan downed two more slices of oily duck breast and then indulged in the surprisingly spicy creamed spinach tarts. At last, relieved of his rapacious hunger, he leaned back in his chair, settling into a lazy sense of satisfaction. He studied Elezar's deft manner with knife and fork. The man ate so neatly. Skellan wondered how long Elezar had practiced to master all the small motions of turning the tines and blade, sliding the tiny edges across, between, and around each other to make it all appear so effortless. He considered his own setting of silverware but couldn't imagine himself managing more than scooping up stew with one of the spoons.

"If I can't manage manners perhaps I will have to change myself into a hound again and play at being your kept creature in Cadeleon," Skellan suggested.

Elezar laughed.

"You are a thousand times more suitable as a man than a dog." Elezar glanced to him from the corner of his eyes and again lowered his voice. "And I wouldn't be half so happy to have a dog share my bed."

"When you put it like that I suppose there will be nothing for it but to master all this tiny cutlery, then." Skellan found it funny how little it took to hearten him today. Just a glance and a whisper and he felt as if he could accomplish most anything. Half of it he supposed arose from the relief of actually surviving his battle against the demon lord. He settled a little more in his chair and let his eyes fall closed.

"Is the count asleep, Lord Grunito?"

Skellan recognized the serving boy's voice but didn't bother to open his eyes.

"No, I'm just…" Skellan drifted, unsure if he'd completed his statement. He thought he heard dishes clinking and clattering. "I'm just resting for a moment…"

"Lady Hylanya sent furnishings from the Sun Palace for the suite upstairs but it's not completely cleaned up yet," Elezar informed him.

"We already have a room." Skellan pried his eyes open and noted that the mess hall looked nearly empty and the many candles had burned lower than he would have expected. He must have dozed off.

"That barren little chamber certainly isn't worthy of Count Radulf," Elezar informed him. Skellan couldn't help but snicker, thinking of the far more squalid domicile he'd claimed at the Rat Rafters. He'd been fine with that room. Certainly he didn't need something so grand as a suite.

"I like our little room," Skellan told him. Honestly, the chair he occupied suited him well enough right now. The padded leather accommodated his bony ass and sharp shoulder blades nicely.

"It will have to do for tonight," Elezar replied.

"Any room will serve so long as I have you in it with me." Skellan cracked his eye open in time to catch Elezar's fleetingly flustered expression and then drifted off again, smiling to himself.

Elezar woke early with a ripple of anxiety. He'd dreamed of the barrow again but the memory had distorted. He, not his brother, had been attacked and mutilated, while another man lay bleeding in a heap of red hair and dog skin.

Elezar's hand clenched against Skellan's chest. He felt ribs rise and fall against his fingers and warm skin lay beneath his palm.

Skellan was fine. They were both safe... for the time being at least.

Faint light edged in beneath the window shutters and lent a soft glow to the simple room. The first morning bell hadn't sounded yet but Elezar felt certain that its toll wouldn't be long off. The crow of a rooster was the only sound that carried from across the garrison grounds but Elezar caught the distinct perfumes of wood smoke and baking bread drifting from the kitchens. The new day was already underway and a multitude of tasks awaited him.

Elezar rolled onto his back and beside him Skellan made a disgruntled sound but then curled his arms around himself and settled back to sleep. Elezar sat up but paused, taking in the sight of his own body stretched alongside Skellan's. Their closeness felt monumental and dangerous and yet what was it really but two men sleeping in easy company? What harm did it really do anyone?

Elezar touched Skellan's cheek lightly, stroking his red gold stubble. He'd need to shave before tonight's formal dinner but Elezar did like the look of him like this. A certain roughness suited Skellan. Or perhaps that was simply how Elezar had grown accustomed to him appearing. As Count Radulf, Skellan would likely have to change some: polish his appearance and manner. Elezar didn't know why but he found the idea somewhat disconcerting.

The sound of bells ringing from far across the city brought Elezar's thoughts back to more immediate concerns. He rose quietly, rinsed himself at the basin on the writing table, and then dressed from his traveling trunk, which Atreau had sent from Bishop Palo's townhouse. His own clothes felt familiar and distinctly Cadeleonian, though Elezar found that they didn't quite fit him any longer.

Still he couldn't go on wearing a Labaran theater costume and expect to command much respect from the men now serving the garrison. Elezar tightened his belt. He'd regain the weight he'd lost in the Mirogoth lands soon enough.

He left Skellan to sleep. Though his first course of action was to assign two men recommended by Sheriff Hirbe as Skellan's guards. The two stocky Labarans had served as personal guards to Skellan's father and both struck Elezar as intensely loyal to the Radulf family as a whole.

With that done Elezar took a brief breakfast and then set to work integrating the assorted Labaran militias and the ragged remnants of the Cadeleonian cavalry into a unified force. He quickly decided that all commands would be issued in Labaran, since the majority of the troops spoke Labaran natively and the Cadeleonians all possessed some degree of fluency from living day-to-day in Milmuraille.

Elezar soon discovered that those who had rebelled against Commander Lecha's corruption belonged to a single cavalry unit, led by a captain called Tialdo. The captain's family had lived in Milmuraille for five generations and owned the Cadeleonian language printing press, which produced broadsheets as well as books. Even haggard, gaunt, and ragged, the captain obviously inspired his men's respect. Elezar didn't forget that Captain Tialdo had already roused his men to mutiny against one commander, so he went to trouble to sound the captain out for any sign of resentment at the thought of taking orders from a man twenty years his junior. Fortunately, Elezar's reputation and noble rank went a long ways towards offsetting his youth. The fact that Elezar had freed the captain and his men from imprisonment and then kicked down a door to rescue the captain's daughter seemed to have made a more powerful impression upon all the Cadeleonian troops than even his suspicious relationship with Skellan.

For the time being at least, they appeared eager to accept Elezar's command and willing to drill with the new Labaran troops. The expertise of the Labarans with their pikes and swords brought out the best sort of rivalry in the Cadeleonian cavalrymen and vice versa. When Javier joined them out on the sandy practice grounds, Elezar and he fenced as they had at the Sagrada Academy. In the years since then, they'd both grown faster and more practiced and much more quick to ignore form and cheat a little. As Elezar parried Javier's blows and drove in with his own thrusts, the memory of his schoolboy attraction rose like the dust swirling around their feet. The longing that had once seemed painfully intense now felt nostalgic and naïve in comparison to the reality of adult desire that he shared with Skellan.

At last, Elezar won their bout by exploiting the moment Kiram appeared upon the grounds and drew Javier's attention. Javier took the fall with a laugh.

Elezar offered his hand and drew Javier up to his feet. The men surrounding them cheered. Afterwards it felt easy and natural to assign the troop practice roster and continue sparring with his captains. Javier took the opportunity to exhibit his and his stallion's prowess in the arena. Cavalrymen drew around him while Kiram struck up a conversation with fellow archers and then the few gunners in the garrison. Though throughout it all Elezar couldn't help but steal the occasional glance to where Bone-crusher slept. The troll shifted and his shadow stretched across the grounds like a mountain's. They would need more men than even these if they were going to defeat creatures as enormous as trolls. Still this was a better start than Elezar had dared to hope for.

By the time Sheriff Hirbe arrived to introduce Elezar to the captains under his command—the fire guard as well as the city guards in charge of the wall, waterways, and harbor of Milmuraille—Elezar felt very much at ease in the company of the men in the garrison. His men saluted him as he passed them as if they had always done so and at the gates of the port-cullis the guards wished him a safe return.

Three hours later Elezar rode through a half-empty dock-side street. Columns of dust rose in his wake. On either side of him, bobbing ships and rambling warehouses whipped back from the line of his sight. He grinned as Cobre carried him ahead at full gallop and cool wind poured over them. Elezar felt the stallion's joy at exerting himself reverberating through his own bones and muscles. For an unguarded moment he exalted in the simple pleasure of riding, fast and unfettered, where he would.

Cart horses and dock workers alike stared as Cobre made a show of clearing the remnants of a fallen bell tower in a soar-ing leap. Earlier, near the west gate of the city wall, Cobre had been shy of the fallen towers they'd crossed, but as they had traveled the stallion had grown accustomed to the spills of blackened rubble. With only a dozen of the city's hundreds of bell towers still standing the burned ruins were a common sight.

"Show off," Elezar whispered to the horse but he wasn't displeased to have so quickly captured the full attention of the guards manning the dock's high tower. They let him pass at just the mention of his name. Elezar took himself up to meet with the captain of the harbor guard—just as he'd already met with the three captains in charge of the city's north and east gates. He left Cobre hitched to a post near an appreciative mare. One of them might as well enjoy the opportunity to so-cialize. Sheriff Hirbe had in fact stayed behind at the east gate with the youngest of his captains to play the game of crowns they apparently indulged in every week.

Inside the high tower Elezar didn't bother much with small talk, nor did the captain of the harbor guard. This captain, like the other two, knew that when an attack came it would fall first and hardest on them and their troops. Chitchat concerning the weather and mustache wax wouldn't alter that.

In this case mustache wax proved even less likely of a distraction since Captain Wirret of the harbor guard turned out to be a sun-beaten blond woman.

Elezar took a moment to come to terms with that—reminding himself that the grimma were women and their sex hadn't stayed them from commanding armies or killing any number of men quite efficiently. Something in the captain's stern demeanor reminded Elezar of his own mother. She'd ruled the Grunito lands in everything but name for all of Elezar's life.

Still Elezar couldn't keep himself from offering her the partial bow he would have executed for any young woman of good breeding. The captain smiled at him; she looked to be a decade his elder.

Elezar informed her of the number of new men-at-arms that she could expect to add to the ranks of those already patrolling the dock and river. The captain shared her maps with Elezar and promised to send the best six of her watch up the river to scout ahead for the advancing line of the grimma's armies.

"They may have a river wyrm in their thrall if the stories of Grimma Ylva are true," Captain Wirret said.

"They may," Elezar conceded. He knew of wyrm only from myths but after all he'd seen last few days he wasn't about to discount the threat of their existence. "We'll need to recruit whale harpooners to patrol the river. Hire them and I'll see to their payroll."

"Here's me not arguing with a Cadeleonian gentleman's right to take the bill, then." She feigned a curtsy and then she and Elezar both laughed.

Then a movement outside the window caught Elezar's attention. A dark green mass broke the surface of the river.

"And we aren't without great creatures of our own." Elezar pointed out the window to the far shore where Bone-crusher rose from the swirling current. The troll dragged the limp body of an immense water serpent behind him, and after crouching down on the bank, he tore into the serpent with his rocky teeth, devouring both flesh and bone.

"War makes for strange allies," the captain said.

"It does indeed."

Elezar offered his goodbyes, leaving the captain to watch Bone-crusher eat while he made his way back to the garrison to face his own dinner and the disconcerting alliances that might be forged there.

"But I've already had a bath!" Skellan objected as Elezar escorted him upstairs and through the doors of a bedroom suite on the second story of the garrison headquarters.

Just entering the room Skellan felt as if he was trespassing. He did not belong in such a place among such costly goods. A dressing table and inlaid wardrobe filled half the large chamber. Just beyond two standing screens Skellan sighted the massive bed and brocade chairs that took up the other half of the chamber. Then he took a gander at a large gilded tub standing on ornate feet and filled with steaming water. It occupied a sunlit corner of the room and appeared to have arrived with two servants of its own.

The immaculately dressed and extravagantly mustachioed young men stood to the side of the tub, tending a cart loaded with a worryingly unfamiliar variety of concoctions and implements.

Skellan frowned at Elezar.

"I've endured two baths already if you count the washing you gave me after we first met at the stable."

The two Labaran men looked up from their bottles and Skellan took in the distinct scents of spice perfumes and musk oil. The men's red uniforms identified them as servants of Count Radulf, but Skellan had no idea what they were doing here in the garrison or when they'd arrived. Elezar seemed to take in their presence without concern.

"That was more than a month ago," Elezar reminded Skellan. "A little soap and warm water isn't going to kill you."

"It could!" Skellan twisted in Elezar's grip to face him. "I could contract leech fever or bath-cough or, or—"

"Or you might not stink like the king of a vulture's ass," Elezar said. Skellan scowled at him but that only served to bring a slight smile to Elezar's harsh face.

"I don't stink," Skellan declared. But then he thought of a better argument. "The smell of me certainly didn't put you off last night."

Elezar's tanned cheeks colored but he didn't release Skellan.

"I don't think much of anything would have put me off you last night," Elezar whispered. "But you're not spending this evening with just me. You're going to be dining with nobles. Lords and ladies, the likes of your father's chamberlain and your half-sister, Lady Hylanya."

The idea of his sister—the fact that he suddenly had a sister—took Skellan off guard. Count Radulf's daughter was famous throughout the county. Skellan could remember the feel of her serene profile stamped on coins he'd filched. In taverns he'd often heard her name spoken warmly by men prone to fantasize about elegant girls and their immense dowries. A wave of dissonance rolled through Skellan at the thought of occupying the same room as the count's daughter, much less sharing a bloodline.

Elezar spun him about and gently pushed him up to the side of the tub. "The least you can do is show them the courtesy of rinsing the sweat, dirt, and medical balms off yourself."

"Lady Hylanya is coming here to meet me?" Skellan said it more to test the idea against his own feeling of uncertainty than for the sake of conversation.

"She's here already. She arrived with her entourage and doesn't seem likely to leave until she's seen you. The duke of Rauma is keeping her entertained for now but even he can only provide so much distraction. Particularly with such a large retinue attending the lady." Elezar offered Skellan a wry smile. He drew the dog skin cloak from Skellan's shoulders and handed it off to one of the servants. "She brought the entire wardrobe that Count Radulf had apparently intended for you."

"A wardrobe?" Skellan repeated. "You mean more togs than I'm already wearing?"

"And then some." Elezar nodded. "I took the liberty of choosing a few of the more simple pieces for this evening."

Elezar indicated the swaths of shining red silk and brocade stacked neatly atop a gold filigree dressing table. Skellan had hardly paid any attention to the costly mass of fabrics when he'd entered the room but now he noted the count's motif of scarlet wolf heads adorned many of them. He felt certain that Commander Lecha would not have left the costly table behind, so it must have accompanied the clothes.

"Looking through the wardrobe, I'd say the tailors, milliners, and cordwainers received very accurate measurements of your height, build, and foot shape."

Skellan frowned. "How?'

"Your friend Rafale would be my guess," Elezar replied. A brief expression of distaste crossed his harsh face but then vanished. "You should get in your bath before the water goes cold."

"Why are there two men standing there behind us?' Skellan asked him in a whisper.

"Your dressers. Brought by your sister." Elezar, too, spoke quietly though he appeared somehow amused to be doing so.

"I don't need one fellow much less two to pull my pants up for me."

"You're going to be wearing more than just pants, I hope. They'll help you with the slashing of your doublet, lacing your boots, and whatever else you should require. And before you argue, keep in mind that all gentlemen of any rank keep at least one personal dresser—"

"Where's yours then?"

"They're back at my home, where, if I were attending a formal supper, I'd expect them to see that I was presentable for my guests."

Skellan wasn't certain that he entirely believed Elezar. He seemed far too wary of his attraction to other men to glibly allow a couple of them to handle his naked body. He struck Skellan as far more comfortable living out of his saddlebags.

But then, Skellan had only known him in his role as a duke's varlet. Who could say how differently Lord Grunito lived in comparison to Skellan's own Elezar.

He eyed the masses of rich cloth again. Materials enough to dress him twice over and Skellan only recognized the barest of them as clothing. He wondered if Elezar really knew about all of this or was having him on.

"What are those short pants?" Skellan pointed to the gauzy silk.

"Those would be your underclothes," Elezar supplied.

"That next to them?"

"Embroidered hose, which will probably look quite fetching on you," Elezar said, sighing. "That is, if you ever do deign to wash."

Skellan scowled at Elezar but not with any real anger and Elezar obviously saw through it. A slight smile curved his mouth.

"Do you want me to throw you in the tub?" Elezar inquired.

"No." At least not in front of these two servants. "Fine. I'll bathe."

Skellan loosened his belt and slid his dirty breeches to the floor. He didn't miss the way Elezar's eyes moved over his naked body or the slight flush that colored his face when he realized that Skellan was grinning back at him. The tub wasn't so small that they couldn't both entertain themselves in its steaming waters.

But to Skellan's dismay Elezar started towards the door.

"Where are you going?" Skellan called.

Elezar stopped and turned back. "I need to assign watch duties and make certain my garrison captains know which new men are serving them now. We've already absorbed an influx of sixty new men-at-arms from the count's holdings. If tonight goes well, we'll need to be prepared to house and integrate even more men. At the very least I'll need beds for them. I should speak with the captains of the city gates as well."

"Oh." Of course he would be busy. They could be at war in a matter of weeks. The thought awoke a restless anxiety in Skellan himself. He ought to be out on the city wall building his wards, not standing up to his shins in a tub of perfumed water.

"Do you truly think that this supper is the best use of my time?" Skellan asked. "If I left now I could begin work on the gates before—"

"The gates will be there tomorrow," Elezar replied. "Right now dinner is more important. You need allies and supporters, you understand that, don't you?"

Elezar waited in the doorway, studying him. Both the servants hovered beside the bath like anxious geese.

"You know I do. If I didn't I wouldn't have appointed your Javier and Kiram to court positions, would I?" Skellan sank down into the water. One of the servants startled Skellan almost out of his skin by running a washcloth over Skellan's bare back.

Elezar smirked at Skellan's alarmed expression. The servant continued scrubbing him down. Skellan didn't particularly like the man's touch—his nervousness all but crawled over Skellan's spine—but he took a kind of amusement noting Elezar's tension in watching the exchange. He lingered at the door as if he couldn't make himself leave. Skellan couldn't say if that was because Elezar—like himself—felt uneasy in the presence of these two strange men or if he feared the Skellan might make some misstep in their company. Did he think Skellan would bite one of them?

"Bishop Palo and his niece will be dining with you tonight," Elezar said, finally.

"Will they?" Skellan smiled at that, remembering the last time he'd dined with the old man. Admittedly, that time he'd been crouching beneath the bishop's table in the body of a hound. But he'd received plenty of fatty scraps from the elderly man's hands.

"Is that going to be a problem for you?" Elezar asked.

"Why would it be?" Was there something terrible about the bishop's niece? All Skellan recalled about the young woman was that she'd come to wed Elezar's duke and that she was said to be demure and pretty. No, Elezar's concern wouldn't have to do with a woman who'd only arrived in the city this month.

Elezar frowned at Skellan meaningfully. The servant at Skellan's back stilled his ministrations. Then a realization came to Skellan.

"You mean because the Cadeleonian church condemns men like me?" Skellan didn't feel overly troubled. After all, the Cadeleonian church claimed no legal standing here in Radulf County. As far as he knew the bishop hadn't ever even attempted to have a man or woman here in the north punished for either witchcraft or their sexual practices.

"There is that," Elezar replied. Even from across the room Skellan could see the muscles in Elezar's jaw flex. He was trying not to let his anger show, Skellan realized. "But there's also the part he played in your abduction. He stole your family and inheritance from you."

No doubt he had. But Skellan possessed no recollection of that lost family and had never known he was deprived of his inheritance. He'd grown up hungry and mostly homeless but so had many other witches, tramps, and thieves. It struck him as more work than it was worth to attempt to set himself up with a grudge against the bishop now.

"We have enough trouble to contend with without digging up the past to make more enemies, don't you think, my man?"

Elezar nodded but looked none too pleased. Skellan wondered if it was possible that Elezar could have taken offense for him. Could he brood on wrongs that Skellan couldn't himself remember?

"If the grimma breach the city they'll do worse to Bishop Palo than any of us. He has to know that," Skellan added. "He needs us."

"For now," Elezar replied. "But I don't trust him."

"He's not as much of a snake as Bois, I don't think," Skellan replied. To his surprise Elezar shook his head.

"Your father's supporters did what they had to in their attempt to bring you home. I don't like the decisions that they made but I understand why they made them. They were loyal to your father and to you."

"The bishop is loyal to his church and his prince." Skellan shrugged again. The servant washing his back shifted to soap down Skellan's shoulder. Glimpsing the young man out of the corner of his eye Skellan noted that he looked bored. Skellan wondered if that was an affected expression or if the man truly could care less about politics.

"I won't try to argue that anyone of that bunch commands the moral high ground," Elezar responded. "I'm just saying that if it comes down to it the bishop has already shown himself willing to make alliances well outside the bounds of his church to keep you from coming to power."

Skellan could have pointed out that Elezar himself seemed to have wandered far from the doctrines of the Holy Cadeleonian Church, but he didn't feel comfortable making such a personal comment in the company of these two strange servants.

And in any case what did it matter? Men strayed from their faiths nearly as often as they strayed from their wives, in Skellan's experience. Most glutted themselves on the forbidden for a time and then found their remorseful ways back. The thought made Skellan suddenly realize that he'd never even asked Elezar if he was married. Did a wife and children await him back in Anacleto?

If so, when this was all done, and supposing they actually won their battle, Skellan wondered if he would have it in him to let Elezar go. He had bound him, body and soul, but there had been few real words between them. No actual promises, really.

"If you would lift your arms, my lord," the servant with the washcloth whispered. Skellan raised his arms and tried not to make a sour face at the servant's thorough mopping of his armpits.

"We need to talk more," Skellan called to Elezar over the servant's bowed head.

Did noblemen really converse like this? It seemed awkward, far too awkward. Then the servant plunged his hand down to Skellan's thigh and Skellan nearly leapt out of the tub. Water splashed across the stone floor.

"What in fuck's name are you trying at?" Skellan shouted. The young man jerked back, slipping in a puddle and cowering at the foot of the tub. "I didn't ask for a wet wank and if I had needed one my own man is standing right there!" Skellan gestured to Elezar.

"I wasn't… I didn't mean…" the servant protested. Skellan read genuine fear in his pale face. "It's just all the dirt…"

"Sorry." Skellan sighed heavily. "I'm not used to having another man's hand on me for any reason other than fucking." This didn't exactly produce the relaxed response that Skellan had hoped for but the young servant did regain his feet.

"I can scrub my own prick well enough," Skellan added. The servant allowed Skellan to take the washcloth from his hand. Skellan looked back to Elezar only to note yet another mortified flush coloring his face.

"Perhaps we can talk more later," Elezar said.

"Later, then," Skellan agreed. Somehow, just trying to take a bath he'd screwed everything up. Elezar executed a quick bow and then made his escape without another word. Skellan slowly sank back down into the tub.

How was he going to manage a dinner, much less a war, when he couldn't even play at being a lord well enough to take a bloody bath?

After making quick work of scouring himself clean, Skellan managed to win a little friendliness from his two servants by making genuine inquiries about the voluminous sleeves of his linen shirt, the gold of his brocade coat and breeches, as well as the all the assorted potions that they insisted on applying to his body.

The men were brothers, Pilife and Roberr—though Skellan wasn't certain which was which, since the elder brother made the introduction for them both. Between them, they'd had served the count nearly twenty years. As improbable as it seemed to Skellan, they both seemed to honestly take great interest in their work. They distilled their own perfumes and had always stitched the count into his clothes to ensure the very best fit.

"Your father, the count, wasn't vain," the older of the two confided to Skellan. "But he understood that his ancestors had blessed him with certain advantages and that failing to exploit his natural endowments would be foolish."

The younger servant nodded and then very gently worked scented oil through Skellan's wild red hair. He trimmed the ends with a pair of silver scissors, then scooped up the fallen locks and threw them in the fire, as if he knew that leaving them lying about for another witch to snatch up would make Skellan nervous.

"A hawk that's ashamed to soar might as well have been born without wings," the older servant went on. "That's what he told me once."

Skellan nodded and willed himself to remember the phrase as appropriately lordly.

"Did he ever say anything about m—" Skellan cut himself off as he realized what he was asking. How pathetic it would sound to these two, or to anyone.

All his life he'd cultivated a defiant pride in being a penniless foundling.

My mother is the South Wind. My father is a stone.
I call the cobbles my friend. And my name is my own.

That was what he'd always said when anyone attempted to make a taunt of his abandoned state. He'd fostered a secret belief in himself that he shared a bond with the motherless elements of the world—stone, water, and wind—and that what others might think a loss was the key to his power.

And yet now he couldn't quite keep himself from feeling the ache that had always lived in him. He'd been so lonely, so desperate for kindness, even from the ragged surfaces of rocks. It embarrassed him beyond words.

"He spoke of you often," the older of the servants said. He met Skellan's gaze briefly as he tugged the white folds of Skellan's shirtsleeve up from between the slashed brocade of his heavy coat. "You were his one and only heir and nothing mattered to him more than bringing you home. Even we who merely served him knew that."

The younger man nodded his agreement.

Skellan tried to call up some feeling for the count other than the natural deference and annoyance of his street witch's upbringing. But he didn't possess a single memory of the man as his father. When he tried to conjure up a sense of being protected or doted upon he recollected Bone-crusher's stony shoulder. He remembered Navet and Merle purposely leaving a window in their stable open for him and laying out a blanket. He thought of Cire scowling at him for missing his rent and then handing a bowl of porridge to him anyway.

"Every year the family celebrated the day of your birth, you know." The older servant knelt and began stitching the seams of Skellan's scarlet breeches to a nearly skintight fit. Skellan watched the needle glint and plunge as the servant plied it with an astounding speed.

"I didn't." How strange must the have been? "Every year?"

Both servants nodded.

Skellan didn't know the exact date of his birth—the year of the wolf, Lundag had told him, and he'd often amused himself deciding that any day of the entire year could be his. How odd to imagine strangers knowing and celebrating the exact day.

"Yes, every summer solstice a place was always set at the table for you at your father's right hand. Year round, rooms were maintained for you in all of his palaces." At Skellan's back the younger servant tugged more white linen up through the slashed doublet.

Skellan thought he should have felt touched by the idea that his father never forgot about him, but he couldn't help but find the extremity of the count's devotion odd. Who maintained a place at his table and rooms in his house or celebrated the birth of a child he had never met? How would it have felt to be the count's daughter, alive and at his side, while he brooded and obsessed on some long-lost son?

"Shall we put on your boots now, my lord?" the older servant asked, proffering stockings. The younger servant turned to the dressing table to scoop up the long, scarlet boots. Laces and leather draped over his forearms. He looked as pleased as a boy cuddling a puppy.

"Here's the trouble with that. No witch worth a turd wears shoes," Skellan said.

"But you are Count Radulf now," the older servant insisted. "And these are cut from the finest leather in three nations."

"And a sight they are indeed. Quite handsome," Skellan acknowledged. Handsome and, no doubt, costly. He shook his head. "But they could be spun from moonlight the gold and I still wouldn't wear them. I need to feel the earth beneath my bare feet."

The two servants stared at him in obvious disbelief.

"But certainly it wouldn't matter for just one evening?" the older man suggested.

"Now that, my friend, is an argument to trick a wolf into wearing a dog's collar if I ever heard one," Skellan replied but he offered the man a smile to soften his refusal.

At the best of times he would have been hesitant to wear even a slipper, but with so much around him feeling unfamiliar and uncertain he refused to cut himself off from literally knowing where he stood.

These two could give him all the wounded glances they liked.

Reflexively Skellan flexed his toes against the stone floor, taking in the faint resonance that played through the sheets of rock. Already the garrison grew to know him. Neither the towering walls nor the wide courtyard woke to his call, but slowly—one flagstone, slate shingle, gate, and archway at a time—the place warmed to him.

"It seems a terrible shame..." The younger servant studied the boot in his arms.

Skellan wondered if he should offer the boots to the servants. They'd probably command a good price in the rough market where Skellan often came by rabbit skins and hides still soft enough to chew.

A strange sensation interrupted his thoughts. A shiver skipped up from the flagstones, sending chills along Skellan's spine. A presence, perhaps a witch, drew near and was coming closer fast.

Skellan spun to the door just in time to hear a loud rap.

The elder of the servants attending Skellan moved quickly to see who called. He blocked Skellan's view as he opened the door, but an instant later the servant bowed and stepped back, holding the door wide open. A lanky adolescent girl swathed in brocaded silk, fox fur, and gleaming nets of rubies and gold thread stared directly into Skellan's face. Her eyes were like chips of jade set in a marble mask. Ruby-studded gold pins held her thick auburn braids up in a coiled crown. Armed guards, silk-gowned attendants sporting brightly plumed hats, and a sister-physician peopled the hallway behind her.

The girl glided into the room without once breaking her gaze from Skellan's.

He knew her, of course, though he thought that the silver coins cast in her likeness must have been minted when she had still been a plump-cheeked child. That, or the artist had taken

GINN HALE

liberties, softening the planes of her long face and hiding the sharp angle of her jaw with decorative cascades of blossoms.

She was not pretty but certainly striking.

"I would know you anywhere," Lady Hylanya Radulf whispered. "You look so much like Papa."

Skellan resisted the reflex to return the compliment. Instead he simply stood before her as she reached out and wrapped her long arms around him and pressed her young face against the brocade of his doublet.

Skellan realized two things at once. First, the aura of magic he'd sensed at her approach radiated from the fatherly blessings placed within each of the bright rubies that she wore. They rang through Skellan's breastbone like the vibrations of tiny bells, each wishing this young girl health, wisdom, and above all, protection.

Secondly, Skellan realized that the count—whom he had never known as a man, much less as a father—had been as dear to this girl as her own heart. Her mourning for him suffused her body. Skellan gently returned her embrace. Famous and statuesque as she was, she was still younger than Sammi and Sarl—just a child who'd lost her family.

Skellan didn't expect to feel suddenly protective of her. Sister or not, he hardly knew the girl, but he understood the strain of being young, alone, and frightened. He returned the girl's embrace. If Milmuraille fell, Lady Hylanya would be among the first captives that the grimma would publicly butcher. She was old enough to know that and yet she'd remained in the city.

After only a moment she released Skellan and he let her step back from him.

"I'm sorry. That was forward of me," Lady Hylanya said, but her gaze continued to move over his face as if she couldn't keep herself from searching his features for another, more familiar countenance.

"No harm done, my lady—" Skellan began.

"Hylanya. You must call me Hylanya," she insisted. "Rafale tells me that you go by the name Skellan."

"Did he?" Skellan asked to hide his momentary dismay at hearing Rafale's name on her lips. But then Skellan caught himself. He'd known of Rafale's dealings with the count and his daughter. Who better for the count to employ as his spy than a playwright from a well-bred family? Rafale could mingle among every class, whether casting for new actors, charming patrons, or making a study of characters as diverse as virgin heiresses and mongrel street witches.

But that seemed so different now that he'd met Hylanya—now that he knew her as his sister, the idea of Rafale sniffing around her disturbed him. The way her eyes lit up when she mentioned the man told him that she was already too fond of Rafale by half.

"Is it true?" Hylanya asked.

"It's true," Skellan went on quickly. "I've answered to Skellan nearly all my life. Though Master Bone-crusher always calls me Little Thorn."

"Bone-crusher? The troll, you mean?"

Skellan nodded. "Everyone else knows me by Skellan."

"Skellan, then." Hylanya said it purposefully as if placing the word firmly in her mind. "Father and I always spoke of you as our Hilthorn..." For just a moment her expression wavered but she drew in a quick calming breath. "But there's no point addressing you by a name you don't answer to, is there?"

"I might be slow to come when you called, if you did," Skellan replied and briefly he remembered the duke of Rauma's efforts to put a name to him. Randy-boy, now that would have been a fine name for a count. Skellan wondered if Hylanya would find the story funny or offensive.

He gazed at his sister and she looked back at him and he thought that she must have been as much at a loss for anything to say as he was. Then she glanced down and laughed. Skellan followed her gaze to his bare feet.

"You don't want to wear those boots, do you?" she asked with a delighted smile. The expression softened her angular face and returned some of the pretty charm that her visage possessed when impressed upon silver coins.

"I'm not so keen on them," Skellan admitted.

"Papa fairly hated wearing shoes." She beamed down at Skellan's knobby, tough feet. "He'd abide them for formal functions but the first chance he got he'd tear them off and hurl them across the room. Anyone truly close to him knew to expect him in his bare feet."

Skellan wondered what it would have been like to commiserate with the count and join him in throwing shoes around. He thought he would have liked that and then felt a disquieting pang of sorrow. What was the point of making himself miss a man after he was already dead?

"Will you wear the boots?" Hylanya asked him.

"Not unless one of these two fellows manages to overpower me and wrestle them onto my feet." Skellan indicated the two servants standing silently to the side. He almost thought that the younger might just take him up on it. Skellan flashed him a wolfish grin and the young man clearly reconsidered.

"No boots," Skellan stated.

Hylanya appeared pleased with the answer and then turned to the two dressers. "That will be all then, I think," she informed them. At once they bowed their way out of the room.

A trim sister-physician bustled past the two of them. Three big men, each blond and tall enough to pass for Mirogoths but clothed in Labaran fencing leathers and wearing costly Cadeleonian swords, followed the woman into the room. Instinctively, Skellan stole a glance to the small slit window at his back. Too narrow by half to squeeze through.

The armed men flanked the door but looked bored—one hid a yawn behind his gloved hand. Skellan relaxed a little. Lady Hylanya doubtless kept guards. Perhaps one of these was even her champion. They all possessed handsome enough bodies.

A veritable throng of other attendants and men-at-arms waited out in the hall, and Skellan half expected them to come pouring into the chamber as well. However the sister-physician firmly closed the door on them.

"Ancestors spare us from all those chatterbox gossips," the sister-physician muttered.

"My nurse, Lady Peome." Hylanya indicated the woman.

Despite the wisps of steel gray hair that escaped her snood, few wrinkles lined her pretty pale face. As Skellan met her gaze he realized that she looked somehow very familiar to him, but he couldn't imagine how or where they might have met before.

Peome turned and curtsied deeply. Skellan wasn't certain if it was to him or Hylanya. She straightened quickly enough and then she withdrew a folded letter from the sachet pocket of her neat red robe. The simple jade rings that adorned her fingers whispered with blessings but so softly and briefly that Skellan thought he might have been mistaken.

"Sheriff Hirbe gave me this," Peome told Hylanya. Then she smiled at Skellan. "And he sends his best to you as well, Count Radulf."

Skellan nodded but blankly, not really certain of what she was talking about but attempting to make no offense. Hylanya opened the letter and after briefly glancing at the contents held the thick page out to Skellan. Skellan guessed that she'd already read it and wondered at this play of opening it in front of him.

He frowned at that.

"Oh! I hadn't thought…" Hylanya said when she saw his expression. "Were you taught to read?"

"Yes, at least well enough to understand this, I think," Skellan replied. He took the letter and studied the elegant Cadeleonian script. He recognized Elezar's name right away. The bounty offered for his head made for a small fortune but didn't come as a surprise. Only grand wealth lured professional swordsmen to risk their lives hunting a man like his Elezar. The description of Atreau Vediya, however, gave Skellan pause.

Atreau.

He'd heard that name now more than once and there was something in the description that turned his mind back to the month he'd spent with the duke of Rauma.

Dark hair, tall and well made, with a handsome face and wastrel's character. Too fond of obscene doggerel and wine, he is commonly found in the company of taproom whores, who indulge his licentious appetites, or in the service of noblemen whose own vices incline them to support Atreau. He is fluent in his mother's Labaran and often wears the rose perfumes favored in the southern counties there.

Awash in rose water, obscenity, and drink… that did describe him very well. And hadn't the duke quoted his mother with a Labaran proverb at the theater?

"You see," Lady Hylanya said, "your Cadeleonian is not an emissary or agent of his prince but a wanted man—a murderer."

Skellan met her eyes and recognized that she wished to see him outraged.

"Elezar already told me all about this," Skellan assured her. Though he recalled that at the time Elezar had been very careful of the details concerning who'd bedded whom. He suspected that he now knew why. He read over the letter again, fusing suspicion into certainty.

The duke of Rauma had not traveled to Milmuraille but instead had sent his old schoolmate, Atreau Vediya, likely in hopes of hiding him here in the north. Yes, that made much more sense and explained all those details of the duke's character that Skellan had found so at odds with the man's history and reputation.

It explained his fevered memory of cracking his eyes to see the supposed duke flushed with fury and declaring all that he would do for Fedeles' sake. Atreau had made other suggestions, ones that warped and twisted in Skellan recollection, but all came to the same point. He'd argued that selling Skellan into the power of the Cadeleonian crown and church could win them all a way home.

Elezar had looked harrowed—Skellan clearly remembered his haunted dark gaze falling over him—but he'd refused, hadn't he?

"It troubles you, I can tell." Hylanya's words interrupted Skellan's attempt to remember exactly what he'd overheard last night.

"This Elezar Grunito is famed for his murderous temper. In Cadeleon he's said to have slain at least six noblemen in petty duels. And here he's already killed another seven commoners—"

"In self-defense," Skellan put in. "He didn't seek those men out. They came after him, drawn by promises like the one in this letter." He could have added that one of those men's deaths had been his doing. The sensation of plunging the long curved hunting knife into the man's back played through Skellan's hand. For an instant that soft noise, almost a gasp, sounded in his mind and he remembered how the man's hot blood had frothed from his punctured lung and looked as if it were boiling up from his wound.

Skellan studied the letter. Strange that just a few passages of ink could cost so many lives.

He didn't want to think of any of those things, much less share them with Lady Hylanya, her nurse, or the three guards who stood watching them in silence.

"Elezar Grunito is the kind of man who attracts trouble," Hylanya went on in a tone of solemnity that struck Skellan as too rehearsed for a girl her age. "That isn't a good trait in any companion, but particularly not in a count's champion."

The nurse nodded at Hylanya like a proud stage mother observing her daughter's first recital. Skellan wondered if the nurse was unaware of her own movement or if she'd grown so accustomed to being ignored by those attending Lady Hylanya that she didn't bother to hide it.

"You've put no little thought into my champion," Skellan replied to Hylanya. "Have you met him?"

Brief uncertainty flashed across Hylanya's face and she stole a glance back to her nurse. The woman gave a quick shake of her head.

"I've not been introduced to him," Hylanya conceded. "But Rafale has described him to me in detail and when I questioned the duke of Rauma this afternoon, even he agreed that it would be better if you didn't take a Cadeleonian lord as your champion."

"Well, the duke wouldn't be terribly happy about seeing himself or his friend caught up in a battle against the grimma, would he?" Skellan replied.

"It isn't their war, is what he said," Hylanya said.

Skellan just smirked and to his surprise Hylanya nodded.

"I know," she said. "Our county is their concern enough for them to insist upon maintaining their own forces here."

"They do seem happy enough to take out butter taxes," Skellan agreed.

"And build their chapels here." Hylanya rolled her eyes in a manner that reminded Skellan of Sammi. "But first sign of trouble and where are all the famed warriors of Cadeleon?"

"I think my man Elezar shares your disgust on that front," Skellan told her. "That's why he's taken on this garrison."

Hylanya caught her lower lip between her teeth and shot Skellan a vexed look. He laughed.

"Tell me, did the sheriff say anything when he sent this letter along?" This question Skellan addressed to the nurse, Peome. His attention seemed to take her aback momentarily. But then she simply shook her head.

"He wanted everything out in the clear," Hylanya admitted. "He said that there should be no secrets between allies in a time of war. I agree with him. I think the sheriff is partial to your man, Lord Grunito. But he would be, wouldn't he? Old sword masters always love young bloods. And Lord Grunito's reputation obviously impresses soldiers."

Good to hear that at least the sheriff realized that this squabbling over who served who in what capacity was only going to help the grimma. Skellan considered his newfound sister.

"But not you?" Skellan asked her. "Here's a man who has outmaneuvered superior numbers of mercenaries and assassins, a man who penetrated the Sumar grimma's sanctum and then walked out alive and free. Do you really think I'd be wise to toss such a fellow's offer to aid us aside and ship him back to Cadeleon?"

"No, of course not, but... but..." Hylanya foundered.

"No one disputes Lord Grunito's prowess in the realm of battle. Certainly, his services should be accepted in some capacity. But such a man might not be best suited to traditional Labaran posts." Peome's voice rose soft and low from behind Hylanya. Her gaze remained demurely angled at the floor. "Commanding a garrison is something very different from serving our own count so personally as his champion."

"Yes, that's it exactly." Hylanya nodded. "Of course we want him to fight for us but your personal champion should be someone... trustworthy. Someone who understands the honor you bestow upon him. A Labaran champion for a Labaran count." Hylanya indicated the three brawny swordsmen flanking the door. Skellan took in their assessing gazes as well as their handsome forms. More than a trace of Elezar's defined muscle graced their bodies and they each bore a comely appearance, but none of them commanded the air of hard-won determination that so suffused Elezar.

A week ago none of these men would have spared Skellan a crust of bread much less come scraping about to share his bed and spill their life's blood at his bequest. But Elezar, without even being asked, had championed Skellan even when he'd been nothing but a filthy dog.

"I'm flattered, gentlemen," Skellan told them. He returned his attention to Hylanya. "Now I've no doubt that you've a fine eye but I don't imagine that you've spent too many evenings roving blooding halls, so may I ask who chose these three handsome fellows?"

"Rafale," Hylanya supplied. "But he didn't find them on the streets! These men are the finest from among Papa's chosen guard."

Rafale, again. He did get around, didn't he?

"The best boots and the finest men." Skellan mused. "It's a pity they are all wasted upon me."

Hylanya glanced back at the three men and then to Skellan.

"But they are perfect…" She looked truly perplexed for a moment then suggested, "They can demonstrate their blades, if you'd like—"

"Oh no, that's not necessary," Skellan replied. "I'm sure Rafale's already taken full measure of their skill with their blades."

Two of the men colored prettily while the third offered Skellan a sly smirk. Skellan did warm to him for it—though not enough to make him his champion.

"Look, Hylanya," Skellan said, "I know that you're doing this because you want to help me. You want to support me as count—"

"Yes. Always. I promised Papa I would." Hylanya nodded and again Skellan thought the girl was looking at him but seeing their father.

"But right now I don't need a new champion any more than I need a pair of boots or a vat of costly perfumes. What I need are the means to defend this city and our county."

Hylanya seemed to consider this, her expression growing graver.

"You aren't as I imagined you would be," she said and Skellan guessed that between the count's obsession and constant reminders of his existence Hylanya must have built up quite the idea of what her lost brother would be like. Probably many of the count's intimate courtiers had constructed some version of Hilthorn Radulf. A cleaner, courtly man of far more reasonable character than Skellan. Few would thank him for dispelling their illusion, but a pliant fantasy wasn't going to keep their county standing or save anyone from being fed to the grimma's wild armies. Hylanya's imaginary brother would do her no more good than red leather boots would do for Skellan.

"I admit you're not what I expected either. For one thing, you're less silver than in your portraits," Skellan replied. "Harder to pocket as well, I'd guess."

A smile flitted across her mouth. She glanced back to the line of swordsman and then to Skellan. "You really don't want them?"

Skellan shook his head.

"Then… Then what can I do for you?" she asked. "How can I help?"

"Support me as I am," Skellan replied. "Help me to win over these people I'm to meet tonight."

Again Hylanya seemed to think hard on the suggestion. Then she nodded.

"I will tell you all I can about them." She looked to her nurse. "As will Peome. She is quite well informed, you know."

"Of that I have no doubt," Skellan replied.

The nurse continued to gaze meekly down at the floor but Skellan didn't miss the very brief curve of her lips. And all at once he realized how he knew her. Years earlier he'd glimpsed her taking her leave of Rafale's study. He'd been naïve enough then to feel jealous but Rafale had laughed and informed him that he might indulge in indiscretions but he drew the line at pumping the cunt of his own half-sister.

"We only want what's best for you," Peome said.

"Then don't let me fail here tonight," Skellan replied. "Tell me what I need to know."

Peome met his eyes then and Skellan felt certain that Rafale hadn't lied about her relation to him. Her gaze could have been the twin of Rafale's.

"If you will not sever your connection to the Cadeleonian lord," Peome said. "Then there are other steps you might take to strengthen your support among the Labaran courtiers. At the very least, you can keep those who would trouble you busy at each other's throats."

Skellan grinned as the nurse went on, calmly and sedately explaining the rivalry between Lord Valscon and his cousin Lord Ruite as well as Guild Master Wauluret's desire for the count's approval to erect a sky-gazing tower on private Radulf lands. Peome informed him of new and old alliances within the court and among the ministers and guildsmen. Hylanya offered gossip concerning Bishop Palo and his newly arrived niece. So many names, titles, and vices floated past Skellan that he thought he'd never remember them all.

But then both Hylanya and her nurse fell silent. Peome looked Skellan over, her expression impassive and cool, and said, "Just remember, young count, at this moment it costs them nothing to call themselves your friends. The lives they will offer up to your service are those of their vassals and guardsmen, not their own. But not one from a hundred will stand at your side if the city walls fall."

After leaving Skellan to his attendants, Elezar made for the stable. Had he wished to bathe, dress, or simply take inventory of the large staff that had migrated from the Sun Palace to his garrison, Elezar could have turned Cobre over to the care of a groom. But he preferred to tend to the stallion himself. A sinking dread came over him when he considered the prospect of attending this evening's dinner. So many of the people invited had witnessed Skellan caress his cheek in the courtyard that morning and all of them would know that he'd become Skellan's champion.

His man, as Skellan proudly informed all and sundry.

The idea elated Elezar and at the same time filled him with horror. The conflicting sensations twisted through him like snakes devouring each other's tails. He'd never known another man as brash or brave as Skellan nor one whose company gave him such pleasure.

At the same time Skellan stood to cost Elezar everything: title, nation, lands, and family. Perhaps even his life. Elezar doubted that Skellan knew the meaning of the word discretion much less how to employ it—or even understood Elezar's need to. If he remained with Skellan much longer, every soul in Labara would know the nature of their relationship and rumors would reach Cadeleon quickly.

He risked being branded both an abomination and traitor. If that came to pass, then it wouldn't just be Lady Reollos offering a bounty for his head. Both the royal bishop and the king would likely pay gold to have him cut down. His own family would have to decry him unless they wished to make enemies of the Holy Cadeleonian Church.

He'd gone through so much to keep Isandro's secret from sullying the family name, but how much worse was his own defiance of holy law?

Elezar touched the charm hanging from his neck and traced its worn surface. Of all his brothers he thought Nestor would understand, but the shame of it would probably break their mother's heart.

Elezar didn't want to think about that. He couldn't and keep going. Instead he focused on the simple task of brushing Cobre. The motions soothed Elezar and the familiar surroundings of the stable lent him a sense of security. No matter where he roamed stables were always much the same, filled with the heat and scents of living animals and sweet fodder. Here, he shared a purpose with every other man and little else mattered. Cobre enjoyed Elezar's care and asked nothing more of him.

"Straight for the stables. We Sagrada men are damned predictable!"

Elezar looked over his shoulder to see Javier leading his lean white stallion, Lunaluz, through the doors. Earlier Javier had mentioned surveying the remains of the sanctum. Elezar guessed from the ash coating Javier and Lunaluz that they'd just returned.

"We do have a reputation to uphold," Elezar called back to him. He spent a moment more with Cobre then left the stallion to his fresh feed.

As he strode to the stall where Javier tended Lunaluz, he recognized the shaggy, scarred horse in the next stall as Kiram's mount, Verano. When Elezar had last seen the piebald gelding he'd been as plump and glossy as a spoiled puppy. Now whip thin and battle-scarred he could have passed for a warhorse twice his age. His battered hide testified to the hardship of Javier and Kiram's lives in exile.

Still, as Elezar drew near, Verano greeted him and seemed happy to have Elezar scratch his shaggy jaw.

"He remembers you," Javier commented as he stripped off Lunaluz's worn saddle.

"Sure he does. He's Grunito stock. Cobre's cousin." Elezar fished through his pocket and found a scattering of oat seed, which Verano quickly took off his hands. "What are these scars on his legs and shoulder?"

"Mordwolves. The grimma aren't all that tolerant of other magic being practiced in their lands." Javier paused in his careful grooming of Lunaluz. Sorrow briefly lined Javier's youthful face. "I nearly lost them both that night."

Kiram would have been riding Verano. Judging from the gelding's scars, it had been a close fight. Bloody.

Elezar met Javier's gaze and for the first time he noticed how changed he was from the youth Elezar had known. His countenance appeared almost utterly unaltered—still strikingly handsome—yet something in the pallor of his skin and the darkness of his eyes seemed to radiate a deathly quality. The very perfection of him struck Elezar as somehow ancient and lifeless as marble.

Elezar had thought the last five years had torn the humanity from himself but now he wondered if Javier hadn't endured far worse.

He wanted to ask, because Javier more than anyone knew exactly what Elezar risked if he kept up with Skellan. But he and Javier had never been ones to talk too much. Certainly they'd never discussed any matter so private or personal, and Elezar didn't think he probably had the right to pry. And yet, he needed to know.

He scowled down at his battered boots.

"I want to ask you something but..." He glanced up to meet Javier's curious gaze but then dropped his own attention back to his boots. Oddly, Javier gave a soft laugh.

"If it concerns oral technique—"

"No!" Elezar felt his face flushing and glared at Javier. "No. Nothing like that."

Javier shrugged, flashing Elezar a wicked smile.

"I just wondered," Elezar said, "if you had known then what you do now, would you still have... gone?"

The smile faded from Javier's mouth and again Elezar thought he sensed that deathly presence floating beneath Javier's flawless pale face.

"Would I still have chosen to live in exile as a Bahiim?" Javier turned Lunaluz's brush over in his hands. "For myself, yes. Even if it had cost me my life I would have made the same choice. But I don't know that I would have asked the same of Kiram."

Javier's gaze flickered to Verano and his voice went a little rough. "Back then, I didn't realize how much I was taking from him. His home, safety, and even a place to practice his mechanisms… I cost him everything."

Elezar hadn't expected that response, but he realized the truth of it. Fleeing with Javier hadn't won Kiram any freedom that he couldn't have claimed as a Haldiim. He'd forfeited an illustrious career as well as his friends and family.

"I'd like to think that if I'd known," Javier murmured, his expression bleak, "I would've had the courage to break both our hearts and leave him behind. I don't know what I would have done without him… but he might have been better off without me."

Elezar had only seen more anguish in Javier's proud features once before, when Kiram had lain dying in his arms. He hadn't meant his inquiry to lay Javier open and he felt embarrassed to witness so much emotion in him.

"He would have just come after you," Elezar said. "Probably would have snatched you up in some ingenious trap and then treated you to a few hours of lecture on the futility of escape."

Javier laughed and looked relieved.

"You could be right," Javier said. "He's tenacious."

Elezar nodded. Javier hadn't given him the kind of answer he'd expected, but he'd told him something that Elezar wouldn't have even thought to consider. He felt awkwardly touched that Javier would be so honest with him.

"Skellan had better be serious about making Kiram his court mechanist," Javier abruptly stated.

"I imagine that he is," Elezar replied. "He's not likely to find anyone better, is he?"

"No." Javier sighed but still seemed troubled. "Kiram needs a place to live, a city and society that doesn't just consist of wild Irabiim, crows, and me. Hell, he needs someone who knows what he's talking about when he starts drawing all those cogs and pipes and talking about melting points."

Five years living in a wilderness, Elezar thought. It was a wonder Kiram hadn't gone out of his mind considering the rich life he'd led back in Anacleto.

"Skellan is a man of his word," Elezar assured Javier.

"Good, because I don't think I've seen Kiram so excited about anything in ages. He's completely changed his mind about evacuating the city. Now he's set on fighting to the very end."

Unbidden, Elezar remembered the last time Kiram had thrown himself into a battle. They had traveled the Old Road to save Fedeles but hadn't been able to reach him through the razor-edged shadow curse. Then Kiram had leapt through and pulled Fedeles free but not without cost. The memory of the bloody chasm of Kiram's mangled torso flared through Elezar's mind.

In the rafters overhead birds called and filled the air with the flutter of their wings but for a moment all Elezar heard was the roar of machinery in his memory. A desolate chill twisted through him as he recollected his own helplessness just standing there beside Nestor watching as Javier hunched in the blood and howled Kiram's name.

"He'll be fine. The city isn't going to fall," Elezar told Javier.

Javier arched a dark brow but he didn't argue. Neither of them needed reminding of all the ways the grimma might take Milmuraille or how easily lives were lost in battle.

Javier returned to brushing Lunaluz's dusty white coat. Elezar straightened. He still needed to change clothes and find the sheriff to discuss the evening's guests.

"I've answered your question. Will you answer mine?" Javier asked.

"All right," Elezar agreed, though something in Javier's tone made him nervous.

"What is it that you're fighting for here, Elezar?"

Elezar scowled. Hadn't Atreau wanted to know exactly the same thing this morning? "Why is everyone so concerned with my motives suddenly?"

"Because you appear intent upon risking so much that it would make anyone wonder what reward you hope to receive."

"I risk no more now than I have in any duel." Elezar shrugged as casually as he could. "There's a fight to be had here and I'm always game for a fight."

Again, Javier's sharp black brow arched skeptically.

"You never were so simple as you would have people believe," Javier told him and then his expression softened and he lowered his voice. "I know you, Elezar. You've always had reasons for the battles you've fought. Even when they were against me."

Elezar couldn't deny that. "All right. I have my reasons. But they're my own and no one else's business."

Javier frowned at the brush in his hands. "I'm not trying to pry into the details of your affections—"

"Aren't you?" Elezar asked.

"No. If I were, I wouldn't bother asking you, that's for damn sure. I'd put my question to Skellan. He doesn't seem to know that he ought to be keeping any of this a secret."

Elezar scowled. He'd been thinking nearly the same thing earlier. "Then what is it that you want to know?"

"I want you to tell me that this isn't just your way of closing shop now that you've avenged your brother." Javier spoke quietly though he all but glared at Elezar.

For an instant, Elezar honestly didn't understand what Javier meant. Then, when he realized, he didn't know how to answer without bringing up an ugly old history between them. A dull ache moved across his chest and he wondered if it was possible for muerate poison to linger in a wound for years.

"I'm not trying to get myself killed," Elezar whispered at last. Hadn't he just had to tell Atreau the same thing? Was there a bleak note pinned to his back? "I mean to beat the grimma and keep Cadeleon from entering a war on Labaran soil. That is what I'm doing here."

"And openly becoming Count Radulf's lover?" Javier asked.

"How could that possibly be construed as an attempt at suicide?" Elezar demanded.

"It will certainly get you killed in most of Cadeleon," Javier replied.

He always was quick in debate, Elezar thought.

"I'm not—I can't think about Cadeleon or the repercussions right now," Elezar admitted. "I can't and still… still do this."

Javier looked like he might argue but then he just reached out and scratched Lunaluz.

"It's hard at first, I know. You can feel like you're utterly alone trying to come to terms with it." Javier glanced back to Elezar. "What you asked earlier, about it being worth all the trouble?"

"Yes?" Elezar felt his pulse pick up.

"It's worth it. I can't even tell you how relieving it is when you realize that you don't have to lie to yourself or anyone else. You can hold your head high and be exactly who you are." Then Javier laughed and scratched a bit more at Lunaluz's flank. "It's amazing really how much anguish and trouble we can put ourselves through just trying to find the kind of peace that any animal worth his hide is born with."

Elezar glanced to Cobre and thought that Javier had a good point. He ought to try and remember that, when he was tempted to berate himself for being nothing more than a beast.

"It gets easier and better," Javier said. "If you let it."

How simple that sounded and how hard it was to actually manage, like refraining from scratching at a scab. Painful to do, maddening to resist.

Elezar sighed and lifted his gaze up to the rafters. Already the fresh straw and grain had attracted a small flock of speckled finches. The tiny birds flitted about, their beaks laden with gleanings. Hard to believe that a day ago only shit, filth, and fly-infested carcasses had filled this same space. Now, nearly two dozen hearty Labaran chargers occupied the stalls and Elezar could hear more horses and their grooms out in the paddocks.

He noted with pleasure that the gray charger that had carried him last night had won the affection of a young flag bearer who'd come along with twelve cavalry men from Count Radulf's country estate in the east of the county. The Labaran youth smiled at the old horse with the kind of expression that most boys probably reserved for their grandfathers.

Across the stable two older Labaran grooms, sporting neat mustaches, laughed at the antics of the rat hound prancing alongside them. Elezar smiled, recalling his comparison of his mother's exuberant little dog to Skellan.

When he caught sight of Atreau coming through the stable doors he almost called out Javier's earlier greeting. But then Sheriff Hirbe and Fedeles' two pages followed him in and Elezar's heart sank. They made a resplendent group, all of them dressed in brocade and fine furs, but that only reminded Elezar of the dinner he would soon be attending.

"You see?" Atreau's voice drifted brightly. "You can't go wrong looking for a Sagrada man in a stable. And here we've found two."

Javier glanced back over his shoulder to offer an offhanded wave before returning his attention to his horse. Atreau led the sheriff and pages to Elezar's side.

"Missed me?" Elezar asked.

Atreau nodded, though his gaze lingered on Javier and Lunaluz. Of all the Hellions, Atreau most mourned the end for their wild schooldays. Then, Javier's power had seemed limitless. They'd all indulged in excess and thought themselves forever sheltered from all repercussions. To Elezar, such assumptions felt absurd now, the naïve fantasies of childhood.

Atreau sighed and turned his attention back to Elezar.

"While the sheriff and I were attending Lady Hylanya," Atreau began, "we had an interesting conversation concerning the traditional role of the count's champion and I thought that we ought to discuss it with you before the dinner tonight."

"Oh?" Elezar glanced to the sheriff. Little curls cascaded down his snow white beard and the rich emerald of his brocade coat seemed to impart a sparkle of green to his gray eyes. He regarded Elezar in return with that disconcertingly warm smile.

"Labaran champions aren't just blades for hire. They are far more tied to their master or mistress than a mere proxy during a trial of combat—" the sheriff began.

"Yes, I know. I read the biographies of the last two Radulf champions when we first arrived here." Both their lives had been short, which had made for quick reading.

Elezar guessed that Atreau and the sheriff still hoped to dissuade him from his alliance with Skellan by now pointing out the status he stood to lose in becoming the count's personal duelist. Elezar added, "A champion swears life to his master, forsaking his own name and family, as I recall."

"Indeed." The sheriff raised his white brows. "So you did know what you were doing."

Elezar nodded and Atreau scowled at him.

"I certainly had not been informed of the extent of all this," Atreau snapped. "And I'm not certain that you're in a position to forsake all other obligations, considering that you're still in my service—and by extension in the service of Prince Sevanyo."

Javier turned back to them at that. "I'm of a mind to agree with you, cousin, and by all means give Elezar a good chewing. But I should tell you that the count has already bound Elezar to him with a web of scarlet spells. It's done."

That Elezar hadn't known himself but he managed not to let it show.

When the hell had Skellan done that? What sort of spells?

Javier might have read Elezar's uneasiness because he added, "As far as I can tell, they aren't spells of thrall or enslavement, but they do bind Elezar and young Count Radulf quite powerfully."

"Why couldn't you have waited?" Atreau's words broke into an inarticulate growl of frustration. "Lady Hylanya has brought three Labaran swordsmen. Three. All of them skilled, good-looking, and more than willing to service the count."

Service? But Elezar didn't rise to that.

Instead he simply resisted the spark of jealousy that lit up in his chest. He knew some grimma and Labaran nobles collected harems of champions—he'd seen the Sumar grimma's champions with his own eyes—but until this moment he'd imagined that the relationship between himself and Skellan was somehow different.

Their intimacy had moved Elezar so powerfully—shaking his very idea of himself—that Elezar hadn't even considered that it might have meant less for Skellan. It wasn't as if Skellan had ever said anything about it and he'd been very honest and offhanded about bedding other men before Elezar.

Elezar knew he had no right to feel so possessive and yet he couldn't stop the hot surge of anger that flooded him and quickened his pulse as if he were about to step into a dueling circle. He knew himself and his capacity for jealousy well enough to feel certain that he wouldn't tolerate another champion.

But Skellan hadn't sent for these men. Elezar reminded himself of how Skellan had snapped at the servant attending him in the bath. *There's my man*, he'd said. At the time it had embarrassed Elezar but now he was glad for it, relieved that he could reassure himself that he wasn't just a passing indulgence for Skellan.

"Three men." Elezar managed to force a bland smile. "What a very accommodating sister."

"Quite open-minded even by Labaran standards," Javier murmured. Sheriff Hirbe frowned at Javier.

"I'd wager that the swordsmen are more Rafale's doing than Lady Hylanya's. He's never been too fond of Cadeleonians," Sheriff Hirbe informed them. He eyed Elezar. "But truth be told, Rafale is far from alone in fearing that a Cadeleonian nobleman of your stature might wield an undue influence over an inexperienced young man like our Skellan."

"*I* would have undue influence over *him*?" Elezar gave a dry laugh. He could hardly convince Skellan to wear pants or take a bath while just a day ago Skellan's company had led Elezar to the brink of treason and heresy.

Undue influence, indeed.

"But things aren't always as they appear," the sheriff added and something in his sympathetic smile made Elezar think that perhaps he did understand. "Even as a youth, our Hallen bent grown men to his purpose. He had his way over us all. If Skellan is even half as willful and irrepressible as his father, then there's probably not a man alive who could dominate him."

"Isn't that obvious? After all, Elezar isn't the one casting spells over Skellan." Atreau scowled at Elezar as if he were attempting to glare the enchantments off of him.

"Oh, I know he's not, but other folk are another matter," the sheriff agreed easily. Then he returned his attention to Elezar. "You present a striking figure and possess quite a reputation, Lord Grunito, while most of the Labaran nobility think only of our Skellan as a stolen youth. Not much of a stretch for them to imagine a man like you seducing and controlling the young count."

"Seducing?" Just then Elezar noticed the two pages stealing furtive glances at him as if they feared he might suddenly lunge out and ravish their scrawny, spotty bodies. Elezar just snorted.

"I'm not arguing that you did," Sheriff Hirbe said. "Only that it's an assumption that's easily made."

"But you have a solution?" Javier didn't look up from where he crouched, inspecting Lunaluz's left leg.

"An idea," the sheriff conceded. "If Elezar were to play up his role as a champion at this dinner, it would go a great way in allaying the fears of many."

"Is there someone in particular whom I should run through at the dinner?" Elezar inquired. Despite his sarcastic tone his mind went immediately to the three other man contending to become Skellan's champions. Was that what it would take? Blood sport as dinner theater?

"Now, that's not for me to say," the sheriff replied. "My hope was that you'd stand guard while Skellan ate. Make it clear that you intend to act as a champion and not as a Cadeleonian noblemen."

Elezar considered the prospect.

"I can do that easily enough, but we will need to discuss the reinforcements for the city walls as well as a communication system across the city now that so many of the bells have been lost. There's also how we intend to distribute pay—"

"Yes, yes. But none of that is likely to come up at this first dinner. These people want to know Skellan and they will want him to know them." Hirbe inclined his head to Atreau. "Wasn't that your thought, my lord?"

"Yes. I've already sounded out a number of our guests and I'd reckon that they fall into two groups. Those who were the previous count's favored supporters intent upon retaining their positions and those who hope to join them in the new count's court. Oddly only a single guild master voiced any concern that Skellan wasn't even the count's child." Atreau shook his head and set the iridescent pheasant feathers atop his cap bouncing. "Not even Bishop Palo seems to think there's a possibility that Skellan could be an impersonator."

"No one who spent any time with the boy's father would," Sheriff Hirbe replied. "The resemblance is uncanny."

"Yes, but I'd think with so many witches in this city alone that there'd be a bit more skepticism when it came to appearances. I mean, the man can turn himself into a dog, can't he?"

"Can he?" The sheriff appeared delighted by this news. "He doesn't use that dog skin cloak of his to turn himself into a scarlet hound, by chance?"

Elezar nodded.

The sheriff grinned and then explained, "The previous count used to regale us all with stories of how his own mother often transformed herself to escape her duties at court. Lundag permitted Hallen to give his child only one gift and he sent his mother's cloak."

"Descended from the Scarlet Wolf, isn't that what's said of the Radulf family?" Javier commented. "A wild foundling calling himself Skellan turns out to have been born from the direct bloodline of Skellan the Scarlet Wolf. That begins to sound a little like one of those Labaran epics of great veis. The lives of heroes filled with fate and prophecies."

"Yes, it does have an epic feel to it when you put it that way. And you're right. A prophesy would round it out nicely." The sheriff gave a nod.

"There's not one though, is there?" Elezar asked.

"No, someone would have mentioned something like that right away if there were," Atreau added. "Labarans love their omens and prophesies."

"Likely it hasn't been penned yet," Javier replied and he exchanged an amused smile with the sheriff, who chuckled.

"Indeed. We'll have to see how things actually work out before the exact words are carved into the old stone of the Radulf family temple. There are always a few spots left empty for just such things."

Elezar wasn't certain if the old man was joking or not.

"Have you always been so familiar with the Radulf family?" Elezar inquired.

"No, not at all. In my youth I was little more than a game house buck. But dueling, I won the honor of schooling with Hallen as his guard. I was well beneath him in rank but he welcomed me as a friend and confidant. Those were the happiest two years of my life until the birth of my daughter." The sheriff's expression turned wistful in a way that reminded Elezar greatly of Atreau when he reminisced upon their Hellion days. The sheriff sighed. "As I said, Hallen had a way about him that inspired men to serve him. Only it didn't feel like servitude with him. It felt like... like love, I suppose."

Elezar almost choked at those words.

No Cadeleonian man he knew of ever spoke of loving another man. Respecting, admiring, envying—even ravishing were more likely to be admitted. Elezar tried not to betray his shock at hearing such an honest confession. The sheriff smiled at him wryly.

"I don't mean I loved him in a romantic sense. Though there were many who did. I mean that he brought out the best in the people around him and we couldn't help but love him for it. Skellan possesses a great deal of that quality too, I think."

Elezar nodded and the sheriff went on.

"Given the opportunity to shine on his own tonight, I have no doubt that Skellan can win the support of his subjects. But that won't happen if a good half of them are distracted by you, Lord Grunito."

Atreau looked as if he might object but Elezar recognized that the sheriff honestly wanted Skellan to succeed and likely he was right about his fellow Labarans.

"All right, I can stand at attention and keep my mouth shut for one dinner," Elezar agreed. "I suppose I should eat something now. I wouldn't want my growling belly to offend some skittish courtier."

"I knew you were the kind of man who could be counted

upon." Sheriff Hirbe smiled at Elezar like a gambler who'd rashly backed a nag only to realize that the animal could really run. And that seemed to settle the matter. Elezar left Javier to the respite of the stables and parted from Atreau, his pages, and the sheriff in the courtyard.

A cold northern wind cut through Elezar's coat and the air rang with honking calls. Elezar craned his head back to see the sky turn snow white as a vast flock of hoar swans passed overhead.

"They're flying south," a young guard commented. "Why are they flying south this time of year?"

"Fleeing the grimma armies," a grizzled old soldier replied.

Elezar thought the man might well be right. He wondered what other creatures the armies might flush out from the wilds. Up on the wall several archers loosed arrows, bringing down a few of the swans. Then the birds were gone and the blue sky gaped open and empty.

Catching sight of Kiram up on the wall walkway, Elezar realized that he'd been among the quick archers. They exchanged a wave as Kiram pelted down the stairs to collect his share of the felled fowl. Elezar counted seven of Kiram's distinctive arrows jutting from the breasts of dead birds. He'd always been good, but apparently hunting for his supper every day had vaulted Kiram into mastery of the bow. He wondered if the Labaran archers at the garrison would appreciate a demonstration of Haldiim techniques.

After that Elezar walked the grounds, inspected the guard posts, and double-checked the duty roster. As he went he caught snatches of gossip from among the men-at-arms. More than once he heard his own name whispered along with some exaggerated number of men he'd killed in combat. Few of the Labaran soldiers concerned themselves about Elezar's relationship with Skellan beyond the few wagers on how long Elezar would last against the champions of the grimma. Elezar bet twenty gold coins on his own success against any challenger.

"My ancestors beat the grimma on this very land once before. I don't mind reminding any challenger of how hard a Cadeleonian can fight," Elezar said. "Though I imagine that many of your Labaran ancestors fought that war as well."

"Now that's the truth, isn't it?" A pikeman grinned. "We knocked the piss right out of those old hags and their beasts back then."

As Elezar turned from the group he noted a change in their demeanors. Most stood straighter, looked more assured, and all of them offered him proper salutes. Elezar didn't know whether he would ever see a copper wolf of winnings but the rise in morale was well worth the money.

Feeling buoyed, he decided to visit the infirmary on his way to the kitchen. There the sister-physicians he'd dined with the night before greeted him warmly and asked after both Skellan and the charming duke of Rauma.

"Both well," Elezar assured the women. The eldest of the two slipped Elezar a sachet of dried lovebright blossoms to place under Skellan's pillow and ensure faithful dreams.

Elezar managed to mumble his awkward thanks. The old woman cackled in response and slapped Elezar's back as if she were a war master sending him into his first duel.

The emaciated girl whom he'd carried from the storeroom had recovered enough to sit up in bed. She remembered nothing of her rescue but her father—Captain Tialdo—did and his gratitude embarrassed Elezar, because really he'd done so little to deserve it. Still he accepted the captain's thanks and spent a few minutes discussing how best to lay pit traps around the city's perimeter.

Then Elezar excused himself and wandered back to the kitchens, where he persuaded one of the eight cooks who'd come from the Sun Palace to slip him a heaping bowl of bream stew as well as two slabs of toasted black bread slathered in butter. Taken with a mug of table beer it made for a good meal.

Clouds of steam perfumed with sharp northern herbs and

costly spices warmed Elezar and clung to him like cologne. At the tables all around him, cooks and assistants worked frantically. Elezar eyed the glistening body of a roasted goose that two women heaved out of a sweltering oven and laid on a board to dress with fennel and honey. He'd miss the opportunity to taste that and the sizzling cakes of river crab that another cook carefully wrapped in strips of bacon before frying.

However, he wasn't disappointed to learn that he wouldn't be feeding on the prized Labaran dish of lemon-poached snails dusted with flakes of gold. Noting that at least six dishes, beautifully garnished though they were, consisted largely of snails, frogs, and dormice, Elezar began to view his deprivations with relief.

At the far side of the table where Elezar ate, a kitchen boy hunched, carefully positioning tiny sugar pearls in a floral pattern across the surface of an ornately cut piecrust. Elezar smiled to himself as he imagined the quick end Skellan would make of all the elegant victuals. Perhaps misreading Elezar's amused expression, the boy cast him a warning glare and drew the fragile pie away from the line of Elezar's sight.

Once he'd downed his food Elezar retreated from the bustling kitchen. He took a few minutes to rinse the dust from his body and dress in the clean clothes that Atreau had sent for from Bishop Palo's townhouse. He took a pleasure in throwing aside his reeking, tattered old boots and donning a fresh pair, cut exactly to fit his feet.

He already stood at the foot of the stairs in the vast, empty entry hall when the guests began to arrive. From a great distance across the city a lone bell tower rang out the twilight hour.

CHAPTER
TWELVE

The upper crust of Labaran society gathered quickly, filling the barren space of the gray stone garrison with expensive perfumes, extravagant cascades of iridescent plumage, and bright conversation. Attendants, clothed in the count's red, darted between clusters of guests, distributing the traditional small cups of butter tea. Unlike the serving Elezar had received at the Rat Rafters, these simple clay cups contained not only a thick curl of butter and warming spices but also a generous shot of strong, woody liquor. After a few cups most in the crowd seemed to grow quite convivial.

Waiting at the foot of the massive stone staircase, Elezar ignored the butter tea and kept his mouth shut, allowing Sheriff Hirbe to act as host while he played the role of a stone-faced guard. When one young dark-haired woman attempted to slip up the stairs for a peek at the new count Elezar halted her with just a glower.

"Oh! I was just curious, but…" The noblewoman brought her pearl-studded fan up to cover her mouth and then scurried back to the two men who'd escorted her in—her brothers, if Elezar remembered correctly. She handed each man a coin and Elezar guessed she'd wagered that a woman could get past him. Had they known anything of Elezar, the older of the brothers would have been a better bet. Not that Elezar would have allowed him up, but he might have let the strapping man fetch him a cup of buttered tea.

The siblings quickly joined another group friends and their interest in breaching the staircase seemed forgotten. They drifted into the rest of the crowd.

Watching them all, Elezar couldn't help but note the difference between these northern Labarans and own Cadeleonian countrymen. Here, merchants and nobles chatted almost as if they were peers, women were announced not just as daughters, widows, or wives, but as scholars and officials in their own rights and the diversity of races made it obvious that—in Radulf County, at least—a Labaran wasn't a breed but an affiliation. The dark-skinned woman who led the Weavers' Guild clearly descended from Yuanese heritage, while her husband, a soft-spoken astrologer, could have passed for a full-blooded wild Mirogoth. Though his extravagantly coiffured mustache and peacock-plumed cap betrayed his nationality in an instant.

Atreau and his pages joined the company, welcomed with hearty greetings from the men and excited glances from many of the women. Elezar noted Rafale among the crowd as well. He flirted in a broad theatrical manner with the wives of several guild masters. The husbands looked on with the indulgent air of men who enjoyed the envy their acquisitions inspired.

That much seemed the same as in the courts of Cadeleon.

When the young footman announced the arrival of Bishop Palo, Elezar tensed and recognized a similar reaction in several other guests, but when the bishop strolled into the hall he received a polite welcome. Not so warm as Atreau's but not the open scorn Elezar had expected to greet a man who had plotted the downfall of the county's new ruler. Though perhaps part of that arose from the fact that the bishop's pretty young niece and her maids accompanied the old man and his attendants. The girls passed Elezar in a cloud of excited whispers, perfume, and pearl-studded brocade.

The bishop's black and violet robes lent a ghostly pallor to his thin skin and short white hair. His attendant priests followed him at a distance, though they stood close enough to one another to form a wall of black robes behind the bishop. Though he mingled with other guests for a time, the bishop steadily made his way to Elezar's side.

"Has he arrived yet? The young count, I mean," the bishop inquired.

"Not yet, Your Grace. He and his sister, Lady Hylanya, are upstairs taking a moment to become acquainted. I expect that they will join the party shortly."

The bishop nodded and tugged at the collar of his holy robe then glanced back at his attendants. Sacrist Bois' shadow fell over the bishop as he moved silently behind the old man. Though Elezar held little warmth for the bishop he couldn't help but feel defensive of the frail old man as Bois' cold gaze settled on him. The sacrist studied the bishop with the eye of a hangman measuring out his rope.

"Sacrist Bois told me that you were the one who found him, Lord Grunito," the bishop said.

"Inasmuch as he was lost," Elezar replied.

Oddly the bishop smiled at that and then lowered his voice.

"It's a relief to know that he survived." A brief frown creased the bishop's face. "A man doesn't disobey his prince. But some commands never sit right, if you know what I mean."

"I…" Elezar understood the bishop well enough, but the implication startled him a little. It made political sense that the order to do away with Skellan would have originated from Prince Sevanyo, but the knowledge clashed with Elezar's ideal of his prince. He didn't want to think of the resplendent man who had once placed a silver circlet on his brow and called him a brave son of Cadeleon as also calculating the abduction and enslavement of a mere child. And yet he'd seen much more of courtly politics since his schooldays and he didn't doubt that Bishop Palo spoke the truth.

What he didn't know was why the bishop would whisper this confession to him of all people.

"If you don't understand my meaning, then that's all for the better." The bishop placed his hand on Elezar's forearm. His grip felt frail as a sparrow's. "A mortal sin, even undertaken for the sake of crown and country, burdens a man's soul and it never leaves him completely. I've lived long enough to know that."

"You would not attempt it again then?" Elezar asked.

"I am not the kind of young man the prince would choose for such thing now." The bishop stared hard at Elezar and spoke in a hardly audible whisper. "The boy has already survived so much and for no greater crime than being born. It would destroy us all if he fell now to the hand of an assassin. I beg you, do not do it."

Elezar blinked at the bishop. Did he really believe that Elezar had been deployed to Milmuraille to assassinate Skellan? Elezar met the old man's dark eyes and knew that the bishop truly expected murder and worse of a prince's envoy.

Maybe if Elezar had really been appointed as an envoy by Prince Sevanyo then he would have been dispatched as an assassin. However, Fedeles had placed no such burden upon him, entrusting him instead to forge a peace.

Elezar shook his head. "I'm not—"

"If my advice means nothing to you, then, as I said, it's all for the better." The bishop's practiced smile returned. "I'm old and not likely to live much longer, but if I could, I would save one other man. It's my calling after all, isn't it?" The bishop laughed dryly at his own words. Then he released Elezar's arm and stepped back from him.

"Best not be seen in my company too long, Lord Grunito." The bishop cast a glance back at Bois. "Funny how God revisits our own sins upon us. He possesses more humor than I think you young people can understand... A dark humor perhaps, but still grand... Oh, I must have one of those cups of butter tea. I'm parched."

With no more excuse than that the bishop drifted after one of the liveried attendants. Bois cast Elezar a suspicious look and Elezar glowered back at him until the sacrist broke away and stalked after the bishop.

"I told you he wouldn't even allow his own holy man past. Pay up." The dark-haired woman who'd earlier attempted to take the stairs accepted several silver coins from her brothers. "He truly is the count's man."

As more trays of butter tea flowed from the kitchen, other

conversations and wagers floated past Elezar while he stood, feeling a growing sympathy for all those trolls that had been frozen alive in stone and made to stand guard for countless years. He glanced to the men-at-arms guarding the entry and exchanged a convivial nod with them each.

Then a series of bright bells chimed from the top of the staircase and twin blond boys dressed in crimson liveries called down: "Announcing Count Hilthorn Radulf and his honored sister, Lady Hylanya Radulf!"

Chatter fell silent and everyone in the hall looked up to see Skellan and his sister descend arm in arm. Elezar stared along with the rest of them.

Skellan's long, angular build lent an appearance of delicacy to his boyish sister while she imparted an air of dignity to him. Side by side, both tall, sharp featured, and clothed in scarlet, gold, and lustrous furs, they looked like bold illustrations from gilded tomes of Labaran history brought to life before Elezar's eyes.

With his gleaming red hair in gold-banded braids, his lean body draped in the richest cloth, and so composed of an expression on his face, Skellan could have been another man entirely: a stranger whom Elezar found breathtaking but knew not at all.

Then he glimpsed Skellan's bony bare feet jutting out from the cuffs of his ornately embroidered hose and he recognized the scarlet fur draped over Skellan's shoulder as that dog skin cloak that he kept with him always. Elezar felt an unnamed tension melt away. The pressure of Skellan's new title and obligations might have moved him to bathe and dress like an elegant stranger, but this was still his Skellan. No doubt about it.

"Elezar, my man!" Skellan flashed him a grin and Elezar couldn't keep from smiling back at the warmth of the greeting. "Come. Meet my sister, Lady Hylanya!"

"It would be a privilege to do so, Count Radulf."

Elezar felt the focus of the gathered guests turn on him

but he didn't look away from Skellan and his sister. The young noblewoman allowed Skellan to lead her to where Elezar stood at the foot of the stair. Behind them a parade of ladies-in-waiting, pageboys, nurses, and guards waited on the stairs. Elezar noticed three well-dressed men carrying dueling blades and wondered if these three muscular blonds were the men Rafale had chosen to supplant him.

"Lord Elezar Grunito." Skellan's amused expression tempered the formality of his address. "I present my sister, Lady Hylanya Radulf. Hylanya, this is my chosen champion Elezar."

"A pleasure." Lady Hylanya's countenance betrayed none of the exuberance or emotion that Elezar expected from such a young girl. Only slight crease of her brow hinted at her uneasiness as she allowed Elezar to take her hand in Labaran greeting. Then she performed a perfect Cadeleonian curtsy, to which Elezar bowed very low.

"Will you join us for our repast, Lord Grunito?" Lady Hylanya asked him. Something in her delivery made Elezar suspect that she'd been instructed—maybe by Sheriff Hirbe—to make the inquiry so public.

The quiet of the hall told Elezar that many of those gathered listened, waiting to weigh his response. Elezar replied with a formality he'd not called upon since he sailed from Cadeleon—perhaps longer even than that.

"Alas, I cannot oblige, Lady Hylanya. My place, as the count's champion, is to stand guard this night. But I do thank you for the generosity of the invitation."

Lady Hylanya responded with a serene nod but Skellan scowled.

"My man doesn't go hungry while I eat," Skellan objected.

"I've already eaten, Count Radulf. You need not feel troubled on my account," Elezar assured Skellan.

He glanced to the three handsome Labaran duelists standing among Lady Hylanya's entourage and Skellan followed his gaze. "Above all else it's my privilege to stand as your champion," Elezar said firmly and Skellan seemed to grasp his meaning.

"Yours and yours alone," Skellan replied. He caught Elezar's shoulder and squeezed. Somehow Elezar felt the heat of Skellan's hand even through his own thick doublet and shirt. For just an instant he saw fine red filaments spark from Skellan's fingers and flit over his own chest. Elezar had to stifle the reflex to flinch back but the only effect of the spell seemed to be a tiny flare of warmth.

"So many people." Skellan looked past Elezar's shoulder, taking in the gathered crowd.

"None you need fear," Elezar whispered. "I'll be at your side the whole night."

Skellan lifted his head just a little.

"Thank you," Skellan replied softly.

Then he continued across the hall with his sister at his side. Elezar fell in directly behind them. Lady Hylanya's guards followed behind him, though not as closely as the slim middle-aged sister-physician whom Elezar guessed served as the girl's nursemaid. A perfume of violets drifted off her and her gaze never seemed to rest but roved like an agitated guard dog's. She spared Elezar only a quick glower.

The group of them snaked slowly through the crowded hall while Skellan received greetings and introductions. As strangers surrounded Skellan, Elezar caught sight of Bishop Palo standing at a distance and pondered the old man's certainty that Prince Sevanyo would dispatch an assassin.

Just because Elezar wasn't such a man that didn't mean someone else couldn't be. But certainly the prince couldn't have sent anyone so soon. Skellan had only been discovered recently... Though, that didn't mean that only the old count's people had been searching for him all this time.

"Duke Quemanor!" Skellan waved Atreau closer. Elezar didn't miss the sly grin on Skellan's face as he reached out and gripped Atreau's hand—if they'd been any other two people

Elezar might have even wondered if Skellan hadn't slipped a note to Atreau in the exchange.

"Now here's a gaffe, eh?" Skellan looked to his sister and then Atreau. "The duke and I have spent no end of days in each other's company already but not once were we formally introduced. I don't think I even caught his first name..." Skellan frowned but went on before either Atreau or Lady Hylanya could answer him. "Was it Atreau?"

Elezar's gut clenched as he noted the slightest flush color Atreau's face but Atreau gave nothing away and Skellan went on, "But no. Forgive me. It's Fedeles. Fedeles Quemanor, isn't it?"

"Yes," Atreau replied quickly. "But as this is your county, Count Radulf, I certainly would be delighted to answer to any new title you deemed to settle upon me."

That won a laugh and a few smiles from those overhearing the conversation. Elezar relaxed only a little. A good time to reveal Atreau's true identity wasn't likely to arise but this moment definitely ranked as one of the worst.

"I think for now I should simply call you Fedeles." Skellan offered his hand to Atreau in Labaran greeting. "I hope you will understand that when first we met the circumstances of my survival required me to disguise myself. There was no malice in my deception."

"Certainly. Every man does what he must to make his way." Atreau pressed his right palm to Skellan's, and Elezar realized that though Skellan had obviously sniffed Atreau's true identity out, he wasn't going to give him away. A wave of relieved gratitude swept through Elezar.

For his part, Atreau appeared just a little awestruck. Elezar doubted that Atreau often encountered anyone so forgiving of his deceit as Skellan seemed to be. He held Skellan's hand longer than mere courtesy demanded and seemed honestly touched when Skellan went on to offer him a Labaran pledge.

"I greet you now in all honesty and truth and offer you my friendship," Skellan told him and then he flashed a sharp grin. "My birth name may be Hilthorn Radulf, but please call me Skellan."

"It is an honor, Skellan," Atreau replied.

Skellan then introduced his sister. More pleasantries and chatter passed as further nobles, merchants, and city leaders voiced their delight at Skellan's return to his birthright. A few young women and men attempted to flirt, but all seemed a little too wary of Skellan to actually hold his attention. Only last night he'd shaken the entire city and slain a demon lord. They all knew that he wasn't quite one of them.

Bishop Palo's pretty, dark-eyed niece only managed to whisper her greeting and curtsy before she began to look faint. Her maids flocked to her, cooing and hurrying her from Skellan's path. She settled on a divan to cast longing glances after Atreau's back.

The older guests cited their great admiration of the previous count and those who could played upon Lady Hylanya's good manners to make their introductions. A few awkward moments arose when Skellan's impoverished upbringing shone through but Skellan made light of them and generally managed to win laughs from those surrounding him.

Elezar noticed that the nursemaid standing to his own left gave a quiet commentary of hushed little clucks and grumbles at the sight of each guest. Her responses gave an uncanny forecast of Lady Hylanya's formality or warmth towards any given person. Elezar wasn't delighted at how both women seemed to brighten at the sight of Rafale. He reminded himself that Skellan needed every supporter and Rafale had proven himself to be that, even if he'd been less than forthcoming about it. Skellan greeted him coolly and Elezar wondered if it wasn't because his sister appeared so taken with the man. Sheriff Hirbe, on the other hand, received a much more friendly greeting from Skellan, which inspired the sheriff to recount the bawdy tale of the previous count's sly exploits.

At last Skellan reached the chamber where an immense oak table stood laden with candelabras of blazing beeswax candles ringed by sprays of fragrant herbs. Dozens of huge silver mirrors, stripped from the Sun Palace, reflected the warm light and filled the otherwise barren walls with echoes of the gathered guests' splendor.

It felt almost like witnessing true magic, seeing the vast panes of gray stone transform into a mosaic of gold, brocade, and spangles of bright blue and green feathers. As more and more people trailed Skellan into the chamber their own opulence adorned the room.

"Is that me... everywhere?" Skellan leaned back to whisper to Elezar. Then he bobbed his head as if attempting to evade his own reflection. Next to him Lady Hylanya adjusted a string of rubies ringing her graceful throat.

"It's all of us," Elezar reassured him. He met the reflection of his own gaze but then glanced over the faces of those gathered behind them. He noted that Lady Hylanya's nursemaid did the same, pinning Bishop Palo with a particular malevolence. Sheriff Hirbe met his glance in the mirror and grinned at him. Elezar smiled back, guessing that this magnificence of gilded frames and refraction had been in some way his doing.

"It's just a trick of polished silver and light," Elezar murmured to Skellan. "You'll get used to it quickly enough."

"I can't see the stones," Skellan replied. A month ago Elezar wouldn't have grasped the implication of that but now he felt a pulse of alarm.

"I can order them taken down—"

"No." Skellan flexed his hands quickly as if he were plucking the strings of a harp. "I've found the silver beneath the glass. It knows my bloodline. And the stone is there even if I can't see it."

"That's good then?" Elezar only now noticed that his hand gripped the hilt of his sword. It embarrassed him to realize how strained his nerves must be that he nearly drew his blade without even being aware of it and that it had been in response to nothing but a wall of reflections.

He exchanged a glance in the mirror with Skellan and without a word it seemed as though they each read the other's uneasiness and the recognition somehow reassured them both. Skellan straightened and smiled.

Elezar dropped his hand from his sword and then followed Skellan as he took his place in the carved chair at the head of the table. From the right of Skellan's chair, he watched as the rest of the guests settled onto the silk cushions of their seats. Behind each guest, a guard, an attendant, or servant of some kind stood. The tableau reminded Elezar of chapel sculptures depicting blessed patrons with guardian saints towering behind them and presenting them to the gates of heaven. Sheriff Hirbe had been right, Elezar decided, to have him stand as the count's champion. Skellan would have seemed deprived if he alone sat without any guardian at his right.

Skellan looked up and down the length of the table. Then he stood, commanding the attention of his noble guests, just as he'd claimed the rapt attention of the witches at the Rat Rafters nights before.

"Promises were made of a great feasting tonight, but before we tear in, I've been advised to bend all your ears with a fine speech penned by our own Rafale." Skellan inclined his head in Rafale's direction and drew out the piece of heavy rag paper. Elezar stole a glance over the clear Labaran script, catching a long list of mythic warlords said to have wrested Labara from the rule of the grimma. The page looked nearly black with tight lines of script. Skellan smiled at the paper.

"This is a princely soliloquy filled with poetry, but the reading of it seems long and likely to keep us all from our dinner. So, let me sum it up. It informs you all of the might of my bloodlines, both Radulf and Sumar, and then reminds you of your friendship to my father and your obligations to my lineage. It goes on a fair length enumerating relatives that I'll admit I never knew were mine, and then concludes with my promise to rule you all justly." The rueful amusement in Skellan's voice carried as if the mirrors reflected sound as well as image. "This is a wondrous speech, one that should be recited up on a stage, by a fellow with a flowing white beard and golden leaves scattered at his feet, but I'm no such fellow, am I?"

Several involuntary laughs erupted from the younger guests while many of their elders watched Skellan nervously. The nursemaid standing behind Lady Hylanya's seat pinned Skellan with a hard glare as if he were a rascal child she longed to smack upside the head.

"I can see that you're hungry and I'd be the last one to keep a grumbling belly from its feed. So instead of reading a more stately man's words I'll give you all my own and have done with it." Skellan returned the speech to the pocket of his doublet. Then he turned his attention to his audience of nobles, merchants, and city leaders and they gazed back at him. "I never knew either my mother or father and I'd feel like a liar calling upon either to justify my right to this county. My right was won in combat the night before last and it's my own deeds—not those of my ancestors—that I stand by. I don't know what any of my ancestors would have done in the face of an invading grimma army, but I tell you that I will fight them with all my power. I will lay them low even if I have to drag every one of those bitches down with me."

The assurance of Skellan's voice sent a shiver down Elezar's spine and at the table everyone, even Atreau and his pages, seemed to feel the certainty in Skellan.

"As for what I would have of all of you." Skellan shrugged. "People don't fight with all their hearts just because they're asked—not even if they're asked by their liege lord. You'll each do as you please regardless of any promises or pleading squeezed from me. So, I would only have you remember that, though we are all dressed warm and about to feed on wine and fat, we aren't alone in this city or in the county. There are other folk, those whose service, labor, loyalty, and taxes put all these goods in our grasps. From mere babes to codgers and crones, they all look to us for justice and protection. That is the only obligation I would call upon you each to answer. Be the champions your people need. Be deserving of the riches of Milmuraille that you now enjoy."

A quiet followed Skellan's words. Elezar wasn't sure if he read awe or confusion in the faces of the men and women seated at the tables, but the vast majority of the guards, attendants, and servants appeared truly taken with Skellan. He might not be who the aristocracy of Milmuraille expected him to be but it seemed he was exactly the count their servants wished for. Skellan himself continued to maintain his smile but Elezar saw the effort of it. It was good he hadn't attempted the long, wordy speech Rafale had prepared for him.

"And speaking of riches to be enjoyed, let us have our supper!" Skellan waved his hand to one of the serving boys who peered in from the kitchen. "I'm done jawing. You may bring on the grub!" He dropped back down into his seat and moments later a train of servers carried out dish after dish of steaming, rich foods. Elezar had seen many of the dishes when he'd eaten in the kitchen and a good number of them hadn't roused much of an appetite in him, but now garnished and plated like fragrant treasures on golden chargers, even the snails looked striking and rich.

Pairs of young women, their dark hair pinned up in maiden's braids, paraded around the table with gold and scarlet flagons of sweet Labaran wine and watered bitters. Glasses filled, drained, and filled again as the guests relaxed in each other's company and indulged in all the food their silver trenchers would hold. Conversation ebbed and flowed from serious consideration of war to lewd jokes and winking innuendos.

Had he been seated at the table, Elezar likely would have grown restless, even bored, if he'd found himself—like

Atreau—seated between two young women who seemed intent upon comparing the quality of perfumes available from Yuan and the Salt Islands. But standing at Skellan's side Elezar felt free to observe anyone he wanted and to listen in on a variety of conversations. He studied the attendants, guards, and companions who stood behind their masters' chairs, considering them as people rather than functionaries for the first time.

Lady Hylanya's nursemaid clearly doted on the girl but also often cast motherly glances to Rafale. The elder of Atreau's pages appeared enrapt by the women chatting with his master while the younger boy eyed their brimming plates of food with a longing that obviously outstripped any other lust. Sheriff Hirbe's companion leaned over the back of another man's chair with the air of a devoted child, whispering in his grandfather's ear. Once he glanced up the length of the table and offered Elezar a conspiratorial wink. Elezar tried not to appear confused and responded with a short nod, which earned him a broad, sympathetic smile. Sacrist Bois, on the other hand, might as well have been a gargoyle glowering down on Bishop Palo from a Labaran temple downspout.

Elezar wondered what others read in his expression when he gazed down at Skellan. Did passing servants easily discern the flush of affection that rose through Elezar's body? Was the pull of longing there for anyone to recognize or did it just feel that way to him? And for that matter, when had he become so fond of Skellan that observing his barbarous attempts at table manners had begun to strike him as charming?

Perhaps charming was exactly the right word—maybe all this heat and longing resulted from the spell Skellan had placed upon him. Elezar wasn't certain if he found that thought reassuring or distressing. He hardly wanted to find himself in the thrall of a witch, but if he was enchanted, then these tender, vulnerable emotions would not have been truly his own.

Watching Skellan tip several pearl onions into the fragrant water in his finger bowl and then toss the concoction back like a shot of liquor, Elezar felt terribly certain that his delight in the other man's unique qualities arose from a genuine affection. How could a man not find Skellan's fearless enthusiasm endearing?

"That was not good," Skellan commented over his shoulder. "I can see why no one else is drinking the stuff in these little bowls."

"It's for rinsing your fingers," Elezar whispered to him.

"Tastes better to suck them clean, if you ask me," Skellan replied. Elezar's skin warmed as he watched Skellan lick the oil from his own long fingers. Poor manners, but so appealing in the most primal way.

A moment later, Lady Hylanya and the two noblemen sitting nearest Skellan noticed his gaffe. The three politely emulated him, quaffing down their perfumed water as well, which in turn inspired a number of other guests all down the length of the table.

Skellan observed them with a quizzical expression. The he muttered, very softly, "Now if I let a fart rip, do you think they'll try that as well?"

Elezar managed not to laugh out loud but not easily. Skellan grinned at him and then turned his attention back to his dinner companions. Elezar listened to their conversation while his own thoughts wandered between the reinforcing the city's defenses and word of his involvement with Skellan reaching Cadeleon.

"It depends on the Sumar grimma," Skellan remarked to the man on his left. He paused to carefully spear a hunk of pork with his snail fork. "If she refuses to allow the other grimma free passage through her lands then they'll be forced to camp their entire army along the river in a narrow band." He wolfed down his meat and the other man nodded. "But as I said, much will depend upon the Sumar grimma and where she places her allegiance…"

With the idea of the Sumar grimma in the back of his mind Elezar stretched slightly, craning his neck back to gaze up into the shadows of the ceiling. There he saw the faintest traces of orange lights. Then they seemed to blink out of existence. Elezar scowled up at the stonework. Another ochre light flickered briefly to life and a reverberating shiver passed over Elezar as if a string of invisible bells rang through him.

At once Skellan's head came up and he followed Elezar's gaze up into the shadows.

"Assassin!" Skellan bounded up, swinging onto the tabletop. Leaping over plates and platters, he raced to the middle of the table. Elezar drew his sword and sprinted behind the chairs of the startled guests to follow Skellan. Up on the table, Skellan swore something in Mirogothic and then made a motion as if he were hurling a spear up into the ceiling. Elezar thought he caught a glint of red light flash from Skellan's hand.

A piercing shriek sounded from high above the table. As Skellan swung his arms down towards the floor, a black eagle with wings nearly the length of Elezar's body was torn from the shadows. Screaming, flapping, and raking massive talons through the air, it tumbled towards the floor but then caught its balance and wheeled towards Skellan's back.

Elezar bounded into the eagle's path and swung his blade with all his strength, severing the bird's huge head. For an instant the eagle's body continued upward, spraying dark blood across Elezar's left arm. The black fluid seared where it struck Elezar's skin and he quickly wiped it away on his doublet. A moment later, the eagle's body plunged down to the floor in a lifeless mass.

A second shriek sounded from overhead.

Everyone in the chamber gaped up at the ceiling as Skellan hauled another eagle out of the shadows on an invisible tether. This time he didn't pull the creature from the air.

"I hear you," Skellan shouted up at the eagle, "and I will break her thrall over you but you must fight her will."

The eagle's scream tore through the chamber and the huge bird flapped and flexed its talons but didn't strike. Skellan muttered something and his hands moved as if he fought with a tangle of knots. Strangely Elezar felt a hot tingling in his own chest, and for an instant he thought he saw not an eagle hanging over them but a thin, naked Irabiim woman. A cloak of black feathers floated out behind her as if suspended in deep water while a tangle of flickering orange symbols glowed up from her dark skin like scales.

With a feeling of dread, Elezar stole a glance down to the body at his feet. Black feathers peeled back, revealing a young man's bare chest. The man's head lay face down, curly blond hair spilling into the pool of his own blood.

Skellan groaned and then wrenched his arms wide apart, tearing something powerful asunder. The force of it rippled through the room and the symbols swathing the Irabiim woman blinked out. She dropped from the air like a stone. It was Atreau who bounded up from his chair and caught the frail woman. Her battered cloak of black feathers spilled apart like scattering ash.

Skellan shoved a candelabrum and two silver platters aside and crouched down on the table.

"Does she live?" Skellan asked.

"She's breathing," Atreau replied. He gazed at the withered woman in his arms with a tender expression, and looking more closely, Elezar realized that the Irabiim woman appeared old enough to be his great-grandmother. Her pale eyes fluttered open but then fell closed again.

"Thank you for your chivalrous reflexes, Duke Quemanor." Skellan bounced back to his feet and looked around at his guests. Most stared at Skellan in return. Bishop Palo's niece had fainted, as was expected of a well-bred Cadeleonian girl. Elezar caught both Rafale and Sacrist Bois studying him and the dead man at his feet. Bois glanced aside when he noted Elezar watching him in return but Rafale lifted his glass as if offering him a mock toast.

All heads turned a moment later when Javier threw open the doors to the chamber and raced in with Kiram and a dozen guards behind them.

"The grimma—" Javier stopped abruptly when he caught sight of the bloody body at Elezar's feet and then took in the emaciated woman in Atreau's arms.

"Bloody mess," Kiram said and he was right. Ugly spatters of black blood dripped down the walls, beaded the table and dishes, and clung to Elezar. Though with the young man now dead, his blood no longer burned but simply congealed.

"His cloak," Skellan called to Elezar. "Give it to me quickly."

Elezar stripped the feathered cloak from the decapitated body. The feathers clung and curled around his arms and hands like wet linen and the warm aroma of a living body rose up from them. Once he'd pulled the cloak free Elezar tossed it up. Skellan caught it and swung the cloak around him far from his own body. The wings billowed like sails catching the wind. Skellan flung the cloak high overhead where it winged in a slow circle as if it were once again a living thing. Though it made an eerie headless silhouette now.

"Return to your maker," Skellan shouted up at the cloak. "Burn the sky with the name of Hilthorn Radulf, who has broken her spells. Go!"

With a gesture Skellan seemed to wave the cloak back into the shadows of the ceiling. For a few moments Skellan simply stood there in silence and everyone else, including Elezar, watched. The air felt still now. The strong metallic scent of blood permeated the room. His fresh clothes had been soaked and his sword would need cleaning again. He fought the urge to look down at the youth he'd killed. He didn't want to see the face.

Skellan hopped off the tabletop to stand beside Atreau and study the tiny woman in his arms. She opened her pale blue eyes and whispered something too quietly for Elezar to hear.

"My Irabiim isn't so good." Skellan looked to Kiram and at once Kiram closed the distance with Javier right behind him. While Kiram went to Skellan and the old woman, Javier stopped and knelt beside the young man Elezar had killed. He laid one hand on the severed head and the other on the ridge of the naked chest. Then he looked up to Elezar.

"He's free," Javier said.

"That's one word for it," Elezar replied.

"Better than having the grimma snatch up his soul to enslave him again." Javier straightened. "We don't always have the option to be merciful, but I think that at least you were swift in dispatching him. Sometimes that's the only kindness a man can offer."

Elezar recognized the truth in Javier's words, but it didn't quite feel like absolution. He guessed that mere words never could do that. If they did, a man might feel righteous in murder far too easily.

"She gives you thanks for breaking Grimma Ylva's spell," Kiram translated as the white-haired woman murmured from Atreau's arms. The woman's gaze flickered briefly to the dead youth and then returned to Skellan.

"He could not resist the spells, but now he will be reborn to freedom," Kiram translated after another string of murmurs. "He is where Ylva cannot reach him at long last."

Elezar took some consolation in that thought. Enough to allow him to turn his mind to the necessities of the evening. In a flurry of action he made sure that the dead man's body was removed to the chapel. Servants cleared away the dishes sullied with blood and a group of sister-physicians came and took the ancient Irabiim woman from Atreau. Javier and Kiram attended her as well.

Labaran wine and strong cider arrived in silver chalices, which were emptied almost at once. Soon inebriated guests toasted Skellan's first victoryagainst a grimma and jested that he'd done it as easily as skinning a rabbit. They reveled in the atmosphere of triumph and Skellan grinned and indulged them with sleight of hand tricks and by making coins seem to appear from his smiling sister's braids. But Elezar noted the tremble in Skellan's hands and caught moments when his grins neared grimaces.

If any of the guests noted the same or worried that the grimma's assassins had penetrated into the heart of the city to strike at Skellan directly, they didn't give voice to their concern. Laughter, congratulations, and toasts echoed through the chamber as servants carried in towering honey cakes and plates of glistening candied fruit. Eventually even the parade of sweets and soft cheeses ended. At last Skellan bid his guests a good night, withdrew, and Elezar followed him up to the suite of rooms that now brimmed with Skellan's new belongings.

Alone in the privacy of the suite Skellan sank down to the floor and bowed his head against his knees.

"What's the matter?" Elezar checked the lock on the door then knelt beside Skellan. As he touched Skellan's shoulder he realized that Skellan was shaking.

"Just the shock," Skellan replied. "Grimma Ylva wasn't so easily beaten as I played at."

"You're hurt?" Skellan shook his head but Elezar didn't believe him.

"You're quaking like an aspen leaf," Elezar told him.

"Fatigue. It was still too soon since I fought the demon lord. I'm done in but I couldn't let them know, could I?" Skellan smiled at Elezar. "That bit with the cloak was a bluff. The thing was coming back to life and if I hadn't let it escape it might well have transformed any one of you and carried you as a slave back to Ylva."

The idea of that chilled Elezar. He'd held that cloak in his hands and felt it grasping at him.

"I didn't think to set wards so high," Skellan murmured. "I should have thought..."

"You know now—" Elezar's reply was cut off by a light knock at the door. Both Elezar and Skellan started like boys caught with their trousers down.

"Can you stand?" Elezar whispered.

Skellan nodded and rose to his feet but only managed a few steps before his legs began to buckle. Elezar took his weight and carried him to the huge bed while two more knocks sounded from the other side of the door. Skellan made an attempt to look at ease on the pillows and silk bedding.

Elezar strode across the room and wrenched the door open to discover Rafale.

"Whatever you're peddling, we have no need for it tonight," Elezar told him.

"Only the count's champion for a day and you're already mistaking yourself for his wife, are you?"

The first response that came to Elezar was just to punch Rafale's teeth in, but he controlled himself. He didn't need any more blood on his hands right this moment. And he'd come to suspect that Rafale's connections with the county's nobility ran far deeper than he'd first thought. The man certainly worked as far more than a mere playwright.

"Skellan is tired and wants his sleep. What do you need?"

"Just to have a few words with him," Rafale replied. He tried to peer past but Elezar positioned his bulk to block the view of the bed.

"Let him come, Elezar," Skellan called from behind him. Rafale grinned, and though it annoyed him deeply, Elezar stepped back to allow Rafale into the room. Elezar took out a little of his frustration by slamming the door shut.

Skellan stretched on the bed like a study in languid repose, his hands crossed beneath his head, his long legs crossed at the ankles. Rafale made a show of admiring him while Elezar did his best to suppress his aggravation.

"I wanted to tell you that you did very well this evening," Rafale said.

"Of course I did," Skellan replied. "Didn't I always say I was meant for greater things?"

Hearing his arroant, assured tone Elezar would never have suspected that Skellan had been crumpled on the floor only moments ago.

"That you did, my love. That you did." Rafale laughed like a man indulging a child.

"So, I'm the darling of the county nobs now, am I?" Skellan inquired.

"Maybe not their darling, but you impressed them no end tonight." Rafale casually dropped down onto the edge of the bed. "That scene with Grimma Ylva's assassins couldn't have been better timed if it had been planned..." He placed a hand on Skellan's knee. "It wasn't, though, was it?"

"Oh, certainly," Skellan replied. "I and the grimma arranged it all as supper theater."

Again Rafale offered Skellan that condescending laugh, which made Elezar want to knock his handsome head in.

"Have you got anything to say that's worth hearing?" Elezar snapped. "Or did you just slither in here to get in a grope?"

Rafale scowled at him but then turned his attention back to Skellan.

"Possessive, isn't he?" Rafale commented.

"But loyal," Skellan replied. "A fellow in my position could do much worse than win loyalty from his man. I might, just for example, end up like Cire and find myself relying on a charmer who'd do me in for a chance at bedding any nob with a title."

Rafale's smile wavered just slightly.

"You're not just any nob, my love," Rafale replied. "And yes, I would do her and anyone else over for your sake. That's my loyalty."

"And you think I should be glad for it?" Skellan heaved himself upright though Elezar could see that it took nearly all the strength he possessed. Exhaustion lent a raw quality to his voice. "You think that I should be well pleased that you plotted to kill Cire, Merle, Navet, and every other one of my friends from the Rat Rafters?"

"We were out of other options—" Rafale began but Skellan cut him off.

"You played it up as if you were offering them a great opportunity and you knew—you had to know—that those coffers would have killed them all—"

"Yes, I knew. But the sacrifice would have been worth it if it had saved you and Milmuraille. Don't you see that?"

"No," Skellan stated flatly. "You had no right to lie to them. No right to decide that their lives were worth less than anyone else's."

"Skellan, I did it for you—"

"For me?" Skellan glowered at Rafale. "I was nothing but a piece of cheap ass for you until you realized I was Hilthorn Radulf. If I hadn't been my father's heir you would have sent me to die right along with Cire. You did nothing for my sake. You only serve a title. You could care less about the quality of man holding it."

There was so much anger in Skellan's expression that it made Elezar's heart ache. It seemed obvious that though Rafale may never have loved Skellan, at one point Skellan had loved Rafale.

"Never, Skellan, my love. I would never harm you." Rafale tried to touch Skellan's shoulder but Skellan batted Rafale's hand away.

"I don't want you here," Skellan said. "For Cire's sake I'm willing to keep your secret but you are no longer welcome in my chamber, you understand?"

"Skellan, don't be childish about this," Rafale said. "I'm better placed than anyone to help you."

"Direct me, you mean?" Skellan glowered at him. "You think I'm going to totter about like one of your actors, spouting words you've written for me?"

"You didn't like the speech I wrote? Is that what this is really all about?" Rafale inquired with another indulgent smile. "I admit it wasn't perfectly suited to you, but I had only a day to compose the thing. You did nicely enough."

"This isn't about a speech." Skellan cut him off. "This is about the fact that you were willing to kill Cire and you seem to think that I should be happy that you'd do such a thing for my sake."

"Were you a little more worldly you would understand, Skellan. A man does what he must. I wouldn't have taken any pleasure in seeing Cire die but if it could have saved the city—and you—it was a small price to pay. I would do anything—"

"When did you know?" Skellan cut him short again. "When did you know who I was?"

Rafale paused and Elezar guessed that he was weighing just how much ignorance he could claim. Skellan clearly read his guilt. His expression turned almost sickened.

"It's been years, hasn't it?" Skellan asked. "You knew for years and you just let me live like…"

"I knew, but you weren't ready for court life, Skellan, and certainly the count's court wasn't prepared for the trouble you would have brought. But I looked after you, didn't I? I gave you monies and treats and if you'd have come more often I would have kept you warm in my bed any night."

Skellan glowered at Rafale with shining eyes and Elezar wondered if he wasn't on the verge of furious tears. Rafale saw it too and his expression gentled. Though there was something almost smug about his smile—as if he took a certain pleasure in knowing that he could disturb Skellan so deeply.

Elezar wished that he could call Rafale out and cut him down in a dueling circle but he knew more bloodshed wasn't going to solve anything.

"Sweetheart, I haven't always done the right thing. I'd be the first to admit as much," Rafale said soothingly. "But I've always acted in your interest. I am ever your truest lover—"

"You aren't my lover! You aren't even my friend! You're just a bastard who fucked me," Skellan burst out. "One of many! I don't want you near me!"

"You can't mean that." Rafale paled as if ill. "I've always been there for you."

"For me? For Vieve, for Mistress Houblon, for Cire, and for my own sister as well! Who haven't you been there for?" Skellan snapped. "You might have charmed me once, when I was a pathetic starveling on the street, but I've grown up and learned what a real friend is, what true loyalty means."

Skellan's gaze shifted to Elezar and his expression softened. It was only a tired glance and a few words, so it shouldn't have moved Elezar so deeply. Yet he found himself staring back at Skellan with a tenderness that unmanned him. Rafale glanced between them and sneered.

"You are greatly mistaken if you think this Cadeleonian is going to stay at your side. He serves another—"

"Oh, for fuck's sake," Elezar growled. "Just shut your mouth and get out. Skellan's done with you."

Rafale's face flushed. He shot Elezar a look of absolute hatred and, for an instant Elezar thought he might draw the ornate dagger that hung from his belt. Instead, Rafale squared his shoulders, stood, and offered Skellan a stiff bow. Then he withdrew with his head held high.

Elezar locked the door after him and then strode to Skellan's bedside. Remembering Rafale's earlier presumption, he didn't seat himself on the bed but found a footstool and settled down on that.

"You're starting to swear like a real Labaran," Skellan told him. He looked as if he might fall asleep at any moment.

"And who shall I blame for that?" Elezar teased.

"It has been my pleasure." Skellan smiled but he looked exhausted. He barely rallied enough strength to pull at the clasps of his scarlet doublet.

"Here." Elezar went to him and drew the doublet off. Then he stripped off the white shirt beneath and noticed a sprinkling of blood and burns marking Skellan's right arm.

"You were hurt."

"You too," Skellan commented.

Elezar glanced down at his own hand, noting for the first time the spattering of burns marking his knuckles and forearm. He'd been so distracted he hadn't even registered them.

Now he saw that the burns almost perfectly matched those marring Skellan's pale skin.

Skellan reach out and entwined his fingers with Elezar's. "Come lie with me."

"Are you sure?" Elezar inquired. "I understand that three quite comely fellows are all vying for the same invitation."

Skellan snorted derisively.

"You mean Rafale's chosen men? He can keep them."

"You weren't in the least bit tempted?" Elezar managed to ask in a light tone.

"They were nice enough to look at but I wouldn't put up with any one of them snoring in my ear all night long." Skellan shifted to make a space in the bed. "The honor of that position is all yours, my man."

CHAPTER
THIRTEEN

In Elezar's opinion, a chasm of disparity loomed between the breezy descriptions of fortifying a city against the onslaught of an opposing army as they appeared in the military histories he had studied at the Sagrada Academy and the reality of the exhausting labor involved.

He remembered thinking that the short lists of precise steps involved in digging out defensive ditches and reinforcing battlements all seemed obvious and simple. He'd wondered why War Master Ignacio had insisted on constantly drilling the instructions into him and every other lordling at the school. At the time, single combat had struck Elezar and his fellow Hellions as the key to battle, greatness, and glory. But now, surrounded by the populace of Milmuraille, Elezar thought he understood.

If one man died on the battlefield another could stand in his place, but if even a foot of the city wall failed then the breach might cost them everything. When thousands of lives depended on every inch of the fortifications holding against assault, then the miles and miles of walls and ditches seemed overwhelming. The work left no room for half-assed guesses. Knowing those exact specifications that the war master had drummed into him offered Elezar his only certainty when all around chaos and complications reigned.

Simply finding suitable materials proved to be hard enough. Hauling stone, iron, and lumber, much of it salvaged from the collapsed buildings scattered across the city, required dozens of teams of draft horses and hundreds of volunteers. After that platoons of masons, blacksmiths, and carpenters transformed the wreckage into new, towering fortifications. Folk all across the city joined the crews moving supplies. Others set to work digging trenches, pits, and the additional wells that would be required to douse fires.

Teams of red-robed sister-physicians streamed in and out of the Mockingbird Playhouse as well as several gambling dens, transforming them into infirmaries for coming casualties. Many of the folk seemed to volunteer for work at the city wall just for the opportunity to gawk at their young count as he strode high overhead, dressed in scarlet brocade and a dog skin cloak, while cloud imps and little gold birds flittered around him.

At least once daily, Skellan walked the entire perimeter of the city, laying spells over each new piece of fortification and searching the sky for signs of his wethra-steeds. Often Javier and Cire joined him while other witches on the streets below drew their own wards across houses, shops, carts, and cobblestones. When he passed the old section of the city, Navet and Merle always called greetings to him and—Skellan had rather proudly confessed to Elezar—they nearly always brought him spicy Yuanese sausages.

In the evenings when sunset colors streamed across the river's sinuous surface and lit up sword blades as well as windowpanes, Elezar often imagined even he could discern wards glimmering up from the masonry of the garrison walls. Recently he'd noticed more and more flickers of magic catching his eye. He wasn't certain if that was due to the sheer number of spells and charms spreading through Milmuraille or an effect of Skellan's constant proximity and the spell binding them. Were those brief flashes of ringing color a hint of how people like Javier, Cire, and Skellan perceived the world at all times?

Only last night Skellan had tried to share some of what he felt in creating his wards.

"It's as if I reach, with my soul, up out of my body and place red constellations overhead. Then I let their light fall down to protect the buildings and streets below. If I don't think about why they are all here, then they're lovely, really. But sometimes I feel almost lost up there." Skellan had leaned into him. "But then I remember the beckoning pleasure of our bed and my soul flits right back down to my flesh to have you warm me up."

The conversation hadn't gone much further, since the bed and its intimate respite held the same draw for Elezar himself. They found as much pleasure as they could in the short hours of the night, but all too soon the sun blazed over the horizon and another day of work stretched before them both.

This morning, like every morning the past week, young men and even a few girls from a variety of backgrounds reported to the garrison expecting to be honed into soldiers fit to defend their county.

The girls, including Sarl, Elezar turned over to the female captain the harbor guard. The garrison had served as brothel too recently for him house these few boisterous girls in barracks brimming with young men. And the garrison barracks were indeed brimming now. Elezar's field captains inducted men and boys dozens at a time. He found that some captains possessed more discriminating taste than others, however.

Only yesterday Elezar had discovered that one recruited youth was all but blind while another he found limping along on only one leg. He'd found them both work in the kitchens, and a few hours later he'd sent a gaunt grandfather back to the care of his wife and children who'd all come searching for him.

Elezar wished sorely that he could have turned more of the recruits away, but the city walls stretched far and protecting them required far more bodies than Elezar commanded, even given the private Labaran infantrymen now serving him in the garrison.

It didn't do to think on that too much.

Still, while riding maneuvers with his best cavalrymen, Elezar glanced out across a regiment of boys attempting to wield heavy pikes in formation. He recognized one shaggy-haired Labaran lad and couldn't help but reign Cobre to a halt. The boy struggled to balance his pike and nearly fell backward onto the taller youth behind him.

"Doue?" Elezar called to him. The innkeeper's son looked up from his pained study of his weapon with a startled expression. Then his face lit up with delight. Elezar noted that the boy had attempted to wax the few downy hairs on his upper lip into a courtly mustache.

"Master Elezar!" He managed something like a salute. "I've joined your army!"

"So I see." Elezar felt the blood draining from his face but he maintained his easy smile. A boy like Doue wouldn't last a moment against a Mirogoth warrior. Hell, the child's older sister, Fleur, would have been more suited to the battlefield.

"Does your mother know?"

"Aye, sir. She and Pa sent me off. Fleur's joined the women in your kitchen."

"The whole family's nearly in then," Elezar responded, just to have something to say. What parents sent their unwed daughter into a garrison full of soldiers? The same couple, he supposed, who imagined that a boy as young and guileless as Doue would survive even a day of battle. Glancing over the formations of fresh volunteers, Elezar picked out a few other youths who appeared as green as Doue. Maybe ten of them looked more boy than man. Too many, and yet he knew that if they were to hold the city walls they would need every body they could lay hands on to maintain a tight line of defense.

"We'll teach those grimma a thing or two," Doue opined.

"We will indeed," Elezar agreed. Voicing his fear for the boy would only spook him as well as many of the other volunteers. Morale had to be maintained. Still Elezar hesitated. He couldn't spare every youth who reminded him of his little brother, Nestor, and expect to win a war. But maybe he could save this one.

"As I remember, you spent a fair amount of time in your father's stables," Elezar commented.

"Yes, sir," Doue replied.

"Well, Cobre's been missing your ministrations, I think."

Elezar stroked the stallion's neck absently. "Tell your officer that Lord Grunito requires your services for his charger. Then go and report to the stable master."

"Truly?—I mean, yes, sir!" A delighted, worshipful grin spread across Doue's plump pink face. Then he bowed to Elezar and then pelted across the courtyard, dragging his pike behind him as he hurried to his commanding officer. Elezar turned away and nudged Cobre ahead. His own sentimentality embarrassed him and he knew that the speculation likely to follow the transfer would do his reputation no good at all. Still, the knot of ice that had seemed to grind in his gut melted away.

Soon enough, battle practice wiped his thoughts of the boy from Elezar's mind completely. He focused entirely on the near impossibility of combating a troll. Towering over him and Cobre, Bone-crusher obliged Elezar and thirty other cavalrymen in playing the part of their adversary.

When he'd first made the suggestion to Bone-crusher, Elezar had been at pains to assure the troll that neither he nor his men would truly harm him. Bone-crusher had agreed to participate but with an oddly amused expression.

Now Elezar understood why. Charging the troll was like riding against a mountain. Swords, spears, and maces only knocked accumulations of mulch and moss off of the troll's rocky hide but hardly scratched him.

Master Bone-crusher easily spun and caught both horse and rider in the stone cage of his fingers. Had he wished he could have crushed any of them, but the troll treated them quite gently. When a horse shied, the troll stepped back and made a soft, small noises, almost like the nickers of a foal, until the mount calmed.

"Tell me, Master Bone-crusher," Elezar called after making another charge behind the troll only to have his spear skid off the troll's shoulder, "is there anything that would penetrate your skin?"

*My own teeth have ground through another troll's throat.
My fists have cracked another troll's skull asunder.*

"I can believe that," Elezar replied. "But is there a weapon that a man like myself might wield?"

The Sumar grimma is said to possess a spell that can transform forged metal into a weapon that will lay open even stone.

Bone-crusher scratched at his mossy backside and then crouched down close to Elezar. Cobre tensed and Elezar felt the stallion's heart pounding beneath him, but he held his position, even as the musky odor of the troll rolled over them. *Our Little Thorn hopes that she will offer it to us along with her allegiance, I think.*

Elezar nodded.

But I do not know that we can depend upon her. None of the grimma are inclined to kindness but I... I hesitate to speak of it with our Little Thorn. I think that deep in his heart he holds a great hope that she will care that he is her child. Bone-crusher cocked his massive head, providing Elezar with a view into the hollows that normally shadowed the troll's eyes. For an instant Elezar felt that he peered through a dark stone keyhole into a whirling sea of molten gold.

"She cared enough to send me to find him," Elezar replied.

Finding him is not the same thing as joining him in battle against her own.

"No, it's not," Elezar admitted. "I suppose that if we don't hear back from Eski and Magraie soon, I'll have to talk to him about it." Tonight, Elezar thought. That was if either of them could manage to stay awake for anything other than sex.

After days spent with Javier, Cire, and a shifting constellation of Milmuraille's street witches weaving together wards from all across the city, likely the last thing Skellan wished to think about would be more magic. Or worse, what tenuous hopes he might pin on his estranged mother's affection. Still, they did need to talk and in the last week it seemed that the only time they could do so alone was in Skellan's bed.

Or perhaps he'd give it another day. Tomorrow night, Elezar thought. He just needed to resist the urge to let ecstasy wash away all the anxiety of the day.

"One way or another we'll fell the grimma's trolls."

Bone-crusher nodded and his eyes again fell into shadow. *A hard fall will crack a troll as well.* Bone-crusher seemed to consider something far off in the direction of the river. *Your cannon shot does bite. Enough pounding in one place might do more than annoy me.*

"How much cannon shot?" Elezar inquired.

Some twenty stones might break my ankle. Then the fall would knock some wind out of me as well.

Twenty shots simply to break an ankle. How many more shots to inflict a fatal wound on even one of the trolls traveling with the grimma?

They were going to need more cannons and cannon balls.

Two days later that thought led Elezar straight into the delicate business of requisitioning ships, their crews, and cannons.

Sheriff Hirbe and Atreau both appeared to appreciate Elezar's company. The dozen cavalrymen whom he'd brought to shadow them certainly didn't hurt when it came to maintaining the pretense of ship captains' voluntarily handing their vessels over to Count Radulf. Only one captain attempted to refuse outright.

The stocky Cadeleonian sneered past the sheriff and looked Atreau over as if he thought him an overpriced trollop.

"So you're the one that's turned bender for Count Radulf, are you, you pretty thing?" The captain took a step closer to Atreau. "You turned whore for the Labarans and now you think you can prance your ass up onto my ship and commandeer it?"

"Actually," Atreau responded with a very tight smile, "the count's champion is my dear friend Elezar here. Perhaps he could better explain why we are requisitioning your ship, crew, and cannons."

Elezar dismounted then and strode past the sheriff and Atreau to stand almost chest to chest with the captain. Bowing his head to glower down upon the man, Elezar noted droplets of sweat rising on the captain's brow. All across the ship's deck sailors went quiet as they looked on.

Elezar wanted to beat the captain down to his knees and make him beg before his men, but he restrained his rage. He'd not come here to avenge himself—or Atreau—upon this lout but to ensure that this ship and its crew defended the city.

So, Elezar caught the captain's dingy shirtfront in his fist and hauled the man up to the tips of his boots. Then he reiterated Atreau's request very clearly and firmly.

He then continued, "Thousands of lives depend upon these ships maintaining a blockade of the river. If Milmuraille falls to the Mirogoths, then Cadeleon will be drawn into the resulting war here on Labaran soil. And no one wants that, right?"

"Of course we don't," the captain rasped. "I see that, now. My ship is at Count Radulf's service."

"Good." Elezar released the captain and strode back to Cobre. He could feel the Cadeleonian sailors—even those on ships docked nearby—gawking at him. Moments later the captain accepted his payment of Labaran silver from Skellan's treasury and signed the contract Atreau had drawn up.

Then their party departed from the ship, leaving Wirret from the harbor guard to decide the best use of the heavy galleon.

"The handy thing about our Elezar is how quick he can loosen a man's bowels with that displeased look of his," Sheriff Hirbe commented to Atreau as they rode. Elezar frowned at the comment as both Atreau and the sheriff looked back at him. Then both burst into laughter.

"That's exactly the face," Sheriff Hirbe said.

Atreau nodded and Elezar had to suppress the reflex to scowl more deeply at the two of them.

"I've grown so used to him," Atreau commented. "I actually find the sight rather charming, but as I recall I nearly did piss myself the first time Elezar charged me in sword practice back in our school days."

"I am right here, you know," Elezar said.

"And happy we are for that," Sheriff Hirbe replied.

While the encounter with the ship captain didn't seem to alter either the sheriff or Atreau's attitude towards him, Elezar did note a slight change in the attitude of his cavalrymen. As word spread throughout the afternoon, the garrison infantrymen warmed to him as well. He'd feared that so open a declaration of his relationship with Skellan might cost him their respect and ruin morale. But the fact that he'd clashed with a fellow Cadeleonian for the sake of Milmuraille—and had won—seemed to far outstrip any a distaste his men might have felt over his sexual preference. More than anything else, Elezar realized, these soldiers all wanted to know that their leader had dedicated himself to their cause and that he'd not tolerate a mere merchant, not even a Cadeleonian one, standing in the way of their triumph.

Not a one of them said so much aloud but Elezar recognized the almost worshipful quality in their gazes and the pride in their expressions when they saluted him. Captain Tialdo—the father of the girl whom Elezar had carried from her prison of a storage room the week before—beamed at him and obviously took pleasure in bringing Elezar news. This late afternoon he found Elezar in the moldering remains of the garrison's war library. Elezar looked up from a water-stained page depicting the mythic beasts that served each of the grimma as champions.

"Sir." Captain Tialdo saluted.

"What is it?" Elezar closed the book. No need for any of his men to see these grotesque sepia images of hulking mordwolves, immense snow lions, huge boars, and slavering bears. Not yet.

"The Irabiim boy—"

For an instant Elezar thought Captain Tialdo meant the youth whom he'd beheaded at Skellan's diner party. But the commander looked too excited and Elezar realized at once that the man had to be speaking of Kiram.

"He's Haldiim," Elezar commented but it hardly seemed to penetrate.

"He's built a trumpet that's gushing out great sprays of flame, sir!"

That Elezar wanted to see for himself.

Out in the yard, not far from the well, Kiram and his strange mechanism had already drawn a crowd of soldiers, kitchen staff, grooms, and sister-physicians. Even Bone-crusher edged near. Blackbirds roosted in the branches of the trees clinging to the troll's back and white cloud imps ringed the ragged horns crowning Bone-crusher's head. The cloud imps swayed on the breeze, each extending only one delicate tentacle to cling to the crevices in the troll's horns.

Infantrymen and cavalrymen stepped aside for Elezar and Javier beckoned him over to where he stood at the edge of the ring of onlookers. Several pails of water and sand sat to Javier's right and a few feet away black scorches streaked the sandy ground in arcs around Kiram's boots.

Kiram raised his head and nodded at Elezar before returning his attention to the neck of his mechanism. To Elezar's eye it looked as if Kiram had strapped on a weird hybrid of two hand bellows and a long-necked hunting horn. Though the bell of the horn tapered in at the very end and a wisp of smoke drifted from its blackened iron mouth.

Kiram himself appeared dressed not to work a forge but to step into one. A thick leather skullcap covered his head and laced over the swath of damp cloth that he'd wrapped over his nose and mouth. A wooden visor, with long slits of smoked glass, shielded his eyes, while a leather coat covered his torso and arms and hung down over his thighs. Even his feet and long hands were protected in thick leather, though his fingers poked out from the clipped tips of his smith's gloves.

He carefully adjusted some small screw in the iron valve that connected the bellows to the neck of the horn. Then, aiming the mouth of the horn upward, Kiram squeezed on the bellows with his elbow—as if he were compressing the air sack of a Salt Island bagpipe—and a fountain of flame spewed up into the air. Onlookers all around leapt back. Some cried out in shock, others in delight. Elezar himself tensed as Kiram turned and the geyser of fire swept past. Javier grinned at Kiram as if smitten all over again and Elezar shook his head. Those two truly were meant for each other if the sight of Kiram scorching the sky brought such an enamored expression to Javier's face.

The blast hardly lasted past a minute. Then Kiram adjusted that screw again and the flames guttered out, leaving only streaks of black around the mouth of the trumpet and a pungent plume of dark smoke.

Kiram pulled the wads of wet cloth down from over his nose and mouth and shoved back his visor. A flush colored his dark skin and made his pale blue eyes seem to gleam.

"Let's see a mordwolf swallow that!" Kiram grinned at both Javier and Elezar.

One of the grooms whooped and then suddenly every man and woman in the courtyard seemed to be cheering. Elezar roared long and loud along with them. Though none of them matched Bone-crusher. The troll's deep laugh swept over them like a wave, almost too low to hear, but they all felt it rock through to the core of their bodies.

"You've set my balls humming like water drums, Master Bone-crusher!" Skellan called into the following quiet.

As a group, the entire crowd turned to see Skellan come riding through the garrison gates. He looked handsome atop his big mount, though Elezar knew that if Skellan could have had his own way he would have been down with his feet on the ground. Behind him came Cire, mounted on a fawn mare that

Skellan had gifted to her along with enough income that she could now dress in gold silk and a cloak of mink. Her familiar, Queenie, poked her narrow face out from between the folds of dark fur and then darted back into the shadows of Cire's lap.

"We saw the flames from the street," Cire commented.

"It would seem that our good count has chosen very wisely when he appointed his court mechanist!" Elezar gave Kiram a friendly pat on the back, which, with the added weight of the mechanism, nearly toppled him. Fortunately Javier caught his arm and steadied him with half an embrace.

Minutes later Elezar and Javier together unbuckled and lifted the mechanism off of Kiram. Then, following his instructions, they very carefully stowed the thing in a sand-filled cask. Elezar seared the tip of his thumb, but otherwise they managed to balance the hot, heavy mass of iron tubes, bellows, and leather buckles easily enough.

With the fire gone the crowd dissipated back to their evening duties.

Skellan and Cire briefly disappeared into the stables, though Elezar expected to see them again soon enough. He turned back to Kiram

"So what are you calling this mechanism of yours?" Elezar asked.

"The Fiery Wind of Our Savior's Flaming Ass," Javier said. He then added to his sacrilege by making the sign of the Holy Cadeleonian Savior most devoutly over his chest.

"That isn't an accurate description in the least." Kiram peeled the leather skullcap off, freeing the riot of his curling gold hair. "It's an incendiary device, fueled by a distillation of marsh pitch. Though that alone isn't really much of an innovation. The royal mechanist in the king's court attempted the same thing a year or so ago but flubbed it and nearly burned his entire study down."

"He's so lovely when he gloats," Javier whispered.

"The trick is in constructing the ignition point and the

valves to keep the flame from flowing back into the fuel bellow and igniting the entire thing," Kiram went on as if he hadn't heard a word. "Valves have been around for ages, of course. Pipers on the Salt Islands have depended upon such things to keep their bagpipes from leaking air for generations. But manufacturing a valve and seals that won't burn or melt represented a serious material challenge—"

"Elezar's eyes are glazing over," Javier broke in, not altogether inaccurately, though Elezar had been attempting to stoke some fascination. He'd certainly appreciated all the fire that resulted from this talk of distillation and valves.

Kiram sighed but then shrugged. "Yes, well, I'm sure the details can keep until I publish. So in short, I'm calling it a pluming torch."

"However it works, you're right that it would be hell for a mordwolf or any man trying to come over the city wall." Elezar studied the homely mechanism where it sat propped in its chest. Who would expect so much ferocity from such a jumble of pipes and leather? Amazing as magic, really. "How quickly do you think you could have more of them made?"

"If I had more time I'd like to test a bit further, but as is, I've already drawn up the plans." Kiram paused and Elezar could almost see him making calculations. "Likely we'll see between thirty and fifty in a week. We'll start training members of the wall watch with them as soon as they're assembled."

More and sooner would have been better, but Elezar nodded anyway. They were damn lucky to possess even one weapon so utterly terrifying.

"Will that be enough?" Kiram asked and all at once Elezar recognized the exhaustion that belied Kiram's confident smile and assured demeanor. No doubt he'd labored over this mechanism for days and nights on end. A week ago only a scrap of paper existed and now a complete, functioning mechanism sat there. Kiram had to be teetering on the brink of collapse.

"Surely it will," Elezar replied. "You've given us something amazing, Kiram."

Kiram looked relieved then.

"Didn't I tell you? You'll save us all." Javier wrapped his right arm around Kiram's shoulder and hugged him. Kiram leaned into Javier, resting his head on his shoulder.

"You should take him to bed," Elezar said.

Javier smiled and stroked Kiram's arm. The naturalness of the action and the intimacy both fascinated and agitated Elezar.

"Did you hear that?" Javier bowed his face closer to Kiram's. "The garrison commander has ordered us to bed."

Kiram muttered something in Haldiim that Elezar didn't quite catch but Javier laughed. Then he offered Elezar a mock salute and took himself and Kiram away.

CHAPTER
FOURTEEN

The next day Elezar hardly saw Skellan, Javier, or Kiram, as one necessity after another arose. He'd not even completed his survey of the city's southern wall of the city when he found himself summoned, as if he were a common man-at-arms, to attend Lady Hylanya at the Sun Palace. Fortunately he'd played the role of a varlet for so many months now that the interruption of his work amused more than annoyed him.

He agreed to go with the three handsome swordsmen who had been dispatched to retrieve him, but only if they could go by way of the Labaran sanctum.

He'd not yet seen the remnants of the Labaran sanctum in daylight and wanted to observe for himself what remained. Most folk rode or walked at a good distance from the collapsed walls and many of them made holy signs or gripped the blessed trinkets they wore. Elezar slowed Cobre slightly.

Wide gaps in the broken walls of the sanctum exposed ragged expanses of the charred orchard and the ruined buildings beyond. Dunes of ash mounded beneath windbreaks formed by the sections of tower walls that still stood. Pools of gleaming obsidian caught the afternoon light like the water of a black stream.

Despite the desolation of the place Elezar noticed shoots of grass already greening swaths of the grounds. New reeds edged the wide perimeter of the water garden pools. The two troll children sheltering in the ruins tumbled together, looking like mossy boulders rolling about. As they wrestled, they produced deep cooing noises that sounded to Elezar like both laughter and the calls of doves. Bone-crusher watched over the two of them while he tore the carcass of a river serpent into three portions.

The big troll glanced up from preparing the troll children's meal and waved a gory hand to Elezar. Elezar returned the friendly gesture. The three handsome swordsmen riding along-side Elezar stared at Bone-crusher with varying degrees of awe and horror in their expressions. Elezar took a little pleasure in the thought that such reactions would have annoyed Skellan had he chosen any of these three men as his champions.

"So, why is it that Lady Hylanya needs to see me so urgently?" he asked.

"It's something to do with Rafale's meddling, no doubt," the youngest of the three commented to Elezar. "He comes and goes like a rash of merrypox. Trades a little much on his sister's position as the lady's nurse, if you ask me. The previous count didn't trust him so much as he makes out—"

"What Master Rafale does is none of our concern so long as it pleases Lady Hylanya." The eldest of the three swordsmen scowled back at his junior. Elezar supposed that Rafale had his supporters among these men. After all, he'd selected them from the multitude of the previous count's personal guards.

The young swordsman bowed his blond head and appeared contrite. Though when neither of the other two watched he shot Elezar a commiserating smile and whispered softly, "Merrypox."

After that they made impersonal conversation, exchanging opinions about exactly what the mythic witch-forged swords might have been and then discussing the merits of newest light armor coming out of Anacleto. Soon the winding streets led them to the gold and scarlet edifice of the Sun Palace.

Both Prince Sevanyo's residence and the royal palace in Cieloalta would have dwarfed Count Radulf's Sun Palace but neither of those two great structures matched this one in rich detail. Everywhere Elezar looked bas-relief scenes of wolves hunting in stylized forest scenes caught his eye. They spiraled up pillars and ran as stone inlay across the worn steps. The motif of red wolves appeared again and again. The creatures ringed the tops of the two bell towers and guarded the eaves of the stables. Inside, they darted across tapestries and formed a mosaic between the fragrant flowerbeds that filled the circular courtyard at the heart of the palace. Wolves peered down at him from the gilded woodwork of the ceilings and they twined their bodies into the knot work that framed the narrow gallery of portraits.

Elezar guessed that even more of the Radulf family symbols decorated the drawing rooms but so many courtiers, guards, and maids filled the one that Elezar entered that he could hardly see the floor or walls for all the richly dressed people waiting in attendance upon Lady Hylanya. Elezar recognized several guild masters and thought he glimpsed Rafale hanging back in the company of four smiling young women. Most of the people gathered chatted or amused themselves with card games but several of the young mustachioed men looked dazed with boredom. One elderly gentleman snoozed in a velvet-backed chair. Elezar hoped he wouldn't be expected to join their number while waiting for Lady Hylanya to call for him.

Fortunately, he and the three swordsmen were shown directly into Lady Hylanya's private chamber where the fourteen-year-old sat in the company of four brunette maids. The women surrounding Skellan's broad-boned sister looked far older than her but also much more dainty—like sparrows attending an eaglet. Two of the maids worked at braiding Hylanya's long red hair while the other two held what looked like pages of correspondence.

At Elezar's entrance, the maids folded the pages away and the eldest of them—a woman of perhaps thirty—stood beside Hylanya. Her delicate hand rested on the hilt of the bejeweled knife hanging from her ornate knife belt. Another maid gripped an ivory comb as if preparing to drive Elezar back with the small tines.

Taking in their nervousness, Elezar stopped far short of Lady Hylanya. He offered her a proper deep Cadeleonian bow, though as he straightened, he couldn't help but search the chamber for some sign of Lady Peome. The nurse was nowhere to be found among the graceful chairs, small tables, and the two large freestanding embroidery frames.

Hylanya must have noticed his search of the chamber because she commented, "Peome has stepped out to settle her dear little niece, Miri. She won't be long."

Something about Hylanya's tone and expression made Elezar think that she'd deliberately waited until her nurse was absent to send for him. Living with nine younger brothers had honed his instinct to recognize youthful waywardness.

"I'm sorry to have missed her," Elezar replied out of polite reflex but he didn't bother with further niceties. "Your swordsmen informed me that you were concerned by an urgent matter that required my attention."

"Yes," Hylanya said. Rather than explaining further she curled her hand into the strings of garnets and rubies hanging around her long neck and fixed Elezar with a stare. Elezar watched her in return, feeling uneasy about the intensity of her gaze. The Sumar grimma had regarded him in the same fashion when she had attempted to pry into his mind with a spell.

Then several red sparks lit the air between them and Hylanya flinched back in her chair, with an expression that reminded Elezar of a startled cat.

"Hilthor—Skellan really has placed you under his protection, hasn't he?" Lady Hylanya said. She heaved a dejected and somewhat dramatic sigh.

"So I'm told," Elezar responded. He tried not to show his irritation but he wasn't pleased to have been summoned from important work just to be toyed with by a teenaged girl. "If that's all you needed to know, then perhaps I should be on my way."

"No, that's not it at all!" Hylanya rose from her chair. "I needed to be certain that someone else didn't have control of you before I trusted you."

"Someone else?" Elezar asked. He didn't particularly like the insinuation that any witch would have control of him, Skellan included.

"One of Skellan's enemies." Hylanya glanced back at her maids and then to the young blond swordsman standing to Elezar's left. Standing there, with her hair hanging half in braids and such a pensive expression, she struck Elezar as very young. Despite her height and striking features she was, in fact, younger than Sammi and Sarl. Younger than even Fleur, he reminded himself.

He let go of his anger. She had, after all, just lost her father and all the protection that he had provided.

"Which of Skellan's enemies are you worried about?" Elezar asked.

"Bishop Palo," Hylanya said. "He's the reason that I had to send for you…" Again Hylanya looked uncertain. "Rafale has sworn that you can be trusted with this and that you wouldn't fail Skellan."

Elezar didn't feel at all reassured by the idea of Rafale handpicking him for anything, but he waited for Hylanya to go on.

"A very reliable source has word that the bishop has been ordered to murder Skellan—"

"What source?" Elezar demanded.

"I will not say his name." Hylanya's pale face flushed. "But he can be trusted."

Bois, Elezar expected. But if he had proof, surely he would have presented it to Skellan or Sheriff Hirbe at the very least.

"Who it is doesn't matter," Hylanya went on. "What is important is that the bishop is plotting again and we must stop him before he can harm Skellan. He must be… dealt with. And you are precisely the man to do it, Lord Grunito."

"Dealt with?" Elezar raised his brows, feeling a little taken aback by Hylanya's sweeping statement. He glanced to the maids but none of them would meet his gaze.

"You could easily enter the bishop's house and you are a skilled swordsman," Hylanya continued with her argument. "You are the perfect man for this and it would prove your loyalty to Skellan beyond any doubt—"

"Just to be clear," Elezar cut her off. "You do realize that entering a man's home and cutting him down in cold blood is murder."

"But he's plotting against Skellan!" Hylanya objected.

"Then lay charges against him and have him declared a traitor," Elezar responded. "You claim that you have a reliable man who can testify to the bishop's scheming. Have him come forward and let this be done legally. Otherwise, what you're doing here, my lady, is plotting an assassination. And that would make you no better than the bishop."

"How dare you!" Hylanya snapped. "I'm trying to save my brother!"

"If that's the case, then expose this plot of the bishop's. Have your source come forward," Elezar stated again. "It does the count no honor to have murder committed in his name when the matter could be brought to trial."

Hylanya glowered at him with such anger and frustration that Elezar almost thought he felt her fury roll over him like a hot gust. The silk hanging from the embroidery frames fluttered and then stilled.

"Is there a reason that this man can't come forward?" Elezar asked.

Hylanya stepped back to her chair and dropped down into it. She glowered at her feet.

"Peome says that it would only cause trouble with the Cadeleonians," Hylanya muttered. "And Sheriff Hirbe says there isn't any evidence for him to act upon. But we all know what Bishop Palo has already done and he deserves to be punished!"

Elezar understood Hylanya's outrage, even shared it in a way. But murdering the bishop would not do anyone any good, particularly not now. With the sheriff already alerted to the matter, likely the bishop's killing would get his assassin quickly executed as well—if only to appease the Cadeleonian population of the city. Even then it might not be enough to keep their fragile alliance from falling apart.

Elezar studied Hylanya and decided that she truly wasn't considering the repercussions of her demand. But he wondered if Rafale might have.

How difficult would it have been for the charming playwright to put this idea into Hylanya's head? He had to have known that Elezar would refuse—any sane adult would refuse. But perhaps Rafale had simply wished to further cultivate Hylanya's distrust of Cadeleonians and Elezar in particular. If that had been his intention it seemed to have worked perfectly.

Hylanya slumped back in her chair, casting Elezar a malevolent glower.

"I'm sorry, my lady, but I cannot rightly murder Bishop Palo," Elezar said with a shrug. "Not only would it be immoral but it would do Skellan and this entire city more harm than good at this point."

"So everyone says. But he isn't safe and I won't lose my only brother." Hylanya clenched her hand around the stones of her necklaces. Her knuckles stood out, turning white with the intensity of her grip. Then she gestured as if waving Elezar aside. "Go now, Lord Grunito. Since you will do nothing to prevent an attempt on Skellan's life, then at least guard my brother, as is your duty."

Elezar made his bow and withdrew. On his way out he noted the sympathetic expressions of the surrounding maids and swordsmen. Or perhaps they were simply relieved to see him go. He closed the door to Hylanya's private chamber with a very deliberate care and did his best to maintain a calm appearance as he worked his way through the crowded drawing room. On the threshold of the hallway, he caught Rafale regarding him from a mirror. Rafale smiled and raised a small glass of wine as if toasting Elezar's departure.

By the time Elezar reached the north city gate he'd ridden off most of his frustration. Lady Hylanya might abhor him but the captains of the city guard and the harbor guard largely welcomed him. They warmed further after he introduced Kiram, who treated them to a demonstration of the pluming torch. After that, discussion turned to how best to position and implement the new weapons. A new division, drawn up from the Labaran fire guard and Cadeleonian gunners, was assembled and began training under Kiram that very day.

Then as the sun sank low and Elezar rode back for the garrison he noticed several Labaran boys hurling cakes of cow dung at the walls of a Cadeleonian chapel. They fled when they saw Elezar and Cobre charging down on them. Though when the priests emerged from the chapel and caught sight of him, they appeared none too happy. One informed him that he was now well-known throughout the city and that no doubt he would be equally infamous in the fires of the red hell.

Elezar didn't slap a nearby mass of dung into the man's face, but only because he didn't want to get his hands dirty. He departed, silently fuming.

Thankfully Cobre made for pleasant company in the garrison stable. As he groomed, watered, and fed the stallion his anger eased. He couldn't allow the remarks of a cowardly priest and the ire of a teenaged girl to diminish all that had been accomplished in Milmuraille over the past ten days. Despite their differences the vast majority of men and women in the city worked together for the common good of all.

As he strolled from the garrison stables he spied Skellan and Cire and felt relieved at their welcoming expressions. He considered what he should tell Skellan of Hylanya's summons. The last thing he wanted was to rouse animosity between Skellan and Hylanya. And in truth, nothing had come of Hylanya's demand. Better to let the matter pass and give Lady Hylanya a little time to cool her temper.

Cire waved to Elezar while Skellan absently licked at something on his thumb. All at once Elezar forgot nearly all the events of the day. He had to look away to keep his thoughts from sliding into obscene recollections of the glorious sensation of that long tongue on his flesh. In years past he'd easily suppressed such thoughts but now, actually knowing the physical pleasure of another man, his desire seemed, at times, to possess him.

Elezar studied Cire like she was an antidote to his rising lust.

Her tiny stature always surprised him, particularly after days spent in company with fighting men and heavy Cadeleonian chargers. She hardly stood higher than Skellan's elbow and most of her height seemed to come from the bright red coils of her glossy braids. Despite her diminutive size she kept pace with Skellan and matched him in exuberant gestures and the burst of her bright, loud laughter. Though old enough to be Skellan's mother she looked and behaved much more like an elder sister.

"Well met, Master Elezar!" Cire greeted him. Then she cast Skellan an exasperated look and elbowed his hip. "Enough sucking your thumb. You'll look an idiot in front of Lord Grunito."

Skellan quickly pulled his finger from his mouth.

"I scalded it," he explained.

"There's a coincidence. I singed a finger as well yesterday," Elezar replied. "I'm not sure what it says about us that we both seem to have penchant for handling things too hot to hold." Though when he looked down at his own hand he realized that his burn had already faded. There was one advantage to his callused fingers, he supposed. Skellan's hands, he knew, were far more sensitive than his own. "Here let me have a look at your burn."

Skellan let Elezar take his hand. His skin felt hot against Elezar's and his long fingers looked pale and graceful in Elezar's thick tanned hand. Two small blisters dotted Skellan's thumb but they faded before Elezar's eyes.

"Now there's a trick I wouldn't mind learning from you." Elezar stroked the back of Skellan's hand once and then released him.

Skellan looked like he wanted to offer a response but then Cire leaned between them.

"Tell him about the frogwives!" Cire said, beaming. Queenie peeked her pointy snout out of the cloak and then scurried up to perch on Cire's shoulder.

"What about the frogwives?" Elezar asked.

"It's a bit long in the telling, and I'm half-famished." Skellan favored Elezar with a coy glance, which two weeks ago would have confounded him. Now Elezar recognized the expression as the half-begging gaze of a man who'd likely spent too many years as a dog, winning scraps from the tables of soft-hearted fellows If Cire hadn't been there, he'd have teased Skellan for it.

"All right, let's make for the mess hall, and see if the cooks won't feed us some of the early servings they're dishing up for the night sentries," Elezar suggested.

Skellan's appearance in the mess brought all fifty of the men on sentry duty up to their feet to salute him, but also sent two kitchen boys pelting back to inform the cooks that they would be serving the count himself. No doubt Skellan would have gladly gobbled down anything they placed on a plate before him but clearly pride required the cooks to serve their count with a number of rich dishes.

Both Cire and Skellan enjoyed the dishes enormously. Elezar gladly handed his appetizer of butter-poached snails over to them. If the day ever came that he managed to get a dish of snails down his throat he supposed he truly would have to consider himself a Labaran. For now he dug into this mutton stew.

"So, frogwives?" Elezar prompted.

"Nearly a hundred of them are swimming down the river to join us against the grimma," Skellan replied. "Their sisters here in the city sent word of me breaking the sanctum's hold over them. And they've come to join our battle for the sake of their sisters still enthralled."

"They think that you're going to free all of their kind?" Elezar asked

Skellan nodded as he chewed an immense mouthful of snails. Then he added, "And I will, if I can. Every creature deserves freedom."

Beside Skellan, Cire stilled, her spoonful of stew halfway to her mouth.

"Not all of them, certainly? Not the trolls?"

"Trolls most of all," Skellan replied. "I wouldn't see a troll enslaved any more than I would allow a man or woman of Radulf County to be stripped of freedom."

"But…" Cire downed her soup and then lowered her voice. "You've not told this to too many folk, have you?"

"No one's asked," Skellan replied. "I've discussed with Javier, though."

"Really?" Elezar found it strange to imagine Skellan and Javier talking, but he wasn't certain why. The vast disparity of their upbringings aside—Javier had enjoyed the wealth and indulgence granted a young duke while Skellan had grown up living like an unwanted dog—they had much in common. Certainly both of them understood the realms of spells and curses as Elezar could never have hoped to.

"Indeed," Skellan replied. "While they were fleeing from Grimma Naemir's lands Javier and Kiram sighted a family of trolls still living wild. Javier feared the trolls would attack them and was shocked when they simply fled into the mountains, abandoning their catch of salmon."

Elezar tried to imagine Bone-crusher fleeing anything. Having charged the massive troll numerous times he couldn't picture it.

"It makes sense that the wild ones would be flighty," Skellan went on. "That's the only way they've remained free all this time. Otherwise the grimma would have already captured them to add to the power of their sanctums."

Elezar nodded as he downed more of his stew, then asked, "Did Javier say what became of the salmon?"

"He ate it, of course!" Skellan grinned. "Can you imagine he'd let a free meal go to waste? I certainly wouldn't have."

"It's all fine and nice for a few trolls to live wild and free in the far north, but this is Radulf County we're discussing," Cire said.

Skellan appeared nonplussed. He scraped his spoon across the empty hollow of his stew bowl. Cire sighed heavily.

"Let me advise you here, because your opinion of trolls is far from the common one." Cire looked to Elezar as if confirming her opinion. Elezar certainly couldn't have argued that point with her, so didn't try. She went on, "Don't breathe a word about it until it's done. Fishermen already like to grumble about freed frogwives raiding their nets. You don't want to have to deal with the entire city getting up in arms at the idea of hordes of trolls stumbling around their neighborhoods, eating up children, and fouling roads with turds the size of houses."

"Trolls bury their shit. And besides that, they don't like our cities. The spaces are too confining," Skellan replied. "They love the high, wild mountains of their births."

"Still." Elezar spoke softly, mindful of the men dining at the tables surrounding theirs. "I think Cire's right about keeping this quiet. Right now the entire populace of Milmuraille is unified to repel an invasion by grimma. If they're told that they're also being asked to risk their lives for the liberty of frogwives, cloud imps, and trolls, it undermines the point they're rallying around. Some will come to fear that you're wagering their city for the sake of monsters."

"They aren't monsters. They're simply creatures from an age before our own: the firstborn of this world. Once all this land and these waters were theirs." Skellan gazed forlornly at his empty stew bowl but then sighed. "I know you're both right. Bone-crusher's told me much the same thing. But I swore to him that I would do all I could to see him and his kind freed and I will keep my word."

Elezar didn't know why Skellan's insistence surprised him, except that such unwavering moral resolve clashed with his idea of a man who'd only survived by resorting to theft, prostitution, and scavenging. He'd been brought up thinking that those born common or deprived of wealth simply could not afford ideals. But more and more he was coming to realize that this, like so much of his early learning, was not true. He'd known dukes, bishops, and princes and couldn't imagine any one of them adamantly championing as unpopular of a population as trolls simply because it was the right thing to do.

"They aren't the monsters folk think them to be," Skellan muttered. "They're just easy to be frightened of."

Elezar nodded and Cire frowned at him.

Labaran lore and history abounded with tales of heroic champions wielding enchanted weapons to slay savage trolls. Few other creatures seemed to represent the enemies of all Labaran civilization and morality.

But the more time Elezar spent in Bone-crusher's company the less he believed those stories and the more he understood Skellan's affection. For all Bone-crusher's terrible strength and size, he behaved neither as a stupid brute nor as a voracious monster. He regularly fed upon the river serpents and freshwater sharks that might have killed any number of sailors and fishermen when doubtless he could have more easily glutted himself on the penned livestock of Milmuraille's meat markets—or even its people.

The last three evenings he'd observed the troll carefully pick his way through the crowded garrison yard and settle down to whisper low and deep to the horses and cloud imps, before moving on to tend to the two troll children sheltering in the sanctum's ruins. Watching the troll in those quiet moments, Elezar felt moved by a greater humanity—for lack of any better word—than he'd seen in many men. He thought he understood why the troll possessed the name of Holy Green Hill as well as Bone-crusher.

"Of course you'll keep your word," Elezar said. "Cire and I are simply advising you not to go out of your way to make it harder for yourself than it needs to be."

"Exactly," Cire agreed. She stroked Queenie and then fed a bit of her buttered bread to the golden rat. "There's no reason to tell anyone about a plan they'll only attempt to dissuade you from, unless you want to be dissuaded, which you don't, do you?"

"No," Skellan stated flatly. "But folk do need to know about the frogwives coming to join our fight."

"Definitely. Captain Wirret of the harbor guard most of all. I think she'll be pleased to have the help." Elezar spent a moment working a stringy bit of mutton from between his back teeth with his tongue. "Are there such things as frog... husbands?"

Cire looked uncertain but Skellan nodded.

"Folk rarely notice them because they're much smaller and so shaggy that they pass for little rafts of kelp and river grass when they're swimming on their own," Skellan said. "Though most of them cling to their frogwife's back once they've mated. They look like little more than cloaks of cascading green kelp. The frogwives carry their frondy little ones much the same way, but often clinging to their chests."

Elezar remembered the brief glimpse he'd caught of frogwives the night Skellan had broken the sanctum. Odd to think that what he'd taken for a few women sporting long weedy tresses must have been mothers and wives carrying their entire families.

"Really? Just like in the stories?" Cire asked.

Skellan nodded and Cire cast an amused glance to Elezar.

"Well," she said, "I suppose we can all feel plenty pleased that we aren't frogwives, then. Can you imagine the pain of having some lazy, hairy fellow clinging to your backside all the damn day through?"

"My Elezar is plenty strong," Skellan replied with a grin. "He hardly minds me humping about on him—" The rest of Skellan's statement dissolved into snickers while Elezar attempted not to succumb to a discomfited flush. Fortunately the past weeks had blunted his susceptibility to embarrassment. Something in Skellan's laughter even pleased him—the freedom of it and the honesty.

Cire rolled her dark eyes but with an indulgent expression. She handed another hunk of buttered bread to Queenie. Elezar surreptitiously observed the three soldiers seated nearest them. If they overheard the comments, they'd not been affected. Their attention seemed entirely focused upon the set of bone dice they tossed among themselves.

"Speaking of taking a man," Cire began, though they'd been discussing frogwives as far as Elezar had noticed. She glanced meaningfully to Skellan. "You know I've had my eyes on Rafale for a while now."

Skellan sobered immediately.

"You haven't placed a claim on him," Cire stated.

"I haven't. I wouldn't," Skellan replied. "There's nothing between him and me."

Elezar guessed that all three of them knew that was a lie but none of them wanted to say as much. Elezar also suspected that he didn't want to hear the rest of this conversation, but he couldn't extricate himself. He didn't know that he could bear to look at Skellan and see his longing for Rafale. Particularly not after the ugly intrigue Rafale had arranged for him with Hylanya.

Elezar bowed his head, making a study of his scabbed knuckles and the bruises coloring the back of his hand. Such blunt hands, certainly not the graceful fingers of a playwright.

"So you wouldn't challenge me if I claimed him?" Cire asked.

Skellan didn't answer at once and it dismayed Elezar that a mere pause could cut through him so deeply. He couldn't keep himself from looking across to Skellan.

"I wouldn't," Skellan answered at last. "But honestly, Cire, I'd be none too happy if that was the choice you made—and not because I hold some torch for Rafale either—but he's trouble and I'd be afraid for you if you decided to tie your own life to his. He's the sort who's going to end up dying with a dagger in his back. I wouldn't want you to share that fate—"

"You don't actually think I would bind my vei to his?" Cire raised her red brows and shot Elezar a quick, amused glance, as if he too should find the idea absurd. "No witch since the ancients has done that. Rafale's a fine fuck but his cock hasn't turned me into some love-struck dunce, Skellan. I mean to bind him to me, not the other way round. I'm certainly not going to waste my power healing every case of merrypox he manages to catch."

Skellan didn't appear much more pleased by this than Cire's earlier statement.

"So long as he agrees, you can do what you will," Skellan replied at last. "But he must agree or I will challenge you."

"You already have one man wrapped around your finger." Cire jerked her thumb in Elezar's direction. "Why shouldn't Rafale be mine?"

"I didn't say he couldn't, only that he must choose you," Skellan replied coldly.

"But he won't!" For an instant, raw frustration contorted Cire's expression. Queenie bristled and glared from her shoulder like an alarmed guard dog. Men at the surrounding tables looked questioningly to Elezar. He gave a shake of his head and they returned to their own business, or at least pretended to.

Cire reached up to stroked the rat's tiny ears. As she calmed the rat, Cire's own agitation seemed to fade. At last she looked back to Skellan. "Rafale thinks he only needs to wait until your Elezar is either run through or sails back to his own land. Then he'll snatch you up and eventually charm you into giving him free run of Radulf County."

Elezar hadn't imagined that Rafale held him in any high regard but hearing that the man pinned so much hope to his departure or death did not bode well for their future interactions. It struck Elezar as dangerous that such a man might already have a firm hold over Lady Hylanya.

"Rafale is what he is and neither you nor I have a right to—" Skellan began but Cire cut him off.

"What he feels for you is nothing but obsession. I'm the one he truly loves." Her expression turned almost pleading as she gazed at Skellan. "If I enthralled him and bound him to me, I could lift all the ambitions that plague him from his mind. I could make him happy. Don't you want him to find his happiness?"

Again Skellan hesitated but this time Elezar watched his face and understood that an immense tenderness towards Cire gave him pause. Then Skellan hardened his expression.

"You would enslave him," Skellan stated. "No slave is happy."

Cire shook her head.

"He isn't happy now so what difference does it make?"

"His vei is his own to forge of his free will." Skellan sounded almost apologetic.

"How can you say that, with your own man sitting here, all bound up in your spells?" Cire demanded.

"Elezar's will is his own," Skellan replied.

Cire's skepticism showed plainly. Skellan frowned at her but she turned her attention to Elezar.

"So?" Cire arched her brows. "Are you free to defy our Skellan just as you please, Master Elezar? Or for some strange reason have you found yourself falling into accord with him as if by magic? Do trolls seem suddenly a proud race? Has

Milmuraille mystically transformed into a wondrous city that you would, of your own free will, sacrifice your life for?"

Elezar didn't answer her but clearly she read uncertainty in his expression.

"Hypocrite." Cire pinned Skellan with an imperious glower. Elezar too studied him.

"I am not. I didn't..." Skellan met Elezar's gaze and his expression turned from offended to injured. "You think I've enthralled you? That I would rail against trolls and frogwives being stripped of their freedom while I enslaved you?"

Elezar hadn't thought so. But Cire's words undermined his certainty. He was not the man he had been when he'd first arrived in Milmuraille. He now teetered upon becoming an outcast, neither truly Cadeleonian nor Labaran. And he had found his values shifting, his appreciation of the strange growing, and his deference to the wealthy and highborn dulling.

But at the same time he recognized in himself the weakness of wishing to evade responsibility for his choices and new values. How simple it would be to place the blame for all his transgressions of holy Cadeleonian law upon Skellan's magic. How easy to blame a witch as so many other men before him had done.

Easy but also, Elezar knew, an act of utter cowardice. Defiance and desire had burned in him long before he'd set eyes upon Skellan. His sympathy for Bone-crusher stemmed from his own reputation as a monster among pretty and proper folk. He knew what it was to be judged a brute on the basis of physical appearance alone.

"If you were in my thrall do you think I'd have submitted to four—no, five—five baths at your insistence?" Skellan sounded aggrieved as only he could be by the imposition of washing.

Elezar laughed in spite of himself and at once his brooding mood broke.

"No, I don't think that you've enthralled me." Elezar had to resist the urge to reach out and pull Skellan to him and press a kiss to his brow. The motions were becoming as reflexive for Elezar as reaching for his sword or soothing Cobre.

The garrison mess hall wasn't the place and there was a matter that he did wish to discuss with Skellan.

"But I am concerned about some trouble Rafale seems intent upon stirring up through your sis—" Elezar abandoned his question as shouts of alarm rose from the beyond the mess hall doors. A roar of Labaran swearing clashed with Cadeleonian curses. The commotion brought Elezar to his feet, ready to draw his sword. Across from him Cire, too, leapt up, her knife drawn, clearly prepared to protect Skellan.

Atreau, his pages, and two brawny Cadeleonian priests burst in, shouting and struggling to drag Bois with them. Blood soaked Bois' cassock and his hands. A wild expression contorted his features almost beyond recognition. He snarled and fought against the ropes binding his wrists behind his back. Atreau kicked his feet out from under him and Bois dropped to his knees.

Atreau appeared nearly as furious as Bois. A red weal marked his cheek and blood spattered the torn front of his shirt. The elder of his pages appeared to be bleeding from a gash in his forearm.

Bishop Palo's niece followed them in. Blood caked her black hair and flecked her shocked, pale face. Her three dark-haired maids hovered around her as if at any moment she might collapse. Guards at the doors closed in around the group and several brawny cooks and kitchen boys armed with skewers and cleavers rushed in from the kitchen. At the same time the soldiers at the surrounding tables bounded to their feet and as one closed in to shield Skellan.

Elezar took in Bois' bloody hands and Atreau's furious expression and knew at once what had happened. It seemed like more than coincidence that Lady Hylanya had urged him against Bishop Palo only a few hours ago and now here was Bois, soaked with blood.

"He murdered Bishop Palo!" Atreau shouted. "Before witnesses and in cold blood. He slit the holy man's throat. He would have slain Palo's niece as well if we hadn't raced across the garden and stopped him."

A sob escaped the bishop's niece and her maids immediately encircled her in a protective wall of yellow silk. The eldest of them glowered at Atreau.

"She should not be here, my lord. Please let us take her away to the safety of her rooms."

For the only time Elezar could remember Atreau seemed utterly unmoved by the sight of a woman's distress. He shook his head.

"We were all witnesses and we have come to testify against this man and see justice done according to Labaran law." It wasn't the maid or even Elezar whom Atreau addressed but Skellan. "I bring four witnesses before you, Count Radulf, and we all will testify against Bois Eyeres—"

"I demand the right to combat!" Bois thrashed violently and nearly threw the priests off of him as he rose to his feet and staggered ahead. He too gazed intently at Skellan. "My blade will prove me justified."

"You cannot challenge a testimony of four or more by combat," Atreau shouted back at Bois. "You will hang! That is the law!"

"Were I a mere murderer you would be right," Bois snapped at Atreau, but then he again swung his attention back to Skellan. He pulled the young priests and Atreau's pages down with him as he dropped to his knees before Skellan. "My count, I have letters sent to the bishop by the royal bishop ordering your assassination. And this evening in the garden—I could bear the outrage of it no longer!" Bois glared at Bishop Palo's niece. "They scheme to have you killed, Count Radulf. Palo couldn't sway your champion to become his assassin so he turned to his niece to seduce Lord Quemanor into the work."

Alarm lit the faces of the surrounding Labaran soldiers, and not a few of them studied Atreau and Bishop Palo's niece with guarded suspicion.

"Lord Quemanor," the bishop's niece cried out to Atreau, "I beg you, do not allow this cur to slander my honor so!"

Elezar wasn't certain what she expected Atreau to do. Clearly neither was Atreau, though his eldest page looked truly pained by the young woman's anguish.

"Ask your champion, my count," Bois insisted. "Ask him about his conversation with the bishop."

Skellan glanced to Elezar, as did nearly everyone in the entire mess hall.

"Did the bishop approach you, Elezar?" Skellan asked.

"No," Elezar replied but then the strangeness of his last conversation with the man returned to him. "Not as such. He seemed to be under the impression that I might have been sent by Prince Sevanyo as an assassin—which I wasn't. I told him as much and he seemed relieved to hear it. He said that he regretted the part he played in your abduction—"

"Fool! He was sounding you out," Bois growled. "Playing the part of the repentant elder while testing exactly where your loyalties lay. His reports back to the royal bishop name you as a traitor to the crown."

"You have these reports?" Elezar demanded. "The letters you spoke of earlier?"

"Some of them, yes. They are hidden behind the portrait of the previous Count Radulf, hanging in the bishop's library." Bois' gaze remained fixed upon Skellan. "Order these dogs off me and I will bring them to you, my count."

"No!" Atreau objected. "This man has murdered a Cadeleonian holy man and attempted to murder a lady of noble birth. He cannot simply be set free on the basis of his word.

I will go—or better yet, Elezar, to find these supposed letters. But Bois must not be released after what he's done! No matter what his motive, he is still a murderer."

Skellan stole an uncertain glance to Elezar.

"I'll go," Elezar offered. Then he added, "If you wish, Count Radulf."

"Yes," Skellan said. He studied the two young priests and pages restraining Bois. "First I would have you take Sacrist Bois into Labaran custody here in the garrison. And we will... offer Lord Quemanor and the bishop's niece our... hospitality, as well."

"I would rather return to my uncle's townhouse—" the niece began but Skellan cut her off with a shake of his head.

"You will stay," Skellan stated flatly.

Before her maids or Atreau could object Cire stepped forward. She offered the bishop's niece a charming smile. "Dear child, the count can't send you back to the very place where you witnessed so terrible a murder and nearly met your own end. What would they say about him back in Cadeleon if he did such a thing? Here you'll be safe and our handsome Lord Quemanor will be close at hand to ensure that all is well. If we are lucky he may even see that we are entertained." Cire shifted her attention to Atreau. "I've heard you could sing a lemon to sweetness, Lord Quemanor. Perhaps after you've all washed and dined you and your companions would do us the kindness of a melody or two?"

Elezar had no doubt that Atreau understood that he was being held here but he still smiled handsomely and agreed as if the invitation had been one he'd long hoped for. He stole a single glance to Elezar and as casually as he could Elezar flashed the hand sign of the Hellions. Then, with a nod, Atreau ordered his pages and the young priests to release Bois and provide company for the bishop's niece.

Elezar signaled four of his own men over to assist him in escorting Bois to the garrison's stockade. Simply crossing the mess hall he became aware of the newly suspicious stares that the Labaran soldiers cast at Atreau and Bishop Palo's niece while the Cadeleonian captains openly sneered at Bois. Likely, word of the murder had already spread from the bishop's townhouse to the streets of Milmuraille. By sundown gambling men would be placing wagers on Bois' guilt and on the brawlers who would argue both sides with their fists and knives.

No matter who was proved correct, Elezar realized that the result would do nothing to unify the city's population or troops. Between them the bishop and Bois might have provided the invading grimma with a greater service than they had rendered to either of their own masters.

Once Elezar had gone, Skellan went to walk the garrison wall.

A wild, warm breeze rolled at Skellan's feet and then swept down from the garrison wall to bluster across the sentries on the grounds below. The yellow flames of torches leapt and spit in wind while the small lights from candles and lamps burned serenely in the windows of the garrison barracks. Those were tamed fires now, Skellan thought, brought inside to grow slow and sleepy behind the protection of costly windowpanes. Those were fires that had forgotten that they'd been wild once, that had forgotten that they did not burn on goodwill alone and soon those flames would allow men to snuff them out with a pinch of damp fingers.

Skellan wondered how many of his guests now enjoying the light and warmth of the household fires, as they bathed and prepared to dine, longed to see him snuffed out as well. More of them than he would have liked. At the moment, remaining inside with them felt like lingering in a trap.

He didn't belong here among so much refinement and formality. Such pretty people who all lied and smiled as if they'd suckled on deceit like mother's milk. He didn't know how to survive among these people.

Give him Clairre, with her scowls and criticisms—damn it, give him a pack of furious feral dogs—at least they were honest in their hunger and rage.

Skellan drew his cloak in close around his shoulders, just to feel the familiarity of it. He paced the wall walkway, trying to ignore the soldiers trailing him: guards, whom Elezar seemed to think he needed. Skellan glanced back and the two sturdy Labaran soldiers saluted him. Skellan nodded to them, though he felt like a fraud putting on airs, as if he were a great lord and master.

Counts, grimma, and warlords of the ancient epics dispatched their enemies without hesitation. They recognized liars and spies in an instant and went to war, thinking of only glory. Certainly they didn't struggle to understand tax reforms—which their teenaged sisters had tried for hours to explain to them. Nor did they feel gripped by utter uncertainty in the face of bloody politics.

A real leader would have known how to respond to the bishop's murder and certainly wouldn't have felt stunned by the thought of Cadeleonian princes dispatching assassins to kill him. He ought to have recognized the bishop and his niece for conspirators when they sat, laughing at his table… if indeed they had been plotting. He only had Bois' word on that. And he did not know that he could trust Bois.

Skellan flexed his toes against the stone and felt the solidity of it. How he wished he could claim that deep, immovable calm. But he didn't possess a sedate nature any more than he could claim political acumen.

He surveyed the chaotic, tangling streets of Milmuraille and took in the shining sparks of spells and wards flickering against the twilight gloom like newborn constellations. Scarlet spells of his own making arched up into the sky like the dome of an immense cathedral, overwriting the moon and stars with Skellan's will to make Milmuraille safe.

There was where his strength lay, in his own witchflame and in the stone, water, and wind that he made his own.

But what good did all that power do him when he would not wield it as those ancient heroes had? Skellan turned back again to his guards. They scanned the darkness, peering through the fluttering shadows cast by torchlight, while Skellan spied owls and creeping mice all illuminated by a heaven set ablaze by his own wards. With a word and little gesture of his hand he could have bent both these two men to serve his will utterly. He could have bound their flesh to forms that pleased him and seared devotion into their minds.

A grimma would not have hesitated. Skellan suspected that even his own father had felt no compunction in casting a thrall over the minds of friends and opponents when it served him. Too many men and women rhapsodized over the charm, wit, and handsomeness of the previous count for Skellan to believe otherwise. Hearing bath boys, guild masters, Sheriff Hirbe, and even Cadeleonian priests recollect the delight of basking in Hallen Radulf's presence, Skellan had felt tempted more than once to turn their wistful gazes to him.

How much more safe would he be if he bent all those near him to love him? How much more happy his court, guards, and Cadeleonian guests would feel, with all their uncertainty and doubts torn away and only the blare of devotion sounding through their minds?

Wasn't that what Cire had suggested? A man might find bliss in the grip of a witch's thrall?

"Lead sugar is no less poisonous for being sweet," Skellan whispered Bone-crusher's words to himself.

"My lord?" one of the guards inquired.

"Nothing, just thinking aloud," Skellan replied.

He turned back to the plain stone face of the garrison headquarters. Firelight blazed from the mess hall where the bulk of Milmuraille's protectors now took their supper. A lulling murmur of low voices drifted through the twilight. Most had volunteered to fight and the valor of that made Skellan's heart ache. What a betrayal then, to strip choice from such men and rend their pride and courage down to nothing but base obeisance.

Out across the grounds Bone-crusher lay curled up and sleeping near the stables. An owl fed her young up in the crooked branches of one of Bone-crusher's saplings while cloud imps drifted over his mossy flanks, hunting mice and beetles. Skellan wanted to go to him, but restrained himself and let Bone-crusher enjoy the dreams that a century of captivity in the Labaran sanctum had denied him.

Instead he took himself up to the infirmary. Near the door a young sister-physician kept a desk and ledger but seemed to generally ignore both in favor of fresh news. This evening the young woman leafed through a Cadeleonian broadsheet with a disapproving expression. She greeted Skellan and his guards warmly. Beyond her, some fifty sickbeds stretched out to the foot of the fireplace. Nearly all lay empty. One emaciated Cadeleonian girl slept with several blankets piled over her.

By the fire, three older sister-physicians tended their cauldrons of bubbling medicines. Three more of the women chatted at an oaken table where they sorted their first harvests of summer herbs and prepared huge rolls of clean bandages for the bloody days ahead.

Pungent salves perfumed the air and dulled the rank odors of sickness and death. The strong scent of cedar and birch oil filled Skellan's nostrils as he made his way past the many empty beds to the one where an ancient Irabiim woman lay curled beneath a cloak of silver owl feathers. Her small, frail frame lent her the look of a child beneath the blankets and curls of her wiry white hair stood out like frost against her dark, weathered skin. She cracked one eye open as Skellan drew near but didn't rise from her bedding.

She murmured something and Skellan listened intently. He'd grown better at understanding her accented Irabiim but certain words still evaded him.

"They are nearer now," the old woman whispered. "I smell Grimma Ylva's bloody breath on the back of my neck."

"She won't find you here," Skellan assured the frail woman. She offered him an indulgent smile. Skellan still did not know her name. She'd lived so long in Ylva's thrall that she couldn't remember it herself. The sister-physicians referred to her as their Little Dreamer because she slept so much.

"She will find us all," the old woman replied. "She is the autumn wolf and her belly gnaws with boundless hunger. She will not cease her hunt until she's had her kill."

The words flowed over Skellan and he nodded, understanding their intent, if not the exact terms. He, too, felt Ylva's presence. Each evening as he studied the northern horizon, her molten orange witchflame spread through the darkness like a wildfire and grew in Skellan's mind. Lundag's voracious Auntie Wolf-Bitch, she filled the air with the scents of fermenting apples and decaying meat. But above all her witchflame seemed to ripple with a relentless rage—a fury that truly seemed like madness.

Unbidden, Skellan remembered Bois' face as the priests dragged him in. But he didn't want to think on that right now.

Instead he turned his attention back to Little Dreamer. A cloak of gray feathers engulfed her tiny body and framed her wizened face.

"Do you like the cloak?" Skellan asked though he knew the change of subject was hardly smooth.

"Yes, thank you." The Irabiim woman's lined face lit up with a grin. "It has brought me good dreams. I fly free with my ancestors across open skies."

Skellan peered back at his guards. They both seemed occupied discussing the Cadeleonian opinions voiced in the broadsheet that the young sister-physician had procured.

Skellan drew closer to the Irabiim woman and lowered his voice.

"The nearer Ylva and the other grimma come the more strange their presences feel to me. They feel immense and... inhuman." Skellan finished because he knew no words in Irabiim, Labaran, or Cadeleonian for the strange quality of the Mirogoth grimma. Neither Lundag nor Oesir had possessed so vast a presence that even from across an entire country Skellan had felt their radiance prickling his flesh like sunlight on burned skin. The Mirogoth grimma pervaded the very air and light with their presence. Skellan could taste them, smell them, even see their witchflames infusing strange colors into the water and wind. They cast their wills before them like mountain ranges throwing whole valleys into shadow.

The old woman nodded.

"They were forged in an age before yours. Before even mine." The old woman paused, staring at Skellan's face as if something in his features disturbed her. "Though you bear a resemblance. You are like the grimma."

Skellan gazed down at the ruby ring that blazed on his right hand like a brand.

"I'm told that I'm the son of Drigfan," Skellan admitted.

"A rare thing then. The old blood does not breed in this new age. They do not flourish any longer but live on alone because they cannot die," Little Dreamer said.

"What do you mean, they cannot die?" Alarm shivered down Skellan's spine.

"Not the Labaran warlords, nor Cadeleonian priests, nor even my own Bahiim could ever destroy the Old Gods completely."

"Old Gods? You don't mean that the grimma are Old Gods?" Skellan wasn't certain that he understood the old woman. Her faded blue eyes focused on his face but then her gaze went distant.

"We broke them apart to make them weak. Obedient—or so we thought! But even broken and bound, the grimma are not meek. They do not forgive and they cannot die." Again she searched Skellan's face. "But you are like them and you know the story."

"No, I'm sorry but I don't know which story you mean," Skellan replied. He still wasn't certain that he understood exactly everything that Little Dreamer said. But the thought that the grimma could be Old Gods both explained the raw power he sensed from them and frightened him deeply.

The Old Gods had been the living spirits of the air, earth, and water whom desperate mystics had embodied in monstrous flesh to drive back invading hordes of demons. Myths abounded of how, after the defeat of the demons, kingdoms had fallen before the Old Gods and entire holy orders had arisen to destroy the mighty creatures.

How could he hope to defeat gods?

"Everyone knows the story. Always the same." The Irabiim woman sighed. "Children rise up to undo the generations before them. We seed the rebellion that brings our own end... We are reborn as the youth that devours the old..."

Skellan frowned, uncertain of what to make of that exactly.

"Do you truly believe that the four Mirogoth grimma are Old Gods?" Skellan asked.

"The daughters of the sky."

Even Skellan knew that was only a myth. The vast spirit of the air broke into four quarters—the winds of the four directions—and those four became immense dragons who each ruled over a season. They were elements, lent characters by storytellers and bards. The immortal four couldn't actually exist anymore than death or life could be embodied in mortal flesh. How could they have become grimma?

And yet even now the vibrance of their witchflames—their souls—played through his awareness. They were no mere witches. Bishop Palo's assassination and Cadeleonian conspiracies seemed petty and small in comparison to the threat of the grimma.

"If they are the daughters of the sky, then how were they ever defeated?" Skellan asked in a whisper. "How did Lundag drive them from this very city a hundred years ago?"

"Has it been so long as that? A hundred years and I have been bound up for all of it." The Irabiim woman lifted her frail hand and studied her withered flesh with an expression of loss. "My children... They will have gone to their next lives already..."

"I'm sorry," Skellan told her. "I didn't mean to pain you."

"None of your doing, child. And soon enough I leave this old husk and sorrow behind to live again, anew."

Skellan didn't know how to respond to the odd mix of

hope and fatalism that seemed to underscore the Bahiim faith. He realized that he probably shouldn't have come here and disturbed her. He didn't know why he had, except that his mind had been so occupied by the temptation of casting a thrall over the men and women around him that he'd needed to see the human cost of it. He wasn't thinking clearly. Likely this talk of the grimma being Old Gods frightened him because he was already agitated. It couldn't be true.

How could it be?

"I should let you rest." Skellan started to stand but the old woman reached out and caught his hand. Her cool fingers felt dry and thin as onion skin. Skellan stilled in her grip.

"It was Zi'sai."

"What?" Skellan thought he must have heard wrong.

"It was Zi'sai, the demon lord. They were gods when they fought the demons but now they are trapped in flesh—immortal flesh—but still their true power is restrained," the Irabiim woman stated quietly. "Lundag's Labaran lover knew where the demon lord's soul lay trapped and threatened to unleash him if the grimma did not cede Milmuraille."

"Her lover?" Skellan asked, though he wasn't certain that he wanted to know.

"Harmund Radulf. Irabiim called him the Childeater."

Skellan nodded. Even he knew of Harmund Radulf, though the man had gone to his grave eighty years ago and supposedly after a falling out with Lundag. She had boasted that her champions had devoured the old count, but later Skellan learned that the man died while pursuing a stag into the Sumar lands. He'd sired an heir and that young man had been Skellan's own father.

The thought of so much history bearing down so close to him made Skellan all the more uneasy. There was so much he didn't know and it all seemed to be closing around him like a trap.

"I remember the day." The Irabiim woman's gaze had gone distant again. "The sky clear for miles. I soared nearly to the black of the stars. Vast armies sparkling below like flecks of mica in a stream. Even so high up, I felt Ylva's fury. But he feared the demon lord more than she hated Lundag. If only by a little."

"Now Zi'sai is destroyed…" Skellan whispered. He felt as if his blood had gone thick and cold in his veins. He had killed Zi'sai and it was because of him that Oesir's witchflame had died out over the Labaran sanctum. He'd brought the grimma marching to Milmuraille almost as if it had been his vei.

"The pact is broken," Little Dreamer said. "Ylva comes for this city with a hundred years of rage in her belly. She does not come alone." The Irabiim woman's fingers slid from Skellan's hand. She sighed heavily. "I hope that I will not live to see her again."

"Don't say that," Skellan said. "Ylva won't take this city from me and she won't enslave you or anyone in my protection."

The Irabiim woman smiled faintly at him, looking almost indulgent.

"I dream of flying free on the summer wind because of you, child." She closed her eyes and pulled her bedding and cloak in close around her small frame. "You need not promise me anything else."

She settled her face deep into a herb-stuffed pillow and her eyes fell closed. A moment later Skellan realized that she'd once again slipped away to sleep.

Distant bells rang from the last remaining bell towers in the city. Skellan left the Irabiim woman to her dreams. As he departed from the infirmary the sister-physicians curtsied to him and his guards fell in behind him like heavy-booted shadows.

He ought to have gone and called upon Bishop Palo's niece or Atreau and his party of pages and priests, if only to feign some trust in his Cadeleonian allies, but he still felt too ill at ease, too tempted to misuse his power to ensure the absolute loyalty of those around him.

As the bells faded he wondered why Elezar hadn't yet returned. Bishop Palo's townhouse didn't lie so far from the garrison that the ride could have taken him long. He'd sent Elezar almost out of reflex, thinking a Cadeleonian nobleman wouldn't encounter resistance at the bishop's townhouse, but now anxiety began to pick at Skellan's assurance. People throughout the city now recognized Elezar, but few greeted him as a noble Cadeleonian. Most knew him as Count Radulf's champion. If the bishop's household had plotted Skellan's assassination, they weren't likely to welcome his chosen man with anything but malice.

Elezar had taken soldiers with him and he was far from helpless. Skellan laid his hand over his chest, feeling the hot pulse of spells. He would know if harm came to Elezar. He would feel it. Mere fear shouldn't distract him so, and yet he found himself striding out into the darkening dusk to once more pace the garrison wall.

His guards huffed and clattered behind him as they charged up the stairs, racing to keep pace despite the weight of their weapons and armor. Skellan resisted the urge to outdistance their noise. He couldn't call himself a count and still slink about like a thief. He straightened, slowed his pace, and greeted the sentries as he passed their posts.

"A lot of folk out and about in the Market Square and the Theater District," one of the sentries informed Skellan. Amidst the long blue shadows of twilight dozens of orange torches burned.

"Someone's found a pearl oyster, do you think?" the other sentry suggested.

"Perhaps. A good omen if that's the case," Skellan replied, but he didn't linger to watch fishmongers and cider sellers mingle with musicians and actors. Elezar and Bishop Palo's townhouse lay out past the far southern wall and Skellan hurried on his way.

When he came around the corner to the southern wall he caught sight of a tall dark-haired man standing with his straight back to the nearby torches. Light and shadow danced along his form and for a moment Skellan thought Rafale waited there. Then the man turned towards the noise of Skellan's guards. Torchlight threw hard lines across his handsome face, etching his concern like years of strain. He squinted through the growing dark, not quite settling his gaze upon Skellan.

"Who comes?" Atreau called and despite his worry he didn't reach for the dagger at his hip. His pale hands rested on the stone of the wall, looking raw from scrubbing.

"Lord Quemanor." Skellan stepped quietly into a pool of yellow torchlight. "You should be at the table with good meat and strong wine, not out here in the dank dark."

"Elezar hasn't returned," Atreau replied. "I thought he would have been back by now."

Skellan smiled slightly. He wasn't alone in his worry at least. He stepped to Atreau's side and stroked the stone ledge. The rock felt half-alive beneath his fingers, almost crackling with the spells Skellan had poured into it.

"I don't know what's delayed him, but I do know he's still well."

"Do you?" Atreau asked. "How?"

This close the perfume of roses and strong wine drifted from Atreau to fill Skellan's lungs.

"He is my man. I'd know if he'd been done over in an alley," Skellan said.

Atreau scowled. "Because you've put a spell on him, is that it?"

Skellan nodded but Atreau didn't appear to take consolation in Skellan's reassurance. He sighed heavily.

"When this is all done..." Atreau paused, his gaze drifting out over the tiny fires that flickered along the heights of the city walls. More torches burned near the Theater District and Skellan wondered if some special performance were underway or if these were the fires of the newly appointed city watch.

"If we prevail here against the grimma," Atreau went on, "you realize that Elezar will need to return to Cadeleon, don't you? He doesn't belong here with you."

"I'm heartened that you are so sure of our success that you are planning beyond it," Skellan replied. He hoped that would put Atreau off. He didn't feel ready to discuss Elezar's inevitable departure. Nor did he like the possessive tone of Atreau's words.

"Will you release him?" Atreau demanded.

"Release him? It isn't as if I've seized him against his will," Skellan replied. "I offered and he accepted."

"I'm sure that's how it seems to you." Atreau frowned. "But you're a Labaran—a northerner, at that. Desire between men isn't new to you. It isn't a terrible weakness that you've spent all of your life resisting and feeling like a monster for possessing in the first place. You can't begin to imagine what it's like for a Cadeleonian to... encounter someone like you. He doesn't know how to say no to it."

"Speaking from experience, Lord Quemanor?" Skellan couldn't help his scoffing tone. He'd spent nearly a month listening to Atreau's memoirs on debauchery. A less repressed man would be hard to come by even in Yuan. Atreau's handsome face briefly creased with some troubled thought. Then he arched his brows at Skellan.

"I know Elezar. I schooled with him, drank with him, and whored with him. I know—" Atreau cut himself off short, his gaze flicking over Skellan's guards. Skellan almost saw the thought cross his face that these were men standing behind them, not mere suits of deaf, mute armor.

"What is it that you would say?" Skellan addressed Atreau in Cadeleonian, though even he could hear the hard edge of his Labaran accent.

Atreau shoved his hands into his sable coat and leaned

against the stone ledge of the wall. Though he likely thought himself hidden in deep shadows, to Skellan's eyes a tapestry of scarlet spells illuminated his expression like embers glowing up from the stonework.

"Has he told you about Javier?" Atreau asked.

"He has," Skellan replied but the intensity of Atreau's expression gave Skellan pause. "All of you schooled together, but Javier converted to the Bahiim religion and had to abdicate his title and flee north with Kiram."

Atreau shook his head but not it seemed in denial of what Skellan said.

"It wasn't supposed to end like that. We were Prince Sevanyo's favorites, the finest sons of our nation. We were destined to be glorious heroes, with Javier and Elezar leading us fearlessly. Whether he will admit it or not, there has only ever been one man who could command Elezar's heart. None of the rest of us could ever have hoped to move Elezar. It has always only been and will forever be Javier."

Skellan hunched in his cloak. He'd seen Javier and Elezar keeping good company over the last week and he would have been lying if they hadn't struck him as a beautiful pair. But he'd not missed the way Javier's entire countenance lit at the mere sight of Kiram Kir-Zaki. Nor was he so naïve as to imagine Elezar as so steadfast that he wasn't capable of finding another man as arousing as the first he'd ever pined for.

"What? Because they shared a hand job in boys' school?" Skellan didn't laugh but only because Atreau looked so deadly serious.

"What was between them was sacred, stronger than brotherhood! We all swore on our lives to protect each other and Elezar's oath to Javier was the heart and soul of us all." Atreau shook his head. "I knew you couldn't understand."

Offense flared through Skellan. He'd sworn his own share of oaths and kept them. Though clearly Atreau couldn't imagine him possessing such integrity or resolve.

"You haven't remained forever faithful to that first girl who lay down with you, so why do you insist that Elezar should never move on?" Skellan asked. "I remember you wrote that you once promised her jewels and cakes, but now you can't recall her full name."

Atreau's brow furrowed.

"That's different…"

"How?" Skellan asked.

"Because promises between men are meant to be kept!"

At that, Skellan did laugh.

Atreau at least possessed the grace to concede. "Not all promises, obviously. But among Javier's Hellions our promises meant more than you can understand. We were closer than brothers, and with Javier and Elezar leading us, all our futures were assured."

All at once, Skellan realized that this conversation had nothing to do with him and little to do with the men Elezar and Javier had grown into.

"You want your heroes to remain exactly as they were in your youth, when you drifted along in their wakes and expected a deference you never earned, is that it?" Skellan felt certain he'd struck his mark from the way Atreau's face colored. "Now you fear they've left you and you stand here facing a vast cruel world all on you own."

Skellan gazed out at the dark horizon where the grimma's witchflames lit the night clouds like roiling lightning. How small and dim all the torches in the city streets seemed by comparison.

"I'm afraid of no such thing," Atreau snapped. "I can't live here in Milmuraille for the rest of my life. I have family—duties back in Cadeleon."

"Then go."

"I can't return alone. I can't lose Javier and Elezar both." Atreau's voice quieted to a savage whisper.

Skellan smiled at Atreau's fierce glower. The expression reminded him so much of one of Sarl's glares that he couldn't help but relent in his annoyance. After all, he held no illusions about the hardship of being isolated and feeling unwanted.

"We are all afraid to be alone sometimes. No one wants to be abandoned," Skellan said with a shrug. "But your friends haven't left you as far as I can tell. They've changed from when you were all spoiled schoolboys, but they've remained true to your friendship, haven't they? Elezar's certainly done all he can to protect you."

"Yes, more than he should have." Uncertainty showed in Atreau's face. He sighed and the anger seemed to drain from his expression. "It's just that Javier has nothing left and now we're caught up in this war—Elezar having to ride out and fight monsters. He shouldn't even be here. It's all my fault."

Skellan didn't know how to answer to that, or if he should speak at all. It wasn't his place to say what was and wasn't another man's vei. In the silence Atreau ran his hand over his face and heaved another deep sigh. Then he lifted his face up to the sky and stared up into the heavens.

"How can the stars be so beautiful even when everything is falling to the hells?" Atreau murmured.

"It's a mystery, isn't it?" Skellan replied. "The terrible and lovely lie together like fleas on a dog's hide."

Atreau smiled slightly and then slipped back into Labaran as if it were his native tongue. "My mother used to say much the same thing. About my father, actually. He was the ruin of her, but she loved him to her dying day."

Studying the man, Skellan thought he could see what it was about him that so attracted lovers. He bore his heart so openly and honestly. It lent pleasing humanity to his polished, handsome presence. Rafale commanded much the same allure but offered his confessions with practiced knowing. Perhaps he'd been much like Atreau in his youth, before he'd honed his charm into an unfeeling weapon. Skellan didn't know, but he perceived a candor in Atreau, which Rafale had long ago shed.

"I know that your loyalty doesn't lie with me," Skellan said at last. "But you're a true friend to Elezar and I don't think you would knowingly send him into danger."

"No. Never. I never meant for any of this. I just wanted to feel what it was that had moved Javier to abandon us. I never wanted to hurt Reollos or for Elezar to—"

"I don't mean the death in Cadeleon," Skellan cut him off. "I mean allowing him to go to Bishop Palo's townhouse if there is indeed an immense plot brewing there."

"The last thing I want is to put Elezar in further danger." Atreau appeared taken aback by the suggestion. "It's a bloody mess at the bishop's townhouse but safe. At least as safe as anything in this wretched city is… God, all that blood… I could use another drink before thinking about it more." Atreau closed his eyes for a moment then returned his attention to Skellan. "I suppose Bois' mad claims of a plot aren't something you're inclined to simply overlook?"

"Only an idiot thinks a snake can't bite him twice." Skellan felt the proverb fit the occasion. "I have to know the truth."

Atreau nodded. "I honestly don't believe that Bishop Palo's niece played any part in any plan. I swear to you that I certainly didn't."

One of Skellan's guards gave a quiet, disbelieving snort. Skellan glanced back to see the second guard nod in agreement with his companion. Still Skellan did believe Atreau's innocence. In part because he'd overheard Atreau's plan to abduct him and turn him over to the Cadeleonian king. Atreau didn't plot murder but escape. His greatest concern throughout had been keeping himself, Elezar, and Javier safe. An assassination now, when the harbor and city gates were heavily patrolled, wouldn't have tempted Atreau. No, that plan would only appeal to someone so fanatically dedicated to the Cadeleonian crown that forfeiting his own life and plunging all of Labara into a war with the grimma would seem a small price.

If Bishop Palo had been such a man, he'd hidden it well. Skellan frowned at his own hesitance to believe that an old man with a kind smile could dupe him. But he knew actors, had seen them strut and weep in perfect deceit. How much more perfect would a spy need to become to have survived so long among so many enemies?

"I suspect that Bois made the accusation to turn you against the Cadeleonians living in the city," Atreau went on. "I think he resents the fact that you didn't execute the bishop when you came to power, and that you appointed Elezar as your champion instead of choosing a Labaran like himself."

"So he murdered the man in broad daylight?" Skellan asked. "Just to lay a false accusation?"

"Desperate men act rashly," Atreau said. "I don't know what was in his mind when he cut the bishop's throat. He looked half out of his head and he was shouting wildly. But I do know that if you absolve Bois of the cold-blooded murder of a holy man, you will infuriate every Cadeleonian in this city."

Politics, Skellan thought with disgust, but he suspected Atreau was correct. No matter what proof Elezar brought back, the murder and accusations were already working like a wedge driven deep into the tenuous unity of Milmuraille's mixed populace.

What would Bone-crusher have made of all this?

"Justice must be served," Skellan said after a moment. "Regardless of whom it offends, no one is above the law and no one is beneath it."

"Easily said, but you aren't in a simple position. Even I understand—" Atreau's words were cut short by a flurry of cries from the sentries at the garrison gates. One of them sighted a party of riders approaching fast, though the agitation in his tone as he called alarmed Skellan.

"Elezar?" Atreau voiced Skellan's own thought. Without a further word they both sprinted along the wall walkway. Skellan's guards fell in behind them. The moment he turned the corner of the south wall, Skellan knew something had gone very wrong.

Made small and indistinct by distance, hundreds of men and women carrying bright torches marched east on the road from the fish market to the garrison, while another stream of torches wound south towards the Cadeleonian district.

On the grounds below, soldiers charged from their barracks, answering the calls of their captains. Archers pelted up to take their posts on the raised walkway, while cavalrymen poured into the stables and foot soldiers marched from the armory with their pikes and spears at the ready.

Cooks and sister-physicians peered from the windows of the main building. Skellan recognized one of Atreau's pages leaning out the kitchen door. A moment later Javier hauled the young man inside only to take his place, watching from the steps.

At the front gates a Cadeleonian captain shouted and his subordinates hauled the gates open in time for two horsemen and a carriage to race into the courtyard.

Skellan didn't have to see the crests decorating the carriage to recognize his sister's presence. He felt her in the flush of ringing charms that lit the air. The carriage had hardly drawn to a halt before Lady Hylanya bounded from it. Her red hair hung in unkempt braids and her clothes looked rumpled.

"Where is my brother?" she demanded.

"Up here!" Skellan called to her and she immediately raced up the narrow stone steps. Her nurse and guards struggled to keep pace with her. Garrison archers stepped aside quickly. When she reached Skellan she threw her arms around him and embraced him almost too tightly for him to draw a breath.

Tracks of tears shone on her cheeks and her hands felt like brands of ice where they clung to his back.

"The bishop tried to kill you!" Hylanya drew in a shuddering breath and then pulled back a little from Skellan. "Rafale told me and I couldn't—I was so scared for you!"

"I'm fine. The bishop never came near me," Skellan reassured her while at the same time he wondered how word had reached Rafale. Had Cire sent Queenie to him? "Bishop Palo was cut down in his own garden by Bois and as of yet there is no proof that he meant me any harm."

"But…" Hylanya drew in another deep breath and then glanced back to the streets of Milmuraille where hundreds of torches blazed. "They are saying that Bois saved you, but that you and he have both been imprisoned by the Cadeleonians in this garrison." Her voice faltered and she looked nearly overwhelmed with emotion. "Hil—Skellan, I was so afraid for you."

"Where in the hells did that story spring up from?" Atreau muttered, but Skellan's attention remained on his sister and the river of torches blazing up from the streets beyond her. Skellan could pick out individual faces in the crowd now, and their voices rose even over the shouts of the garrison guards who raced to secure the gates.

"Free our count! Free our count! Free our count!" boomed like a battle cry.

Skellan had to raise his voice to ensure Hylanya heard him. "If you and that crowd have come to rescue me, where are the others going?"

"To tear down the bishop's townhouse and punish his conspirators," Hylanya shouted back.

"Oh God." Horror showed starkly on Atreau's face. Skellan felt as if he might be sick.

Elezar found the bishop's body slumped across a bed of vibrant blue gentians. A spray of his congealed blood speckled leaves and blossoms like a dark dew. The old man's throat gaped wide and seemed to almost ripple with the iridescent bodies of flies. The heat of the summer evening lent a disturbing warmth to the dead flesh and the bishop's gaze almost appeared contemplative in its fixed study of the sunset-streaked sky.

Elezar noted the clean stroke of the single deep wound. Muscle, bone, and cartilage lay exposed, leaving only a few inches of flesh still attached to the bishop's black-robed remains. Bois had struck hard and fast with a blade as sharp as a razor.

Elezar's old instructor, War Master Ignacio, would have been impressed by the skill if not the deed itself.

Fanned around Elezar, ten of his cavalrymen eyed the corpse and empty grounds with expressions of dismay. Flowers fluttered in the warm breeze and a fat squirrel bounded up the trunk of nearby tree where it chattered its annoyance at Elezar and his men. But no other sentry had been left with the bishop's corpse, nor were any of the household's priests on hand to whisper prayers over the old man's fallen body.

No one had greeted Elezar and his men at the townhouse gates and only three boys had been on hand at the stables. And yet the townhouse was far from silent. Alarmed and angry voices rose from the house itself, carrying from an open window on the second floor.

"Should we take His Grace—his body—to the chapel?" a young Cadeleonian cavalrymen asked.

Elezar shook his head and straightened from where he'd knelt beside the bishop's remains.

"We'll leave him until Sheriff Hirbe arrives. He'll need to see where the man fell." Why the sheriff, or at least one of his deputies, wasn't already here Elezar didn't know, but it added to his uneasiness. This murder warranted men of the law. Yet it seemed no one in the household had summoned anyone.

Elezar had already dispatched two of his own men to bring the sheriff, but he didn't know how long that might take, particularly with the night gloom encroaching upon the winding streets.

After a moment of thought, Elezar pulled off his cloak and laid it over the bishop like a shroud. "Go in peace to God's salvation," Elezar said and his cavalrymen repeated his words, though all but two of them belonged to Labaran temples.

"Right now, I'd say we'd best find out what the entire staff is doing up in the main house," Elezar decided.

He and his men slipped into the stately, sprawling townhouse unannounced and found beautifully decorated room after room abandoned. Beeswax tapers burned in silver candleholders, linens spread across the dining table, and a roast pheasant lay on a cutting board with only a plump black rat making any attempt at carving it.

Elezar wondered if it was one of Cire's. If that were the case, maybe she'd know what happened here. But no, if Cire had witnessed anything of the murder through one of her rats she would have said as much even before Atreau had dragged Bois into the garrison.

Men's voices drifted down from the staircase as did the distinct scent of smoke. Elezar started up the steps, but then one of his cavalrymen gave sharp whistle for his attention. Elezar joined the cavalryman to peer through a crack between the ballroom doors. Inside, bowed as if in supplicant prayer on a bare wood floor, nearly the entire house staff knelt in an eerie silence while a group of six priests paced around them like group of seething schoolmasters preparing to mete out punishment.

The moment Elezar and his men pushed open the double doors wide, maids, cooks, pages, grooms, and groundsmen looked up at them with expressions of obvious relief. The priests appeared startled and distinctly guilty. One young acolyte reached for his pen knife, but then, catching Elezar's glower, he dropped his hands before him and bowed his head.

"Lord Grunito, I'm afraid it is not a good time to come calling." A brawny priest drew a step closer to Elezar. "Bishop Palo has been slain and his household is mourning his passing with prayer."

Elezar didn't even bother arguing with this obvious lie.

"You'll release these people at once," Elezar stated.

"No!" Alarm rang through the priest's voice. He held his hands up to Elezar in supplication. "Please. If these Labaran servants summon the sheriff, all our lives could be forfeit. Sacrist Bois will charge that we have all been in league against Count Radulf, and every scrap of paper and letter will be read for signs of our guilt. Lord Grunito—"

They were buying time to destroy evidence. Elezar didn't wait for the priest to finish his plea for Elezar's complicity.

"The sheriff has already been summoned," Elezar addressed the gathered servants. "You are all free to leave this room, but remain on hand to answer the sheriff's questions."

Elezar left four of his men to ensure that the staff weren't intimidated further and that the priests also remained on hand. Then he bounded up the stairs. There he found a dozen priest in the midst of tearing apart both the bishop's library and his private rooms. They dumped armloads of letters, books, and parchment scrolls into blazing hearth fires. One priest hurled a gilded history book at Elezar and another drew a dagger against him but Elezar dealt both men hard blows with the flat of his sword and knocked them to their knees. The rest of the priests went still as startled deer. They dropped to their knees as Elezar ordered, but the fires they'd stoked had already consumed most of the bishop's correspondences.

Elezar pulled what he could from the sweltering flames with a poker and doused the fires, but his reward for singed hair and scorched fingers amounted to little more than scraps of correspondence amid a mountain of char and ash.

Elezar swore and had to fight the urge to smack the grin off the face of one particularly gleeful priest. If he let himself strike the man he very well might not stop at a single blow.

"You're idiots! Do you realize what you've done?" Elezar glowered at them. "You've managed to make yourselves all appear guilty." He didn't have to take in the faces of his own Labaran cavalrymen to know the truth in his own words. They, and likely the majority of the city's Labaran population, would now suspect some widespread Cadeleonian conspiracy.

And, God help him, Elezar wasn't that far from drawing the same conclusion himself. Except that when he leafed through one of the steaming tomes he'd pulled from the flames he found only a history text, which the bishop had notated.

An illustration of wolves wrapped in a briar of Mirogothic knot work spread beneath Elezar's fingers, the fine lines and jewel-like colors ruined by burns and soot. The zealotry and stupidity of the destruction angered Elezar almost as much as the idea of a Cadeleonian cabal.

"Take these priests to the chapel and see to it they do not leave until the sheriff has spoken to them." Elezar sent four of his men—sturdy Labarans—who quickly complied, herding the priests and driving them to the chapel like sheep.

Elezar and his remaining two men continued to search the upper floors.

All of the portraits from the library lay in a heap and though Elezar did discover a niche in the wall where the miniature of the previous count once hung, only a few torn scraps of a letter remained crammed into the very depths of the narrow crack. Elezar picked out a few complete words written in the indigo ink of a bishop. They read:...*he is no longer his master's man, though he does not seem to realize as much...*

Elezar felt a chill as he remembered Bois' claim that Bishop Palo had decried him to his royal masters back in Cadeleon.

But one phrase taken out of context proved nothing and the second remnant said: *wonderful soup! The flesh these northern gourds is without question a delight.*

The backsides of both tattered pieces revealed another of the bishop's favorite soups, this one eel, and the phrase: *the dog that bites his master's hand must be…*

"… slain or he will turn the entire kennel mutinous and savage," Elezar whispered the rest of the scripture to himself. If he had been the subject of the letter then this was not the most pleasant quote to encounter, but still a far cry from evidence of an assassination plot against Skellan.

Elezar scowled at the wrecked library and when he walked through the bishop's suite of private chambers he found worse. Nearly every piece of paper and parchment had been burned. The smell of smoke hung heaviest in the bishop's bedroom and Elezar noted that one of the priests must have thrown the windows open to keep from choking while he and his brothers shredded and burned everything.

"Sir?" The Cadeleonian captain, Tialdo, spoke softly. "What are we to do?"

"We keep looking. If there's nothing to find then so be it, but we can't have it said that we made no attempt."

"Yes, sir." Captain Tialdo nodded, though Elezar caught the slightest hesitance in his expression.

"We're not trying to prove the bishop guilty," Elezar assured the man. "We simply need to know the truth. Most importantly, we can't open this up to accusations of complicity among Cadeleonians."

"I know, sir. It's just the girl, his niece, she's my daughter's age…" Captain Tialdo didn't go on. Elezar didn't need him to. Likely it would mean the death of the girl if any evidence was discovered to back Bois' accusations. But that didn't make it anymore right to allow Bois to be executed for murder if he had indeed stuck against assassins intent upon killing Skellan and dooming all of Milmuraille.

"The priests weren't in her rooms, were they?" Elezar said.

"No, sir. They weren't."

"Let's have a look for ourselves then." Elezar added for Captain Tialdo's sake, "We may well prove her innocence."

"Yes, sir."

The young woman's gold-draped rooms were strange to Elezar, filled with a delicate maze of small furnishings, countless fragile vials of perfumed toiletries, inexplicable varieties of clothes, and a large collection of painted lutes. A search through her writing desk revealed long sheets of musical scores in various states of completion, blank sheet music, and a nearly empty ink bottle, but not a single letter.

Her cherry wood wardrobe gave up a bounty of minks, sables, and silks, as well as several pretty embroidery projects, each depicting a holy star wreathed in blossoms. Her dressing tables and jewelry boxes abounded with baubles, ribbons, combs and dozens of glittering pendants, broaches, and hairpins. Still no letters.

The Labaran cavalryman found a frightened puppy cringing beneath the young woman's downy bed between her chamber pot and a basin of scented water. Elezar had the man take the puppy down to the kitchen to be fed. Then he and Captain Tialdo paced through the three adjoined rooms yet again.

"I'd rather have found letters with nothing in them than to have found no letters at all."

"Indeed." Captain Tialdo nodded but then he shrugged. "Some girls don't write—"

"—and are never written to?" Elezar shook his head. "I know for a fact that Lord Quemanor wrote to her recently. He's wooing her."

"Love letters?" Captain Tialdo's expression brightened. "Those would be a very different thing, I can promise you." The man strode jauntily to the bed. He tossed a pillow aside gently and then flipped back the first layer of goose down mattress. At once Elezar spied a gold silk sachet and snatched it up. A floral perfume drifted up from the papers folded within the sachet.

"How did you know?" Elezar asked.

The Cadeleonian captain laughed and tossed the mattress back down and then carefully smoothed out the bedding.

"My daughter did the same with the love letter she received last year," he explained. "With the garrison the way it was under Commander Lecha, I wanted to keep her away from certain types of men so I spent some time rooting it out. A father has to look after his daughter, you know."

Elezar nodded. Before his brother Nestor's marriage he'd not really cared for any girls, but as he'd grown fond of his sister-in-law, Riossa, he'd found himself looking more protectively upon most women. Cadeleonian girls from good families in particular seemed to be raised in a state of ignorance, confinement and docility that rendered them extremely vulnerable to the will of any man who could lay hands upon them.

Though perhaps Lady Oasia Reollos could have argued otherwise. Her very vulnerability would seem to have made her quick and lethal in protecting her standing. Meek, sweet, and harmless might be how their men liked to see them, but not every Cadeleonian woman obliged.

With that thought Elezar opened the sachet and pulled out a thick sheaf of folded letters. The first five Elezar recognized as the products of Atreau's elegant script and poetic turn of mind. For his part Elezar hadn't noticed the bishop's niece as possessing "*eyes as deep as the night sky*" nor a "*voice that would call all of nature to life even from the depths of winter,*" but then he wasn't inclined towards such observations.

Another letter bore Fedeles' unmistakable clean script and in no way matched Atreau's worshipful tone.

Duty to my family title requires me to produce a legitimate heir, which I cannot accomplish without a wife. Your cousin has assured me that you are in good health, well proportioned for birthing, and not averse to becoming a duchess…

Elezar cringed as he read Fedeles' blunt proposition. "Proportioned for birthing" wasn't likely to win any young woman's heart. Still there was an honesty to the entire thing that was very much like Fedeles. Certainly the single letter from Fedeles wasn't dripping with the kind of overheated innuendo that the three letters from Commander Lecha reeked of.

Had those been the only missives in the satchel Elezar would have been well pleased. But last among the letters was one penned in the dark indigo ink of a bishop but the writing wasn't Bishop Palo's. The ornate watermark and indigo seal of Royal Bishop Nugalo filled the last third of the second page of fine paper.

"Shit," Captain Tialdo whispered the moment he glimpsed the seal. "How bad is it?"

Elezar scowled at the tight lines of furious script.

"The first page appears to be written in some kind of code but the second is a writ of absolution and pardon for mortal sins committed in service of the Holy Cadeleonian Church and crown."

Captain Tialdo looked even more horrified. He lowered his voice to a whisper. "What do we do with it? The girl's only nineteen, for God's sake."

Elezar nodded, though at nineteen he'd slain two men and had already dedicated himself to ensuring the deaths of another six. He cherished no illusions about the tender innocence of youth. If anything, he'd found himself growing more merciful as the years passed and he witnessed the consequences of righteous deaths and merciless justice. The lives he'd taken for his brother's murder hadn't eased his own guilt nor brought his brother back to him.

At nineteen he would have offhandedly condemned the bishop's niece. Yet he now hesitated, feeling a sorrow at the thought of yet another death that would do no one any good.

"I've had some practice with ciphers." Elezar considered the first page of the letter. "Before we assume these are orders for the count's assassination, I'd like to have a go at seeing what is truly written here."

"I've used a few codes as well," Captain Tialdo offered.

"We could do worse than try to crack this letter and have the truth. Who knows? Perhaps it's not so incriminating as it looks."

Captain Tialdo nodded, though Elezar could see that he didn't hold out much hope for the girl's innocence. Still, he brought Elezar clean paper, scribe's ink, and a quill from the library. Then the two of them hunched at the niece's small writing desk, in the midst of all her musical notations, and began picking apart the letter.

After attempting a few substitutions, they realized that the words meant to be read were those that corresponded to the musical notation of the holy song mentioned in the first line of the letter and which the bishop's niece had written out on sheet music.

Elezar tapped the notes out and wrote the words from the letter, while Captain Tialdo read them aloud.

"Defend our holy nation, virgin, and embrace sacrifice. Wed the lord. Enter his house. Serve us there. Turn his heart, prove treachery, or slay the man. Ensure no heir survives. His fall lights the path for a holy man to reach the throne. Bless you." Captain Tialdo frowned at the choppy message. "Wed lord… slay the man. Did the bishop mean her to wed and murder Count Radulf?"

Elezar considered the possibility of that and read the words over.

No, he realized, this didn't likely have anything to do with Skellan. And in a way this was much worse, because if bespoke of a greater rift between the royal princes and their supporters than Elezar could have imagined.

"I think the royal bishop meant that she should accept the duke of Rauma's marriage proposal and serve as a spy or even assassin if and when called upon."

"Kill the duke? Fedeles Quemanor?" Captain Tialdo raised his brows. "What in God's name had he to do with all of this?"

"Nothing. Look at the date of the royal bishop's letter. Written early last winter, well before Hilthorn reclaimed his birthright."

"But why plot the murder of Lord Quemanor?"

"That's a very long story, but short answer is that five years ago he and his cousin, whom you know as Javier the Bahiim, made the royal bishop look a fraud. Also Fedeles is the last of the Tornesal bloodline. If he dies without heir the vast holdings of Rauma will fall into the royal bishop's possession." Elezar resisted the urge to crush the letter in his fist. It was evidence that Fedeles would need to see.

Captain Tialdo rolled up the sheaf of sheet music and re-tied the silk ribbon around it. His expression turned soft and melancholic as he straightened the bow.

"So, the bishop's niece wasn't plotting against the count."

"It doesn't seem so," Elezar replied. "Though scheming to marry and murder a Cadeleonian nobleman is hardly an harmless pursuit."

"We don't know that she agreed to it."

"The fact that she kept the letter and writ imply that she meant to use them for something." Elezar folded the letter but didn't return it to the silk sachet along with the others.

"Such a young thing, and so pretty. It's a pity." Captain Tialdo eyed the pages in Elezar's hands. "It doesn't prove Bois' claims against her but neither does if prove her a meek innocent."

"No, all of this only bends us over a barrel to get fucked from both ends, doesn't it?" Elezar replied and Captain Tialdo looked briefly surprised at Elezar's turn of phrase but then laughed.

"It does at that," Captain Tialdo agreed. "It won't please our Cadeleonian troops to know that they're fighting for a count who condones the murder of a holy man."

"Skell—Count Radulf isn't likely to condone Bishop Palo's murder. I think he liked the old man. I don't really understand how, but he seems to have found it in himself to forgive the bishop's earlier treachery against him."

"Earlier treachery? What has the bishop ever done to the young count?" Captain Tialdo appeared truly perplexed.

"You really don't know?" Elezar raised his brows.

"No. I mean aside from preaching against the practices of witchcraft and... unnatural carnal desires." Captain Tialdo winced as he said the last two words and then added quickly, "He wasn't outspoken on either subject. It's Labara, after all."

Elezar let the comment pass. Larger matters were at stake than dogmatic definitions of what was natural. The fact that his own men didn't seem to know what had happened in the city they were defending worried him far more.

But then how could Captain Tialdo know? Skellan's entire existence had been kept from the Cadeleonian population by Labaran nobility intent upon forging an alliance with the Sumar grimma. Elezar shook his head. How were they all ever going to work together with so many lies and so much misinformation between them?

"You knew that the previous count's son had been abducted, yes?" Elezar asked.

Captain Tialdo nodded.

"Well, it was Bishop Palo who helped Grimma Lundag steal Hilthorn. She held him ransom and as far as I can work out she kept him as a dog. She literally turned him into a dog and then made a ritual of torturing his father once a year as the price of keeping the boy alive."

"Bishop Palo..." Captain Tialdo's expression turned from perplexed to horrified. "How long did this go on?"

"Eight years. Hilthorn escaped when he was eleven and lived as a street witch for the next ten years." Elezar remembered Skellan joking about nearly being thrown into a dog fight and his hungry days of whoring, but those were not confidences that he wanted to share. It was enough that Captain Tialdo understood that Bishop Palo had played a part in Skellan's deprivation of family, wealth, and safety.

Captain Tialdo's horror seemed to deepen as the full implication of Elezar's words sank in.

"I'd heard whispers but—I mean, there were rumors concerning Hallen Radulf's missing son, and we all knew that Grimma Lundag had abducted children for ransoms but..."

"They kept it a secret," Elezar explained.

"Why?"

"Because Hilthorn's mother is the Sumar grimma and how happy do you think that would have made the royal bishop?"

Bleak comprehension lit Captain Tialdo's face.

"And the Labarans know all of this?" Captain Tialdo asked.

"Not all of them or all of it but enough of them know most of the story. So you can see why they might not look upon Bishop Palo's killer as a monster so much as a righteous avenger."

"I knew Commander Lecha was a corrupt bastard but I never would have guessed that Bishop Palo..." Captain Tialdo's expression turned bleak. "No wonder the Labarans are so cold to our priests. The Cadeleonian population needs to know about this."

"They do, indeed," Elezar replied.

"It will take a few days but I could see to it that the story is told," Captain Tialdo offered.

"I'd be glad if you'd spread the story anyway you could." Elezar knew enough of Captain Tialdo's involvement with the Cadeleonian broadsheet to feel certain that the man could ensure that word traveled swiftly through both troops and Cadeleonian civilians. Knowing of the wrongs dealt Skellan might serve to lessen the outrage most Cadeleonians would feel if Bois walked free.

"I will, sir." Captain Tialdo grinned and opened his mouth to add something more when the cries of a cavalryman interrupted him. The young Labaran rushed into the room.

"Lord Grunito! Sheriff Hirbe has arrived and would have words with you."

Elezar stood, tucked the sachet of perfumed letters into his coat, and started for the door. He turned back at Captain Tialdo. "Coming?"

"Yes, sir."

As soon as Elezar stepped off the stairs and glimpsed Hirbe he knew something had gone wrong. Hirbe's bright, quilted cap hung askew and fine locks of his white hair drifted around his weathered face in disarray. Road dust blanketed his clothes and cast a dull gray tone to the bodies and faces of the six deputies who'd accompanied him. But more than anything else it was simply the expression on the slim man's face that alarmed Elezar. He'd spoken to the sheriff with dead bodies at his feet and when the entire city seemed on the brink of crumbling in the coils of a gigantic, fiery serpent, and always Sheriff Hirbe maintained some trace of a smile, some air of calm.

Now worry lay stark upon his face and he glanced back over his shoulder out the wide window with apprehension.

"They are coming to tear this place apart and likely kill anyone they can lay their hands on," Sheriff Hirbe announced. "We have to get the staff and priests out. But I don't think we have time..."

Elezar's stomach clenched into a hard knot, his thoughts leaping immediately to the grimma and their armies.

"Which grimma is here? Do you know?" he asked, praying it was the Sumar.

"Not the grimma. It's a mob of Labarans from the Theater District," Sheriff Hirbe went on. "I have no idea how they got word about Bois and the bishop—I heard it myself from them well before your man reached me. The gossip on the street is a far cry from what your man said. The mobs believe that

Hilthorn and Bois are being held prisoner at the garrison on the bishop's orders and they are out for Cadeleonian blood."

Elezar couldn't quite grasp how so many details could have gotten so garbled, reversed, or clearly fabricated in so short a time. Under other circumstances he might have questioned the sheriff in more detail but that could wait. A furious Labaran mob certainly wouldn't.

"How far behind you are they?" Elezar looked past the sheriff's shoulder to the window. Now he could just pick out the distant flickering lights of torches. They were still back on the hill but racing down fast. From the growing glow of light Elezar realized this wasn't a crowd of a few dozen, but hundreds.

Elezar turned to his Captain Tialdo. "There's a back gate behind the chapel. I want you and the other men to evacuate the staff and priests to the garr—"

"—not the garrison," Sheriff Hirbe cut in. "The larger crowd is there already. They think they're freeing Bois and the count from you. I don't think it would be safe to take a Cadeleonian priest anywhere near the place just now."

Two mobs? That struck Elezar as disturbingly planned. He remembered Hylanya's insistence on disposing of the bishop but this seemed far beyond the machinations of a teenaged girl.

In any case, now wasn't the time to brood over it. He watched the approaching throng with a desperate need to escape that quashed all other questions. Captain Tialdo stood beside him, peering out the window and whispering a string of obscenities like they were prayers.

"Take the priests to the docks," Elezar decided. "Get them onboard the duke's ship and keep them safe. Hell, sail out of the harbor, if you must. We need to find out all we can from these people if we're going to hold anything resembling a fair trial and get this city back to order."

"Yes, sir. You'll ride with us?" Captain Tialdo asked.

"No, I'll do what I can here to buy you time. Now go."

Captain Tialdo saluted and then turned and raced away. Elezar heard his voice echoing in the halls of the house as he called his fellow cavalrymen and the lingering members of the household staff to him.

Sheriff Hirbe eyed Elezar. Behind him his six deputies stole uneasy glimpses at the open street out the window.

"Buy them time? You think you can hold this townhouse with just that wrought iron fence out front and a few yards of drive?" Sheriff Hirbe scrubbed at the dust clinging to his curling white brows. "You won't last the time it takes to pass water, Lord Grunito."

The sheriff's assessment was likely correct. One man couldn't hold back a mob. He wished he had Kiram's pluming torch. The sight of all those flames gushing up would likely have stilled a mob. Inspiration came to Elezar.

"I don't need to hold the townhouse I—we—" Elezar met the sheriff's gaze. "We only have to keep the crowd's attention away from the south gate long enough for my cavalrymen to get the household out of here. Then we'll fall back and let the mob have this place. No one needs to die for a pile of wood and rocks."

"So that's all *we* have to do, is it?" A wry smile curved the sheriff's lips. Glimpsing amusement in the sheriff's countenance, Elezar felt heartened.

"That, and keep everyone on both sides from getting killed," Elezar added.

"Oh yes, that." Sheriff Hirbe gave a dry laugh. "You have a plan, I hope?"

"Ever heard the Haldiim saying of 'fight fire with fire?'"

"I haven't, and I'm not certain I'd call it sound, having doused a number of house fires," Sheriff Hirbe replied.

"I never had much use for it myself until exactly this moment. But now I think it's inspired genius." Elezar studied the growing sea of torches lighting up the northern street. The crowd moved more like a marching phalanx than a mob and oddly didn't appear interested in looting any of the surrounding Cadeleonian homes, which Elezar found surprising.

Then he noticed that all six of the deputies, as well as Sheriff Hirbe, were watching him in silent expectation.

"There's a hay cart filled with baled, dry straw in the stable and at least five casks of Cadeleonian seed oil in the kitchen cellar," Elezar went on. "We'll want to barricade the front fence with straw and soak the bales in oil. We don't light anything until the crowd is nearly on top of us. When the fire goes up, hopefully it will throw the mob into confusion and buy us enough time for the house staff to get well clear. Straw isn't going to hold anyone at bay long but it won't do them any harm either. If we build it up on this side of the gate, it ought to provide a spectacle without tumbling down on anyone. What do you think?"

"I think we'd best get to it then," the sheriff called to his deputies. "The four of you, to the stables and fetch that hay cart—"

"And my stallion, Cobre," Elezar added. If this all went wrong he wouldn't leave Cobre locked in a stable.

"You don't want to fetch him yourself?" Sheriff Hirbe asked.

"I'll be of more use hauling oil casks. They're heavy and have to be heaved up a flight of stairs from the cellar."

The sheriff's brows rose sharply and he nodded. "Right. I'll bring your Cobre myself." He turned back to his deputies and pointed to the two brawniest men. "The two of you help Lord Grunito with the oil. We meet at the front gates. Quick as rabbits!"

Elezar charged down to the cellar and all but hurled the oil casks up to the deputies. They took turns rolling the heavy wooden casks down the long sandy drive to the front gates. Elezar hauled the last cask up himself.

Outside, a warm tumbling wind carried the chants of the approaching crowd like the hot breath of a roaring beast. Hundreds of torches threw back the gloaming shadows and set the street alight as if the sun still burned behind the black silhouettes of the nearest houses. Elezar caught sight of a young couple fleeing from one of the two grand houses across the way. Servants quickly followed, lugging baggage and making for the grand Cadeleonian chapel further south of the bishop's holdings. In the other Cadeleonian townhouses staff bolted the decorative gates and retreated to the main buildings where they simply snuffed their lights and drew their curtains. Elezar hoped that the vast grounds of the bishop's townhouse would keep the mob occupied.

Then Elezar caught his first clear glimpse of the nearing mob as they passed through the dark gaps between the nearest backlit houses.

"Traitors! Traitors! Traitors!" The accusation hammered the air and sent a chill down Elezar's spine.

He reached for his sword then stopped as he realized that he could clearly pick out the faces of individuals in the mob. The flickering light and their open fury distorted their features. Still Elezar thought he recognized old Ogmund as well as several merchants from the fish market. There was the elderly woman whose cider pot had stilled a man who would have murdered Elezar only a few weeks before.

These weren't people he wanted to harm, much less kill.

The sheriff and his deputies arrived with the hay cart, their own mounts, and Cobre. The deputies set to work throwing the bales of straw up against the tall wrought iron fence. They blocked the largest gaps between the decorative iron rungs but didn't even attempt to barricade actual gates. On the off chance that anyone got through, the last thing they wanted was to trap anyone under a tower of flaming straw and oil. One young deputy slid the iron crossbar of the gate in place, but Elezar didn't expect it to hold long against the number of furious people marching for them.

"You can go if you want," Sheriff Hirbe told Elezar. "There might still be time for you to get clear. Keeping the city law isn't your duty."

"It would be my honor to help you, sheriff. And those oil casks aren't getting any lighter." Elezar patted Cobre once but then turned and set to work hefting the casks up to douse the costly Cadeleonian seed oil over the rickety towers of baled straw. Wind rolled over Elezar, engulfing him in the smoke and heat of the nearing torches.

"Traitors! Traitors! Traitors!" The chant drowned out the words Sheriff Hirbe shouted to Elezar and his deputies.

Elezar leapt down from several bales of straw and swung the last cask of oil up. His greasy fingers slipped on the bronze rim of the wooden cask but he kept his grip. He charged up the last tier of bales and poured the fragrant oil across the already glistening straw. Streams of oil drizzled down to the cobblestones, ran beneath the gates, and formed glistening pools between the street cobbles. The blaze of torches danced in the slick puddles like a premonition of the flames to come.

Elezar bounded down from the doused straw and then withdrew several steps to where the sheriff waited beside the horses.

"With all that oil on you, you smell as sweet as an almond lamp, Lord Grunito," Sheriff Hirbe shouted. "You'd best get back a bit or you might light up like one when we set flame to that lovely tower of ours!"

Elezar backed away a few steps. Cobre followed him, his dark eyes wide, nostrils flared, and his whole body trembling with tension.

"You remember our great ride through Anacleto?" Elezar whispered and stroked the stallion's jaw and Cobre snorted. "We'll give them hell again if we have to."

Elezar swung up into his saddle and felt a kind a prepared calm come over Cobre's muscular frame, as if the stallion were giving his might over to Elezar. Silently, Elezar accepted the responsibility for them both. He gripped his reins in one hand and curled his fingers around the hilt of his sword with the other. He didn't want to hurt anyone but he wouldn't allow harm to befall the sheriff, his deputies, or Cobre.

Ahead of him, the sheriff and his men also mounted up. Neither trained for war nor tested in battle, the Labaran horses whinnied and pranced nervously across the sandy grounds of the drive. The sheriff chided his plump gelding and the deputies slowly brought their mounts to attention. But even through the dark, Elezar noticed the flash of the whites of the animals' wide eyes. These were not animals prepared to charge the crowd, though Elezar felt they would certainly carry their riders away from the torches fast enough.

Through the bars of the fence, Elezar studied of the closing mob and felt his heartbeat quicken.

Human bodies surged like a rushing wave of seething humanity. Labaran men, women, and a multitude of excited youths shouted in time, as if answering the furious beat of a war drum. Many wore theater masks and odd costumes. Those on the edges of the group carried the torches while many in the midst of the horde gripped knives and hammers and axes. The torches cast bizarre shadows up the walls of the surrounding houses.

Their sheer number didn't unnerve Elezar nearly as much as the way the entire group moved together. He'd seen church parades display more rowdy, chaotic behavior. None of the of young men hurled stones against the costly windows that they marched past. No one broke off from the group to attack the open gardens and overhanging trees of the Cadeleonian houses on either side of the street. They chanted and marched upon the bishop's townhouse with a singular, focused purpose.

This wasn't a mob so much as a militia. But how? He couldn't imagine Ogmund being a part of any organized event, much less one that required military precision.

Then first line of men and women caught sight of the sheriff on his horse awaiting them behind the barred gates of the bishop's townhouse. Abruptly, their shouts and howls lulled and something like confusion showed on several faces.

"What you do here, now, is unlawful and no good to your

new count's cause!" the sheriff shouted. "You have been lied to and misled! The count is safe—"

Elezar narrowed his eyes. He spied a faint thread of greenish light curling through the crowd and entwining bodies like some strange bindweed. It flared and then flickered out before Elezar was certain of what he'd seen.

"Traitors! Traitors!" One young man's voice rose from far back in the mass of bodies and torches. Another green thread flared and faded and the young man's words seemed to spark through the rest of the crowd. The momentary calm shattered into a wild frenzy of screams. "Traitors! Traitors! Traitors!"

The crowd charged the gates and on the sheriff's signal two deputies hurled their lamps into the straw bale. Cascades of orange fire gushed up and still the crowd surged forward. A stocky Labaran man hurled himself against the wrought iron bars even as flames rolled over his bare hands. His face contorted with agony and still he slammed his body again and again against the searing metal. Beside him a young woman shrieked, her hair and shirt crawling with flames as she clambered up the bars of the fence. Three young men shoved an old woman aside to throw themselves against the front gates. Oil fires flashed to life at their feet, but the youths didn't relent.

"They're under thrall!" Sheriff Hirbe shouted, his expression horrified. "They can't stop themselves and they can't be reasoned with."

The nearest deputies fell back behind the sheriff. The youngest looked sick.

The entire mob heaved into the flames. Their weight rocked the gates and sent burning bales tumbling down into their midst. Smoke poured up in black plumes as men and women, their clothes smoldering and their faces scorched and blistered, fought their way to the gates.

Elezar had seen brutal and violent deaths before, but this was worse, sickening to witness. Screams and cries tore the air. The smell of burning flesh and hair churned in clouds of black smoke. Hundreds of people—some of them folk Elezar recognized and could remember laughing with—helplessly pushed themselves and everyone before them into the fire. A blaze Elezar had hoped would stop them, a fire of his own devising.

When he saw Ogmund push towards the growing flames he knew he had to act. He couldn't allow these captive people to remain trapped by the gates as flames engulfed them.

"Make for the south gate," Elezar shouted to Sheriff Hirbe. Then he urged Cobre forward between the arching bales of burning straw to the iron lock of the front gate. Elezar reached out and threw the hot lock open. The metal scorched his palm but he hardly noticed. He wheeled Cobre about. As the gates started to swing inward, Cobre leapt forward, barely carrying Elezar clear of the hands that grasped for his arms and legs.

Cobre raced up the drive and the mob came pouring into the grounds. Elezar felt the grit of sand flying over him as it whipped up beneath Cobre's hooves.

Behind them, the mob roared and shouted like tormented creatures. Ahead of them Sheriff Hirbe and his deputies urged their own mounts up the drive, intent upon the southern gate. The sheriff craned his head back, his face drawn and pale as he took in the horde at Elezar's back.

"Traitors! Traitors! Traitors!" The chant boomed. Elezar felt something small and hard slam into his back. Another heavy blow struck against his shoulder. Stones, Elezar thought.

He stole a glance back over his shoulder and caught sight of a young man hefting an ax after him. Elezar nudged Cobre and the stallion swerved mid stride. The ax blade whistled past Elezar's face.

Then, just as Elezar had before briefly glimpsed that pale green thread, luminous scarlet symbols—curling, scribbled strange tangles of letters and forms—rose up from the stones of the drive, from the paths of the garden, and even from the walls of the townhouse. They swung over Elezar, sending shudders through his body as they brushed his skin, and then fell upon the mob like wind-blown leaves.

The mob at Elezar's back went suddenly silent. He stole another glance back over his shoulder. The entire crowd stood still, as if frozen.

The few red symbols rising from the bishop's house were faint reflections of the massive constellations of scarlet symbols that lit the whole city. The entire skyline of towers, temples, and aqueducts shone with rising red symbols. The brilliance of them burned Elezar's eyes and threw the dazed, silent crowd into shadow.

Not far ahead of him, Elezar heard the sheriff swear, "Mother's blood preserve us."

Spells, these had to be spells.

Despite his urge to flee, Elezar slowed Cobre and turned him to take in the sight of the entire city blazing with blood red spells. Countless symbols swirled into the air like swifts taking flight. They rose, twirling and flocking into a great mass over the tall walls of the garrison. The wind churned and throbbed with their motions. Elezar felt the hairs raising across his arms and across the back of his neck. Cobre snorted and shivered.

Then as the spells coiled and turned, Elezar recognized the form they created: an immense, fiery wolf. The moon hung in the shadow of one eye. The other appeared blacker than even the night sky. Elezar had seen such an image in ancient texts and had thought it a flight of fancy at the time. But here blazed the raw aura of a grimma—a witchflame surging up so powerfully that even common folk could see the true form of the witch's soul.

A terrible dread gripped Elezar. Had Grimma Ylva found a way to reach across the miles and strike directly at Skellan?

The apparition opened its black maw, exposing teeth as white as stars. To Elezar's shock the low voice that boomed over the city rang with Skellan's intonations.

"You will lay down your weapons! My good folk, you have been taken in thrall and led wrong in my name and I will not have it!" The words pulsed gently over Elezar, but the people standing on the drive swayed and fell to their knees as if struck by a strong current.

"Lies have gripped your hearts and minds, but I tell you, I am safe. I tore apart a demon lord and broke a sanctum! I cannot be taken captive in my own city!" Skellan's words gentled a little. "Return to your homes and be at peace this night."

As Skellan's voice faded, the scarlet spells forming the vast, looming wolf broke apart, scattering like autumn leaves back to the walls, stones, and cobbles from which they arose. Several swept past Elezar, warming his skin and burning bright as embers. Where the spells fell they dulled to darkness in a matter of moments.

The crowd, that seconds before seemed murderous and mindless, resolved into confused, injured, and frightened individuals. More than one turned to Elezar for answers and he explained what he could. Shortly after that, the sheriff and his deputies wheeled back and rode down from the gardens to help. The youngest deputy lit out to fetch sister-physicians from the nearest temple.

"You saved more than a few of these folks' lives with that foolish stunt of opening the gates, you know," the sheriff commented to Elezar.

"It was I who endangered them in the first place."

"No. You weren't the one who enthralled them. That's the one who's to blame here."

Elezar nodded. It had to have been a powerful spell to have enthralled so many people, but he had no idea who had crafted it. The memory of the pale green thread came to mind but in a city so populated with witches he doubted that alone offered much to go on.

"You were near at hand when it started, weren't you?" Elezar asked the sheriff. "Did you notice anything…" Elezar trailed off, having no idea of what might implicate the person—or people—behind this mess.

"I could make a few guesses but they'd be no more than that. No evidence." Sheriff Hirbe scratched his beard. "I think she contrived for Bois to move against the bishop to set this all in motion. Though I don't think she reckoned on our Hilthorn taking control of the entire city so fast."

"She?" Elezar asked and he thought again of Hylanya and the way her scorn had seemed to sear the air around him.

The sheriff shook his head.

"Pure speculation on my part and too dangerous to chatter on about. That sort of thing can get the blameless killed all too easily."

Elezar started to object but then remembered the letters hidden away in his own coat. The sheriff had a point. Accusing the innocent would do no good. And yet...

"What worries me most right now," the sheriff went on. "Is Bois being executed as a murderer when the entire city thinks he's only guilty of loyalty—"

"Not the entire city," Elezar cut in. "Certainly not all the Cadeleonians."

The young deputy returned with several sister-physicians and both Elezar and the sheriff hastened to aid them in tending the injured. They carried a good number of men and women to the bishop's townhouse and soon transformed his lavish ballroom into a temporary hospital. Elezar brought water from the kitchen well, carried great rafts of bedding down to the sisters, and managed not to trip over Ogmund's distressed badger as the grizzled animal raced to its master. When two deputies rolled out a huge keg of table beer, Elezar was heartened to see Ogmund, his left hand bandaged and his badger snoring on his lap, accept a mug of the brew with a smile.

Nearly an hour later, Elezar stumbled down the drive to the hitching post where Cobre awaited him. Small oil fires still flickered along the periphery of the iron fence and smoldering bales of straw scented the dark. Elezar greeted Cobre and indulged the stallion with an expensive cube of sugar, liberated from the bishop's kitchen.

Then the light of a lamp fell over him and Elezar turned to see Sheriff Hirbe approaching him.

"I hoped we might share a few more words, Lord Grunito."

"Certainly."

The sheriff stroked his beard and drew near enough that Elezar could smell the wool and pick out the pattern of blue flowers on his patchwork hat.

"How badly do you think they would take it if Bois were absolved?" the sheriff asked in a whisper. It struck Elezar as telling that the sheriff didn't ask how poorly he, as a Cadeleonian, would take such tidings. At the same time Elezar knew that his personal feelings didn't reflect those of the majority of his countrymen. Perhaps the sheriff suspected the same thing.

"Very, very badly. Even the most loyal of my Cadeleonian captains would find it hard to fight for Hilthorn if he openly exonerates Bois after he murdered a bishop."

"And if he's not freed then the Labaran population is bound to think that Cadeleonians are exerting control over the count," the sheriff said. "So we're fucked."

"That thought had occurred to me as well," Elezar agreed. Despite the grim prospect he smiled.

"We'll find a way through it," the sheriff said after a moment and then he held his hand up. Out of habit, Elezar placed his hand to the sheriff's as if making a pact with him. The older man's fingers felt as rough as Elezar's own.

"We will," Elezar agreed. He had no idea how they would but he knew, as the sheriff no doubt did, that they had to find a solution. If they didn't then the factions might tear the city apart before the Mirogoths ever got the chance.

Elezar closed his eyes. If only Bois had possessed the sense to recognize that he was committing a murder and plan an escape, they wouldn't be facing this problem. If only the idiot hadn't thrust his fate into Skellan's hands…

"It would appear that your escort has arrived, Lord Gruni-to." The sheriff's words interrupted Elezar's train of thought and he opened his eyes, half-expecting to see Captain Tialdo. Instead the sheriff gave a nod of his head in the direction of the smoldering main gates. Master Bone-crusher towered over the iron and flickering flames. He stepped over the gates and crushed out an oil fire as easily as a man might snuff a candle flame.

Elezar wondered what it said about these last days that he could now find such a sight reassuringly familiar.

CHAPTER
SEVENTEEN

The vast crowd closed in.

Skellan didn't have the time or desire to take to the pinnacle of the sanctum to work his spells as a grimma would have. Instead from the meager height of the garrison wall he threw his senses and witchflame into the blazing wards he'd strung across the city and the sky above. His flesh felt molten with the power. His breath rolled up, a roaring wind rising from his lungs as he stretched his witchflame across the sky. From a height far beyond the shell of his body, he gazed down.

Great bridges and towers spread beneath him like exquisitely carved toys. Hundreds of human beings appeared small as fleas, their multitude of torches little more than flecks of light. Winding around them, the faint jade spell of another witch hung, small and dull as a thread of weather-worn yarn.

Skellan snarled at it and with a flex of his witchflame tore the spell to shreds. He devoured the frail remnants of broken power, making them his own. Then he called down to the small people gathered beneath him. But even as he spoke, his senses soared higher and further, reaching up into the warm night winds, tasting primrose blossoms and honey. Turning his gaze beyond the scarlet, webbed walls of Milmuraille, he winced at the blazing emerald fire that raged over the forest beyond the river.

The Sumar grimma's witchflame rose up before him, immense and monstrous as the ancient dragons of Bone-crusher's stories. Membranous wings spread, engulfing the black sky in the fragrant green light of long summer days. Her huge coiling body stretched like a river, far more vast and shining than the dark ribbon of the Raccroc. Her massive talons reached down to the land below, not seeking its support, but holding miles of wilderness in an unyielding grasp.

Skellan shuddered, feeling suddenly like a pretender,

perched here in his tiny domain.

Then the dragon's head lifted on a long serpentine neck and eyes that blazed like suns seared into Skellan. He forced himself to meet her gaze. Her power rolled over him like scorching flames.

"Do I frighten you, my child?"

Her words thrilled through Skellan like wind rippling a candle flame. He was gazing up into the soul of the Sumar grimma. His mother.

"No. I'm not frightened," Skellan answered though he knew she felt the lie in his words as much as he did.

"You would be wise to fear the sight of a grimma, child of mine. Our wrath and avarice bears down upon you." She beat her vast wings and Skellan hunched against the force that shredded through him. He needed to drop back down beneath his wards and yet he could not bring himself to flee like a whipped whelp. This was the mother he'd never known—the mother whose absence he'd felt as long as he could remember. He needed to know something of her and more importantly he needed her to know the strength of his will.

"You should know that I am not bred from those easily defeated," Skellan replied.

"No. But you are an infant pitting himself against immortals. We will tear you to pieces if you stand against us. So, come, bow down in obedience to your mother and I will take you beneath my wing. Come to me and I will protect you."

"And Milmuraille? Radulf County?" Skellan demanded.

"What do you care of that foul nest of forged metal and mortal filth? That place was your prison. Now you are free. Come home to my forests and I will gift you with mates of every form and champions beyond compare. I will keep you safe, my own child. The Cadeleonians will not lay their filthy hands upon you again. Leave Milmuraille to its fate and I will see that it is returned to the forest it should be."

Skellan knew he could not agree and yet he hesitated. Fear

and the terrible, childish desire to please her twisted in him. But neither were stronger than his certainty that he couldn't abandon his home.

"I will protect you for all of time," she added softly.

"No. I have promised to defend the peoples of these lands. I will not let you, or any grimma, take them."

"Your promise is a child's! How will you keep such an oath when Naemir, Ylva, and Onelsi make war against you? They will torture and defile you! They will not show you mercy even if you are our son. I would show you greater kindness by devouring you myself than if I let them take you alive!"

Her words tore through him, splintering his grasp on his own wards and sending the red spells scattering back to the city below. Stripped, his soul exposed, Skellan burned beneath the green flames of her stare and the raw power of her voice.

"I will not lose you again! Come to me and bow down to my protection!"

Skellan fought to keep from crying out in pain but he would not submit to her demand.

"No!"

"Obey me!" Her jaws dropped wide and a wall of blinding green fire roared over Skellan.

He could withstand no more. He fell from his height, his soul and senses collapsing back into the fragile shell of his living flesh. All at once agony flooded his body. His legs gave out and he felt hands grip him and pull him back to his feet.

His ears rang and his sight flickered with the afterimage of too much light.

"Hilthorn?" Hylanya sounded far away.

"Count Radulf?" Atreau asked. Skellan wonder which of them supported his body. Perhaps both did.

He clenched his eyes closed, though the Sumar grimma's flames still smoldered beneath his lids. Every secret fantasy he'd harbored of a gentle, adoring mother died within him. In their place a dread took root.

He was fighting Old Gods for Milmuraille, Little Dreamer had told him, and now Skellan knew she had been right. He dragged in a breath, held it, and slowly exhaled. Another breath and the deafening ringing in his ears quieted. Living feeling returned to his limbs.

The night air felt soothing against his skin. He steadied and took his own weight. As he opened his eyes he realized that it had been Atreau who caught him. In the harsh lamplight his face appeared ghostly pale.

Hylanya held Skellan's hand between hers and whispered a blessing to him. Her words hardly formed spells but the intent was strong and easing to Skellan's battered senses. The two guards whom Elezar had assigned to protect him looked on with frightened expressions. One gripped his spear while the older man beside him held up a lantern against the darkness.

Beyond them the crowd of Hylanya's attendants, guards, and nurse stood between formations of soldiers who'd gathered to defend the garrison. All of them seemed to stare at Skellan. Hylanya's nurse, Peome, gazed at him with particularly uneasy expression, as if she thought he might turn suddenly feral.

Self-consciously he straightened and drew his cloak closer around his shoulders as he gazed down to the street below. The enthralled mob that had pounded at the front gates had already broken apart. Now Skellan only caught sight of a few individuals slinking back to their homes or the taverns that offered them the greatest comfort. The spell that had enthralled them had been powerful and yet so fine that nothing of it remained now but the faintest whisper of jade. That, too, dissipated in an instant.

Skellan tried to reach out and find any remnants of the spell but the moment he pushed his witchflame from the center of his body a sickening exhaustion washed through him. He swayed against the stone wall.

A cold hand steadied his back.

"Count Radulf, are you unwell?" Atreau asked quietly enough but the still of the night seemed to carry his words. These gathered folk could not know how hard he'd been thrown down by the Sumar grimma's mere gaze.

"I'm fine. Truth be told, I fear I'm brewing some foul wind in my bowels after choking down too much of this evening's stew." Skellan pulled a grin and hoped it didn't appear too forced. "Thank you for asking, Lord Quemanor. I'll warn you if I feel a volley coming on."

Atreau laughed but Hylanya only gave a slight shake of her head.

"I felt her too, Hilthorn," Hylanya whispered.

Atreau and the guards looked confused. Skellan felt certain that if he looked beyond them he would recognize the same expression on many other faces of those standing nearby.

"Felt who, my lady?" Atreau asked.

"The Sumar grimma," Hylanya replied, though she cast Skellan a questioning glance. "I think she's very near."

Skellan shrugged. It wasn't that the Sumar grimma had drawn nearer to them so much as the whole force of her attention now focused upon them. Shudders slithered down Skellan's spine and he had to fight to keep his dread from showing on his face.

"She is quite a ripe old thing." Skellan kept his smile wide and his voice bright. "Probably the smell of her put me off my digestion. Still, I don't think she's going to arrive tonight. No point in all of us standing around in the dark. Hylanya, you should join the duke here for supper."

Hylanya stared at Skellan and then looked to Atreau with great uncertainty.

"But what about Bishop Palo's plot?" Hylanya spoke softly, as if somehow Atreau might not hear her.

Skellan felt too beaten—almost broken—to bear thinking of the bishop's brutal murder or all the possible conspiracies he might have inspired. He wanted only to escape and lie down somewhere dark, soothing, and safe. Instead he braced himself against the wall and managed an offhanded shrug.

"I've been assured that the man is dead, so I don't think he's much of a threat today. And I've sent my champion to look into Sacrist Bois' accusations. In the meanwhile, the duke and the bishop's niece are my guests and I would be honored if you, my dear sister, would do me the kindness of playing host in my place."

Skellan read the objection rising in Hylanya's expression and went on before she managed to speak. He lowered his voice only a little.

"I'm not certain that it's only airy farts pounding at my back end, if you take my meaning, and I think it would be poor manners to make the duke wait while I fight it all out in the shitter. Still, that makes for a finer repast than me taking a chance at passing wind in the dining hall and blowing out the ass of my pants with fiery shits, don't you think?"

Atreau actually blanched at the comment, but Hylanya regarded Skellan much more seriously. Then, at last, she nodded.

"Very well," she said. "I have no wish to embarrass our family. I will gladly stand in as your hostess, but promise me that you will feel better soon."

"I swear it," Skellan replied, because he felt certain that he couldn't feel much worse and go on living. "I'll be on my way to the shi—er—privy to get it all settled first thing."

The majority of folk gathered about him made their excuses and descended from the wall walkway as quickly as possible. Hylanya allowed Atreau to escort her down, though her guards and her nurse looked none too pleased. Skellan remained on the raised walkway until the courtyard cleared. Across the grounds he saw Bone-crusher watching him. More than anything Skellan wanted to rush to the troll and curl up on the safety of his mossy shoulder. But Skellan's guards tromped after him as he started down the steps and he couldn't stand the thought of them looking on as he came all to pieces.

So Skellan turned and made his way to a line of soldiers' privies at the back of the courtyard. His guards stopped outside the wooden door as Skellan pulled it shut.

Inside, Skellan threw up his dinner, and then shaking and miserable, he pulled his cloak in around himself and willed himself to melt into the numb of animal flesh. The repellant stench of vomit, piss, and shit grew overpowering to his canine sense but also lost much of its repugnance. As Skellan settled into the comforting body of a lanky red dog, he found the latrine's pungence strong and earthy and only rebelled at the closeness of the walled confines.

The cutout at the back of the privy, which allowed in moonlight and breezes, hung low enough and large enough for Skellan to leap up to and crawl out from. Then, dropping to the ground, he slunk away from his bored guards and scampered to Bone-crusher.

A little bird startled from the branches overhanging the troll's broad shoulders and a cluster of cloud imps drifted just beyond the easy reach of Skellan's long muzzle as he bounded over the troll's gnarled feet and clambered up onto one outstretched thigh. Bone-crusher leaned forward slowly and bowed his huge face down next to Skellan's. His corbelled, mossy brows rose slightly, sending a mouse scurrying for another shelter.

The Sumar grimma found you, didn't she, Little thorn. Bone-crusher cocked his head slightly. *I felt her words like thunder falling across the far mountains. I feared that she would take you... or tear your soul from your body up there among the clouds.*

Skellan hunched against Bone-crusher's rocky flesh. He had feared the same, perhaps worse, and he still didn't feel secure. He hadn't eluded her or driven her away. She'd allowed him to fall free from her. Next time she might not. Then what would become of Milmuraille and Radulf County? What would she do to Elezar, Bone-crusher, and Hylanya—or to

Cire, Navet, and Merle? Javier and Kiram might escape back to the Irabiim, but Skellan felt certain that neither Atreau nor the pages who attended him would survive. Very few in the city would.

And it terrified Skellan to think that there was nothing he would be able to do about it. A miserable whimper escaped him and he buried his head in the tangle of ivy and long grass clinging to the crags of Bone-crusher's thigh.

She hurt you, didn't she? Bone-crusher sighed and his breath smelled of clay and the riverbanks. *I'm sorry. Not all mothers can be as kind as mine was. But you're safe here and now.*

Skellan nodded but returned his head to the mass of leaves and grass.

A few moments of quiet passed. Skellan curled his body up in one direction and then another but couldn't seem to find comfort. His nerves still sung with terrible agitation and every screech and scrape of night noise set his heart racing.

Then Bone-crusher reached out and gently cupped his body in his big hands. He leaned forward, lifted Skellan high, and then set him down in the shadow of the garrison well.

I am not the one you need now, Little Thorn. Mine is not the comfort you seek.

Then Bone-crusher straightened and strode from the garrison, leaving Skellan to solace he could find in the dank stones of the old well and the mocking warmth of the dancing summer wind.

CHAPTER
EIGHTEEN

After the crowds, fires, and noise earlier, Elezar found the garrison courtyard relieving in its stillness. As always, the darkness agitated him but not so badly as it might have months before. He knew the garrison and the men well enough to recognize his surroundings from dim forms. Ahead of him, a few torches lit the grounds and the faint melody of a Cadeleonian lute drifted from one of the open windows in the headquarters. Sentries at the doors called to him with welcoming expressions and saluted as Elezar drew near them. Bone-crusher stood over them all as the sentries reported the events of the evening to Elezar. One young Labaran, whose blond beard and stout build betrayed a recent Mirogoth ancestor, looked almost giddy as he described the majesty of their count's witchflame.

"You should have been here, sir! With a flick of his hand our count summoned a Scarlet Wolf vast enough to devour the moon and he put down the entire mob gathered at these gates. They know why he's called Skellan now, don't they, sir?" The young man grinned.

Elezar simply nodded.

"I reckon the count's wolf will put the fear into those grimma too." The second, more fine-boned, sentry beamed at Elezar. "Everyone was in awe of him. I even saw, up on the wall, the duke of Rauma throw his arms around our count and embrace him, he was so thankful for the count's protection."

"Really?" Elezar asked. Both men nodded.

The sentries assured him that they'd witnessed both Lady Hylanya and the duke embracing Count Radulf. After that, their entire party withdrew to the main building to celebrate.

"Though I don't know that the bishop's niece ought to be allowed, if I may say so, sir," the blond sentry added. "Her, or those priests that came with her from her uncle's house."

"That will be for the count to decide," Elezar responded. "But not tonight, I think."

The tone of finality in Elezar's voice conveyed well enough that both sentries saluted him again. Elezar left them and called one of the messengers to him. Cobre snorted in annoyance, having stopped short of the stable, which emanated the scent of both his supper and fellow horses, but Elezar took his time ensuring that the swarthy messenger understood the orders he would carry to Captain Tialdo.

"First thing in the morning he should return to the garrison with the priests and household staff. They are not to be treated as criminals, but they are not to be allowed their freedom until the count has seen them," the messenger repeated.

Elezar sent the messenger on his way.

Then he stabled Cobre and took time to make certain that the stallion had not suffered any burns or injuries when they had charged the burning gates. Thankfully Cobre looked fine. Elezar left him to feed and rest in Doue's care.

When he stepped out from the stables and started for the main building, Bone-crusher knelt down and blocked him. Again, Elezar thought he glimpsed molten gold swirling deep down in the hollows of the troll's eyes as Bone-crushed bowed his face down to Elezar's height.

He needs you, but he'll not be found among the folk feasting and singing in the hall. He waits by the well.

"The well?" The thought worried Elezar. He'd imagined that Skellan had remained inside accepting toasts in his honor and congratulations for his quick action and impressive display of power. Elezar would have liked to offer such a toast himself. Skellan had saved lives this night. Elezar would have liked to put his arms around him and tell him how proud he felt of him, how amazed. "Why is he at the well in the dead of night?"

Bone-crusher sighed and in the dim light Elezar wasn't certain if the troll's craggy expression was one of sorrow or dismay. The troll turned up the mossy palms of his hands and shrugged, sending cloud imps flapping from his shoulders.

He needs you.

That was all Bone-crusher needed to say. Elezar raced through the fluttering torchlit shadows of the courtyard to the cool corner where the well stood. A large, dark animal burst up from the shadows, slamming into Elezar's chest. A long hot tongue lapped his face as the big dog keened and nuzzled at him in a frenzy. Its tail wagged and it bounded around Elezar, rubbing against him and jumping up on him with an excitement bordering upon mania. The whimpers that escaped the dog disturbed Elezar greatly.

He gripped the shaking beast's chest, holding the animal as he stared into its pale green eyes.

"Skellan?"

The dog nuzzled his hand.

"Why in the name of God—" His words were cut off as the hound lapped at his mouth and nose. Elezar turned his head aside. "Why are you a dog again?"

Bone-crusher reached them and carefully lowered himself to the ground in a crouch. Elezar looked to the troll for some explanation but Bone-crusher's attention focused on Skellan.

I've brought him, Little Thorn. Your champion is here to comfort you.

Skellan butted his head into Elezar's hand and reflexively Elezar stroked and patted him. Skellan quieted enough for Elezar to inspect him for injuries as best he could in the poor light. As Elezar ran his hands over the hound's body Skellan seemed to relax more. He leaned into Elezar's touch and his breathing calmed. Skellan appeared in perfect condition—other than being a dog. Though Elezar found that alarming enough.

Particularly when Skellan made another attempt to lap his mouth and Elezar realized that the witch was trying to kiss him. Elezar drew back.

"No, that's as far as that goes while you're…" Elezar gestured at the whole of Skellan's animal form. "While you're like this."

Skellan responded with that sad, begging look that so suited a hound's features. Despite how disconcerted he felt, Elezar laughed. Skellan's brows rose hopefully and Elezar shook his head.

"No. You come out of that dog skin cloak. I'm not going to pretend that you're exactly as I would most want you when you're walking around on all fours."

Skellan hung his head so forlornly that Elezar reached out and stroked his ear before he could stop himself. Skellan sighed as if the weight of the world were upon him.

"What is it?" Elezar asked. "Did the mob frighten you? Bois' accusations?"

Skellan gave a shake of his head.

"What then?" Elezar knelt down and took Skellan's face in his hands so that he could look him in the eyes. "I can't help if I don't know what I'm up against here. Come, Skellan, talk to me as a man."

Skellan went very still. Then Elezar felt a powerful shudder pass through him and the soft fur and thick skin beneath his fingers crumpled. The bright eyes staring out from the hound's skull went black and hollow. The warm, living face that Elezar had gripped in his hands crumpled like cloth as Skellan ducked out from beneath the skin. He leaned forward, pressing up against Elezar's chest and the hound's body fell behind him in a cascade of supple cloak.

Skellan's clothes reeked like a kennel and the costly fabrics looked thin, almost eaten away. Though his rings appeared unchanged by the transformation. Perhaps this was the reason most powerful witches eschewed clothes, adorning themselves instead in furs, costly metal, and strings of jewels.

Skellan bowed his head against Elezar's chest, leaning into him. Elezar embraced him. The heat of his body radiated through Elezar and he felt his heart pounding so strongly that he knew Skellan could feel it as well. For a few minutes they remained close and silent. Then Elezar drew back slightly.

"Where are your guards?" he asked and he could just pick out Skellan's scowl in the gloom.

"I lost them at the privies. I don't imagine that they think I'm still there... Maybe they're looking for me."

Elezar suppressed the urge to lecture Skellan—as he'd done more than once already—on the necessity of protecting a man of his station. That could wait.

"Why did you leave them? Why hide here, as a dog?"

Skellan sniffed and then rubbed his nose. Elezar kept his arms wrapped around him and waited.

"Did you see when I broke the thrall cast over the folk from the Market and Theater Districts?"

"You were magnificent," Elezar told him.

"It wasn't all that difficult to manage." Skellan sounded oddly shy. "But afterward I felt something above me. Something radiant shining beyond the wards I've laid across the city—"

"And you went after it." Elezar shook his head at Skellan's disregard for his own safety. His boldness might well be the undoing of him.

"The Sumar grimma... my mother, she reached out to me..."

Skellan went very still in Elezar's arms. Elezar waited for him to say something more but he only bowed his head back down against Elezar's chest.

She is not a gentle creature. Not accustomed to being refused. Bone-crusher's words drifted over Elezar like the murmur of distant winds.

"What happened?" Elezar asked.

"She demanded Radulf County." Skellan didn't lift his head. "When I refused, she threw me down from the heights."

Elezar didn't know exactly what that meant but he felt certain that it couldn't have been pleasant. "How badly did she hurt you?"

"She hurt me plenty but not deep," Skellan replied. "She could have killed me."

"Killed you?" Waves of dread and then relief washed over Elezar. Skellan could have died and there would have been nothing he could have done. Elezar glared up at the dark vault of the night sky. Not since he was eleven years old had he felt so incapable of laying out an enemy.

"I wasn't disturbed by how much she hurt me exactly..." Skellan trailed off, staring down at the ring shining on his finger. "I imagined—more hoped—that she'd... care."

Elezar had no answer for that. When he'd stood before the Sumar grimma he'd taken her fury as a sign of how deeply she felt the loss of her beloved only child. She'd seemed so intent upon recovering Skellan. How could she then nearly kill him? Elezar couldn't imagine even his own stern mother so completely repudiating one of her own children.

Elezar glowered at the distant northern constellations.

"I don't know how I'm going to..." Skellan's words died to silence and Elezar dropped his gaze back down to look at him.

"What?" Elezar asked.

"I can't make myself greater than she is and she's only one of the four of them. This entire county looks to me to save them all but I don't—I can't..." Skellan clenched his jaw against the rest of his confession. He sounded broken and Elezar didn't know what to do about that.

He stroked Skellan's lean back, feeling the hard angle of his shoulder blades and tracing the line of his spine. Skellan relaxed into his arms. The entire night seemed empty but for the two of them. Then a guard called out the change of the watch, and Elezar noticed the soft coos of the cloud imps clustering around the crown of Bone-crusher's ragged skull.

In the calm darkness, Elezar contemplated the nearly unbearable thought of defeat—the loss of the city, the fall of the county, the deaths of all the people surrounding him, and above all else, the sickening possibility of Skellan's death—and knew that he could face anything other than that.

Even cowardice.

"We could leave. Fall back to the south," Elezar said.

Skellan lifted his face, looking desolate.

"Milmuraille is mine to protect. I won't abandon it." He ran his long hands over his face. "But you don't need to stay, none of you…"

"Don't be an idiot," Elezar replied. "I've only just found you. I'm not about to leave you."

Nor will any of us old ones, Little Thorn. Bone-crusher lifted his huge hand as if to touch Skellan's cheek and the perfume of wild flowers swirled in the wake of his motion. Two ghostly white cloud imps drifted down, their tentacles twining and twisting like sea-tossed ropes. One dropped a dead mouse at Skellan's side. The other laid a shining heap of crushed beetle casings at his feet.

"Thank you." Skellan smiled and took both the rodent carcass and the glossy insect remains, secreting them away into the threadbare pockets of his once resplendent brocade coat. No doubt Skellan's two fastidious dressers would be delighted at finding those, Elezar thought for a briefly amused moment.

"I don't want anyone to die for my sake." Skellan hung his head.

"I know you don't." Elezar stroked his cheek, coaxing Skellan to look up at him. "But that isn't your choice. We each of us choose for ourselves what it is that we'll fight for—die for, if it comes to it."

Skellan shook his head. His long red hair fell across his face.

"No one wants to die for me. No one wants to die at all. They want to win," Skellan replied. "They think I can win for them but I don't know that I can and I—"

Elezar caught his chin and lifted Skellan's angular face.

"You can't take responsibility for all of the people who might be killed. No one in this city is in your thrall. You aren't forcing them to stay and fight." Elezar held Skellan's gaze, willing him to accept the certainty of his words, because this was one thing Elezar understood intimately. "The decision to stand and fight is one each of us has made of our own free will, because there are things here that each of us feels are worth fighting for—even worthy of dying for. But that choice belongs to every individual and it's part of what makes us each who we are—something that gives us pride and stands at the very heart of who we choose to be."

Skellan's wide, mischievous mouth flattened and Elezar recognized the expression as a guarded uncertainty. He wanted to believe Elezar but hesitated.

Elezar kissed him once lightly, tasting the salt of sweat. Skellan's hands dug into the folds of Elezar's clothes.

"Have you ever heard about the Siege of Anacleto?" Elezar asked him.

Skellan shook his head.

"It took place long ago, even before the Mirogoth invasion and the Battle for Milmuraille. The king of Cadeleon decided to purge the Haldiim peoples from his lands and ordered them executed. The earl of Anacleto—"

"A relation of yours?"

"Far back, yes," Elezar acknowledged but then he returned to his story. "The earl refused to turn over the Haldiim population in his lands and so the king sent an army to seize the city and destroy the Haldiim sheltering there. But when the king's army arrived they found merchants, sailors, farmers, and even barmaids and beggars armed and standing against them, as well as the earl. That motley militia fought the king's army for every foot of their city and finally at the walls of the Haldiim district, they and the Haldiim archers broke the king's men. Nearly half the city's defenders died, including the earl."

Elezar paused a moment as he always did when he thought of his ancient, headstrong ancestor: an infamous ruffian and brute but somehow one of the only noblemen willing to stand against the king's cruelty. Who could say what capacities dwelt within other people?

Elezar went on. "The reason I'm telling you this isn't only because they won the city, but because the motivations of so many of the defenders are mysteries to this very day. Only a minority of the populace were Haldiim and, considering the times, most of the Cadeleonians probably didn't think any better of them than did their king. Yet bigots, body slavers, and even priests fought alongside the Haldiim to protect Anacleto. Who can say what roused so many of them to give their lives? I used to wonder how they all held together without a single unifying cause. But now I think that their individual motivations must have been part of what made each of them fight so hard and so valiantly. No one fell back. No one deserted the fight. Every one of them must have had a personal reason—something, maybe someone—they cared for and wanted to protect even at the cost of their own lives. They fought as an army but really each of them must have found their own path to courage."

Skellan looked thoughtful then nodded.

"Each followed their own vei," he said. "Like you and I do now."

"Yes. I suppose that's exactly it," Elezar agreed a little ruefully. "I guess I'm telling you something you already know then."

"I hadn't thought of it in that way, though." Skellan stared out into the darkness of the courtyard and then turned back to Elezar. "They truly fought against their own king's army?"

"Against church and crown." Elezar nodded.

"And they won?"

"They did." Elezar felt a rush of pride and a twinge of homesickness as he answered. "The Haldiim district still flourishes. Our master mechanist, Kiram Kir-Zaki, grew up there."

"It always sounds so easy in stories of times past." Skellan dropped his hands into his pockets. Then, frowning, he pulled out one of the beetle shells. Elezar smiled at the thing but Skellan contemplated it with a rather serious expression.

"At least we know that this city and others have held against superior forces," Elezar said. "We just need to find a way to do it again."

"I suppose you're right." Skellan turned the glossy shell over in his hand. "And we all take strength from different sources and in different forms. I can't draw power from those I've imprisoned in a sanctum, as Lundag did, nor can I call on centuries of wards spread across entire forests like the grimma will do when they come. I have to find a different way to be stronger than they are."

"You did just kill a demon lord," Elezar reminded him.

"Yes, I called the nothingness of the Black Fire."

"Can you try the same thing on the grimma?"

Skellan nodded slowly, hesitantly, and Elezar remembered how he'd found Skellan laid out like a corpse up on that pinnacle at the end of the battle. Oesir had sacrificed his life so that Skellan would survive.

"It will kill you to do it again, won't it?" Elezar realized.

"Likely it would," Skellan said. "And if it didn't your Javier would slay me."

"What?" Elezar scowled at the suggestion and a low growl rumbled up from Bone-crusher's massive chest.

"I swore to him that I wouldn't call the Black Fire again," Skellan replied with surprising equanimity. "He has to live by his oaths and I must live by mine."

"He wouldn't—" Elezar began but then cut himself off. Javier took his vows as a Bahiim seriously, he knew that. "I wouldn't allow him to harm you."

Skellan smiled indulgently at Elezar.

"I won't pit you against your dear friend, Elezar. I promise." Skellan returned to his contemplation of the beetle shell again. "Master Bone-crusher? Do you remember the story you told me of Skellan the Scarlet Wolf and the great gold wyrm?"

Aye, Little Thorn. I remember it.

"The gold wyrm was a hundred times stronger than Skellan…"

Yes, yes, a good tale, that one. The great golden wyrm crushed a dozen little kingdoms in its desire to rule all the northlands.

Neither mordwolves or great bears could fight it. And soon it neared the home of the Scarlet Wolf—Skellan, your namesake, Little Thorn. Bone-crusher smiled craggy boulders at Skellan. *After much thought, Skellan asked his witch to turn him into a swarm of fleas and throw him upon the wind to fall across the wyrm's hide.*

There he bit and bled the beast both day and night, growing stronger from feeding upon it as he kept the wyrm from even a wink of sleep. At last, at the very gates of Skellan's home, the wyrm begged the fleas for peace. Skellan gleefully extracted a pact from the great wyrm demanding everlasting peace between them. But then he became a man again and held the wyrm to its promise for all his witch's lands. What a rage the wyrm felt! It roared and gnashed its teeth but was bound by its word. In the end all it could do was slink away after blessing all of Skellan's descendants to always carry his greatest weapon.

And that, Little Thorn, is why all dogs have fleas.

Skellan scratched his shoulder and then laughed. He offered Elezar a shy smile. "I always loved that story."

Elezar smiled back, happy to see Skellan's mood lighten.

He'd encountered a number of adventures attributed to the mythic warlord, Skellan the Scarlet Wolf. Most were bloody, brutal tales of conquest and murder but scattered among those there were always odd, funny stories like this one. Elezar wondered which, if any, captured the true character of the warlord.

"I can't become a great wyrm but fleas aren't beyond me." Skellan lifted the beetle shell up as if to block out the moon with it. "I've called down the vast emptiness that devoured the demon lord but until just now I hadn't noticed all the tiny emptinesses... voracious as fleas. If I found a way to set them loose..."

Bone-crusher looked as puzzled by Skellan's pondering as Elezar felt. Though having asked Skellan for explanations in the past he knew that he wasn't likely to actually grasp much of the magical realm that Skellan seemed to so seamlessly navigate.

What are these emptinesses, Little Thorn? Bone-crusher asked.

"All around us..." Skellan waved his hand but then frowned as if he'd been asked to define something utterly intuitive, like water. "We and everything all around us are made up of countless grains of creation—tiny pieces that once fell from the stars. They're like the sand that forms a riverbank. It looks whole, feels whole, but each grain is actually separate and between every one of them lurks a hollow." Skellan shivered. "A hungry nothingness, like that of the Black Fire but not vast as the night sky. These are smaller than an eye can pick out and locked up between all the grains that make up us and the whole world around us."

Elezar studied his own hand and tried to imagine how it could be made of only tiny grains and the spaces between them. He couldn't see it, quite literally, but looking to Skellan he thought that maybe his witch could. Only a foot away Bone-crusher too appeared to study the stony mass of his folded thighs. The troll rocked his big head from side to side as if hoping to catch a glimpse from a different angle.

"So, how do we use these tiny emptinesses, then?" Elezar asked.

"I'm not certain that they can be used. I need to take a little time to think upon very, very small spells. Maybe brew a potion of cricket breath and flea farts." Skellan laughed and then returned the beetle casing to his pocket. "But not tonight. Tonight has been too long already."

Skellan drew in a deep breath and then leaned forward and snuffled Elezar's neck. There was a certain pleasure to the sensation of Skellan's warm breath on his skin. He wrapped an arm around Skellan's shoulders.

"I didn't realize it before, but you smell like you rode here straight out of a smokehouse."

"Something like that," Elezar replied. "We set a fire to distract the mob at the bishop's townhouse, but it didn't go exactly as planned…" Elezar quickly related the events of his evening. When he came to the bishop's niece he paused, torn between reluctance to condemn the girl and his desire to speak honestly with Skellan. At last he simply told Skellan everything.

"Well, that's awkward," Skellan commented after Elezar described the message he and Captain Tialdo had deciphered. "I can't endorse her plotting against the duke of Rauma but at the same time I've got enough trouble already. The last thing I want is to stumble into the midst of a fight between a Cadeleonian duke and his royal bishop."

"You would be wisest to pretend that you knew nothing of it. Leave the bishop's niece to Atreau and me."

Skellan considered the offer then shook his head. "I'm loathe to look aside while the girl is throttled in some back garden."

"I'm not going to kill her," Elezar reassured him. He wouldn't speak for how Fedeles might choose to punish the girl once she returned to Cadeleonian soil. That would be months from now and well out of his hands. "I simply mean to warn Atreau and have him keep her out of trouble."

"Very well," Skellan agreed. Then he cocked his head. "But you found nothing to support Bois' accusations against her or Bishop Palo?"

"Nothing," Elezar admitted. "However, considering how much the priests burned, I can't say that there wasn't anything to begin with. I did find the niche behind the portrait of the previous count. Letters had been hidden there. I found shreds of them, but how incriminating they actually were and of whom…" Elezar trailed off with a hopeless shrug.

Skellan scowled but Elezar couldn't produce evidence— one way or the other—where none existed.

"I can't just release Bois," Skellan muttered. "He murdered a man in cold blood."

"True enough," Elezar agreed.

"If he was in possession of all this proof, then why not bring it to me? Why lash out so suddenly?"

Elezar couldn't speak for Bois but the man hadn't ever struck him as the sort to simply lose his wits and cut a man's throat for no reason at all. After all, Bois had infiltrated the bishop's home years ago and doubtless he could have contrived a better opportunity for both an assassination and his own escape.

Hadn't Sheriff Hirbe commented along the same lines, earlier this evening?

"Could he have been under a thrall?" Elezar asked.

"Maybe," Skellan replied. "He did seem somewhat shocked by his own actions at first but then if anything he seemed to think he'd acted rightly, as if he were a hero."

"He's not the only one with that opinion it would seem," Elezar conceded. "After all, he was acting out of loyalty to you—"

"Yes, both he and Rafale seem to think that so long as they're plotting murder and slitting throats on my behalf then they ought to be elevated above all law." A disgusted grumble rose from Skellan's throat, sounding suspiciously like a growl. "It makes me all the more angry knowing that the bishop was killed in my name as if I haven't the wits or honor to protect myself in any manner other than resorting to assassination."

Elezar studied Skellan through the gloom. Cadeleonian princes and lords employed assassins against their enemies as a matter of course, almost as a right of their noble births. Had he possessed a different temperament—less need to take his vengeance with his own hands—Elezar might have dispatched his own assassins to do away with his brother's murderers. Doubtless he would have seemed more of a cultured gentleman to his fellow Cadeleonians if he had.

Up until now Elezar would have probably thought them right. But, with the memory of Bishop Palo's dead body in the back of his head and the smoke of too many fires saturating his cloths, Elezar could see Skellan's point. What good had Bishop Palo's murder accomplished that couldn't have been achieved in a court of law?

"I can't simply let him go," Skellan said. "He must answer for his crime."

"He should, but this is a case where you must tread carefully. Many Labarans feel that Bois was justified and acted out of loyalty to you and the county. I don't like it, nor will most Cadeleonians, but perhaps extending him some form of mercy—"

"If I'm seen taking Bois' hand and giving him amnesty what will folk make of it but that I'm condoning the murder of the Cadeleonians under my own protection?" Skellan glowered at Elezar but at the same time gripped his hand as if he feared to let him go.

"I don't know that there is a right way out of this mess with Bois, but something must be done and quickly or the matter will undermine all the work we've done to create a unified force to defend this city." Elezar couldn't help but think that Sheriff Hirbe had been quite right in cursing Bois for not at least having the sense to flee. If they could have been rid of him, without Skellan having to publicly take sides... But no, they were burdened with Bois when they least needed him.

Something had to be done and Skellan couldn't be involved, Elezar realized.

"We're not likely to find an answer tonight." Elezar returned Skellan's grip and rose to his feet, drawing Skellan up with him. "But you should be seen with your guests, so that they can toast you and take confidence from your power."

"But I'm not—"

"I know you took a hard blow today, but morale matters and right now people need to believe that you are powerful." Elezar felt a warm flush rising across his cheeks. "And honestly, Skellan, you are powerful. I can't tell you how wondrous it was to see that wolf of yours. You're amazing."

Elezar knew from Skellan's embarrassed expression that he sounded like a gushing idiot, but the fact was that he'd been astounded by Skellan. For all his fear and uncertainty, a faith had grown up in him. Not the oppressive faith in an all-knowing and condemning Cadeleonian God, but a fledgling belief that together he and Skellan could save this city.

Skellan frowned down at his own feet then lifted his face to regard Elezar.

"You really believe that?" he asked.

"I do."

Skellan's gaze remained on him for a few moments as a lilting melody drifted through the night air and a guard called the changing of the watch. Elezar didn't know what Skellan saw through the gloom but at last a smile lit his face and that truly smug, mischievous glint seemed to light his pale eyes. He straightened.

"For you, my man, I shall be wondrous and astounding."

CHAPTER NINETEEN

Elezar knew that he would have to take action, even if it meant betraying Skellan. He suspected that the knowledge had lurked in the back of his mind from the first moment that he'd seen Atreau dragging Bois into the mess hall. But he'd avoided acknowledging the decision all through the evening. He'd wanted some other option.

But as he watched Skellan carefully lay his collection of beetle casings on his windowsill while his two dressers looked on in utter dismay, he realized that Skellan was too true to himself, too committed to his own values, to be swayed by anyone else's opinion. That trait made him honest and refreshing, but it also rendered him nearly incapable of negotiating the ugly and underhanded dealings of politics.

The younger of the two dressers picked up Skellan's tattered coat then gave a gasp when he discovered the dead mouse in the pocket.

Skellan glanced to the man and shrugged.

"Cloud imps," Skellan said as if that explained everything. Then he returned to his study of the night sky outside his window.

The attendant grimaced at the tiny, stiff body in his hand and then sidled to the fireplace and hurled the mouse into the flames. The second dresser approached Skellan.

"Would you rather wear emerald or scarlet for this evening's gathering, Count Radulf?"

"I put my full faith in you, Pilife, to make me seem a sophisticated fellow." Skellan favored the man with a smile.

"Yes, sir." The dresser straightened slightly and Elezar understood his pride. It felt touching and breathtaking to have Skellan's complete trust. "The scarlet then, sir. You will look majestic."

Skellan broke into a wide grin then looked to Elezar. "I'm going to look majestic, my man! You'd best prepare your mind for my most amazing transformation yet!"

That won a laugh from both dressers and they set to work at once while Elezar looked on. He'd grown so comfortable and so fond of the sight of Skellan—so attached to touching him and taking both pleasure and comfort in holding him in his arms every night—he didn't want to think that he could sacrifice all of that. Yet something had to be done with Bois and it had to be done fast before he lost his nerve.

Elezar didn't linger overly long amidst the dancing and chatter of the garrison's impromptu guests. Once he'd escorted Skellan—dressed afresh in scarlet and gold—to be welcomed, toasted, and share jests with Cire and Lady Hylanya, he excused himself. He cast a stern glance to Skellan's personal guards. They saluted but then returned to tracking Skellan's quick motions. Both men now eyed Skellan like a pair of young gamblers who'd just realized they'd taken on a cardsharp.

Elezar had been tempted to commiserate with the two of them—knowing that Skellan wasn't the sort to make their positions easy—but he couldn't set a precedent for overlooking failure. They'd each lost a day's pay and taken a knock to the back of their fool skulls. Elezar had no doubt that his own mother would have punished them much more harshly, but the men were Labaran and already angry enough with themselves for failing.

Across the room the three handsome swordsmen who'd become attached to Lady Hylanya's immense retinue drew close to Skellan as Elezar fell back. They laughed at some comment Skellan offered and Elezar fought the urge to glare at them from across the room. Cire claimed Rafale's hand for a dance and several other courtiers and ladies-in-waiting joined them.

At the edge of the group the bishop's niece plucked bright melodies from a lute but only managed a few wan smiles as

Atreau's pages and several of Hylanya's musicians paid her compliments. Her maids attended her like watchdogs, glowering with particular fury when a neatly coifed and ornately mustachioed Labaran gentleman sidled up beside her to sing.

If he hadn't known better, Elezar would never have guessed at the alliances and animosities within the gathering. Such, he supposed, was the illusory world of etiquette and courtly accomplishment.

Atreau drifted through the room, charming men and women and winning far more than his share of wine from a besotted-looking serving girl. Elezar caught his attention with a Hellion's hand sign and Atreau casually crossed the room to where Elezar stood in the shadows of the doors. Along the way Atreau claimed a second glass of pale gold wine, which he presented to Elezar.

"Is that soot you're wearing in your hair, Lord Grunito?" Atreau inquired.

"Indeed. I've decided to sport a slightly charred style so as to stand out from all the well-dressed gentlemen vying for the count's favor."

Atreau smiled but a hardness edged his expression. As he took in the red, scorched streaks marking the back of Elezar's hand even his firm smile faltered briefly. Then he raised his glass and his voice. "We must toast to Count Radulf's steadfast integrity then."

Several Labarans near them hurried to raise their drinks as well. Elezar nodded and drank along with them. Sweetness suffused the wine, almost hiding its alcoholic bite.

"Looks like you do have some competition for his attentions." Atreau nodded meaningfully to where Skellan stood, surrounded by handsome courtiers and the three brawny swordsmen.

Elezar couldn't help the stab of jealousy he felt, but he fought against giving it reign over him. He was the one Skellan trusted, the one Skellan confided in, and beyond that neither of them had promised each other anything. Elezar had no right or reason to glower at those swordsmen or the charming courtiers surrounding Skellan. Still, he found it easier to look away than to attempt to twist his expression into some benign smile as one of the swordsmen took Skellan's hand and bowed to kiss his fingers.

Elezar frowned at the delicate wineglass in his hand. Next to him Atreau shook his head.

"Aren't you going to run the interloping whelp off?" Atreau asked.

Five years ago Elezar might have run the man through, but now he shook his head.

"Skellan can rebuff him if and when he wants. And if he doesn't..." Elezar paused as Skellan's laughter filled the room. Both Elezar and Atreau looked to see Skellan grin and playfully cuff the swordsman away from his hand.

"Any more of that and I'll think you're trying to tongue the ring off my finger!" Skellan wiped his hand across the leg of his silk breeches. "And really, you have no idea the places this hand of mine has been. I'm not famously keen on washing, you know."

Elezar laughed despite himself and he wasn't the only one. The swordsman managed a stiff smile in response and stepped back, allowing Skellan to continue his conversation with his sister. When Skellan did briefly look his way, Elezar raised his glass to him but remained where he was. Skellan turned back to his sister and her entourage.

"You see, he's not a faint-hearted maiden who needs keeping up in a tower. And I'm not the one who ought to be worrying now in any case." Elezar lowered his voice as he went on, "When I searched the bishop's townhouse I found something in his niece's room—"

"The letter from the royal bishop?" Atreau asked. For a moment Elezar simply stared at him.

"You already knew of this?"

Atreau nodded, shot a smile to one of Lady Hylanya's ladies-in-waiting, and then returned his attention to Elezar.

"She showed it to me two days after we met," Atreau responded as if nothing could be more obvious. "I told her to keep hold of it so we might deliver it to Fedeles—"

"Fedeles?" Elezar barely managed to keep his voice lowered. He took another quick sip of his wine. "So she knows that you're not…"

"She's not an idiot," Atreau said. "The man who wrote to her was obviously a very different fellow, if you understand me."

Having read Fedeles' letter to the young woman, Elezar did understand.

"So I took a chance and confided in her and in return she confided in me." Atreau finished his wine and turned the empty glass in his agile hand.

"You didn't think to tell me any of this?" Elezar asked.

"You weren't here to tell. You were off in the Mirogoth forests," Atreau replied. "And when you did at last come back the whole city seemed to be on the verge of being destroyed, so I was a bit distracted."

"Yes, but Fedeles may still be in danger from the royal bishop. I doubt that Bishop Palo's niece is his only agent. He needs to be warned—"

"He was. I sent word to him at once." Atreau gave Elezar a level gaze. "I've written to him since and told him everything else as well, you should know."

Elezar took a moment to consider that. He couldn't know what Fedeles would make of the news that he'd become Skellan's champion—or even if Atreau would have worded the information so euphemistically.

"What will Count Radulf do to Abea—the bishop's niece?" Atreau inquired in a whisper.

"Nothing," Elezar replied. "He's agreed to leave her fate to Fedeles' discretion. As far as he's concerned she's done nothing to him."

Atreau frowned as if he'd prepared himself for any response but this one. Elezar drew the letter from his coat and slipped it into Atreau's empty hand.

"You make certain this gets to Fedeles," Elezar said.

As Atreau secreted the letter in his own coat, his expression remained uncertain. He studied Skellan from the corner of his eyes.

"He will acquit Bois then?" Atreau asked.

"He doesn't want to," Elezar replied and again Atreau appeared flummoxed.

"But his Labaran supporters…"

"Skellan doesn't view it as Labarans against Cadeleonians." Elezar couldn't quite hide the frustration in his voice. "He just sees this as the murder of an elderly man. Bois is likely to hang."

Earlier Atreau had called for that exact punishment for Bois, so Elezar didn't expect him to look so troubled by the pronouncement now. But his handsome brow creased.

"It was murder. A brutal murder," Atreau asserted. "But Skellan must not execute Bois. Too many of the Labarans believe he was justified and that the bishop planned to have Skellan killed. Likely they were right."

"There's a quick change of tune for you," Elezar remarked.

Atreau shrugged. "I was protecting Abea and myself earlier. I didn't want her or me dragged into accusations against her uncle. Since she and I are safe I see no reason to hang Bois. It would only splinter the factions of the city further. I did see the mob outside the garrison, you know. That's the last thing we need now."

"I know," Elezar said.

"Can't you make him understand the situation?"

"He understands it. He simply doesn't value political alliances over justice." Elezar frowned at his wineglass. It struck him as too delicate for his hand.

"But if Skellan hangs Bois—"

"He can't hang a man who isn't here." Elezar hardly voiced the words—not wanting to admit to the intentions behind them, not even to Atreau.

"What are you going—no, never mind." Atreau sighed. "Just tell me if there's some way I can help."

"Keep Skellan and his guests entertained. I'd rather they didn't notice how long I'll be gone."

Atreau nodded and turned back to the crowd. Elezar left his empty glass on a small sideboard table and then slipped away.

He climbed the steps to the garrison's sumptuous west tower rooms, hoping to find Javier there. Instead Kiram sleepily advised him to check the kitchen.

"He's never been able to resist the temptation to filch a pie." Kiram yawned and made an effort to open his eyes all the way. "Is something wrong?"

Elezar considered telling him about the assassination and the mobs, but if Kiram had managed to sleep through all of that he was likely bone tired. Better to let him sleep.

"No, I only wanted to ask him a question."

"The kitchen," Kiram repeated. "He's had his eyes on the pies. They've been baking all day."

After that Elezar wished Kiram a good sleep and took himself off to the steamy, hot confines of the kitchen. He discovered Javier playing with the fat mastiff pups still sheltering near the ovens. Javier's gaze shifted from the pups to the large rack where dozens of pork pies sat cooling. Javier took a casual step nearer the rack only to have a young Labaran woman, with her hair in looping braids, turn and flash her cleaver at him. Elezar recognized the girl as Doue's sister, Fleur, and was glad to see that she appeared well.

"Now how can such a lovely girl be so very heartless," Javier asked. "Who's going to miss one little pie among such a bounty?"

"Our blessed count!" Fleur replied. "We'll not have the lurking likes of you snatching meals from his table. And don't you try looking big eyes and hungry at me. I know well enough you've already connived two pastries off of the spit boy with your good looks, you bottomless pit."

Javier's attempt to appear wounded was badly undercut by his guilty grin in response to Fleur's last accusation.

"Well called, Fleur," Elezar said.

Fleur spun round and flushed as she recognized him.

"Master Elezar." Fleur gave him a rough curtsey. "This lout is after the count's supper."

"I'll see him out of the kitchen, shall I?" Elezar offered. Fleur brightened while Javier planted his hands on hips and offered Elezar a challenging grin. For old time's sake Elezar simply caught Javier at the waist and hefted him over his shoulder. He wasn't certain if he'd grown stronger or if the last five years had stripped Javier down, but he felt lighter. Or maybe Elezar had just grown used to the feel of Skellan's big-boned frame.

Javier laughed but didn't put up a fight as Elezar carried him out to the stone steps outside the kitchen and then deposited him on the ground. Light from the distant torches up on the garrison walls cast long shadows but Elezar didn't miss the gleam of Javier's white teeth as he grinned.

"I still say you missed your calling as a cart ox, Elezar," Javier told him.

"You missed yours as a magpie," Elezar replied. He glanced behind them and then across the grounds to make certain that they weren't being watched. "I need your help."

Javier's playful expression sobered.

"Is it the Sumar grimma?" Javier asked. "I felt her at a distance but then she withdrew."

"Not yet." Elezar explained all that had happened with Bois, Bishop Palo, and his niece.

"I heard a version of all this from the kitchen gossips. All of them seemed to think that Bois ought to walk free," Javier confirmed. "But I'll warrant that few, if any, of the Cadeleonians in the city would agree with that."

"Few indeed," Elezar replied. "Sheriff Hirbe got it right. If Bois had truly wished to serve Skellan he should have had the sense to make an escape, rather than force Skellan to make a ruling over him."

"Pity it's too late for that," Javier commented.

Elezar said nothing but continued to stare at Javier and almost instantly Javier's expression lit with understanding.

"You're serious?" Javier asked.

Elezar nodded and Javier stood still and silent for a few moments. Then he lifted his gaze to Elezar. "If he were to somehow escape, where would he need to go?"

For a good part of the evening Elezar had pondered the same question.

"The Theater District. The Mockingbird Playhouse," Elezar said. "Rafale, the owner, is a compatriot of Bois' and possesses the resources to disguise him, get him out of the city, and spread word to the right folk that Bois is alive and well."

"But will he?"

Elezar couldn't say for certain.

"I think he will, for Skellan's sake. Or at least to impress Lady Hylanya." Elezar broke off as two of the men on the night watch paced past them. They would check in on Bois in the stockade next and then make the full circle of the garrison grounds again before the next hour ended. Elezar listened as the sound of their footsteps faded.

"If you don't want to do this," Elezar said, "I can find another way."

"I most assuredly want to do this," Javier replied. "I owe you that much at the least for Isandro's sake. I made you a promise and never kept it."

"There's no need to repay me for that. We were children. I had no right to ask so much of you." Oaths were so easily offered and extracted by twelve year old boys. What had either of them known of their futures then? "It was right that I did it on my own," Elezar said and he meant it.

Javier drew in a thoughtful breath then said, "Well, this you don't have to do on your own. I can open a way through the Old Road, but you'll need to keep Bois from falling into the grip of the creatures there."

All too well Elezar remembered the monstrosities lurking in the endless darkness of the Old Road—devils of the Sorrowlands. He shuddered, recollecting the vision of his mutilated brother calling to him, begging him for his help. He still suffered nightmares at the thought of the Old Road, but there was no other way to travel into the garrison stockade and across the city without being seen by a single soul.

"You open the way and I'll see to it that Bois gets through," Elezar assured him.

They walked in silence to the squat stone building that served as the garrison's stockade. Four Labarans stood guard and greeted Elezar as he passed.

Just beyond the building, sheltered from torchlight by the shadows of the stockade itself, they drew to a halt and Javier turned in a slow circle. Tiny, white lights rose from his pale hands like mist drifting from the surface of a lake. Streamers of light traced the motions of his hands as he reached forward and gripped the empty air as if he were catching a velvet black curtain.

The air around them crackled. Javier spread his arms the way he might have thrown curtains wide. A seam of flat blackness split open like a wound in the night air. A sickly, stale breeze seeped from the opening and brushed over Elezar with a caress of cobwebs. Revulsion rippled up from Elezar's memory and his heart began to kick hard in his chest. The same moldering odor had pervaded that ancient barrow. Elezar's throat tightened against the breath he drew into his lungs.

He'd sworn he would never walk the Old Road again— promised himself that he would never endure this place again.

Javier stepped forward. The seam swallowed him utterly.

Elezar gripped his sword hilt—though he knew it would

not serve him here—and forced himself to follow into the grasping dark. Ahead he could see only the light rising from Javier—a white halo outlining his form—but not even the blaze of the white hell that Javier called up seemed capable of illuminating more than a few feet of featureless ground. A short ribbon of dull gray surface stretched between Javier and Elezar. Elezar's footsteps made no sound against the surface and a strangely hollow sensation met each of his steps, as if he were walking across a shell of ice.

At first the dark enclosed them utterly, but then Elezar noticed a faint blue light flickering at the edge of his sight. He didn't look at it, but kept his attention focused on Javier's straight back and long, black braids. Another faint blue form glimmered to life ahead of them.

Isandro hunched, blood pouring from the chasm torn from his gut to groin. He clutched at his belly, as if trying to hold in his intestines then lifted his pale face to stare desperately at Elezar.

"Help me," Isandro gasped. "Don't leave me like this."

It wasn't Isandro, Elezar told himself. The devils of the Sorrowlands lured wandering souls from their paths with visions and lies. It wasn't Isandro.

Still the sight tore at Elezar's heart and filled him with a terrible self-loathing for so callously walking past. Isandro's mutilated form faded as Javier and he walk on, but then came glimmering up from the dark ahead of them again. This time much closer.

"Elezar." Isandro's voice trembled with desperation. "Help me. For the love of God, help me."

Swathed in white light Javier seemed to take no note, but Elezar could barely drag his gaze from his brother's face. He'd died younger than Elezar was now. Died needlessly and horribly. The urge to reach out and offer even the smallest comfort to his brother felt overwhelming.

Elezar's fingers slid from his sword hilt. He lifted his hand out into the inky dark.

Then a hot red spark flashed up across his chest and flew from his hand into the blackness to burst like a cannon shot. Javier spun back as red light bloomed through the dark.

For only an instant Elezar glimpsed weird, floral forms rising up over them from deep roots in the dark. Massive blossoms of jaws bowed from spindly stems, while a twisted blue vapor drifted out from between foot-long teeth.

Then the dark snapped back over them and slowly the flickering blue image of Isandro rose again. Though now Elezar could see that the face wasn't quite solid and that the faint, flickering quality of the form hid far more than it revealed.

"What did you just do?" Javier demanded.

"Nothing. A spark just leap up—"

"Skellan, then. Protecting you, even here." Javier scowled and the blaze of white light surrounding him seemed to crackle and spit.

"What are these things in the dark all around us?" Elezar asked.

"Seedlings from the demon realms, according to the Bahiim. Devils planted by God to test the souls of the dead according to the Cadeleonian church. I don't think anyone really knows," Javier replied. "But they can't bear light, so keep close."

Javier turned and again led the way through the dark, though now Elezar knew that despite the featureless quality of the Old Road, they walked barely beyond the grasp of countless hungry, strange creatures. He didn't look at any of the blue forms as they wavered up at the edge of his vision. Even knowing them for illusions, he still didn't want to revisit the tortured end of his brother's life.

After only moments Javier again split open the dark and the warm glow of a distant lamp streamed in over them. The odor of sweat and piss that saturated the stockade cells seemed almost refreshing after the rank decay of the Old Road. Elezar stepped out into the small cell where Bois lay curled on a narrow cot. Shafts of light from the lamps out in the hall fell across his calm, weathered face. Dark spatters of Bishop Palo's blood colored the front of his cassock but he seemed to have washed his tanned hands and face clean. He folded his hands over his chest and gazed up at the ceiling of his cell with a cool, resigned expression that Elezar knew well. He could almost feel it upon his own face.

As Javier followed him, Bois looked up. His eyes darted from Javier to Elezar and his face paled but his expression remained calm—resigned. He sat up and squared his shoulders.

"I suppose there's no point in calling for help," Bois commented. "All these guards are in your service."

He thought they'd come to kill him in his cell, Elezar realized, and he had to grudgingly admire the calm with which Bois faced such a death.

"If I wanted to kill you I'd have called you out into a dueling circle and made a proper end to you," Elezar said. "We've come to get you out."

Bois brows rose. "Why would you want to do that for me?"

"Because right now morale is more important than justice," Elezar replied. "I'm not going to allow your execution to shatter the unity of our troops."

"The count wouldn't have me executed—"

"He would and he will," Elezar told him flatly. "The priests at the bishop's townhouse burned whatever evidence there might have been for your defense."

Bois looked like he might argue but Elezar cut him off.

"How could you have been so sloppy? Not only killing the bishop in broad daylight but to do it before securing any evidence? What were you thinking?"

At this Bois scowled as if the question troubled him more than it did Elezar. "I heard the guards talking about the mobs. Was anyone harmed?"

"Of course people were harmed," Elezar snapped.

"We need to go," Javier whispered.

Elezar read the distrust in Bois' expression still rose and strode without hesitation into the deathly black of the Old Road.

Though once engulfed in the darkness, Bois went still and stiff. Shock showed on his face as he stared at a distant form. Elezar took in his own dying brother as he followed Bois' gaze but knew that Bois perceived something quite different.

Elezar caught hold of the stocky man's shoulders.

"Stay in the light. No matter what you see, you must stay in the light."

"This is the Sorrowlands," Bois whispered.

"The Bahiim call it the Old Road," Elezar told him. "Someday this place may lead you to the three hells, but today it's the path to your freedom. So walk!"

Bois moved after Javier, but didn't seem able to keep himself from staring out at the flickering blue phantoms that rose out of the darkness.

"Hallen!" Bois shouted at one point and Elezar barely caught him before he bounded out of the circle of Javier's shining white light.

"It's not him!" Elezar wrenched Bois back and held him so tight that he could feel the other man's heart pounding frantically in his chest. The pungent odor of dried blood wafted up to him from Bois' clothes. "The count isn't here. These are only illusions."

Boise clenched his eyes shut and to Elezar's shock the man shuddered in his grip as if he were fighting to hold in a sob.

"Pull yourself together," Elezar snapped. He didn't want to feel any sympathy for Bois and he certainly didn't want to have to attempt to comfort the man.

"We must not linger here." Javier glanced back over his shoulder. His face appeared radiant and hollow. His eyes were black as pits.

Bois drew in a deep breath and nodded curtly. Elezar released him and they continued walking single file through the featureless expanse of darkness. It felt like hours had passed while they merely walked in place.

Twice more as they walked Bois flinched back from whatever visions his own guilt and sorrow conjured.

"I had orders," Bois murmured. "Exact orders."

Elezar frowned at the back of the other man's head.

"Orders from whom?"

"Hy—" Bois began but then said, "I received the orders through Peome's familiar—"

"Her familiar?" Elezar asked. Bois didn't answer. Silence stretched between them. Elezar fought down a surge of frustration. "Orders or not, you had to know that killing the bishop would leave Skellan in a terrible position. You had to know it could split the population precisely when we most need to be united."

"I knew. But I had no choice," Bois said. "You are a bound man as well, you must understand."

A bound man.

"You mean a witch holds thrall over you?" Elezar asked.

Bois nodded and again silence stretched between them. Distantly, Elezar heard an apparition moan and whimper in his brother's voice.

"She keeps a gold finches and a squirrel," Bois said. "She might have other familiars but those are the ones she used to contact me."

"Peome?" Elezar asked.

Bois nodded but stiffly. Elezar scowled at the other man's straight back.

Peome had struck Elezar as dangerous and manipulative but not as the kind of woman to take action without regard for repercussions. No, a woman as mature and clever as Peome would have well understood the kind of damage the bishop's murder might do to all of Milmuraille.

But a teenage girl—a girl mourning the death of her father,

and aware of the part the bishop played in stealing her brother from her—might not think so far ahead.

"Are you lying to me because you can't tell me the truth or is it because you're hoping to protect her?" Elezar asked. Bois nearly stumbled and knew he'd guessed correctly. "You're in Lady Hylanya's thrall, aren't you?"

Javier cast Elezar an approving glance but then turned back to forging their way. Bois appeared all at once exhausted.

"Her father gave me to her on his deathbed," Bois said at last. "She didn't mean to harm Skellan or to endanger the city. But she hated the bishop so much. It was more than I could control or resist. I tried but..."

Elezar understood all too well the blind, murderous rage that could so easily fill an adolescent heart. He could see how that fury might even overwhelm the control of an adult—particularly one who shared that hatred.

He had no idea how he was going to share this news with Skellan. The last thing he wanted was to pit brother against sister muchless set himself up right in the middle.

"But what about the mobs?" Elezar asked.

"That, I suspect, was Peome," Bois replied. "Her familiars in the bishop's garden would have shown her what Hylanya and I had done and she would have known at once what would happen to the city's unity if it came to a trial. If Skellan had to judge in favor of one side or the other—"

"And so she made a show of force for the Labaran side?" Elezar couldn't keep the disgust from sounding in his voice.

"No—at least I don't think that was her driving motive." For the first time Bois stole a glance back at Elezar. He lifted his right hand to display the small black vial cupped against his palm. "Muerate poison. While Skellan and the garrison guards were distracted by the mobs, Peome's familiar brought it to me."

For an instant Elezar wondered how the poison was supposed to help Bois escape from the stockade but then he realized the purpose of the fragile vial.

"So you kill yourself and there's no trial," Elezar said.

"And no need for the count to publically take one side or the other." Bois nodded then turned his attention back to the path Javier led them along. Elezar followed him.

"Would you have taken it?" Elezar asked at last.

"Yes, I meant to wait until sunrise and do it then."

"Why?" Elezar asked.

"I've always loved watching the sun rise," Bois said, with a shrug.

They didn't speak again until Javier brought them out into the summer air of the narrow alley behind the Mockingbird Playhouse. After the deathly hush of the Old Road the voices of revelers boomed from the street and the peals of theatric music seemed to pound from the walls of the playhouse.

"Will you be safe with Rafale?" Elezar asked. He didn't want to care about Bois. He would much rather have retained his disdain for the man, but there had been something in the dignity with which he'd faced his own death and his dedication to the Radulf family that Elezar found touching.

"I'll manage." Bois started for the side door then paused to look back at Elezar and Javier. "Thank you. I know this was for Skellan's sake, but thank you." He didn't wait for their responses but knocked hard against the door. A moment later, Clairre peered into the alley. A halo of gold light framed her gaunt form. Elezar smelled tallow candles and eel stew. After only a few words with Bois she allowed him in. She paused to scowl at the dark shadows of the alley then she pulled the door closed.

Javier shot Elezar an amused look then they returned to the Old Road. Their passage felt like it had lasted days but when they emerged Elezar knew from the position of guards making their rounds that mere seconds had passed since they'd first begun.

Had they returned any sooner they might well have seen themselves departing the grounds of the garrison yard. Elezar frowned at the strangeness of that idea, but then let it go. What a relief to be free of those terrible visions and stale reek of death. Elezar drew in a deep breath of the fresh air.

However when he looked to Javier he recognized concern in his expression. He followed Javier's gaze up to a wide ballroom window. Cheery gold candlelight shone and strains of lute music drifted to them. The bright forms of dancing couples swirled past.

Skellan stood at the glass, glowering down directly at Elezar.

For the amusement of all those gathered in the stately room, a slim courtier sporting extravagantly coiffed hair and a thick mustache of glossy black ringlets performed the wind walk dance backwards and blindfolded. Bishop Palo's niece plucked the accompanying melody from a lute while Atreau gamely attempted to sing the lyrics to the tune backwards as well. Laughter and applause rewarded the three of them, and Skellan clapped as hard as anyone.

After the trouble of the day it felt delightful simply to laugh along with everyone else gathered in the room. Skellan even relented in his anger at Rafale, offering him a smile after he led the gathering through a harmlessly bawdy ditty about a virtuous vixen and a lusty drake. After that Atreau and Rafale sang a hilarious rendition of a love duet.

Though Skellan had to work at keeping a smile on his face as a sudden sharp stab cut through his gut. His toes and fingers burned and then went cold as a chill seemed slither down his chest to curl up in the pit of his belly.

"What a lovely voice the duke possesses," Hylanya commented to him. She cocked her head studying Atreau. "He isn't at all how I expected. Nothing like that wretched Bishop Palo or Commander Lecha."

"That's comparing raisons to grapes, isn't it?" Skellan managed to reply though his stomach rolled and for an instant he thought he might bring up the little he'd eaten.

Skellan clenched his jaw and the nausea passed but his feeling of uneasiness lingered. Perhaps it was a remnant from his encounter with the Sumar grimma, or maybe a lingering ache from breaking Grimma Ylva's thrall the week before. Though something in the numbness reminded Skellan of the deep wounds the Black Fire had dealt him. He exhaled a slow breath and to his dread he tasted moldering, deathly must rising from his own lungs.

Alarm shot through him and though it embarrassed him he reached reflexively, through the weave of spells saturating the grounds for Elezar. In response he felt nothing, not the faintest lingering of Elezar's living presence anywhere in the garrison or the streets beyond.

What could have happened to him? He'd only walked out the doors minutes ago.

Skellan's heart picked up its beat. Could one of the grimma have snatched him up—No, Skellan would have felt that. The whole sky would have blazed with awakened wards and rung like countless tower bells. Instead a sickly chill pooled in Skellan's stomach and his mouth tasted as if it were filled with rotting mushrooms.

The air of death.

Skellan exhaled the foul taste, only to feel it seep back up his throat. This wasn't his own breath, he realized. It had to belong to Elezar. How could his man be breathing the black breath of the dead into his lungs? He would have to be walking the paths of the underworld. The answer came to Skellan suddenly. The Bahiim, Javier.

"—don't you think, Hilthorn?" Hylanya's question sounded in his ears but Skellan could hardly make sense of it.

"I—Sorry. I think I've had a little too much wine," Skellan replied. Then as worry showed on Hylanya's face he added. "I'm fine, really. Just not accustomed to such good grog."

"You've been overworked. Today has been so trying for us all." For no reason that Skellan could understand Hylanya's gaze fluttered to her nurse, Peome. The nurse sighed like a woman of long suffering. One of the swordsmen standing near them seemed to take note of Skellan's uneasiness as well. He started forward, hand outstretched as if he expected to sweep Skellan up in his arms. Skellan's scowl brought the swordsman up short. The last thing Skellan wanted was more attention drawn to how unwell he felt.

He didn't know what Elezar had done but the wards and spells Skellan had wrapped around him bled Skellan cold to keep his man safe. Cire would have laughed at him, if she noticed—or maybe she'd have been horrified at his stupid sentimentality.

"Do me a favor, will you?" Skellan asked the swordsman. "Fetch Javier the Bahiim here to me."

"Aye, my lord." The swordsman's expression brightened. He bowed and made a speedy exit.

"The Bahiim?" Hylanya asked.

Skellan nodded. Hadn't Bone-crusher warned him that the Bahiim were trouble? He couldn't imagine why Javier would whisk Elezar away to the paths of the underworlds.

"I thought it might be good fun to have an Irabiim dance. He's most likely to know the steps, don't you think?"

Hylanya considered Skellan with a skeptical gaze. What she might have said was interrupted by the approach of the handsome courtier sporting the perfectly curled hair and mustache—the son of a baron, though Skellan couldn't recall which one.

Even so, Skellan nodded approvingly when the man asked Hylanya for a dance, and for her part, Hylanya seemed to forget all her earlier concerns as the courtier executed a truly elegant bow before her and then took her proffered hand as if it were a sacred relic. Seconds later, the two of them whisked around the room, keeping step with a bright Labaran tune. Other couples joined them but to Skellan's eye none looked quite so striking as his angular sister and her beaming partner.

The sight made Skellan wish Elezar were here to take in his arms—but no, that would be too easy a thing, wouldn't it? No, his man had to be out and into trouble. As if the day hadn't brought them enough of that already.

Skellan skirted the other folk in the room, declining several offers for more wine and walnuts, and made his way to the dark window. He studied the grounds below, moving his mind over wards as if he were stroking harp stings and feeling them resound back through him. Bone-crusher shifted in his sleep but didn't wake.

Then Skellan felt the air in his lungs alter. Near the squat building that served as their stockade, Elezar stepped out from emptiness. The instant his boot touched the garrison grounds dozens of spells sang to life around Skellan, assuring him that Elezar had come back to him unharmed.

He and Javier looked smug as thieves. He wondered if either of them knew how clearly he could see them in the glow of all his own wards. Skellan's fear for both of them soured to annoyance.

As if sensing his ire, Javier and then Elezar looked up to where Skellan stood and both pulled faces like boys caught with their greasy fingers in a butter crock. Elezar straightened and lifted his hand, offering Skellan a hopeful wave. Skellan clenched his fist to keep from returning the gesture. He couldn't let this pass easy as a piss.

Whatever the two of them had gotten up to, they damn well should have informed him. Elezar should have told him—warned him. And why did Elezar look so damn guilty? What exactly *had* they slithered off to do?

The swordsman Skellan had sent to fetch Javier jogged across the grounds and spoke to both Elezar and Javier. Soon enough all three of them returned to the main building and then came into the room.

Javier drew the most attention with his entrance. Between his Bahiim dress and his striking features he was not a man easily overlooked. Though it was Elezar whom Skellan watched. The guilt he'd revealed at first glance had gone. Now he offered only that indifferent frown that graced the faces of all those carved saints in Cadeleonian chapels. The swordsman escorting the two of them to Skellan appeared a bit too pleased with himself, but Skellan let that pass and thanked the man with his best smile before dismissing him to enjoy himself with the rest of the party.

"Which of you wants to tell me what you've been up to?" Skellan asked once the swordsman strode out of easy hearing. If the whirling dancers and noise of the party didn't absorb Skellan's guards completely they at least maintained the pretense of ignoring his private conversation.

Elezar met Skellan's glower but then bowed his head and said nothing.

"Out for a little wander," Javier said.

"A wander? Do you take me for a fool?" Skellan asked.

"Not at all," Javier replied. He cast his gaze meaningfully across the couples dancing just beyond them. "But this seems the wrong setting for detailing our dull sojourn."

Fuck keeping up appearances, Skellan thought and he only just managed not to say as much. Instead he drew in a deep breath and then said softly. "I know where you were, well enough. Next time you tell me before you go on another such jaunt."

"Should the occasion arise I will make my best effort to inform you." Javier offered him the broad, charming smile of a man who felt in no way beholden to his own word.

Elezar, on the other hand, frowned quite seriously down at his big hands. Bruises, scrapes and burns colored his fingers. Skellan bore many of the same marks, but he kept his own hands shoved deep in his coat pockets.

"I didn't realize that it would disturb you." Elezar met Skellan's gaze and Skellan thought he read genuine concern behind Elezar's stern expression. "Did it cause you much... trouble?"

Had they been alone, Skellan might have told him exactly how horrified and frightened he'd felt, not only of the decaying sensations of the Old Road creeping through him, but during that time when he'd realized that he couldn't find Elezar. But with Javier standing there looking so smug and merry couples dancing past them, Skellan felt too exposed and too likely to say the wrong thing. He simply shrugged.

From across the room Cire caught his eye and then turned to saunter past, with the air of a mother goose watching her gosling's first encounter with a cat. She stilled next to Skellan and craned her head back to study Javier.

"Now where have you left that handsome man of yours, Master Javier?" Cire fiddled with one of the long, silver pins holding her red braids atop her head. "I'd hoped he'd be joining us for the dances."

"He's sleeping, I'm afraid—at least I hope he still is." Javier looked to Elezar questioningly.

"I think he might be waiting for you to come back with a pie for him," Elezar replied. For his part Elezar seemed distracted. His gaze followed Peome for a moment then shifted to Hylanya.

"Oh yes, I was after a pie." Javier laughed at that, though Skellan couldn't guess why.

"The smell of soot and seed oil led you to my Elezar instead, then?" Skellan inquired.

Javier's sharp brows rose at Skellan's words. Elezar frowned but his dark eyes continued to study the surrounding guests like they were troubeling sums.

"Other way around," Javier replied with a slanting glance at Elezar's profile. "Our Elezar came looking for me amongst all the fragrant pies. And well, you know how hard he is to refuse."

Skellan didn't like the tone of that, and apparently neither did Elezar. His attention whipped back to Javier whom he regarded with a deep scowl.

"What in the hells—" Elezar began, but Javier cut him off.

"The two of you might want to retire to a more private setting to have this discussion." Javier's smile struck Skellan as immensely self-satisfied. "I'd hate to have Elezar air my youthful secrets to all the on-looking world."

Cire as well as several other guests looked between Javier and Elezar with curiosity and speculation. Cire shook her head, clearly unable to picture the pairing. Skellan didn't suffer from a similar difficulty. Elezar's strength and stamina struck him as more than enough to tempt any man prone to appreciate such things and Javier was certainly so disposed.

Oddly, Javier's flirtatious tone and Elezar's exasperated response put Skellan a little more at ease. If he'd been inclined to worry about a romance rekindling between the two of them, that look of Elezar's assured him that nothing could have been further from Elezar's thoughts. So then, what had they been up to, really?

A serving girl holding a sliver tray drifted closer to them and past her Skellan noted both his own sister and Atreau moving between the dancers, intent upon approaching them. Javier was right; the last thing Skellan wanted was more company.

"You are wise beyond your years, Master Javier," Skellan said. Then he caught Elezar's hand in his own. "Come walk with me, my man."

He started for the door, Elezar in tow. When Skellan's guards closed behind them Elezar dismissed them.

"I'll keep the count's company the rest of the night," Elezar informed them and despite the difficulty of the day Skellan smiled to himself. Only a week before Elezar would have said those words as if he were confessing a mortal crime. Now other troubles distracted him and the words seem to come as naturally as the weight of his hand in Skellan's own. The guards saluted and stepped back.

Skellan led Elezar up to the enormous bedroom they shared most nights. Elezar kept his own much smaller private rooms on the floor below but hadn't spent an entire night there since Skellan first invited him to share his bed the previous week. Over the course of the last few days, more and more of Elezar's simple belongings had come to rest among all the absurd and ornate frippery brought from the Sun Palace.

As they strode in past the silk tapestries depicting hunting scenes and several silver mirrors, Skellan's dressers caught sight of them, offered a brief greeting. Though it seemed to require only a glance at Skellan's expression before both of the young men made themselves scarce.

Skellan felt very aware of the still and silence between Elezar and himself. Any other night and they might have raced out of their clothes—Elezar teasing Skellan for his bare-footed advantage as he tossed aside his heavy boots—and made directly for the bed. Skellan frowned at the velvet-backed chairs surrounding the gilded dressing table. His own troubled face glowered back at him from a mirror. He glimpsed Elezar's rugged profile and dark downcast eyes.

"I didn't realize that the Old Road would affect you—" Elezar began. "Are you hurt?"

"Oh, no worse than a mouthful of road dust," Skellan replied. He kicked absently at one of the thick rugs. Now that they were alone he found that he didn't want to work up an annoyance with Elezar. Time seemed too short, and he could just pick out the melody of another song straining up from the floors below. He squeezed Elezar's rough callused hands and then placed his own pale fingers on Elezar's hip and leaned into him.

"Did you dance many evenings away back home in Anacleto, Lord Grunito?"

Elezar gave a soft laugh at the idea. He appeared relived at the turn of subject, and Skellan realized that he, too shied from an argument. They hadn't grown so familiar with each other that they knew how the other fought or how much hurt they could inflict or endure.

"Surprisingly, I was not the beauty of the ball," Elezar replied with a wry smile.

"I am surprised, you know." He couldn't imagine that a man as physically skilled as Elezar wouldn't be a joy to dance with. Skellan swayed with him and Elezar wrapped his arm around Skellan's shoulder. The comfort of simply holding him and being held in return amazed Skellan. His aches and exhaustion seemed to diminish. He felt the iron tension of Elezar's body relent beneath his hands. Elezar sighed and bowed his head to rest his brow against Skellan's shoulder.

"It's been a hell of a day," Elezar murmured.

Skellan nodded. So many hard and harrowing days had filled the last two weeks that it had felt like an entire year—like he and Elezar had survived ages together. But really they hadn't even heard each other's names six months prior.

"I honestly didn't think you could be hurt if I went in..." Elezar confessed in a low whisper.

"I believe you," Skellan replied.

For a moment he wanted to leave it at that. They were both exhausted and not long from facing a war. What good would it do to dig at something that they both knew could ruin the easy communion between them?

But he had to know—they had to have this discussion. Again silence stretched between them. Elezar lifted his face. His expression seemed resigned, though Skellan couldn't be certain.

"Why *did* you take the Old Road?" Skellan asked.

"I didn't want to get you involved..." Elezar paused seeming to search for the right words. He shook his head. "You're not going to like this."

"I guessed that much," Skellan replied. He wanted to be able to laugh but Elezar's drawn expression filled him with dread.

"You told me that you couldn't release Bois—"

"Of course not. He murd—"

"I freed him," Elezar said it fast and firmly.

Skellan stared at him in disbelief. Somehow of all the things he could have imagined Elezar getting up to, securing Bois' freedom had not once occurred to him.

"Why?" Skellan demanded. "Why would you?"

"Because you couldn't but it had to be done. For the sake—"

"It did not have to be done!" Hot anger flooded Skellan

and he drew back from Elezar's arms. "He is a murderer by his own admission!"

"I know, but—" Elezar began but Skellan didn't want to hear it.

"A murderer!" Skellan shouted and Elezar winced at his booming voice. He held up his hands as if to quell Skellan's anger. Who knew who might be in the hall, listening.

"Skellan, try to see reason here." The soft exaggerated calm in Elezar's voice only annoyed Skellan all the more. What was he, a skittish horse? But Elezar went on, "If you had executed him every Labaran—"

"I understand the situation! I understood it the last time we spoke of it," Skellan snapped. "And I credited you with brains and honor enough to have understood my decision to uphold the law."

A dark flush colored Elezar's cheeks and Skellan felt sure that his barb had dug deep. The line of Elezar's mouth cut down into a scowl and anger smoldered in his dark gaze.

"Someone had to be sensible," Elezar began coldly.

"And that was you, was it?" Skellan demanded. "Because you're so much more wise in the ways of the world than me, are you?"

"I sure as hell know more than you do about governing a city," Elezar returned.

"You mean the sort of governance that got us all in this shit pit of a predicament in the first place? Secret alliances, lies, and murder?" Skellan drew himself straight and sneered at Elezar's hard demeanor. "Well, murder—yes, I'm sure you know more about that!"

"I did what had to be done," Elezar growled out between clenched teeth and Skellan felt a furious pleasure in knowing he'd again hit his mark. He was in the right and they both knew it.

"That wasn't your decision to make—It was mine!" Skellan thumped his fist against his own chest. "You serve me!"

He saw Elezar's jaw flex and caught the twitch of Elezar's sword arm. If he'd not been furious he would have taken warning or at least stepped back farther out of Elezar's reach. But outrage and justification made him want to press that point home. He drew closer to Elezar and glowered into his hard face.

"So long as you are here in my city—my county—you serve me! You understand?"

"I do," Elezar replied, though anger rumbled through each clipped word. His eyes narrowed at Skellan. "The one who doesn't understand is you."

With shocking speed he caught hold of Skellan's shoulders and all but pulled him up off his feet as he glowered down at him.

"You think I freed Bois because I wanted to—that I took some pleasure in freeing a man who butchered a defenseless old bishop? I did it and I would do it a hundred times over for your sake!" Some terrible, intense emotion seemed to grip him and his words came out as ragged whispers. "You have no fucking idea of everything I've done—everything I've compromised for your sake! For you!" Elezar's fingers dung into Skellan's arms like iron bands and then suddenly he released Skellan, shoving him back from him. Skellan stumbled but caught himself. His heart pounded wildly in his chest.

"I choose to serve you but I am not a mindless minion," Elezar growled. "And we both know that Bois' execution would wreak havoc on our unified troops. Hell, his honorable release would have done the same."

Skellan couldn't argue that point. Even he recognized that people would have taken offense over Bois. He would've done what he could to make it clear that it was a matter of justice and law. But he did know that there were those who wouldn't accept any explanation. Still, he didn't want to concede his honor to such folk.

Elezar went on.

"People, both Cadeleonian and Labaran, look to you as a symbol of this city and its survival. You mean more to them than just one man." This wasn't a direction Skellan had expected. He opened his mouth to object but Elezar spoke over him, in an insistent low tone. "Whether you like it or not, you had to be protected from blame for Bois' fate. You had to be kept above it, whether I released him or murdered him in some back alley. You have to be able to swear before common men and witches alike that you played no part in it. And you didn't play a part in it."

Skellan reluctantly accepted Elezar's words. Certainly, Elezar believed them. But the presumption still angered him.

"You went behind my back and acted directly against my will." Skellan realized that this was what bothered him the most about the entire thing. He knew he wasn't a clever politician nor an experienced leader, but it still hurt him that Elezar had moved against him.

Elezar stood very still for a moment then nodded.

"How can I trust you?" Skellan asked. "How can I call you my champion when you betray me like that?"

"I did not—If you think I would betray you then you have no fucking—" Elezar clamped his mouth shut against his own words. He seemed to struggle in some inner argument then he shook his head. "If you really don't trust me then you should release me. Choose another champion."

Skellan stared at him, feeling almost sick with both anger and confusion. Minutes before they'd been in each other's arms. How could a few words have crumbled everything between them?

"You truly mean that?" Skellan asked.

Elezar didn't meet his gaze. His attention rested on the mirror behind Skellan. He breathed slowly and deeply through his flared nostrils, his mouth clenched shut in a hard line. He nodded curtly and kept his gaze averted.

Suddenly Skellan remembered the night he'd seen Elezar rip a bear claw from the inflamed flesh of his own calf. He'd worn a similar expression and maintained near silence. Until this instant Skellan hadn't realized that he had any real ability to cause Elezar pain. Between his imposing physical presence and his Cadeleonian stoicism he'd seemed as invulnerable as the statues of the Cadeleonian saints he so resembled.

Even now he stood straight and stern with his battered hands clenched at his sides, as he suppressed everything wild and alive about himself. He hardly blinked and yet immense, obvious tension played through his entire being.

Skellan drew in a slow calming breath and forced himself to think of everything at stake for them both and to remember Elezar coaxing him from his dog skin with so much care and concern. Elezar had defended him when turning Skellan over to his own royal bishop would have profited Elezar and his friends greatly.

Anger still smoldered in Skellan's chest, but a great part of that, he realized belatedly, arose from how accustomed he'd grown to Elezar serving him unquestioningly. He'd come to count upon Elezar to give everything and ask nothing in return but the pleasure of their shared bed. Well, that and the occasional bath. But for a man who was a lord in his own right, he'd gone to great lengths to reassure Skellan and most of Milmuraille that he did not aspire beyond the role of an obedient champion. He'd played the part so perfectly that Skellan had almost forgotten that Elezar—and any free-minded person—could and would hold his own opinions and take his own actions.

Chagrin moved through him as he understood that for all his arguments with Cire, he'd secretly grown to expect Elezar to behave as if he were enthralled. But here Elezar stood now, a free man, whom Skellan did believe had acted to protect him but in the most aggravatingly independent manner.

"I don't want any other champion," Skellan admitted at last. "I'm just frustrated and vexed. But likely I'd get over it fast enough if you had the common sense to say you're sorry, my man."

Elezar couldn't hide the relief in his expression, though he tried.

"I am," he blurted and then catching himself he clarified. "I am sorry. But I didn't betray you—I wouldn't..."

Elezar was no master of eloquence but his response went a long way to salving Skellan's pride after being defied and—if he had to admit it—at being made fully aware of his ignorance of political machinations.

"I wanted to protect you," Elezar said. He scowled at his own hands then looked back to Skellan. "If you wish it, then I'll arrest Bois again."

No doubt that offer cost Elezar some pride and it moved Skellan. He shook his head. It wasn't as if he'd wanted to stand as judge over a contentious trial on the eve of a war.

"No. What's done is done." Skellan reached out and took Elezar's right hand in his own. "You could have done far worse than to have protected me by showing a bastard a bit of mercy."

Elezar pulled Skellan into his arms and held him tight. Skellan closed his eyes and returned Elezar's embrace. He rested his head against Elezar's thick shoulder, taking in the scent of sweat and smoke clinging to him. He couldn't have said why but feeling the strength of Elezar's body pressed against his own offered him more reassurance than anything either of them could have said.

Skellan wondered if sometimes talk didn't do men more harm than good. All their attempts to make bits of noise serve to convey intent only confused the simple truths that their bodies already grasped.

"I've never known anyone like you," Elezar murmured. His breath tickled the nape of Skellan's neck. "I wish..."

Skellan lifted his head, taking in Elezar's uncertain expression.

"I want this—" Elezar seemed to wrack his mind for a suitable word but find none. "What's between us, I do want this but I'm worried that I'm not the right sort of man. I've no art or poetry in me and I'm hardheaded as the red bull of my family crest… I don't know that I can give you what you need."

"I don't need anything from you. But I want your company," Skellan replied. Then he couldn't help but add, "Well, that and a happy fuck, but there I give as good as I get, don't I?"

At first Elezar went so still that Skellan worried that words had once again muddled the communion between them.

Then Elezar sought Skellan's mouth and kissed him very gently, almost as if he were afraid of breaking him. His chapped lips and rough beard delighted Skellan's tender skin. As he drew back Skellan caught Elezar's lip between his teeth very briefly and then released him with a grin.

"Tease me much more and I'll have you, soot-streaked and all, my man," Skellan informed him.

Elezar smiled looking almost sly in return. Then he kissed Skellan again but this time with a hard yearning that sent arousal surging through Skellan. What little though he'd given the ash clinging to Elezar's hands and clothes, Skellan forgot. He slid his hands down the planes of Elezar's body, massaging and caressing taut muscle. He delighted in felling Elezar's flushed response as he slipped his tongue between Elezar's lips and teeth to invade the heat of Elezar's mouth.

Their tongues lashed, slid and traced each other. Elezar tasted rich and smoky. His arms curled around Skellan, clasping him closed but for all the power of Elezar's embrace, it gentled at once and released then instant Skellan stepped back.

Such naked longing showed in Elezar's tanned, lined face that Skellan felt both flattered and moved. A drowning man couldn't have wanted air more than Elezar seemed to want him at this moment.

Skellan caught the clasp that held Elezar's heavy cloak and with a well-practiced motion loosened the heavy garment and tossed it aside onto one of the ornate chairs. Then he took Elezar's hand and led him back to the bed. Elezar followed him with the silent intensity of a cat stalking prey. Though when Skellan turned to pull Elezar's linen shirt over his head he felt Elezar's heart pounding wildly through his powerful chest.

Had Elezar been another man Skellan might have teased him for that or his shaking hands and unwavering stare. But oddly Elezar's intensity touched him. For Skellan, sex could be ardent or a mere amusement to pass the time in pleasure but it never seemed so inconsequential for Elezar. He fucked the way holy men prayed: giving all his heart and soul to it.

Still Skellan couldn't suppress his own sense of play. The back of Skellan's calf bumped into the bed behind him and he drew Elezar near.

"Well, here's us and our costly bed." Skellan raised Elezar's callused hand to his lips and ran his tongue over tender skin of Elezar's wrist before dropping back to the downy mattress and splaying his legs wide. Leaning back on his elbows, he grinned up, seeing Elezar's breath catch and his dark eyes dilate.

"But how will I ever get out of these silk breeches with both my attendants gone?" Skellan rocked his hips, and the gold needlework decorating his scarlet breeches glinted in the lamplight.

The corner of Elezar's mouth quirked up then.

"They do appear too tight for you," Elezar replied. But he didn't join Skellan on the bed. Instead he knelt at the bedside and ran his long fingers up Skellan's legs and over his hips. He reached the line of gold buttons that secured the crotch of Skellan's breeches. The heat and weight of his hands brushed across Skellan's skin. Anticipation flooded Skellan's groin and all at once the silk and gold thread clothing his flesh did feel far too binding.

Elezar couldn't fail to notice Skellan stiffening beneath his touch and yet he worked the small buttons apart with a slow, painstaking care. Skellan rocked his hips into Elezar's hands, groaning. Another brief smile flickered over Elezar's mouth.

"Easy now." Elezar slowly unfastened another button. "You don't want me to tear your fine raiment."

"Damn the trousers!" Skellan groaned.

Elezar gave a soft laugh. He pulled apart the last buttons in fast succession, freeing Skellan. Then he lowered his head, taking Skellan between his lips and lapping him with his tongue as if he were a sweet. Pleasure flooded Skellan as Elezar bowed down deep over him. Skellan could think of nothing but how wonderful this felt. Ecstasy rolled through him and his body arched and pushed for more of the wet warmth of Elezar's mouth. Instinctively he curled his hands into Elezar's thick dark hair. He dug his fingers in and Elezar allowed himself to be led.

A glory more warming and joyous then the most powerful spell rushed from Elezar's compliant lips and hot mouth flooding Skellan's groin with mounting waves of ecstatic sensation.

But then Skellan took in the view below him and realized that Elezar still knelt on the floor. Though pleasure dulled his mind, Skellan knew enough of Elezar to understand that the servile position meant more to him that mere happenstance. Skellan had been pushed down to his knees, himself in his youth and he remembered too well the demeaning expressions of the men who'd so enjoyed having him down at their feet.

That wasn't what he wanted of Elezar.

It took all of Skellan's self-control to drop his hand to Elezar's jaw and lift Elezar's face from his groin. His lips were flushed and the rough hair of his beard sent shivers of delight coursing through Skellan as he raised his head.

"You shouldn't—" Skellan managed to whisper.

"I want to." The admission came out rough and quiet.

And Skellan wanted him to continue as well, but he pressed on.

"Not down on your knees." Skellan ran a coaxing hand down the nape of Elezar's neck. "Come up and join me on our bed where I can give as good as I get, my man."

Elezar paused for less than a heartbeat, but then rose, joining Skellan. Together they tossed aside their clothing and then surrounded by pillows and silk bedding they knelt together. Elezar gamely allowed Skellan to roll him onto his back.

Then, lips to groins they united their bodies, both giving as much pleasure as they took. As scarlet spells lit the stones around them and Skellan shook with a rushing climax, he wasn't certain if it was his own or Elezar's—or the bursting of a far greater pleasure they'd forged between them.

Afterwards they lay gasping together. Elezar turned, clumsy in the aftermath of climax and dropped down to wrap his arm around Skellan's shoulder. He nuzzled his head against the side of Skellan's and a feeling a sated happiness filled Skellan's chest. A tenderness stronger than any he'd even imagined feeling before came over him and he felt embarrassed for it.

"My prick's cold without your mouth on it," Skellan said, because he couldn't bring himself to express any of foolish promises or admissions drifting through his mind. He didn't want Elezar to turn terse and tense again. He'd already asked and received so much from Elezar. He didn't want to press his luck by bringing up a future neither of them might live to even see. What they had here and now was enough.

"Ever the romantic, aren't you?" Elezar snorted but then he shifted his hips allowing Skellan to press his flaccid cock into the damp warm curls of Elezar's groin. Skellan reached out and caught the edge of one of the rumpled blankets. He pulled it over them both.

"Romantic enough." Skellan yawned and then he let his eyes fall closed. He felt Elezar's lips press against his brow and then slipped into sleep.

Broad green leaves spread over Skellan's head, filtering the sunlight into a warm emerald glow. Skellan blinked, feeling dazed and uncertain of how he'd come to lie on a bed of soft moss with a vast bower of leaves and blossoms curling over him. The perfume of ripe fruit drifted over him. A languid fatigue suffused his body. He was dreaming again.

Distantly he became aware of vines curling around his naked arms and legs.

The sensation alarmed him. He managed to kick once. His muscles flexed and pulled with the slow weight of honey pooling from a spoon. He attempted to jerk his arms free but only slowly raised one hand. His strength failed almost at once and all he could manage was to catch the velvety edge of an immense leaf directly above him. As his arm collapsed he drew the leaf down.

And he wished that he hadn't.

It wasn't the light of the sun that blazed above him, but the fiery eyes of a giant green dragon. Cascades of verdant leaves, grasses and vines adorned each of her scales, spreading and tangling down her body like wilderness cloaking the vast expanse of a mountain. Blue sky spread behind her and thick white clouds clung to the forested crown of her long skull.

She was a world in her own right.

Skellan blinked up at her from the cradle of her upturned palm. She bowed her head and through the walls of birch trees, ferns and briars her eyes shone like the molten forge at the heart of the earth. And suddenly Skellan realized that he'd been too right in thinking her a world of her own—she wasn't a woman or a dragon cloaked in illusions of wildflowers and woods. No, he gazed upon a vast wild, landscape curled, compressed and barely contained by mortal forms.

"I'm dreaming of you," Skellan whispered to the Sumar grimma.

"No, child of mine." Her voice rolled over him like a perfumed summer wind. "You are my dream. Here, at last, I can hold you safe."

Skellan wanted to shout in frustration at her words. Would everyone he met justify their actions with good intentions? He could damn well keep himself safe. Yet he didn't have the strength to say as much. He felt so warm and tired. He tried to glower up into her strange face but then simply yawned.

Honeybees hummed past him to plunder the cluster of rose blossoms drooping over his shoulder. Far up on the slope of the grimma's neck, where stands of beech cropped from amidst the fir trees, Skellan thought he glimpsed a herd of deer.

"I lost you once," the Sumar grimma whispered and her words curled around Skellan, blowing his hair in gusts. "You grew up among strangers, so we know nothing of each other and now I fear I will lose you all over again, my own Hilthorn."

"How can you fear losing a son you never knew?" Skellan managed to ask. "Why should you care at all?"

"Why does a hawk tear the plumes from her own breast to warm her clutch? Why would a mother bear fight to the death for her newborn cub? I don't need to know you to want to keep you from harm." As she drew closer the heat of her gaze seemed to pour down upon Skellan. "You are all my hopes, all the best of me brought into this world."

"If that's true then actually help me!" Skellan shook his head and fought to keep his tired eyes from falling closed. "Stand with me against the other grimma."

Suddenly the sleepy warmth drained from the air. The Sumar grimma's eyes flicked closed, plunging Skellan into darkness deeper than if the sun had simply gone out. In a moment the hot gold blaze once more flared to life.

"I cannot make war against the other three anymore than the full moon can kill the crescent. Even we are bound by the laws of our creation." She turned her huge head so that the fire of only her right eye burned above Skellan's head. When she spoke her voice sounded strangely soft and sorrowful. "Why won't you simply come home? I would never let you come to harm again, if only you would return to me."

"I am home," Skellan stated firmly. "Milmuraille is where I was raised and grew up. I'm no longer yours. I am my own man."

The Sumar grimma arched her neck and for an instant Skellan thought that she would strike him down again. He didn't know how he could defend himself. But then she sighed a hot, shaking wind. Leaves and blossoms twisted and fluttered wildly around Skellan.

"You will always be my child. Even when you are no more than bare bones." The Sumar grimma pinned him with her bright gaze and Skellan forced himself to stare back at her, though it burned his eyes and made the skin of his face feel raw and wind-chaffed.

"How willful you are, Hilthorn."

"Couldn't I say the same of you?"

"Yes, my child. We are of a kind."

She closed her eyes, plunging him into darkness. Then Skellan felt himself falling from her grasp, plummeting.

He woke with a gasp, his heart racing.

Beside him Elezar groaned and pulled a blood shot eye open to squint through the faint dawn light. A questioning grumble escaped his lips.

"A dream." Skellan's heard the relief in his own voice. "Only a dream."

Elezar offered him a groggy swipe of his hand, which Skellan took for a pat. Skellan sat up and ran his hands through his hair, trying to scrub his earlier fear from his head. Just a dream, he reassured himself, but then he caught sight of the gold ring on his right hand. A spark of green light glinted from the red depths of the ruby. Skellan drew his hand nearer to him to study the ring, but found nothing altered in the stone.

It shone scarlet and, as he curled his hand over it, is sent a hum of warm comfort through him. The stone and gold felt as much his as the stones of the garrison.

Skellan sighed at his own nervousness.

"There's soot on your back," Elezar murmured.

As Skellan glanced over his bare shoulder, Elezar reached out and ran a thick finger down his flank. His warm hand left a faint gray trace of soot. Elezar laughed sleepily. Though Skellan did note that several other such smudges covered his body from the night before. Elezar himself bore light charcoal gray smears all across his shoulders, chest and hips, though his thick dark body hair camouflaged the full extent of the streaks.

Elezar licked the pad of his thumb and scrubbed it across Skellan's cheekbone then he gave a wry smile.

"I think I made it worse," Elezar admitted.

Skellan caught a clean edge of one of the flaxen sheets and wiped his face.

"Now is that anyway to treat the spell I was writing on you?" Elezar yawned, presenting Skellan a view of his white teeth and pink mouth. Skellan's gaze lingered. Elezar had mastered several lovely tricks with that mouth of his in the last two weeks.

"And what kind of spell would you cast over me?" Skellan asked belatedly.

Elezar's mouth fell back into its natural solemn line but warmth still lit his gaze as he glanced to Skellan and then made some pretense of contemplating the question while he stared up at the painted ceiling above their heads.

Skellan looked up as well. He'd not ever paid much attention to the adornments of the chamber. More often his mind focused on the spells he'd placed deep within the stone and wood.

A faded blue sky spread across the plaster interrupted only by the chipped gold image of two stallions rearing over a dull ochre crown. The crest of the Cadeleonian king floated over them, Skellan realized. It made sense. Cadeleonian crests decorated much of the garrison. Still it felt a little odd to recognize one directly over his head. How much more disconcerting for Elezar to lie here in bed with him and stare up at this symbol of his distant home?

Between cracks and the age of the paint it looked more battered than resplendent.

Skellan wanted to say something but felt at a loss when he took in Elezar's contemplative face. Who could know what thoughts filled his mind? Did he desperately miss his home? Did he revile himself for the pleasures they shared? Was he thinking now about his large family and the lush holdings he risked? Or perhaps he turned over utterly different concerns of armaments and battle plans.

A troubled furrow creased his heavy brow.

"I think I'd place a spell on you to undo the wrongs others have done you," Elezar said at last.

The tenderness of the answer both surprised and embarrassed Skellan.

"And here I was thinking you were wishing two more pricks on me," Skellan teased.

"You're trouble enough with only the one," Elezar said, laughing.

Skellan pretended to consider the matter for a moment then conceded, "I suppose you're right. Can you imagine the mess trying to aim all three in the piss pot with only two hands?"

"You'd just lean out the window and let loose all over the flowerbeds," Elezar replied but he appeared amused. He yawned then slowly his frown returned.

"Bois said something last night and I meant to tell you about it but I was distracted by..." Elezar's gaze moved over the twisted, soot-traced sheets and a slight flush colored his tanned cheeks. "In any case, Bois said that Hallen Radulf turned him and the rest of those bound to him over to your sister, Lady Hylanya."

Skellan frowned. He'd suspected that his father had held a number of his subjects in thralls but he'd hoped that their subjugation had ended with the count's death.

"Bois claimed that killing Bishop Palo was Lady Hylanya's will and that Peome was responsible for rousing those mobs last night. Apparently, she used the confusion to slip a vial of muerate poison into Bois' cell in hopes that he'd kill himself and save you from having to condemn him publicly." Elezar paused as if weighing whether to go on. "I don't know if any of that matters to you but I thought you ought to know."

Skellan nodded, though he really would rather have not known. He didn't relish the thought of confronting his sister or her formidable nurse. He flopped back into the soft mound of his goose down pillows.

He'd not known Hylanya long enough or well enough to guess how poorly she'd react to him reprimanding her. She commanded far more loyalty among the Labaran gentry than did he. If he lost their support it might cost him militia, gold and morale. As much as he wanted this to be a simple matter of right and wrong, he recognized that it wasn't. He couldn't expect Hylanya to simply obey him. And if she didn't, then what would he do?

Skellan pressed his hands over his eyes.

He couldn't just go charging in to the Sun Palace, making demands and threatening dire consequences. He needed to think about this. Needed to figure out some way to manage it with sensitivity. Unfortunately, neither tact nor courtly discretion numbered amoungst his strengths. He was going to have to take time and think hard on how to handle his sister. Which meant doing nothing for the time being at least.

Elezar studied him questioningly.

"I'm attempting to console myself with the thought that at least we all have a common enemy to unite us," Skellan remarked.

Elezar laughed and added, "When you put it that way, we are indeed blessed."

Skellan smiled despite himself. He started to reach for Elezar's bare shoulder but the piercing clang of alarm bells brought both himself and Elezar up to their feet. Skellan reached out to his wards and found them undisturbed, while

Elezar snatched up the white bearskin from the foot of the bed and strode to the window to peer down to the grounds below.

"The stockade." Elezar relaxed. "It looks like the guard taking Bois his breakfast noticed he's gone missing."

Skellan dropped back down to his bedside and pulled his dog skin cloak around his naked shoulders.

"I suppose I should send for the sheriff... I mean, after I'm informed that Bois has broken free."

"After would certainly seem much less suspicious than before." The morning light burned away the stern shadows of Elezar's face lending a boyish mirth to his grin. Skellan tossed a pillow at him, just to indulge himself in the sight of the bearskin falling from Elezar's body as he reflexively knocked the pillow aside.

There were worse ways to start a day, Skellan supposed.

Between them, Elezar and Sheriff Hirbe spent the better half of a day leading their Labaran and Cadeleonian troops on a thorough and perfectly fruitless manhunt. As far as Skellan could tell the result seemed to allay the tensions of nearly the entire populace of the city. Certainly the priests who'd been apprehended at Bishop Palo's townhouse appeared to be relieved when they discovered that they would not have to endure the profane tortures they had envisioned Skellan employing to interrogate them. Though they did suffer several loud dressing-downs from Elezar and two days in the garrison stockade before housing could be secured for all of them.

In the meantime a number of Labaran courtiers who'd previously regarded Skellan with aloof uncertainty now offered him knowing smiles and even winked at him. The master of the Brewers' Guild sent Skellan twelve barrels of his own table beer as well as two cases of sweet butter without any explanation. Not to be outdone, the master of the Butchers' Guild delivered a wagonload of smoked ducks, stuffed geese, sides of boar, and mutton.

Skellan wasn't certain if he or Javier regarded the vast store of meat with greater desire as the heavy wagon rolled across the garrison grounds. The second time they bumped into each other outside the kitchen they'd both been amused to discover the other had stolen a savory pie from the cooling racks. They crouched on the steps, grinning at each other like conspirators as they wolfed down pilfered pasties.

"That was some trick, reaching Elezar on the Old Road," Javier commented to him.

"Not so daring as opening the Old Road to begin with, I'll give you that." Skellan nodded, chewing, and then inquired quietly, "Kiram know you did it?"

"Well, it hasn't really come up in the course of conversation." Javier offered him a guilty smile. "Maybe after all this is over with, I'll mention it."

Skellan had seen enough of Kiram's worry for Javier—not to mention his concern over every detail of the production of fifty pluming torches—to understand the hesitance to add to the master mechanist's tension. Even now Kiram stood before a circle of smiths beside the armory, demonstrating some intricate assembly of tubes and valves. His voice and body conveyed absolute assurance but also the tension of a man who knew that lives, and perhaps an entire city, would depend upon his perfectionism.

Skellan downed the last mouthful of his savory pie, trying not to burn the inside of his mouth on the steaming mushrooms and meat. Javier watched him with such an amused expression that Skellan expected him to add one of the sly teasing remarks that he'd already become known for.

Instead Javier said, "I didn't see it before, but Kiram's right. You do bring out the best in Elezar, you know?"

Skellan hadn't known. He felt his face flushing slightly.

"When he and I kept company, we indulged in more drinking than contemplation and fought simply for the pleasure of beating another fellow down." Javier's gaze drifted from

Skellan to Kiram. His adoration showed clearly. "I'm glad we found other influences in our lives."

Skellan wondered if Elezar would have agreed but thought better of asking. He decided to accept Javier's compliment and enjoy the fact that Javier seemed willing to move beyond the earlier rivalry of their previous conversations.

Though, the change of opinion that startled Skellan most came about much more slowly. He noted it first in one of Elezar's devoted Cadeleonian captains. Normally the man spoke, looked to, and responded only to Elezar. He never displayed open contempt toward Skellan but his actions made it clear that he regarded Elezar his master and endured Skellan's presence out of respect for Lord Grunito. Many of the Cadeleonian soldiers emulated him. Skellan hadn't begrudged them for it. He wasn't their king or commander.

But after Skellan offered both the duke of Rauma and Bishop Palo's niece full run of his Sun Palace and made it clear that he would not forgive any reprisals launched against any Cadeleonian in his county, Captain Tialdo and others like him seemed to go out of their way to offer Skellan greetings and salute him as he passed. The change somewhat unnerved Skellan, and he couldn't help but think he was being set up to be the butt of some practical joke. But the joke never came and twice now Captain Tialdo had actually knelt before Skellan and reported directly to him in Labaran.

Skellan found it amusing to discover that the captain possessed a more refined accent than his own. A day later Elezar mentioned that the man came from a family of scholars and owned the press that produced the Cadeleonian broadsheets for Milmuraille.

"Isn't that the publication that reported me as a half-wild cur?" Skellan asked. He hadn't been offended. It was a fair description.

"I don't think those were the exact words." Elezar scratched at his dark beard. "Yesterday you were designated 'a noble youth of honorable qualities far surpassing the savagery of his ancient bloodline.'"

"What does that even mean?" Skellan asked.

"It means that they're warming to you," Elezar assured him.

The notion reassured him that someday all might be well in his diverse city. He tried to think on it while working himself up to confronting his young sister and her nurse. He'd already allowed himself the excuse of several hectic days to put it off.

And the days as well as most evenings were busy, indeed. He constructed more and more deadly wards, witnessed the new fire guards' first exercises with the flaming geysers of Kiram's pluming torch, greeted a great flotilla of bracken green frogwives, and offered sanctuary to the tribes of Irabiim who fled ahead of the grimma's advancing armies.

Further complications sprouted up from each new occurrence. The Irabiim refugees offered their services as archers but that required troop captains to now communicate not only with Labaran, Cadeleonian, and Mirogoth soldiers, but in Irabiim as well.

The frogwives gladly patrolled the river. However their flagrant pilfering of fish from lines and nets belonging to Milmuraille's fishermen required Skellan to approve compensations from the treasury. That had brought Skellan his first meeting with his own pinch-faced needle of a treasurer.

The pluming torches functioned perfectly but in testing the range of the tremendous flames several of the fire guard nearly incinerated two storehouses of costly silks. Skellan found himself calling upon his treasurer yet again and wondering if the fellow could unclench his jaw enough to eat anything but broth and wafers.

The hectic nature of the last four days had excused his delay in speaking to his sister about freeing her enthralled minions. Up on the city wall in the late afternoon, he told Elezar as much, though Elezar hadn't asked about it. As soon as the words were out of his mouth Skellan felt himself being assessed with a long look.

Beyond the city wall workmen covered the last of the large pit traps that they'd excavated in the open ground between the river and the city. Elezar carefully marked the map he'd drawn up before the workmen hid the traps from sight. When they finished Skellan would weave spells over the chasms and long iron spikes, hiding them from even the gazes of witches.

Elezar wiped the tip of his quill clean and sealed up the bottle of ink that the Sheriff Hirbe had given him. Skellan studied the map and thought, not for the first time, that no matter how rough Elezar might appear the perfection of his script betrayed his cultured upbringing to anyone who cared to take note.

Three men of the city guard passed them on the wall walkway and saluted. Skellan nodded to them but then frowned out at the rolling green waters of the river and the dense forest beyond.

"If you don't want to stop her then you don't have to," Elezar said at last. Skellan took a moment to recall who Elezar might have been talking about then shook his head.

"No. Radulf County and all of Labara is a land of free folk. We may not all speak the same tongue or worship the same gods as but this one thing we all agree upon. No one has the right to enslave another to his or her will." The words came more easily to Skellan than they might have if he hadn't been mulling over ways to broach the subject with his sister.

"Plenty of people seem to think that you have that right," Elezar replied.

"But I shouldn't," Skellan objected. "No one should. That's the letter of the law. More than that it's simply what's right."

A sudden warm wind swirled over them and Elezar stilled the fluttering edge of his map with his hand. A workman on the ground below lost his hat and barely caught it before the breeze carried it out to the river. Skellan watched as the wind tumbled through wild grasses before it turned to whip back up through the dark trees of the Sumar grimma's domain. Everyday strong hot winds rose from the forests of the north and lingered longer. This afternoon sweat prickled beneath Skellan's cloak. Elezar wore his coat open and perspiration beaded the tanned base of his throat.

"If it's the law and your wish as well, then that settles it, doesn't it?" Elezar said. "So what is it that you're afraid will happen?"

Skellan felt the muscles of his jaw flexing. He didn't want to admit his answer. In part because he didn't want to hear it himself. He knew it was foolish.

"It'll be just like Sarl," Skellan muttered. He stole a glance back at his two guards but both seemed far more interested in the armed men of the watch passing near them than in Skellan's confession.

"Just like Sarl?" Elezar prompted.

"Three years ago she took a liking to brewer and somehow managed to addle him enough that the man couldn't recollect where he lived or his name." Skellan could still remember the raw yearning in Sarl's face as she gazed at the befuddled young man. "She kept him in an alley for nearly two days before her sister came and told me. She didn't want to get Sarl in trouble with their father..."

"And?" Elezar clearly wished to suppress his alarm at the idea but the studied calm in his voice gave him away to Skellan.

"She cried," Skellan admitted. "Not a mere tear or two, but truly wept as if I'd ripped her heart in two when I broke her spell. Then she was furious. Spitting curses at me, wishing me dead, and then bursting into tears every time I tried to explain. It was months before she could bring herself to even smile at me and I'd known Sarl for years. Think of how much worse Hylanya might take me doing much the same to her."

"Well, she's not likely to be happy about it," Elezar replied with a shrug but then he looked troubled. "What became of the brewer? Did he regain his senses?"

"He recovered quick enough and staggered back home to his wife with the usual story of being snatched by a witch. He's still well as far as I know."

Skellan supposed he ought to have paid the fellow more mind, but he'd had his own share of troubles at the time. Food had been deathly scarce that winter and Cire had threatened to toss him out if he'd even thought of downing one of her many plump rats.

Elezar folded his map of the pit traps and slipped it into the pocket of his coat. Then he carefully tucked his quill pen into its case and secreted that away too.

"I just have to do it." Skellan resolved though he couldn't muster any enthusiasm.

"Does it have to be you?" Elezar asked.

"What? Who else would tell her?"

Elezar shrugged, which Skellan felt wasn't the most useful of responses.

"I won't profess to know much about the mysteries of young women's hearts," Elezar said. "But it seems like someone closer to her might know better how to talk to her. Her mother—"

"Dead. Long dead," Skellan informed him. "And she's just lost her—our—father. And he's the one who gave these people over to her in the first place, which is another reason I can't imagine her taking this well."

"I know the woman who birthed her died," Elezar replied. "But having watched her and Peome, I'd say that the woman who raised her is still very much alive. If anyone holds greater sway over Lady Hylanya than her father, it would be Peome."

Skellan paused to consider that.

"Maybe…" Skellan conceded. He rested his distracted gaze upon the long shining red strings of spells woven across the wood and stone of the walls surrounding them. "It's a lot to ask."

"A less daunting task for the woman who brought Lady Hylanya up than it would be for you. Lady Hylanya's poise at such a young age speaks of someone holding her to a stringent standard. I'd wager that Peome's already well versed in dealing with her," Elezar replied. Then he added, "Half of good governance is knowing what to delegate to whom."

"There's a clever proverb," Skellan said. "Or did you make it up for the occasion?"

Elezar shook his head. "It's one of my mother's favorite sayings."

❧

.Peome met Skellan several hours later at the eastern watchtower of the city wall, where Skellan leaned out, studying the wild clouds and bolts of brilliant lightning that lit the horizon. The light of witchflames gushed up in brilliant geysers as Onelsi and Ylva drew near and the warm winds of spring clashed with wet storms of autumn. Not far behind them, great banks of sleet and snow swallowed sky and land, turning everything barren white.

No wonder the Irabiim fled.

Soon, he expected, wild beasts too would take flight before the violent storms and some no doubt would be driven straight at the fortifications of Milmuraille. Catching brief flashes of the three grimma's witchflames made his eyes burn and set his ears ringing in a way that made his teeth ache.

At his back an entirely different sensation shivered up his spine. The deathly whispers of Bahiim magic swirled through the waters lapping the city docks. He trusted Javier and recognized that he was most qualified to waken the ancient Bahiim ward that once protected the harbor. Still it felt unnerving to have the white flames of Javier's shajdi twining through his own wards like a spider creeping across his skin.

He wasn't in the best state to meet with Hylanya's nurse.

He noted that she'd gone out of her way to appear even more unassuming than usual. Neither bright plumes nor shining metal threadwork adorned her simple russet dress and scarlet robe. The jade rings encircling her thumbs comprised the only jewelry she wore. Even the delicate silk shawl draped over her shoulders boasted only a trim of needlework. Her steel gray hair glinted like brushed pewter beneath the brown weave of her woolen snood.

"You sent for me, Count Radulf." She curtsied gracefully.

"I did. Look out there." Skellan gestured to the east and Peome gazed out with a grim expression. Despite the afternoon heat she drew her shawl closer around her shoulders.

"If we cannot find a way to defeat them soon their mere presence may destroy many crops," Peome commented.

Skellan hadn't been thinking of farmlands or crops, but he realized at once that Peome had aptly assessed the situation. The thought that he might not only be facing the grimma's armies but that he and his people might well starve come winter did little to lift Skellan's mood.

"I have enough hardship to contend with just preparing for them," Skellan said. "I don't need assassinations and half-mad mobs tearing the town apart on top of everything else."

Peome's calm expression didn't alter. She simply inclined her head in the slightest of nods. Which, as responses went, Skellan thought, didn't give him much to work himself up against. Still he pushed on.

"I won't have citizens of my county enthralled, not even by my own sister. Is that understood?"

That at last sparked a response. Peome leveled a cold stare in his direction and very deliberately turned the jade ring on her right thumb. The air between them trembled with the faintest vibrations and the fine hair along Skellan's arms and neck rose with prickling alarm.

"I'm not certain that I know what you mean, my lord. But I am willing to accept whatever punishment you feel is fitting."

"For fuck's sake," Skellan growled. "Can we not waste time playing nob games, pretending like we're talking about some other bunch of people or speculating about what might happen if someone doesn't do what someone else wishes? I'm putting this to you upright and honest."

Peome opened her mouth as if to argue but then pressed her lips closed and simply nodded.

"I truly like Hylanya. I don't want to hurt her," Skellan said. "But I will if I have to."

Peome straightened, her hands lifting slightly from her side as sparks of magic hummed up from her hands and set her rings glinting. Elezar had called it right enough. The look she gave Skellan was as ferocious and any devoted mother's. In that moment Skellan felt no doubt that Peome would fight him even to her dying breath if she thought he meant to harm Hylanya.

The challenge should have outraged him, but instead a strange ache, half admiration and half envy, filled him. Hylanya inspired such devotion in a woman who was not even her own flesh and blood while his own mother had threatened to devour him hardly a week past.

"I don't want to hurt Hylanya. That's why I've summoned you, Peome," Skellan said in a more casual tone. "I need you to break the thralls. Free the folk—"

"You would have me strip her of her defenders!" Peome's outrage rang clearly enough to draw the uneasy attention of Skellan's two guards. Peome seemed to catch herself at the very same time. She averted her angry gaze from Skellan's face, pretending to straighten her shawl.

"She has defenders," Skellan said. "She is genuinely loved and cherished far beyond anything that a thrall could inspire. You know that."

Peome plucked at the delicate pattern of green vines and red wolves stitched into the edge of her shawl.

"If I refuse?" Peome asked.

"Then I will tear the spells to shreds myself," Skellan said and that brought Peome's head up fast. Skellan thought that she searched his face for some sign of a bluff.

"I know that would hurt her," Skellan repeated before Peome's horror could flare to anger. "That's why I'm asking you to do this. Or better yet, to convince her to release them willingly. If she did that then she wouldn't suffer any ill effects and she could feel proud that she did the right thing and gave those entrusted to her their freedom."

"You really think that anyone with the power to enthrall another would choose not to? How do you imagine your ancestors built this entire county? How do you think your own father ruled over so many people?" Peome shook her head. "How can you, of all people, be so naïve about the importance of protecting the heirs of this county?"

"I'm not naïve," Skellan replied coolly. He doubted that Peome could truly understand. She'd not grown up among the powerless on the streets of Milmuraille. She'd not heard the raw sorrow reverberating through Bone-crusher's lullabies nor witnessed the desolation that remained of Little Dreamer's life.

"I've seen what a thrall steals from brave, proud folk," Skellan said. "And I think that Hylanya deserves to know that she is worthy of real devotion, gladly given."

To her credit, Peome seemed to consider this last suggestion. Skellan pushed on.

"A thrall can be broken or even turned by another more powerful witch. But real devotion—devotion like yours—is strong enough to fight even the commands of a thrall. I don't think that even if they took this city the grimma could turn your heart against Hylanya. But if it were merely a thrall that commanded your loyalty then I have no doubt that the grimma could use your hands to slit my sister's throat."

Peome paled slightly.

Skellan gestured to the writhing clouds in the east.

"Even if you don't give a piss for me or the common law, think about the danger Hylanya will be in. What good will sea of enthralled defenders do her when the grimma turn them into wolves slavering for her blood?"

Peome's gaze remained fixed on the eastern storms. She shuddered as if already feeling the force of those driving winds and walls of sleet.

"You want to protect her." Skellan closed his eyes against the flare of an immense bolt of gold lightning. He focused on Peome. "I want that as well, but enslaving men and women isn't the way to do it."

Slowly, Peome pulled her gaze from the eastern horizon to study Skellan. He wondered if she actually saw him or if afterimages of lightning danced through her vision.

"I will have her release those enthralled to her," Peome assured him.

"Thank you," Skellan said and he meant it.

Peome gave a soft indignant sound under her breath and then executed another perfect curtsy. Skellan suspected that a less refined woman would have told him he could go fuck himself and his thanks.

Well, she didn't have to like him, so long as she did right by Hylanya.

"If I may be so forward as to inquire," Peome's tone and expression were again proper as prayers, "when do you plan to release your champion, my lord?"

Skellan frowned at the smug smile Peome allowed herself.

Why did everyone assume that Elezar was in his thrall? Was it so inconceivable that a man of Elezar's qualities could simply care for him?

Probably.

Skellan exhaled heavily, trying to put his annoyance aside.

"I do not hold a thrall over Elezar Grunito or over any other man or woman," Skellan informed her and she did look surprised. Out of the corner of his eye Skellan thought he noticed one of his two guards shoot the other the pleased grin of a man who'd just won a wager.

"But he *is* bound to you," Peome stated. "You can't be such a fool as to allow him to range freely."

"He chose to be my champion of his own free will. Beyond that, what we share is no one else's business," Skellan replied with finality. If he hadn't been able to bring himself to admit to Cire about the old spells he'd woven between himself and Elezar, he certainly wasn't going to confess to Peome.

She contemplated him and then her gaze shifted, moving around him as if tracing his outline against the afternoon sky. Skellan didn't know what she discerned, but her expression softened very slightly.

"As you wish, my lord." She curtsied again, sinking low.

Skellan wished that she'd simply leave him alone. They weren't either of them enjoying each other's company. Then he recalled that it was his responsibility to dismiss those he'd summoned. He bade Peome farewell. It was only as he watched her descend down the stone staircase and cross to her carriage that he recognized the finely attired man awaiting her. Skellan met Rafale's gaze and the two of them stared at each other for a few still moments.

Anger still churned through Skellan at the thought of all the lives that Rafale had been willing to sacrifice, but at the same time he missed the other man's easy company and wit. Years of friendship couldn't simply be wiped from his heart and mind. He couldn't help but notice the way Rafale's expression brightened at the sight of him. It was almost painful to recognize so much longing in his handsome face.

Perhaps Rafale, like Bois, had been controlled by the will of another—maybe Peome or even Skellan's own father. Maybe Rafale wasn't—

Skellan realized he was making excuses for Rafale and stopped himself. He knew Rafale too well to believe that he was anyone's pawn. He'd witnessed Rafale smiling and flirting with Cire while luring her into a trap. Rafale had told him to his face that he would have seen Cire and the rest of the street witches dead if Skellan hadn't killed the demon lord. He hadn't been a man fighting a thrall with all his will.

No, there was no excusing the man, no matter how fond of him Skellan felt.

As soon as Peome took note of the two of them, she caught Rafale's sleeve and pulled him toward the carriage, shaking her head and muttering words that Skellan imagined were none too flattering to himself. Then Peome cast a quick glance back at him and to Skellan's surprise she sent a blessing whirling on the air to add to those already protecting him.

❧

Standing at the water's edge in Milmuraille's harbor, Elezar did his best not to laugh. A particularly persistent frogwife had been attempting to coax Kiram into climbing onto her broad, yellow green back for a swim for the last two hours. She floated lazily alongside the pier where Kiram and Elezar crouched. Some forty feet out Javier's small boat bobbed on the deep emerald water. The frogwife grinned with teeth like fishing hooks and the membranes covering her bulging yellow eyes flickered against the bright afternoon light.

"You are so slender, and I am powerful as a waterfall," the frogwife teased. "I could carry you and your husband down to find the best oysters and fattest toads."

"Tempting, but I don't think your other mates would appreciate my company, much less my husband's." Kiram nodded to the three kelpy masses clinging to leathery skin of the frogwife's muscular back. A head as delicate and small as a cat's raised up, blinking at both Kiram and Elezar, and bared rows of tiny, sawblade teeth before settling back down into the shadows of the frogwife's cascading green hair. The frogwife produced a series of burbling sounds, which Elezar had learned were a kind of laughter. She took the pulley rope Kiram held out for her and dove beneath the dark waves. Seconds later she surfaced alongside the prow of the skiff on which Javier knelt. Captain Wirret herself steadied the narrow boat while Javier skimmed his hands over the water.

After a few words with Javier the frogwife and several others of her kind dived down into the depths below. Pulley rope spooled through Elezar's gloved hands as the frogwife swam deeper. All along the pier, other men and women of the river guard fed out similar lines.

Cire knelt ten feet behind Kiram and Elezar, listening to the squeaks of the dozens of dock rats that crept to her from beneath the pier like nervous informants. Elezar found it strange to observe the sheer volume of rodents that came and went around Cire. They'd been invaluable in searching through the hundred-year-old remains of abandoned dock buildings as well as the more recently collapsed bell towers and warehouses. The rats in their hundreds had located the eroded markers of an abandoned Bahiim holy circle as well as the more recent Cadeleonian carvings of four-pointed stars.

Cire rewarded each of the rats with seeds as they swarmed around her feet and then skittered away.

Behind that strange scene numerous Irabiim gathered and gazed out at Javier. Others stood on the city wall with their bows. A number of curious Labarans congregated along the dockside street also, as did a variety of bored sailors. Even one of the Cadeleonian priests who had served Bishop Palo stood amidst the crowd. His black and violet robe looked odd paired with his muddy green fishing boots and the Labaran tome clutched in his knobby hands.

The balding priest gave an encouraging nod when he noticed Elezar looking at him. Elezar returned the homely fellow's smile, relieved that this one priest, at least, was not intent upon wishing him straight to the three hells.

Strangely, this Cadeleonian priest had been the one to suggest their enterprise. Under Bishop Palo's direction he'd spent the last thirty years studying the mythic history of Milmuraille's waterways. He'd never discovered proof of the Holy Savior's presence in Radulf County as the bishop had hoped, but he had come across several detailed descriptions of an immense golden seal that previous priests had placed in the harbor to suppress the shining power of an ancient Bahiim holy circle.

While his fellow priests had been burning letters in Palo's townhouse, this single priest had apparently been holed up in a Labaran rain temple, poring over ancient tomes and mapping out the markers that would reveal the location of the gold seal.

Something about the priest's guileless smile and political obliviousness reminded Elezar a little of his own father and restored a bit of Elezar's pride in his fellow Cadeleonians.

From time to time Sheriff Hirbe or one of his deputies broke up a scuffle amongst the folk gathered along the dock road. Most quarrels seemed to be between vendors selling snail skewers and table beer. The majority of the onlookers remained rather subdued. Some even wandered off to the nearest taverns. Elezar didn't blame them. So far all they'd witnessed had been a flurry of rats, followed by dozens of men and women spooling out huge lengths of rope to be fed through pulleys. The highlight of the day so far was likely Javier directing frogwives but even their work took place deep at the harbor's floor far beyond the sight of common folk.

Kiram yawned and beside him Elezar did too.

"It could be interesting to see how the Bahiim power resurfaces once the seal is lifted, I think," Kiram commented.

"Will it?" Elezar asked. "You think we'll see anything?"

"Not as much as Javier will or your Skellan might. At the very least we ought to witness a few sparks when the old Bahiim power is freed." Absently, Kiram scratched at a bit of rust marring the pulley wheel. Machine oil spattered his dark brow and glistened from several of his short gold curls. He'd likely come straight from his workshop to assist Javier.

"What I find fascinating is how power in so-called holy places can often be stored for years on end without any worshipers or practitioners maintaining it," Kiram stated and his bright blue eyes seemed to gaze far past Elezar. "I assert that the very fact that a wide variety of different religious and mystic groups tap into the same sources of power demonstrates that there's a universal, physical source. Which I suggest indicates that what we think of as spiritual forces are in fact natural aspects of our world. If I'm correct, then they could be harnessed by mechanical means and put to work for populations regardless of their religious practices."

Elezar spent a while blinking as he tried to understand Kiram's beyond-blasphemous line of reasoning then commented, "It's good to know that five years traveling with Javier hasn't made you any less of a mechanist."

"Thank you," Kiram said, grinning. Then his gaze shifted to Elezar's collarbones. "What about you?"

"I never was a mechanist," Elezar replied.

"No, but you weren't so inclined to wear pendants last I saw you," Kiram commented.

Elezar wasn't certain of what he meant until he realized that the pendant Nestor had given him showed where he'd opened the front of his shirt. Elezar lifted the charm and turned it once from the four-pointed Cadeleonian star to the Bahiim tree and then let it fall back against his skin.

"I haven't attended chapel in five years. Nestor gave me this."

Kiram's expression warmed at the mention of Elezar's closest brother. The two of them had been best friends at school. Nestor often spoke of Kiram and had made a habit of visiting the Kir-Zaki family regularly since Kiram and Javier had fled Cadeleon.

"He converted secretly," Elezar whispered. "He and his wife Riossa both took oaths before you uncle's partner, Alizadeh."

"Why would they?" Kiram looked startled and then concerned. "That could prove extremely dangerous for them both."

"If the wrong person found out, yes." Elezar hated to think of that but he took consolation in the relative permissiveness of his native city. "But since the night the Circle of Red Oaks lit up with Bahiim blessings things have been changing some in Anacleto. A good number of Cadeleonians have gone to the

Red Oaks, witnessed some miracle or received treatments, and then secretly converted. It's becoming fashionable in a number of wealthy circles."

"Fashionable? Really?" Kiram frowned and then turned his attention to Javier. "But legally a converted Cadeleonian could face charges of heresy."

"Unfortunately, yes." Elezar fed out another yard of rope then glanced to Kiram's solemn face. "At least things seem to be changing, if only slowly."

"True, true," Kiram said. "Do you think that by the time you become earl the laws will have altered enough to allow Javier to go home again?"

Elezar felt the responsibility behind Kiram's question. He rarely considered himself as a future earl because he took no joy in pondering his father's demise. He was a simple man but also kind and unabashed in his affection for his wife and children. Still, Elezar owed Kiram an answer.

"If they haven't, I'll change them myself," Elezar answered. "I'll do everything I'm able to ensure that you and Javier always have a home."

He wasn't so naïve as to imagine that holy law could be easily altered nor that the royal bishop wouldn't bring the full power of the Holy Cadeleonian Church against him and his holdings, but Anacleto had stood against church and crown before. And in any case he knew that if he didn't challenge the heresy laws then Nestor would. Elezar didn't want to leave such a battle to his gentle younger brother.

Kiram interrupted his thoughts with a dry laugh. Elezar turned to Kiram and saw that he still watched Javier but now with a grin. On the skiff Javier looked to be whiling away his boredom by blowing into the wings of a little cloud imp that appeared intent upon sticking a tentacle in his nostril. Another cloud imp nested in his long black braids.

"Likely one week after returning home he'd be packed up and riding north again to play with everything wild and ancient here," Kiram commented.

Remembering Javier's earlier comment that he would have chosen a life of exile even knowing the hardship of it, Elezar thought that Kiram was likely correct.

"And there's my position to consider at well. Our townhouse here is actually wonderful," Kiram went on. "A little plumbing and I might even be able to convince my relatives to pay me a visit someday."

There was that. Kiram's brother owned a merchant ship and Kir-Zaki candies sold well here in Milmuraille.

"You find a way to install plumbing here in the north and you'll likely be the richest man in Radulf County."

"That does appeal, I must admit—" The rest of Kiram's musing was cut short by an excited shout from Javier as all six frogwives resurfaced. Having secured their ropes to the seal buried in the muck at the floor of the harbor, they swam back to the pier. As soon as they were clear, Elezar and the rest of the river guard set to work at the pulleys.

At first Elezar felt as though he strained to haul an entire ship up from the bottom. Then, with a jolt, the weight far below gave way. Pulley wheels creaked as soaking rope rolled through them. Elezar heaved hand over hand, feeling the resistance grow lighter as the seal rose through the water. At last he and a dozen other men and women hauled the huge, filthy disk to the surface.

It looked only a little larger than the lid of a beer keg, but its incredible weight betrayed the pure gold from which it had been cast. Silt and kelp dribbled off as it rocked between the four lead ropes, which had been threaded through four rings on the edges of the disk. At last the seal slammed to rest on the pier. As it struck the wooden planks hunks of gray mud fell away, exposing a gleaming design of raised stars and ornate Cadeleonian script.

Doubtless the value and beauty of the seal would have held the attention of everyone gathered if it hadn't been for the radiant burst of frothing white light that shot up from the harbor only an arm's length from where Javier stirred the waters with his hands.

The light flared. As Elezar stared down, the murky waves of the harbor turned perfectly clear. Hundreds of fish darted and scattered. A small, speckled ray fluttered from the muddy floor and drifted into the shadow beneath a moored ship. The light radiated from a ring of shining green coral. Frogwives dived down and chased each other between the arching branches of the coral as tiny gold lights drifted up from the water like a school of luminous jellyfish.

Similar golden lights had fallen from the sky to illuminate Anacleto five years ago when Javier had ignited the Circle of Red Oaks in the sacred grove there.

"Blessings! That one is for strength and I think the other means wisdom." Kiram leaned over the edge of the pier and scooped up two of the bright symbols in his cupped palm. The signs glowed against the dark skin of Kiram's hand as he reached out and carefully poured the shining symbol for wisdom into Elezar's palm. It trembled against Elezar's skin, shining brightly, but then stilled and seemed to fade into the calluses of Elezar's hand. Mere months before Elezar knew he would have been horrified at the thought of the tiny, foreign blessing dissolving into his flesh, but now he accepted the small spell for the gift it was.

Beneath the water, frogwives captured the drifting gold symbols by the dozens and soon the blessings glinted all across their green bodies. Two frogwives swam to Javier's skiff and splashed shining symbols up onto him. He retaliated but with a broad grin.

Elezar squinted down at the circle of coral as it dimmed and shadows of the harbor closed back over it.

"Who makes a holy place that far under water?" Elezar wondered aloud.

"Frogwives," Kiram replied. "According to Javier, back before the Mirogoth invasion several tribes of frogwives were converted by Bahiim. They created their own holy circles in rivers and lakes as well as this on here in the harbor of Milmuraille."

Elezar wasn't certain why but it had never occurred to him to wonder about the religions that mythical creatures might follow. He supposed it was because he was used to thinking of them a symbols of religions themselves.

"Strange," Elezar said.

"I know, I thought so too," Kiram agreed. "But Javier seems to have been right, and since the circle is now reignited, it should protect the harbor and the mouth of the river at least."

Elezar wondered what Skellan might make of all this. He'd probably be far less surprised than either Elezar or Kiram. Though, the sheer volume of gold they'd managed to haul up from the bottom of the harbor would likely please him—or at least please him in that it would offer him some respite from the long-suffering expression of his treasurer.

Elezar walked back to where the seal lay. Thick as his forearm and as wide round as a shield, the thing likely weighed more than Elezar could hope to lift on his own. Though he supposed if he could leverage it up onto its narrow side he might simply be able to roll it along like a wheel. He noticed Sheriff Hirbe standing beside Cire, eyeing the seal as well. The breeze rolling off the water tousled his white beard.

"I've sent for an oxcart," Sheriff Hirbe called.

Elezar nodded.

Then alarmed shouts arose from the crowd gathered on the road alongside the dock. Both Elezar and the sheriff turned to look. People darted and pulled one another aside as four roan horses pulled a stately scarlet and gold carriage through their midst. The carriage hardly stopped before Hylanya bounded from it, followed directly by her three strapping swordsmen. Two ladies-in-waiting trailed them with nervous expressions.

Hylanya appeared furious, a snarl on her angular face and

her hands clenched into fists. She stalked straight for Elezar. The swordsmen behind her moved oddly to Elezar's eye and their expressions seemed a strange mix of confusion and anger.

All of them clutched their sword hilts, though the youngest of the three gripped his sword arm with his other hand as if fighting to restrain it. The other two men were red-faced and sweating profusely.

"My lady—" Sheriff Hirbe bowed low but Hylanya swept past him, her glower fixed upon Elezar.

"Where is Lady Peome?" Hylanya demanded. "What lies have you told Hilthorn that he's summoned her from me?"

"I've told no lies, my lady." Elezar resisted the reflex to bow. He wasn't about to expose his neck to this seething girl and the three swordsmen clearly in her furious thrall. "Skellan only wished to speak with Peome—"

"Don't lie to me!" Hylanya's pale eyes glittered and Elezar realized that she was on the verge of tears. "She only acted to protect me and this city! But you told, didn't you?"

Elezar wracked his mind to work out what confidence she thought he'd betrayed but the flash of the eldest swordsman's blade distracted him. Elezar's own hand went to his sword hilt. He read horror in the other man's sweat-beaded face.

Something tiny and furry skittered behind Hylanya's party but Elezar didn't dare look away from any of the three swordsmen. He heard Kiram rise behind him but didn't look back.

"I called you to me in confidence." Hylanya jabbed a long finger at him. "I trusted you not to tell—"

"I've not betrayed your trust," Elezar insisted. The only confidence she'd trusted to him had been her wish to have Bishop Palo murdered. Elezar lowered his voice because the last thing he wanted was for Hylanya's or Peome's involvement to be exposed to every gawker on the street behind them. "Peome is not being punished for anything. Skellan—Count Radulf only wants to speak with her."

Hylanya shook her head. Her long braids glinted in the sharp sunlight like copper. Something—or more likely someone—had stoked her fear and outrage to a murderous fury. Elezar thought he understood the ferocity of emotions lashing through her young heart and he recognized how truly deadly she might become.

"I don't believe you," Hylanya snapped. "I might be young, Lord Grunito, but I am not without my resources. I have been warned against you and I will not allow you to harm those I love!"

The second of her three swordsmen drew his blade with a shaking hand.

Elezar's pulse doubled, pounding feverishly through him. He didn't want to kill these men, but neither was he willing to be cut down. He drew his own sword. He'd be wise to charge now and cut down the other man while he still struggled. Elezar knew as much but he couldn't bring himself to act.

Then at the edge of his sight he noted dozens of rats scurrying between the swordsmen's boots. They gnawed furiously at something, but Elezar couldn't see what. All at once both the older swordsmen staggered and stumbled. One fell to his knees while the other dropped his sword and clutched his chest as if he feared his heart had been torn from it. The youngest of the three swordsmen bounded between Elezar and Hylanya with his hands thrown out wide. He dropped to his knees before Hylanya and bowed his blond head.

"My lady, Lord Grunito speaks the truth. Rafale has misled you with whispered rumors and petty insinuations. Lord Grunito is not your enemy. He has done nothing to threaten your brother or this city."

Hylanya's pale gaze darted from the kneeling young swordsman to Elezar and then back.

"I beg you, Lady Hylanya, do not use us to harm an innocent man," the young swordsman said. "If you do, justice will rule against you and we will be cut down to a man. Please, my lady, have mercy."

"How can he be right?" Hylanya demanded, jabbing her finger again at Elezar. Tears spilled down her cheeks, but it was frustration that rang through her voice. "How can you take his side against me? Stand up and obey me! Do as I command!"

"Forgive me," the young swordsman murmured. "But I will not."

"How..." Hylanya began but then her voice trailed away as she looked down in horror at the pack of rats fleeing from around her feet. They raced back to Cire, who shook her head at Hylanya. Then she squared her tiny shoulders and strode to Hylanya's side.

"I am truly sorry for all that you've endured, Lady Hylanya. But no man, not even as charming a scoundrel as our Rafale, is worth losing your honor and dignity over. He's definitely not worth making an enemy of your own brother for."

"I don't..." Hylanya appeared suddenly at a loss. "I haven't—"

"Oh, I know you mean no real harm. Your heart is in turmoil and you've just lost your dear father. The whole city has been in such a state of confusion that I doubt anyone told you that your brother cannot abide the holding of any creature in a thrall." Cire cocked her head slightly at Hylanya's shocked expression. "It's as I thought. You've not been properly informed. I'm sure our Rafale means well but sometimes he exaggerates for dramatic effect and can give a lady something of the wrong impression."

Hylanya towered over Cire and yet she allowed Cire to take her hand. Cire smiled up at her with a sympathetic expression.

"Let's the two of us have a more private talk, shall we?" Holding Hylanya's hand, Cire turned her away from Elezar and led her back towards her carriage. "Now I've known both Rafale and Skellan for years, my dear, and I think there are a few details that must be cleared up. I'm sure the Lady Peome will join us shortly and we can make an evening of it." Cire glanced over her shoulder to the swordsmen and called, "Gentlemen, come along. Count Radulf's sister should not travel unguarded."

At that the three of them roused themselves and hurried to the carriage. They and the ladies-in-waiting followed Cire and Hylanya back into the carriage and they rode away, just like that.

Elezar stood, stunned by the sudden dissipation of what he'd thought would be a mortal threat. Across from him Sheriff Hirbe too looked dazed as he watched Hylanya's carriage disappear around a corner.

"What on earth was all that about?" Kiram asked.

Elezar turned back and to his surprise noted that not only had Kiram drawn his own short sword but that Javier had joined him in guarding Elezar's back. Water dripped from his hair and clothes. He pressed his pale hands together and the white light shining in his palms faded.

"That girl is going to be a very powerful witch when she's full grown," Javier commented as he squeezed excess water from one of his thick black braids. "If Cire hadn't begun the delicate work of unraveling the spells, I don't think I could have broken the thrall Hylanya held over those three men without killing them or her."

"I'm not sure that Count Radulf would let us keep our townhouse if you killed his sister," Kiram remarked.

"You're the one who drew a blade," Javier replied. "You even beat Elezar to it, I might point out."

"Well, a Hellion doesn't let another stand alone, does he?" Kiram sheathed his sword with a self-conscious speed. Javier grinned at Kiram as if he'd just won some old and long-ranging argument.

Elezar wouldn't have blamed Kiram if he had left him to fight alone, but it touched him that Kiram hadn't. He could hardly credit that Javier had obviously dived from his boat and swum the harbor to come to his aid. Belatedly Elezar realized that he'd grown so accustomed to facing threats alone that he hadn't even considered that he might call upon allies. He shouldn't have felt so moved—except that for years he'd lived knowing he'd wronged both Kiram and Javier and feeling certain that neither of them would ever forgive him, much less defend him.

"You've made Elezar blush!" Javier laughed and Elezar felt his face heat further.

Fortunately Captain Wirret's expansive swearing drew attention from him. She tied off her boat and then climbed up onto the pier. She pinned Javier with a disapproving glower that would have done Elezar's mother proud.

"Next time give us a warning before you bound off the prow and completely off balance the boat, will you, Master Bahiim?"

"My apologies," Javier replied. "I was rather caught up in the moment."

"Mother's blood, did you really think that you were the only one who could come to our Elezar's rescue?" Captain Wirret jerked her thumb to the harpooners and sailors still standing ready in their boats. Elezar recognized Sarl among them. Then Captain Wirret pointed up to the line of archers on the wall. "That young swordsman of Lady Hylanya's spoke the sure truth when he said that he and his fellows would be struck dead if they moved against our count's man."

Then to Elezar's surprise Captain Wirret threw her arm around him and offered him a bracing, brief hug. The scent of smoked kelp and leather drifted off her.

"No one does our count's man in while I and my troops are on hand. Never you fear, lad."

"Thank you," Elezar managed. He hadn't been called a lad since he'd been twelve years old. Captain Wirret released him with slap on the back and the sort of encouraging grin she might have offered to reassure a boy after he'd skinned his knee in a fall.

Beside them Kiram pulled Javier's soaked cloak off his shoulders and set to work wringing the water from it while Javier peered down into the harbor.

"I might as well dive down now. I'm already wet," Javier said. "I'd love to touch the holy circle and feel how it reaches through the waters."

"If you must," Kiram replied. "But if you're carried off by a frogwife don't expect me to come dog-paddling to your rescue."

"You know you would." Javier shot Kiram an arrogant and self-satisfied smile. He caressed Kiram's cheek. Then he stepped to the edge of the pier. With a motion of his hands he lit a halo of white light around his body and dived in, moving through the water like a falling star streaking into the darkness of the night sky.

"Well, that's certainly a man with no fear of contracting leech fever." Sheriff Hirbe strode to join them. "Mistress Cire wasn't half-daring either, was she?"

"I think she saved several lives just now," Elezar agreed. Though he still felt mystified as to exactly what she'd done. Had she placed some kind of spell on Hylanya or had her sisterly warmth and certainty won the girl over?

"I'd hoped to have a word with her about a couple thefts—" Sheriff Hirbe cut himself off as he noted the concern in Elezar's expression. "Not because she's a thief! No, no. It's simply that there's hardly a move made in this city that one of her rats hasn't witnessed. She's already proved very helpful to me and my deputies."

"She's pretty as a painted doll and ripe for a rich man's wedding bed as well, if her old uncle tells true." Captain Wirret grinned at the sheriff and to Elezar's surprise the old man's cheeks colored slightly.

He drew near to Elezar and dropped his voice low. "Do you want me to send my deputies to charge Rafale with conspiring against you? If so we'll have to act fast before he can gather his friends and their wives to his defense."

Elezar hadn't even thought to press charges. Briefly he entertained the image of Rafale tossed on his overconfident ass in a jail cell. But he doubted that retaliating would do anything except bring Rafale more attention and allow him to stir up further trouble. And the last thing Skellan needed was to have his exhausting work building wards around the city bogged down by the petty rivalry of his lovers. Hells, the last thing *he* needed was to have the city gossips making even more of his relationship with Skellan than they already had done.

"No," Elezar decided. "It would cause more trouble than he's worth as far as I'm concerned."

Sheriff Hirbe looked like he might argue but then nodded.

"Wise choice, I say," Captain Wirret put in. "When we're on the brink of war the last thing any of us wants is trouble amongst ourselves. You'd think Rafale would realize as much."

"Aye, you'd think." Sheriff Hirbe pushed back his bright cap and ran his fingers through the curling shock of his thick white hair in a hopeless attempt to smooth it down. "But then you'd imagine that with the threat of the grimma overrunning our city, folk wouldn't bother with murdering and robbing each other, but I can assure you they still do."

"People rarely change their characters even when they do themselves nothing but harm," Kiram said. Then he looked up from the water to Elezar. "A history teacher of ours used to claim that war and hardship always brings out the best in men and women, but I've not found that to be particularly true. From what I've seen, times of crisis simply strip a person's character down to its purest qualities. Some people prove themselves to be self-serving khivash while others reveal truly courageous natures."

"Aye," Sheriff Hirbe agreed. "That reminds me of a saying my own mum used to quote to no end. '*When you can least afford to be brave that's when it's most important that you are.*'"

"A fine proverb, that," Captain Wirret said. "But I'd counter it with my own dear, departed mother's wisdom. *There's no philosophical conversation that doesn't go down better with a round of beer.*"

Sheriff Hirbe conceded that the captain's dear, departed mother had been a wise woman indeed. And that he could use a table beer if the captain was paying. Kiram demurred, prefering to await Javier's return. Then they turned expectantly to Elezar. Eyeing the two of them, Elezar got the distinct feeling that they would drink him to a state of incoherent admissions.

Thankfully Elezar's cavalrymen arrived moments later, summoning him at once to Count Radulf's side.

"With allies like these…" Skellan muttered as he watched Peome's carriage pull away. He lifted his gaze up to the breaks of blue sky overhead. Something flashed like a fleck of mica. Then a second glint lit up. In an instant the tiny flashes arced and split like forks of lightning. They struck the ground below Skellan with a thunderous boom that brought watchmen and Skellan's guards to attention.

The older of Skellan's guards lunged in front of him, shielding Skellan with his own body, while the younger man bounded to the head of the stairs to block any attack from below.

All of them stared down to the grounds, as the clouds of dust settled to reveal Eski and Magraie mounted atop their shining wethra-steeds. Both riders lifted their faces to Skellan. They looked hollow eyed and weary.

"The Sumar grimma is coming," Eski called.

A sickening chill clenched through Skellan's guts.

"When—where is she?"

"Now!" Magraie pointed to the north. "We could only keep an hour ahead of her. She'll be at river any time."

Skellan heard the whispered oaths of the men around him and he shared their dread but refused to let it show. If she crossed the border of the Raccroc River, a hundred years of truce would be broken. Once she set foot upon Radulf land, her very touch would begin to turn the wood, water, and stone against him. He had to stop her if he could and as soon as he could.

"Call my champion to me at once," Skellan decided. "Tell him we will ride out to meet the Sumar grimma."

"No." Elezar glowered at Skellan like he'd suggested sending infants and ducklings into battle. "Milmuraille is secure and fortified. Riding out from the city to meet the Sumar grimma's forces on open ground is madness."

"She hasn't reached the river yet. If I can get there first—"

"No!" Elezar's voice carried across the wall walkway. Guards, cavalrymen, and even a young girl on the grounds below looked up at them. Elezar lowered his voice but his expression grew all the more dark—late afternoon shadows etching the hard planes of his face into a mask of disapproval. "We'll send scouts to discover the numbers, formations, and kinds of troops we're up against. Then we can decide how best to fight her. Blindly running out there is sheer folly. You could be up against—God knows what. Armed men, bears, wolves, and probably trolls! Skellan, you're too important to risk—"

Skellan didn't want to hear all the reasons Elezar felt he ought to be treated like a precious eggshell. He needed to protect his claim over the Radulf lands. He had to keep the Sumar grimma from setting foot on his soil. Just looking at Elezar's strained expression Skellan knew he wouldn't understand why he could not let any of the grimma set foot here. In fact, hearing Elezar speak, Skellan wondered if Elezar wouldn't rather have trussed him up, carried him back to the garrison, and secured in some padded cupboard for the rest of the war.

Elezar didn't seem willing to acknowledge that only Skellan stood any chance of driving the Sumar grimma back before she or her forces forded the river. Arguing only wasted time.

"I'm going," Skellan stated.

"I can't protect you out in the open. Please—" Elezar's voice softened, but Skellan didn't have patience to listen. They'd squandered too much time already.

He pulled his cloak close and called up the molten heat of his witchflame. Spinning from Elezar's reach, Skellan leapt past his personal guards and the men of the city watch. The muscular flesh of a lean hound enfolded him and carried him down the wall walkway's stairs in great bounds. He hit the grounds and raced out to the open street.

The scents of the surrounding city washed over him, as did the distant sounds of immense timbers across the river cracking to splinters. Something dark and pungent perfumed the northern shore.

Trolls. The Sumar grimma had brought battle trolls.

Skellan raced for the city gates, his muscles drinking power from every cobble his feet lighted upon. He dodged between carts and mounted riders. Upon the walls he heard men shouting from the watchtowers. His nose filled with the sulfurous edge of black powder casks being hauled up the cannons on the wall.

Behind him he heard Elezar swearing and then the thunder of hooves. He didn't look back but threw himself forward, willing the earth and wind to carry him farther and faster with every leap. Skellan cleared the city gates and rushed into the open meadows of wild grasses that rolled from the high ground of the city down to the wide riverbank. Dense walls of dark forest lined the other side of the river.

Ahead of him Skellan saw tall pines shuddering. From behind he felt the ground reverberating with the fast impact of hooves.

"Skellan!" Elezar roared from behind him. "Are you out of your damn mind? You can't fight her alone. At least wait for Javier and Cire!"

Glancing over his shoulder he caught sight of Elezar atop his black charger and signaling to the thunderous line of his cavalrymen. They closed in around Skellan, flanking him, but Skellan didn't slow. Elezar urged his mount up beside Skellan and Skellan feared Elezar might attempt to snatch him up off the ground. But instead Elezar urged his mount ahead. Great clods of grass and mud flew through the air in his wake. The other riders fell in, and Skellan realized that they rode like an arrowhead, before and beside him, with Elezar driving ahead at the very tip.

Before them the trees lining the far bank of the river shook, groaned, and then shattered as two jade green trolls smashed them down. Weedy brush clung to their jagged skulls and carpets of wild grasses flowed over their shoulders. The harpoons and chains rising from their backs shone as if still molten. Both trolls let loose with bone-shaking roars.

Skellan flattened his ears but even so the wave of sound struck him like a burning wind, filled with the thick odors of decaying wood and fermenting fruit. He nearly stumbled but managed to keep moving.

All around him cries of alarm escaped horses and several slowed their gait or turned aside, tossing their heads. Their riders swore and struggled to bring them under control. Only Elezar's black stallion, Cobre, appeared unmoved. He didn't miss a step and from his back Elezar belted out his own frustrated roar, calling his men back to order. The cavalrymen pulled back into formation.

Skellan sprinted onward, praying that his momentum wasn't greater than his abilities. No turning back now. He tore over the warm, grassy earth drawing all the strength he could from it.

The two big trolls hunched like craggy hills at the rolling water's edge. Smooth river stones cracked beneath their weight while tattered branches of broken trees tumbled down from their jagged heads and tangled amidst the harpoons and chains jutting from their backs. Then six snow white bears strode out from the shadows behind the crouching trolls. They prowled up to edge of the riverbank where the soil turned muddy and reeds grew in thick mats.

The bears stared at Elezar, as did the trolls. Skellan felt terrified for him. One blow from those stone fists and Elezar and his mount would be crushed. Neither his sword nor the spear hanging from his saddle would penetrate the hide of a troll.

"If you are going to do something, Skellan, now would be a good time!" Elezar shouted back at him.

And Skellan realized that Elezar didn't have a plan of attack. He and his men had charged out from the protection of the city walls to shield Skellan as best they could. Fear and frustration rolled through Skellan. Why couldn't they have simply let him come alone? Why did they all have to endanger themselves?

"Skellan!" Elezar called again, alarm rising through his voice.

Another troll, this one with nearly twice the bulk of the other two, even heavier than Bone-crusher, strode over the splintered timber. High on the troll's back, with her hands braced between jutting harpoons, stood a lanky, pale woman. Her hair blazed red and rose around her face as if swimming up through a breeze. Skellan knew her at once: his mother, the Sumar grimma.

Polished stones and shining enchantments wreathed her throat and cascaded down her full, naked body like strings of chain mail. Even at a distance and dwarfed by trees and trolls, she seemed to burn against the dull afternoon sky. Halos of emerald light radiated from her like rays of sunlight.

Riders all around Skellan threw their hands up to protect their eyes. Their mounts stumbled and turned their heads away from the ferocity of the Sumar grimma's witchflame. Even Elezar pulled his charger to a halt and shielded his eyes. Cobre snorted and bowed his big head.

"Skellan, we must fall back, now!" Elezar shouted.

Skellan said nothing. The form he wore suited stealth and speed but not speech. His animal body also muted the blaze of his witchflame, but now that he'd gotten this near the Sumar grimma he no longer needed the disguise. Skellan called up the molten heat of his soul and then pushed himself up onto his hind legs. For an instant his bones felt as fluid as fire, burning beneath his flesh. Then the hide and muscle of the hound fell back into the recesses of his cloak and Skellan caught his own weight and felt the full blaze of the Sumar grimma's witchflame beating against his exposed skin.

His fine raiment hung again in tatters and the ruby ring on his index finger vibrated like a bell reverberating with the Sumar grimma's presence.

She had called him her child and sent the ring he wore to him. He wanted it to matter to her that it was him, not some anonymous soldier, who stood before her. But as her witchflame roared down, he realized that his presence meant nothing. She would not stop unless she was driven back.

He dug his feet into the rocky soil and hurled his own witchflame ahead of him, slamming it into the Sumar grimma's. The impact jarred them both and sent plumes of scarlet and green flames bursting through the air. Skellan ground his teeth and pushed harder against her, driving her ferocious soul back. Every sinew of his body strained. He took a slow step then another. Steadily, he forced the Sumar grimma's witchflame back as if he were shouldering a boulder out of his way. His muscles shook and a lingering canine instinct brought a low snarl to his lips.

At last, Skellan reached the riverbank. His feet sank deep into the mud, each footstep driven down by the resistance of the Sumar grimma's witchflame.

"Won't you bow down before your mother?" Mockery colored the Sumar grimma's tone as she suddenly she drew her witchflame back to the far bank of the Raccroc River. Skellan nearly overbalanced into the water when her resistance dissipated. He staggered and caught himself. The Sumar grimma's laughter rippled through the air.

Skellan pulled his feet free from the grip of the sucking mud. He resisted the urge to look back to see if Elezar and his cavalrymen had recovered from the radiance of the Sumar grimma's witchflame. Instead, he concentrated on her. She smiled at him like a child grinning at an ant she intended to rip the legs from.

"Is this the welcome you offer your mother, my monstrous child?"

He felt foolish and angry for imagining, even silently and secretly, that when they finally met in the flesh it would matter to her that he was her son.

"If you came here acting as a mother ought to, then I would welcome you. But I will not allow you to claim the land I defend."

"And how will you stop me, my Hilthorn?"

The trolls across the river glowered and the white bears leered, gaping their sharp teeth at him. Skellan felt the ground behind him thump with horse hooves as Elezar and his cavalrymen rallied behind him. Relief swept through him, though he didn't dare to look back to see the expressions on their faces. Likely Elezar glowered at him as hatefully as the trolls across the river did.

But he hadn't asked Elezar or his men to follow him and he refused to feel guilty right now.

The huge troll carrying the Sumar grimma strode nearer. Waves of woody, fungal odors rolled off the creature, and flocks of birds winged from the twisted old pines that clung to the troll's ragged shoulders. Stones and shrubs tumbled loose from the creature's back and pelted the land below like landslides. It must have been centuries since this troll had been roused from his earthy dreams. He'd plainly grown immense in that time. With each step he seemed to grow even larger.

Cold dread shivered down his spine but Skellan forced himself to clear his mind. Even the greatest creature could be brought low. He merely had to think how. The troll took another step and the water of the river crested and broke with the force of its footfall.

Skellan glanced down to the murky hole he'd pulled his foot from moments ago. He remembered beetle casings and the tiny hollows between even the finest grains of sand.

Realization came to him and at once he plunged his witchflame into the far bank of the Raccroc River. He felt the thick walls of clay and stone. He tasted the matrix of rich minerals and dark water. Something light and shimmering white rolled through the waters like radiant streamers. When he pushed his witchflame into the soil of the banks, opening millions of tiny holes, the white light seemed to pour around him as if to shield him in its cold radiance. This was some Bahiim spell that protected the river from invasion, Skellan realized. He focused on opening up the tiny spaces within the structure of the clay and allowing the river to flood in.

Instantly the solid ground supporting the grimma's trolls and bears squelched and burbled, turning to soft, sucking mud. One of the trolls gave a shocked howl as the ground suddenly gulped it down to its chest. The second troll stumbled back, sending the bears scattering away from its flailing limbs.

The troll carrying the Sumar grimma pulled to a halt and then took two pounding steps back.

Over the rumbling whimpers of the sinking troll and the angry snarls of bears, the Sumar grimma's laughter sang out.

"Well done, my child. But are you truly so cruel as to drown a hapless beast held in my thrall?"

Skellan hated her for so adeptly pricking his conscience. The trapped troll across the river continued to thrash and cry, but it only succeeded in loosing more of the ground beneath it and sinking further into the muck. The smaller troll nearest it called, long and low, like a howling wind. Then to Skellan's horror it lunged forward into the sinking mud attempting to grasp its fellow and drag it free. They both foundered. The pleading terror of their calls tore at Skellan. He couldn't keep from thinking of Bone-crusher and knowing that his friend, too, heard these agonized death cries.

"They're yours to protect! Help them!" Skellan shouted at the Sumar grimma. "Save them!"

"Were they yours, would you?" An unconcerned, almost curious tone rang through her question.

Skellan couldn't stand it. He felt like a fool but he couldn't just allow two hapless enthralled trolls to die like this.

"Skellan, don't..."

He didn't hear the rest of Elezar's words. His thoughts dived into the murky sludge of the far riverbank. He wrapped his will around the immense weight of the two trolls. Their bodies crushed down upon him. The blazing white streamers fought him, dragging at the trolls, intent upon drowning them. Skellan groaned against the Bahiim spells and the sheer weight of earth and water. He flexed with all his might, hurling the trolls up onto the stable ground behind them. They slid and skidded several feet before coming to a halt near a crushed heap of shattered pines.

Under other circumstances Skellan might have found their surprised yelps amusing—high-pitched, tiny sounds escaping giant bodies. But now he couldn't even keep his balance. He swayed and gasped for air as the dissipated power of his witch-flame sputtered and attempted to rekindle inside him. He felt cold to his bones.

He fell to his knees in the river reeds and dug his hands into the muddy bank, searching for the strength he needed to raise a ward before the Sumar grimma struck against him.

A dark shadow rolled over him and he looked up fast only to see Elezar, dismounted and leading his charger up to him. Elezar gripped his sword in one hand and held Cobre's reins in the other. His gaze seemed fixed upon the Sumar grimma and her servants across the river.

"Can you stand?" Elezar whispered.

Skellan pushed himself back to his feet and Elezar gave a slight nod.

"Can you get into Cobre's saddle?" Elezar's attention remained pinned on the Sumar grimma as he stepped forward, leading Cobre up beside Skellan. He continued to speak in a furtive whisper. "Ride for the city and I'll do what I can to distract—"

"I won't run from her," Skellan said flatly.

Looking at Elezar's back, Skellan easily read the frustration coursing through him. He said nothing. Doubtless he knew as well as Skellan that this was neither the time nor the place for an argument between them.

Skellan flexed his bare feet against the earth of the river-bank and willed it to give him strength. He hadn't made this land his, but he knew it belonged in his protection. Somewhere deep in within the black silence of long buried, ancient stones he felt a response. Old prayers and forgotten magics stirred. Had his witchflame blazed around him he would never have felt the answer of the very land itself. But now dust that had once been golden blessings and the pebbled remains of immense guardian cairns awoke to his plea and warmed him.

Across the river the two muddy sodden trolls slowly regained their feet. Sludge, reeds, and river grass dripped from their hulking forms. The Sumar grimma's bears gave them a wide berth, now keeping close to the walking mountain that carried their grimma.

"You will not cross this river!" Skellan shouted.

Again amusement lit the Sumar grimma's pale face.

"Then come, my own Hilthorn, stop me!"

Without warning she took five fast strides and launched herself from the troll's rocky shoulder. Her witchflame lit the air and Skellan again caught a glimpse of that immense dragon, spreading its shining membranous wings. She grinned at him as she glided up over the river. Then, as she dipped towards the river's rolling surface, stones seemed to stretch up to meet her feet. One after another the boulders of the deep riverbed stretched up as if molten to form half of an arching white bridge. The waters spit and flashed with a shining white froth but could not reach her. More stones rose slowly, closing the bridge and reaching out for the shore where Skellan stood, shaking.

Never in his life had Skellan sensed such power. Solid stone flexed to the Sumar grimma's whim—not like an object in her grasp but as if it were an extension of her. She moved the very earth as if she were twining a lock of hair around her finger.

He couldn't best that, not even if he burned himself to a cinder. Raw fear surged through Skellan and he almost reached out to pull himself into Cobre's saddle. But where would he ride to? What wall would stand against her once she stepped onto Radulf land and lay claim to it all? Right now he still could call the strength of Milmuraille's past guardians to his aid, if nothing more.

If she could be stopped it had to be here.

He launched himself forward, not knowing what he would do but so desperate that it didn't matter. He couldn't wait to know how to fight her, because likely that wisdom would never come to him. All he could hope was to strike fast and hard and do her harm enough to give her pause. Even if it killed him, he meant to make her hurt for every bit of his land that she took.

As he ran he pulled every shred of strength he could from the surrounding land and then leapt for the rising stone of the Sumar grimma's bridge.

He slammed into the shifting rock and cracked it wide in his rage. He leapt again as the rock splintered. As he charged the Sumar grimma the stones behind him crumbled and crashed back down into the foaming river. Red flames rolled up from Skellan and, halfway across her bridge, the Sumar grimma stilled.

Her cold green eyes lit with a terrible delight and she threw her arms wide as if preparing to pull all the strength of the living world into the forge of her witchflame. Skellan threw himself at her, praying to take her before she could call more power down.

He slammed his witchflame against the shining spells woven over her heart. Precious stones shattered, throwing splinters into his hands. Shards of diamonds, rubies, jade, and emeralds fell away but more rose up from beneath, growing up like scales. His fist should have been in the hollow of her chest but he found only more spell-etched stones beneath his fingers.

Then her arms closed around him in a crushing grip. Her skin felt thick as saddle leather and her yellow fingernails sank through his tattered clothes like hawk talons. Skellan tried to fight against her grip but sedating warmth enfolded him. The perfume of honey and grape vines filled his lungs and languor poured through him. All his fury dulled, leaving him hanging against the Sumar grimma as she rocked him in her arms.

"To hold you again at last, my child." The words touched Skellan with a surprising tenderness.

He lifted his head to look into her face.

Up close he could see the weird, waxen quality of her features. Shadows flickered and rolled behind her skin, as if something much more alive and radiant burned beneath her flesh. Her green eyes shone so bright that they seemed to glow far beyond the orbs of her skull.

Skellan remembered his dream of her—that huge dragon that was itself a summer kingdom and all at once he knew that Little Dreamer had been right. The Sumar grimma was no more a human woman than he had ever been a hound. Mortal flesh bound her, much as goatskins had served to lock away Sammi and Sarl's natural powers from the hunger of the demon lord.

Suddenly Skellan wondered how powerful—how terrible—the Sumar grimma's true form might be.

"What are you?" Skellan murmured.

"I am your mother and you are my lovely abomination. My one child and my last hope for freedom."

"I'm not your hope or an abomination." Skellan felt sluggish, almost half-asleep in her grip. He tried to call up his witchflame to push her back from him, but the red flames only seemed to curl and dance around her head like wraiths.

"You were born to be both, my Hilthorn. Yours is the vei I cannot walk myself. You will free me."

"You are free," Skellan groaned.

"No, my child." A knowing sorrow drifted over Skellan. "You do not even know what true freedom feels like, but I will show you."

All at once he felt his witchflame rise on a warm breeze. All the pain of his body melted away as he whirled into the open sky. He became wind—pure motion freed from all confines of living flesh. Effortless joy suffused him as all sense of care and even time fell away from him.

But he couldn't simply leave everything behind, he reminded himself. No matter how relieving it felt to escape, he had to resist and return to the body that still hung in the Sumar grimma's arms. He had to defend his home and friends.

He concentrated and a frail red spark shone far below him. He hurled himself down to it. He plunged back into his body, suddenly aware of the weight of his flesh and the chaos of his living senses. The river waters pounded his ears. Birds shrieked in the trees. Light and color hammered through his eyes, dazing his thoughts. Scents churned over him—sweet, sickening and endless. Even his skin seemed consumed by the constant crawling sensations of air churning around him.

He shook in the Sumar grimma's grip as he struggled to reclaim the comfort he had always known inhabiting his own body.

"There is more than one way to make a prisoner of a god, my child. More than one way to strip the wind of its freedom and chain it to the earth. You cannot understand because you have never known what it is to be beyond the grasp of living flesh. Even those who should remember have forgotten, but I can still recall what was taken from me.

"When this world was young I existed, whole and free. For ages I was all the sky. Rain, wind, sun, hurricanes, and snowfall. I was my own realm and I was at peace even in the fiercest storm.

"But then mortal creatures called me down, cut me asunder, and trapped me in horrific flesh to make war against the demons who would have claimed their lives and lands."

Looking at her, Skellan once again sensed that immense emerald dragon arching up over him, wings unfurled to fill his entire horizon and its eyes flashing like lightning.

"They tore me into four quarters to make me weak. And each part of me learned pain, and rage, and hatred. We made so fierce a war against the demons that the skies blackened and the land burned. We fought them by the thousands and though we screamed with suffering, we could not die."

This, too, Skellan felt rocking through him.

Burning spears drove into his chest. Blades and teeth ripped him open even as he thrashed and tore at his hideous enemies. He sank his teeth into flesh and for the first time tasted blood. He shook with shock and pain. A desolating exhaustion sank into the marrow of his bones, but the battles went on and on. Mountains crumbled and vast plains burned to ash.

At last he collapsed atop the ruin of his last enemy's broken back and looked out over a stinking field of rotting remains. A dead world spread before him and for the first time he understood both the cost of victory and defeat. His own body grasped him in a cage of agony, skin ripped to raw muscles, bones riddled with cracks. His breast lay gashed open, exposing the shudders of his pounding heart. A desolate, soulless wind scratched him with the stench of burning bodies.

He gasped in agonized breaths and fought desperately to return to the respite of the breezes. With all of his being he yearned to shed this horror of flesh and reunite his mutilated soul with the heavens high above him. He'd known those skies so well once, but now he could only recall the loss of what he'd once been. Every breath he drew stank.

Then out the corner of his one remaining eye he spied little creatures—ugly, stupid human beings clutching charms and bones, painted with mud and wearing animal carcasses, as if they could disguise their devious intentions. They encircled him, edging slyly closer, whispering their gibberish and thinking him theirs to name and command. They crawled over him, like flies suckling at an open wound.

Incandescent fury lit his soul. They had done this to him—butchered his spirit, stolen his peace, and forged him into this agonized creation of their own need. He wanted nothing but to punish them. And he now knew enough of war, of pain and cruelty, to make them suffer.

Skellan flinched from the taste and sensation of men and women thrashing against his massive jaws. They shrieked and pleaded as he swallowed them alive.

"All of that ended long ago. The demon lords are all dead now and the Old Gods have been put to rest." Skellan whispered the words not only to the Sumar grimma but to reassure himself as well. In the back of his mind he could still feel her violent anger shuddering through him. "All that has been over for hundreds of years."

"It serves priests and Bahiim to think it over and done with. They imagine we are all at rest in ancient wood, sealed beneath the oceans, and locked within the confines of our sanctums. But we, whom they called down—we who became their first gods, their Old Gods—we are still here. They may have bound us up in the skins of their own kind, walled us into great temples and sanctums, and filled our prisons with sacrifices, but we remain with you even now. And we still rage—" Some bitter thought seemed to come to the Sumar grimma then. She scowled and corrected herself. "I still rage. Others have grown content, playing warden over lesser creatures, but I have not forgotten what I once was."

Anger smoldered through her tone and even distorted the blaze of her witchflame. Skellan felt it ripple past him to settle on Elezar and his cavalrymen.

From within the sphere of the Sumar grimma's soul, he glimpsed the men as she saw them: greedy-eyed, devious savages. The stunted flames of their souls contorted and flickered like twitching insects. Their bodies and faces smeared through constantly shifting caricatures of fear, hate, greed, and lust. Their mouths hung with hunger and reeked of lies, their hands twitched as if possessed with relentless, grasping avarice.

Next to them their mounts stood, souls laid bare but with a simple purity.

With such a warped perspective it was no wonder that the grimma placed thralls over the humans who served them and surrounded themselves with beasts. But Skellan refused to share the grimma's point of view. Even through the waves of her witchflame he recognized Elezar. He concentrated on the truth he knew of the man and he pushed his own vision through the Sumar grimma's.

Elezar was brave and dedicated, surprisingly patient, and capable of immense tenderness. Of course, he was also capable of feeling greed, ambition, lust, and rage. No doubt he could practice deceit. But none of those qualities made him a monster. They were what he overcame with his sense of humor, his kindness, bravery, and loyalty.

The Sumar grimma scowled at the clear vision Skellan held up before her, and he realized that something in Elezar's countenance struck a chord of recognition in her. She didn't want to remember him but she did: the lone Cadeleonian envoy who'd breached her sanctum, promised to find her child, and kept his word. A flicker of uncertainty played through her face. Skellan seized upon it.

"The people before you now aren't the same ones who wronged you so long ago," Skellan told her. "These people have never done you any harm and you have no right to invade their homes and enslave them."

Skellan felt the change in her before he saw it. A shudder passed through the radiance of her witchflame and the furious, incandescent creature trapped beneath her skin dimmed. An almost human warmth colored her cheeks and her eyes dulled to a sage gray.

"Have I invaded?" the Sumar grimma asked. She lifted her talon-like nails from Skellan's tattered clothes and very carefully released him. "Have I yet set even one foot upon the land you call your own, my child?" This time her bemused expression seemed to suit her face and an almost charming gleam came into her eyes.

Despite himself Skellan smiled back at her wryly.

"You expect me to believe that if I hadn't stood against you here on the river you wouldn't have invaded?" Skellan asked.

The Sumar grimma's thin lips parted to reveal a much too toothy grin.

"If you hadn't stood against me, then I would have known that you were not ready to face the other three. I would have invaded and crushed your city walls and carried you back home with me."

"But I do stand against you. So is it still your intention to destroy my lands and people?"

The Sumar grimma laughed and Skellan frowned. He'd not thought this an amusing question.

"What do I want of more lands? What use is all the dirt of every kingdom when none of it can ever set me free?" She gazed down at the cascade of cracked stones and enchantments adorning her chest. Then she looked to Skellan. "I needed to know if Lundag succeeded in breaking your vei when she stole you from me. I only wish to see if you still harbor the hopes I whispered over your infant body."

Skellan didn't know how to respond to that. More than once she'd called him her hope—and a part of him still pined for a mother, longed to somehow be all that she wished for. At the same time he couldn't imagine that what the Sumar grimma hoped for would be anything he could bring himself to take part in. He'd felt her furious satisfaction all too clearly in her memories of ages when she'd marauded villages and cities, wrecking her vengeance.

She might once have been benign as a breeze, but she'd left that behind long ago.

"And am I still your hope?" Skellan asked.

"You are not broken, my child... not yet. Who knows what the other three will do to you. If they knew..."

"Knew what?"

The Sumar grimma didn't answer immediately but instead peered back over her shoulder to the white bears gathered at north bank of the river.

"There are those who hold to the truth of their natures no matter how deeply or long they are transformed." The Sumar grimma looked to Skellan then. "You and I are strong in that way—uncompromising."

Skellan nodded. He didn't know how the Sumar grimma surmised this of him but she wasn't wrong. Though, he thought that Little Dreamer, too, must possess such a nature to have returned to her humanity after more than a hundred years under Ylva's thrall.

"But even gods can be seduced by the luxurious senses of new flesh. They learn to thrive upon the petty pleasures and ambitions of mere monarchs, and so they grow more and more like the mortals who imprisoned them. Ylva now relishes ruling the sanctum that binds her to her body. She doesn't remember the time before we were called down to the flesh of gods. She hardly even remembers that in those first bodies we protected this earth and its most ancient creatures—we did not merely rule it. Our war, and all we suffered, was a means to a greater peace." The Sumar grimma gave a dry laugh. "Sometimes even I forget that."

"What of Onelsi and Naemir?" Skellan knew little of the northern grimma except that she dwelt in a kingdom of ice and snow, keeping only beasts for company. For a brief time she'd held Kiram Kir-Zaki captive, demanding that he craft an astrolabe for her. But she'd released him when the device was completed.

Of Onelsi he knew only the ferocity of her sulfur yellow witchflame and stories of her cruel whimsies.

"Onelsi is as a child playing at Ylva's knee. She makes war against you because it will amuse them both," the Sumar grimma said. "And Naemir comes because she is bound to answer her sisters. In truth, she cares only for the heavens that we lost so long ago—the stars that were ours. She watches the night sky and from time to time attempts to take her own life, just to see if it might be possible yet."

"I'm sorry," Skellan responded in spite of himself. Naemir might be his enemy but he couldn't help but feel sympathy at the thought of anyone so desolate as to attempt suicide.

The Sumar grimma's expression softened further, her smile turning warm in a way that reminded him of Cire.

"Yes, that is the nature of your father's flesh, such capacity to place your sympathy where you will. It makes you as unpredictable as a mere mortal. You can lie and love as you please. All of that makes you an abomination among our kind, a dangerous half-breed possessing a god's power and a mortal's will."

Silently, Skellan thought that she had no idea of what she was talking about. He possessed a powerful witchflame but he certainly wasn't a god—not even one whose power was restrained by much weaker flesh. Never could he have summoned river rocks to form the bridge that now supported them both. The best he managed had been shattering the second half of the bridge. That, he suspected, had been the doing of all those ancient spells scattered across the land.

The Sumar grimma cocked her head in an oddly animal manner, then as if sensing his thoughts, she said, "Don't look so uncertain of yourself, my child. You are young, not yet in the full bloom of your power. Even so you already defeated a demon lord whom we—locked in these human bodies—could not have fought."

He wanted to tell her that he'd nearly died in that battle. Only Oesir had saved his life. But he hardly knew her, and though he yearned for the affection and acceptance of a mother, he didn't trust the Sumar grimma.

"If you think me so capable then why are you so certain that the other grimma will defeat me?" Skellan inquired and not out of idle curiosity. He could hope that she might offer him some insight into his weaknesses and how the other three grimma might exploit them.

"You were born free of the bonds that restrain and also sustain us. There is no sanctum that you must defend nor is there one for you to draw strength from. You must forge alliance where your heart lies." She turned back to the two trolls whom Skellan had thrown from the river. "You are susceptible to mercies that we cannot feel. To me another grimma's troll is only a heap of rock that she has enthralled. I see the people and creatures bound to her only as extensions of her—dolls, dressed in her colors and filled with her intentions."

"But they aren't dolls—"

"Not to you." The Sumar grimma stole another glance back at her own gathered trolls and bears. "Those in my own thrall seem... alive. There are some I even feel fondness for. But those that are not tied to me are nothing."

Skellan couldn't imagine how that could be possible. But meeting her gaze he believed her. She cared for her own. When she looked at him with such warmth it was because he, too, was hers—her only child, born of her blood, body, and will. She didn't know him or like him for the man he'd made himself. Her attachment to him arose from a primal impulse to protect her own: a drive almost as ancient and primitive as she was herself.

"If you didn't come to conquer, and you aren't going to carry me away, then why are you here?" Skellan asked.

She didn't respond at once and her pause made him wonder if she truly knew herself.

"I do not want you to be destroyed," she said. "But I cannot fight against other aspects of myself. Not even for your sake..."

Skellan waited for her to come to some conclusion. He watched as her gaze lifted from him to take in Elezar and his cavalrymen, mounted at the river's edge. Elezar gripped his sword in his right hand and glowered back. Skellan couldn't help but feel proud of them all—awaiting only his command to charge into the deep waters, though they had to know that they would die at the hands of the Sumar grimma.

She cocked her head again in that animalistic way. "How is it that frogwives, cloud imps, and even a troll all serve you of their free will? The wethra-steed you sent to me were not enthralled but chose to serve you. Even the Cadeleonian—"

"Elezar," Skellan insisted.

"Yes, your Elezar is free."

"Isn't that the vei you wanted for me? Didn't you wish that I would bring freedom?" Skellan asked. Her bewilderment struck him as amusing given how insistent she'd been earlier about her own need to reclaim her liberty.

"But how do you command them? How will you make them stand and battle?"

Skellan understood her incredulity. He'd suffered uncertainty about his own ability to inspire loyalty more than once. He'd even been tempted to enthrall those around him. But now he remembered the story that Elezar had told him about his home of Anacleto. How the citizens there had each of their own volition stood against their own king and his mighty army. Suddenly a realization came to him.

"I don't force them to fight. That's why they choose to," Skellan told her. "Milmuraille isn't a domain that I rule like a sanctum. It's a homeland to countless free creatures. And this battle against the grimma, it's not only mine to fight. It's all of ours. That's why they choose to stand with me."

The Sumar grimma stepped back from him. He felt that immense, incandescent emerald presence rise up from her to stare down upon him from a great height. Her eyes lit and her expression went distant. Then, in a breath, her witchflame collapsed back down into the shell of her body and she regarded him with a new expression, both sly and affectionate.

"I did wish that you would bring freedom... I see it now. That is the vei you have forged of all my hope and spells. Until this moment I hadn't seen the full form of it." A smile twisted her thin mouth then. "What is bound to a grimma cannot be used against a grimma. That is the law. But that which is free may choose to follow you."

"A free creature can choose any—"

"You are flesh of my flesh and I will not make battle against you." She cut Skellan off, reaching out for him. Skellan held his ground, though he dreaded being taken in her grasp a second time. But she only laid her hand lightly upon his shoulder. A warm breeze rippled through his hair and caressed his cheek. "Take what I leave and find a way to end my captivity. Become my hope, even if it means the doom of us all." Then she let him go easily.

She turned and strode across the remnants of the bridge to the far side of the riverbank. The two younger trolls groveled low on the ground before her when she stopped in front of them. Skellan dug his feet in against the twisted rock of the bridge supporting him, preparing to pull what strength he could from it to stop the Sumar grimma if she lashed out against her enthralled trolls.

To Skellan's shock the Sumar grimma threw her arms wide and in a burst of brilliant green flame she burned away the chains and harpoons buried deep into the troll's shoulders and backs. Both trolls stumbled and peered around them as if waking from a dream. As the Sumar grimma strode past, her great white bears closed around her, nervously chuffing and growling. She stroked their hides almost absently. With a kick of her foot she flew up to land on the ragged shoulder of the largest troll. She touched one of the harpoons and it melted away like frost beneath the warmth of her hand. The remaining harpoons disappeared in moments and the lengths of chain fell from the troll's body, breaking into shimmering dust before they reached the ground.

The Sumar grimma leapt into the air and at once a dozen eagles launched themselves from the surrounding trees to circle beneath her feet. Halos of green fire ringed her.

"Let them choose!" Her voice boomed across the sky, but Skellan knew she spoke to him. Then her attention shifted and Skellan turned to see the line of her sight fall directly upon Elezar. He scowled back at her with fearful uneasiness.

"Elezar!" She shouted his name as if they were familiar. "Your reward."

She tore a white charm from her breast—a bit of carved ivory—and hurled it down. As it flew from her hand the tiny shard twisted and stretched. Terror seized Skellan. He turned and threw himself towards the south shore. As if by instinct his witchflame rose around him, hurtling him farther than he'd ever leapt. He all but flew to the shore and still he wasn't fast enough. The ivory charm fell like lightning, searing the air as it streaked down.

To Skellan's shock Elezar didn't flinch but blocked the shining lance with his sword, as if he were in the habit of fencing with lightning bolts. A shower of white sparks arced into the air and for an instant Elezar's sword shone bright as molten steel. Then it darkened and coalesced to glassy black. Its edge gleamed and faint golden blessings winked from beneath the surface. A spell-forged blade, Skellan realized, a weapon made to slay even the most powerful of creatures.

"Don't die before you can use it," the Sumar grimma called. Oddly, Elezar offered her a salute. The Sumar grimma turned in the air, eagles rising around her, and then without another word she made the slightest motion of her hand and soared from sight, leaving Skellan with six bears, some ten eagles, three trolls, and a glowering champion.

CHAPTER TWENTY-THREE

As he rode back to the city, the very heavens seemed to reflect Elezar's mood. Towers of black clouds filled the eastern skies, churning and flashing with furious bolts of lightning. Yet the afternoon winds buffeting Milmuraille rippled with summer heat. Sweat bees and flies crowded the air. Cobre slashed his tail in annoyance and Elezar slapped away some biting gnat.

Normally he wouldn't have taken much note. Flies seemed a small price for all of summer's bounty, but at the moment he felt that he'd endured all the irritation as he could abide.

Still, he suppressed his seething temper for the entire journey back to the city, through the crowded streets, and into the garrison courtyard. The strangeness of finding himself and his cavalrymen now escorting bears and trolls while flanked by massive eagles distracted him from his ire to some extent.

Watching Skellan revealing the true forms of the enthralled beasts proved fascinating enough. Certainly he'd not expected to discover that while five of the bears were enthralled Mirogoths—four dazed blond men and one woman—the sixth turned out to be a strapping young Labaran trader who'd gone missing some thirty years earlier and now appeared half the age of his younger brother, who still served as a watchman at the city gates. Both men wept upon recognizing each other. The trader seemed at a loss seeing all the changes wrought by the decades he'd been gone. He cheered, however when he learned that the infant daughter he'd left behind now held a revered position as a sister-physician.

Skellan also released an Irabiim mother and her three children from the bodies of the eagles. To everyone's surprise, though, the remaining seven raptors turned out to be genuine eagles, albeit deeply confused and distressed eagles. All of them perched around the Irabiim mother and called to her like loyal pets or, more disturbingly, like the young born of the body she'd been entrapped by for years.

Of all the creatures abandoned to their care by the Sumar grimma, it was the trolls, for all their towering bulk and greenery, who inspired the least confusion. They were just what they appeared to be, nothing more and certainly nothing less. They'd drawn awed crowds in the streets and inspired cheers from onlookers who seemed to think Skellan had won them.

Cire met them shortly after they reached the garrison and embraced Skellan like a proud mother. Elezar noticed Rafale among the gathered onlookers who threw flower petals down upon Skellan. He couldn't be certain, but he thought he saw Skellan offer Rafale a warm smile.

That did little to improve Elezar's rotten mood.

Once Skellan had finished releasing the bears and eagles, Bone-crusher approached. He greeted the other three trolls in low rumblings that sounded to Elezar like great rock slides and the deep tones of groaning ship timbers. The four trolls embraced and then Bone-crusher informed Skellan that the three newcomers were willing to fight if Skellan swore never to enthrall them.

Before a crowd of soldiers Skellan gave his word to the massive trolls and they, in turn, knelt and swore loyalty to Skellan. Then Bone-crusher led the others out to the river docks to hunt freshwater sharks and river serpents. The folk gathered in the courtyard of the garrison watched them retreat in awe. On his own Bone-crusher dwarfed most common houses, but in the company of three other massive, bramble-carpeted trolls, the sight of them moving was like watching an entire swath of countryside strolling through the narrow city lanes.

In the midst of it all Javier sidled up to Elezar to ask him if he knew what had happened to his sword. Overhearing the question, Captain Tialdo cast Elezar a curious look as well. Elezar didn't know and he'd been doing his best not to brood on what might have become of his sword. So Javier's inquiry only added to his general annoyance at the day's events.

"The Sumar grimma threw a charm of some kind at me and when I blocked it with my blade, it... changed." Elezar frowned down at the sheathed sword hanging from his hip. Javier eyed the weapon like a cat considering a ball of yarn. "She told me not to die before I had a chance to use it."

She'd offered him much the same advice when she'd thrown Skellan's ring to him months before.

"She's placed some kind of blessing upon it, do you think?" Captain Tialdo asked quietly.

"That is not a blessing." Javier shook his head, his expression thoughtful. "No, this feels much more malevolent... brooding..."

Captain Tialdo made a holy sign to ward off evil. Elezar supposed he should have followed suit but in truth he felt more aggravated than afraid. In any case, making signs and appearing terrified of his own weapon would hardly instill assurance in the crowd surrounding them.

While the vast majority of the garrison's troops watched after the retreating trolls, a few attempted to make conversation with the newly freed bears and eagles. Amongst the throng of kitchen women Elezar caught sight of Fleur as she shyly offered bread to the brawny, nearly naked Mirogoths. Many of Elezar's cavalrymen hung around Eski and Magraie as they tended their radiant wethra-steeds just outside the stables. Grooms also lingered, praising and soothing the cavalry horses for their bravery in charging both trolls and bears.

Cobre nudged Elezar's shoulder and he stroked the stallion's neck but hung back from the stable. He wanted to wait until the majority of men and women cleared off, so that he might tend Cobre in quiet. He needed time and solitude to alleviate his own aggravation.

"I thought the plan was to have Skellan wait until I could join you at the city gates," Javier said.

If Captain Tialdo hadn't been standing there with his glossy stallion, Elezar wouldn't have stopped himself from saying that apparently there weren't any fucking plans where Skellan was concerned. Instead Elezar gave a terse shake of his head. Javier's brows rose but he offered no further comment on Skellan's mad dash from the protection of the city walls. Instead Javier's gaze drifted past the groups of jubilant men and women clustered around Skellan and his entourage of newly liberated, bearskin-cloaked Mirogoths.

Elezar followed his gaze across the grounds and noted Kiram holding out a map and chatting with two of the older Irabiim. Eagles settled on the garrison stonework all around them. Doubtless Kiram hoped the Irabiim's previous aerial perspectives would aid in discerning just how close their enemies were.

"You can't say he's not practical," Elezar murmured to himself.

Skellan, on the other hand—

Elezar could feel his fists clenching as he took in his rangy witch's careless grins and caught phrases of his pleased chatter with soldiers, Mirogoths, sister physicians, and kitchen staff. Like the rest of the population of the city, most the folk gathered on the sweltering open grounds of the courtyard appeared under the delusion that Skellan had bested the Sumar grimma.

Sheriff Hirbe stood to one side of him smiling but with a kind of fatherly worry deepening the lines of his brow. Skellan laughed and gave a flourish of that damned red cloak of his.

Observing him, anyone would think that they all just returned from a pleasant evening's ride. Which, admittedly, inspired higher morale than the reality that their entire party had only survived to ride back through the city because the Sumar grimma allowed it. Out in the open, beyond the range of cannons, archers, and even the wards protecting the city, they'd been utterly at the Sumar grimma's mercy. If it had come to it, Elezar knew he couldn't have saved himself much less Skellan or his cavalrymen.

His fury and frustration at finding himself so helplessness still burned in his gut.

"There's something fascinating about this sword." Javier's words drew Elezar's attention back from Skellan. "I wonder…"

Javier dropped to a crouch and reached slowly for the sword. Elezar felt a vibration hum through his hip and then the hilt all but jolted up to Elezar's hand. Emerald sparks spit from the pommel, flying at Javier. Javier jerked back, almost fell, but caught himself and rose quickly back to his feet.

Elezar couldn't help but angle an aggravated glance at him. Did every man he'd ever found attractive have to be an impulsive idiot? What was he thinking, just grabbing for Elezar's blade like they were still boys sharing their toys?

"It certainly doesn't want anyone but you touching it." Javier pinched out a smoldering corner of his coat cuff. "It feels nearly alive with power. They say steel reforged by a grimma's witchflame can cut through anything—even slay a troll."

"Like the sacred blade wielded by Our Holy Savior?" Captain Tialdo asked. His expression betrayed a disbelief that Elezar himself shared. He doubted very much that the sword he now gripped would draw poison from wounds or make fertile a once-barren battlefield.

"Oh no!" Javier laughed. "Nothing holy about it. The blade certainly seethes with power but it's the weapon of a destroyer, not a holy man."

"Is it evil, then?" Captain Tialdo asked, though even he seemed to recognize the strangeness of asking such a question of an infamous heretic. Still Javier, like the captain and Elezar, had grown up in the Cadeleonian church and understood the dogma like instinct.

"No." Javier paused a moment, seeming to consider his burned cuff. "Spell-forged blades are said to take on the character of their masters. So likely it will become whatever Elezar makes of it."

Both men looked to him questioningly. Elezar frowned back at them. What did they want, a sermon? Some promise of his virtuous heart and righteous spirit? He didn't have anything like that in him.

"It's a weapon to wield against our enemies. That's all I need it to be and all I intend to make of it." Elezar released the warm hilt, allowing the blade to slide back into its sheath.

Captain Tialdo nodded but still eyed Elezar's sword warily. Beyond them, the infantry captain on duty and the chief cook called those under their commands back to their work. The courtyard soon emptied of most everyone but the company of pikemen training on the grounds. Skellan remained with Kiram and two of the Irabiim while Sheriff Hirbe strolled across the grounds to greet Eski and Magraie. Elezar caught a bit of conversation about the stone of passage Naemir had given Kiram.

When the man in charge of the evening sentries wandered past, Elezar called him over to quickly check the night's active duty roster. All their men were well and accounted for.

After that Captain Tialdo and Elezar turned their discussion to the practical subjects of where to house these new allies—the ruins of the sanctum offered far more open space for the trolls than did the crowded garrison grounds—and how best to integrate them with established troops.

By the time a groom took charge of the captain's mount he seemed again at ease, offering his usual crisp salute to Elezar before he took himself off to share his dinner and the day's events with his daughter up in the infirmary. A few minutes later the kitchen bells clanged. Javier, too, took his leave, hurrying to join Kiram and Skellan who had both turned to take their supper in the common mess.

Skellan cast a questioning glance back to Elezar but clearly recognized Elezar's annoyance, and tugging his cloak close around his mud-spattered shoulders, he slunk into the garrison headquarters. Elezar felt a brief but nearly overpowering urge to charge after him.

He forced himself to turn away. The anger in him felt righteous but Elezar knew himself well enough now to understand that he made very poor decisions in fury.

He swatted a fly away from his face and then led Cobre to the stable. Doue met him inside, beaming with excitement and casting looks of worshipful longing back to where Eski stood brushing down her wethra-steed.

"She's beautiful, isn't she?"

Elezar wasn't certain if Doue meant the girl or her mount. From the way Doue's gaze moved over them both, Elezar thought that perhaps Doue didn't really know which he admired more himself. Despite his own foul mood Elezar smiled.

"Her name is Eski," Elezar informed the young man.

"You know her?" Doue regarded Elezar with an expression of wonder bordering upon awe. He didn't think he could have impressed Doue more if he'd claimed to be a close friend of the South Wind.

"I've had the honor of traveling with her through the Mirogoth lands," Elezar replied. "Shall I introduce you?"

Doue flushed to the roots of his hair but then nodded.

Elezar made the introduction and he thought it did him some good to witness the quick camaraderie that sprung up between the two. How easy it seemed for children to accept each other. Beyond Eski and Doue, Elezar noted Magraie, looking hollow eyed but happy. Sheriff Hirbe threw an arm around his shoulders and invited him, and by extension his wethra-steed, to dinner at his home. Such relief at the sheriff's kindness showed on the young man's face that witnessing it embarrassed Elezar.

The sheriff extended his invitation to Eski and she accepted with her usual glee.

"It's warm enough that we can eat out in the garden with your companions," Sheriff Hirbe commented.

Elezar left them to their plans, while Doue attempted to

tempt Nottsol with a hunk of apple. The shining gold we-thra-steed regarded him with an expression of equine amusement but wouldn't accept feed from any hand but Eski's.

Elezar withdrew back to Cobre and occupied himself in the calming routine of brushing the big stallion down, picking his hooves, and then indulging him in feed. The quiet calm of Cobre's company allowed Elezar to relax and set aside enough of his anger to let himself think past it. He touched the hilt of his sword and noted the hum of excitement it sent up the length of his fingers.

While Cobre chewed through his fill of summer grass, Elezar retreated to an empty corner of the stable and drew his sword to examine the gleaming black blade. Though it looked strange, the weight of the blade still felt familiar—still felt good in Elezar's hand.

He swung it through a practice of parries and thrusts, fencing his own long dark shadow as it darted between tall bales of gold hay. Fast motion and exertion soothed Elezar, like a favorite melody flooding his body and setting his heart pounding. His bones and muscle flushed with an assurance and strength. Steadily his troubled mind stilled. He moved faster, pushing himself to beat his own darting shadow. His blade whipped through the air, the unforgiving edge embodying all of his will.

Sweat poured down his back and arms, but he hardly noticed. The air whined as his sword slashed through beams of afternoon light. He thrust, leapt back, and then lunged forward to slash shining motes of dust into a whirling storm. He pivoted back, feinted left, and then with a powerful thrust skewered a bale of straw. Pure physical pleasure flooded him as he drove the blade in deep.

Then, to Elezar's horror, golden stalks all around the blade blackened as if burning away. Elezar jerked his sword free. But the corrosive charring didn't stop until the entire bale crumbled to a heap of dark ash. Elezar stole a guilty glance back over his shoulder in time to catch several horses as well as the Labaran head groom staring at him. At the door of the stable Skellan stood, still dressed in velvet rags and spattered with flecks of river mud.

Elezar felt his face flushing and his earlier annoyance flooded back to him. The groom he ignored and the fellow did Elezar the same courtesy. But Skellan came padding up to him as if he hadn't just witnessed the bare blade gripped in Elezar's hand turn some three stones' weight of hay into ash.

There's a brilliant instinct for survival. Come running to the angry man holding a smoking black enchanted sword.

Elezar just kept himself from voicing his unkind thoughts. He sheathed his sword and realized belatedly that he'd missed some of what Skellan was saying to him.

"—and then Cire said that Hylanya was so mortified that she released all of the folk she held in thrall this afternoon. I'm sorry that she caused such a scene at the dock."

"Shouldn't you be eating?" he asked as Skellan drew near to his side.

"I have done," Skellan replied with a pleased smile. "I can make fast work of a plate of sausages when I don't have to use all that silver nob cutlery."

Often Elezar found Skellan's lack of table etiquette amusing—the honesty of his hunger and appreciation of his food could even seem refreshing in comparison to the complaints of spoiled lordlings—but now he found it aggravating. Just another example of Skellan's brash ignorance.

"You certainly wouldn't want to master a fork and confuse us all," Elezar snapped. Then something else, something far more enraging, occurred to him. "Where are your guards?"

Skellan pulled a sour expression that made Elezar want to grab him by the shoulders and shake him. Why couldn't he grasp that he had to be protected? Elezar felt his hands clenching and obviously Skellan read the anger in his expression because his cocksure smile fell and an uncertainty lit his eyes.

"'They're just outside the stable." Skellan gestured back to the twin shadows falling across the afternoon sun that flooded in from the open stable doors. The men themselves stood just out of sight. "I thought they should keep watch since I'd be protected more than enough in your company in here."

Somehow the reasonableness of the response only irritated Elezar all the more.

"So you can think about keeping a watch at the doors now, when you're surrounded by your allies, but two hours ago with the Sumar grimma coming for you, you couldn't even be bothered to get behind a God-damned bush?" The words came out harsh and loud.

Skellan's shoulders rose and he drew back, scowling at Elezar.

Beyond him Doue and another stable hand gawked. The head groom immediately called to the youths, ordering them out to other duties elsewhere, and then made his own escape while muttering something about locating more neatsfoot oil. After that only the horses remained, watching Elezar and Skellan.

"I didn't mean to vex you, my man," Skellan went on. "I just didn't have time to waste—"

"Time to waste!" Elezar didn't even try to temper his outrage. "You didn't want to *waste* time planning when you could get right down to letting the Sumar grimma rip you apart?"

"I'm not ripped apart." Skellan drew himself up straight in indignation and threw his arms out wide as if displaying the tattered wreck of his clothes in any way validated his argument. Elezar's gaze settled on the half-scabbed gashes marring both his arms where the Sumar grimma had held him. Skellan glanced at his shoulders too.

"I'm hardly even scratched," Skellan stated.

"By sheer fucking luck!" Elezar roared. Anger coursed through him like a great wave. Horses other than Cobre startled but Elezar couldn't care about that now. He glared at Skellan. "You are only alive right now because the Sumar grimma chose not to kill you. If she had decided otherwise not only would you and I be dead but the entirety of Milmuraille would now be stripped of all the wards protecting it! Everyone in this entire city would be hers for the taking."

"But I wasn't killed," Skellan objected.

And for just an instant Elezar wanted desperately to kick him across the stable just to prove to him that he could be hurt, that other people could and would harm him. Elezar's right hand clenched in a hard grip and he realized that instinctively he'd grasped the hilt of his sword.

Horror at his own reflex flooded him.

He released the sword hilt and stepped back from Skellan. He wasn't thinking clearly, he realized. Too much anger and worse, fear at the prospect of his own powerlessness to protect Skellan, still suffused him. He turned away, trying to reclaim control of himself. He watched line upon line of horses in their stalls feeding, drinking, and observing him in return. His own Cobre rubbed his flank against the boards of his stall wall. Further along, Javier's brilliant white stallion, Lunaluz, lifted his head and cast Elezar the sort of appraising look that his master often wore.

Elezar could almost hear Javier chiding him. *Really, Grunito, that temper of yours would only be a credit to distempered dogs and infants trapped in soggy diapers.*

Elezar heard Skellan creeping after him and he knew the moment Skellan halted, well out of arm's length. Elezar was so aware of the other man that he thought he could almost sense the radiance of his body raising the hair at the back of his neck.

"What are you so angry about, my man?" Skellan asked softly.

Elezar didn't know if he could stand to face Skellan and respond. He wasn't sure the question even deserved an answer. Did Skellan really lack the imagination, or maybe common sense, to see how his charge on the Sumar grimma might enrage a man entrusted with his safety?

Instead he stared ahead to the heaping sacks of grain that the stable hands had only begun to store away in the rafters. A dozen little birds flocked around the spills of kernels left where previous sacks had torn.

"What do you think I'm angry about?" Elezar replied at last.

"I... I don't know, except that... perhaps you felt obligated to protect me but when you rode out you couldn't..."

Certainly much of Elezar's frustration did stem from that, but did Skellan really not see that there was far more to it? Elezar stole a glance over his shoulder and caught Skellan staring at his back with the forlorn expression of a lonely dog. The reflexive pity Elezar felt at the sight made Elezar curse his own pathetic heart. He returned to glowering at the grain sacks while he pushed clumsy words around in his mind, attempting to work out some way to convey his frustration to Skellan—other than throttling him.

"You are Count Radulf. Don't you understand what that means? You are the embodiment of all your lands and people." Elezar spoke carefully. "If you are taken, then so is all of Radulf County. If you're killed, then all the work, all the preparations that every man and woman in this city has undertaken, will be undone."

"That can't be true." Skellan sounded uncertain. "There would still be other witches and Lady Hylanya—"

Elezar spun back on his heel, enraged that Skellan could even suggest that he might be so easily replaced. But when he caught sight of Skellan's expression his anger dulled. He looked so utterly at a loss and so obviously confused by Elezar's mood. He didn't even have the sense to cringe from the violence Elezar might inflict but instead stared at him as if Elezar held some prize that he longed for but couldn't grasp.

Elezar sighed heavily.

"I'm beginning to think that you might be the greatest threat to your own survival that I have to contend with," Elezar stated.

"I'm sorry." Skellan looked all the more downcast and nodded as if this were an unavoidable truth of the world. "I didn't mean to endanger you or your men. I just knew that I had to act… The Sumar grimma had to be stopped."

"She did," Elezar acknowledged. "But certainly not in some reckless, haphazard sprint to a completely exposed position on a riverbank."

Skellan opened his mouth but then to Elezar's relief he shut it again, with an unusually subdued expression.

They both stood quietly and for the first time Elezar noticed a cloud imp flitting after mice in the hayloft. He glanced back to Skellan and suddenly felt adrift. How far his life had strayed from his Cadeleonian heritage in such a short time. It was as if he'd stumbled into some other man's life and had just taken it up.

Skellan smoothed a ruffled edge of his cloak and Elezar wondered if he wasn't trying to soothe himself—perhaps stroking that animal part of him that so often took shelter within that hide.

"I'm not good at being Count Radulf," Skellan said. "In all truth, I'm a little afraid of becoming good at being the count. I don't want to be the sort who'd send men to fight battles I'm too much of a coward to take on myself."

"Trust me, you're in no danger of that," Elezar replied. "Why in the three hells did you think that you had to be the one to challenge her?"

"Because…" Skellan frowned down at the ring on his index finger. "Because she's my mother and I… I wanted to meet her. I wanted to show her that I wasn't a coward."

Elezar hadn't expected that. Skellan so rarely acknowledged his parentage that it was easy to forget. This would have been the first time he'd met his mother since he'd been an infant.

"I can see how facing her might have seemed important. But you must understand that in both battle and governing we all play different parts. You shouldn't throw yourself into the role of a foot soldier any more than I should decide to carry Cobre to battle on my back, just to be fair about things."

Skellan laughed.

"The bridle might suit you though," Skellan said but then his expression sobered. "But I do see your point there."

The tension gripping Elezar's body seemed to ease at that. As obstinate and brash as Skellan could be, he did seem willing to hear Elezar out. This didn't have to be a battle of unbending wills.

"There are other people in this world better trained and more suitable for certain work. You just have to use them," Elezar said.

A slight frown curved Skellan's lips.

"It's hard to imagine... Not that there are others better with a sword or on the back of a horse than I am—I do know that much. Only it's strange to think that such folk should be answerable to me. I'm used to being on my own, doing what I must for myself. Six months ago all these guildsmen and soldiers wouldn't have spared me a splash of piss. It's hard to think that now they want to lay down their lives at my order."

The idea of that had never occurred to Elezar. It should have, but it hadn't.

Now, for the first time, he considered the sort of absolute self-reliance Skellan's life must have required. Had there ever been a time when anyone would have given him anything simply because he asked—simply because he was himself? Hell, half the Labaran soldiers now serving Skellan were probably the same men he'd spent a decade hiding from. As far as Elezar could tell, Skellan's experiences with the merchant classes seemed to have ranged from prostitution to nearly ending up in a dog-fighting pit for their amusement.

For all Elezar's secrets and sense of isolation, his own upbringing had brimmed with favors, gifts, and the implicit understanding of his elevated position in the hierarchy of Cadeleonian society. Even throughout the last five years of drinking and dueling, his excess of violence had been largely indulged in deference to his rank. He'd lived a rough, hard life, but of his own volition, and he'd always been free to return to the comforts of his noble entitlements. In a way he'd spent five years playing at the brutal existence that Skellan had faced from the time he was eleven.

It occurred to Elezar that he, at the same age or even much older, with his sense of lordly privilege and social conformity, would not have survived all Skellan endured. Certainly he wouldn't have adjusted easily to the sort of intense deprivation that had made up a full decade of Skellan's youth.

So, how fair was it to expect Skellan to adapt perfectly to the noble world in a matter of weeks?

"All right. I can see your point on that as well," Elezar admitted. "Sometimes I forget that all of this is new to you."

"It is." Skellan gave a shrug. "But complaining about it is a bit like moaning about how long it takes to count all the gold in my treasury."

Elezar nodded and considered Skellan's bedraggled form anew. He'd come so close to dying today and they weren't even at war yet. It had scared Elezar so badly, so deeply, that he still felt the fear of it like the reverberation of a bell ringing on and on through his whole body.

"Just so we're clear about this though," Elezar said. "When the other three grimma arrive you *will* stay behind the city walls, inside the wards that you and Javier and every witch in this city have erected. You are the key to those wards and all Radulf County. You cannot be risked."

Skellan offered no reply but a familiar and obstinate line creased his red brows. Either he didn't want to hear this or he didn't believe it. Perhaps that was another aspect of his youth. He'd grown up a foundling of no importance to anyone but a troll. He didn't seem able to easily accept that now he commanded an importance beyond even his own desires.

"You *must* let soldiers fight for you when the time comes," Elezar insisted. "Skellan, I'm not joking. If you're… lost, then everything is lost. You aren't just an anonymous nobody who can do what he wills with his existence. You're the living embodiment of Radulf County and as such you cannot indulge in foolhardy acts. Accepting the sacrifices of those who serve you to protect the greater domain is the burden of ruling."

"But it doesn't seem right to ask so many other people to risk their lives while I huddle behind the city walls," Skellan replied.

"Maybe not." But since when did fairness have anything to do with warfare, Elezar thought but decided not to say. Instead he responded, "But I promise you, it's worse to the risk the entire county and all the folk living here just to assuage your private sense of what's equitable."

"But we Labarans are equitable," Skellan replied. "We believe in parity and freedom and—"

"I know, I know. Those are all fine ideals for a time of peace. Fine ideals with which to rule your own subjects. But you aren't going to be fighting your own subjects nor are your enemies going to respect your sense of honor." Elezar cut him off but softly, understanding that Skellan really did hold himself to these ideals. "Look, there's a reason that Cadeleonians are famous for winning wars. It's not just our horses and cannons. We are honest enough about ourselves and each other to recognize that while many among us can become outstanding warriors, our prowess and skill means nothing unless we protect the very few who are worthy of fighting for. You are one of the few, Skellan."

"I doubt that many folk would agree with—"

"Now's not the time to indulge your insecurities," Elezar stated. "Your people are willing to kill and to die for you. I will fight to the death for you. That's the truth of the matter. The worst thing you could do now is to betray their loyalty and mine by getting yourself killed."

Skellan's expression strained with thoughts that went unspoken. Elezar stared back until Skellan bowed his head.

"I'm not trying to get killed," Skellan said at last. "And just so you know, the fact that I went out to meet the Sumar grimma when I did was the only thing that kept her from coming to take the city."

"Of course it did." Elezar felt a little of his old annoyance creeping back over him. "Why would she, or anyone, bother to siege a well-defended city when you run out and present yourself to her? You might as well have stuffed an apple in your mouth and laid down on a silver platter in front of her."

"You don't understand. It was a test," Skellan insisted.

"A test?" Elezar could hardly believe it. A rush of outrage swept through him at just the thought. "A test of whom? Me? My men? What were you testing us for? Whether we'd really die to protect you from your own bad judgment—"

"It was the Sumar grimma's test of me!" Skellan eyed Elezar like he truly might be an idiot and Elezar's temper foundered into confusion.

"Why on earth would she test you?" Elezar asked. How did marching on Milmuraille just to test Skellan make any sense, when the Sumar grimma might just as easily have seized the entire county for her own?

Skellan shook his head, ambivalence plain upon his angular face.

"She said that she wished to prove my courage in the face of an attack from a grimma. She wanted to witness the strength of my conviction to free those enthralled."

"Why would she, of all people, care about that?" Elezar had seen the hundreds of Mirogoths the Sumar grimma had kept enthralled as deer and the others she had turned into bears and set to guard those deer. As far as he'd seen almost no one within her holdings had escaped the Sumar grimma's thrall.

"When we were up on the bridge, she showed me her life in an age long past." Skellan's hands curled into his cloak and despite the heat he pulled it closer around him. "I think that in some way she and the other grimma are themselves enthralled. They weren't born into the bodies that they now inhabit."

"What do you mean?"

"They aren't human beings. Or they weren't originally. They've been locked up in the bodies of women so long now that I think maybe they've become a little more human than they once were. I think that's the only reason the Sumar grimma cares that I'm her son, but they still aren't..." Skellan trailed off as if uncertain of how to sum up all the humanity that the grimma lacked. Having met the Sumar grimma, Elezar needed no further explanation. Instead, he tried to think of a way that this new information might serve them in their future battles.

"If you could break the spells enthralling them would they be more vulnerable?" Elezar wondered.

"I don't think so." Skellan shook his head. "They were locked up in human bodies to restrain their power. But before that they were Old Gods, the four daughters of the sky."

Elezar frowned, trying to recollect that Labaran myth. Then he remembered a brilliant illustration of four gigantic dragons, one for each of the four directions of the wind and embodying the four seasons. He recalled thinking it a pretty image, befitting a costly compass perhaps.

Then he remembered that huge snarling form that had flickered before his eyes as the Sumar grimma had clutched Skellan. That immense emerald creature with its long coiling tail, scaled body, vast membranous wings, and gaping reptilian jaws had seemed to block out the sun. Elezar's entire body went cold as ice.

"You're joking..." Elezar managed to get out.

"I'm not," Skellan said.

"But how could they..." He didn't know why it seemed so hard to believe. He'd seen children transformed into rabbits, bolts of pure lightning that became shining horses, and full-grown Irabiim who slipped from the folds of feathered cloaks that had once trapped them in the bodies of eagles.

Hell, he'd charged trolls and faced down griffins in the city streets. It wasn't that he couldn't believe that the monstrosity he'd glimpsed was indeed real. No, Elezar realized. He simply didn't want to know that he and all of the city's defenders might soon be facing three much more fearsome creatures.

"So, unless the spells enthralling them are maintained, we could have three dragon goddesses to contend with?" Elezar inquired.

Skellan nodded but he looked distracted by some other thought. Elezar wasn't certain that he really wanted to ask if there was something more to this.

"But even those weren't their first forms." Skellan sounded thoughtful.

"No?" *Could it get worse?*

Skellan gazed up and Elezar followed his stare to the flecks of dust and gold straw wafting through the bright shafts of afternoon light.

"Before they were broken apart and given bodies they were a single spirit. The soul of the sky: Wind."

Elezar heard the words and yet his mind gave an odd lurch as he attempted to truly grasp their larger implications. He didn't know what to think of that information or how to respond.

Wind.

How did someone fight wind? Could any man—even one armed with a spell-forged sword—hope to defeat a raging storm? Did it even have to be battled or would it simply carry itself away into the high reaches of the heavens? Elezar did not know, and more than that, he had no way of even hazarding a guess.

"You know, my man, if you defeat one, you'll be my Champion Wind-breaker."

Elezar blinked at Skellan in a sort of stunned confusion. Then a shout of laughter burst up from him. How relieving it felt.

"How could you promise me such a grand title?" Elezar asked. "Particularly in the company of all these handsome steeds each perfuming the air with the great volleys that mere men can only stand in awe of… Or in horror of, depending on just how close a fellow stands."

Despite the stupidity of the entire exchange, Elezar smiled, pleased and relieved to see Skellan snort and grin like a schoolboy.

Elezar continued, "So does any of this information about the grimma mean anything new for our defense of the city?"

"I don't think it changes anything. The Sumar grimma wanted me to know my heritage, I think. And she wanted me to understand that once all four of the grimma were one ancient spirit. That's why she can't join our side against them." Skellan's expression turned wistful. "I think that, as my mother, she truly doesn't want harm to come to me but she's powerless to stop the other aspects of her own spirit from attacking."

Elezar considered that and then nodded. It made sense that she'd freed her trolls, bears, and eagles if that was the only way that she could offer any protection to her child.

"Did she say anything else?" Elezar asked.

"Not much." Skellan bowed his head as if attempting to hide his wistful smile. "I know it means fuck all to the defense of Milmuraille but… I think that by the end she realized what I was doing and was proud of me. I'm not the child she would have raised but she still gave me her blessing."

That's why Skellan had been so giddy on their return, Elezar realized. He'd been acknowledged by his mother.

Elezar felt like a clueless clod. How had he failed to realize how much it would mean to Skellan to face the Sumar grimma in person? She wasn't just a powerful opponent to him but also the woman who'd given him life. Of course he'd raced to meet her and delighted in receiving what motherly affection she could offer.

Elezar could almost feel his own mother's hand slapping the back of his head for being such a dolt.

Quiet settled around them but it was a comfortable quiet, interrupted only by the soft noises of the horses and the occasional brief squabble between little birds. Skellan stepped up to Elezar's side.

"I am sorry about earlier. I didn't realize how it would affect you or your cavalry," Skellan said. Then he added, "I won't do it again."

Elezar nodded his acceptance of the apology and then slid his left arm around Skellan's shoulder and hugged him to his chest. Skellan leaned into him.

Stripped of his anger, an uneasy sense of vulnerability crept over Elezar. He could armor and arm himself all he liked, but Skellan still remained exposed. He felt so lean in Elezar's grip, not fragile, but stretched thin and hungry by constant exertion Elezar could see Skellan's pulse jumping in the long line of his throat. The bones of his hard shoulders dug into Elezar's chest and arm. It seemed a wonder that so much strength and power inhabited such a wiry, wild creature as his Skellan. Stranger, that he felt so much simply standing with him like this.

He wished he possessed any gift with words, because there was something in the turmoil of his thoughts that he wanted to tell Skellan, but language eluded him. He might jabber on, trying to tell Skellan how like a physical pang Skellan's mortality felt to him. How beautiful and somehow rare Skellan's pulse seemed to him in this moment. But he knew his own tongue would turn clumsy and trite. So he simply held Skellan.

"You want your supper yet?" Skellan asked. He sounded sleepy.

"Food can wait," Elezar decided. "Right now I just want to take you to our bed."

"Indeed." Skellan grinned at Elezar.

Elezar woke to a cracking, fast rap against the door. He lurched from the comforting weight of Skellan's sleeping body. Long shafts of dawn light filtered in from between the curtains. He snatched up his breeches and staggered across the room, buckling his belt. He jerked the door open before the guard outside could land another loud rap against the oak paneling.

"What?" Elezar demanded. Even as he asked, he took in the figures gathered in the hall and their expressions: four alarmed garrison guards and an exhausted woman wearing the emblem of the river guard scouts. All at once he felt wide awake and knew exactly why they stood before him. He'd hoped for more time.

"The grimma's forces?" Elezar met the scout's gaze. "Where?"

"The main armies are still four days off but advanced parties have reached the river. Packs of mordwolves. They're raiding mills and farms." The tanned young scout looked haunted as she spoke the last words. "We sighted a group of farmers fleeing for the city, but I don't think they'll make it here before..."

"How many and how far are they from us?" Elezar asked.

"Some fifty folk, from gray-hairs to infants, as well as live-stock," the scout reported. "They hadn't reached Southbend Mill when we passed them in our skiff maybe two hours ago." The young woman's lip appeared to tremble. It might have been nothing but a flicker of the torchlight. "We couldn't help them. The skiff can only carry the two of us and we couldn't..."

"You did the right thing," Elezar assured her and he meant it. The tiny, swift Labaran scouting skiffs could carry the weight of one man or two slender women at most. Loaded down with refugees, a scouting skiff stood more chance of drowning everyone involved than ferrying anyone to safety.

Still if he and his cavalrymen mounted up now and rode hard they stood a chance of reaching the mills that populated the river's bend. The thought of facing the mordwolves he'd glimpsed in the Sumar lands sent a shiver through him, but someone had to go.

"Our captain wants to know if the count will allow her to send two boats upriver to try and pick up the farmers, but they'd need an escort."

"Yes, to both," Elezar responded. He turned back to snatch up his discarded clothes. From the bed Skellan shook his head but with an amused expression lighting his sharp features. He bounded up from the bedding and strode, naked, towards Elezar.

"You're thinking of riding out there yourself, aren't you?" Skellan shoved a thick tangle of his red hair back from his face. "And after all that yesterday about important people not rushing off to recklessly face their doom."

"We can't just leave them."

"Oh, I agree with you on that account." Skellan traipsed up beside Elezar. He looked to the scout. "Tell Captain Wirret that I'll call Bone-crusher and his new companions, Iron-step, Grind-stone, and Hill-fist, to clear the ground ahead of her boats. Trolls can cross the ground fast as horses and mordwolves will just break their teeth if they try for a bite of Bone-crusher..." He trailed off as he seemed to take note of the guards and the young scout all staring at him.

"Pants," Elezar whispered to him. Skellan sighed as though burdened by outlandish prudery, but then turned back and swept up his dog skin. The scarlet cloak covered some of his nudity as he strode back toward the bed. He turned in a circle, raising his arms high. Then he called out long low notes that seemed far below the range of any human voice. The sound carried through the air, as if echoing across a vast canyon. Elezar felt the tones reverberating through his chest and loins. Next to him the guards rocked back from the door as if pushed aside by the escaping song. The scout shuddered and hunched as notes rolled over her.

Skellan quieted but remained standing with his arms raised and his head lifted. Elezar felt aware that he, the four guards, and the scout all stood listening intently along with Skellan for some reply. For a moment Elezar thought he only heard a distant wind whispering over the garrison walls but then he realized that he recognized Bone-crusher's voice.

We go now to make a meal of the mordwolves, Little Thorn.

Skellan smiled and turned back to the party assembled at the door.

"They are on their way now," Skellan announced. He cocked his head and eyed Elezar. "You see, I'm delegating. What of you? Will you wait here or will you join Bone-crusher?"

Anticipation and dread circled through Elezar, stirring up that familiar surge of resolve. Part of him would rather never lay eyes on a mordwolf again, but he wouldn't acknowledge the chill of fear coiling in his gut; the same sensation always came over him just before a duel. Mortal fear, like the scar bisecting his thigh and the memories of his brother's bloody murder, could not be expunged or outdistanced. Yet the desire to do so often drove Elezar to prove his own courage and strength again and again.

Elezar wondered if there wasn't something truly perverse about him that the horror of his youth inspired him to seek out violent confrontations. Or perhaps it was simply that he knew no way to silence his own uneasiness other than to throw himself into action. He wanted a taste of what he and his men would face when the full might of the grimma's armies arrived. He needed to test his own resolve.

Perhaps that made him as reckless as Skellan, in his own way. But he thought better than to admit as much. In any case he was more practiced at battle than Skellan and certainly more dispensable.

"I'd best go. I should see how mordwolves attack," Elezar said.

A brief frown creased Skellan's mouth but then he nodded.

"Keep safe," Skellan said.

Elezar readied himself and rode out ahead of the two riverboats that Captain Boski had dispatched. He and Cobre kept back behind the trolls but also upwind of them. Their massive feet tossed up huge clouds of dust, in places obscuring the road and vast fields of green crops and wildflowers. All along the road, abandoned gardens stood ripening while flocks of wild birds fed freely. Here and there Elezar spied plump hares lazing among carrots and longpeas.

Beyond the verdant fields, the eastern sky filled with dark storm clouds that turned the rising sun red orange as a sunset. Walls of lightning flashed in the distance, the crack of thunder sounding long after the light died. Elezar took in the ominous sky and for just an instant he allowed himself to feel dread, knowing all of that darkness, power, and rage would soon fall upon Milmuraille.

But then he turned his concentration back to the road ahead.

Soon enough they came upon the bright red waterwheels of the mills that populated the riverbank along the south bend. The waterwheels splashed and creaked in rhythm to the flowing waters but out of time with each other. Elezar thought he heard sheep bleating but his view wasn't clear. The massive green mounds of the trolls moved like hillocks between him and the river.

Elezar came around a wide bend in the road and all at once took in the sight of a pack of eight mordwolves, feeding upon two fallen oxen and the herder who had been leading the animals.

The shaggy mordwolves were not so tall as Cobre but they certainly would have made Skellan's red hound look like a fine-boned lapdog. Splashes of blood colored their gaping muzzles and speckled their gray hides. Their saber-like canine teeth glistened in the light, extending well past the animals' lower jaws. One of the mordwolves wrenched a leg from a dead man's body while others tore at the bellies of the oxen.

Unlike common wolves or dogs the mordwolves ate in unnerving silence, issuing neither whines nor growls. The crack of bones shattering in their jaws and the wet rip of rending flesh was the only sound of their feast.

Then three of the mordwolves lifted their bloody heads from the chasms of the oxen's gaping bellies. Silently, they barred their teeth at both the trolls and Elezar. The other five mordwolves immediately looked up as well.

Cobre snorted and Elezar felt the stallion's heartbeat hammer through his own legs. If any people or livestock sheltered among the mills Elezar didn't see them. All of his attention locked onto the mordwolves. He gripped his sword.

Just ahead of him Bone-crusher let loose a roar and lunged forward. The three other trolls followed his example, howling like windswept thunder. The mordwolves scattered, though one didn't get quite clear. Bone-crusher stamped down hard atop the beast's back, crushing the mordwolf as if trampling a rat. A pitiful, nearly human scream escaped the mordwolf. Bone-crusher kicked it aside and it slumped into the dirt as lifelessly as a rag.

The seven remaining mordwolves leapt and dodged between the trolls, nearly causing Bone-crusher and the hulking Hill-fist to collide as they gave chase. Iron-step crushed another of the beasts but slid in the slick mass of its spattered entrails and went down hard on one knee, almost knocking Grindstone down as well. Tufts of greenery and shards of the troll's stony hide cracked away upon impact.

What looked like panic on the part of the mordwolves almost appeared to be genuine cunning as they darted between the trolls' feet. With the trolls nearly tripping over each other, the surviving six mordwolves stood a chance of escaping back across the river and into the forest.

Elezar urged Cobre ahead, circling wide around the trolls to cut off the escape of the two mordwolves closest to the riverbank. Cobre closed the distance, swinging Elezar alongside the nearest mordwolf. The beast's shoulder rose nearly to Elezar's knee and at close range he could smell the blood and gore caking the mordwolf's bristling gray coat. Elezar shifted, and as Cobre bounded ahead, he swung his sword down across the back of the mordwolf's neck and skull. The blade seared through the flesh as if it were cutting through water. The mordwolf's heavy skull tore free in a bloody arc and for several moments the immense beast's huge body continued to run. Then suddenly its feet tangled and its body slumped into the ground.

Elezar raced after the second mordwolf and again Cobre ran the creature down. Elezar took aim at the mordwolf's skull. But then the creature turned its head and called, "No!"

It was the voice of a girl—a child.

Despite himself, Elezar hesitated and in that moment the mordwolf sprang at him. Hot breath and teeth like daggers came at his face. Elezar drove his sword into the mordwolf's throat, burning through flesh in a single stroke. Still, the hulking body slammed into him with the force of a battering ram. Elezar fell from his saddle and hit the ground with half the mordwolf's dead weight atop him. The severed head gaped a hand's breath from his face. The jaws snapped once, sending a jolt of terror through Elezar. He hurled the bleeding carcass off him and leapt to his feet.

Just ahead of him, Cobre swung around, placing himself between Elezar and two mordwolves charging up from the riverbank. The instant Elezar had fallen the beasts must have turned from their flight to close in on him.

The bastards don't miss a beat.

The larger of the two lunged at Cobre and the stallion reared back, landing hard kicks down across the mordwolf's head. The mordwolf fell back, drawing Cobre after while its companion slunk to the left and charged Elezar.

Elezar's pulse pounded wildly but his grip on his sword felt steady. He brought the long black blade up before him and it sang with the fury pounding through Elezar's body. The mordwolf's grizzled form seemed to shudder as the waves of heat rolling off the sword distorted the air. The charging mordwolf veered to Elezar's left. Elezar pivoted, keeping his blade between them. Then his boot heel struck the severed head lying at his feet and he stumbled. The mordwolf pounced.

Its body blotted out Elezar's view as it hurtled at him. Elezar drove his blade up and into the mass of the mordwolf's body. They fell together, Elezar going down backwards with the mordwolf tearing through his coat and light leather armor even as its weight drove Elezar's blade deep into its chest. Teeth grazed Elezar's left shoulder, but it was the crushing weight on his chest—the rancid mats of hair filling his mouth and nostrils as he fought to pull in air—that nearly overcame him. A piercing pain shot up from his chest as he felt a rib crack. He shoved with all his strength but couldn't budge the dead weight suffocating him.

Then suddenly the mass lifted and Elezar found himself gasping up at Bone-crusher. The troll studied him for a moment then lifted the mordwolf up to his craggy mouth and bit the head off.

Elezar rolled to his feet and stumbled towards Cobre. The stallion met him with an anxious nicker and snuffled Elezar's bloody left shoulder.

"Just a scratch." Elezar stroked the stallion's jaw as he surveyed the open fields and wide road. The only remaining mordwolves appeared to be those the trolls had crushed or now gulped down their gullets. Six dead, Elezar counted, which meant two had made it across the river. Looking out at the dark woods of the far banks, Elezar felt the distinct uneasiness of being studied in return. On the near bank, moored to one of the mill launches, he caught sight of a riverboat. Guards escorted humbly dressed folk and their small herds of livestock aboard.

One slim blond guard waved and Elezar realized that it was Sarl. She looked taller and more tanned than he remembered, but she still flashed the same charming, wide grin. He waved back. Then both of them returned to their own business.

Elezar led Cobre to the road and inspected him there, reassuring himself that Cobre had come through the fight largely unharmed. Like Elezar, he bore a few scratches, but none looked deep or serious. Still, Elezar drew water from the river and rinsed the mud and blood from Cobre's cuts before washing them with coinflower and comfrey oil. The last of the antiseptic oil he rubbed into his own slight wounds. It stung but certainly smelled better than the mordwolf blood caking his clothes.

From the higher ground of the road he watched the riverboats pull away from the launches, ferrying people and animals. A troop of glistening green frogwives swam alongside the boats and from time to time Elezar noted the glint of the harpoons that they carried.

Behind him the trolls finished the last of the mordwolves and their low voices rolled and rumbled in a debate over the oxen that the mordwolves had already killed. At last they tore those apart and devoured them too, leaving just the mutilated body of the herder for Elezar to bundle in a saddle blanket and carry back to Milmuraille.

As he rode, he glimpsed shadows slinking beneath the stands of fir trees across the shore. The flash of wild animal eyes met his gaze and then vanished.

Skellan strode over the same stones that he must have paced across a hundred times in the last month. He lifted his hand, stroking the taut lines of power that wove the vast tapestry of wards blanketing the city. He plucked a fine scarlet string and it sent a shiver vibrating down his spine. Was this how a spider felt in the heart of her web, he wondered.

Ahead of him, Javier and Cire leaned against the battlements, gazing out from between the stone merlons. A little ahead of them Kiram Kir-Zaki had actually climbed up into the empty space of a crenel to peer out at the river using a spyglass of his own making. Ringlets of his gold hair fluttered around his face as the wild winds rising from the east swept over him.

Cire rose on the tips of her toes to study the long swath of green fields and open road spreading beneath them. Queenie poked her nose out from one of the pockets of Cire's golden silk shift. Standing so close, Javier, with his long lean form, dwarfed Cire. He, too, studied the view but not so intently. Instead he glanced often to his right where Kiram perched with his spyglass.

"Anything?" Javier asked.

"Eight mordwolves that I can see," Kiram called over the churning wind. He didn't look away from his glass. "They're fast."

Javier squinted into the distance and then turned his attention back to Skellan, offering him a wry smile.

"Elezar's got some gall criticizing you for brash attacks, doesn't he?" Javier asked.

Skellan laughed but shook his head. "How could I expect him not to ride out? He's good at this kind of thing."

"True. If any man could take on a pack of mordwolves I'd put my money on Elezar," Javier agreed but he didn't look exactly pleased. Doubtless he wondered why Elezar hadn't taken his full cavalry with him. Skellan could have told him that Elezar hadn't wanted so many horses getting under the trolls but that wouldn't have done anything to alleviate Javier's concern for his friend.

Though he did wonder if Javier couldn't see that he stood ready, fingers curled through his wards, prepared to draw all the power of his witchflame and feed that force into Elezar. The way his dark gaze flickered over Skellan's hands made Skellan think that Javier did sense something but neither of them spoke of it.

Skellan tugged anxiously at a line of spells, feeling them pull against his fingertips like taut strings of a lute. Whispers of power and purpose hummed against his palms.

It didn't matter that Elezar rode into danger, Skellan assured himself, because he wouldn't allow his champion to come to harm. Particularly not after last night. Standing in the stable he'd seen the bare honesty in Elezar's face when he had demanded that Skellan use him, even sacrifice him. He'd promised his own life, just as simply as he'd handed his knife to Skellan earlier, but for the first time Skellan realized that Elezar understood full well what he offered up. Likely he understood it better than Skellan did himself.

Since Skellan had become a count, numerous people had blithely assured him of their loyalty and made meaningless pledges, but Elezar alone had spoken the truth and meant every word.

I will fight to the death for you.

Those words, spoken so frankly, had pierced Skellan to his heart. He didn't think he'd ever felt so moved by another man in his life. Certainly not by a man who was all but shaking with fury at him. Somehow even Elezar's frustration had only made a greater testament to the conviction behind his commitment. He'd never known anyone who so clearly wanted to wring his neck and despite that anger would still insist upon laying down his own life for Skellan's sake.

And somehow, knowing that Elezar meant exactly what he said, Skellan wanted nothing but to ensure that he would never fulfill his promise.

"Elezar will be fine," Skellan said as much to himself as to the others gathered on the wall with him.

"Probably. Though even the best man can make a mistake." Javier stepped forward to catch the back of Kiram's coat as the other man leaned out further over the battlement, utterly enrapt with the view captured by his spyglass. "Or get carried away," Javier added over his shoulder to Skellan and Cire.

"I'm not carried away," Kiram responded, though he didn't waver from his spyglass. "I'm focused."

Cire shot Skellan an amused glance and Skellan felt certain that despite the damage done to the Rat Rafters she'd grown fond of the two men. She enjoyed teasing them about giving up a dukedom for the joys of living on squirrel meat and pine cones. Dramatic gossip concerning their romance had spread all through Milmuraille now that Kiram was becoming known for his pluming torches. If they all survived the war, Skellan imagined that Rafale might pen a play about the two of them.

"So how are Skellan's trolls working out as rescuers?" Cire inquired. "Anyone been squashed yet?"

"No, it looks like the trolls are leaving the rescue to the river guard. They're pursuing the mordwolves. But they're grouped too close together. The mordwolves can run them into each other. Wait, Elezar's charging. That sword of his is something—" Kiram broke off his commentary with an abrupt Haldiim curse. "Khivash!"

Javier's grip tightened as Kiram leaned out further and Cire straightened. Even Skellan's two guards tensed and looked to Kiram for further news.

Skellan gripped the threads of his wards and relaxed as best he could, readying to take on the worst injuries that might come. For several moments, he sensed nothing through the shared bond but the whisper of Elezar's hammering heartbeat. Then a jarring sensation slapped his back. If Skellan hadn't been concentrating on it he likely wouldn't have noticed at all. The lash of teeth slicing across his left shoulder however caught him off guard and then a much sharper almost crushing pain bit into his ribs. A faint but distinct odor rolled through his mouth and his lungs burned for fresh air.

He could feel Elezar's heart and his own falling into a single rhythm. Skellan drew in a deep breath, sharing it with Elezar. And then suddenly the pressure lifted from his chest and Skellan glimpsed the faintest image of Bone-crusher gazing down at him. He resisted the temptation to follow that vision and see through Elezar's eyes.

The ground seemed to roll as Elezar rose to his feet and Skellan staggered in the grip of a strange feeling of vertigo as he disentangled his own senses from Elezar's.

Cire and Javier had both turned to stare at him. Queenie even clambered up to Cire's shoulder to flick her whiskers at Skellan.

He smiled at them and in truth he felt good. He hadn't needed to call up the power of his wards at all. Elezar's injuries were relatively slight. Even the hairline cracks in his ribs diminished as Skellan drew them into his own body and his witchflame melted them away.

"He's up and he looks fine!" Kiram called. "His left shoulder is bloodied but he's moving it easily. I think it's just a—" Kiram stopped short as he turned to address Skellan. Then he, like Cire and Javier, stared at him. Skellan glanced behind him but only found his guards.

"Skellan," Cire said, "your shoulder is bleeding."

Skellan glanced down to see two splotches of bright red blood soaking up through the costly white silk of his shirtsleeve. He scowled. Another absurdly expensive shirt ruined. Really, he didn't see the point in being dressed in all these fine togs when he just wrecked them.

"My dressers are going to want to kill me," Skellan muttered.

"What happened to your shoulder?" Cire demanded.

"Nothing." Skellan shrugged, but feeling the sting of the cuts, he drew his cloak over his shoulder. "Just a scratch."

"You weren't scratched a moment ago." Cire frowned at him as if she suspected him of indulging in some wild recklessness the instant her back had been turned.

"But then moments ago neither was Elezar." Javier arched a brow and very carefully reached out and brushed his hand through the shining red beam of one of Skellan's wards.

Skellan felt the pure white chill of Javier's curious fingers. He traced the curves and curls that Skellan had strung like bells, each cast to resonate with a different power and purpose. Unlike his previous contact with Skellan's spells, this time Javier didn't attempt to pull anything asunder but instead carefully and cautiously traced the forms before him like a blind man feeling his way through a glass shop. Skellan heard the faintest whispers, echoes of his own voice, murmuring promises of devotion, protection, and shy affection. An embarrassed flush climbed up his face.

Javier's expression softened. He drew his hand back and said, "One of my ancestors once shared a blood oath not unlike this one you've crafted. We've all heard stories of ancient witches who shared their power with the champions that served them as warlords. Still, I hadn't thought anyone forged such bonds in this day and age."

As he spoke, a look of horror came over Cire. On her shoulder Queenie arched in alarm, but then unable to find a threat, resettled with her whiskers twitching nervously.

"Skellan, tell me you didn't!" Cire demanded but Skellan couldn't deny the truth and she saw as much in his face. "You hardly know him. How could you be so foolish?"

Cire probably thought him a romantic moron—likely Javier did as well. Maybe he was, but Skellan couldn't regret his decision. It hadn't been clever but it was right and fair.

"If Elezar is willing to act as my champion then the least I could do is lend him my protection," Skellan replied and he hoped that it sounded like something he'd thought out, perhaps even a philosophical decision, and not an impulse of pure sentiment. He wanted to steal a glance back at his guards, just to assess what they made of all this. But gawking behind him would only have made him look all the more hapless and guilty to Cire.

"Lend him your protection?" Cire asked. "That's exactly what you don't do for your champion! It defeats the entire point of having him fight and die in your stead if you're taking on his hurt. For fuck's sake, Skellan! How can you still be so naïve—"

"I beg your pardon." Kiram lifted a callused hand in the Irabiim gesture of peace as he interrupted. "But am I understanding this correctly? You, Skellan, have cast a spell that transfers Elezar's injuries to your own body?"

"Yes—" Cire snapped.

"—No," Skellan corrected.

"No?" Cire raised her brows. "Then what's the blood on your shoulder from?"

"Ah, I believe I can answer that." Javier appeared rather pleased with himself and cast Kiram a self-satisfied smile. "I think that Skellan's spell acts like a release valve. It doesn't transfer all of Elezar's injuries to Skellan, but rather takes on the excess of them so as to mitigate their extent."

"That sounds more like the function of an overflow drain than a release valve," Kiram commented.

"Yes, well, you get the idea," Javier replied. "If Elezar is injured badly enough, then a certain amount of that injury will flow to Skellan… I suppose it *is* like a drain to some extent, but that sounds so—"

"Stupid?" Cire suggested.

"Commonplace, I was going to say," Javier responded.

"No form of plumbing is commonplace here," Kiram muttered. But then his gaze shifted to Skellan and his expression turned serious. "Considering how hard and often Elezar fights, aren't you taking a rather formidable risk?"

"Yes, he is," Cire answered. She glowered at Skellan. "What if one of those trolls had fallen on your Elezar? Or a mordwolf took his head off?"

Skellan had no answer for that any more than he'd had an answer for Elezar when he'd shouted about the possibility of the Sumar grimma killing him. Who could know what would happen or how ruin might come? But cringing in fear from every threat of death and failure hadn't been how Skellan had ever lived his life. He didn't see the point of starting now.

"They didn't. And if you're going to harangue me about everything that could possibly go wrong, why don't we start with the likelihood that this wall could collapse under us or maybe the sun will burst apart, plunging us into a world of endless night—"

"Stop being absurd," Cire snapped. "You're arguing like a little child."

"I'm arguing like a man who's made up his mind," Skellan responded. "And no amount of nagging can change what's done. I've made my decision."

Cire didn't have an answer to that. She looked almost taken aback then simply shook her head.

"Elezar doesn't know, does he?" Javier asked.

"He knows that I forged a bond between us," Skellan replied.

Javier's keen dark eyes narrowed and Skellan found that he couldn't quite hold Javier's stare.

"I don't think that he needs to know. It would only burden him with a sense of more responsibility," Skellan admitted. This time he did look back to assess his guards' reactions. How would fighting men respond to the idea of the bond he'd forged between himself and Elezar? They both studied Skellan with expressions that he didn't quite recognize but had seen holy men sometimes cast up at the stars shining overhead.

Perhaps he struck them as unknowable.

"I don't want news of this to bother Elezar, not while we're still facing the threat of three grimma armies." Skellan eyed his guards first but then turned back to Cire, Javier, and Kiram. "I'll explain it all to him when we're through this. Is that understood?"

All three agreed, though Kiram asked, "But you will tell him, won't you?"

Skellan nodded his assent but thought to himself that, more likely than not, he wouldn't. Because how could he admit that he'd tied himself to Elezar's fate when all that Elezar would be thinking of was his imminent return to his family and homeland? How pathetic would he seem to Elezar then?

A piercing trumpet note sounded from north gates, announcing Elezar's return to the city. Skellan wanted to race across the battlements to welcome him back. But first he needed to change his bloodied shirt. As he turned towards the garrison, he caught white forms flashing across the dark clouds like lightning, but they neither cracked apart nor faded. Instead the sky filled with the shining forms of wethra steeds charging out from the dark clouds.

The great mass of the grimma armies still lay days away but, Skellan realized, their assault had already begun.

For an instant Skellan simply stood in awe, taking in the sight of hundreds of luminous wethra-steeds galloping across the sky.

Terrifying and majestic, just as the old stories had claimed. The wethra-steeds blazed brighter than stars, their equine forms throwing off bolts of lightning as their hooves struck the clouds. Their golden riders urged them on, howling war cries that rocked the air like thunder.

Steeds and riders arced high and then suddenly dropped to smash against Skellan's wards with the fury of lightning strikes. They burned themselves apart as they ripped into the weave of spells. One after another, they crashed down from the skies above Milmuraille, hammering Skellan's will and wracking his body with shocks. Mirogothic voices roared hate and rage into his ears. Blinding light seared up inside Skellan's skull and he stumbled. He knew that one of his guards caught him, kept him from toppling from the height of the battlements, but he didn't see which of them saved him.

Skellan's awareness soared with his witchflame up from his prone body to the heights overlooking Milmuraille. There, he crouched atop the dome he'd woven from wards to shield the city. Below him the Sun Palace looked like an ornate miniature and the tiny specks of the people scattered as if blown aside by a great breath.

As a second wave of wethra-steeds lit the dark storm clouds, Skellan bounded up. He raced across the scarlet weave of his wards, covering miles of the city below as he charged to meet the assault. The wethra-steeds arched over him, dazzling his vision. Then they lanced down. Skellan leapt up to meet them in the air. He engulfed all their beauty and grace in the voracious jaws of his witchflame. He devoured them and fed the wild excess of their power out into the vast fabric of his wards.

Yet for every one he consumed in his witchflame another two slammed into the wards, steadily tearing deeper into the web of spells protecting the city below. The attack sickened Skellan with its utter disregard for the lives of the wethra-steeds and their riders. Their loyalty and valor deserved better but he couldn't afford to think on the horror of so many deaths of such rare creatures. He couldn't even afford to offer them mercy.

As dozens more descended from the sky, Skellan drew in the stored force of his wards as if he were taking in a deep, smoldering breath of flame. White hot power flooded him. He knew that far below his body writhed and convulsed, but here in the heights his witchflame felt immense and his senses sang with joyous strength.

The wethra-steeds dived and Skellan hurled all his fury and force in a vast wall of fire, devouring them. He rushed onward, burning through the dark storm clouds and throwing down sheets of sleet and rain in his wake. From the icy heights he glowered down and for the first time took in the long, dark columns and herds of wild creatures that made up the front lines of the grimma's armies. Tiny flags fluttered on pine poles and ranks of Mirogoths, dressed in furs and leather, gawked up. Skellan hung over them, lighting the sky with the image of his scarlet wolf. But the grimma themselves were still hidden from him.

Skellan sent his anger flying into the storm winds and booming out over the dark forest and craggy mountains, hoping that it reached the grimma lurking beyond his senses.

Lay on all the might and lightning you will. Come to me and I will burn all your armies to cinders!

He hurled down a second wall of fire. The men and women beneath him screamed, attempting to outrun the flames. Animals shrieked and bolted. Despite his anger Skellan couldn't bring himself to pursue them to their fiery deaths. Once again he drew the flames back as if he were inhaling fire. He bounded back to the familiar sky hanging over Milmuraille just in time to see two great dragons rise from the eastern edge of the forest. One shone bright as the rising sun and the other smoldered like a sunset. Both of them swung their huge heads in Skellan's direction, and almost acting as one, they threw open their gaping jaws, hurling flames and torrents of ice across Skellan.

He didn't attempt to fight them from the heights but instead dropped like a stone, releasing all the strength he'd gathered back into his wards.

He half-expected the grimma to follow after him. He hoped that they would, so that he could draw them into the web of his wards. He would fight them here and now and be done with the waiting. They could fight each other—witch against witch—instead of sparring with armies and at the cost of so many lives.

But instead they merely spat curses after Skellan, throwing a flurry of embers and ice over the city.

Skellan plunged into his living flesh with the grace of a diver striking bare stone. His entire body clenched in on itself like a fist and his ears rang with the sound of his own ragged howl. Nerves from the soles of his feet to the crown of his skull ignited like seams of black powder. Skellan fought his own clenching jaw to gasp in a deep breath of sweet summer air. He held it in his lungs—silencing the animal cry that had escaped him. Still curled into a ball, he cracked his eyes open.

Ribbons of smoke and ash plumed across the blue sky while gusts of snow drifted like mist, melting away before reaching the ground.

The younger of Skellan's two body guards leaned over him, cradling Skellan's head in his lap. Cire knelt beside him, her small warm hand pressed against the skin of his throat. He could feel the outline of her fingers as his pulse pounded against them. Skellan's second guard stood, grimfaced and gripping his spear, as if expecting an army of enemies to materialize before him. Only a few feet away Javier and Kiram looked on.

Kiram frowned but not at Skellan. He called out something in Irabiim and Skellan realized that his collapse had drawn the attention of the group of Irabiim archers positioned on the east wall. After a few more words from Kiram the archers returned to their posts.

Javier glanced up to the now invisible wards overhead and offered Skellan a commiserating grin.

"Well done. You're nothing if not quick to take up the fight," Javier commented. "Though next time you might want to sit down before you abandon your body to the care of your guards. Or better yet you might ask Cire and me to assist. We are actually rather skilled, you know."

Cire shot Javier a look of long suffering but then returned her attention to Skellan.

"Are you hurt?" she asked. Belatedly Skellan realized that Queenie had dropped down to press her tiny body against his chest. Skellan wanted to pet her but didn't yet trust his hands.

"No. Sorry for the surprise." Skellan's voice felt raw and the words came out rough. He cleared his throat and then forced himself to straighten his limbs. "I'm fine. You might want to call Queenie back."

Cire nodded and Queenie instantly scampered up from his chest to Cire's outstretched hand. A chill crept over the warm spot she'd abandoned.

As he spoke, it occurred to him that he could hear fire bells ringing. The smoke streaking the sky didn't just trail behind falling embers but drifted up in plumes from the city. Several of the grimma's cinders must have fallen through the holes the wethra-steeds had punched in Skellan's wards. Thatch roves and wooden buildings would be burning. He wondered if he ought to do something to assist Sheriff Hirbe and his fire guard, then he wondered if he'd even be able to stand on his own just yet.

He tried and found that he could, though he didn't rise with any particularly grace. His body felt foreign to him, one leg dragging with numb while the other twitched as if trying to dance to a rhythm only it knew. Once Skellan managed to stand and take a few steps, his sense of belonging in his own body returned.

"I'm fine," he repeated as much to himself as anyone else.

"Those were wethra-steeds that we saw burning apart, weren't they?" Kiram asked. His expression seemed a mix of wonder and sorrow.

Skellan started to answer but then realized that the question hadn't been addressed to him.

"Yes, beautiful, weren't they? I never thought I'd see so many at once." Javier's youthful face lit with delight for an instant but then turned grim. "It seems a pity that they should all have to die. But then that's the nature of war. And this will only be the beginning."

Skellan didn't want to think on that because he knew Javier was right.

Elezar charged through the city gates as balls of fire rained down from the sky. He jerked Cobre's reins and the two of them lurched to the right as a flaming mass slammed into the road beside them. It looked no larger than Elezar's fist but hissed and screeched like a dying boar as it burned out. The smoke rising from the remaining glassy black lump smelled oddly fragrant, almost like copal resin.

A pair of boys dressed in oversized wall watch uniforms wearing brass helmets raced from the nearest guardhouse. One youth upended a bucket of sand and dirt over the seething remnant feet from Elezar, while the other pelted onward with his head cocked back to follow the blazing decent of another fiery mass. Elezar's breath caught in his chest as he, too, took in the trajectory and realized that it threatened one of the wall watch armories. If those flames tore through the thatched roof, who knew what they might ignite? Both black powder for cannons and marsh pitch for Kiram's pluming torches were stored there.

He nudged Cobre and the stallion charged past the boy. Elezar snatched the sand-packed bucket from his hand and raced to the very door of the armory. The men standing guard blanched at his charge but to their credit they held their ground.

"Take cover!" Elezar shouted. With all his strength he hurled the bucket up at the incoming missile. It struck clean and hard. The flaming mass burst in a geyser of orange fire. Smoking black shards rained down along with a spray of smoldering tin and sand. Not a sliver reached the armory door.

Elezar craned his head back, expecting another volley of fire, but none came. Then one of the wall watch called the all clear.

Around Elezar merchants, peddlers, and guards crept from the shelter they'd taken. Two elderly woman scuttled from beneath a milk wagon and right away set to teasing the brawny smith who peered out from beneath an upended wheelbarrow. He did rather resemble a shy tortoise emerging from its shell.

As Elezar rode past, a flock of paunchy gray geese honked at him from eves of a thatch roof. The herder boy in charge of the birds wondered aloud how such fat birds had managed the flight. Then he gaped in surprise when the girl standing near to him pointed out four of her white milk goats perching in the branches of an overhanging apple tree. Elezar couldn't help but stare as well. Adding to the strangeness of the scene, a flurry of beautifully formed snowflakes swirled through the tree branches, glazing the leaves, fruit, and wood in a filigree of frost.

Then the ground rocked beneath them all. Cries of shock and alarm rang out. Goats bleated and geese hissed and honked. Elezar gripped his sword and turned Cobre around to face the city gates. The smith scurried back beneath his wheelbarrow and both of the wall watch youths ran to the cover of the guardhouse.

The earth shuddered again.

Bone-crusher and the other three trolls appeared over the city wall. They came pelting past the gates, moving with alarming speed for such gigantic creatures. They took little notice of Elezar or the surrounding populace on the street. Though, they managed not to crush anyone in their passage. But one of the goats toppled out of the apple tree. The trolls bounded over courtyards and cleared whole buildings as they raced for the east wall. Elezar guessed that Bone-crusher feared for Skellan. Elezar did as well.

He and Cobre followed after the trolls.

They had all witnessed the ranks of wethra-steeds burn across the sky like a wall of lightning. Skellan's giant scarlet wolf had bounded up from the city, devouring them with fiery jaws. Elezar could only guess at how many had died but it had seemed that Skellan had torn through dozens at a time.

Then Skellan had charged into the distant dark storm clouds only to turn back and sink into Milmuraille as a volley of fire and ice flew after him. Elezar hadn't known what exactly that exchange had meant but he couldn't keep from remembering the night he'd found Skellan hiding and shaking with hurt. Then it had been the Sumar grimma he'd faced and she'd not intended him real harm, but this time…

Elezar didn't allow himself to think further on what harm could have befallen Skellan. No, he reassured himself, Skellan would be safe and well. He just had to see him to know as much.

He reached the first guardhouse for the east wall only moments behind Bone-crusher and the other three trolls. Sweat trickled down his back and his muscles ached with the tension of his anxiety. He swung down from Cobre, securing him to a hitching post, and then raced up the stairs to reach the wall walkway. At the top of the stairs he nearly trampled Javier and Kiram as they started down.

Behind them he caught sight of Skellan and Cire as well as the two guards. All of them appeared unharmed and in good spirits. Skellan peered down to where Bone-crusher stood near the wall, his head not more than twenty feet beneath. Something in Skellan's appraising expression gave Elezar the impression that he contemplated the leap from the wall walkway to Bone-crusher's craggy skull.

"Did we get in the way of your blind charge up the battlement, Grunito?" Javier commented with a dry smile. Elezar didn't even mind Javier's mocking tone. Almost giddy relief at the sight of Skellan looking so well filled him.

"Sorry, Tornesal, you've just gotten so tiny that I mistook you for a sprite fart," Elezar returned. "Imagine my shock when you started talking! Speaking of, one of the mordwolves called out when I ran it down. I'd swear it sounded like a little girl calling to me."

Skellan frowned, as did Cire, but Kiram's face lit with recognition.

"I told you I heard them talk that night," Kiram addressed Javier.

"They weren't speaking, then or now. They just parroted a sound as they'd been trained." Javier looked to Elezar. "I believe that Grimma Ylva teaches them all to squeak out pathetic-sounding cries. It's exceptionally disturbing and easily throws a man off. I would have mentioned it to you, but you were gone before I had the chance, weren't you?"

Elezar favored him with the Mirogoth shrug.

Javier continued, "I don't think they can manage more than 'no' or 'oh no.'" Javier glanced to Kiram. "That's what that fucker said to you, wasn't it?"

"Oh no! Oh no!" Kiram mimicked in a sweet falsetto. "And then the stinking beast leapt onto Verano to rip my throat out."

"Aren't they enthralled people, though?" Elezar asked.

"Not all of them, my man," Skellan answered. His voice sounded strained—raw. "Nothing in Grimma Ylva's old creatures but mordwolf meat."

"Well, it might be worth mentioning to the rest of the troops." Elezar brushed past Javier and Kiram to reach Skellan. His concern must have shown on his face because Skellan assured him that he was fine before Elezar even asked.

"You might worry a bit more about your own injuries," Skellan told him as the group of them joined the waiting trolls on the grounds below.

"Just scratches," Elezar said. In truth he'd expected more pain from his ribs. He would have sworn two had cracked when he'd gone down under that mordwolf's weight. He drew in a deep breath and then prodded his own chest, but discovered none of the familiar stabs of pain that had previously accompanied cracked and broken ribs.

Cire cast him an odd look but he didn't know what exactly to make of it and when Sheriff Hirbe arrived a few minutes later he forgot about the matter altogether. Soon he turned his attention to drilling his infantry and cavalry with their new troll allies, while Skellan gave leave for the two old river bridges to be pulled down. Better to destroy them than allow them to serve their enemies.

CHAPTER TWENTY-SIX

That night Skellan lay in bed but his senses soared, restless and anxious. All day he'd paced the city walls, reinforcing his wards, and yet the thought still nagged at him that a weakness remained. That weakness was himself—if he failed, then so would his wards.

Floating high in the night sky, he studied the scarlet tapestry of spells and took in the fragile city below. Hundreds of other small wards lay beneath his own, glinting like beads dangling from the trim of an immense tapestry. Individually not one of those small blessings would deter the grimma but if they could be lent the glamour of a great unity, then perhaps.

His gaze fell upon the ornate spectacle of the Sun Palace and he reached down to the flickering ruby fire curled around the young girl seated on a balcony. Hylanya worried a piece of rose soapstone, unconsciously crafting something very like a spell as she dug into the soft pink surface of the mineral. Reaching down to the stone, Skellan momentarily shared Hylanya's awareness of the swordsman who lounged beside her card table and the bickering words passed between Lady Peome and Rafale. He sensed her realization that she did not know the full truth of the events surrounding her and her first suspicions of the motives of the adults whom she'd once trusted implicitly.

She crafted something very like a candor stone, Skellan realized. He marveled at how innately magic came to his sister. As he traced the lines of her building spell he realized that it was Elezar whom his sister contemplated.

"He fought bravely for Milmuraille by the river. We all saw him." Hylanya rolled the soft stone between her long fingers, digging a line through the surface with her nail. She scraped an impression of a bull's horns. "Mistress Cire even claims that one of the actresses at the Mockingbird saw him deliver Bois to safety."

The blond swordsman nodded, but neither Rafale nor Peome noted Hylanya's comment. They continued to grumble at each other. Since Rafale had taken up residence in the Sun Palace Hylanya had slowly come to notice that Peome was far more often grim faced and short-tempered.

Rafale hated Elezar Grunito and given the chance happily mocked the other man's brutish appearance and Cadeleonian prudery. Peome, on the other hand, did not trust him or any Cadeleonian completely but on more than one occasion now she had scolded her brother for stirring trouble where none was wanted and spreading lies.

Now the two of them argued in hushed whispers over whether his death in the coming combat might serve Radulf County for the worse or the better. Hylanya might have taken Rafale's side a month ago, thinking that the Cadeleonian's presence among Labaran courtiers an affront and his demise all but overdue. But recently Mistress Cire had pointed out the shy affection in Elezar's expression when he looked at her brother.

And she could not dispute Mistress Cire when she argued that Lord Grunito had already risked his life for Skellan's sake while Rafale, for all his poetry and flattery, had not once come to the count's defense. In addition, the charming swordsman at the card table had spoken approvingly of Lord Grunito on several occasions.

So now Hylanya toyed with the thought of defying both Peome and Rafale's opinions. She considered liking Lord Grunito, despite his ugliness and despite his nationality.

She lifted her head as she felt Skellan's presence and she curled her hands over the piece of soapstone.

Skellan hadn't meant to intrude upon her private thoughts but he felt relieved to know that Hylanya was warming to Elezar. The last thing any of them needed was another incident like the one at the harbor. Though that had not been his reason for reaching out to her.

Hylanya, I must ask a favor of you. If it weren't so important I wouldn't, but you're the only family I have here in the city.

She seemed to understand that Skellan wanted to keep this matter between the two of them and so turned just a little on her divan so that her face could not be easily seen by anyone else.

"What do you need?" Hylanya whispered.

If my wards are seen to waver or fail then the grimma will not hesitate to enter the city. So, if I am injured or... gone for some reason, I need you to maintain the illusion that the wards still burn over Milmuraille.

The two of them had not known each other long or well and yet Hylanya's expression still softened with sorrow. Skellan feared he'd chosen poorly and that she might burst into tears, or worse, refuse. But Hylanya drew in a steady breath and after stealing a glance over her shoulder she nodded her agreement.

"Show me and I will do all I can. I'll make you and Father proud, I swear."

Skellan reached down to the soapstone and caught the curling weave of Hylanya's beginning spells. A short laugh escaped Hylanya as if he'd tickled her.

Come on, let's get out of this dull place.

Skellan gripped the spells as if he were taking his sister's hand. Rich red curls of her witchflame flickered up and returned his grasp. Then Skellan bounded up from the balcony and felt Hylanya's awareness rise along with him up the height of his wards.

He felt Hylanya suck in a startled breath as she took in the clear view of both the city at their feet and the vast army besieging them.

Don't worry. The grimma can't pick your witchflame out from mine at this distance. You're safe. Now what we're going to do is weave an illusion from all those tiny spells beneath us. You see? You won't need to actually alter them. We'll just lay glamour over them so that they all appear bright scarlet. Like they're all one huge spell. Even the witches who built the spells won't notice what we've done but to the grimma it will look like a vast spell woven by one very powerful witch.

Skellan felt Hylanya's giddy excitement radiate from her witchflame.

Together they dived back down into the city breezes. Like a pair of nighthawks they winged through empty streets, whirling around the tiny blessings that hung over pumpkin patches and flowerbeds as well as the grander enchantments strung across the steeples of Cadeleonian chapels and Labaran temples. Red across the holy gold stars. Red over sacred names. They colored the spells as if painting them over with fingers dipped in scarlet dye. Then they winged away, leaving no one the wiser, except perhaps a canny alley cat or two. Despite the past days of dread Skellan felt his sister's delight in their prankish adventure wash over him. The playful joy that once came to him so easily reignited and for the first time in months he let himself soar and dive as if carefree.

At last they came full circle and he returned Hylanya to her divan. She straightened from where she'd seemed to nod off. Her swordsman came to her side at once, asking if she wasn't cold, and Skellan left her to his handsome company.

He returned to his own chilled, still body and curled his arms around Elezar.

CHAPTER TWENTY-SEVEN

The next morning the dawn sky darkened with huge flocks of songbirds, crows, ducks, grouse, and even hawks—all abandoning their nests in the forest as if fleeing before a great fire. Their shadows fluttered and rippled across the city, setting dogs barking and inspiring a few fat geese to join their immense migration south. Archers felled many birds but hardly seemed to impact the vast numbers soaring overhead.

Soon Elezar ordered them to cease, for fear that the archers stood to loose every arrow they possessed before all the birds flew out of range. Even so, numerous larders no doubt would fill with doves, ducks, grouse, and buntings.

Soon other wild creatures followed, fleeing the grimma's armies and the rising storms. Many plunged heedless into the river and others fell into the pit traps that surrounded the walls of Milmuraille. Deer, boar, glossy ermine, and entire warrens of rabbits forded the river and then flooded across the open fields of abandoned Labaran farmlands.

Behind them marched the grimma's armies. Ranks of gray mordwolves, huge white snow lions, and shaggy brown bears flanked entire tribes of big-boned Mirogoths, armed with bows, spears, clubs, and heavy axes. Most the Mirogoths walked, but several hundred rode astride giant bucks. Behind the thousands-strong armies of men and beasts, Elezar counted some fifty trolls. Huge eagles circled them as if soaring on the wakes of their giant strides. Elezar shadowed his eyes but still couldn't look directly at the three largest trolls. Brilliant light flared from their shoulders and he guessed that the grimma rode them like generals overseeing the forces below.

As early afternoon sun filtered through the growing clouds, the first ranks of the invading army plunged into the river. Long-limbed, razor-toothed frogwives and as well as a flotilla of harbor guard harpooners attacked them, spearing and drowning dozens at a time. Thin ribbons of radiant white light lashed up from the choppy waves, slashing beasts and Mirogoths, and filling the air with the stench of burned skin and hair. The battle churned up the rolling waters to a dark red froth.

Bone-crusher and his fellow trolls wrestled long black wyrm from the river while harpooners brought down Mirogoths as well as mordwolves and snow lions. And yet thousands of men, women, and beasts plunged into the frothing bloody waters and swam across the currents, driving on for the far shore regardless of the violent deaths surrounding them.

The mindless quality of their advance unsettled Elezar as he and his cavalry waited at the crest of the far riverbank. The grimma's troops pushed each other onward as relentlessly as great herds of migrating elk.

They charged up the banks, all but throwing themselves onto the pikes and spears of the cavalry. Elezar drove his spear through the heart of an immense boar but he hardly jerked the weapon free of the dying creature before another charged him. Cobre hammered the beast with his steel-shod hooves and Elezar speared it through the neck and spine only to find an third and then a fourth boar storming him. Tusks slashed through his leather armor. Their advance seemed endless.

All down the line, every one of Elezar's cavalry battled the same onslaught.

The grimma's troops swarmed up through the mud and reeds by the hundreds. They climbed over the corpses of their fallen comrades, fought tirelessly, and even died in near silence. The men and women as well as the animals betrayed no emotion either in triumph or defeat. Inevitably they broke through.

A pride of snow lions ripped through five of Elezar's cavalry. Captain Tialdo ordered men in and closed the gap. An instant later, further upriver, mordwolves mauled horses and devoured their riders. Elezar swung back behind his own men to butcher the surging pack of mordwolves before they could circle around behind the cavalry. But even as he slashed through the wolves, boars smashed through the cavalry line at three different points. The huge animals impaled and gutted anyone in their way. The rest of the grimma's forces poured through the gaps in the defensive line.

Elezar knew that neither the harbor guard in their small boats nor his own cavalry could hold the entire length of the river. But they meant to take as great a toll upon the invading force as they could while they retained the advantage of high ground. If only the losses affected the grimma's warriors in any way.

Elezar remembered the helpless push of the enthralled crowd that had assaulted the fiery gates of the bishop's townhouse and recognized at once that these forces, too, obeyed wills other than their own. And he knew those who controlled them cared little for their lives. That understanding made killing them seem all the more terrible and also necessary. Watching them drag themselves from the water and mud and then march on like soulless slaves, Elezar truly understood the reality of what Skellan railed against. This was why he absolutely rejected the power to hold others in thrall.

Their sheer numbers exhausted the harbor guard and overwhelmed even the merciless green frogwives. At last, as sunset spread over gasping, bloody riders, harpooners straining to hoist their weapons, and frogwives struggling in tangles to drag mordwolves and snow lions beneath the water, Elezar heard the captain of the harbor guard order her troops to fall back. Elezar called the same to his cavalry. Darkness would soon strip them of them the small advantage their superior positions granted.

They'd done all they could.

Elezar himself bled from a several gashes in his forearm and another two just below his right knee. A hot trickle of blood dribbled down his ear, but he couldn't remember when or how the injury occurred. He felt tired to his bones and Cobre's black hide looked dull gray with sweat.

Leading the retreat, Captain Tialdo hunched in his saddle, bracing the wreck of his left arm, while behind him four young Labaran cavalrymen swayed in their seats, their faces bloodied and ax wounds gaping across their legs and backs. Some forty other cavalrymen bore equally ugly wounds and at least another twenty lay dead—most alongside their warhorses.

Elezar and the strongest of remaining cavalrymen swept up their wounded and unhorsed. Elezar took up a young man who'd lost his helmet and likely his right eye along with it. The young man pointed deliriously at the torn remains of his fallen friend but Elezar shook his head. What light and time remained had to be used wisely. They could only carry the living back to the protection of Milmuraille. Elezar left the dead to the grimma's troops.

The young Labaran drooped into Elezar's shoulders. His body felt limp and cold as ice but his grip on Elezar's waist remained strong.

A wind rose behind them and as they raced for the torches lighting the east gates, rain poured down from the gray sky. Elezar glimpsed gored and drowned corpses littering the banks all along the river. Inside the city walls, he learned that more bodies had washed up along the river docks, most unrecognizable as the remains of enemies or allies. Volunteers had spent all the day dragging the dead from the waters and preparing them for burial. Excited guards exchanged news of a sailor who'd hauled a deathly cold harbor guard girl from the water only to discover that she still drew breath.

Elezar thought of Sarl, but he refused to imagine her among the dead.

"She and eight others revived! Ancestors blessed them no doubt."

Elezar didn't catch the other guard's response over the crack of thunder, though it heartened him that the stories being spread were of triumph. Right now he still had his own men's survival to ensure. Shouting folk out of his way as Cobre thundered down the streets and the cavalry rushed behind him, Elezar led his men to the nearest infirmary.

Several of the theaters near the east gate had already been converted into hospitals. There, Elezar discovered the gilded tiers and costly private boxes of the Mockingbird Playhouse now packed with awaiting sickbeds. He thought he glimpsed Clairre among a group of actresses, tearing old curtains into bandages. Up on the stage, benches laden with herbs, poultices, leech pots, and bandages surrounded several tables that Elezar guessed were intended for surgeries.

A team of stocky sister-physicians took the young man Elezar carried. In soft voices, they assured him that the youth would be well looked after, just as other clusters of red-robed sister-physicians murmured the same words to other cavalrymen carrying in their wounded comrades.

Elezar turned. Horses still needed tending. As he started for the ornately painted doors the weight of a small hand settled on his wrist, stilling him.

"Do your own injuries need treatment, champion?" A white-haired sister-physician craned her lined face back to look him in the eye. Elezar shook his head but then paused a moment as he realized that he recognized the woman. She'd been one of the sisters who'd first come to the garrison to treat Captain Tialdo's daughter among others. She'd played at flirting with Atreau but for all her lighthearted manner she'd saved many lives that Elezar had feared lost. Just meeting her gaze now he felt more reassured that his men would recover.

"Just scratches," Elezar told her. She frowned at the cracked chain mail and tattered leather armor hanging from his arm, but Elezar hadn't lied to her. Earlier he'd thought his injuries far worse—they'd hurt deeply enough when first inflicted—but now they seemed little more than a few deep scrapes.

"He's a lost cause, Mother Solei."

Elezar knew the man's voice but it struck him as so out of context that he didn't quite recognize it.

Atreau grinned at him then jumped down from the raised stage and strode up to the sister-physician to proffer a jar of salve to her.

"What are you doing here?" Elezar asked.

"Whatever I can." Atreau shrugged. "I may not be the most deadly swordsman Cadeleon ever produced but having traveled with you I have learned a few things about patching such men up."

Elezar hadn't expected anything like this from Atreau and felt a little ashamed of himself for underestimating his friend. Atreau had his failings—who didn't—but he didn't disert his friends. And he certainly possessed a charming bedside manner.

Atreau glanced at Elezar's forearm and then crouched down to inspect his leg. He tugged a broken curve of a snow lion's claw from the ragged links of Elezar's chain mail.

"You're a devil of a lucky man, you know that?" Atreau studied the claw.

"Half my luck is down to the prowess of my horse," Elezar responded. Though, as he caught sight of two more of his cavalrymen being carried in, he added, "The other half is my brilliance in choosing to fight alongside the best men in Labara."

Despite their wounds, the men grinned at him proudly.

Atreau arched a brow but didn't argue. They both understood the importance of maintaining an air of assurance in the face of the exhausted, injured troops as well as the chatty sister-physicians and surrounding actors and stagehands. Despite the anxiety gnawing at him, Elezar took time to walk among his men, encouraging and congratulating them as his eldest brother had once done for him.

He went out of his way to find Captain Tialdo and then crouched down beside the man's cot. Captain Tialdo lay very still, dark blood already seeping through the masses of bandages cocooning his left arm. His face looked pale as porcelain, his eyes glassy from fever and pain. Elezar followed the captain's gaze up to the ceiling where sheets of rain washed across the skylights. The downpour threw strange undulating shadows over the gilding that adorned so much of the theater. Two snow white cloud imps sheltered together amidst the ornate reliefs.

Captain Tialdo's eyes flickered to Elezar briefly before returning to the ceiling.

"We gave them hell, didn't we?" the captain asked.

"We did. They paid in lives for every foot of Radulf territory they touched."

Captain Tialdo smiled then and nodded.

A young sister-physician approached and Elezar helped her lift the captain upright so that he could drink from the cup she proffered. A few minutes later the captain fell into a sedated slumber. Two more red-robed sister-physicians approached. They waved Elezar aside while they examined Captain Tialdo's arm and discussed how much he would lose beneath their bone saws.

Though Elezar had inflicted far worse injuries upon his enemies, he found that he couldn't stay to watch this.

Outside rain pelted him. He found Doue along with a number of other stable boys from the garrison already tending to the horses and sheltering them in the wall watch stables.

Elezar looked Cobre over, inspecting Doue's treatments for the many cuts and scrapes that slashed across the stallion's right flank. None looked too deep but still Elezar hated the sight of them. He spent a few minutes afterwards allowing Cobre to nuzzle him in return and steal tufts of sweet grass from his hands. Then Elezar left him to feed and sleep.

He took himself up the heights of the wall. Wind and rain buffeted him, but he wasn't alone on the battlements. Four guards nodded their greeting as they paced past him on their watch. Further on Elezar picked out the four captains of the wall watch inspecting the lines of glossy cannons. The gunner teams tended their weapons. Many crouched beside the huge barrels, using their own bodies to protect their casks of black powder from the rain.

A party of nobles stood at a distance as well, observing the progress of the grimma's armies and speaking in grim whispers. Far fewer men and women attended Lady Hylanya today than on any other occasion that Elezar could recall. Still she was far from alone. Rafale stood near her, looking handsome and oddly untroubled. The youngest of her swordsmen remained as well. He held up his cloak to shield Hylanya from the worst of the rain and seemed to take little note of anything other than Skellan's sister. Peome glanced back from Lady Hylanya's side. She offered Elezar a slight smile but didn't call out any greeting.

Elezar left them all to themselves.

Soon enough the captains and the nobles departed to take their suppers, leaving Elezar and the teams of gunners to the gloom and rain. Elezar leaned into the slight shelter of a merlon and studied the river and farmlands to the east. He closed his eyes and for a time exhaustion overtook him. When he looked up again he thought less than an hour could have passed, still he felt more rested.

Steadily, through the twilight, the remaining armies of the grimma crossed the river, marching over the bodies of their own dead. They made camps outside the city walls, well out of range of any cannon shot. Hide tents spread across acre after acre of fields and pastures. Their presence transformed the verdant land into miles of strange gray shadows and gleaming animal eyes. They blotted out the horizon in their numbers.

So many, Elezar thought.

A tremor rose up from deep within him and the horror and dread he'd held back all day gripped him. He'd slain men and beasts before. He'd witnessed and inflicted terrible, bloody deaths. But never before had he battled through a sea of enemies, never before had other men looked to him and paid for his failings with their lives.

He didn't want to think of Captain Tialdo nor of the many lifeless forms washed up along the riverbanks and yet the memories clung like cobwebs, filling him with a useless guilt. He could regret the cost of defending the Radulf lands but abdicating responsibility would alter nothing and refusing to defend Milmuraille certainly wouldn't save any lives. He knew that.

If only knowing could banish the regret and anxiety that haunted him.

He wished he had it in him to pray, either for guidance or respite from his own immense sense of responsibility. But five years of killing men of far greater devotion than himself hadn't instilled much faith in him. Still he found his hand curling over the pendant he wore. He traced the star on the face and the Bahiim tree etched into the gold back and thought briefly of his younger brother, Nestor.

No doubt, had he stood here beside Elezar now, he would have been terrified and miserable in the cold rain. But likely he would've also felt fascinated as well. Elezar smiled a little, imagining Nestor hunched against the foul weather and attempting to sketch the strange creatures filling up the fields and farmlands.

Elezar turned his attention back to the grimma's three camps, taking in the strange, almost beautiful quality of so many huge beasts lying down together while Mirogoths tended the huge animals' injuries. He watched the figure of a slender woman combing the shaggy back of a bear with her fingers. At last she pulled what looked like the tip of a spear free.

The sight made him very aware of how far from home he stood. But it also reminded him of the vulnerability and mortality of his foes. They, too, hunched beneath the wind and rain. They, too, suffered losses—far more than Elezar's cavalry or the harbor guard. They could be defeated.

It just wouldn't be easy or without cost.

The grimma crossed the river last, riding amidst their escort of harpooned and shackled trolls. When they reached the river's edge an icy white fog rose up from the waters and rolled across the fields. As the trolls set foot upon the shore, walls of black clouds whirled up behind them and then surged towards the city. Elezar shuddered as the frigid wind slashed across the battlements.

Lightning wracked the sky and sleet fell like blades.

Then suddenly the sky overhead flared with twisting scarlet designs. Forms like curling ribbons and vines climbed into the black clouds, burning them away and opening the clear night to a warm summer wind. The rain stopped. Brilliant stars spilled across the heavens. Several of the gunners cheered and called out blessings to their count. For the first time Elezar noticed that images of the Radulf family's red wolves decorated the cannon barrels.

Elezar straightened and gazed up at the clear constellations. He wondered if Skellan looked up at the same stars as well.

He'd be in the ruins of Oesir's sanctum, with his circle of fellow witches, Javier, several other rangy Bahiim, and the trolls. They'd all spent the last three days planning for the attack doubtless still to come in the depths of the night. Elezar and the spell-forged sword he now possessed had a part to play as well.

Considering the number of huge nocturnal animals the grimma commanded, a night assault on the city seemed inevitable. The grimma's forces could exploit their greatest advantages during the dark, when guards were most likely tired and Milmuraille's defenders would hardly be able to see beyond the small gold pools of lamp and torchlight that glimmered here and there among the battlements.

Elezar glared into the waning light. Already, the vast majority of enemy troops had faded into the gloaming. Rarely, he caught a glimmer of eye shine. Snow lions' eyes glinted as yellow green as burning copper, the mordwolves' eyes gleamed turquoise, and the glowers of bears' eyes caught the torchlight from walls of Milmuraille with flickers of red. Twin pricks of deep gold glowed from much higher as the grimma's trolls paced the perimeter of the east wall. For now they remained out of range of both cannons and archers.

"Ah, and here he is, brooding into the night," Atreau called from behind him. Elezar turned into the glow of lamplight to see Atreau striding up the stone steps. Behind him came Kiram, dressed in the heavy leathers that he wore when deploying his pluming torch. His blond hair still hung loose while his cap and gloves dangled from his belt.

"Well, if you're going to brood, this certainly seems a good night for it," Kiram commented. Then he smiled at Elezar. "Quite the fight you led this morning."

Elezar smiled at the sight of the two of them and nodded. They joined him at the battlement wall. Atreau set the lamp in the niche of a crenel and then produced three fragrant, linen-wrapped buns from his coat pocket.

"I imagine you're hungry."

"What Grunito isn't always hungry?" Elezar accepted the warm pasties. In truth, he'd been far too sickened to feel any appetite while amidst the wounded men of his cavalry, but now as the rich buttery scent of the buns wafted up to him he grew ravenous. He devoured two of the large pasties, hardly tasting the goose fat and eel. But he savored the third, noting the sweet green peas and shallots amidst the thick cuts of meat.

"This is wonderful. Thank you." Elezar managed between the last few bites. The buns changed nothing of their military position, but Elezar found that he felt better for having enjoyed them—more ready to face a second battle.

"Compliments of the count's kitchen," Kiram replied. "The cooks in the Sun Palace and at the garrison made some magnificent number and sent them out to the harbor guard and wall watch as well as the hospitals."

Elezar nodded. He remembered Lady Hylanya discussing some sort of arrangement with Skellan days ago but hadn't really considered what a difference such a small luxury could make.

"Considering how many Javier filched over the past three days I'm surprised they had any left." Kiram leaned against the stone lip of a crenel and squinted into the darkness beyond the city walls. Atreau also peered out at the grimma's camp.

Elezar almost followed their gazes but a motion on the steps caught his attention. He glanced back to see Javier padding up towards them. In the dark, his pale skin appeared nearly luminous, and his figure seemed slim and long as a shadow. Three faint spheres of white light floated a few feet ahead of him. He offered Elezar a silent grin as he crept up behind Kiram.

"Next you'll be summoning the sheriff out to have me in shackles for gluttony. And after I offered you a share of my takings," Javier teased.

Kiram spun back and the look of pervading affection that passed between them both fascinated and embarrassed Elezar. Javier threw his arm around Kiram and the two of them kissed. Elezar felt his face flushing at the sight. Atreau studied them as if witnessing a startling sleight of hand. Then he peered sidelong to Elezar. Elezar looked down at his feet and wondered how Javier had grown so at ease with his own desire.

Then Javier drew back a little from Kiram and the two of them joined Elezar and Atreau at the edge of the battlement.

Elezar found himself thinking of the last time all four of them had stood on great battlements. Then they'd been boys schooling in the old fortress of the Sagrada Academy. Then warfare and invading armies had been the realm of history classes and games played out for the pride of their instructors and war masters.

"I can't help but think that Master Ignacio would be appalled at how underdressed and dowdy we all are." Javier's tone was wry and Elezar nodded. Obviously he wasn't the only one reminded of their schooldays. All those bouts in dueling circles wearing heavy decorative armor bore so little resemblance to the speed and chaos of an actual battle. Yet that had been where he'd honed his skills and where all four of them had forged their friendships. It felt like ages ago, like a time of myth that he could only half-recollect.

"I think he'd be rather proud of his best and brightest sons of Cadeleon," Kiram replied. "The defense of the river was a classic high-ground maneuver."

"It was, wasn't it?" Atreau's expression brightened briefly but then he sighed. "It's so clean and simple in texts that one hardly recognizes the reality of it. The riverbank looked like blood and madness from up here. And the infirmary... I can't help but feel glad that Fedeles isn't here. Though I could damn well have used Morisio's help bandaging wounds."

"No hope for that. Last I heard Morisio and my brother were nearing the Jade Islands. Morisio has been penning notes concerning the various beak shapes of the island parrots." Kiram's expression made Elezar suspect that Kiram found the studies fascinating, though Elezar couldn't imagine why. Kiram added, "I suppose they're trading spices in Yuan by now. That should earn them both a pretty sum."

"Life at sea does seem to suit Morisio," Atreau admitted. "I have no idea how. I couldn't keep much more than a few biscuits down the entire time I was aboard the *Red Witch*. The voyage from Cadeleon to Labara wasn't any better for me either. Give me a horse and solid ground."

Javier nodded with an expression of profound agreement and Elezar wondered if he also suffered from seasickness. He vaguely recalled Javier as a young boy objecting loudly to boating, but he'd not thought much of it at the time other than how charming Javier could seem even when he behaved like a brat.

"I suppose it's for the best that he's happy and thriving." Atreau scratched his arm then sighed again. "I miss him though. The card games and dice and all."

"I know what you mean," Kiram agreed. "I miss Nestor, but I'm glad he's not with us now." Elezar shared that sentiment.

"Elezar, on the other hand..." Javier didn't bother to finish the sentence. Both Atreau and Kiram laughed lightly and Elezar smiled. If he had to be known as a violent brute at least his reputation could lift his friends' spirits.

A companionable quiet settled over them. Javier rolled his flickering spheres between his fingers absently. Kiram watched him but also glanced from time to time to the few young men and women marching up the steps hauling crated pluming torches. He nodded greetings to those who noticed him but let them attend their business otherwise. Elezar surveyed the flickering lamps and torches below them where members of the wall watch gathered and discussed the doubling of the guards. The captains had all well in hand. Atreau stared out from the battlements.

"They're going to send those fucking giant trolls against us, aren't they?" Atreau asked at last.

"Yes. Tonight or tomorrow night," Elezar agreed. "Most likely tonight in hopes that we won't have had time to mount a strong enough defense to stop them."

"But they can't know that we have Javier and the white hell with us." Atreau looked to Javier and the gold lamplight lent an almost worshipful softness to his expression.

"I don't think that they'd care if they did know." Javier's assured tone belied his words. "Still it does serve us well that I remain hidden beneath Count Radulf's wards until the time comes for battle."

"And then?" Atreau inquired.

"Then the darkness in which they have hidden their monstrosities shall be thrown back." Javier nodded to Elezar. "And we will ride forth in such light as will lay our enemies low."

Elezar nodded but Kiram gave a derisive snort.

"You're quoting Bishop Seferino completely out of context now."

"Some wisdom transcends mere context," Javier replied with a self-satisfied smile. The tiny sparks of white light brightened as if shining with amusement.

Kiram rolled his eyes and pointedly looked to Atreau.

"From what I understand. The plan is to send out spies to assess the exact movements of the grimma's troops in the dark. When they charge, Skellan and Javier will work together to stun them with light and our forces here on the walls and a select few on the ground will hit them as fast and hard as is possible." Kiram nodded his head in Elezar's direction.

"The trolls in particular must be killed before they can breach the city walls," Elezar added and his fingers curled around the hilt of his sword. The plan had not pleased Skellan but even he had accepted it.

"What spies are going to risk their lives out there, though?" Atreau asked.

Elezar opened his mouth to respond but a horn sounded from the grounds below announcing Count Radulf's arrival. Both Eski and Magraie rode their blazing wethra-steeds alongside the glossy red carriage. At the same instant, low vibrations shuddered through the wall walkway and black silhouettes eclipsed twinkling constellations as Bone-crusher and his fellow trolls marched behind. Sheriff Hirbe and Skellan's two personal guards followed, though their roan mares neither flashed nor gleamed like fallen stars. Cheers rose from the men and women on the grounds and up on the walls. Elezar went to the steps for a better view.

Skellan alighted from his carriage and then helped Cire down after him.

It was then that Elezar noticed the tiny patches of dark forms scrabbling from the shadows of every building, storeroom, and stable. They converged like a black river that flowed toward Skellan's carriage.

Rats. Hundreds upon hundreds of them poured across the grounds, following Skellan and Cire to the eastern gates of the city walls. Then they came climbing up over the stairs, squeaking and scuttling over each other in their multitudes.

The first wave surged up onto the battlements. Dozens of the grizzled beady-eyed creatures scurried over Elezar's boots. Their advance elicited a disgusted groan from Javier and several gasps and curses from both Irabiim archers and the gunner teams. Still more rats flooded the walkway and then clambered down the opposite side of the battlements with a fearless drive. They descended, spilled out to the open fields, and raced to where the grimma's armies camped.

"I believe these are our spies," Kiram muttered to Atreau. Both of them appeared none too delighted as the rodents swarmed over their feet. Kiram shook off a confused rat as it started an ascent of his trouser leg.

"No one ever mentions this sort of thing in the great epics," Atreau remarked.

"Perhaps you can correct the oversight in your own memoirs," Javier suggested, though he aimed a repelled scowl at his own foot. Elezar couldn't keep from laughing when he noted the two fat rats pausing atop Javier's boot to copulate. Seconds later they scampered away, leaving Javier to eye his boot leather as though the all the muck of an open sewer could not have fouled it worse.

"What was it that Bishop Seferino wrote about great men inspiring the ardor of those all about them?" Kiram said, laughing. Elezar and Atreau exchanged amused grins. Elezar wondered if any of this would one day grace one of Atreau's memoirs. Perhaps if they actually survived it would.

On the grounds below, Cire and Skellan mounted the steps amidst a flowing stream of vermin. Skellan held Cire's small hand and led her like an attentive brother. She seemed hardly aware of her surroundings. She gazed ahead as if blind. Her favorite rat, Queenie, draped over her shoulder like a skinned stole. Only Queenie's quivering whiskers betrayed that the tawny rodent still lived. Skellan's guards followed while Sheriff

Hirbe, Eski, and Magraie remained below chatting with the captains of the wall watch.

"Just a little further," Skellan coaxed at the top of the steps. Elezar stepped out of the way to allow them past to the crenel where Atreau's lamp flickered.

"Here we are." Skellan lifted Cire's fingers from his own and braced both her hands on the stone. He drew the lamp back and Atreau stepped forward quickly to take it. Light flickered and jumped, making the last waves of rats seem to swell and swerve with their distorting shadows.

"You're on the battlement of the east wall," Skellan informed her. "My man Elezar is here and so are Javier and Kiram as well as the duke of Rauma."

Cire nodded but didn't glance to any of them or offer them greetings.

"Yes, I know their scents." Cire blew out a long breath and leaned against the stone wall, gripping the surface as if clinging for her life. Rats rushed around her, racing in dark masses over her feet and legs, rubbing across her hands and emitting countless tiny cries as if singing to her.

"The land is so open here... Yes, I see the trolls... smell all those nasty creatures. I want to bite them, bleed them..." On Cire's shoulder Queenie barred her teeth and snapped her jaws once before quieting again.

Skellan crouched down at Cire's side, studying her face.

"Do you know where you are, Cire?" he asked.

"I am spread across a thousand hungry bodies racing over miles of soft earth. I'm sniffing out stores of sweet grain to make my own and I'm pissing in my enemies' drinking water. I nip their feet and fingers and gather to wait and watch." Cire blinked slowly, as if it required all her will to close her eyes even for an instant. "I am on the battlements of the east wall looking out through a thousand eyes and I see everything. Yes, I know where I am, Skellan. It's not me you should fear for. So long as these battlements stand I'll be safe."

Skellan nodded and straightened but his expression remained concerned. He glanced to Elezar, pulled a smile, but looked all the more exhausted for the attempt. The last three nights he'd hardly slept. Instead he'd paced the city walls at all hours, reinforcing his wards and muttering to himself. Elezar stepped up to his side and to his surprise Skellan leaned into him. Skellan bowed his head against Elezar's chest and closed his eyes.

Despite the surrounding men and women he wrapped his arms around Skellan. If Javier was going to be bold enough to kiss in public it seemed the least he could do. He held Skellan, offering what he could of his own strength. And when Skellan's witchflame rose up and his legs wavered, Elezar held him all the harder.

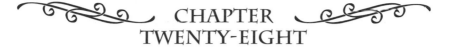

Skellan knew he stood atop the worn stone of the city wall. He felt the night air rolling over his bare face and bringing to him the perfumes of lands that should have been too distant to sense. Impressions of evergreen and ice, ripe apples and delicate crocuses rose from blazing witchflames like breath drifting through cold air. The ground heaved with the pounding hearts of thousands of enthralled bodies. Skellan felt them all, like flies crawling across his skin.

He even thought he knew the hour. Certainly he sensed slivers of moonlight falling through the darkness like a faint mist. Stars tugged at him from the heavens, shifting through his wards ever so slightly with each passing moment. Had the power been his, he would have reached up to those distant cold stars and anchored the whole world to this minute, when Elezar wrapped his arms around him and they were all of them still safe.

But he couldn't stop time any more than he could step off the path of his vei.

Even as he longed to hold back the advance of hours, even as he leaned into Elezar's embrace, part of his awareness already rode far above his body, crouching at the edge of his wards and glowering out at the three grimma facing him down.

They remained atop their trolls. Skellan didn't know if they feared him enough that they refrained from setting foot directly upon land he claimed as his own, or—more likely—they could not yet decide among them which had first right to lay claim to Radulf lands.

Onelsi and Naemir hung back, their witchflames burning upward into the heights of the heavens and stirring up wild winds where they met. Spring and winter clashed without rage or intent but simply due to their innate natures. Thaw and frost crackled through the clouds in volleys of lightning and shrieking gales. Rain and snowflakes fell in turns.

Dark haired and spindly, Onelsi leaned on her shaggy troll, child-like in her stance and petulant expression. In comparison Naemir appeared gaunt and white-haired as a crone atop her hoary troll. Cascading strings of silky blossoms clothed Onelsi while only scales of frost-etched ice lay like jewels over Naemir's pale, naked form.

At the head of the camp, flanked on the ground by ranks of saber-toothed mordwolves and in the sky by dark eagles, Ylva returned Skellan's glower from the right shoulder of her iron orange troll.

The human guise that locked away her true nature stood tall and willowy, swathed in strings of gold. Her long toes dug into the shoulder of her enthralled troll and her graceful hands gripped gold chains like reins. Her rust blonde hair and perfect porcelain face reminded Skellan of Lundag. Though even at the height of her power and anger, Lundag could never have radiated such raw disdain. Ylva's witchflame roared and lashed across Skellan's wards. Her pale gaze focused, unblinking, upon him across the miles.

Pathetic mongrel. Your frail city will not stand a day against the grimma. We will gut you and let crows feed upon your eyes. Your servants will be nothing but game for my wolves. Bow down now and I will deliver you a merciful, swift death.

A thick odor of blood seemed to roll off her and Skellan shuddered.

Skellan held his wards and let them shine as if they were the only lights in all the night. Ylva narrowed her eyes against the blaze but continued watch Skellan.

"You shouldn't be here on the wall," Elezar told him. At first Skellan didn't quite understand the words, but then he recollected where his mortal body stood.

"If one of those trolls does breach the gates, you can't be here," Elezar continued in a low whisper.

"They won't get through," Skellan replied.

The hard line of a scowl creased Elezar's mouth.

"But if they do—"

"Then I have to be here to hold the grimma back from setting foot within my city," Skellan replied. No matter how badly Elezar wished it he wasn't going to cower back behind the walls of the garrison. Doing so wouldn't save him if the city fell because he would be the first target every troll, mordwolf, snow lion, and enthralled Mirogoth would seek to kill. And if they'd breached these city walls, the garrison wasn't going to fare any better.

"Skellan—" Elezar began but Skellan cut him off.

"You won't let them get through, my man," Skellan replied lightly as he could. "You and Bone-crusher and our friend Javier will knock them on their hairy asses."

Even as he spoke on the battlements, he took in the full extent of the armies gathered to tear down Milmuraille and he knew that he was lying. These thousands of enthralled creatures were never going to relent, nor could they be terrified into breaking ranks. They might not seize the city tonight but sheer endurance would not save the city from them.

He had to find a way to break the thralls that the grimma held over their minions. He couldn't do that while hiding. He needed to feel the raw power the grimma extended and face it straight on.

I will find a way, Skellan promised in silence.

"They are moving," Cire called suddenly. "They plan a direct attack against the east gate with all of their might. They mean to end this tonight."

Skellan could see that she was correct. Out in the fields and trampled pastures the grimma's armies were moving and Cire's rats raced ahead of them. Skellan spread the fingers of his right hand, tripping a tiny line of spells, and a bell sounded, calling Milmuraille's defenders to arms.

"It's time for me to go," Elezar whispered into his ear.

"I know," Skellan replied but he leaned in against Elezar's steel breastplate.

"I won't let them reach you," Elezar murmured. Then he drew away from Skellan, leaving him to look on from the cold heights of his wards.

Mossy cliffs and ragged crags surged through shafts of torchlight as enemy trolls charged the eastern wall. Elezar glimpsed carved stones and swaying tree branches, a huge snarling mouth. Their silhouettes eclipsed the stars as they closed in. Exposed on the ground in front of the city gates, Elezar fought the instinct to flee back to the protection of the walls behind him

The ground rocked as immense footsteps hammered into the earth and sent sprays of dirt and grass flying. The pungent musk of the huge bodies poured through the air like a thick fog and somewhere up on the city wall one of the gunners coughed.

Crouched a few yards left of where Elezar sat atop Cobre, Bone-crusher and Hill-fist remained so still they could have passed for hillocks. Further on his right Iron-step and Grind-stone hunched, heads bowed low, thighs and shoulders tensed. They waited like racers at their starting lines.

Cobre stamped and blew a hard breath.

Elezar calmed the stallion as well as he could. Though waiting in the darkness outside the city gates as the ground shuddered beneath him, Elezar shared Cobre's agitation. A roar like the thunder of a rockslide tore through the night. Somehow the high-pitched squeals of the surrounding rats carried through the deep cacophony. Elezar couldn't see them—could hardly see anything but brief flashes from the few torches shining high on the battlements—but he knew they skittered past him in droves. Cobre snorted his displeasure as they scurried over his hooves.

Javier's white stallion, Lunaluz, answered Cobre with a soft nicker. The city gates threw deep shadows across Elezar's right side so he couldn't pick out even a hint of Javier but Elezar knew he waited there. He heard him murmur to Lunaluz. On the battlements overhead, Eski and Magraie stood ready among flocks of shadowy, winged creatures, teams of gunners, Irabiim archers, and Kiram's torch brigade. Behind Elezar rose the gates themselves, towering and heavy but also the weakest point in the entire wall.

Elezar's whole body tensed as the trolls closed in. He clenched the hilt of his sword and felt Cobre's trembling beneath him.

Where was the signal—the spell that Javier and Skellan had so carefully blessed the city's defenders against? It had to come soon. Now. Or they would all be crushed while they waited, blind in the darkness.

If something had gone wrong—

Then a scarlet light streaked up from the city wall like meteor and exploded into hundreds of brilliant flares, illuminating the sky in a red glow. Instantly Javier threw his arms into the air and the red lights turned to blinding white.

The blessing placed over Elezar's brow tingled. He hardly noticed as he took in his first clear sight of the attacking army. A wall of trolls, followed by the vast sea of thousands of snarling, giant beasts. The ranks of charging trolls stumbled back, flinching from the burning illumination. Several crushed the mordwolves at their feet. Others threw their mossy arms up to shield the pits of their eyes and charged onward blindly. Mordwolves and snow lions hunched and tossed their heads as Javier and Skellan's spell seared into their eyes like acid. Boars squealed.

Animals and trolls veered from their courses and yet many still charged straight for the city gates.

With a roar, Bone-crusher sprang up and sprinted to attack the nearest enemy troll. The other three trolls followed his lead and Elezar and Javier too charged ahead. High overhead Eski and Magraie leapt from the walls, leading eagles down upon their blinded enemies. Bone-crusher slammed a smaller, ruddy troll to the ground, sending saplings and shards of stone flying.

Elezar veered from the rocky shrapnel and narrowly missed being trampled as a half-blind troll stamped at him. Cobre stumbled but caught himself and swung Elezar around to the troll's calf. Elezar slashed through the steely tendons and rocky flesh with a stroke of his black blade. The troll howled and staggered. Elezar's heart hammered as the troll's shadow lurched over him. He reined Cobre around fast and galloped across the open ground to severe the troll's other tendon.

Molten gold poured from the wound like blood as the troll collapsed onto its side. Elezar swore as droplets seared his thigh and burned into his armor. The troll thrashed and Elezar raced between the troll's pounding fists to reach the exposed stretch of its prone back. He plunged his sword in between the massive jutting rocks of vertebrae. The black blade burned through the troll like an ember melting through wax.

The troll screamed and Elezar bowed his head against the wrenching wall of breath and sound that poured out. Cobre kicked as if trying to knock the piercing noise back. Then the troll went still and silent, crumpling into the dirt. A stream of gleaming gold pooled out from its body.

To Elezar's left, Bone-crusher wrenched the head from his opponent. A geyser of gold sprayed from the gaping throat as the decapitated body fell to the ground like a massive rockslide. Huge plumes of dirt filled the air and more terrible roars rose, echoing through the clouds of rising dust.

To his right Elezar could just make out the fiery white flames of Javier's sword as they leapt up to consume another troll. Just ahead of him he made out the silver forms of Magraie and his wethra-steed, Rigni, plunging down upon an enemy troll and striking its skull like a bolt of lightning. The gigantic troll stumbled and then toppled across two blinded snow lions. Eski swept over Elezar, charging a troll who'd nearly reached the gates.

Cannons boomed from the city walls. The shot only scratched the enemy trolls but killed dozens of mordwolves, snow lions, boars, and elk. Others tumbled down into the chasms of pit traps, dying on spikes and spears.

And still the grimma's forces raced for the city walls—blinded, battered, and yet relentless. They advanced like the waters of a flood.

Elezar slashed and gored mordwolves, boars, and snow lions. He blocked the blows of heavy antlers with his shield while Cobre delivered violent blows with his steel-shod hooves. For each creature that fell another charged forward. Elezar tore through the flesh of beasts and trolls until his arms ached and his hands blistered as if he were a mere boy still struggling with the weight of his own blade. Cuts, scrapes, and shallow gashes bled all across his body and sweat soaked him. Beneath him, Cobre gasped, near exhaustion.

Bodies littered the ground, transforming the landscape from an open plain into ragged hills of troll carcasses and muddy valleys of gore, blood, and gold. Elezar could hear eagles shrieking overhead, but dust and cannon smoke turned the sky a murky gray.

Elezar urged Cobre up onto the slumped carcass of a troll, searching for better view of the fighting all around him. In the shadow of the troll's sprawled arm Javier wheeled Lunaluz about to face a herd of big, bristling boars. Javier hurled a stream of blazing white light into their midst. The animals shrieked as they burned. Outlined by the blaze of their bodies Javier appeared gaunt, his face hollow as a dead man's and beneath him Lunaluz looked almost skeletal.

Just beyond Javier, Hill-fist staggered and fell to his knees before a huge ice-crusted troll. The gaping chasm where Hill-fist's arm should have hung glowed as a brilliant river of gold poured from the troll's side. The icy troll hefted Hill-fist's severed arm up like a club. Bone-crusher broke through the clouds

of smoke and dust to tackle the enemy troll and they fell together in a snarling tangle that rocked the ground. Hill-fist
staggered back to his feet and stood swaying. Then he stumbled
forward to block the charge of yet another hulking troll.

Flames gushed from the city wall, illuminating the shapes
of several snow lions as they scaled the wall.

"Shit." Elezar reined Cobre after the beasts though he
feared he was too late to bring the two cats high on the wall
down. Above him he recognized Kiram driving the fiery
mouth of his pluming torch into the face of a giant cat. The
snow lion fell burning from the wall but another clawed its
way up the stone face. Its head and shoulders bristled with Irabiim arrows. Kiram and several others poured fire over the
snow lion, blackening the air.

As he closed in Elezar realized that a pride of the cats were
using the fallen bodies of two trolls to reach the higher lev-
els of the city wall. Two of them still crouched on the trolls.
Elezar cut one of the beasts down from behind but the other
turned on him. It glared at Elezar from the slit of one blistered
eye. Then it launched itself from the promontory of the troll's
shoulder.

The big cat's teeth punched through his shield and its
weight threw Elezar back from his saddle. He and the snow
lion hit the ground together. Pain jolted through Elezar as his
shoulder cracked down against the rocky limb of a dead troll.
The snow lion bounded up but Elezar only managed to get to
his knees. The big cat leapt for him and Elezar brought up the
remains of his shield. The cat struck with brutal force, shattering the shield.

Then suddenly Cobre's black mass reared up. The cat
snarled and slunk back as Cobre kicked at it and advanced to
protect Elezar.

Elezar forced himself up, though his limbs felt leaden.
He stumbled forward as the cat pounced onto Cobre's back,

digging its claws into the horse's flanks. Cobre screamed and bucked wildly. The snow lion sank its claws in all the more deeply and clamped its jaws down into Cobre's back.

Horror and fury surged through Elezar. His exhaustion and pain meant nothing. He leapt forward to reach Cobre. The stallion's hooves slashed past Elezar as he lunged in closer. The snow lion snarled and snapped but Elezar jerked back from its jaws and turned with Cobre. Then he dived in, driving his sword up into the snow lion's chest. Briefly he saw the wound burn black. Then Cobre lurched, knocking Elezar aside. He tumbled and rolled to his feet as Cobre at last threw the dying snow lion from his back.

Blood poured down Cobre's sides and Elezar's saddle hung in tatters of leather where the snow lion had clawed and bitten through it. Cobre gasped, his eyes showing white with fear. He reared and trampled the fallen snow lion. Then he spun back on Elezar.

Cobre looked so terrified that Elezar feared the stallion couldn't recognize him through his panic.

"Cobre." The surrounding roars and cannon fire swallowed Elezar's voice. Still he held out his hand and called again. The stallion drew in several fast hard breaths. Then Cobre turned alongside Elezar, just as he'd been trained to do, protecting Elezar and allowing him to remount. Elezar caught his reins and then swung up into what remained of the saddle. Cobre twitched as Elezar remounted but betrayed nothing more of his pain.

No man could have been more brave, Elezar thought. His own fear and exhaustion would have shamed him had he possessed the time to think on it. But already a pack of mordwolves closed in, obviously intent on reclaiming the elevation of the two troll carcasses. Weeping blisters sealed their eyes but they seemed to sniff Elezar and Cobre out.

Elezar drove them back, but both he and Cobre were bloodied and badly outnumbered. The mordwolves dodged and circled around

Then Bone-crusher thundered into their midst. Thin streams of gold poured down the troll's body like waterfalls. His jaw hung, looking broken. Still he kicked and crushed the life from the mordwolves. Two dim lights swept through the sky above them. It took a moment for Elezar to recognize them as Eski and Magraie. They appeared almost tarnished as they hunched against their wethra-steeds. Elezar could hardly make out Eski's face for the dark blood dribbling from her scalp. They both dropped to the ground near Elezar, taking up defensive positions near the city gates. A moment later Javier joined them. His flesh appeared insubstantial as smoke rising off his bare bones. Battered and caked in dirt, Iron-step and Grind-stone followed. Seams of cooling gold streaked their bodies like immense scars.

Elezar scanned the battlefield for a sign of Hill-fist and then realized that Hill-fist's corpse tangled with the remains of another troll only a few yards from him. The burned bodies of snow lions lay scattered across them.

"I'm not sure how much longer we can last out here." Javier's voice sounded hollow and yet he managed a smile. "But it will be interesting to find out."

Elezar nodded his acknowledgement. He wasn't about to call for the gates to be opened for their retreat. Javier, Eski, and Magraie could retreat through the air or Sorrowlands. But he and the trolls had to stay until the grimma's forces fell back and the gates were no longer under threat.

Far fewer of the grimma's army stood now. Heaps of broken and burned corpses carpeted the ground. Many beasts charged and turned upon each other in their blinded confusion. Others seemed lost and staggered to the river where frogwives awaited them in the dark waters.

"Madness," Elezar muttered. Bone-crusher groaned in reply.

Then through the chaos more than two dozen trolls rose up, advancing from the grimma camps. Elezar had no doubt they'd been held in reserve for just this moment, but it depressed him nonetheless. The clouds of smoke and dirt drifting through the sky shielded them from the worst of the searing light that Skellan radiated over the battlefield.

Another low groan escaped Bone-crusher as the wall of fresh enemy trolls closed in upon them.

"Eski, Magraie," Elezar called back. "Can you clear the air a little to allow Skellan's spell to hit these trolls?"

"Rigni thinks he and Nottsol might be able to whip up a breeze." Magraie's voice sounded rough and dry. A black bruise colored his right eye and most of his nose as well.

"We'll do what we can." Eski straightened and wiped the blood from her eyes.

The two of them ran their hands over their mounts and then in an instant the wethra-steeds bounded up into the sky like flashes of lightning. They circled each other as they rose through the clouds and steadily drew a dark spiral of dirt and smoke in their wake. Shafts of red and white light speared the battlegrounds. Several of the advancing trolls roared with pain as the light struck them. But as before they continued forward.

"Bone-crusher." Elezar stole a glance back at the troll and felt a pang of sorrow just seeing the profusion of his wounds. He'd fought so hard already, but he was the strongest of their trolls and the most fearless. "Hold the gates. If any of them get past the rest of us, you have to stop them."

Bone-crusher nodded and squared his stance before the gates.

As Elezar gripped Cobre's reins he felt the stallion's tense dread like his own. Still he urged Cobre ahead and the stallion charged. Javier rode out at his side. Iron-step and Grind-stone flanked them. The four of them tore into the first two enemy trolls but other trolls raced past them. Eski and Magraie dived after two of them but another three veered past their fallen comrades. Elezar turned Cobre back and chased the advancing trolls.

As he rode, he felt the shadow of another enemy troll fall across his back. He stole a glance over his shoulder and realized that another three trolls were nearly on top of him. Two of the trolls ahead of him slammed into Bone-crusher. The air filled with furious agonized roars. Out of the corner of his eye Elezar saw a huge ice-caked troll reach up and swat Magraie and Rigni from the sky. They crashed to the ground along with the blackened shot of the city's cannons. He heard Eski scream his name.

Killing the trolls that surrounded Bone-crusher was more critical than answering the call of a young girl far back in the midst of the battle. He knew that. Still he wheeled Cobre around, dodging between the stamping feet of trolls. He'd been entrusted with Eski's welfare and he'd brought her into a war. He couldn't just leave her to die.

Ahead he saw another of those damn ice and snow capped trolls holding Eski and Nottsol between its cupped hands, attempting to crush them like insects. Nottsol threw off waves of sizzling light, which chipped and cracked at the troll's rocky flesh. But steadily the troll's hands closed around the two of them.

"Elezar!" Eski howled as the huge, stone fingers curled over her.

He couldn't reach her in time and yet he urged Cobre ahead. He glimpsed Javier riding for Eski but then a pack of mordwolves swept in upon him. Javier burned several of the huge animals to bone but still they harried him, snapping at Lunaluz's gaunt belly. They forced Javier to circle and fall back.

A snow lion charged Elezar. He hewed through the animal's skull and neck. Cobre bounded ahead.

And then to Elezar's horror the sky lit with the silver and gold flashes of attacking wethra-steeds. In an instant some thirty wethra-steeds and their Mirogoth riders descended like falling stars. Four swept past Elezar, shooting straight for the city gate and Bone-crusher.

Almost at once, the grimma's trolls fell, their skulls cracked open or immense chasms torn through their chests, exposing luminous gold organs. Two radiant steeds smashed through the chest and back of the troll holding Eski.

Stunned wonder filled Elezar. He couldn't understand why these wethra-steeds had turned on their own forces until he saw one of the gleaming riders and realized that he knew the man. Jarn, Eski's uncle. These were the Sumar grimma's emissaries or had been—since she would have had to free them for them to join this battle. A rush of giddy hope lit Elezar's chest.

Seated behind Jarn, Eski's angular mother drew the string of her bow taut and sent an arrow hurtling into the throat of a mordwolf. A moment later Elezar recognized Elrath mounted behind another of the Sumar grimma's emissaries. She bounded from the back of the wethra-steed as it swept close to the ground. Barefoot she charged across the open battlefield.

Elezar reached Eski first. He swung down from Cobre and knelt over the girl's battered, prone body. Nottsol stood only a hand's length from her, flickering like a dying candle.

"She's breathing," Elezar shouted as Elrath sprinted over the mound of three dead mordwolves. She looked more like a wild thing than she had even in the forest. Her hunting spear appeared blackened with blood. Dirt streaked her face and long white braids. Tenderness transformed Elrath's snarling visage as she reached out and touched Eski's cheek.

"She needs a physician, but…" As he spoke Elezar realized the stupidity of the thought. In the midst of a battlefield, Eski was lucky just to have been spared trampling—certainly no physician was going to appear from the heaps of corpses to tend her.

Elrath gave a curt shake of her head and then extended her bloody right hand out to Nottsol. The wethra-steed staggered and flickered to her side. Elrath looked back at Elezar.

"We will protect her here." Elrath hefted her spear. "You hunt these trolls. Use your black blade. Cut them down!"

Elezar almost felt Elrath's fury light through him. Perhaps it was only his own guilt but a surge of angry strength ignited in him. He left Eski with her and mounted Cobre. He assaulted the nearest trolls, letting his anger, guilt, and despair drive him. He butchered mordwolves and snow lions in his fury and slaughtered trolls. His black sword rang like a bell as it ripped through stone bodies and spilled streams of molten gold.

In the air, Jarn and his fellow emissaries felled trolls, one after another, and on the ground, Javier, Iron-step, and Grindstone regrouped at Bone-crusher's side, defending the city gates.

Elezar pushed deeper into the grimma's forces and the trolls seemed to back away from him. He didn't quite trust himself to believe what he thought he saw. But soon it became obvious that the grimma's forces were falling back—retreating. Delirious relief crept through Elezar, but he didn't dare glory in the triumph yet.

The knowledge that the grimma's enthralled forces were not moved by their own fear or losses nagged at him. If these trolls and beasts withdrew, it was not to flee for their lives but because one of the grimma willed them to fall back. That, all too easily, could draw Elezar and the city's defenders to pursue them into some trap.

Elezar wondered how he might warn Jarn and the other emissaries high above him. Then as he cleared the fallen remains of another dead troll, he saw Rigni. The wethra-steed hunched on the ground, pale and nearly as translucent as a veil of mist. Beside him Magraie's body sprawled across the remains of a snow lion. A brilliant shaft of white light shone down across him. Elezar couldn't help but see the broken bone of his right calf jutting up through the rags of his boot. A series of deep gashes had laid the youth's chest open. He lay too still for a living man.

Rigni lifted his head as Elezar neared them and to Elezar's shock Magraie blinked and opened his mouth. Elezar couldn't hear his words but Rigni rose like an apparition and suddenly Elezar felt a boyish voice rush over him.

"I cannot lift my Magraie to my back and he will not stand."

Elezar glanced across the rutted torn grounds for any lingering snow lion or mordwolf but they'd all withdrawn further east. He swung down from Cobre and very carefully reached out and lifted Magraie. The young man's blood streamed down his wrist and a gasp of pain escaped him as Elezar shifted his weight up onto Rigni's back. Magraie clutched at the wethra-steed's mane. As his hands touched Rigni, the wethra-steed grew more substantial and radiant.

"Take him to the sister-physicians in the city," Elezar said.

Rigni cocked his head and met Elezar's gaze.

"We must all ride for the city's wards." Rigni's voice sounded stronger and much more mature now. "She is unleashing the winter against us."

"She…" Elezar began to ask but then he felt the deathly cold wind sweep down from the grimma's camp.

He turned to see immense waves of snow and ice flooding across the land like a surging tide. Fields of verdant crops and bountiful apple trees froze into tangled sculptures of frost. The ground rumbled as crystals of ice burst up, encasing everything in a white filigree. The river crackled as huge panes of ice split the rolling water, turning crests, waves, and even flying droplets solid in seconds.

Overhead the Sumar grimma's emissaries fled for Milmuraille. The city gates swung open for Bone-crusher, Iron-step, Grind-stone, and Javier. A flash bolted up from the battlefield and Elezar briefly recognized Elrath and Eski mounted on Nottsol. Then they were gone. Elezar swung up onto Cobre's back and Rigni bolted ahead of them.

Cobre galloped hard, gasping, on the verge of collapse, as all around them fingers of ice clutched the ground and frosted the air. A frigid wind crawled over Elezar's back. But he and Cobre kept moving, even as the ice broke the ground before them. Snowflakes poured over Elezar and hoarfrost grew through Cobre's mane. But the cold couldn't seem to claim them.

As Elezar raced through the city gates he realized that Skellan stood atop the battlements, driving the killing winter back.

CHAPTER THIRTY

Skellan swore and snarled, restraining himself until the gates closed behind Elezar. Then he hurled all his frustration and fury out against the encroaching onslaught of wind and ice. His rage exploded in vast arcs of flame. He reached out and ripped the icy clouds from the sky, hurling them to the dirt as violently as he'd witnessed the grimma's mindless slaves hurl Hill-fist's body aside.

And what they'd done to Bone-crusher—

Skellan growled with anger at the memory and at his inability to protect his own. But now none of his people remained upon the fields and in this moment, Skellan didn't give a shit for the hapless pawns of his enemies.

Rage eclipsed all thought of his wards and the city they protected. He called on every spell and charm in his grasp, willing them against the grimma's armies. The city at his back went suddenly dark, while the grounds of the battlefield before him shuddered. Ancient stones and deep, deep fires answered his roaring cry.

Jets of shattered rock and flame erupted and the city walls trembled. Seams across miles of land threw up swirling pyres. They grew into a whirlwind of fire, churning across the field of corpses to rise like a typhoon over the grimma's followers.

The grimma sent sheets of ice and rain against him but Skellan batted them aside.

He felt hollowed out by the scouring power coursing through him. Still he pushed farther.

Geysers of flame erupted all across the grimma's camps. Men, women, children, and animals were engulfed. Their cries filled the air. Abandoned farms and empty mills crumbled before the insatiable conflagration. Miles of farmland and orchards blackened.

Skellan shook with anger and exhaustion. Feverish tremors rocked his mortal flesh.

"Let them all burn!" Skellan snarled into the vast blazing landscape. Smoke billowed over him and tears tracked down his cheeks. The men surrounding him on the battlement stared and many backed from him. Gunners bent their heads against the smoke. Cire started to reach out to him but then pulled her hand back and simply withdrew down the stone staircase.

Some corner of his mind knew that his guards gaped at the sight before them and that the Irabiim archers made holy signs over their hearts. Kiram Kir-Zaki slid his smoked glass visor back down over his eyes and whispered, "Khivash."

None of it meant anything to Skellan. He was a destroying flame. He was the Scarlet Wolf risen up to devour his enemies in the fiery jaws of a red hell. He blazed with a rage so intense that his flesh seemed hardly able to contain it.

Little Thorn. Don't. Bone-crusher's low aching groans felt like ice water against fevered skin. *All you'll accomplish is your own exhaustion. You cannot hurt them by killing their slaves.*

Skellan tore his attention from the burning plain before him and spun back to see his battered friend crouching on the grounds below. Seams of cooling gold crisscrossed his arms and chest. His thick coat of moss, grass, and saplings bore wide scrapes, exposing the bare granite of his body, as if he'd been flayed. He supported the left side of his jaw with one hand.

You swore you would free my folk.

Suddenly, all Skellan's rage turned to sorrow.

Burning pain rocked through him as he clamped down upon the fires he'd brought to life. His witchflame seemed to lash against him as he forced it to relent and recede into his body. His arms and legs trembled and a sheen of sweat covered his face and chest. Gently Skellan reached out and the wards over the city reignited.

Then he stumbled down the stairs to Bone-crusher's side.

The troll bent low, encircling Skellan with his huge, gashed arms. Skellan threw himself against the troll's shoulder, and though it mortified him, he wept into the soft moss.

He was acting like a scared child, and he ought to have known better, but it had broken his heart to witness the beatings Bone-crusher and Elezar had taken, and to see Hill-fist die. He hadn't felt so torn up even when Oesir murdered Lundag and all of her wolf champions. But then, that hadn't been his doing. Tonight, he'd been the one to send Hill-fist, Bone-crusher, and Elezar out into danger. He'd ordered Iron-step, Grind-stone, Javier, Eski, and Magraie into a brutal battle and deluded himself that somehow no harm could befall them.

As much as he hated the grimma for the hurt they'd done to the folk closest to him, he also hated himself for sending them out to suffer, fight, and die.

"I'm sorry," Skellan whispered. "You're so hurt and I..."

I know, Little Thorn. It is a terrible thing to make war. Bone-crusher's breath wafted over Skellan like the gentlest embrace. *But you cannot let it change you. You must not become like the grimma.*

"I couldn't even if I wanted to," Skellan muttered.

But you could, Little Thorn. You're the child of a grimma. Her power and ferocity lies within you. But your heart would be the price.

Skellan wouldn't have understood what Bone-crusher meant before tonight, when he'd felt fury obliterate his compassion. He'd teetered on the brink of pure rage and immense power. The experience offered an unnerving insight into a grimma's perception of her world. Theirs was a realm of brilliant and absolute godly power. The world they sensed radiated with the brilliance of eternal stars and the fires of the deepest earth. From within such vibrant enormity the existence of any mortal creature became a dim, ephemeral mote.

Bone-crusher had it all too rightly.

No matter how many of the grimma's folk he killed, it wouldn't disturb any one of the grimma the way it tore at Skellan's heart seeing his own people suffer. The grimma were hardly more capable of caring for mortal lives than was a river capable of mourning those drowned beneath its waters. That was part of what they were and also the price of their immense power.

But it wasn't what Skellan wanted to become.

He leaned into Bone-crusher, drawing in deep breaths of the troll's soothing, earthy scent. Caring and compassion weren't meaningless. Mortal creatures might be ephemeral and small in comparison to the magnificent power of the earth, oceans, and stars, but only mortal caring inspired the courage and will to challenge those immense powers—to defeat them even at the cost of pain and death.

Don't let the lure of that power destroy who you truly are.

"I won't," Skellan promised. His faint tone embarrassed him. He wasn't a child—he might feel like one but he couldn't go on acting like this. He scrubbed the tears and soot from his face then slowly stepped back from the comforting familiarity of Bone-crusher's chest.

"Shall I tend to your jaw, Master Bone-crusher?" Skellan managed a somewhat jaunty tone.

Save your strength, Little Thorn. It's nearly set on its own. All the tending I need now is to sleep beneath your wards. Iron-step and Grind-stone are going to the broken sanctum to calm the children and take our rest. Tomorrow we will sing our songs for Hill-fist.

"Take your rest then and sing to Hill-fist for me. You have my word that I'll not become a heartless grimma in your absence."

Bone-crusher opened his arms and straightened. As he drew back Skellan noticed Cire waiting with Queenie a few feet from him. His guards stood on the battlement steps and his master mechanist, Kiram Kir-Zaki, eyed him from a walk-way. Skellan felt a flush rising across his face and wondered if there would ever come a time in his life when he appeared in public without making a scene worthy of some half-mad character from one of Rafale's plays. Certainly not today. He almost thought he ought to take a bow but resisted. They really would all think him deranged if he did that.

As Bone-crusher stood and started back to join his fel-low surviving trolls in the ruins of the sanctum, Cire strode to Skellan's side.

"Skellan, that fire just now—"

"I know, I didn't mean to scare everyone. I'm sorry."

"Sorry?" Cire's pale eyes widened with baffelment. "I could give two turds about being scared. I thought you were going to kill the grimma. It was amazing! Why'd you stop?"

Skellan shook his head.

"I was only killing innocent people and creatures under a thrall. They're the ones I promised Bone-crusher that I'd set free. And I wasn't." And there was more to it. Even as he con-sidered the price of killing the grimma, Skellan felt a revelation that he'd not recognized at the time suddenly become clear. His aching fingers twitched as he remembered hammering at the Sumar grimma. He'd shattered the spell-etched stones ar-moring her—splintering and burning into the hollows where her heart should have beaten—only to feel others rise to take the place of the ones he destroyed. And she'd shown him the mortal wounds she'd suffered battling demons, but no hurt had ever released her spirit from the flesh that caged her.

His flames this evening could have consumed earth and heavens alike but still wouldn't have killed the grimma.

"No matter how ferocious, an attack against a grimma's physical body is never going to kill her." Skellan muttered the words to himself as much as Cire. "Even if I seared their flesh away they would just grow new skin beneath. Their sanctums wouldn't release them from this realm so easily…"

Cire frowned at him.

"How are you going to defeat them, then?" she asked.

Skellan shook his head but not in reply to Cire. His thoughts raced back to his battle with the demon lord and the life he'd experienced through the Sumar grimma.

He'd made a mistake by thinking of the grimma as beings like Lundag, who had raised her own sanctum. In truth the grimma were far more like Demon Lord Zi'sai, whose body had been trapped, undying for ages, by the sanctum. The Sumar grimma had said it herself. Their sanctums were their prisons.

Skellan couldn't hope to defeat any of the grimma so long as sanctums held them, because in keeping them restrained in the bodies of women, the sanctums also continuously regenerated and healed their flesh, granting them immortality.

Skellan scrubbed at his brow, willing himself to resist the encroaching confusion of exhaustion. The sanctums' hold over the grimma had to be the key to their defeat. He knew that. If only the sanctums didn't lie hundreds of miles away and hidden by countless spells. If only he could somehow get inside one and feel all those ancient spells.

"If they are bound to the sanctums, then the spells binding them can't only exist within the sanctums..." Skellan muttered to himself. "A bond has two points. One will lie in the sanctum, the other in the grimma."

"In the grimma?" Cire asked.

All at once the strain of the calling so much power and then abandoning it rolled over him. He felt dumb, clumsy, and cold with fatigue. He closed his eyes and found the effort of opening them again nearly too much.

"If you drop over I'm not sure I can catch you," Cire commented. "Maybe you should sit down."

Skellan nodded but before either of them could say anything more, Javier charged into the grounds upon his shining white stallion. He bounded from the horse's back and raced up the stone steps to Kiram.

"I felt an old power awaken—" He went silent as he took in the view of the lands beyond the city wall.

"It was Count Radulf," Kiram said. "I thought he'd opened the Cadeleonian red hell."

Javier turned to pin Skellan with a hard stare. Skellan gazed back at the pale Bahiim. He didn't need to chastise Skellan aloud—his disapproval appeared obvious, just as it had after Skellan awoke the Black Fire.

"Fear not!" Skellan managed to call out to him, and the men and women of the wall watch as well. "I'll not engulf the world in magma and flames. I only wished to show the grimma what they were truly up against." That was a lie but it sounded so much better than the truth. Javier's expression remained suspicious, but many of the surrounding guards, gunners, and archers seemed to relax. Several even looked heartened.

Skellan continued to consider Javier. Typical of a Bahiim to condemn a witch for dabbling in dangerous realms when he and his kind regularly traveled the paths of the dead and underworlds filled with demon seeds. The thought of the Old Road made Skellan shudder, and yet it was said to span all mortal realms and carry travelers hundreds of miles in minutes.

No sanctum would be too far for the Bahiim to reach, though all of them would still be impossible for him to find, much less breach, without a stone of passage.

"Skellan?" Cire's voice scattered his thoughts and startled him in a way that assured him that he'd all but fallen asleep on his feet.

"Yes? Sorry. What did you say?" Skellan couldn't recollect his own earlier thought, much less Cire's comment.

"I asked if you wanted to visit the infirmary and see how the others are doing." Cire frowned at him. "Though I think that perhaps you might want to claim a bed there yourself for a few hours at least. Really, Skellan, you look ready to drop."

"I'll see my man first and the wethra-steeds and riders who came to join him on the battlefield." He owed them his thanks. If they hadn't arrived when they did, most likely the battle would still rage but up here on the walls.

Cire nodded but then glanced behind Skellan to his two guards.

"If he topples over, one of you will catch him, yes?"

"Yes, ma'am," the older of the two assured her.

"Jarn and the others are tending Eski and Magraie's wounds. They've taken over most of the stable across from the Mockingbird Playhouse." Javier strode down the steps, still watching Skellan too closely. Kiram followed him, though he appeared less suspicious than soot-stained and tired. He and his torch-bearers had been brilliant, Skellan thought, and he told Kiram as much. Kiram accepted the compliment with a gracious smile.

Skellan said his goodbyes to Javier and Kiram, though in the midst of it somehow the two of them ended up coming along. Kiram—at Javier's insistence—to have a cut in his forearm treated. And Javier came—at Kiram's insistence—to get some rest because he looked, literally, like Death. He mounted his white stallion and rode alongside the magnificent gilded carriage that Skellan had inherited from his father.

The Mockingbird Playhouse wasn't far and at this late hour the streets stood nearly deserted. Still Skellan managed to nod off before the sudden halt of the carriage woke him.

"Behind you, my man," he muttered as he came back to consciousness. He felt certain that he'd dreamed something disturbing and important but as his senses turned from the realm of dreams to waking his memory faded back like a morning fog in the rays of the sun. "He held a knife, I think," Skellan muttered to himself.

"Knife?" Cire asked.

Across from him Cire and Kiram exchanged a glance.

"It's nothing," Skellan assured them. The range of skeptical gazes his claim inspired embarrassed him. Couldn't any of them pretend to believe him, at the very least? Despite the heavy languor of his limbs, he made a game leap from the carriage. His guards swung down from the footmen's perches on either side of the carriage and started after Skellan.

From the door Cire leaned out and called after him.

"Where are you off to in such a rush so suddenly?"

"To find Elezar." He couldn't recollect the details of his dream but a sense of dread and prophesy clung to him.

"Who knew he'd come over so smitten?" Cire murmured. Skellan guessed the comment was meant for Javier and Kiram. Though perhaps it had been addressed to Queenie or another of the dozens of rats that now crept from the shadows to lurk like tiny attendants at the wheels of the carriage.

Skellan started for the infirmary but then turned to the stable across the street. He might not know Elezar perfectly but he'd seen enough of the man to guess that he'd still be tending his warhorse. Caring for the stallion always seemed to restore his composure. And Javier had mentioned that the wethra-steeds and their riders had gathered at the stable.

A watchman with an anxious hound at his side nodded as Skellan entered

Inside a few lamps lit the stalls and strange flashes of light shuddered and flared like an approaching lightning storm. Skellan almost expected to hear the crack of thunder, but instead an eerie silence pervaded the stable. A tone, too deep and low to hear, rolled through the air like a wave. Skellan felt it rocking through his bones and muscles. All around him horses craned their heads over the doors of their stalls, their eyes wide and their ears pricked. A mare briefly rolled her dark eyes Skellan's way as he and his guards passed but most of the horses took no note at all of his presence

Skellan followed the leaping flares of light and shadows to the back of the stable. Sackes of feed hanging from the rafters cast eerie shadows. He reached an open area where bales of hay served as makeshift walls. There, a dozen shining wethra-steeds and their riders formed a circle around two prone bodies. Eski and Magraie lay unmoving on beds of animal skins as two strange figures knelt at their sides. Skellan recognized them as Rigni and Nottsol, as he had first seen them in the skies above the garrison: stripped of flesh and flickering in and out of existence within the mortal realm. Their many long distorted limbs crackled and split like tongues of lightning as they sank down into the bodies of their chosen companions.

Whether they meant to save Eski and Magraie or to die along with them Skellan didn't know. A new rush of guilt flooded him. He couldn't bring himself to intrude. Instead he averted his gaze from the crackling light the two gave off. He backed away.

Skellan turned and as his eyes adjusted to the darker shadows of the stable he realized that some dozen wild Mirogoths hunched in the shadows of the stable's oak support beams. The strands of lichen in their hair and their stillness lent them the presence of trees or stones. A pale woman who reminded Skellan of Eski nodded to him but offered no other greeting. She and the rest looked tired and intent upon the circle of wethra-steeds.

Amongst the Mirogoths Skellan recognized Sheriff Hirbe. His bright cap and sweet cologne stood out from the dirty, dull-dressed Mirogoths like a lark's song splitting the silence and yet he was as grim faced as any of them. The older man shielded his eyes with a hand as he gazed at Magraie's beaten, bloody body. Skellan wondered if he should go to the sheriff, but he didn't know what he would say. He'd been the one to send the youth into battle. How warmly could he expect the sheriff to welcome any consolation he offered?

Then from behind him Cire appeared. She took the sight in and immediately went to the sheriff's side. Where Skellan would have stood feeling guilty and doubtless looking uneasy, Cire simply knelt beside the sheriff and took his free hand in her own. She said something and a little of the sorrow seemed to lift from the older man's face.

Skellan realized that he could do nothing here. The we-thra-steeds would save Eski and Magraie if it could be done. And those gathered would mourn them if it could not.

He turned away and stumbled from the flashing light. He wanted to find Elezar. Following the streaming light of a lamp, Skellan felt relieved that his intuition had led him rightly, though a jolt of horror struck him the moment he took in all the blood caking Elezar's hands and arms.

The boy, Doue, stood to the side of the paddock. He gripped the handle of a pail brimming with medicinal-smelling liquid. Elezar whispered to his stallion and washed the ugly wounds torn across the animal's flank and legs. The horse snorted as if still winded and swayed. Even through the flickering lamplight Skellan recognized the anguish in Elezar's expression. He pressed a fistful of bandaging against a wound in the stallion's chest but blood soaked through and trickled down Elezar's arms.

With a groan the horse's legs folded and he collapsed to the straw. Elezar dropped to his knees beside his stallion and continued to press his hands over the stallion's wound.

"No," Elezar whispered. "You can't give up… Please, Cobre."

Skellan didn't know if it was his own exhaustion and sorrow or Elezar's that shook him, but all at once he felt raw inside, as if someone had dragged a knife across his bones, stripping the muscle and sinew from his ribs, and torn his heart away.

Beside him, Doue snuffled and shuddered as tears dribbled down his face. He sucked in a sob but continued to clench his pail with both hands. Then he looked to Skellan. He didn't have to speak. Skellan understood the plea in his expression at once.

Skellan's legs shuddered. His mind felt like a burned-out hull. A wise man would take the long view and recognize that one horse didn't matter, not if its salvation came at the cost of Skellan's own safety.

But he couldn't let Elezar lose the stallion that had carried him into battle and stood with him so bravely.

He dragged his witchflame up, though the effort almost toppled him. He caught the wood of the paddock and steadied himself as his senses reached into the stallion. He felt the huge heart pounding like his own and absorbed the sense of yearning. How desperately the horse wanted to rise as Elezar asked it to. But all the heat and strength of his body spilled from that tiny, deep hole in his chest. He felt cold. His tongue lay like a slab of lard in his mouth. His eyes dried to stiff, listless orbs of glass as he tried to focus his gaze on Elezar's drawn face.

Skellan poured the strength of his witchflame into the wound, closing it and filling the stallion with his own living warmth. He felt the horse draw an easy breath and he pulled back from the animal.

Strangely, the terrible cold and sick weakness followed Skellan back into his own flesh. He swayed and toppled. The boy, Doue, cried out in alarm.

One of Skellan's guards caught him but he didn't know which one. He couldn't make his eyes focus. His mind drifted.

He thought he might have been floating through a cold stream, but then he caught a trace of that familiar scent. He managed to open his eyes briefly as Elezar lowered him to a soft, creaking surface. The Mockingbird Theater's gilded ceiling reliefs haloed Elezar's grim face. His eyes were red-rimmed and Skellan though he must have wept for his horse.

"He'll live," Skellan tried to reassure him, but the words escaped him in a groan.

"Idiot," Elezar said fiercely, but he stroked Skellan's face with a tenderness that Skellan hadn't expected. The heat of his fingers seemed to sink into Skellan, soothing him.

He let his eyes fall closed again and something deeper, more lasting than mere sleep enfolded him.

CHAPTER
THIRTY-ONE

Elezar stood beside Skellan's cot, spent to his bones but too anxious to sleep.

The sister-physicians had given Skellan one of two cots high on the balcony in what had been a private box seat. The other cot lay empty and ready for Elezar. He couldn't bring himself to even sit but instead he turned to pace the narrow balcony. On the floor below hundreds of cots spread out in the tight columns, reminding Elezar of infantry formations, but also of graves filling a churchyard. Most of the injured lay unnaturally still, drugged into the deep sleep induced by duera. If the sister-physicians were right, it would keep fever from taking many of them as well as slow the flow of blood from the worst wounds.

Up on the stage four weary sister-physicians tended to the latest influx of wounded: Irabiim archers and men of the wall watch who'd driven back snow lions and enemy eagles. Only eight looked badly hurt—though Elezar's eyes felt so tired and his mind so fatigued that he knew he could easily have miscounted

Kiram sat on a stool amidst them while Javier stood at his side, throwing off small flares of bright white light. In the near silence of the late night Kiram's soft admonishment for Javier to stop blinding the sisters carried even to Elezar. The young sister-physician stitching up Kiram's arm gave a quiet laugh. Javier extinguished the sparks and laid his hand against Kiram's back. He stroked Kiram's spine as the sister-physician tied off the last of her stitches and then wrapped the wound with duera-soaked bandages.

Elezar glanced down at his own arm. He'd lost his leather gauntlet somewhere outside the city walls—torn away by a snow lion or mordwolf. His armor hung in tatters and yet only the finest scratch marred his tanned forearm.

Where deep burns from molten gold should have disfigured his thigh and shoulder Elezar sported little more than a few pink blisters. Even the bruises from his fight this morning at the river had faded instead of darkening to the black masses Elezar had expected to see.

Elezar only needed to glance down at Skellan's limp forearm and see the fine line of a matching scratch to confirm the sickening suspicion coiling through his gut. Skellan had taken his injuries, endured as much pain as Elezar himself, and as if that weren't enough, the idiot had driven himself to collapse to save Elezar's horse.

Not that Elezar wasn't grateful. He'd felt gutted when he'd discovered the deep wound in Cobre's chest—when he'd known the stallion had given the last of his life to carry him to safety. He'd silently begged any spirit or God for Cobre's life. But he hadn't thought Skellan would answer his prayer or that he'd pay such a terrible price to do it.

Elezar frowned down at Skellan's still body. His chest hardly rose to draw breath and his skin looked deathly white. Even his lips appeared waxen. By comparison his red hair and scarlet cloak spilled out around him like blood. Neither the sister-physicians nor Javier had been able to wake him.

Not even Cobre's salvation should have come at this price.

Elezar scrubbed at his tired, stinging eyes and sank down to crouch at Skellan's bedside. If he'd not been so tired, he suspected he would have raged at Skellan—and himself—for not realizing sooner what Skellan had been doing. Had he possessed the strength for fury, likely his anger would have sheltered him from the desolate fear that now gripped him.

"How could you do this to yourself?" Elezar lifted his hand to touch Skellan's but stopped himself. His fingers were filthy with dried blood. Wiping them against the dusty, torn sleeve of his shirt hardly made an improvement. "Please don't make me the death of you. Skellan, I..." Elezar's voice failed him and he fought to keep his composure.

But he couldn't bear it.

He'd only just begun to know how truly happy he could be—begun to hope that that his entire existence could amount to more than a battle of revenge, rage, and shame. For the first time since he'd been a child he'd felt joy unfettered by self-recrimination. The guilt of surviving his more worthy brother as well as lusting with such violence after his friend, Javier, had faded. These last months he'd taken pride in his place at Skellan's side, not just as his champion, but also as his man—his lover.

Elezar shoved his face into the bedding and wrapped his arms over his head to muffle the sounds of his grief. Skellan's limp hand fell against his arm, seeming cold and lifeless as ice. Elezar fought with all his will but he couldn't keep himself from weeping. He clawed at his own hair and half-smothered himself against the mattress of the cot, trying to mute the pathetic, low sob that escaped him.

Minutes later, he regained some of his composure. He wiped his wet face with his sleeve, doubtless tracking dirt across his cheeks, and then straightened from beside Skellan's cot. For a while longer, his attention remained focused upon Skellan's motionless form.

Then he noticed the figure standing in the shadows of the velvet curtains at the doorway.

"Who's there?" Elezar demanded and Atreau stepped forward, holding a silver tray in his hands. The sympathy in his expression embarrassed Elezar and assured him that Atreau had witnessed him at his weakest.

"I brought wash water and a cloth," Atreau said.

"Thank you." Elezar couldn't meet his gaze for the sense of mortification building in him. His face felt hot and he hoped the shadows hid his swollen eyes.

"Come wash up. You'll feel more yourself." Atreau set the tray down on an absurdly ornate table that sat beside Skellan's cot.

Elezar nodded. Droplets of astringent oil perfumed the water and it stung the tiny cuts and scrapes that marked his face and hands. But as he'd rinsed away all the blood and grime he reclaimed his composure. A sense of desolation still filled his chest, but he refused to fall apart in front of Atreau again.

Atreau fixed his gaze on Skellan and said, "They're saying that he turned the battlefield into a wasteland after you left it. He threw the grimma's storm aside and killed thousands of their troops."

"Did he?" Elezar stole a glance to Skellan and had no doubt that the reckless witch had battled the grimma without a thought for his own life. Plainly without a thought for how precious his life might have become to Elezar, damn him.

Elezar had to look away, for fear of emotion unmanning him once again. He scrubbed the washcloth hard against his face and wrung it out as if he were twisting the life from it. When in the three hells had he become such a sop?

A spark of frustrated anger lit within him, but it guttered at once, offering him no relief from the raw ache of his heart.

"Elezar..." Atreau began and then fell silent.

Elezar couldn't think of anything to say either. He stared down at the murky water filling the porcelain wash basin. There was a comparison to be made there between the beauty of the vessel and the ugliness of what it contained but Elezar didn't have the heart to think on it. Nor did he wish to consider his part in spoiling the once pristine water. He ruined so much of what he touched, it seemed.

"The count—Skellan isn't dying, is he?" Atreau asked.

"He wouldn't dare," Elezar replied. "No, Javier and the sisters say he's gone deep within but he will recover if only we keep him protected and let him sleep. Though they have no idea how long that may be."

"Then why were you—"

"You wouldn't understand if I told you."

Offense lit Atreau's expression. "You really think me so petty a friend that I wouldn't understand what it is to love someone? Or to fear losing him? You have no idea—"

"No, that's not what I meant. I have no doubt that you know more of both love and compassion than do I, Atreau. But this..." Words failed him.

"What then?" Atreau's affronted expression melted to curiosity. He looked to Skellan and to Elezar's surprise caught the corner of a blanket and pulled it over Skellan's bare shoulder.

"Those scrapes and bruises on his arms and the welts and blisters on his hands and legs," Elezar confessed, "they are all my doing."

Atreau's brow furrowed and he cast Elezar a disbelieving look.

"You beat and burned him?"

"No. He took on my injuries." Elezar indicated the expanse of his own unmarked thigh that showed through the burnt gaps in his breeches. Atreau leaned close then glanced back at Skellan.

"The two of you are sporting matching bruises on your cheekbones as well... But how?"

"I don't know. But I think this is how he bound us together. I knew he hadn't made a slave of me but I had no idea of what he'd done to himself. For months now he must have endured all the discomforts of my wounds and said nothing. Now the idiot has taken blows that should have laid me dead on the battlefield tonight. I would have gladly died for him but instead he's made me the cause of his pain—" Elezar felt his voice giving out and clenched his jaw shut. He had no desire to humiliate himself with another maudlin display.

To his surprise Atreau reached out and wrapped an arm around his shoulders. Elezar might have taken offense at being offered comfort as if he were a love-struck milkmaid but just now he felt far too tired to make a show of masculine vanity.

He accepted the embrace and found it comforting. It reminded him of the farewell embrace his brother Nestor had offered him years ago, when he'd left the Sagrada Academy.

After a moment Atreau drew back and sighed. "As much as it pains me to say this I think your young count must truly adore you, Elezar."

"I don't want him to adore me at the cost of his own well-being," Elezar snapped. "He had no right—"

"You can't command how someone else loves you," Atreau replied.

"Now that's a line to whisper to blushing maids if ever I've heard one."

"No, it's a truth that I've learned at great cost," Atreau answered. "Honestly. Longing and love take their own forms in each of us and no matter how powerfully you might wish it, you cannot alter the form of another man's desire."

"Oh?" Elezar couldn't help his skeptical tone.

"You did not see how Morisio and I parted," Atreau replied. He stepped back into the shadows and sank down onto the edge of the empty cot. "I could not love him as he would have wished but neither could I command him to love me less... We quarreled and when I quit the ship he refused to follow me, since my company would only break his heart. He was the dearest friend I've ever known... But I lost him."

Elezar stared at Atreau's shadowed face. He'd never suspected anything of the sort from Morisio—or Atreau, for that matter. Suddenly, Atreau's attempted dalliance with Lord Reollos made a sad sort of sense. And so did Atreau's advice.

Skellan might be infuriatingly unaware of his own immense value and beauty but at least he returned Elezar's desire. At least he could accept Elezar as a lover.

Elezar sank down to the edge of the bed beside Atreau.

"I had no idea... Morisio..." Elezar's strongest memories of Morisio were of his grinning freckled face peering over a hand of cards or looking up from some dull tome of botanical writings. He'd been one of so many youths attracted to Javier's company. But also one of the very few who'd stood with him against the royal bishop's men.

Atreau pulled a wry smile. Then he flopped back onto the cot to stare up at the gilded ceiling overhead.

"He was hardly alone among the Hellions, you know," Atreau replied. "Javier and you made such a striking pair. You two seemed fearless, defiant, and so powerful. Many joined the Hellions just to be near the two of you—"

"Javier, perhaps, but I—"

"Don't be coy." Atreau rolled his eyes. "Nearly every lad so-inclined probably jacked himself off imaging the cruel pleasure of being yours. You were a man among boys and we were all of us in awe of you."

Elezar felt his face flush. He'd been so distracted, so focused upon his own fears and desires, that he'd never considered that there could have been others like himself so close at hand. He'd thought himself a single aberration for so long. Even after he'd realized that Javier and Kiram shared desires akin to his own he'd not imagined that any number of other men could.

He realized now how absurd the thought had been but at the time it had seemed a special affliction bestowed only upon a very rare few. If nothing else, his time in Milmuraille's more seedy taverns had taught him otherwise. Men like him numbered in the hundreds and arose from all walks of life.

"I didn't know," Elezar admitted.

"Of course you didn't, but you see that's my point, isn't it. If any one of those youths could have willed your affections to take another shape, you would have learned soon indeed. But none of us have that power. If Skellan loves you so much that he would lay down his life in place of yours, you have no right to say he should feel otherwise. You can only reject him or accept him and honor what he offers you." Atreau smiled and pushed himself upright with a tired groan. "Though now that you know what he's willing to do for your sake, perhaps you might do him the kindness of taking a little better care of yourself."

Elezar studied his friend's handsome face and then said, "You're quite insightful when you're sober, you know?"

"A little too well," Atreau replied. "Why do you think I drink so much?"

There was a question but Elezar wasn't up to asking it. He'd had too many revelations and horrors already today.

"You should sleep," Atreau said and he rose from the bed.

But guilt flickered up in Elezar. After speaking so plainly with him and giving him such a leading response he owed it to Atreau to ask. Though he hardly knew how.

"Atreau—"

"It's nothing to look so grim about," Atreau responded. "I'm a wastrel because it suits me to be so. If I wished I suppose I could place the blame at the feet of my father and say that my drunken scandals are my means of humiliating him for whoring me out to win himself a handful of powerful friends. But that was long ago and I've been truly happy these last years wandering between you and Fedeles." Atreau picked up the silver platter and filthy wash basin. "It's probably more honest to simply say that I drink and whore because I enjoy wine and the company of women."

Elezar nodded and let him go at that. Every man had his own troubles and weaknesses, he supposed. His was the impossibility of remaining awake even a moment more. He dropped back into the cot.

Brilliant sunlight warmed the wide streets of Anacleto and all along the walkways almond and cherry trees perfumed the air with their blossoms. Before him rose a huge wrought-iron gate with two red-enameled statues of Grunito bulls flanking either side. Elezar leaned forward and peered in between the bars.

Elezar knew at once that he dreamed.

The gates he leaned against had been broken down by soldiers serving the royal bishop years ago. Now, far-heavier gates now protected his family's townhouse but these were the gates of his childhood. They stood slightly ajar, inviting his return. A sense of comfort and belonging washed over Elezar.

On the wide green lawn Nestor and his wife Riossa played with their two little babies while his parents, Lady and Lord Grunito, looked on. Elezar heard his other younger brothers teasing each other, though he could not quite see them through the rows of flowering cherry trees and lush beds of allspice blooms.

Elezar started forward but then a thin, pained cry turned his attention from his family home. He looked back and realized that the buildings across the street did not have the familiar gilded granite of Anacleto but towers of dark limestone carved with grotesque and beautiful reliefs of mythic creatures. Banks of black clouds seemed to rise from between the close-packed line of weathered buildings. Oddly, not a single structure sported a door and all the windows were barred and bolted closed. Elezar smelled roasting meat and heard laughter drifting from the buildings but the streets stood empty.

Only the narrow black cavern of a dark alleyway gaped before him.

Again he heard that thin plaintive call.

He stole a last glance back at his beaming brother and his parents and then turned and plunged into the darkness. As he walked small sparks lit the cracked cobblestones before him, lighting his path as stone of passage had shown him the way to the Sumar grimma's sanctum. He followed these through the dark and frigid maze. Heaps of refuse and banks of soot-caked snow lined his way.

It was not a place that Elezar had known in his life but he suspected that Skellan knew it too well.

"Skellan!" Elezar called because now he felt certain that

it had been Skellan who'd cried out. He turned a corner and suddenly an immense fiery wolf blazed before him.

Elezar stopped in his tracks.

"Turn back!" the wolf growled. "I am the death of any man who draws near me."

He was a terrifying sight, made entirely of flames and distorting the air around him with the radiant heat of his shining body. But Elezar knew his voice.

He took a step forward.

The wolf shrank back and dimmed as he did so. He barred his teeth.

"I will ruin you! Destroy everything you cherish!" The words should have threatened but something in the tone told Elezar that this was a warning and that the wolf feared its fruition more than Elezar did.

Again Elezar strode forward and the wolf backed away, shrinking down and growing dull and dirty. Elezar pounced forward. When he caught the beast he found that he held a battered, emaciated hound in his arms. It shook from cold and Elezar could feel each of its ribs as it gasped for breath in his grasp.

"I'm only trouble, Elezar. You should get as far from me as you can," the hound growled. "You deserve better."

"I don't believe that," Elezar replied. It struck him as strange that such an idea could even arise from one of his dreams. Nor had Skellan ever appeared in an animal guise in his dreams. To Elezar's mind he was always a man—a proud, sensual man with a teasing smile.

Then Elezar wondered if this was his dream alone. How deep did the bond between himself and Skellan reach?

Elezar stared down at the starving, cold creature and noted the stitching that ran along his skull and down his chest. He lifted his hand and pushed back the tattered fur. It fell away from Skellan like a dropped cloth, leaving him handsome and naked in Elezar's arms.

"I know who you are, Skellan, and I'm not afraid."

"So you say but you will grow to hate me." Skellan reached out and caught his tattered cloak. He pulled it back up around his shoulders. As the fur brushed over Elezar's hands he felt a wet heat and smelled blood. "You will abandon me just as I'm always abandoned."

A cutting wind lashed across them and heavy flakes of snow tumbled down. Skellan shuddered in his arms.

"They were right to throw me away," Skellan whispered. "I've only brought suffering and loss to the people around me. I'm an abomination. My mother told me —"

"No!" Elezar dug his hands into Skellan's shoulders. "No, you've been my salvation. You set Bone-crusher free and you've even done right by the men who kept you from safety and comfort all of your life. Skellan, you weren't thrown away, you were stolen. You were precious and loved though you did not know it—you still are."

"How can I be when I've caused so much harm?" Skellan lifted his hand and almost warily stroked Elezar's cheek. "I know how badly you've suffered to uphold my commands."

"You only know because you've taken more of my pain than I've even felt myself."

Guilt showed on Skellan's angular face.

"Why didn't you tell me?" Elezar demanded.

"I don't want you to feel beholden," Skellan said. "I just wanted to keep you safe."

"So you've called me your champion but all the while you've been mine?" Elezar frowned at him. "Do you know what you've done to yourself for my sake?"

Skellan pressed his face into Elezar's shoulder, hiding from his gaze.

"This bond between us, can it flow both ways?" Elezar asked. He thought that it must, otherwise they would not have been sharing this dream between them. "Can I give you my strength as you've taken my injuries?"

Skellan gave a brief, almost reluctant nod, then lifted his face to meet Elezar's gaze. His skin showed nearly as pale as the snow falling all around them.

"Then you must take my strength. You are too important to sacrifice yourself—"

"I don't want to be like the grimma—"

"You aren't!" Elezar couldn't stop his flare of frustration. Despite his anger he only held Skellan's body closer to his own. He lowered his voice. "For fuck's sake, Skellan. What in the hells is so damn hard about accepting the strength and protection that I freely offer you?"

"Sometimes I... I know I'm a bothersome stray. I cause no end of trouble and sooner or later you'll have had your fill of me. That's just the nature of things, don't you think?"

Bothersome? Elezar shook his head. The bravest, most fair-minded man Elezar had ever met, and Skellan thought himself bothersome. Elezar could hardly credit it. Not for the first time he wondered at just how deeply it had scarred Skellan to grow up believing himself abandoned and unwanted. The years he'd spent alone on the streets of Milmuraille certainly wouldn't have led him to expect much tolerance from other folk either.

It was no wonder that his mind conjured this dark winter alley when Elezar dreamed of the resplendent comfort of an Anacleto summer.

"After everything we've been through, do you really believe that I'm the kind of man who'd abandon you just because I felt a little irritated?" Elezar asked the question more in disbelief than any kind of outrage.

Skellan studied him in silence while snowflakes, as ornate as lace, swirled around them. A faraway bell rang out low mournful notes.

"You will leave me someday," Skellan said softly. "You have family and an earldom back in Cadeleon."

"I do," Elezar admitted, though he hated to think about his obligations to either and knew himself unready to weigh them against the pleasure he'd found with Skellan. "I can't say what the future will bring. But right now I am here with you of my own will and there is no one else I'd rather be with."

Skellan said nothing but there was a touching kind of hopefulness in his expression.

Elezar pressed on, "Let me truly be your champion and give you the strength you need. Come with me."

He rose, took Skellan's hand, and drew him back along the trail of shining cobblestones. The icy, soot-stained walls of the alley widened and Elezar found himself standing at the gates of the Cadeleonian garrison.

"It's closed," Skellan said.

"Don't worry. I have the keys," Elezar said. He didn't use them though. He gave a slight push and the heavy gates swung open. Rather than being in the courtyard they walked directly into the room they shared there. Inside the painted ceiling had become open summer sky.

The stone and timbers walls had turned to stands of beech trees and fruit-laden brambles of thimbleberry. Moss grew between the cobblestones. Hares flushed from the brush and bright songbirds took flight before them. Where the bed had stood, a hill of soft moss rose. Fragrant branches of elderflowers formed a bower overhead.

Elezar drew Skellan down to the soft sun-warmed ground. He kissed him carefully first but as Skellan responded, nipping his lip and sliding his tongue into Elezar's mouth, a deeply as ravenous lust overcame Elezar's caution. In the way of such dreams Elezar found himself all at once naked and Skellan stretched out before him.

"Come to me." Skellan held out his arms.

Elezar knelt beside him, stroking the smooth skin of his slim chest and pale stomach. Sweat rose across his shoulders and chest. His entire body felt hot and hard. He fought the rush of animal lust that urged him to throw Skellan over, spread his long, limber legs, and take his pleasure in a feverish frenzy.

Ever so carefully he bowed his head, kissed Skellan's throat and shoulders, and then flicked his tongue across his nipples.

Skellan's wanton gaze nearly undid all his self-control. Elezar started to draw back but Skellan wrapped his arms around him and held him with grinning wiry strength.

"You're always so careful."

"You're precious to me," Elezar replied, though he never would have said as much had he been awake. "I want you, but it would kill me to think I hurt you for the sake of my lust."

"Oh, but I'm stronger than you imagine, my man." Skellan ran his cool, pale hands up over Elezar's shoulders and then down along the line of his chest, down to his groin. "And haven't you promised to give me everything?"

Elezar's entire body seemed to rise to Skellan's knowing touch and hungry gaze. Skellan rolled over onto his knees and cast Elezar an inviting glance over his shoulder.

"Come and give me all you have."

Arousal rolled through Elezar so intensely that it made him ache. He moved over Skellan's exposed body. His hands shook as he fought to control his own desperate wanting. Despite Skellan's provocative words he invaded the delicate, velvet heat of his body slowly. Beneath him, Skellan shuddered and gasped. He stretched like a calfskin glove and Elezar felt the pounding of Skellan's heart as if it were throbbing through his own body.

"Are you all right?" Elezar asked as he ran a hand down Skellan's sweating flank and stroked Skellan's hot flesh to a proudly flushed erection. Skellan bucked back against Elezar's hips, drawing him in with the rhythm of Elezar's hand.

"You'll drive me mad if you hold back any longer."

Elezar needed no more invitation.

He plunged into Skellan, rocking deep and fast, with the hard rhythm that seemed to possess them both. Skellan arched and pushed to meet him. Elezar gave all of his strength with every thrust and felt Skellan pulling at him, drawing him in, taking what he needed—what Elezar offered with mounting, fevered ecstasy. The world around them fell away, leaving only their desperate union and its gushing, shaking climax.

Then they lay curled together, slick and sticky, in a musky darkness. Elezar dragged in a breath, feeling utterly satisfied and at the same time completely spent—like a stallion that had been ridden to height of his strength and the limit of his endurance. Skellan brushed a damp lock of Elezar's hair back from his face and pressed a gentle kiss against his brow. Elezar took gratification in noting the healthy glow of Skellan's flushed skin and the lively shine of his green eyes. Overhead tiny white stars bloomed like fragrant jasmine in the darkness.

"Thank you," Skellan whispered.

"My pleasure," Elezar replied.

"And mine as well." Skellan settled down next to him. Their bodies pressed bare skin to skin, close and comforting. Elezar found the weight of Skellan's hand on his chest reassuring. The sound of his breathing was as soothing as the rhythm of a distant sea. All at once Elezar marveled at how perfect this felt—how good and right.

Once he'd feared such a union as nothing but bestial, cruel lust. He'd been taught that the desire he felt made him a monster and would destroy any man so unlucky as to submit to him. But nothing could have been further from the truth. He'd given all of himself to Skellan and in doing so sustained him. What the priests of his family chapel would have condemned as an abominable sin, Elezar now realized could in fact be uplifting, freeing, and even a means of salvation. He smiled to himself at the thought, and because it was a dream, he belatedly realized that those were holy stars shining above him like blessings.

CHAPTER THIRTY-TWO

A jubilant cockerel in the courtyard below crowed raucous broken notes and would not be silenced by either barking dogs or laughing maids. The cacophony woke Elezar with a start. A few shafts of wan morning light played over the gilding and vibrant paint of the walls, illuminating ornate patterns of bas-relief beasts entwined.

Remembering last night, Elezar curled his hand to stroke Skellan's shoulder and then jolted up in alarm when his hands cradled only damp sheets. Elezar pulled himself free from the tangled bedding and staggered the few steps to Skellan's bedside.

To his relief, a healthy flush colored Skellan's cheeks and his sleeping breath came in a deep, even rhythm. Elezar wasn't certain if he only imagined it, but he thought that the bruise on Skellan's cheek had faded while his hair had taken on a deeper luster. His eyes fluttered open as Elezar knelt beside him.

"I had a wonderful dream, my man," Skellan murmured groggily.

"Oh yes?" Elezar smiled at him. "Was I in it?"

"In it indeed." Skellan grinned. Then he closed his eyes and his smile faded to the soft expression of sleep. Elezar let him rest. He felt certain that if a need arose someone would come for Skellan. Better to let him sleep while he could. Had the cot offered a little more room Elezar might have curled up beside him, but as it was he feared the cot would likely collapse under their combined weight.

Elezar stood and stretched. Glancing down from the balcony he noted that most of the men below still slept. Only two sister-physicians patrolled between the beds. Though as Elezar looked closer he realized that a great number of the beds were now empty. Sheets and blankets lay in tidy folds at the foot of many of the mattresses. He didn't know if he should be relieved or disturbed. Had a remarkable number of men recovered in the night or had a horrific percentage of them died of their wounds?

He picked out Captain Tialdo among those still abed and sleeping. But neither Kiram nor Javier seemed to be there. Elezar decided to believe in the skills of the sister-physicians and hoped that most of the men and women who'd suffered wounds defending Milmuraille had recovered at least enough to return to their own homes.

His own injuries appeared largely faded while Skellan's seemed completely gone. In fact the red gold stubble of his beard seemed to have grown quite a bit. Elezar resisted the urge to run a finger across Skellan's cheek.

He didn't want to wake Skellan. And in any case he needed a piss.

He ducked past the velvet drapes and slipped out the narrow door to find two of Skellan's guards engaged in a subdued discussion of wrestling holds. They greeted Elezar and asked anxiously after Skellan.

"Well," Elezar assured them. "He's resting easily now. I imagine he'll be up as soon as he catches a whiff of morning sausages."

"They should be frying some up anytime now, I reckon," the elder of the two guards commented and the younger nodded. Elezar found the relief in their expressions touching if a little amusing—it wasn't every day that two brawny Labaran soldiers reminded him so much of hens worrying over a precious egg. He suspected that he looked much the same.

He made his way to the reeking closets that served as privies for the balcony floor and held his breath while relieving himself. Kiram wasn't alone in missing the plumbing of Anacleto. Having added his contributions to the refuse heap a story below, Elezar started back through the narrow corridor that wound around the private box seats. On the way he came across Sheriff Hirbe, who appeared a little shocked and at the same time reassured to see him.

"So you're up!" The sheriff smiled but the warmth didn't quite reach his eyes. Gauging by the shadows beneath the older man's eyes and his unkempt hair, Elezar guessed that he hadn't slept much if at all.

"How is our Skellan?" the sheriff asked.

"Good," Elezar assured him. Then, though he dreaded the answer, he asked, "What of Eski and Magraie?"

"Young Eski is up and about, though she's sporting a black eye and split lip that would put most prize fighters to shame. Magraie..." The sheriff's wan smile faded and Elezar's hope fell.

"I'm so sorry," Elezar said and he meant it, though he knew his words were little consolation.

"He isn't dead. That's what we have to remember," Sheriff Hirbe said. "Rigni carried him up into the realm of the heavens to live on with him. We'll not see the boy's mortal body again but... But Magraie's spirit rides the clouds even now. He's still with us."

Elezar couldn't think of a response. Fortunately the sheriff didn't seem to need one. He sniffed hard and then shook his head.

"We'd feared that the same might have become of the count when he and you both slept an entire day away, but the Bahiim—Javier—assured us that you were both still among the living. Some healing spell passing between you, he said—"

"Wait. We've slept through an entire day?" The empty beds on the floor below and the great relief the guards had expressed made much more sense but the thought still alarmed Elezar. "What of the grimma's forces? How have you held the walls?"

"The grimma and their armies have remained in their camps licking the wounds Skellan dealt them the night past. But more mordwolves, elk, and boar are fording the river by the hour. Summoned by the grimma. They're likely still too few to take the city but soon..."

"We need to strike before they can recover."

"That is the general consensus." The sheriff offered Elezar a brief smile. "But the fact is that our forces are pretty battered themselves. Though if the count is feeling up to it we could certainly profit from another attack like the one he unleashed earlier."

Elezar hadn't witnessed that attack, only felt the force of it shake the ground beneath him and tasted fire and searing flesh on the air as he drew breath. He felt certain that the attack had left Skellan shaken and not just from the effort of it.

"We'll have to see once he's woken," Elezar replied.

"But you think that will be soon?" the sheriff asked.

"As I told his guards, get sausages frying and he's likely to come bounding straight to you."

Sheriff Hirbe laughed harder than Elezar expected the joke merited. Though he guessed that after Magraie's death the sheriff was relieved just to find anything amusing.

"I'll see that the kitchen fires are stoked and have food sent up to the two of you directly," the sheriff said.

"Thank you."

"You might warn him that his sister has been anxious as a hare in a kennel on his account. Lady Peome only just got her to sleep in the hostel three doors down. Cire made her a draught."

"I'll tell him."

The sheriff started to turn for the stairs but then glanced back. "In truth Lady Hylanya asked after you as well. I think that she's warming to you, Lord Grunito. Most here are."

It was an easy remark and it shouldn't have moved Elezar greatly. After all, at least the Labarans ought to have warmed to him after he'd ridden into battle against mordwolves, snow lions and trolls twice in one day. But not even that cynical thought dissipated Elezar's pleasure at the sheriff's words. Lady Hylanya, the sheriff, and likely nearly every soul in Milmuraille knew him as Count Radulf's lover and yet they did not disdain him for it. They recognized his prowess and accepted him in a way he could never have dreamed of being accepted even in his own home. He felt his face warming with an embarrassed flush.

God's blood, he was turning as sentimental as his father, and he couldn't even claim a head injury as an excuse.

Sheriff Hirbe grinned as he noted the blush but did Elezar the mercy of making no comment. With that they parted and Elezar returned to find Skellan still dozing.

He cracked one eye when Elezar entered the small space of the private box but didn't rouse himself.

Elezar went to the richly carved rail of the balcony and gazed down at the floor below. Captain Tialdo's daughter sat on a stool at her father's side. She said something and the captain smiled in response. He looked a little better this morning, though still pallid and weak.

"I dreamed that I'd figured it all out," Skellan murmured.

"Oh?" Elezar glanced over his shoulder to where Skellan remained sprawled with his eyes closed. "And how did your dream manage that?"

"I can't remember it all now." Skellan remained quiet for a few moments then added, "I had to hide you and your sword in a bearskin so that the grimma wouldn't know what sort of weapon you brought against their champions and... we won the war somehow, but I can't remember that part. And afterwards the dream turned odd and I was with you in Anacleto. Only I had to play at being your dog and wear a collar and... and I think someone stabbed me..."

"I can't say I like the sound of that," Elezar said.

"Not the stabbing, no. But the part earlier." Skellan paused for a gaping yawn. "The first part. Disguising you in the bearskin and then using the stone of passage that Kiram Kir-Zaki was given to breach Naemir's wards. That might work. But I have to figure out how to get at the bonds holding the grimma..." His voice trailed off and after a minute his breathing deepened. He'd returned to his dreams, perhaps to interrogate them.

Elezar watched him, pondering what he'd said. At first, it seemed the result of whimsy and worry tumbling like clouds in the wind. But Elezar knew that many of Skellan's dreams were much more than mere fantasies. Even the dream they'd shared the previous day, for all its fantastical trappings, had produced real results.

Skellan seemed to use his dreams the way other men employed pen and paper to work out complex figures. He could well be onto something, particularly with the stone of passage that Naemir had gifted to Kiram. Elezar had forgotten about that. He decided to send the bored guards at the door to fetch Kiram as well as the bearskin from Skellan's bed in the garrison.

"Just ask his dressers. They'll know where it is right away," Elezar assured them. Then, noting their hesitance, he added, "I'll personally keep watch over the count until you return."

That seemed to relieve their worry and the two of them set off at once. Elezar didn't know how long they'd already been standing in the dim hallway but he imagined it had made for a dull duty.

He returned to the room and his study of the sickbeds below and pondered how much longer the grimma would hold back before their next assault upon the city walls. He ought to send someone to check on Bone-crusher and the other two surviving trolls. Also he would need to meet with Jarn and the other emissaries whom the Sumar grimma had released. Likely many of them knew the other grimma from traveling to their sanctums. Maybe they'd noticed weaknesses that no one in Milmuraille could guess at. As he tried to organize all that he felt needed doing—visiting Cobre after he'd made certain Skellan was well guarded would be the first matter—he heard someone open the door behind him. The scent of fried meat and onions rolled in and Elezar's stomach growled.

He turned back. For just an instant the soft shadow of the velvet curtain allowed Elezar to mistake the well-made man for Atreau but his sneering expression destroyed the illusion at once.

"Well, you certainly are the watchdog, aren't you, Lord Grunito?" Rafale greeted him. He set the tray of bread sausages and gravy down on the small table at Skellan's bedside. His disdainful expression turned soft as he glanced down at Skellan's sleeping face. He reached out to stroke Skellan's cheek.

"Don't," Elezar warned.

Rafale turned and cast him a murderous look.

"You think you can keep him from me, don't you?" Rafale demanded in a low voice.

With a single stroke of his blade Elezar certainly could have kept Rafale from laying a finger upon Skellan ever again. But he resisted the petty temptation to say as much.

"I don't have to keep him from you," Elezar replied. "He knows what you are. That you could have taken him to his father anytime and relieved his misery but it suited you to keep him cold, starved, and isolated from the court where he might have made friends other than you."

"Is that what you've told him?"

Elezar sighed. This felt beneath both him and Skellan.

"Honestly, you aren't important enough for me to bother discussing with anyone," Elezar said.

"I don't believe you. I've seen the way he looks at me—"

"No, you just remember the way he used to look at you. But he's learned better. I think a lot of people have."

Rafale looked as if Elezar had knocked the wind out of him but he recovered quickly. His handsome features furrowed with anger.

"First Skellan and now even Lady Hylanya. You really think I'll allow you to worm your way into my place?"

"I've no desire to take any worm's place, Rafale," Elezar replied. He didn't have the time or strength to jab and posture with the man. "If the count and his sister tire of you, don't blame me. Likely they've seen you for the conniving sycophant you are."

Rafale's face went scarlet with fury. Elezar shook his head. He'd been so jealous of the man at one time but now he just found him pathetic. Elezar turned away from him.

The doors opened on the floor below, throwing an arc of light across the empty beds as Kiram and Javier strode into the theater. Elezar lifted his hand and waved.

"Elezar!" Skellan shouted.

He spun to see the tip of Rafale's dagger raised to plunge into his chest. His shock seemed to stretch the moment. Elezar recognized the wet black gleam of muerate poison along the blade. Rafale's teeth showed in a snarl of fury.

But strangely Rafale didn't drive the dagger down. He stood as if frozen and Elezar wondered if Skellan's call had stilled his hand. Rafale tottered a step to the side and collapsed. Then Elezar saw Skellan standing, looking pale and horrified, as he stared at Rafale's shaking body and the hunting knife jutting from his back.

Rafale went very still. Elezar crouched down, and placing his fingers to Rafale's neck, felt his pulse slow and then stop. Carefully, Elezar pulled the bejeweled dagger from Rafale's stiffening hand.

"Is he—did I…" Skellan stepped back from where Rafale lay. He bumped against his cot and sat down heavily.

"You saved my life," Elezar told him. And then it struck him that likely Skellan had saved them both. Muerate made for a powerful and fast poison and it would have flowed from Elezar's blood to Skellan's had Rafale managed to drive his dagger in.

"Skellan…" Elezar wanted to offer comfort but couldn't think of how. Despite all he'd said to Rafale he didn't imagine that Skellan had so hardened his heart to the man that he could feel nothing at having killed him.

He recalled the shattering horror that had stricken him when he'd thought he'd killed Javier in a rage years before. He'd been utterly inconsolable and filled with self-loathing. Elezar studied Skellan's face. He appeared shocked but not broken, not utterly devastated by what he'd done.

"It was my dream… I realized that it was you, not me, who was stabbed and I woke up to see Rafale," Skellan said. "He saw me too, knew I was awake and still…"

Elezar nodded. He heard the knock at the door—likely Kiram and Javier—but ignored it.

"Are you all right?" Elezar asked.

Skellan drew in a slow steady breath but didn't answer. He dropped his gaze to his long hands.

"Skellan, I know that he and you—" Elezar began but the desolate expression on Skellan's face cut him off short. What could he hope to say?

"How could he imagine that I would allow him to murder you?" Skellan asked quietly and Elezar didn't know how to answer that.

Another knock sounded at the door, followed by a third much more insistent rap. Skellan pushed a strand of hair back from his eyes. He lifted his face, his expression sorrowful but composed.

"Will you send for Sheriff Hirbe or should I?" Skellan asked at last. "We'll have to settle this legally before we can hope to push on."

CHAPTER THIRTY-THREE

So many people crowded into the theater box that Skellan wondered that the whole balcony didn't break off and drop them all into beds on the floor below. Javier and Kiram stood back near the velvet curtains. Kiram held the bearskin that had been delivered earlier. Javier rolled the white polished stone of passage between his fingers as if practicing a trick of stage magic. Past them and just behind Skellan, Elezar loomed, solemn and silent as a professional mourner.

At Skellan's feet Rafale sprawled, his corpse dividing the space so perfectly it looked almost like stage blocking. Two deputies knelt beside the body while the sheriff and Lady Peome looked on. The sheriff's mournful expression showed every one of his years. Lady Peome clenched a white kerchief over her mouth. She hardly blinked as she stared down at her brother's waxen face.

A sense of unreality clung to Skellan. Even as he watched Sheriff Hirbe's men wrap Rafale's body in a blanket and then heft him up and out of the theater box, he still felt as if he lingered in a dream. A dream of one of Rafale's plays wherein Rafale had cast himself as the tragic hero and chosen Skellan for his murderer.

It just didn't seem possible that Rafale could be dead.

Then his gaze fell upon the jeweled dagger that Rafale had nearly plunged into Elezar's back. Muerate poison still blackened the blade. Tiny emerald studs glinted from the pommel—and Skellan wondered who had gifted the costly dagger to Rafale. Some guild master's wife or courtly lady? Would her heart be broken at the news of his death?

Skellan feared Cire would be devastated and she would have every right to blame Skellan. Only he hadn't wanted to kill Rafale—hadn't really meant to, except that Rafale had gone too far to be stopped any other way.

Maybe he should have allowed Cire to enthrall Rafale. Maybe that would have saved him from this end. But as Skellan stared at the knife on the floor he decided no. Shifting the object of Rafale's obsession wouldn't have changed the man he was— had been. Ruthless ambition had been innate to his character, as well as charm and wit. Inevitably he would have overstepped himself at some point or made too dangerous an enemy. Had he been given his life to live over a dozen times likely he would have died violently every time. As with every man, woman, and child, the core of his character shaped his vei. His fate was inevitable because an inherent character lay behind all the varied choices that created each cobblestone of the path that was his destiny.

Still Skellan wished it had been otherwise.

Just at the edge of his hearing he caught the sounds of Cire and Clairre engaging in some small bicker. Their voices rose and then faded as they wandered back towards the dressing rooms on the floor below.

"This far north muerate poison is a rarity." Javier broke the silence in the theater box. "I wonder where Rafale came by so potent a dose?"

Skellan glanced back in time to catch a meaningful nod between Javier and Elezar. Lady Peome straightened.

"I gave it to Bois." She looked with pleading eyes to Skellan. "I would never have supplied it in the service of an assassination, Count Radulf."

"I know," Skellan said. Not that he thought Peome incapable of plotting an assassination. Quite the opposite. She would have planned something far more subtle and effective than this. He felt certain that she would not have acted against Elezar at a point when so much of the city's defense rested with him. Nor would she have employed an agent or a poison so easily traced back to her.

No, this entire scene bore all the hallmarks of a tragic disaster of Rafale's own making. An act of passion and drama that worked so well on a stage, where the fallen dead only held their breath and everyone got up afterward to take a bow. But in life no one got up. Applause didn't ensue. It all just made for a sick atmosphere of guilty horror and left a room full of grim people staring helplessly at a poisoned dagger and a pool of drying blood.

Skellan's stomach clenched and rolled briefly and he pulled his gaze from the seams where Rafale's blood seeped between the floorboards.

"This won't go over well." Sheriff Hirbe met Skellan's eyes but then flicked his gaze to Elezar. "Rafale is—was—a rogue, but a well-loved rogue. Folk won't like hearing that his end came at the count's hand."

The line of Elezar's mouth tensed.

"My doing then," Elezar stated just like that. Not a moment's hesitation. He simply accepted the blame. Skellan marveled at him, at his bloody-minded gallantry. Cadeleonian or not, Elezar could have been a great champion summoned to life from one of Bone-crusher's stories. What wouldn't he sacrifice of himself if it were asked of him?

"No," Skellan cut in. "My standing will not come at the cost of Elezar's."

"It would be better—" Elezar began and Skellan opened his mouth to cut him off.

But Kiram Kir-Zaki beat him to it.

"Does anyone other than those of us here now know of the exact events that led to Rafale's demise?" A moment of perfect silence followed Kiram's question as its implications took root.

"No, but two deputies have just carried his body out. We can hardly claim he's left the city on a southern tour," Sheriff Hirbe responded. Beside him, a little life seemed to return to Lady Peome's dazed expression.

"It's not the fact of his death that needs… reconsidering, but the cause of it. If a more acceptable reason could be found, one that would unify rather than divide our supporters…" Lady Peome said.

Skellan frowned at the idea of making up some lie. It wasn't as if the wound in Rafale's back could be passed off as a natural occurrence. He hated plotting, though he supposed he liked it better than Elezar taking the blame for killing Rafale and earning the animosity of a third of the women in the city. Hylanya and Cire counting among that number.

"You can't expect people to believe he just tripped and fell on my knife," Skellan muttered.

"The best courtly obfuscations are so near the truth that they could pass for him with his wife." Javier tossed the stone from one hand to the other with a particularly cunning smile. "So the events stay the same. It remains Rafale falling beneath the count's blade." Javier held up his hand when Lady Peome and the sheriff both looked like they might object. He appeared quite pleased with himself as he plunged ahead, "However, it isn't because Rafale seethed with jealousy but instead... Shall we say he'd fallen under the thrall of one of the grimma?"

"Ah, I see where you're going with this," Kiram said. "It's a bit of a melodrama but it would fit. Imagine. Rafale, in the throes of a thrall, is sent to murder the count—"

"But resists enough to turn his blow from Skellan towards Elezar." Javier nudged Elezar as if tapping him in for a round of drinks. "Skellan has no time to break the thrall but instead is forced to slay Rafale. But before he passes on, the count frees him of the thrall that took hold of him..." Javier glanced to Skellan. "Not only does that cast everyone in a good light but it rather sets the groundwork for you to enforce your bans against the use of thralls."

Again they all fell briefly quiet.

"It could work." Lady Peome's controlled expression wavered. Then she pulled a sad smile. "It's just the sort of story Rafale would have loved."

Sheriff Hirbe nodded. He looked between Skellan and Elezar questioningly.

"I don't like lying," Skellan began.

"Says the man who passed himself off as my dog for a month," Elezar whispered so quietly that Skellan just caught it. Had they been alone Skellan would have spun around and licked his face just to see shock replace Elezar's doubtlessly composed expression, but as was, he restrained himself.

"But even I can see the need to do so on this occasion," Skellan finished. "Sheriff Hirbe, will you have the news of the tragedy officially announced? Lady Peome, will you please tell my sister? I don't want her finding out through some gossip and not knowing what is and isn't true."

The two of them agreed. The sheriff took Rafale's dagger as evidence. All conversation ceased when three novice sister-physicians arrived and cleaned away the blood with practiced speed. They bowed to Skellan and took their leave like excited birds.

Then after a few more words, Lady Peome and Sheriff Hirbe departed as well.

Skellan watched the curtains fall closed behind them. He thought that this was likely the first time he'd truly acted in the manner of a Radulf count, not just a foundling impersonator or a pawn of more worldly courtiers' schemes. Now the schemes were his own. Only a month ago he might have bristled at the mere thought of dealing in such complete deceit, but witnessing the horrifying losses of open, honest warfare had tempered Skellan's enthusiasm for absolutes—even truth. Better he learn to use lies than he cost other folk their lives.

He wasn't certain if that made him wiser than he'd once been or simply more compromising.

⁂

Skellan turned his attention to Javier and Kiram. At his request Javier handed over the stone of passage. The pebble was clear as a piece of glass but held a brilliant blue sphere at its heart. It felt like ice against Skellan's palm.

"She told me I'd want the stone of passage one day soon," Kiram said as he laid the bearskin over Skellan's cot. "Not that I believed her. I was only too happy to get out of that icehouse."

Javier nodded and rested his hand on Kiram's shoulder protectively. Beside them, Elezar took up the bearskin and studied it.

Skellan rolled the stone over his palm but his attention drifted to the murmurs and whispers rising from the floor below. Already news of Rafale's enthralled demise spread through the theater. He recognized Clairre's shout of horror and Cire's cry, and he felt like a monster for his part in their losses. Though belatedly he realized that if they believed Rafale to have been enthralled, at least they could each mourn, curse, and toast Rafale while still believing him faithful and brave in his own way. They, if not Rafale, deserved that. Their grief at least wouldn't have to be a source of shame.

"So then?" Elezar's voice brought Skellan's attention back. "Is there some way you think you can use the stone to breach the Naemir's wards?"

Skellan glanced to him and read the intense concern in his shadowed, dark eyes. He supposed his man thought he mourned Rafale too. Elezar wasn't the kind of man who'd discuss his fear for another in company, but Skellan didn't care if Javier and Kiram overheard the truth.

"You needn't look so worried for me, my man," Skellan told him. "It wouldn't have been my first choice to kill Rafale but it's not in me to regret choosing your life over his. I'd do the same a thousand times over."

As he expected Elezar's tanned face colored at his blatant statement. Javier grinned at him aprovingly. Kiram nodded as if he'd predicted Skellan would say as much, though his attention remained focused upon the stone in Skellan's hand.

"So the stone?" Kiram asked.

"Naemir meant it to bring you to her," Skellan told Kiram. He closed his eyes and cupped his hands over the stone. Cool blue symmetry coiled at its core, vibrating like a clear note and shining like a distant star. Skellan lifted the stone to his mouth and drew in a deep icy breath. "She admired your understanding of the invisible truths. Cold numbers and the movements of stars and…" Skellan felt a frigid longing rise to his lips. He tasted desiccated flesh and the dust of bones. "Death. She longed for you to bring death to her… She hoped that your Bahiim might be the one to unmake her—to free her from the cage of immortal flesh."

Skellan looked to Javier but today he hid his deathly countenance too deeply beneath a pale mask of youth for Skellan to discern. Yet he had glimpsed the Bahiim's true face and suspected that Naemir must have as well.

"If she wanted me to kill her why did she release Kiram at all?" Javier asked.

"I think it must have been because she knew you couldn't do it alone," Skellan answered. Clear indigo notes still whispered through his mind. "You are part of a solution, as is Kiram, but not the entire thing. So she gave Kiram this stone of passage to bring you back to her when the time came."

"She had some kind of premonition that all of this would come about and hoped that they'd end her?" Skepticism edged Elezar's expression.

"I don't know if she had a premonition or if she sent this stone away with Kiram in hopes of setting her demise in motion." Skellan frowned, not thinking of just this stone of passage but of his own birth and coming of age. "Naemir and the rest of the grimma are ancient—born with the first breath of the wind, before the mountains of the north rose from the earth. Their experience and grasp of the workings of the world must be immense by now. With such a vast perspective and so much time, who knows how easily one of them could craft a small spell that given ages could proliferate powerful changes."

"So by giving me a stone of passage she ensures that when someone does find a means to end her life the tool to reach her is already out in the wider world?" Kiram asked.

"I think so," Skellan replied. "Nothing is preordained but every choice made, every action taken, builds a stepping stone in a vei. With enough patience and persistence even blind luck can be crafted into something like a fate. And the grimma are in a better position than most to use their time and power to shape events."

Javier nodded but appeared troubled. He said, "Following that reasoning, you realize it bodes particularly ill for any plan we might attempt set in motion against them? Who knows what spells Onelsi and Ylva have concocted ages ago to defeat us?"

"Well, yes," Skellan admitted. "But our advantage is that— if I'm right—we're exploiting the plans of two grimma against the other two." Skellan felt the ring on his finger warming each time he rolled the stone of passage over its band. The stone grew cooler in response. Summer and winter. Opposing sympathy resonated between them, intensifying the power of both.

One brought a new life into the world and the other courted a cold death but their motives were the same. He and this cold stone had both been crafted to serve the grimma even if that meant destroying them.

"I'd thought before that we'd just been uncommonly lucky to get hold of a stone of passage," Skellan continued. "But holding it now I feel certain that Naemir meant her stone of passage to come to Milmuraille and to bring about an end to her existence. I'm almost sure that even her march here was meant to bring her and the other grimma closer to the demise she and the Sumar grimma created for them all."

"If she is really that suicidal why bother with all these elaborate machinations?" Elezar asked. "Why doesn't she just kill herself?"

"She can't." Skellan's answer came in the same breath as Kiram's. Skellan let Kiram explain.

"Twice while I was held prisoner in her sanctum she threw herself from the highest tower." Kiram swallowed hard as if fighting back sickness. "Her body was... everywhere. But she didn't die. She came back together like pools of bloody water pouring into each other."

"None of them can die," Skellan added. "They're bound by the power of their sanctums to remain trapped in human flesh. And in any case, it's not actually death that she and the Sumar grimma are seeking. It's their freedom from the flesh that's bound them for ages—"

"Because they're the daughters of the sky?" Elezar provided.

Both Javier and Kiram turned to Elezar as if startled by his capacity for speech. Elezar shrugged. "Skellan told me this bit earlier. After the Sumar grimma told it to him."

"*The* daughters of the sky?" Javier asked.

"The very same," Skellan said.

"So their original state of being is that of a single fluid wind spirit?" Kiram asked.

"Yes, I suppose that's how they could be described." Skellan nodded. It was nice, if a little surprising, how quickly Kiram seemed to catch on. "Their realm spanned the world and reached up to the very edge of the stars. They were completely unfettered by flesh. But then—"

"Then if I remember my Mirogoth mythology correctly, the Age of the Demons came," Javier interjected, his expression bright. Skellan got the distinct impression that he was showing off for Kiram's benefit. "They would have numbered among the wild primal spirits that the first witches called down into the flesh of the Old Gods. So the grimma once fought and defeated demon lords, did they?"

Skellan nodded. "But they weren't women then."

"No?" Kiram asked.

"Dragons. Fucking gigantic dragons," Elezar supplied. "I didn't see it long or too clearly but for a moment when the Sumar grimma met Skellan at the river, I saw the thing—her." He spread his muscular arms wide. "Like an entire mountain charging down and blazing green."

"Old Gods," Javier said quietly and though he said nothing more he studied Skellan with an assessing gaze. Maybe he wondered how the son of such a creature could present so common a figure. Skellan resisted his feeling of self-consciousness and pushed on with his explanation.

"After the demon lords were driven out by the Old Gods the human population found themselves left with a world of wild gods of their own making but beyond their control." Skellan tried not to worry about Javier's frank, assessing gaze. "I think every culture in every land shares some story of driving back or defeating Old Gods."

"Some of us have many," Javier said. "But yes, even Cadeleonians preach of their Holy Savior's battles to drive the old heathen gods up here into the northlands."

"In the case of the grimma, I suspect that none of the witches who bound them up were still living by the time the demon lords were destroyed. No one knew how to release them so an enterprising coven of witches tried to trap them in the mortal flesh of human beings to limit their power and ferocity. By necessity, a spell powerful enough to manage that had to be anchored in something immense."

"The size of a sanctum?" Kiram asked. "Naemir once said that her throne served as her prison. I thought at the time she was speaking symbolically."

"She wasn't. As best as I can tell—" Skellan glanced down to his ring and the stone of passage in his hand and he felt certain. "The sanctums draw on the power of all those souls trapped in their walls, all the trolls and wethra-steeds and other wild beasties that those early witches could enthrall. All that power—all those suspended lives—rings the grimma in radiant energy but every thread of it also confines them inside a living body."

Kiram frowned and Skellan could almost see him trying to mentally diagram the construction of such a trap.

"Think of it this way. You have a dog on a leash and you can drag it about pretty easy and set it on whomever you want. But the more leads in your hands, the more each spirited hound pulls, dodges, and wraps the leash about your legs. You have an entire pack in your hands, but it takes all of your concentration to manage them."

"So they'd just need to release control of the sanctums to be freed?" Kiram asked.

"Exactly, except they don't know how to release the sanctums. My mother said Ylva and Onelsi don't even remember that they had an existence before the sanctums."

"And if they do break free of the sanctums we'll have four gigantic dragons on our hands. Correct?" Javier put in.

"A gold star for you, Tornesal," Elezar replied.

"Dragons..." Kiram scratched his head as if trying to massage the idea into his skull. "That's just so... I mean, it sounds like something from an age of myths."

"It ought to, since that's the time they come from." Skellan couldn't help how it sounded. It was the truth. "You likely didn't give much thought to the existence of trolls either before you came north but they were always here."

Kiram considered him then said, "That's true."

"I don't know that I'm up to taking on four dragons." Javier's earlier grin fell away to an expression nearly as solemn as Elezar's. "I could open the shajdi completely but with so many people so near I might kill everyone in Milmuraille before I brought down the four—"

"No, that's the mistake." Skellan cut him off with a shake of his head. "The answer isn't to attempt to summon a greater power than theirs. Power is their realm. They may not look it but they are still Old Gods. We must bring their battle into our realm."

"Witticism and card tricks?" Javier suggested, arching a black brow skeptically.

Kiram laughed but Elezar cuffed Javier in the head.

"Don't be an ass just because you don't have the answer and Skellan does."

"We're good, my man," Skellan assured Elezar though secretly it pleased him that Elezar so quickly took his side. "We use the Old Road to slip past the other two grimma into Naemir's camp. There the stone of passage will offer us some safety—particularly if Kiram carries it. Once I'm there I draw a ward ring and issue a witch's challenge—"

"Your plan is to duel a grimma alone?" Javier objected.

"Not just my plan," Skellan replied. "It's my vei. It has been since I came of age. Only I had the wrong grimma at first."

He saw Elezar's mouth press to a hard line as though he were forcing himself to keep his mouth closed. If they'd been alone, Elezar would have argued with him, he knew. But now he understood that his man's true loyalty would prevent him from opposing Skellan in public. He hadn't meant to use that against him but secretly was glad Javier and Kiram were present.

Javier, on the other hand, narrowed his gaze and said, "If you're planning to unleash the Black Fire again—"

"Nothing so grand, I swear." Skellan held up his hands. Though it had been his experience in the grip of the Black Fire that had awoken his senses to the power of emptiness and absence. "I told you it's not in the kingdom of the vast forces that this battle can be won, but in the humblest and smallest of realms. I plan to break their power by infiltrating the invisible motes between the grains of creation. I will be a flea biting the great wyrm to bits."

"I have no idea what you're talking about." Javier's brows furrowed and he looked questioningly to Kiram.

"Don't ask me. I'm just a mechanist."

Skellan wasn't surprised neither of them could guess his intention.

Only he had opened the huge emptiness of the Black Fire and seen it tear spells and mortal flesh down to those tiny grains of existence. Though he'd been wracked with pain and near death himself he'd witnessed the Black Fire expose the minute structures at the core of all creation. Forces too small and too silent for mortal senses to detect had been laid bare before him. Since then the idea of them had remained, turning through his thoughts: those seemingly insignificant, invisible motes from which all the world arose.

"Unless," Kiram said suddenly, "there is an obscure Yuanese mathematical theory that holds that all things, no matter how solid they seem, are actually built up from discrete assemblies of smaller and smaller structures. You know, the way a city is made up of many buildings, and each building is made up of individual timbers and every timber is made up of wood fibers. They infer that pattern repeats all the way down to the very smallest possible particles. We cannot see them but the vagaries of their structures are what underpin the variety of life and material all around us. At least that's the theory."

Skellan stared at Kiram in awed silence. No wonder Naemir had been so fascinated by the brilliance of his mind. Was there nothing he couldn't comprehend? Nothing he didn't know about? "Yes, that is exactly the realm where I think I'll find the undoing of the grimma."

"So, it really does exist?" Kiram's expression lit up.

"I've seen it," Skellan said.

"When we're through all this the two of you will have to pen a treatise together," Javier commented. Skellan thought he was joking but Kiram nodded quite seriously.

"But, for the matter at hand." Elezar gave Skellan a direct and assessing look. "You think you really can beat the grimma in a challenge?"

Skellan straightened and returned Elezar's stare.

"I can," Skellan said with all the assurance he could muster. He had to defeat them, because if he couldn't then more bloody battles would ensue and countless innocent lives would be lost. He had to beat them.

"All right. So Javier sneaks you into Naemir's camp where Kiram and the stone of passage will ensure that you aren't attacked. From the protection of Naemir's camp you plan on making your challenge. Have I got that all correct?"

"Exactly."

"So what am I to do with this bearskin?" Elezar asked.

"You and your sword are going to come along to get us out of there if I'm wrong about Naemir or anything else," Skellan replied. "And I could well be wrong."

Elezar ran his hand along the white fur. "But you don't want Naemir or any of the others to feel the presence of my sword so you want to hide it, and me, in this animal body?"

"If you'll consent to it."

Elezar frowned down at the long white cloak of bearskin. Skellan knew he asked no small measure of trust from Elezar. If something went wrong Elezar might find himself living as a white bear for the rest of his years. Though if too much went wrong none of their lives would last long enough to worry over.

"I'm probably enough of a beast that I won't even notice the difference." Elezar smiled wryly then asked, "So when do we do this?"

"As soon as I've had a piss and eaten those sausages," Skellan replied. He didn't know why but that earned him a laugh from all three other men.

CHAPTER THIRTY-FOUR

For all the times he'd been called a beast and had even thought of himself as one, Elezar had never imagined how truly strange it would be to inhabit the surging senses and powerful flesh of an animal. Scents rolled over him in rich rushes, filling his mind with flashes of bodies and stores of cured meats. At the same time the words to describe them dulled and fell from his grasp. Colors faded from his vision but sounds welled forth.

He didn't need to see the horses in the stables to recognize their scents and pick out each of their distinct voices any more than he needed to look to know that Javier stood behind him, sweating as the noonday sun beat down upon the garrison grounds. Kiram held their mounts a few feet further back in the scant shadows of the stable. Up on the walls soldiers looked on and Elezar tasted their nervousness as the breeze swept the smell of them down to him.

"Elezar," Skellan called his name and Elezar lifted his massive head. Skellan stood only a yard from him but downwind and ringed in pale red streams of light. The sight of him drew Elezar like a powerful need. The intensity of feeling welling up shook Elezar as did his difficulty in ignoring it. He bounded forward on all fours, his whole body trembling with excitement and joy.

Skellan stiffened but didn't bolt back.

Elezar managed not to bowl him over but couldn't stop himself from lowering his head and nuzzling Skellan's face and chest. He wanted to throw his arms around him but as he lifted his hand, a dissonance stopped him.

It wasn't a hand but a massive white paw tipped by five long black claws. Elezar stared at the monstrous paw then lowered it back to the ground and turned his head to actually take in the stunning mass of his transformed body. He dwarfed

Javier's stallion, Lunaluz, outweighing the horse by a hundred stone and towering five hands taller while still down on all fours. Standing upright he realized he could reach the second story of the central building. His hide shone bright white in the sun and looked as incongruous in the garrison courtyard as a glacier. The sandy ground behind him bore deep ruts and gouges from where his claws had torn up cobblestones and earth in his explosive rush to Skellan.

Elezar tried to tell Skellan that he hadn't meant to startle him, but only a distressed groan escaped him. Skellan's expression changed but Elezar couldn't read it as he once would have. Fear shivered through Elezar as the realization of just how much of a beast he'd truly become closed in upon him. How much more of his mind might he lose with each passing moment?

Skellan raised his arms and reached up to stroked Elezar's cheek.

Just that touch eased Elezar's distress. He felt the muscles of his shoulders relax and the stiff hair all along his back and forearms settle into silky white waves.

Skellan leaned his head into the thick muscle of Elezar's neck.

"I know it's fearful and strange at first. I do know. But I swear that you're safe, my man. I'll not allow anything to do you harm."

Elezar heard the words and understood them but it was Skellan's voice, the feel of his weight, and the strong smell of him that truly soothed. Elezar drew in a deep breath—tasting the tang of Skellan's sweat and the licorice root musk of his skin, the perfumes of magic and flesh—and again that surge of joy set his body humming with excited delight. He resisted the ferocious intensity of the longing surging through him only by forcing himself to recall the first six stances of a Cadeleonian swordplay. He focused with difficulty upon the words, on names of the swordsmen who'd made each form famous, on history and dates that he'd not recollected since his school days. Steadily the raw emotion of his animal body quieted.

"Is all well, my man?" Skellan asked.

Better, Elezar thought the word just to maintain his grip on language though he couldn't say a thing. Skellan lifted his face and then nodded as if he'd understood him.

You hear me? Elezar focused hard on the question and again Skellan went still and drew a deep breath like a hound catching a scent on the wind.

"Yes, I hear you."

Elezar found the thought almost absurdly comforting. He hadn't realized how deeply isolating it felt to be stripped of the ability to communicate. Again, he reflexively nuzzled Skellan's face and chest. Skellan leaned into him, stroking his head and neck and then giving a laugh as Elezar nosed his armpit. He was aware that he shouldn't behave like this and yet the happiness that filled him seemed nearly impossible to deny.

"All right, all right!" Skellan caught hold of his ears and whispered. "I adore you too, but right now we must make our way across the Old Road. Are you ready for that, then?"

Elezar got control of himself and stepped back from Skellan. He nodded then glanced back to Javier and Kiram. Kiram led their horses closer with great caution, murmuring soothing sounds, which Elezar found relaxing as well. Javier peered at Elezar then quite purposefully strode across the grounds to his side. Unlike Skellan, he radiated vibrant tension and smelled sharp as fresh-cut grass—anxious, Elezar realized.

"I thought you were absurdly big as a man," Javier muttered. He held out his hand as he might have for a horse or hound to take his scent. "But this is beyond all reason. You're fucking gigantic, Elezar!"

Elezar shrugged, though the motion felt odd in this new body. Javier jumped a little and then seemed embarrassed of the reaction. He angled his gaze to Skellan.

"Did you have to make him so damn huge?"

"That's only half my doing. Elezar's strength brings out the best of the bearskin's potential. He's made to be mighty whatever his form." Skellan smiled at Elezar. "Even in a mouse hide, my man would likely stand tall as a draft horse."

"Not exactly subtle," Javier commented. "Particularly not if we have to make a fast break from the grimma camps."

"Oh, I don't know. He's hardly as big as a troll. And I'd guess he can move quick enough." Kiram coaxed the horses alongside Elezar. Their nervousness perfumed the air like the scent of roasting meat. Elezar's mouth watered and he resisted the urge to lunge forward for the kill. He knew these horses and liked both of them greatly, he reminded himself. Focusing on that attachment, his hunting instinct receded. He kept his gaze averted from them, giving them time to grow a little more comfortable with his smell and proximity.

Kiram handed Lunaluz's reins to Javier and then, he reached out and placed his hand against Elezar's ribs. His fingers trembled as he first patted Elezar but then grew steadier.

"Your coat is quite soft, Elezar," Kiram commented.

"Really?" Javier asked. Then he too reached up and stroked Elezar's shoulder.

How strange was that, Elezar thought.

He couldn't imagine any other circumstance when Kiram and Javier would stand so close to him, caressing his body without even a hint of sexual overture. Nor could he think of another circumstance when he would have felt so utterly relaxed accepting the intimacy, but as was, a contented sigh escaped him as well as a pleased, rumbling thrum.

"It really is still you, isn't it?" Javier laughed softly, sounding relieved.

Elezar nodded.

"Of course it is," Skellan replied. "Why would you think not?'

"Kiram and I have both encountered men who were lost in the bodies of ravenous animals." Javier drew back to stroke

Lunaluz's nose. Kiram's gelding snuffled his hand as well, taking the scent of Elezar's new body from his palm.

"I'd not allow that to happen," Skellan assured Javier and Javier made some response but the words drifted past Elezar. He shifted just a little to allow Kiram to scratch just under his rib. Kiram obliged him with enthusiasm.

That was certainly nice. Elezar hadn't before taken much note of Kiram's hands but now he had to admire their dexterity. Elezar stretched. Kiram scratched along his flank, the sun warmed his back, and he found himself giving into a lazy yawn. The idea of an afternoon nap drifted through him.

Skellan smoothed his own scarlet cloak and after another moment cleared his throat.

Elezar looked to him at the noise.

"If we've all settled in, I'd say we'd best be off. The grimma will only send more reinforcements across the river the longer we linger."

"Yes, of course." Kiram patted Elezar one last time then returned to Javier and the horses.

Elezar straightened, his languid mood slipping away as he reminded himself that he still faced the journey over the Old Road. He shivered and hair bristled along his spine. He edged closer to Skellan and knelt.

They'd agreed earlier that the easiest way for Skellan to keep pace with Javier and Kiram's horses would be for Elezar to carry him. Now Skellan grabbed handfuls of his hair and hide and scrambled up onto his back. Elezar felt Skellan's weight and heat as he might have sensed a sparrow hawk alighting on his shoulder. He glanced to Javier and Kiram, both of them atop their mounts, and it struck him that they were all of them fragile creatures. All precious to him. A wave of protective tenderness welled through him.

Had he been in his own body he wouldn't have acknowledged the affection that kindled in him but now he couldn't seem to shield himself from it. For the first time he felt relieved to be bereft of speech, if only to save himself from babbling his loyalty and friendship like a sloppy drunk.

Javier sat up very straight in his saddle and raised his arms high above his head. He paused with the natural dramatic flair of a stage performer.

Soldiers, kitchen women, stable boys and even men on guard duty all stopped their work to stare at Javier in expectation. The entire garrison fell so quiet that for the first time Elezar picked out the chirps of cloud imps from the building eaves and the very distant rumbles of sleeping trolls.

Sparks leapt from Javier's fingers. Then he threw his arms wide and streamers of white light rose from his hands. He glowered at the empty air before him. Elezar caught the scent of sweat rising on his skin though Javier gave little outward sign of the intense strain he endured. Javier clenched his hands and with a violent sweep of his arms tore the air asunder, opening a gaping archway of darkness before them. It hung like an immense pane of black glass, appearing no thicker than a coin, and yet Elezar knew the thin stretch of darkness hid a vast realm within.

Gasps rose from all around but Javier seemed to take no notice. He nudged his stallion ahead and disappeared into the dark. Kiram followed, looking calm but gripping his reins with white-knuckled fists. Elezar strode after them, feeling Skellan's body tense against his back. Stale rafts of dry air drifted from the dark archway. Just as Elezar reached the arch a small golden creature scurried ahead of him as if to block his path with its tiny body. Elezar snorted, taking in the rat's scent. Queenie, Cire's familiar.

"I must go," Skellan said.

The rat squealed piteously.

"I'm sorry, Cire, but this is my vei. I must take this path." Skellan leaned over Elezar's shoulder and lowered his voice. "But in my absence I need you to stay and help Hylanya hold the wards protecting the city. Please, will you do that for me?"

GINN HALE

The rat didn't budge. Elezar suppressed the creeping urge to snap her up in an easy mouthful. He'd never credited how powerfully the drive to hunt and eat ran through animal flesh. It made his own most base urges seem quite restrained.

At last Queenie lifted a small paw as if offering a farewell gesture to Skellan and then she scuttled aside.

Elezar took a last breath of the fresh, warm air and then plunged himself and Skellan into the desolate gloom of the Old Road. Ahead in the gray expanse Javier and Kiram waited. Radiant white light blazed from Javier and cascaded over Kiram. But as Elezar closed the distance he noticed the red glow that surrounded him. And for the first time on the Old Road the mutilated form of his brother didn't rise before him.

Instead red-lit tangles of tendrils and roots coiled up overhead like a labyrinth of briars. But where Elezar might have expected thorns or blossoms clusters of long glossy teeth gaped and snapped. A faint blue vapor drifted from between sets of fangs.

"Oh no," Skellan muttered. "We'll not be taken in by lies and pity."

Skellan leaned forward on Elezar's shoulders and made a motion as if he were fanning the air. Red gold light shot ahead of them. All at once a breeze rose and dissipated the coiling masses of blue vapor.

"Thank you a thousand times over for that!" Kiram called back, though he didn't turn his gaze from Javier's shining form.

"Welcome," Skellan shouted in reply but then he fell silent.

He ran his hands along Elezar's back with a nervous energy that Elezar understood all too well. Even devoid of haunting figures, the dark realm reeked of fungus and dry rot. The catacomb of snarling briars stretched out endlessly in all directions. They walked on and on but nothing changed. Hours could have passed and Elezar wouldn't have known if they'd traveled miles or merely yards.

Then at last an arch of blue sky opened ahead of them. Elezar raced after Javier and Kiram to reach fresh air. The frigid wind pouring in caught in his lungs. As he bounded out from the Old Road, Elezar narrowed his eyes. All around him sunlight flared off hills of snow and icy spires. A chilling wind hissed and spit fragments of sleet against his advance. Kiram and Javier hunched on their horses and Elezar felt Skellan curl down against his back as winter enfolded them.

Only days before fields and orchards had spread, resplendent with the gold and green bounty of summer, but now a vast courtyard of polished ice, carved snow, and frost towered around them. Sprays of yellow grain, blossoming flowers, and entire trees gleamed as if encased in glass. To the north Elezar caught a glimpse of the broken remains of a waterwheel half submerged in the icy river. And with a glance over his shoulder he realized that the stormy camps under Onelsi and Ylva's rule spread between him and the walls of Milmuraille.

Before him walls and arches of wind-sculpted snow encircled what looked to Elezar like the peak of a glacier, except that he could just make out a lanky, pale figure seated amidst the crusts of snow and sheets of ice as if brooding upon a throne. She sat so still and appeared so colorless that Elezar almost thought her carved from the snow drifts surrounding her.

Then she opened her eyes to glower at their party. Her white lips parted exposing a wide red maw and ragged yellow teeth. Little more than a sigh rose from her but all at once sleek white forms burst from the surrounding snow. Nearly two dozen snow lions stalked towards them. Their padded paws hardly made a sound as they moved across the fields of snow but the pungent scent of their bodies seemed to hiss through Elezar's brain.

A booming roar escaped him. One of the lions yowled its displeasure. Kiram's gelding, Verano, stamped and snorted and then backed just a little closer to Elezar. Javier reined

Lunaluz nearer to Kiram, forming a defensive front. Plumes of white breath rose in rapid puffs from the horses. Skellan dug one hand into Elezar's coat and from the way his weight shifted Elezar guessed that Skellan had drawn his knife.

Then Elezar heard the soft crunch of ice-crusted snow cracking behind him. He wheeled around, snarling. The two snow lions hissed but backed from him in low crouches. The blood and muscle of his bear's body surged with the desire to pursue and kill them. But Skellan jerked at him and he quickly restrained himself. He needed to keep close to Kiram and Javier and protect their backs.

The snow lions gathered and circled them slowly. The hair all across Elezar's body rose. Agitation churned through him, heating his muscles but also dulling his thoughts to the need to protect his own and tear these threatening animals to pieces. Snarls rose from him as two of the big cats stole small steps closer.

"I'm not one to tell you your business, but now would be a fine time to throw that stone of passage, my master mechanist," Skellan called over the whistling wind.

"Throw it?" Kiram sounded disbelieving.

"It will ignite the path of our safe passage," Skellan replied. "Throw it and be ready to follow the light that will make our safe path to Grimma Naemir!"

Elezar didn't look to see Kiram's response. He couldn't drag his attention or anger from the two snow lions slinking closer. Everything about them infuriated him, from the sly way they crept between snow banks to their smug scents. Even the way the tips of their long tails flicked irritated him. Elezar's body shook with the desire to charge. His muscles blazed and his heart drove his pulse to a double tempo.

"Don't let them bait you," Skellan told him firmly but Elezar hardly heard the words over the pounding of his heart and the fury buzzing through his mind.

Then the snow beneath him lit with a brilliant blue light. Heat rolled up through the thick pads of Elezar's feet. The surprise of it undid some of his anger and let him think. This path shone and warmed him exactly like the one that had led him to the Sumar grimma's sanctum.

The nearest snow lion snarled, showing Elezar her long fangs and challenging him to charge her. Instinctively, his body flexed in response but his own memory as well as Skellan's terrified grip stilled him. The Sumar grimma's champions had attempted to lure him from safety the same way. His calf throbbed with the physical memory of how near that had come to killing him.

"I know you do not want to but we must turn our backs to these snow lions, my man," Skellan urged. "We must follow Kiram and Javier to the foot of Grimma Naemir's dais before the light of safe passage fades. We have to go, Elezar!" The words hardly penetrated but Skellan's urgent tone galvanized him.

He whirled around to see a curving avenue of shining blue light illuminating Kiram and Javier as they led their horses over the ice towards the jagged dais where Grimma Naemir now stood. As Kiram advanced the trail of blue light behind him dimmed and faded. If Elezar remained standing his ground, in a matter of moments he and Skellan would be completely exposed.

At once, Elezar charged after Javier and Kiram. He leapt, throwing all of his anger and strength into motion. The raw force and speed of his body surprised him. He closed the distance of some thirty feet in two powerful bounds. Skellan swore but clung to him with his whole body as they soared and sprang over the ice. As much as Elezar's strength surprised him so did his new mass. He hit the ice a few feet behind Javier and Lunaluz but didn't stop. He slid across the slick ice like a battering ram plowing through silk curtains. Instinctively, he sank sharp black claws into the ice, ripping deep furrows as he skidded several feet. He stopped just short of Lunaluz's braided tail. Javier glanced back over his shoulder and offered Elezar a strained smile.

"Never underestimate the grace of a Grunito, that's what I've always said," Javier commented.

Elezar tossed his shaggy head as a rumble purred up from his chest in place of a retort. Behind him he heard the snow lions growling their annoyance and he smelled them closing in to follow.

"So long as we remain on the path they can do us no harm." Skellan leaned forward so that his head pressed close to Elezar's ear. "It's only Grimma Naemir we have to worry about. At least until the other two notice that we've invaded their camp, that is."

Elezar nodded and turned his attention to the dais before him.

When he'd entered the Sumar grimma's sanctum he'd not only found it at odds with the season but that the grimma had seemed subtly inhuman. With Grimma Naemir there was no subtlety about either. The closer they drew to Naemir the colder their surroundings grew. Kiram shuddered from the chill and Javier rubbed his gloved hands together to raise some warmth. Even Skellan, who he'd seen walk through icy mud barefoot, shivered. Wrapped in the blazing thick flesh of this massive bear, Elezar only truly felt the driving cold when he drew a breath. Then he tasted winter ice deep in his throat. His exhalations billowed up like smoke.

Snowflakes as large and ornate as medallions swirled on the frigid winds and the wan sunlight glinted off their edges as if gleaming across knife blades. Grimma Naemir stood at the very heart of all the cold.

At a glance she might have passed for a naked, wild-haired crone. But after only an instant of studying her Elezar noticed that the cascade of glassy stones, falling from her throat to her groin, were not mere jewelry but icy scales erupting from her frost white skin. Her hands and feet, like her broad mouth, seemed proportioned for a much larger creature. Her eyes looked like black pits dug out from the cracked and deeply eroded surface of her gnarled face.

She pulled thin white lips back from bloody red gums to expose a grin that reached nearly to her tattered ears.

"So you return to me after all, Kiram Kir-Zaki." She didn't raise her voice to be heard over the wind. Instead the wind lifted and hurled her words down upon them. "And not only do you bring me your deathly little prince but the son born of my other self."

Kiram and Skellan both straightened at Grimma Naemir's words. Javier slouched in his saddle like a surly youth at roll call.

Then Grimma Naemir's gaze fell upon Elezar. She blinked and cocked her head like an owl appraising a shrew. She extended her hand, crooking a bony finger and its cracked, yellowed nail.

"Come, bear. Bring our child nearer. Let me feel the fire of his soul burning up through that shell of mortal flesh."

Her words resonated through Elezar but he refused to obey her command. His claws flexed into the ice as if resisting a physical pull.

"It's all right, my man. Take me to her." Skellan's voice sounded assured but his hands shook against Elezar's shoulders. "This is why we have come."

Elezar snorted his displeasure but padded forward, carrying Skellan to the foot of Grimma Naemir's icy dais. To his surprise the grimma dropped down onto all fours and slunk—like one of her snow lions—down to the second lowest step. She straightened in a motion as fluid as a snake rising to strike. Elezar tensed, his black claws cracking the ice beneath him.

But Grimma Naemir's expression had gone soft and the faintest warmth seemed to color her cheeks. She held up her hands as if warming them before a fire.

"Child of mine." Though Naemir spoke, Elezar could have sworn it was the Sumar grimma's voice he heard. "My beautiful abomination. Have you come home to me at last?"

Skellan's entire body seemed taut, his hands and legs clenching against Elezar.

"I have come to free all the old spirits now held captive and to make you whole again, mother of mine."

For just an instant Naemir gazed at Skellan with an expression of such pride that she seemed nearly human. Then a cruel laugh rattled up from her bony chest.

"You've killed a demon and you think yourself a god to decide the fate of the grimma? You filthy mongrel!" Her voice had changed again, gone soft and velvety as if a much younger, more arrogant woman spoke through her. Ylva perhaps. "We were the true gods. We devoured armies of demons while your father's ancestors cringed in their own shit. We are not so easily undone as mayflies, boy! We will make a ruin of you and all your mortal realm. We will reclaim our rightful places as gods and you mortals will again learn to cower in terror. You, mongrel, you would be wise to tremble before me!"

"Were I the son of a lesser mother I would tremble," Skellan shouted back. Elezar felt the tremors that shivered through Skellan but he gave none of his fear away as he extended his hand over Elezar's shoulder and displayed the Sumar grimma's ring. "You may posture and threaten me as you wish. But the truth is that I am a blade forged by your own hand. I am the vei you have crafted for yourselves and I have come to claim you."

Elezar didn't know if it was his own building agitation or simply the absolute resolve of Skellan's words. But a booming roar tore up from him and he slammed his massive paws down and cracked apart several feet of the dais step. Grimma Naemir's gaze flicked to the crumbled hunks of ice and then to Elezar's face. Hot breath poured over his bared teeth. And he barely stopped himself from slamming his massive paw across her skull.

"Don't," Skellan intoned, but it wasn't his command that stilled Elezar this time. It was the hopeful, almost delighted excitement lighting Grimma Naemir's expression.

"Such fury." Age and exhaustion now filled her wistful tone. And Elezar felt almost certain that she must be mad or possessed by the other grimma. "You really do mean to murder me—"

"Free you," Skellan cut in.

Naemir rolled her eyes.

"Name it as nicely as you like, dear child. I don't care. But can you truly do it? Can you?"

"I can."

Naemir studied him. "You cannot know how many before you have tried and failed. Arrogant men who thought they could slay dragons with slivers of steel. Ambitious women who connived to seize the power of witch queens with poisoned knives. There have been so many before you who claimed they could kill us. We—I—have hoped and waited and faced every one of them, only to endure pain and rage without end—"

"Not without end," Skellan replied. "Not after today."

Again, that look of rapturous joy lit Grimma Naemir's weathered features. Then she drew in a long breath and seemed to calm herself. She retreated up two steps.

"You don't come before me without cause. If you could do this thing without my aid it would have been done already." Grimma Naemir made a motion of her hand and the wind whipped up, to spatter them with sleet. "Tell me what do you need of me, little murderer?"

"Only this place to stand and draw my ward ring," Skellan called into the wind and his voice broke through it. Naemir's hands went still.

"You mean to make a challenge against a grimma?"

"I mean to best a grimma and claim her sanctum," Skellan said. "I mean to break the thrall of that sanctum and all others after it. I meant what I said, Naemir. I have come to free every wild spirit and every ancient creature."

Grimma Naemir contemplated him and the wind calmed.

"Then I offer you and yours sanctuary within my camp. Issue your challenge from this place. If you win, you will prove yourself truly our—my—precious child. If you fail..." She shrugged and spared Kiram and Javier a glance. "My champions will dine well, I think."

Skellan drew his circle with care. Crouching, one hand outstretched to trace the icy ground, he turned, calling up the power of old stones and transforming their raw material into shining scarlet wards. One after another they rose up through the ice and snow like burning blossoms. Skellan closed the circle, pressing all his will to survive and save his home into every ward.

Just beyond him Elezar paced, restless as the anxious animal he appeared to be. From time to time he stood his full ten feet and studied the lines of distant storm-wracked tents belonging to the other grimma. Such wariness showed on his face that Skellan thought he could almost peer through the thick white hide and see Elezar's serious countenance.

Two of Naemir's snow lions watched Elezar but kept their distance. The others settled down to maul the carcass of an ox. One aged lion sprawled atop a snowy rise, snoring.

At the very foot of Naemir's dais Kiram and Javier calmed their horses but kept them saddled and ready to take flight. Skellan didn't blame them for their lack of confidence in him. He could hardly credit his plan himself. But it was the only way he could think of to bring a swift end to this war.

It hadn't put anyone at ease when Naemir crawled down near Kiram. Skellan watched the plumes of her deep blue witchflame unfurl around her like huge, tattered wings. He missed the words she exchanged quietly with Javier and Kiram. But then she wrenched her head violently back, snapping her own neck. Her body spasmed, then swayed as if about to slump into Kiram's arms. Suddenly her spine jerked straight, whipping her head upright. Blood dribbled from one of her nostrils but she seemed hardly aware of it.

"You see," she muttered to Kiram. "It's no use."

"Well..." Kiram seemed at a loss.

"Don't let it ever be said that you didn't try your hardest," Javier put in.

"No," Naemir replied. "I have tried. Not just breaking bones but with blades and by fire as well... Have you ever smelled the fat of your own flesh searing away?"

Skellan paused, reflecting on Naemir's pitiable state. He realized that he hadn't truly understood the harm done by quartering a single spirit and then trapping those torn remnants in flesh until now. By comparison, the Sumar grimma seemed to have adapted to her transformation, though she raged against the freedom she'd lost. But Naemir could not break herself away from the other aspects of what had once been her whole spirit. She had gone mad and Skellan felt a deep pang at that realization. She suffered as much as any cloud imp or troll. She was as trapped in a body she despised and rejected as was any man or woman imprisoned within the flesh of an elk or wolf.

Skellan pulled in a breath of the frigid air and turned his concentration back to the last of his wards. He laid his hand down on the ice and called. The stones beneath answered and rose, melting through ice and frost to shine as luminous scarlet wards.

He had to win this challenge. Not just for himself and his people but for the grimma as well.

Onelsi arrived first, swinging her legs from the shoulder of a battered, sulfur-colored troll. Elk and boars frolicked beneath her, though the nearer the party drew the more forced and maniacal the animals appeared. They leapt and bounded, with tongues lolling from their mouths and terrified wide eyes. Threads of Onelsi's lemon yellow witchflame jerked them like marionette strings. Up on the shoulder of her troll Onelsi grinned, tiny and childlike, and she tossed a bevy of spring flowers onto the wind. The petals slapped across Skellan's cheeks.

He brushed them away and his wards seared them to perfumed smoke.

Onelsi giggled and then threw herself from her perch. Her witchflame burst up into pale yellow wings, catching her and holding her in the air as she swirled and spun, dancing her way to Skellan.

Elezar bounded forward and bucked up onto his hind legs. He flexed his massive paws as if preparing to swat the grimma from the sky. Both Javier and Kiram raced to stand at Skellan's back.

To Skellan's surprise Grimma Onelsi stilled, hanging in the air. She grinned indulgently at Elezar but then cocked her head to peer past him to Skellan.

"So, here's the creature we birthed. How ugly you are!" She sounded like a child taking glee in her own revulsion "You're like a stillborn calf!"

Elezar growled but Skellan just laughed.

Onelsi was hardly a beauty herself, at least by any human standard. Her large head and spindly body lent her the look of a child but up close Skellan could see cracks in her skull, arms, and legs where bits of a horn punched through her human guise. Her large eyes appeared to drift further and further apart the longer Skellan looked at her. What he'd taken for flowers cascading down her naked chest and thighs he now realized were tattered membranes of glistening pink and yellow flesh.

As much as Naemir's mind seemed broken, Onelsi's body appeared incapable of settling into a single, comfortable form.

Onelsi swirled up several feet in the air, surveying the circle of Skellan's wards.

"But those are well made and handsome as little suns! I've not seen their like before but they are so very beautiful. They're so pretty!" She drifted, her dirty bare feet rising up until she hung upside down but still stared at Skellan's wards. Her eyes fixed upon the names of the wind and the promises of freedom that Skellan had forged into his wards. "Once I was even more lovely than those wards... I was light as breath and brilliant as a sunrise..." She sounded slightly unnerved as if the memory had just returned to her. The horns protruding from her skull stretched like a chick struggling to break free of an eggshell. Skellan heard bone cracking. Onelsi curled her hands over the side of her head, clenched her wide, wandering eyes closed, and drifted back upright.

"We mustn't remember or we'll be no better than Naemir." Then her voice dropped. "But we are Naemir… We all are— No! That was long ago. That is done. We do not remember it at all."

She opened her eyes and this time her gaze darted away from Skellan's wards. Though, one of her eyes seemed to drift through the flesh of her face like the moon moving through clouds. It focused again upon Skellan's wards.

Skellan wondered if it would be possible to win her over without resorting to a battle. If he could remind her of the joy she lost perhaps she would be willing to trust him.

He concentrated on that delighted free sensation that he'd so briefly shared with the Sumar grimma. He held the feeling and focused the blaze of his witchflame into capturing its essence. A swirling scarlet bead coalesced just above his ruby ring. It flashed as if winking at him. Skellan blew on it and it drifted, light as a feather, to Grimma Onelsi. She jerked back but when the bead simply continued to flash and float she reached out and snatched it to her. All at once her cheeks flushed and a smile spread across her face. She cradled the charm until it died like an ember in her cupped hands.

"What's the point of fighting a war to seize more land and enslave more peoples when all you truly want is to be freed?" Skellan asked her.

"We can't be freed," Onelsi snapped. Her expression turned petulant. "We are forever and nothing can cut us out of these cages of bone and meat!"

"I can," Skellan replied. "I can free you if you let me."

Onelsi's entire head seemed to shudder but then she spun in the air turning her back on him.

"You are made of mortal flesh and fashioned to lie."

"I'm not lying!" Skellan called. He'd seemed so close to solving the entire matter. "If you allow me access to your sanctum—"

"You would enslave us even further. Turn us to stone and plunder our wild forests—"

"No. I swear. I can free you!"

"Then free us. But I'll not be made the fool of mortal enchantments again." She refused to look at him and with a flash of her bright wings she flew back to the shoulder of her troll. The elk and boar beneath her suddenly stilled and dropped to the snow, blanketing the ground like abandoned toys. Only the faint plumes of their white breath reassured Skellan that the enthralled creatures still lived.

Skellan couldn't look at them without feeling furious and frustrated with his own helplessness to release them.

He had to challenge one of the grimma and finish this. If it killed him, then that was a price he would pay. He forced himself not to look to Elezar. He'd not betray Elezar's trust and loyalty with death. If he suffered a mortal wound, Skellan promised himself that he'd cut the bond between them. Oddly that thought calmed Skellan's nerves. It reminded him that he'd already made his peace with the idea of dying in a duel against a grimma.

It wasn't a matter of whether he could make himself issue the challenge, just a matter of whom he'd issue it against.

He scowled at Onelsi's back and the yellow horns studding the line of her naked spine. He wished that he could drive all shreds of sympathy for her from his heart. He needed to be able to fight with fatal intent.

But she looked so small, as broken in body as Naemir was in mind.

Then the earth trembled with the thunder a huge troll racing over the ground and the howls of mordwolves filled the cold air. Skellan's attention shifted immediately. Naemir's snow lions rose to their feet and encircled her dais while Javier and Kiram led their horses to Skellan's left, opposite of where Elezar already stood, baring his teeth.

A rich autumn wind tossed aside the winter chill as Ylva appeared over a snowy hill. She stood on the shoulder of a ruddy troll, holding a chain in her hand as if it were the leash of a dog's collar. Unlike the other grimma she held her witch-flame close, almost corseting her body with its burnished gold tones. From her thick blond hair, smooth features, and long legs she looked very much like a beautiful woman of perhaps forty. Resplendent gold charms armored her breasts and a belt of gold beads draped down her thighs. She wore a knife at her hip and the hilt looked as if it had been carved from human bone.

Her mordwolves ran at the troll's heels like a hunting pack and the sunset colors of her witchflame turned their gray coats gold and red. They drew to a halt only yards from where Skellan stood inside his ring of wards. Onelsi spared Ylva a glance but then returned to sulking with her head nestled against her troll's bright yellow earlobe.

From behind Skellan, Naemir called out, "Come no further, Grimma Ylva. You are already too much in my mind this day!"

Ylva shook her head but made no motion to advance.

"I'm not here for you, you mad old hag!" Ylva shouted back.

"We shouldn't fight!" Onelsi turned back and frowned at Ylva, who offered her an indulgent smile.

"It's not fighting if I simply state what we all know to be more true than the North Star."

"My head hurts," Onelsi groaned. "He made my head hurt."

"Never you fret, my little Onelsi." Ylva's gaze slid to Skellan and he felt the force of her attention like a molten brand held next to his skin. The Sumar grimma, too, had struck him with the power of her intent but she had restrained herself. Ylva's anger smoldered over him.

"I am Hilthorn Radulf, son—" Skellan began his formal challenge only to have Ylva cut him off.

"We know what birthed you, whelp! And we have come to put our abomination in its grave."

Skellan decided that he held no hesitance in crushing this one grimma at all.

"I challenge you!" Skellan shouted. "Victor takes all that the other possesses!"

"As is only right, and I do take up your challenge," Ylva agreed.

She turned and the symbols carved into her troll's shoulder lit up around her, forming her circle of wards. Then an arc of her fiery orange witchflame shot from her outstretched hand. Skellan hurled his own witchflame to meet and bind hers. The contact shocked through Skellan and though she hid it well he saw Ylva rock on her heels as she felt the impact of his will. They were locked in their challenge now and only conquest would release one of them to do what he or she wished with the other.

Skellan rolled his shoulders and flexed his bare feet against the icy soil beneath him. A kind of assurance seemed to fill him despite the terrible risk of this duel. This was his vei, he felt sure of that. This was the moment all his life had led to and he would be victorious. His confidence flared through his witchflame and Ylva scowled.

"But mine is the right to name the terms," Ylva called suddenly.

Skellan didn't feel as if he could have heard her correctly. Terms? What terms could there be between witches... other than—

"I choose duel by champions," Ylva announced and the arc of her witchflame split like fingers of lightning to illuminate the bodies of six of her mordwolves. "Call your champion to meet mine, mongrel!"

Skellan's heart lurched in his chest and he felt the blood draining from his face.

No. This wasn't how it was meant to happen. He couldn't accept.

Standing on his hind legs, Elezar towered over even Ylva's mordwolves, but they outnumbered him six to one. They would tear him apart. Like an old injury breaking open, the terrible image he'd seen in his dream threatened to become reality.

His Elezar bloodied and encircled by six wolves.

No. He couldn't let that happen.

But if Skellan refused, then everything—Elezar, Milmuraille, all Radulf County—forfeited to Ylva.

Skellan's hands shook. He couldn't make himself accept or refuse.

Then Elezar stepped forward. His eyes met Skellan's and his voice filled Skellan's mind.

If this is what it must be then let it be. I am your champion and I won't go down without a fight!

Out of the corner of his eye Skellan glimpsed the horror on Javier and Kiram's faces. Javier flicked his fingers nervously as if attempting to catch open the Old Road for them to escape through. But wards were drawn and the challenge issued already. A witch's word would bind him even on the Old Road. Ylva would claim them even there and kill them like cowards in the darkness.

Skellan refused to die like that.

"Duel by champions, then," he replied. His witchflame jolted and spit as if it hated this as much as Skellan did. Then it split to throw a shining halo over Elezar. Skellan felt sick but Elezar bounded forward, the blaze of Skellan's witchflame turning his white coat a bloody scarlet.

A strange unity of mind and muscle gripped Elezar the instant Skellan agreed to the duel. The man he was understood dueling with a certainty that matched perfectly to the impulses of the bear he'd become. A raw, savage drive flooded him like fire surging through his veins. He embraced both the power and rage. He tore across the cold ground, throwing back masses of snow in his wake.

The six mordwolves stood in a semicircle a few paces ahead of Ylva's troll. Just from the scent of them Elezar knew that the two largest beasts at the center were a breeding pair, likely the leaders of this pack. The other four moved ahead just a little, beginning a flanking maneuver as Elezar charged their center of their line. The largest male mordwolf snarled at Elezar while his mate bared her teeth.

Elezar understood by instinct as much as intellect that he couldn't allow the wolves to close ranks around him and attack him as a pack. He had to destroy the advantage of their numbers before the large male and his mate got their teeth into him or he'd die like a gutted doe.

Ripping into the ice-slick ground he suddenly pivoted left and hurled himself onto the smaller female mordwolf slinking up alongside him. She gave a startled whimper before Elezar caught her neck in his jaws and tore through her spine. Her fur and blood filled his mouth with the wet heat of raw meat. Murderous joy filled his body, though a corner of his mind flinched.

Her closest companion raced for Elezar, howling like a man gone half-mad. Elezar met his charge with a brutal rake of his long black claws, gashing his skull open from the left eye and flaying his nostrils. Elezar crushed through the wounded mordwolf's throat with his second blow.

Then the remaining four mordwolves fell upon him.

The big male narrowly missed Elezar's face as he lunged in at him. His mate took advantage of Elezar's distraction to clamp her jaws into his left arm. Her teeth sank deep into skin and muscle as she jerked violently against Elezar's attempt to pull his arm free. The two smaller mordwolves raced to circle behind him. Sharp teeth nipped at the back of his leg. Elezar roared in pain and fury and swung round, dragging the big female mordwolf off her feet. Her mate and the two smaller wolves darted back from him while the female continued to grind into his left arm.

Agony flared through him as she cracked into bone and tendon. Elezar jerked against her, only sinking her teeth deeper.

Elezar realized that his resistance only served to aid her in shredding his flesh from the bone. Fighting the urgent instinct flooding him, he forced himself to plunge his left arm into her gaping mouth and down. He hammered the full weight of his body against the tendons of her lower jaw. Cartilage and bone snapped beneath his assault. He wrenched his ragged arm free as the mordwolf shrieked and her jaw tore. Her blood and Elezar's steamed as it poured across the snow.

The large female attempted to retreat from Elezar's reach as her mate charged. Elezar caught her with his right arm and jerked her into his jaws. She clawed at his gut, kicking hard, but she couldn't keep him from tearing out her throat. He dropped her still-shaking body as her mate plowed into him. His weight knocked Elezar off balance and when the other two smaller mordwolves leapt onto him he fell back and slammed hard into the icy ground. The big male crouched on Elezar's chest, crushing the air from his lungs. Elezar lashed out at him with his right arm but the male still sank his teeth into Elezar's shoulder. The other two mordwolves attempted to pin and mangle his right arm as the male on his chest tore a mouthful of muscle from Elezar's left shoulder.

Horror and agony wrenched through Elezar.

He slammed his skull into the large male's. His vision broke into flashes but he felt the male sway and his jaws released. Elezar could hardly think but a decade of drilling kept him fighting. He managed to jam his right leg under the stunned mordwolf and kicked the wolf into the smaller mordwolves. They slammed into each other and slid on the ice.

Elezar lurched to his right and shoved himself back up to his feet. He slipped in the slick pools of blood surrounding him and nearly fell. Only yards from him the mordwolves regained their footings.

He knew he should charge them now, before they could organize themselves. But his muscles felt like lead weights and as hard as he gasped he couldn't seem to get enough air. Flesh and muscle hung in strips from his left arm and he couldn't stop his body from shaking with pain.

Then he caught sight of Skellan, pale and bleeding as well. Beside him Javier and Kiram looked on in helpless horror. All their lives depended upon him now. He couldn't stop.

With a bellow he charged the mordwolves.

Skellan could hardly stand the pain, and he knew that what he felt was only a fraction of what Elezar endured. He only half-heard the words whispered between Kiram and Javier.

"Can you... I don't know, reach in there and help him?" Kiram asked.

"Too many wards." Javier sounded furious and frustrated.

Skellan shared his anger, though he turned it upon himself. Why hadn't he realized that this could happen? Why hadn't he planned for it? His clever plot for unweaving the spells binding the grimma was meaningless when all he could do was to absorb a little of Elezar's agony while his man battled for his life. Skellan pushed more of his strength into Elezar but that only served to prolong the brutal combat.

Warm droplets of blood dribbled down Skellan's own left arm and spattered on his bare foot.

Perched in a circle of wards carved into the shoulder of her troll, Ylva stood over them all and smiled as if she already claimed victory. Three of her champions lay mutilated and still she could smile. Skellan hated her for that. He wanted nothing more than to leap up and hurl her down into the blood soaked snow. But he couldn't. Until the challenge ended both he and she were physically confined to the circle of their wards.

Skellan's only bridge beyond the circle was his bond to Elezar, just as the thrall Ylva cast over her champions linked them to her. If only he could reach her directly, then he'd tear that smile from her face.

Then he realized that there might be a way if he was willing to place his soul beyond the protection of his wards. It would leave his abandoned body defenseless. But he couldn't allow Elezar to suffer like this any longer.

He knew what he needed to do: reach out through Elezar to breach Ylva's champions and attack her through the links of the thrall she cast over them. His heart raced in his chest. Shifting all of his strength to hurl his witchflame so far would dim the ring of wards encircling him, alerting Ylva to his plan and leaving his body exposed. If Ylva noticed, doubtless she'd strike him dead.

He needed a means to maintain the brilliant illusion of a blazing ring of wards.

Skellan stole a glance to Javier, but it was Kiram who noticed and elbowed Javier to look Skellan's way.

Moving as quickly as he dared, Skellan slid his foot through droplets of his own congealing blood and pushed a bloody streak out to breach the edge of his wards. Javier frowned briefly and Skellan didn't blame him. But then to his relief Javier suddenly glanced to where Elezar lashed out against one of the mordwolves while the other two circled him, snapping and biting his legs and back.

Javier very casually shifted his weight to set his foot in the wash of Skellan's blood. He dropped his hands to his sides and tiny flares of white light flicked from his fingers and fell like snow.

Skellan at once felt Javier's cold power rush through his wards. And then he felt something else, smaller and yet still intense and potent. He glanced down to see Queenie crouching at the edge of his wards with her tiny pink paws pressed into his blood. She must have followed them all the way across the Old Road. The power she funneled to Skellan was slight and yet it heartened him immensely.

He didn't close his eyes, but his lids drooped. As his witchflame rose from his body his vision followed. As he forced his soul past the ring of his wards, he lost all feeling of his body. His awareness coursed across the chill air following his bond to Elezar. For a moment he shared Elezar's struggle, fighting free of the jaws of a huge, rank-smelling mordwolf. The big creature's teeth punched through the thick bear hide at Elezar's hip while the other three wolves dug into his right leg. Curled so close around Elezar, Skellan felt as though the pain might tear him apart.

At the same time he sensed Elezar's determination to endure. Elezar pounded his claws into the big mordwolf's side, wrenching away flesh and exposing bloody ribs. The mordwolf jerked violently at Elezar's hip, trying to topple him.

Elezar needed a better weapon than mere animal claws.

Skellan reached around him and with a flare of searing energy he jerked Elezar free of the bear's body, just as he'd freed himself so many times from his own dogskin cloak.

Elezar slid nearly a foot across the ice while the bear hide collapsed and all three of the mordwolves tumbled into the bloody cloak.

Elezar's clothes hung in damp rags and he still bled from a dozen wounds but not so badly as he had before. The pounding of his pulse hammered through Skellan and he felt as though they were both drenched in sweat. High above them Ylva snarled and swore.

The mordwolves ripped through the cloak and briefly snapped and snarled at each other in their confusion. With a roar, Elezar drew his sword and launched himself upon them. Skellan rode like a falcon crouched on his shoulder. As Elezar brought his black sword down to sever the head of the largest mordwolf, Skellan leapt from him to one of the smaller wolves.

For a sick, disoriented moment his senses went dark and dull. Then he saw the bright orange threads jutting up from the shadowy form of the mordwolf. Skellan caught one thread. It seared into him but he didn't release his grip. He scrambled up the cord as if climbing a burning rope. As he ascended the golden orange blaze around him grew and in response he condensed his witchflame down into a speck—an insignificant mote so small that it slipped between Ylva's vast wards like a flea climbing through a keyhole.

And suddenly his witchflame was inside the ring of her wards.

Ylva spun around. Her hands spread, raking the air to catch him. He slipped between her fingers and swirled around her like a fleck of dust. Up so close, she shone radiant as a star. Brilliant binding spells swathed her in halos of light and burned at Skellan as he circled, searching for a way past them to the core of her. He would find the oldest spells there. Among them would be those that bound her to her sanctum.

He needed to reach those spells and break them.

Golden flames coursed over him and threw his senses reeling. Still he circled Ylva. Spinning, she hunted him in turn. She hadn't yet guessed that he'd abandoned the security of his wards and left his body. But she would soon.

She snorted in annoyance and Skellan realized how he could penetrate the flesh binding her and reach through all of her spells to the very core of her. He waited until she inhaled and then gave himself up to the breath she drew in.

He whipped past the ivory gates of her teeth and fell into a strange world within the grimma. Beneath the shell of her flesh, he found no sign of the blood, muscle, and breath of a mortal creature. Instead he seemed transported into a realm as strange as the Old Road.

A vast sunset sky stretched over him and a black sea of thorny branches rose up from beneath him. Winds seemed to thrash and toss the branches. Only, Skellan suddenly realized, they weren't mere tree branches. Every twig and thorn was a binding spell. Millions of them wound around each other to grasp the air. The wind wasn't blowing through them. They jerked and shook the sky the way a cat might sink it's claws into a silk veil.

Skellan stared at the imense horizon of black binding spells. He'd known that the enchantments binding something so vast as the heavens would have to be large but he'd never imagined anything on this scale. This was an entire world folded up inside the grimma.

How could he hope to destroy so many spells?

Then Skellan noticed the small, shining white sphere floating directly above him. He could have taken it for a full moon. But then he felt a tremor ring through it and saw the black spells below all pulse with the same resonant tone. The force shook through Skellan with a deeply familiar rhythm. A heartbeat.

Skellan shuddered. Winds buffeted him as he ascended to draw nearer the immense white heart.

The nearer he came the more he realized that the entire thing was a mesh of ancient spells—hardly words at all, but cries of fury and howls of rage bound up in molten silver and consecrated in blood. This was the work and will of a hundred witches. It reverberated and rang out flashing thousands of silver white threads, each knotted and wound around another. And it drove all the millions of spells below.

Ylva's very heart was the trap binding her to her sanctum and mortal flesh. It whirled like a weathervane caught in a relentless wind.

As it spun, it revealing a second, third, and fourth face like a moon turning through phases. Each side shone white but at the center of every face different symbols shuddered and pulsed. Skellan read the names of the four directions.

He stared as the burning white symbols whipped past him, hammering out the four pulses of a steady heartbeat. One heart, divided into four chambers, he thought.

One divided into four.

With a rush of excitement he realized that this spell had to exist in each of the grimma, linking and dividing all of them, making four aspects out of a single spirit. Where the threads of this spell braided together the grimma still bled into each other, still shared a resonance. This was why they could never truly be torn asunder and how even across leagues and ages they still felt each other.

It had to be the sanctums that fed the tireless pulse and rotation of this immense spell.

Skellan rose like a moth fluttering to a full moon. He reached out, not to the shining spells, but into those infinitely small spaces between them. He touched emptiness and opened it. Tiny hollows gasped wide. Miniscule darknesses pockmarked the shining facets of the immense spell. Skellan concentrated with all his will on the silence between pulses. He fed his strength into a thousand hollow motes, expanding their reach and cracking the edges of the blazing spells. He felt his own being shaking and shivering in the cold dark but it still wasn't enough.

He called the last of his witchflame out of his own body, forgoing his own heartbeat and breath for the sake of awakening this consuming dark hollow. Everything he possessed, he hurled into nothing.

Then at last the entire shining white sphere shattered apart like a burst dam. The black spells beneath Skellan shredded to mist. Skellan thought he felt Ylva shudder. Then everything around him suddenly exploded apart into a flurry of wild, shrieking wind, rain, and golden light. Skellan felt himself thrown high, his senses lurching sickeningly.

An instant later Onelsi shot apart, hurling out raindrops as she formed a shining yellow cyclone, and swirled up into the tumbling clouds. She spun around Skellan, flowing into the storm wind that had been freed from Ylva. Another explosion ripped through the air, sending sleet and hail up like a geyser. Then a fourth tore through the air, filling the sky with summer radiance and the scent of blossoms. Skellan twisted, tumbled, wrenched ever higher in the midst of their wild exultations.

He tried to reach for the earth far below where he knew his body lay sprawled across the melting snow. He glimpsed Elezar staggering from amongst the dead bodies of the mord-wolves, dripping with blood. He fell to his knees just outside the circle of Skellan's wards, where Skellan's body lay. Javier swore and tore at the wards surrounding him while Queenie squealed in distress.

I'm here. It's all right. Skellan strained to make the words sound. But not even Elezar heard him.

Skellan felt suddenly very afraid.

Then white clouds and a warm comforting wind closed in around him, lifting him still higher. He thought he heard laughter and felt gentle hands stroke his brow. The clouds broke apart before him and he continued to ascend until he found himself cradled in the curve of blue darkness at the very edge of a vast field of shimmering stars. Planets glinted like polished stones and moons danced around them. Distant suns plumed golden arches into the deep darkness and lit swirling clouds in vibrant colors.

The beauty of it stilled him and filled him with wonder. Yet all the grandeur and mystery laid out before him shone deathly cold and lifeless.

***

Elezar carried Skellan's body. Around them the hills of ice crumbled. Dazed Mirogoth men and women struggled out from the hides of snow lions, wolves, elk, and boars. Trolls stood, as if stunned, and then several turned and charged north towards the river as if fleeing for their lives. Tree branches and great slides of mud and rock fell from them as they ran. The ground trembled.

Elezar kept walking. He found the road in a daze.

Javier shouted something at him but Elezar didn't hear it. His ears rang and his muscles felt numb. Rivulets of blood marked his trail as he stumbled onward. Far ahead he glimpsed the walls of Milmuraille. Riots of wild animals and fleeing trolls filled the miles in between. But Elezar kept walking towards the city gates. Pain shot through him with each step and his left arm was too mangled for him to bear to look at. Yet he kept moving, holding Skellan's cold body to his chest.

Get him back to Milmuraille, to the stones that he loved and the land that would protect him. That was all Elezar could think—just to carry Skellan home. The chaos and confusion of hundreds of abandoned Mirogoth troops hardly registered. In the back of his mind he dimly absorbed that Kiram raced ahead of him to summon help while Javier rode behind him. Queenie skittered between his clumsy steps, screeching and squeaking as if warning him of pebbles scattered across the road.

Under other circumstances Elezar would have found himself absurd. Had he been a man watching himself he would have wondered what madness had seized that bleeding, mutilated wretch, driving him to stagger towards a distant city with a dead body cradled in his arms. But he couldn't seem to make himself stop any more than he could keep from whispering Skellan's name and begging him to breathe.

An escort of armed riders met them but Elezar couldn't bring himself to give up Skellan's corpse and so they let him ride in a requisitioned hay cart and hold Skellan. At last Javier rode up beside where Elezar leaned, stroking Skellan's cold cheek.

"He can't be dead," Elezar whispered.

"He's lost but not gone into the next world, not yet," Javier replied. Elezar barely made out his words over the roar in his ears. "But you're the one I'm worried about, Grunito. By the three hells you've lost enough blood to fill a moat and your hand…" Javier looked sickened. "You must let someone tend your wounds."

"As soon as Skellan wakes…" Elezar replied.

Javier shook his head.

"I'm sorry," he said. Then he reached out and fiery white sparks skipped from his fingers to Elezar's brow. Elezar crumpled, still holding Skellan's body.

Skellan threw himself free of the gentle, supporting wind and plunged downward. Gusts raced after him, buffeting his descent and defending him from the surges of lightning and the hungry creatures that flew through the banks of clouds, hunting. Vast wings swept past him, chasing a wild charge of ball lightning. Skellan thought it might have been Wind-eater but he couldn't be certain.

He gazed down through drifts of clouds and miles of sky to the lands so far below him. Forests and mountains spread out like a beautiful stitched tapestry. Rivers appeared little more than ribbons pinned to a vast spill of green satin. A flight of geese passed beneath him, followed by hundreds and hundreds of wethra-steeds and their grinning riders. Skellan had never seen so many riding the sky before. Then he realized that these steeds and riders must have been released from the sanctums. And as he continued to fall he picked out the massive forms of trolls traveling north through dense forest. Hundreds of them threaded their ways back towards the ancient mountains that had been their homes in the age before they themselves had been relegated to realms of myth.

One figure struck Skellan as familiar. As Skellan fell faster and faster the large troll turned and raised his hand. A terrible pang shot through Skellan as he recognized Bone-crusher's rocky face. A deep rumble rolled up to Skellan and shook through him like a long, low note of farewell. Then Bone-crusher turned to lift and carry two much smaller trolls across a river.

He deserved to return home after so long in exile and Skellan knew he had no right to try and lay claim upon Bone-crusher. But seeing his retreating form, Skellan couldn't keep from feeling a deep loss. He couldn't remember a time in his life when he hadn't had Bone-crusher.

For the first time he noticed dozens of Cadleonian ships sailing from the Milmuraille's bay. How many of is friends populated those boats? He didn't want to think Elezar numbered among them but fear of having to face that abandonment, shook him.

At once the wind enfolded him and stilled his fall.

My child, do you truly wish to rejoin that realm of flesh and sorrow? The shining heavens are still open to you.

So much compassion reverberated through the question that Skellan briefly hesitated. But then he shook his head. Whether heartbreak or joy awaited him, the world below was his home.

It's not in me to be satisfied drifting among the stars, no matter how perfect and beautiful they are. I'm a creature who's happy down in the dirty world.

A whisper of breeze caressed him with an almost sad sigh and then the wind released him to fall long and hard into the bruised, cold body he'd abandoned.

<hr />

Skellan woke, staring up at a ceiling he didn't recognize. Stylized scarlet wolves chased plump deer across a gilded woodland of bas-relief flowers and fruit trees. Sunlight glinted across the gold work and Skellan felt a warm ray shining across his cheek. An afternoon breeze drifted from an open window, carrying the scent of costly perfumes, but also stirred up the odors of sweat and dry blood. Skellan turned his head slightly and took in the red silk coverlets of the down bed where he lay. Scarlet and gold pinstripes flashed from the surrounding walls and a stunning array of carved pillars, inlaid tables, ornately framed paintings, and embroidered silk screens dazzled his torpid senses. His surroundings seemed too bright and strange to him.

Then he caught sight of the startled faces of the three richly dressed women at his bedside.

"Skellan!" Cire bolted up from her chair, looking both overjoyed and also on the verge of tears. She bounded across the few feet of marble floor to his bed.

Hylanya, who already sat at his bedside, seemed to brim with delight and even Peome appeared deeply relieved.

For a few moments he continued to search the airy room, but Elezar was nowhere to be seen. A vague anxiety gnawed at Skellan's gut. He wanted to ask for Elezar but as the words formed he suddenly felt too afraid of what he might be told. His heart hammered in his chest and he took a moment to calm himself. He decided on a question he felt prepared to hear the answer to.

"Where am I?" Skellan's voice came out in a dry rasp. His throat felt desiccated and his tongue slapped like a piece of dried apple against his chapped lips.

All three woman answered him but with different responses.

"Home," Hylanya assured him, and he belatedly realized that she had been holding his right hand in hers. The silken nightshirt that he'd been dressed in had made his own arm seem like a stranger's at first glance.

"You're in the master chambers of your Sun Palace," Peome clarified from behind Hylanya. She turned, taking up a pitcher and a glass from a heavily carved sideboard.

"Safe," Cire said. Queenie scampered down her arm to hop into the silken coverlets and survey Skellan from the vantage point of his knee. Then she skittered quickly back to Cire, settling down on her shoulder.

Peome brought the pitcher to Skellan and filled the ornate glass for him.

Skellan tried to sit upright. His muscles responded slowly and clumsily. Reaching for the glass he missed it once before having to use both hands to grip it and draw the cool surface to his mouth. He drank carefully, not quite trusting his throat to swallow though his thirst felt desperate. Peome refilled the glass and Skellan drained it again. Then he simply grasped for the entire pitcher. As he attempted to lift the pitcher his left hand failed him with a sharp shot of pain. Peome caught the pitcher and held it steady to his lips.

"Not too fast at first," Peome said quietly. "You've been lost to us for a fortnight."

As Skellan drank, Peome's words sank into his mind.

Fourteen days. His soul had been lost among the stars and clouds while his body lay lifeless as a discarded coat. He emptied the pitcher and wiped his mouth with his right hand.

"The grimma's troops?" he asked.

"Fled back north. A dozen or so joined the city guards here but most dispersed back into the forests," Cire informed him. "All of the trolls as well as the wethra-steeds and their riders abandoned the city also. It's been strange to go days without sighting a troll's head moving across the skyline."

Skellan nodded and was pleased to note that his head no longer felt like it might topple right off his neck.

"I saw them departing from the sky," Skellan said. "The trolls far below me and the wethra-steeds flying through the surrounding clouds." It had been a breathtaking sight and yet Skellan's heart ached just thinking of it.

"Bone-crusher mentioned glimpsing you among the stars," Hylanya said. "He said that you were with your mother at last."

Skellan frowned down at his silken coverlet, remembering the sight of his friend traveling north, back to his ancient homeland. His eyes pricked but he held the emotion in. He had no right to begrudge Bone-crusher his freedom or mourn his leaving. He ought to be happy for him—for all the enthralled creatures who now were free.

He felt ashamed at the sorrow that welled up within him and again his mind flitted to Elezar. He flinched from the contemplation. Bad enough that he had to face Bone-crusher's departure. He wasn't ready yet to think on Elezar's. In fourteen days a ship might have already carried him back to the shores of Cadeleon.

Skellan still felt too wrecked and groggy to face that, though he knew he would have to. But not just yet.

Slow aches wakened in his legs, and the more his senses cleared, the worse the pain in his left arm grew. He glanced down at his hand. The skin looked almost black with bruises and two of his nails were cracked down to the pink. A raw red scar ran from between his second and third fingers to his wrist. As he turned his hand he saw that the scar bisected his palm as well. No wonder he hadn't been able to grip the pitcher. Far more surprising was the fact that it had taken him this long to notice the injuries.

Gingerly he slid his arm out of the left sleeve of his loose nightshirt. Hylanya gasped as Skellan exposed the ugly expanse of black bruises and thick scabs running from his shoulder to his hand. Clearly she'd not been the one who'd washed him and dressed him in the nightshirt.

"You're healing quickly. Just as your father always did," Peome commented.

"Still, hardly the nicest bit of skin to flash," Cire teased him.

"Consider yourself lucky that I didn't decide to examine the bruises on my bare ass," Skellan replied.

Cire laughed and Hylanya grinned in scandalized delight, though Peome appeared unamused.

"The sheriff and your entire court are awaiting word of your recovery," Peome said. "Shall I let it be known that you've awakened?"

The woman was all business, wasn't she? But then someone had to be, Skellan thought, and odds weren't good that he'd rise to such an occasion.

"Let them know that I'm awake and well, but if you can put off any visits for a day or so. I'm not…"

"I'll make sure you're given the time you need," Peome said.

"Thank you, Lady Peome," Skellan responded, sensing that Elezar would have expected him to behave respectfully. To his surprise Peome's expression softened just slightly. She placed her hand lightly on the corner of his bed.

"You must take care of yourself, my lord. We have lost too many of our best folk already. We need you to stay with us."

Skellan recognized the edge of sorrow in her gaze and he felt an ass for indulging in such grand flights of self-pity. He wasn't the only one to suffer losses and his were far from the worst. This hadn't ever been his private war no matter how much it had felt like it at times. He glanced to Hylanya and then to Cire. None of them had been untouched—likely every citizen of Milmuraille had known terrible fear and sorrow this year.

"Thank you," Skellan said again and this time he meant it truly.

Peome's stern expression didn't shift but a little color came into her cheeks.

"Come, Hylanya." Peome started towards the grand gilded doors where ruby-eyed wolves howled at twin moons. "It will hearten the courtiers and guild masters to hear of your brother's recovery from you."

Cire stood too, though she looked a little torn about leaving.

"I was wondering, Peome," she called, "if perhaps you wouldn't mind if I informed the sheriff of Skellan's improvement. After all you and Hylanya will likely be quite occupied answering all the questions Guild Master Manie will want opinions upon. And the sheriff and I have gotten to know each other over the last few weeks—" Cire stopped suddenly and arched a brow at Skellan. He did his best to suppress the lewd grin curving his lips.

"He's a very, very kind man," Cire stated with uncharacteristic primness.

"Of that I have no doubt," Skellan replied and he meant it. "And quite a catch even with his white hair and beard."

"There's nothing of the sort between us." Cire's cheeks flushed nearly as red as her hair. "But I have grown fond of him."

"It would be much appreciated if you would speak to the sheriff, my dear. Thank you for the offer." Peome broke in, saving Cire from any further teasing. "Come along, Hylanya."

"But…" Hylanya's objection trailed off as she studied Skellan. He guessed that he looked half-dead because she gave in. "We'll talk after you've rested."

"Tomorrow," Skellan assured her.

"I hope you'll be willing to teach me more of how to create wards the way you do," Hylanya added as she stood and smoothed the lines of her resplendent scarlet dress.

"So long as you promise to show me how to handle those snail forks," Skellan agreed.

Hylanya nodded and then hastened to join Lady Peome and Cire as they departed. While the guards in the hall held the doors open for the three of them, Skellan caught a brief view of the clots of courtiers and ministers clustered just beyond the doors of his chamber. He recognized his treasurer and one of the barons among those gathered but didn't catch so much as a glimpse of Elezar.

The doors fell shut and Skellan flopped back into his absurd abundance of pillows. His arm hurt. And of course Elezar wasn't up and waiting at his door. Skellan's own injuries were mere echoes of the wounds Elezar bore. Likely—if his Cadeleonian friends hadn't sailed away home with him—he was still under the care of a sister-physician.

Another pang flared through Skellan's arm, this time causing his fingers to twitch and his skin to tingle. Though afterward he thought the bruises across the back of his hand had faded a little. Skellan frowned. If he'd been feeling better he would have reached out and found Elezar. But he hadn't been in his own flesh long enough to feel comfortable leaving again.

He needed to rest. He closed his eyes and took in a deep breath.

The scent of his own sweat rose over him. Elezar would have called a bath for him. He tried to relax in the large empty bed but found himself staring up at the golden ceiling. Briefly he counted all the wolves over his head. Twenty-eight. He closed his eyes.

He needed to piss.

He rolled clumsily out of the bed and stared beneath it but didn't see anything below or on the surrounding tables that he felt comfortable pissing in. Was everything in the place covered in gold and jewels? Then he noticed the curtains drifting in the afternoon breeze. He went to the open window and peered out from the third story into a pretty flower garden. The windows of chambers across from his own stood open but Skellan didn't see anyone at them and no one appeared to be in the garden beneath him.

Using only his right hand he hiked up his nightshirt and leaned up to the sill to send his own golden stream splashing across a bed of daisies and roses. Relief washed through him. After several protracted moments he grinned to himself, marveling at the volume he was passing. It had been a fortnight but still this was something of a wonder. He'd give a mule a run. He sighed, feeling more himself than he had in days—weeks.

Some commotion sounded beyond the doors of his chamber but Skellan didn't give it much mind. He was committed to his present endeavor and turning around at this point would only serve to ruin a costly floor tapestry.

The doors swung open just as Skellan gave himself a shake. He turned to see Elezar. Bandages hung in disarray from his bruised bare chest and left arm. A deep scrape ran from his cheekbone to the bridge of his nose and black stitches arched over his right eyebrow. He looked like he hadn't shaved in a week or washed in days and yet Skellan thought he was the most beautiful thing he'd ever seen in his life.

His wide smile and the open joy that lit his dark eyes set Skellan's heart pounding.

"I've never been so damn happy to see a man pissing out a window in my life." Elezar closed the distance between them in a breath and pulled Skellan to him. Skellan returned his embrace with fierce joy. It didn't matter how badly it hurt his arm, Skellan held Elezar to him.

Elezar murmured his name as if it were a prayer. A certainty that had eluded Skellan opened in him. Despite his restraint Elezar cared for him deeply and passionately. But he was a proud man and stronger than Skellan could have ever imagined any man to be. If he decided that he had to return to Cadeleon, Elezar possessed the self-control and determination to break his own heart—and Skellan's as well.

It didn't matter if Elezar would eventually leave him for Cadeleon. It didn't matter if losing him would one day destroy Skellan. No matter the cost, this embrace was worth it, Skellan realized.

"I'm here," Skellan replied.

Silently he promised that he would always be there for his man. No matter where Elezar wandered or what battles he fought, here in the north Skellan would carry his knife, share his hurt, and keep a place for him.

"Don't leave me like that again," Elezar whispered.

Skellan almost laughed at the thought that he would abandon Elezar.

"Never," Skellan promised.

"I won't let you go," Elezar murmured. "I'll hold onto you forever if I have to."

"Good," Skellan replied. "Hold me."

Elezar almost crushed the air from his lungs but Skellan took reassurance in that ferocious grasp. For the first time he allowed himself to imagine the life they could have together if Elezar chose to stay with him. It seemed so little to ask, that he simply stay here where he could live in freedom. But Skellan knew the decision wasn't so simple nor would it be a small sacrifice for Elezar to abandon his home and family.

I choose you, first before all others, Skellan thought as he leaned into Elezar and drew in a deep breath of Elezar's body. *I know it's selfish, but please choose me in return.*

"It's all right now." Elezar drew back a little. His eyes gleamed and Skellan wondered if they were bright with unshed tears or just fever. "I'm going to be here for you, Skellan."

"Well, obviously!" Javier's voice rose from behind Elezar's back.

Skellan looked to Javier and noted that he held a roll of bandage in one hand.

Javier cast Elezar a peeved glance. "Damn it, Grunito! I hadn't finished treating your arm, you're not wearing any shoes, and..."

Elezar waved his hand as if shooing away a fly. Then he returned his attention to Skellan. Very gently he stroked Skellan's cheek and then leaned forward and kissed him.

"Oh, go on then," Javier said, sighing. He drooped against the doorframe. "I suppose you've earned this, both of you."

Skellan heard Javier retreat and pull the doors closed behind him but he didn't pay any attention to it. Everything that mattered to him now was in his arms.

Early spring sun reflected across the harbor waters, casting ripples of light up over the pier. Emerald masses of kelp-like strands broke the waves as two frogwives surfaced to catch lines thrown from a smaller fishing skiff. They expertly hauled the boat past two harbor guard cutters. Elezar thought he glimpsed Sarl crouched near the prow, angling her harpoon for some fat fish.

When she noticed their party gathered on the pier she waved. He and Skellan waved back but didn't interrupt her fishing further.

Beyond the harbor guard's skiffs, the dark outlines of larger ships rose, slowly closing the distance to the pier. Elezar lifted his hand to shade his eyes and paused for just a moment at the sight palm He'd grown so used the wide, flat scars that carved through the skin and muscle of his left hand and arm that he now rarely considered the impression they might create at first sight. But as the two ships neared the port, he dropped his left hand and lifted his right instead. With its flocks of cloud imps darting though the sky and crews of frogwives plying the waters as stevedores and harbor pilots, Radulf County presented more than enough shocking sights for Skellan's Cadeleonian guests to take in all at once. Elezar didn't need to add to the number.

Skellan tugged at the velvet collar of his costly scarlet coat.

"I look like a stuffed bird all dressed like this," he muttered.

"You look like what you are, a handsome, powerful count who's come to greet his future allies," Elezar reassured him.

"Just so long as they've not come to try and take my champion from me," Skellan replied.

"Never," Elezar said. Skellan grinned at him and then seemed to relax.

Javier brushed against his shoulder as he tried to find a better view of the ships making port. Behind the three of them Atreau paced to their hitched horses, then turned to pace back to them as if the huge vessels could have docked already without him noticing. Kiram maintained a cool expression. Though the fact that he'd made a daily journey down to the docks to peer through his spyglass for the last week undermined his aloof pretense.

"Skellan, you were right. It's definitely their ship," Kiram announced. He adjusted some brass screw and returned his attention to the view in his spyglass.

As the vessels drew nearer, Elezar felt a fluttering in his chest. Excitement and nervousness tangled up inside him. The nearest of the two ships flew the black sun of Rauma and he now recognized Fedeles standing at the starboard railing. His black hair fluttered in the wind and he brushed it back from his face. In the year since Elezar had seen him he seemed to have filled out across his shoulders and put on more muscle. He caught sight of Elezar and raised his hand in the Hellion's sign as a greeting.

Elezar, Atreau, Javier, and Kiram all returned the gesture and then they all laughed with Fedeles across the distance. Someone on the deck called Fedeles away as the ship drew up to the pier. He turned away and disappeared from sight.

"He looks…" Javier frowned as if searching for just the right word.

"Like a grown man." Kiram lowered his glass. "He's done well. Married and become a father."

"Yes," Javier said, but he didn't sound completely settled with the idea.

Elezar held his own reservations about Fedeles' plunge into marriage and fatherhood. But it wasn't his place to disparage Fedeles' choice of bride, much less voice a question about the timing of their heir's conception.

"Of all the women in Cadeleon," Atreau muttered, "why Lady Reollos?"

"Lady Quemanor, now," Elezar corrected him and Atreau made a sour face.

"A man's heart can't be governed by reason," Kiram offered. He glanced to Javier and received a broad grin.

"Thank the stars," Skellan added gamely.

Elezar nodded, though he suspected the match had less to do with Fedeles' heart than his cunning. He'd read the letter Fedeles had penned to Bishop Palo's niece when she'd been his prospective bride: *Duty to my family title requires me to produce a legitimate heir, which I cannot accomplish without a wife.*

The cold pragmatism of those words made Elezar wonder if it hadn't simply served Fedeles to take a wife who was already with child—very likely Atreau's babe, if Elezar counted the months correctly.

If such was the case, then the match would also have indebted Lady Reollos to Fedeles for protecting her reputation and that of her firstborn child. Making her a duchess might have even allayed her need to see Atreau and himself killed. No mercenaries or assassins had come hunting for either of them since the engagement had been announced. And the charges against them both had been discreetly dropped the day after Fedeles' wedding.

Or maybe Elezar was just letting his imagination carry him away. There was no judging what another man might find utterly compelling about the object of his desire. Kiram had that right.

"You're an uncle now, you realize," Kiram informed Javier.

"Yes. Strange, isn't it," Javier responded but he sounded distracted. When Elezar glanced to him he realized that Javier was searching the ship deck for another glimpse of his cousin. How easy it was to read the excitement and tenderness in his expression. Elezar suspected that the same could be said of himself.

A year living in Radulf County had dispelled much of the studied indifference that both of them had once cultivated. Here it mattered very little if those around them knew whom they cared for. In fact, Elezar suspected a few of Skellan's courtiers of going far out of their ways to reveal themselves as men of broad experience and diverse tastes in hopes of currying favor. Had they known Skellan better they simply would have offered him sausages and smoked eels.

As sailors hurried to secure Fedeles' ship, Elezar peered at the smaller Haldiim trading vessel, the *Red Witch*. There was a fitting name for a vessel visiting Radulf County. Though, now that he thought about it, Elezar remembered Atreau mentioning that the ship had been named by her Mirogoth navigator, so perhaps it wasn't such a coincidence.

"Nestor's with them!" Kiram lowered his spyglass for a moment to share a wide grin with Elezar. Elezar squinted at the small figures on the deck of the merchant ship. He searched for a moment but then quickly picked out the broad shoulders of his younger brother. He wore his hair down to his shoulders in the same style Fedeles sported. A tiny figure leaned against him, swathed in gold. Nestor wrapped his arms around the woman, and though her back stood to Elezar, he knew that she had to be Nestor's charming wife, Riossa. No doubt the two of them would be delighted with all the oddities of Milmuraille—likely they'd spend weeks drawing everything they laid eyes upon.

Elezar laid his hand against his chest, feeling the pendant beneath his shirt. Out of everyone arriving, Elezar felt certain that Nestor and Riossa would genuinely adore Skellan and celebrate all that he'd become to Elezar. The knowledge of that reassured Elezar immensely.

"Is Morisio there as well?" Atreau slid up next to Kiram. "Can you see him?"

"No—wait. Yes! He's just climbed down from the rigging. He's gotten as tan as a Haldiim. Oh, and it looks like he's explaining something to the Mirogoth navigator,. I wonder what tongue they all speak in onboard?" Then all pretense of calm reporting slipped from Kiram's voice and bearing as he caught sight of his older brother, captain of the *Red Witch*. "There's Majdi! Holy shit, I think he's brought Dauhd and my parents as well!"

Kiram actually jumped up and down on the balls of his feet and waved wildly at the approaching merchant vessel. A seeming multitude returned his gesture, Morisio and a tall Mirogoth among them. For just a moment Elezar envied Kiram's closeness with his family. They knew exactly who he was and accepted that in a way that most of Elezar's own relations probably never would.

But then he looked back to Nestor's joyous face and realized that he couldn't have hoped for more.

The following vignette was written as a small holiday gift. The events take place after the last chapter of this book but before the epilogue.

I hope readers will find it fun and not too self-indulgent.

All my best,
—Ginn

RING IN THE
NORTHERN NEW YEAR

Music filled the ballroom with tones as bright and rich as the perfume of beeswax and spiced wine. Guests, dressed in costly silks and furs, chatted, laughed, played cards and sipped drinks. But mostly they danced to rolling, sweet melodies.

Skellan watched couples swirling in circles beneath the gleaming of light of the gold candelabras and sighed. The joy in their expressions and enthusiasm of their motions lent even the most elderly and plainest of them a kind of grace. The beautiful amidst the gathering appeared almost luminous. His lanky sister, Hylanya, grinned in the arms of her favorite swordsman. Atreau Vediya led a pretty, love-struck woman in a lively promenade, while Kiram beamed in Javier's embrace.

Skellan had enjoyed a number of dances himself already. He'd accompanied his sister and Cire across the inlayed dance floor twice each. Two charming young courtiers had made for pleasant partners as well but he'd not felt the thrilled delight that he recognized on the faces of so many of the people he saw around him. Of course, plenty of flushed glows arose from the wine as much as romance.

But Skellan had only to glance to Kiram and Javier and take in the way they seemed so enraptured with just each other—smiling those knowing smiles and hardly taking their eyes off one another—to feel certain that neither of them wanted to greet the New Year with anyone else. For them, no one else in the entire grand ballroom—or even the palace itself—mattered. They didn't even have to know about the Labaran tradition: that those who greeted the New Year together would remain together.

Though clearly Cire had it in mind, from the way she lingered near Sheriff Hirbe at the card table. The sheriff appeared to share the idea and even lured Cire's rat, Queenie, to him with a trail of nuts and seeds.

"So there's joy awaiting the sunrise," Skellan murmured to himself. He slugged down another gulp of wine. The spices danced across his tongue. A year ago he could only have dreamed of swilling such costly grog. In fact a year ago he'd been dressed in rags, hungry and alone. Now he wore scarlet silk, supped on the finest meats and stood in a chamber sweltering with the heat of all his cheerful company. He'd been toasted and paid tribute in several absurdly heroic verses earlier in the evening. He could hardly move without guards flanking him and folk all around smiling at him.

Still, somehow, he felt unknown and alone. He knew that he had no right to—had no reason to—but the previous decade of isolation seemed to rise up like a ghost, enfolding him in a melancholy chill.

The musicians struck up a new melody and someone at one of the dozen card tables let out a cheer of delight. New couples took to the dance floor and a few retired to the tables to drink, gamble, gossip and flirt.

Across the room, towering up from amidst a group of high-ranking military men, Elezar stood. He'd donned Skellan's colors—scarlet and gold—and Skellan couldn't keep himself from watching him. Even among his own broad-shouldered, straight-backed countrymen, Elezar presented a powerful figure. To Skellan's eyes he was the most handsome man in the entire ballroom, regardless of his scarred hand and stern features.

From time to time he returned one of Skellan's glances with a brief smile, but then his attention turned back to a trim Cadeleonian named Captain Mequero. The sea captain would be sailing the Duke of Rauma's ship back to his home country with the new day's tide. Captain Mequero possessed the lean, strong features that Skellan knew Elezar favored—he and the one-armed cavalry captain, Tialdo, both did. They made good company for Elezar as well, all three of them speaking low and intently as if choosing between the white and red wines required the organization of a scouting party and deadly political maneuvering to accomplish.

Skellan smiled at the thought and, catching Elezar's eye once more, raised his glass to him. For a moment he thought he noticed color rise across Elezar's tanned cheeks. Then Elezar and all the Cadeleonians surrounding him toasted Skellan in return. How like Cadeleonians to leave the words unspoken and rely on gestures alone.

In that case, Skellan wondered what he should make of the small, ivory box that Elezar passed, so very carefully, to Captain Mequero. If he hadn't been watching closely Skellan might have missed the captain's momentary pause in accepting the carved box, as if Elezar offered him too precious a treasure. Beside them, Captain Tialdo's smile slipped and his brow creased.

Skellan strained at every magical ward wafting on the air to catch Elezar's response to Tialdo's unspoken question.

"I'm certain," Elezar said. Then to Skellan's annoyance, their conversation turned to horses. Cadeleonians as a race were apparently bred and born with strong opinions concerning horseflesh—even life-long sailors. While one dance ended and another began the group debated and as far as Skellan could tell, no one among them altered the others' preferences a bit.

Skellan downed the last of his wine and turned to one of the many arched windows lining the wall. Patterns of frost traced the glass with frigid beauty. In the night sky, flurries of snowflakes whirled on the hot breath of fiery torches, shining in the light and then burning to vapor. Skellan laid his hand against an icy pane. Somewhere far to the north and high in the mountains the great troll Master Bone-crusher sang a low, rumbling lullaby. Skellan closed his eyes, feeling the faintest echoes of that distant melody as it drifted through the wards he'd hung across the earth and sky. The troll's voice rumbled, deep and low, promising sweet dreams, just as he had years before.

But Bone-crusher protected other children now—orphaned trolls. Their voices rose to accompany Bone-crusher's before they drifted to sleep. This song wasn't meant for Skellan and he drew his hand back. Droplets of melted frost fell from his fingertips like tears.

Skellan grimaced at his own maudlin turn of thought and absently wiped the condensation across the thigh of his silken breaches. If he was turning snuffly and morose over a damp window and the groaning wind then he'd either drunk too much wine or not enough. He wasn't certain which.

"Something troubling out there?" Elezar's voice sounded from just behind Skellan.

He whipped around and found his man contemplating him thoughtfully before turning his solemn gaze to the blustering snowstorm outside the window.

"Only the wind making merry, tossing snow about," Skellan replied. "The weather will hold for your Captain Mequero's departure."

"He's hardly mine," Elezar replied. The idea seemed to amuse him and that alone brightened Skellan's mood greatly.

"Well, that's his loss then," Skellan replied.

Elezar laughed softly at the suggestion but then fell quiet. Skellan eyed him. Elezar commanded as varied a range of silences as did his horse. He held himself with the confidence of a swordsman and yet Skellan recognized something like nervousness in his lowered gaze. He'd clearly crossed between courtiers and dancing couples to reach Skellan but couldn't bring himself to say why.

A foolish hope fluttered through Skellan's chest. He ignored the longing, knowing how uneasy Elezar still felt in displaying his affection publicly. With Cadeleonian captains looking on he'd be all the more on his guard against giving away anything he deemed a weakness. They might dance, but well after the new year began. Perhaps when they were alone in their shared bedchamber.

And yet he'd come to Skellan. That meant much. Even if they weren't in each other's arms, they could be together when the city bells rang out the first hour of the New Year. Skellan wondered if it would be too much to take Elezar's hand in his own. He glanced down at Elezar's long, callused fingers.

"You're not wearing your signet ring." Skellan knew that Elezar sometimes removed the emblem of his noble rank during sword practice but at formal gatherings the red bull always gleamed on his right hand.

"No, I'm not." Elezar replied. Though as far as advancing the conversation went, Skellan felt it wasn't much better than saying nothing. Elezar ran his hand through his dark beard. If Skellan hadn't known better he would have said Elezar was embarrassed.

"Did you lose it up a horse's ass?" Skellan asked as quietly as he could.

"What? No! Where do you get these ideas?" Elezar shook his head and gave another soft laugh. "I gave my ring to Captain Mequero."

"Did you?" Skellan raised his brows. "That's uncommon generosity."

"Not like that." Elezar's lips curled into a wry smile. "You know, in Cadeleon we mark the first day of each New Year by swearing a resolution?"

Skellan hadn't known, but he did now, so he nodded.

"After thinking on this a good while I've decided on mine." The smile fell from Elezar's expression and Skellan read a faint pain in his gaze. "I've realized that I needed to commit myself to my home."

All at once Skellan felt afraid to hear anything more. He didn't want to know what Elezar might have resolved to do and how it involved the ship that would be setting sail for Elezar's homeland tomorrow. Skellan's breath caught in his throat like splintered glass.

"I'm sending my signet back to my family," Elezar spoke the words with a quiet intensity. "I'm relinquishing my claim to the Grunito earldom in favor of my brother, Nestor."

The confession fell so far from what Skellan had expected that for a moment he couldn't seem to grasp what Elezar meant. Then he realized.

"But your family—"

"My family will always be my family—for my part at least," Elezar said. "But I'm not returning to Cadeleon. My home is here. With you."

A grin that doubtless looked half-crazed broke across Skellan's face. His blood felt as if it had gone from ice-cold to molten as dread burned away to radiant joy.

Outside, the first of twelve bells rang out and in the ballroom the musicians struck up the traditional Labaran New Year's tune. Couples all through the chamber rushed to take the floor.

"Will you dance with me?" Skellan asked. A second wave of bells rolled from the city's towers.

Elezar's lips parted but he said nothing.

Instead he simply took Skellan's hand in his own and led him onto the dance floor. Bells rang, music rose and doubtless numerous onlookers murmured. But for Skellan, he and Elezar may as well have been alone, holding one another as the past fell away and the beginning of a new life arose in the grace of their shared embrace.

ABOUT
THE AUTHOR

Ginn Hale lives with her lovely wife and two indolent cats in the Pacific Northwest. She spends the many rainy days tinkering with devices and words. Her first novel, *Wicked Gentlemen*, won the Spectrum Award for best novel. Her most recent publications include the *Lord of the White Hell* books, The Rifter trilogy: *The Shattered Gates*, *The Holy Road* and *His Sacred Bones*, as well as the novellas *Things Unseen and Deadly*, from the *Irregulars* Anthology and *Swift and the Black Dog*, from *Charmed and Dangerous*.